The Destroyermen Series

DESTROYERMEN

PASS OF FIRE

TAYLOR ANDERSON

ACE
New York

ACE
Published by Berkley
An imprint of Penguin Random House LLC
penguinrandomhouse.com

Copyright © 2019 by Taylor Anderson
Penguin Random House supports copyright. Copyright fuels creativity, encourages
diverse voices, promotes free speech, and creates a vibrant culture. Thank you for buying
an authorized edition of this book and for complying with copyright laws by not
reproducing, scanning, or distributing any part of it in any form without permission.
You are supporting writers and allowing Penguin Random House to continue to
publish books for every reader.

ACE is a registered trademark and the A colophon is a trademark of
Penguin Random House LLC.

ISBN: 9780399587559

Ace hardcover edition / June 2019
Ace mass-market edition / April 2020

Printed in the United States of America
1   3   5   7   9   10   8   6   4   2

Cover art by Liddell Jones / American Artist

To Dad

ACKNOWLEDGMENTS

Thanks, as always, to my agent, Russell Galen, and my amazingly supportive editor, Anne Sowards. I appreciate you both more than I can say. I don't have a swarm of proofreading pals to help me pick through things before I submit a manuscript, and Anne is usually the *first* person to wade into the jumble of what I've written, instead of the second, third—or thirtieth. All the more reason I'm indebted to her. That said, there is a fair-size pack of people who bounce things around on my website, and whether the story is ever actually inspired by what they post or not, *I'm* inspired by their imagination and dedication to the yarn. Thanks (in the order their names pop into my head) to William, Lou, Charles, Matt, Don, Steve, Nestor, Clifton, Matthieu, Alexey, Doug, Paul, Joe, Justin, Owain, "The General," Henry, Jeff—and I'm sure I missed some more again. Sorry. If nothing else, you guys have kept me as consistent as is probably possible, and you do remind me of things that likely require revisiting from time to time. Special thanks to technical advisors Cap'n Pat Maloney, who also recently sent me a special artifact I'll always treasure, and Mark Wheeler, who "keeps 'em flying." From a pure "inspirational antics" standpoint, I can't forget to thank Dennis Petty, Eric Holland, Fred Fiedler, and Mark Beck. Good friends all. Oh, and of course there's Jim Goodrich, who's always ready—after the fact—to point out where I goofed stuff up. Thanks, buddy. Time to rub out the character based on you! In that same vein, I'm tempted to stop thanking Dave Leedom, though he still helps with the flying too. I think he's gone, I don't know, maybe a little funny in the head, and I may just be encouraging him.

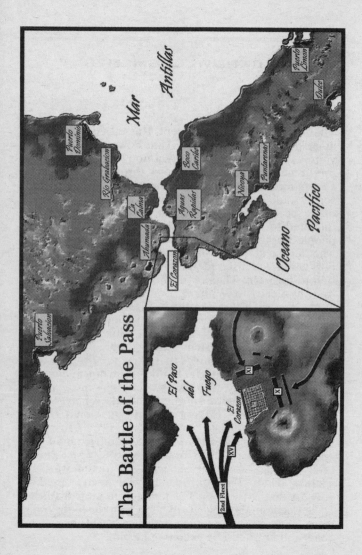

The Battle of the Pass

Mar de Antillas

Oceano Pacífico

Puerto Limón
Dulce
Puntarenas
Nicoya
Boca Caribe
Aguas Rápidas
Puerto Dominio
Río Grahaminn
La Calma
Alumada
El Corazón
Puerto Salvasieu

El Paso del Fuego
El Corazón
2nd Fleet
XV
X
XI

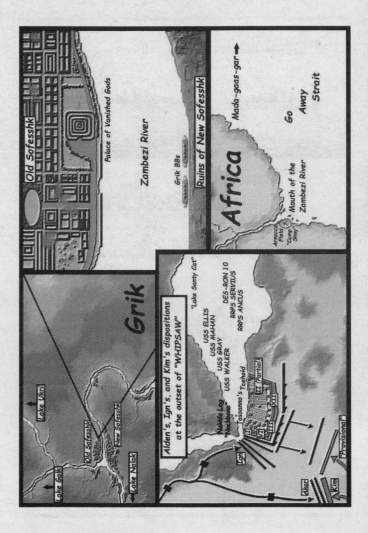

Recognition Silhouettes of Allied Vessels

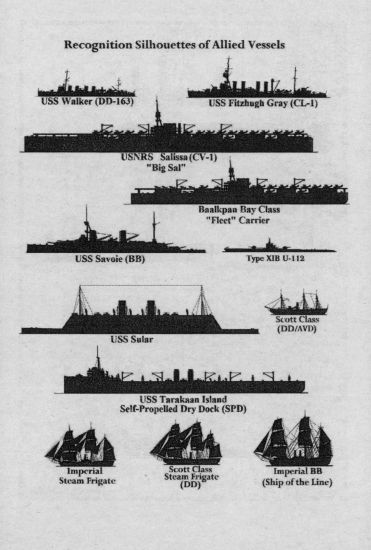

USS Walker (DD-163)

USS Fitzhugh Gray (CL-1)

USNRS Salissa (CV-1)
"Big Sal"

Baalkpan Bay Class
"Fleet" Carrier

USS Savoie (BB)

Type XIB U-112

USS Sular

Scott Class
(DD/AVD)

USS Tarakaan Island
Self-Propelled Dry Dock (SPD)

Imperial
Steam Frigate

Scott Class
Steam Frigate
(DD)

Imperial BB
(Ship of the Line)

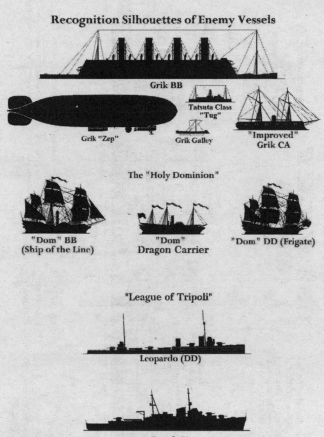

Recognition Silhouettes of Enemy Vessels

Grik BB

Grik "Zep"

Tatsuta Class "Tug"

Grik Galley

"Improved" Grik CA

The "Holy Dominion"

"Dom" BB
(Ship of the Line)

"Dom"
Dragon Carrier

"Dom" DD (Frigate)

"League of Tripoli"

Leopardo (DD)

Ramb V

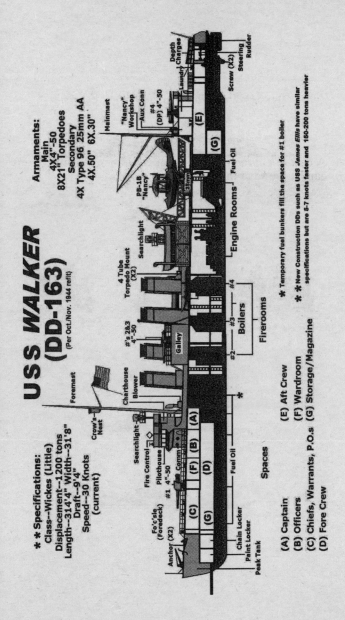

USS WALKER
(DD-163)
(Per Oct./Nov. 1944 refit)

Armaments:
Main
4X4"-50
8X21" Torpedoes
Secondary
4X Type 96 25mm AA
4X.50" 6X.30"

Specifications:
Class--Wickes (Little)
Displacement--1200 tons
Length--314'4" Width--31'8"
Draft--9'4"
Speed--30 Knots
(current)

Crow's-Nest

Foremast

Charthouse

Blower

Searchlight

Fire Control

Pilothouse

Comm

#1 4"-50

Fo'c'sle (Foredeck)

Fuel Oil

Chain Locker

Paint Locker

Peak Tank

Anchor (X2)

Galley

#'s 2&3 4"-50

4 Tube Torpedo Mount (X2)

Searchlight

PB-1B "Nancy"

25mm

Mainmast

"Nancy" Workshop

Aux Conn

#4 (DP) 4"-50

Laundry Room

Depth Charges

Screw (X2)

Steering

Rudder

Boilers

#2 #3 #4

Firerooms

Engine Rooms

Fuel Oil

Spaces

(A) Captain
(B) Officers
(C) Chiefs, Warrants, P.O.s
(D) Fore Crew

(E) Aft Crew
(F) Wardroom
(G) Storage/Magazine

* Temporary fuel bunkers fill the space for #1 boiler

** New Construction DDs such as USS *James Ellis* have similar specifications but are 5-7 knots faster and 150-200 tons heavier

AUTHOR'S NOTE

A cast of characters and list of equipment specifications can be found at the end of this book.

OUR HISTORY HERE

By March 1, 1942, the war "back home" was a nightmare. Hitler was strangling Europe and the Japanese were rampant in the Pacific. Most immediate, from my perspective as a . . . mature Australian engineer stranded in Surabaya Java, the Japanese had seized Singapore and Malaysia, destroyed the American Pacific Fleet, and neutralized their forces in the Philippines; conquered most of the Dutch East Indies; and were landing on Java. The one-sided Battle of the Java Sea had shredded ABDAFLOAT: a jumble of antiquated American, British, Dutch, and Australian warships united by the vicissitudes of war. Its destruction left the few surviving ships scrambling to slip past the tightening Japanese gauntlet. For most, it was too late.

With several other refugees, I managed to board an old American destroyer, USS Walker, *commanded by Lieutenant Commander Matthew Reddy. Whether fate, providence, or mere luck intervened,* Walker *and her sister* Mahan, *their gallant destroyermen cruelly depleted by combat, were not fated for the same destruction that claimed their consorts in escape. Instead, at the height of a desperate action against the mighty Japanese battle-cruiser* Amagi, *commanded by the relentless Hisashi Kurokawa, they were . . . engulfed by an anomalous force, manifested as a bizarre, greenish squall—and their battered, leaking, war-torn hulks were somehow swept into another world entirely.*

I say "another world" because, though geographically similar, there are few additional resemblances. It's as if whatever cataclysmic event doomed the prehistoric life on "our" Earth many millions of years ago never occurred, and those terrifying, fascinating creatures endured, sometimes evolving down wildly different paths. We quickly discovered "people," however, calling themselves Mi-Anakka, who are

highly intelligent, social folk, with large eyes, fur, and ex-
pressive tails. In my ignorance and excitement, I promptly
dubbed them Lemurians, based on their strong (if more
feline) resemblance to the giant lemurs of Madagascar.
(Growing evidence may confirm they sprang from a parallel
line, with only the most distant ancestor connecting them to
lemurs, but "Lemurians" has stuck.) We just as swiftly
learned they were engaged in an existential struggle with a
somewhat reptilian species commonly called Grik. Also
bipedal, Grik display bristly crests and tail plumage, dread-
ful teeth and claws, and are clearly descended from the
dromaeosaurids in our fossil record.

Aiding the first group against the second—Captain
Reddy had no choice—we made fast, true friends who
needed our technical expertise as badly as we needed their
support. Conversely, we now also had an implacable en-
emy bent on devouring all competing life. Many bloody
battles ensued while we struggled to help our friends
against their far more numerous foes, and it was for this
reason I sometimes think—when disposed to contemplate
destiny—that we survived all our previous ordeals and
somehow came to this place. I don't know everything
about anything, but I do know a little about a lot. The
same was true of Captain Reddy and his US Asiatic Fleet
sailors. We immediately commenced trying to even the
odds, but militarizing the generally peaceful Lemurians
was no simple task. Still, to paraphrase, the prospect of
being eaten does focus one's efforts amazingly, and dire
necessity is the mother of industrialization. To this day, I
remain amazed by what we accomplished so quickly with
so little, especially considering how rapidly and tragically
our "brain trust" was consumed by battle.

In the meantime, we discovered other humans—friends
and enemies—who joined our cause, required our aid, or
posed new threats. Even worse than the Grik (from a moral
perspective, in my opinion) was the vile Dominion in South
and Central America. A perverse mix of Incan/Aztecan
blood-ritual tyranny flavored with a dash of seventeenth-
century Catholicism and more advanced technology
brought by earlier travelers, the Dominion's aims were

similar to the Grik: conquest, of course, but founded on the principle "Convert or die."

I now believe that, faced with only one of these enemies, we could've prevailed rather quickly, despite the odds. Burdened by both, we could never concentrate our forces and the war lingered on. To make matters worse, the Grik were aided by the madman Kurokawa, who, after losing his Amagi at the Battle of Baalkpan, pursued a warped agenda all his own. And just as we came to the monumental conclusion that not all historical human timelines we encountered exactly mirrored ours, we began to feel the malevolent presence of yet another power centered in the Mediterranean. This League of Tripoli was composed of fascist French, Italian, Spanish, and German factions from a different 1939 than we remembered. They hadn't merely "crossed over" with a pair of battle-damaged destroyers, but possessed a powerful task force originally intended to wrest Egypt—and the Suez Canal—from Great Britain.

We had few open conflicts with the League at first, though they seemed inexplicably intent on subversion. Eventually we discovered their ultimate aim was to aid Kurokawa, the Grik, even the Dominion, just enough to ensure our mutual annihilation, thus removing multiple future threats to the hegemony they craved at once. But their schemes never reckoned on the valor of our allies or the resolve of Captain Matthew Reddy. Therefore, when the League Contre-Amiral Laborde, humiliated by a confrontation, not only sank what was, essentially, a hospital ship with his monstrous dreadnaught Savoie, but also took some of our people hostage—including Captain Reddy's pregnant wife—and turned them AND Savoie over to Kurokawa, we were caught horribly off guard. Tensions with the League escalated dramatically, though not enough to risk open hostilities that neither we nor they were ready for. (We later learned such had already occurred in the Caribbean, between USS Donaghey and a League DD, and that 2nd Fleet and General Shinya's force had suffered a setback in the Americas at the hands of the Dominion.) But we had to deal definitively with

Kurokawa at last, and at once. As powerful as he'd become, and with a battleship added to his fleet, we simply couldn't risk our invasion of Grik Africa with him at our backs.

Captain Reddy conceived a brilliant plan to rescue our friends and destroy Kurokawa once and for all, and in a rare fit of cosmic justice, the operation actually proceeded better than planned, resulting in the removal of one long-standing threat forever, and the capture of Savoie herself. The battle was painfully costly, however, and the forces involved too exhausted and ill placed to respond when word came that the Grik were on the move. It became clear that all our hopes for victory depended on a heretofore reluctant ally; how quickly we (and Shinya) could repair, reorganize, and rearm; and the insanely, suicidally daring defiance of some very dear friends aboard the old Santa Catalina. Under the command of Captain Russ Chappelle, the ancient armed merchantman steamed up the Zambezi and fought the Grik Swarm to a standstill, ultimately blocking the river with her own half-sunken hulk. Even then her fight wasn't finished, and as reinforcements trickled in, the battle raged on. Finally blasted to utter ruin and with the Grik surging aboard, Commodore Tassanna brought her massive carrier Arracca to evacuate survivors, but Arracca was fatally wounded and forced to beach herself.

Thus, most awkwardly, began the Allied invasion of Grik Africa. Captain Reddy and our Republic allies to the south (with whom, incidentally, I was tagging along) lashed everything at their disposal onward to support our people marooned behind Grik lines. Through daring, terrible suffering, and sheer force of will, "Tassanna's Toehold" held off the Grik until help arrived and the bloody beachhead in Grik Africa, from which we could finally strike deep against the ancient foe, was secured.

At the same time, on the other side of the world in the Dominion, the vile Don Hernan and the League's equally unpleasant Victor Gravois were finalizing a treaty of alliance, while General Shinya was surging north through the devastation left in the wake of Don Hernan's General Mayta. Both were racing to reach the city of El Corazon *and secure it—and the fabled El Paso del Fuego. Mayta got there first and began fortifying El Corazon in preparation for Shinya's and High Admiral Jenks's inevitable assault. . . .*

Excerpt from the foreword to Courtney Bradford's
The Worlds I've Wondered
University of New Glasgow Press, 1956

PROLOGUE

Grik Persia

*T*he sun was falling toward the distant western end of the narrow land bridge—barely three miles wide in places—connecting the convoluted coastlines of Persia and Arabia. Colonel Enaak of the 5th Maa-ni-la Cavalry (composed entirely of Lemurians from the Fil-pin Lands) was intrigued by the very different reflections the sunset cast on the great Western Ocean to his left, and the equally endless (from his perspective) but more placid Lake Sirak to the right. Enaak made a trilling sound and Aasi, his viciously protective me-naak mount, ambled forward to lap water from the lake. It was a bit salty but fresh enough to drink, and despite the land bridge, it served as the boundary between General Regent Halik's Persia and the various Grik viceregencies of Arabia. The border north of the great lake wasn't as well defined, but few Grik lived that far from the coast and borders hardly mattered. A dozen troopers accompanied Enaak on this jaunt, not really a scout, just an opportunity to get away from his HQ for some air and exercise and see the sights for a while. Even for that, however, in this land, nobody went alone. His guard detail moved up and allowed their me-naaks to drink as well.

Superficially, me-naaks, or "meanies," were like giant, long-legged crocodiles with thick hides and long jaws full of razor-sharp teeth. They also wore an almost impenetrable, semisegmented protective case covering their spines and vitals. Large eyes on the sides of their heads and narrow snouts allowed excellent forward vision and depth perception. They were fast, too, as fast as the horses Enaak had heard about, serving as cavalry mounts for the Repubs from southern Africa and for the Second Fleet AEF far to the East. Having never seen a horse, Enaak could only guess which animal had greater stamina. But with their claws and teeth, a well-trained meanie had to be a better battle mount. And at least here, against the Grik, the enemy had nothing like them, and Allied cavalry enjoyed a mobility Grik could only envy.

The troopers sat their saddles, shifting and looking around for threats while their animals slurped cloudy water. Enaak trusted their diligence and allowed himself to contemplate more general matters. Arguably, he commanded the most precariously extended land force in the entire Grand Alliance. *A few ships at sea might be more isolated,* he reflected, *but we've still got the weirdest, most indefinite aassignment, on the most aam-biguous front in the waar.*

Originally detailed to observe the Grik General Halik's retreat from Indiaa into Persia and make sure he kept on going as promised, the 5th Maa-ni-la and Colonel Dalibor Svec's Czech Legion, as his Brotherhood of Volunteers still called themselves (despite retaining few actual human Czechs or Slovaks—whatever *they* were, and wherever they'd come from), had shadowed Halik far longer and farther than ever expected. And they hadn't just watched him. On numerous occasions now, they'd actually scouted for him and occasionally even fought the same Persian Grik. That happened most recently when Halik's army conquered the dead Persian Prime Regent Shighat's capital at Sagar. Enaak and Svec used their mounted agility to harass attempts to reinforce the city, and lobbed exploding case shot over the walls with their stubby mountain howitzers to break up concentrations of troops behind the gates.

Despite that, Colonel Svec still vigorously rebelled against any notion they were "allied" with Halik—or any Grik. Enaak couldn't blame him. Svec's Czechs and their still-mysterious continental Lemurian brothers and sisters had been fighting a guerrilla war against the Grik in Indiaa for decades, the 'Cats having been driven out centuries before. But as long as their vague "treaty of nonaggression" with Halik held, Svec was willing to be selective about which Grik he killed. Enaak was glad. He technically commanded the combined force, but Svec's people hadn't joined the United Homes and even their connection to the Grand Alliance was tenuous. Enaak sensed a palpable paranoia on Svec's part about alliances in general, based on a very old betrayal. But until they reached Sutkag, on the extreme southwest coast of Persia, and Enaak's 5th Maa-ni-la was finally reinforced (and resupplied!) by ships from Madraas, he'd been significantly outnumbered by Svec's detachment of the Czech Legion. If Svec had chosen not to honor the treaty, there wasn't much Enaak could've done. Now the 5th had swelled to almost four thousand troopers—brigade strength for a regiment—and combined with the Czechs (human and Lemurian), Enaak practically had a division. But that still didn't make Svec any easier to handle.

Enaak glanced northeast, back in the direction of their large, isolated encampment several miles away. Field fortifications surrounded the neatly ordered lines of tiny tents. *The laand here isn't thaat different from places in the Filpin Laands,* he mused wistfully, taking in the tall-grass savanna, interspersed with large clumps of high, narrow-trunked trees. There were hills nearby, and hazy purple, snow-capped mountains brooded in the distance. Closer, a small column of Svec's troopers could be seen; one of the official scout details. They were angling closer, the lumbering gait of their tall kravaas belying how quickly the big herbivores could move. Kravaas and me-naaks didn't like each other, but given their size and power, and the long horns kravaas wore all over their bony heads, the outcome of any duel between one of them and a me-naak was always a toss-up. Since most of those present had been around each other awhile, few such altercations occurred. They remained wary, cooperative adversaries. *Kind of like us and Haalik,* Enaak mused.

He resumed daydreaming of a home he hadn't seen in two long years. *I'm told it's more thaan six thousaands of miles away,* he thought. *And though I've certainly traaveled it, I caan't even imaagine such a distaance.* He gazed back at Lake Sirak, its waves glistening under the dimming rays like those of Maa-ni-la Bay, and stretching beyond the horizon to the northwest. *Svec says this lake was paart of the ocean where he came from. Something caalled the Persiaan Gulf.* He sighed. He'd seen a lot of the world in the past two years, a world infinitely larger and more complicated than he'd ever suspected. Particularly when informed by the perspectives of those who'd seen another one entirely.

Aasi raised her head and snorted, water dripping from long teeth. Snorting again, she stepped back from the shore. Preoccupied, Enaak assumed she'd had her fill. Few things frightened me-naaks, but no land animal tarried needlessly long near water on *this* world. Virtually everything beneath it was dangerous—as were some things that had adapted to hunt from it . . .

"Col-nol!" came a cry from Enaak's right. He spun to look at one of his troopers and immediately realized his mistake. The cav-'Cat already had his carbine up and was pointing it at the water. Aasi crouched, jaws agape. None of the 5th burdened their mounts with muzzles anymore; their meanies had grown too attached to them to eat them, so why sacrifice one of their best defenses? Fully half of Enaak's troopers fired at the sudden explosion of spray in front of them, proving they'd remained more alert than their commander. Dashing out of the splashing cascade up on land was what looked very much like a me-naak—only it was easily three times as big and had eyes on top of its head. That's how it crept so close unseen.

It had also just shrugged off half a dozen hits from .50-80 caliber Allin-Silva carbines as it lunged with open jaws for one of the troopers. As quick as the monster was, however, the meanies' reflexes were faster and they bolted from the attack. Apparently even less attentive than Enaak, though, one trooper tumbled from his saddle and dropped to the ground in front of the beast. It began to stoop. A second flurry of shots distracted it—and the trooper's own mount slammed into it with the force of a torpedo, jaws snapping closed on a longish neck. To survive in the water, however, the creature's hide must've been at least as tough as a me-naak's case, and it batted the smaller attacker away. It hit hard and rolled, knocking down another me-naak and its rider, who screamed when his leg was crushed.

Enaak now had his own carbine up, aiming at the thing's eyes, but they were relatively small and in constant motion. "Baack!" he roared. "Fall baack!"

"But, Col-nol!" First Sergeant Liaa-Binaa cried help-lessly, firing again. They had people on the ground in front of that thing!

"Fall baack fifty tails. Thaat's an order. Then keep firing," Enaak insisted. He finally fired himself, missing the eye, but probably hitting the thing somewhere in the head. It screeched and turned to face him. The .50-80 cartridge the Grand Alliance adopted for its standard Allin-Silva "trapdoor" infantry rifles and carbines was a potent round; very accurate out to two hundred, even three hundred tails (or yards) in thc hands of any well-trained troop. Many soldiers could double that, and a talented few could triple it. Its big, heavy bullet would normally get good penetra-tion on large, dangerous beasts and often killed multiple Grik in massed formations.

But this thing seemed particularly well armored, quickly flattening the slugs on impact and preventing them from going deep. *And its head must be extra haard!* Enaak thought as he flipped the breech of his carbine open, eject-ing the spent shell over his shoulder and quickly inserting a fresh one. He cocked the hammer and aimed again. Aasi stood rigidly beneath him while the rest of her kind and their riders loped a short distance to the rear. Enaak felt a surge of gratitude and affection for the animal that had tried to eat him when they were first paired.

The first fallen trooper had taken his chance and scampered to join the others on foot, but the other was trapped under his fallen me-naak, struggling to rise under the weight of another that was dead or stunned. The 'Cat screamed as his mount writhed in panic atop his shattered leg. Dropping back on all fours, the water mon-ster surged toward the wounded prey. Unaware of the firing that resumed behind him or the *vip* of bullets whiz-zing past—and sudden shouts that refused to penetrate his concentration—Enaak led the predator's protruding eye just a bit. When he squeezed the trigger, the carbine bucked against his shoulder and the monster squealed horribly with a terrible volume. It spun toward him again, its left eye popped like a bloody bubble. A long red crease across the top of its head showed Enaak he'd nearly wrecked both eyes. The shouts intensified even as the monster charged toward Enaak—and a large brown blur smashed into its side, flinging it to the ground.

Enaak blinked incredulously as another big brown shape—*a kravaa!*—barreled in and slammed its long, forward-facing phalanx of horns into the monster's belly. The beast squalled and rolled, vaned tail flailing, and tossed the second kravaa and its unsettled rider away. The Lemurian rider landed on his feet, his own tail whipping, and the kravaa rose a little dazedly, two of its horns snapped off. The first kravaa had quickly backed away but charged again, just as two more converged and impaled the monster. That seemed to do the trick, finally, and the beast convulsed and thrashed while blood jetted from gaping wounds. The kravaas and their riders cautiously moved a short distance back.

Colonel Enaak lowered his carbine and shouted, "Cease firing," even though no one was shooting now. That's when he noticed his hands shaking uncontrollably. Quickly slinging the carbine, he crossed his arms over his chest, clenching them tight, and tried to control his blinking. "Col-nol Svec," he called as severely as he could as the second kravaa trotted toward him. It was huffing and blowing, sides heaving, horns and ugly face covered with blood. The big man with the long, bushy beard sitting atop the animal had quite a bit of blood on him as well, though his strong white teeth gleamed through and practically glowed in the gathering twilight. "You and your ani-maal just . . . raammed that thing yourself. I *saaw* you!" Enaak continued. "I insist thaat you refrain from such irresponsible aacts in the future. Whaat would haappen to the Legion here, and our joint efforts, if something haappened to you?"

First Sergeant Liaa was shouting for troopers to help the wounded 'Cat, and some of Svec's people were dismounting to assist. Several kravaas and me-naaks, left

unsupervised side by side, sniffed one another disdain-
fully, but there was none of the usual jostling. Colonel
Dalibor Svec laughed, glancing back at the monster,
which was only twitching now. "I must ask the same of
you, Colonel Enaak," he replied. "In my case, *Major* Svec
would seamlessly continue our association." (Major Ondrej Svec was Dalibor's son by a mother whose origin was
just as murky as that of his Lemurian troops.) He chuckled darkly. "You, on the other hand, are the only one who
keeps me and my Volunteers from killing every Grik we
see. If that *voda plazivy* got you while you sat waiting for
its jaws to snap your *hloupy* head off, who'd replace *you*,
whom I've learned to respect?"

Svec had a point, and Enaak shifted uncomfortably in
his saddle, his tail, somewhat embarrassingly frizzed out,
whipping behind him. A lot of the 5th's experienced officers had been shipped south to join Colonel Saachic for
operations against the Grik capital at Sofesshk, up the
Zambezi River. Their replacements, arriving with the reinforcements, had little combat experience. Enaak's new
XO, Major Nika-Paafo, had seen a little action in the New
Ireland campaign, but was wounded there and had been
an instructor at the Maa-ni-la ATC ever since. Enaak still
wasn't sure how well Nika would adjust to their . . . unusual circumstances here.

A loud groan interrupted them and the two downed
me-naaks finally rose and stood a little uncertainly. The
one must've been merely stunned after all. 'Cats picked
up the wounded trooper. His leg looked bad, but it was
probably a miracle from the Maker that things hadn't
gone much worse. "Still," Enaak continued to Svec, "I
wish you'd stop paarticipating directly in these scouts.
Even without Haalik's aarmy trying to kill us, there are
maany Grik here who not only haaven't joined his Hunt,
as they say, but don't even know about him. Or us, for that
maatter. This is a perilous laand."

"As we were just reminded," Svec agreed. "And again,
I redirect the admonition to you," he countered, now impatient. "That you lead from the front is one reason I like
you. But as I pointed out—and for other reasons—you're
even more indispensable. And if *you* personally lead each

scout, how will your replacement officers gain the experience they need?"

Enaak started to object that *he* wasn't scouting . . . but wasn't that the very definition of "seeing the sights"? He sighed. "Very well. Perhaaps we both might be more careful." He glanced at the horizon, then back toward their encampment. The sun now gone, twinkling campfires were sprouting like tiny orange stars on the prairie. "I must be getting baack. I haave a meeting with Gener-aal Ni-waa and Gener-aal Shlook," he said, an edge returning to his voice. "You couldn't know, because you were already gone when they asked for it. I waas actually raather vaguely looking for you, as a maatter of faact," he added wryly, "because I'd like you there. Ni-waa rarely requests meetings on such short notice, and I suspect he has maatters of importaance to discuss."

"My troopers . . ." Svec began.

"Are in capable hands," Enaak countered. "Come baack with me." He paused. "And thaanks."

General Orochi Niwa, Halik's co-commander, was Japanese. He was thin but hard, and wore brass-studded Grik-style leather armor altered to fit a human over a long, dingy brown smock not unlike the tie-dyed camouflage smocks the Allies had adopted. He carried no weapons and entered Enaak's command tent a little self-consciously. That may have had to do with the minor deception he'd inflicted on Enaak. Warned only moments before by a runner from the detail escorting the visitors, Enaak, Svec, and their most senior officers saw for themselves that General Regent Halik himself and not General Shlook had accompanied Niwa, when he strode through the tent flap behind the Japanese "Marine."

This could be good, Enaak thought, *or very, very baad.* Everyone stood, since there weren't any of the saddle-like chairs Grik could use. Niwa stepped aside and Halik moved to stand in front of Enaak and Svec. Almost as tall and massive as the Czech, with muscles bulging under tight, feathery/furry skin crosshatched by the scars of many fights, Halik dwarfed Colonel Enaak. His leather armor was battered and hard used, and a few daggerlike teeth were missing from his long, savage jaws. Even his high, bristly crest had taken battle damage it hadn't fully recovered from. He wore no cape, like other Grik generals often did, and his tail plumage flared out to the sides. Without any affectation of finery, Halik remained the most impressive Grik Enaak ever saw.

He'd been a warrior and sport fighter before his elevation, and those experiences added not only to his military talent, but also his understanding of what warriors could endure. To say he was physically frightening, with his wicked teeth and claws and obvious power, would be an understatement. But he'd come alone with Niwa and really did have every reason to appreciate the . . . nonaggression and grudging support of the Allies.

He and Niwa were an odd pair. Niwa had been a member of a detachment of Special Naval Landing Forces aboard *Amagi* when the battlecruiser followed USS *Walker* and USS *Mahan* to this world. Sent to Ceylon with Halik as an advisor, Niwa and the Grik commander endured a great deal together, and actually became friends. Friendship was a concept no Grik had ever been exposed to, much less understood, but there was no doubt Halik grasped it now, along with many other very un-Grik-like notions. And Niwa was important to Halik in other ways. He'd taught him everything he understood about the Allies' position and perspective and had certainly made Halik a more formidable opponent, but he'd also taught him things like honor, mercy, and, apparently, ambition.

Key to the latter had been Niwa's influence in turning Halik from a traditional Grik general with no regard for the lives of his warriors into a commander, now regent, whose underlying purpose had become the survival of his warriors—his people—and what they'd become. He led a Grik army that, for the first time in history, was almost entirely composed of sentient, thinking Hij, and not just mindless Uul. Enaak had reports that other Grik were "getting wise," having been trained to think and fight as soldiers virtually from hatchlinghood, but Halik's army had been the first, and learned what it knew the hardest way imaginable.

Part of Halik's mechanism for accomplishing that had

been simply preserving his army long enough for its warriors to reach mental maturity instead of destroying them when they "got old" and learned to think too much. He himself had been surprised to discover that warriors past the age of three or four tended to elevate themselves to a degree and only required education after that. So, by saving his army—something *it* was highly conscious of—he'd instilled another previously unknown concept within its ranks, one that made him a leader to his people instead of just a general to his troops: loyalty. And it wasn't blind, instinctual loyalty like they'd owed to the Celestial Mother or General Esshk; it was earned. Motivated by that special, *different* loyalty, his troops actually trained and fought harder now to please their general regent and preserve his cause. Particularly since his cause was them.

On one hand, Enaak, Captain Reddy, even Chairman Letts applauded that, but they knew Dalibor Svec was right to remain wary. With a proper army of disciplined soldiers now almost two hundred thousand strong, Halik was on his way toward remaking all the Grik in Persia, perhaps beyond. He appreciated his unusual relationship with the Allies—for now—but what if his own loyalty to General Esshk, pushed by his new sense of honor, pitted him against them once again? Especially at this critical time? Henry Stokes, Letts's head of intelligence, constantly prodded Enaak and Svec to evaluate whether Halik could be trusted to stick to the deal or was already more dangerous than ever before.

"Greetings, Colonel Enaak, Colonel Svec," Halik said in Grik. Then he lowered his muzzle in the direction of the other officers, few of whom he knew. Enaak and Svec understood him, just as Halik understood English, but none could really speak the other's tongue. Niwa, as always, would try to clarify any misunderstandings. "I hope you're enjoying your stay in my new regency," Halik continued, "won with your assistance in no small part. The weather is certainly preferable to that which we endured to get here." That was undeniable. It got bitterly cold in the mountains to the east, and Grik were particularly susceptible to cold. Svec and his people might actually find it rather hot and humid here, but Enaak's troopers were

reminded as much of home as he was. "And you're satisfied with the provisions?" Halik pressed. The majority of
their meat came from foodbeasts supplied by the Grik
themselves, though the arrival of Allied supplies had
come none too soon. Humans and Lemurians both required a more diverse diet than Grik and almost nothing
had been coming up behind them across the vast expanse
of Indiaa, and now Persiaa as well. They'd also been extremely low on ammunition, which gave them the willies,
despite Halik's apparent benevolence.

"Quite saatisfactory," Enaak assured, "though I hope
you haaven't depleted your neekis herds too greatly," he
probed. Obviously, neither Svec's nor Enaak's troops
would eat dead Grik—a food source in great abundance
of late, which the Grik themselves were happy to consume. But Halik's Grik had recently adopted other uses
for neekis, a type of plains hadrosaur, and were training
them as beasts of burden. Neekis would never be cavalry
mounts—they were too big and Grik weren't shaped to
ride them—but they were biddable and could pull much
greater loads (including artillery) than paalkas or suikaas. Needless to say, they'd added a lot to Halik's ability
to project power, each able to perform the labor of a hundred warriors—now free to swell his combat ranks.

"Not at all," Halik denied, waving it away. "The herds
here are massive and had been underutilized."

"I'm glaad to hear it," Enaak said.

"So, *plazivy*," Svec said rather pleasantly, considering
his name for Halik meant, roughly, "creepy reptile" in
Czech. "What brings you here, and why the deception?"

Niwa looked pained but Halik nodded as a human
might. "I thought it only right to inform you myself that
we've reestablished communications with First General
Esshk. Perhaps you saw the airship that passed overhead
and landed at Sagar? It was one of many dispatched to
find us, but was the only one to arrive." Halik bared his
teeth in a frightening manner, but for him it was almost a
grin. "I'm sure the rest were forced down by distance, or
searched the wrong direction."

Enaak hadn't known about the Grik zeppelin, though
he had no doubt his scouts would bring the report from

Sagar. As for the others, they'd probably been shot down by prowling planes from AVDs offshore. He was sure Halik suspected that too.

"In any event," Halik continued, "the airship brought tidings of the great war between our peoples—of victories and defeats." He glanced at Niwa. "The latest was of a terrible defeat suffered by General Niwa's people in their Sovereign Nest at Zanzibar. General of the Sea Hisashi Kurokawa is no more." If anything, Halik actually seemed pleased by that, as did Niwa, but Niwa doubtless mourned his other former shipmates.

"We had reports of that as well," Enaak confirmed. Halik knew all about radio and wireless communications, whether he had them or not. Denying they had more up-to-date news than Halik did was pointless—just as pointless as Halik asking for news beyond what was offered. "We also learned thaat quite a few of Gener-aal Niwa's people survived," Enaak conceded. "Some were taken prisoner and will be sent to the Union State of Yoko-haama, where others of their kind reside. Some haave joined our cause," he added pointedly. "*All* will be well treated." He looked back at Halik. "Some of your people helping Kuro-kaa-waa also joined us, much like a few of Regent Shighat's waarriors joined your hunt when he was defeated." He glanced at Svec. "I confess we were all surprised to hear of thaat."

"That *is* . . . interesting," Halik agreed, then waved it away. "But it appears, with Kurokawa gone, our peoples are free to focus on one another again—at least on this side of the world," Halik continued, rather bitterly it seemed, and Enaak felt a chill. The zep must've carried information about the war against the Doms in Central and South America. Possibly about the League of Tripoli as well, which had aided Kurokawa. Keeping the Grik, and Halik in particular, from knowing how thin the Allies were stretched had been of the utmost importance. How would their "arrangement" be affected now that the truth was out? They didn't have to wait long to find out. "Most significant to my army and me, however," Halik added slowly, "the airship also brought a summons directly from First General Esshk and the Celestial Mother herself."

"A summons?" Svec asked darkly, and Halik looked at him.

"Yes. A command that I come at once. First General Esshk requires my army." He looked searchingly at Enaak. "Whether he needs it to join an offensive or aid his defense against one launched by your Captain Reddy, I do not know."

Enaak knew it could've been either when the message was dispatched. Esshk had loosed his Final Swarm down the Zambezi to cross the Go Away Strait and overwhelm the Allied toehold on Madagascar. The only thing that slowed it was a desperate act by Russ Chappelle and his old *Santa Catalina*, which steamed upriver and plugged it up. *Santa Catalina* had been destroyed, as had an awful lot of good people, but they bought time for Captain Reddy to assemble what was left of First Fleet, three corps of the Allied Expeditionary Force, and finally land in Grik Africa itself. Their position remained precarious, but they were within eighty miles of the Grik capital of Sofesshk and the Army of the Republic was churning up from the South. Enaak expected the worst fighting of the war would come in the next weeks and months, but they had a chance, at last—and *he* was stuck up *here*!

"So, *plazivy*, what will you do?" Svec asked, voice still mild, but there was a growing cloud behind it. Halik hesitated, then let out a long breath.

Before he could respond, Niwa shook his head. "He *must* go," he said. "He has no choice. As I—and you—have long understood the concept of honor, his more recent appreciation of its importance is no less sincere. As Emperor Hirohito represented the, ah ... Maker of All Things to me on the world I came from, so does the Celestial Mother command Halik's devotion. And General Esshk *made* him. He can't ignore that." Svec started to interrupt, but Niwa held up a hand. "Nevertheless, General Regent Halik"—he smiled wryly—"the 'King of Kings' fully recognizes the way he forges here, with your help, isn't Esshk's way, and he doubts Esshk can fully approve of what he and his army have become. Esshk might even *destroy* him and all he's done because of it. If not on sight, then very possibly after Halik serves his purpose."

Halik was nodding. "I *must* go," he said, almost pleading, "but I won't take all my army. I can't risk everything to destruction by your people *or* mine, and General Shlook will stay with half my force to hold what we've gained and continue our efforts."

"Half or all, we caan't let you join Esshk," Enaak said softly, but the resolve in his voice was clear. Even half of Halik's army would outnumber his own force more than ten to one.

"I understand," Halik acknowledged, "but you miss our point. I must go, as I told you fairly, but I can't tell you now whether I go to *join* First General Esshk—or fight him."

Enaak's wide amber eyes practically bulged, and even Svec was taken aback. "So . . ." Enaak ventured.

"So," Niwa said brusquely, "we came to invite you to join the campaign as before, though perhaps we shouldn't expect you to scout the quickest paths. None of us have ever traversed the vast distance ahead, across Arabia and down the east coast of Africa, and it would be a simple matter for you to lead us astray. But you'd be with us, watching—reporting on us, no doubt—and this serves two functions. First, we won't join Esshk without first informing you. On this you have our word of honor. Perhaps that might prevent your First Fleet from decimating our advance from the sky as we proceed down the coast—or even landing troops in our path."

Faat chaance of the latter, Enaak thought. *Everybody's pretty busy right now. But* they *caan't know thaat—yet. And the first notion's pretty shrewd. Our planes might slow Haalik, bleed him, but they caan't stop him, so Henry Stokes and his snoops will want word of his every move. We caan give him thaat.*

"Second," Niwa went on, "as General Regent Halik said—and another reason your air power might leave us to our business and we'd be glad of your company—it's possible we may have to fight First General Esshk." He glanced at Halik again. "We have no military alliance, nor are we ever liable to. Halik's people and yours . . . such a thing would be difficult to imagine after all that's passed between you. But we've cooperated against common enemies, and if it comes to it, we'll gladly do so again. After all," Niwa continued in a strange tone, "whether you believe it or not, or can even imagine it, General Regent Halik considers *you* his friends as well, as he understands the term. He *will* kill you if he must," Niwa warned, "though he'd much rather not. If that time comes, however, he'll give you sufficient warning to prepare for death—or escape. Your choice. On that you have *my* word."

"What do you think?" Svec asked after Halik and Niwa left the tent. "Will your Henry Stokes approve *this* insane scheme?"

Enaak blinked deep deliberation. "He didn't aapprove us following Haalik all the way across Persiaa or helping him against his enemies, but it seemed a good idea at the time. And our aactions were at least aaccepted. But we must evaal-uate this, and quickly. I believe Haalik will move very soon."

"Do you trust him?" Svec growled, raising a wide-mouthed cup of seep. Seep was a spirit distilled from pur-plish, pear-shaped polta fruit. Tasty by itself and full of many vitamins humans and 'Cats required, it was also pre-pared into an analgesic, antibacterial paste. Recreational spirits weren't allowed to members of the 5th Maa-ni-la, however, and Enaak insisted his officers abstain as well. The Czechs had no such restriction.

Enaak looked thoughtful. "Oddly, yes. I mean, I cer-tainly trust him to crush us if we make a nuisance of our-selves, but I suppose I also believe him about the rest."

Svec gulped his seep and made a sour face. "I must agree. Granted, he mainly wants us close to shield him from your planes. But without us along, your planes would have a harder time finding him." He shrugged. "If he wasn't sin-cere, why not crush us now? He'd never catch us all, but we'd be no threat after that. I have to say I believe him."

"We must report this to Chaar-maan Letts at once," Nika warned skeptically. "I doubt *he* will trust the honor of a Grik or Jaap!"

"You might be surprised," Enaak said, looking at his XO. It was the first time Nika had ever seen Halik or Niwa, and he was clearly a little shaken by the experience.

Letts—and Stokes—had been reading Enaak's reports for a long time, however. They may not trust Halik, but they had faith in Enaak's assessments. "I think they'll go for it," he decided. "If nothing else, they'll always have a good idea about when Haalik's army *might* join Esshk, and we caan feed them reports about its strength and disposition along the way. Stokes in paarticular will consider it too good an opportunity to paass." He blinked a little nervously. "Unless he decides *we* should try to stop them, somehow." He looked at Svec. "What about your leaders? What will they say about you draagging so much of their military even faarther away?"

Svec grinned, partially at Enaak's probing. He'd never even confirmed he *had* a leader. His people obviously had territory beyond Indiaa, where they'd already begun to return, since there were men in his force too young to have come from that other world when he did, and there were few Lemurian females in the Legion. "Halik's the greatest threat to my people. Keeping eyes on him—and helping you—is the best service my military can perform."

Major Ondrej Svec leaned forward. He had darker hair than his father and his sudden laconic smile compressed his narrower eyes into slits. "So we either go along, or try to summon sufficient transport to pull us out—precisely when such transport is desperately needed elsewhere. We should agree to Halik's terms." He glanced at Enaak. "Tag along, as you say. And there's another thing to consider: if we go, we won't just be sitting here anymore—and we may get into the fighting to the south after all, one way or another."

"True," Enaak agreed. "We might well be in at the finish." He looked back at the younger Svec and blinked irony. "One way or another."

CHAPTER
1

////// *El Corazon*
Near El Paso del Fuego (The Pass of Fire)
January 14, 1945

*Mountain Fish, Island Fish, Ulaagis, Leviathans—they're
all the same: the largest living things we know of on this
world. Far larger than anything where we came from.
They're generally solitary, highly territorial, brooding
beasts, feeding on anything that will fit in their monstrous
maws, including adolescent interlopers of their own species. They're equally dangerous to "trespassing" ships,
and only extremely annoying acoustic assaults can reliably discourage their attention. I hope to study them in
greater detail someday, but for now I can only wallow in
ignorant awe of their proportions. They're ancient things,
perhaps almost timeless—though not deathless, certainly,
since they can be killed, and we know they somberly mi-
grate from all over the world (at least once) to die in the
Sea of Bones northwest of El Paso del Fuego. Paradoxically, however, they also congregate in their multitudes at
the pass itself to breed and calve, and at that one place in
all the world, they coexist in perfect amity toward each
other and all around. Perhaps they must be on their best
behavior to win a mate? Imagine, then, the double irony
that these ordinarily belligerent beasts should witness the
visitation of such appalling carnage upon their singular,
peaceful preserve.*

From Courtney Bradford's *The Worlds I've Wondered*
University of New Glasgow Press, 1956

*T*he evening sky was a weird, almost neon orange, shot with blue-gold streamers as the sun sank toward the red-purple sea in the west. What looked like a vast bay ringed by high mountains intruded on the land to the north, and the distant shore was dominated by the tallest mountain of all. It was a "vol-caano," like many of the others, and though presently deceptively quiescent, its indistinct flanks were wreathed in smoke and steam. And the bay itself was deceptive as well, since it was, in fact, the gaping western mouth of what became a narrow, tide-scoured passage between the Pacific and Atlantic oceans. The local name was El Paso del Fuego, and it ran just about down the middle of where Costa Rica would've been on another Earth.

No one knew what caused it. There were a lot of little differences on this world besides the people and wildlife. According to Courtney Bradford, the Australian naturalist/engineer fighting Grik with the Army of the Republic in southern Africa, a moderately lower sea level resulting in different coastlines was probably the result of some phase of an ice age. Sometimes there were islands where there shouldn't be, or none where there should, and there was a cluster of whoppers around latitude fifteen south where there should've been only the tiny, scattered Samoa, Fiji, Santa Cruz, and New Hebrides islands.

Adventurously seagoing as Lemurians were, they'd never ventured that far into what they called the Eastern Sea before the war. Imperial explorers discovered them during one of their periodic fits of geographical curiosity, but found them unusually dangerous even for this hostile world. Now the Impies stayed away, and little was known about the islands.

But El Paso del Fuego was a bigger difference, for a variety of reasons, and theories about what caused it abounded. Most naturalists in the NUS agreed that all the volcanoes in the region blew it out, and the crazy tidal race eroded a navigable channel over time. Others—and

Courtney was increasingly in this camp—thought some great heavenly body, like a comet or asteroid, whacked the place thousands, maybe millions of years ago. That might not only have caused all the volcanoes in the first place, but could explain a lot of other things, such as why this world had taken such a different evolutionary track.

While perhaps intellectually stimulating, such speculation had little bearing at present. What really mattered was that the Pass of Fire was even more strategically important than the Panama Canal would've been, on a world where the Drake Passage between Cape Horn and Antarctica was too choked by ice to use. There might be brief, occasional spells during which a ship might pick its way through, but the storms were even worse than those off the cape of Africa, and no one ever tried.

Unfortunately, the Pass of Fire was controlled by the Holy Dominion, a human civilization so depraved that the western members of the Grand Alliance were already at war with it before they even knew the pass—and so many threats beyond it—existed. Most pressing now, the treacherous League of Tripoli, composed of fascist French, Spanish, Italian, and German forces from a different past, had made an alliance with the twisted Dominion and might soon bring enough power to bear to prevent the Western Allies from linking up with new friends bordering the northern Gulf of Mexico and Caribbean. The New United States were descended from other Americans that arrived in the 1840s, and would be a big help if they weren't isolated and conquered. Finally, Dom-League cooperation could stop the Allied campaign against the Dominion cold. Without victory there'd never be peace, and time was running out.

Major Blas-Ma-Ar and General James Blair sat on a pair of beautiful black horses, captured from the Doms no doubt, in front of two hundred Imperial dragoons arrayed behind them. Blas was a brindled Lemurian "'Cat" Marine representing the United Homes and the American Navy Clan. She wore the tie-dyed camouflage smock and green platterlike steel doughboy helmet that was standard combat dress for all the Allies, except the Republic of Real People, arrayed against the Doms, Grik, and maybe the League. The only remaining variations were that humans wore trousers and boots or shoes, while 'Cats wore kilts and sandals. A few 'Cat Marine officers and NCOs still wore blue kilts, and the occasional battered set of once-white rhino-pig armor was also seen. Blas wore hers now, as commander of the Sister's Own Division in all but name. Composed of what was left of the 2nd (Lemurian) Marines combined with a growing number of human Ocelomeh (Jaguar Warriors), as well as a heavy brigade of former Doms and local "true Christian" volunteers calling themselves El Vengadores de Dios, the Sister's Own had seen more action than any other division in the Second Fleet Allied Expeditionary Force.

General Blair commanded X Corps, and was General Tomatsu Shinya's XO. Like many officers of the Empire of the New Britain Isles, he still wore his red coat with yellow facings, black piping, and brass buttons for occasions such as this. Like his tall black shako, however, the coat had seen much abuse, and he no longer had a pair of white breeches. Camouflage trousers were tucked into knee-high boots. He still wore long Imperial mustaches, but had also cultivated a thick black beard, something only seen before in the lower ranks. The new style was catching on.

"I don't know whaat the hell's the point of this," Blas grumbled sourly, tail whipping behind her. She blinked something akin to irritated futility as she and Blair urged their mounts forward and they proceeded alone. Half a mile below, down a gentle grade, lay El Corazon del Fuego, one of the principal cities of the Holy Dominion. The outskirts of the city, once a sprawling community of shops and apartments, were abandoned now; many of the buildings torn down or burned by the inhabitants to improve fields of fire in front of a fairly new and substantial-looking wall. An older wall incorporating a pair of impressive tower fortresses protected against a seaborne assault. The recent addition, encompassing the rest of the older, richer part of the city, had apparently been built to stop them.

Halfway between the dragoons and exactly two hundred Dom lancers arrayed at the foot of the wall was a large, parti-colored pavilion with fluttering scalloped edges. Two forms could just be seen in the gloom underneath.

"The point, Major Blas," Blair began with exaggerated patience, "is the same as when we agreed to a similar meeting with General Nerino before the battle at Guayak. We learned quite a bit about our enemy that day."

Blas snorted and her gaze returned to the lancers. They were Blood Drinkers, members of an elite, fanatical military order directly serving "His Supreme Holiness, Messiah of Mexico, and, by the Grace of God, Emperor of the World." The pretentious title would've made Blas laugh, but there was nothing funny about Blood Drinkers at all. They looked fraudulently festive in their yellow coats with red facings. (Blas was darkly amused that Impie Marines had traditionally worn uniforms of the same, but opposite, base colors, and wondered if that was deliberate.) Riotously feathered helmets and the brilliant brass cuirasses of the officers still glowed under the setting sun, and long, intimidating lances stood erect from saddle boots. Bloodred ribbons fluttered near razor-sharp tips.

Impressive, Blas conceded to herself, *an' very pretty in their evil way. Make our draa-goons look downright dingy in compaar-ison.*

Imperial Dragoons had been lancers themselves, earlier in the war, and once looked just as fine. The problem was they hadn't been as *good* as the Doms. Against considerable opposition, General Shinya sacked a lot of officers, issued the troopers the same combat dress as everyone else, and took away their lances. Now they carried Allin-Silva carbines, fought on foot more often than not, and were infinitely deadlier than their Dom counterparts. *Even so,* Blas imagined irreverently, *I bet a few draa-goon officers wish they still haad helmets with faancy feathers stickin' out.* "Nerino learned about us, too," she pointed out, returning to the argument.

"Sadly for him, less than he might have." Blair smiled ironically. "More specifically, that he should've left us alone. Perhaps this new General Mayta has taken a lesson from that and will be easier to reason with."

Blas snorted again. "Reason? With a *Dom*? Whaat war *you* been fightin', Gener-aal? Not the same one I been in. You fought Griks at Sinaa-pore, right? Doms're just as crazy. Maybe worse. I hear some Griks'll surrender now."

"As will Doms, as you know. You command some who have."

"Regu-laars an' conscripts, maybe, given a chaance," Blas conceded, but her tone darkened. "Not them goddaamn Blood Drinkers." She flicked her ears at the pavilion ahead, though her helmet hid the gesture. "I'm sure May-taa learned a *lot* from Nerino an' Don Her-naan. Baad thing is, I figure it was stuff *not* to do. He already knew, or picked up enough, to lead me all through the mountains by the nose an' then haammer you on the maarch. He ain't nothin' like Nerino. An' our roles are baackwards this time. Nerino had to come to us—twice—an' we broke him both times. May-taa knows how we did it, an' now we haave to go to *him* in a position he's had all kinds o' time to prepare. I think taalkin' to him's stupid."

Blair coughed. "It was General Shinya's and High Admiral Jenks's orders that we should." He tensed, wondering how Blas would react. There'd been bad blood between her and Shinya ever since the hellish battles around Fort Defiance, far to the south, but they seemed to have gotten over it.

"Yeah," Blas grumped, tail flipping noncommittally. "They're both great men, smaart men. Don't mean they caan't be stupid too. Least neither of 'em came. Thaat would'a been *real* stupid. Shin-yaa went with us to meet Nerino, remember? Whaat if he'd just rubbed us all out? We might've lost the baattle—not thaat *we* would'a cared."

"We've all . . . become better soldiers," Blair agreed tightly, as close as he'd come to criticizing their commanders, then darted a glance at Blas. She'd certainly become the most formidable combat leader in his X Corps, and he knew what that had cost her. There were rumors. . . . He shook his head. "And General Shinya's now fully aware that he's not expendable."

"Like us?"

Blair laughed. "Nonsense. Mayta can have no motive for treachery here. He seeks intelligence, as do we. We'll all be trying to kill one another soon enough." He stopped and considered. "Though Mayta *did* request General Shinya by name"—he glanced at Blas—"as well as you, my dear. Perhaps he would've set his lancers on us if Shinya came, but he has to know our dragoons would slaughter them—and him—in that event. Honestly, I expect we're safe enough."

They were nearing the pavilion now and the two men standing, waiting for them, were resplendent in the ornate finery of Dom general officers. The most highly decorated was surprisingly tall for a Dom, probably as tall as Blair, though his skin was very dark. He was dressed as a "regular," in bright yellow coat with perfect white facings. Gold lace practically dripped from the uniform, and he clutched a large, equally ornate black hat under his arm. A gorgeous sword with an elaborate golden guard and scabbard, with a hilt of carved ivory or bone, hung at his side, glittering against the silver-white knee breeches, stockings, and black shoes with big gold buckles.

Blas recognized the other man as a Blood Drinker. Like the lancers, the primary difference in his dress was that his coat facings and knee breeches were a dark bloodred, of course. *Which is May-taa*? Blas suddenly, fervently wanted to know.

"Maybe *we're* safe," Blas whispered as they stopped their horses, stepped down, and tied the reins to a picket line where two other horses already stood. It had been agreed there wouldn't even be servants at the meeting. "But if one o' those ass-holes really *is* May-taa, we should'a bombed 'em or shelled 'em."

"Please refrain from such comments," Blair murmured through clenched teeth. "General Mayta is reputed to speak excellent English."

"I have sufficient English for our purposes today," said the tall officer in the regular uniform, "and quite good hearing, considering my somewhat . . . raucous profession." He smiled, and Blas suddenly realized he was *young*. So was the Blood Drinker, though he didn't smile. He was glaring at her with an expression of utter loathing. *Fair enough,* she thought. *I feel the same about you!*

Blair stepped forward and saluted; he'd discussed this

with Shinya beforehand. "General James Blair, at your service," he said. "I'm honored to command Tenth Corps, the *initial*"—he stressed the word—"force investing your city—for Her Majesty Rebecca Anne McDonald and the Grand Alliance. Do I have the privilege of addressing General Mayta?"

"You do," Mayta replied, returning the salute and ignoring—as Blair did—that neither Blas nor the Blood Drinker saluted. "General Anselmo Mayta, at your service, and the privilege is mine entirely. Until the current conflict, only once before in history had the armies of His Supreme Holiness met another upon our own sacred soil—a terrible thing, to be sure," he added with a glance at his seething companion, "but also a fascinating opportunity for those, like myself, who make the study of war their life's pursuit."

Blas was blinking something at the Blood Drinker that Blair couldn't see, but her tail was whipping like a snake preparing to strike. The Blood Drinker couldn't know what the blinking meant, but the hostility of her posture was clear. His hand snapped to his sword and he took a step toward her. Almost gleefully, Blas reached for her cutlass. Blair quickly put a hand on her shoulder just as Mayta restrained his man.

"General Allegria! Control yourself!" Mayta said forcefully, glancing at Blair to ensure he'd stopped Blas. He sighed. "Here, I think, lies the root of our conflict on display. Hatred can be so distracting to the professional! Please forgive General Allegria—for that is his name. I had not even introduced you yet!" he scolded the man lightly, and looked back at Blair. "General Allegria is one of many . . . supplementary sons showered upon my lord, His Holiness, Don Hernan de Divina Dicha. As such, he has only the one name until he distinguishes himself sufficiently for God to bless him with another. One of many reasons, as you might imagine, he's quite as passionate as his father about protecting our home from spiritual—and physical—corruption."

"I'd aar-gue, *Gener-aal*, thaat your murderin' faith is whaat corrupts this laand!" Blas seethed.

Mayta looked at Blas with delight. "Ah! And you're

undoubtedly Major Blas-Ma-Ar! I *can* hear you speak! I'd heard it was so but am astounded nonetheless." He looked at Blair. "The truly faithful can't be induced by a demon. They can't even hear the demon's attempts. But it became apparent that some demons—some *Lemurian* prisoners we secured—*could* be heard by the faithful." He laughed. "You might be amused to learn how many guards were . . . inadvertently crucified as heretics when they reported this." He cocked his head to observe Blair's reaction but saw none. "And the truth was difficult to determine, since the captives refused to speak in front of a Blood Priest, regardless of the . . . incentives. I think it entertained them that we were slaughtering our own! But truth always rises and was eventually recognized— grace be upon those who were not believed," he added piously.

Blas blinked confusion through her anger. "So whaat's your point?"

Mayta regarded her with surprise. "Why, only that we now know, whatever you are, Major Blas, you're no demon! Not human, of course, and therefore unsuited to receive God's Grace," he qualified, "but a mere animal, without corruptive, otherworldly powers. Clearly, you're the most *intelligent* animals yet encountered, but animals nevertheless."

He looked at Blair. "Imagine my distress for the souls of your people. As far from God as they are, many do at least know him—which made me wonder how demons could control them in battle unless they possessed them utterly. I'm tremendously relieved for you, General Blair. You and your people can *still* know God's grace—and I'll endeavor mightily to deliver it to you." He beamed.

"Then I'm sure you'll take it as a favor if I try as hard to do the same for you, General Mayta," Blair said dryly.

"Of course," Mayta agreed. Then he turned back to Blas. "Forgive my digression. You fascinate me, and I'm so pleased to make your acquaintance at last." He spoke aside to General Allegria. "Is it not amazing to be able to converse with animals? Perhaps they might make suitable slaves. Even pets!"

Blair cleared his throat irritably. "So I gather you

asked us here to exchange insults?" he snapped. "If so, I have to wonder why you didn't wait for our great guns to speak for us."

"No, no, not at all," Mayta denied. "On the contrary! You know of our tradition of exchanging . . . pleasantries before battle, and I'd also like to compliment you on all you've achieved so far!" He smiled at Blas. "And you! Your skillful chase through the mountains had me quite convinced your entire army was on my heels." He frowned, but his expression quickly brightened again. "I confess, based on your uncanny deception, accounts of your un-natural prowess in battle, and that you utterly destroyed General Allegria's entire division of Blood Drinkers with the meager force I now know you had, I believed you *must* be a demon." He smiled even more broadly. "I'm so glad that's not the case."

Blas looked at Allegria and conjured an evil grin that displayed sharp canines to best effect. "*Your* Blood Drink-ers? How nice. I wonder why you weren't with 'em when they got *their* 'grace'?" She faced Mayta. "But I don't get how, just because you caan hear me, I ain't a demon. Your dopey, cracked-up religion says so? Thaat's a laugh." Her grin turned predatory. "I *gaar-aan-tee* your faith's gonna take a beatin' under the hell we throw at you!" She laughed. "An' you won't be *able* to hear me then, 'cause your ears'll be blown out!"

Mayta's smile only broadened. "*Que detalle!*"

Blair sighed. "Enough of this. You asked for this meet-ing, General Mayta," he reminded, "and it's just as well, since I've been empowered to offer honorable and gener-ous terms under which any commander in your isolated position would have to consider surrendering his army and the city he defends. Your situation is hopeless; you're outnumbered, cut off from supply by land and sea, utterly at the mercy of bombardment by air and our artillery placed advantageously on the heights. If you force us to reduce the city, we can't possibly discriminate between your troops and the civilian population. The effusion of their blood will be entirely on your hands. In the name of humanity, I beg you to yield."

Mayta glanced down as if considering the offer, but when he looked back at Blair, his smile was gone—as was all pretense at geniality, however bizarre. "I did ask you here," he agreed, "though I'm not as anxious as you to avoid effusion of blood." He shook his head sadly. "You really don't understand the One God and his requirements at all. Let me speak plainly: blood and suffering are the price of grace. They're the *toll* for salvation and paradise! All who suffer in God's name, or bring the suffering of heretics in His holy cause, will join Him in His glorious realm below! What possible inducement could you offer me to surrender *that*? Something else you might consider: I'm not General Nerino. You fooled me once and it won't happen again. Also, unlike the unfortunate Nerino, I won't be surprised by your new and wondrous weapons. I've seen them, appreciate them, and can respond with certain . . . curiosities of my own. Additionally, in spite of your amazing flying machines and superior communications, I probably have a stronger grasp of the situation than you—here and elsewhere. I'm *not* outnumbered, I have sufficient supplies to last a great while, and there are no civilians, as you imagine the term, in El Corazon. All who were are now part of my army, and every man, woman, even the smallest child able to bear arms, is anxious to crush the heretic invaders." He glanced at Blas. "And their Godless . . . familiars."

"So, I'll make *you* this offer," he said with a shrug. "Go away while you can. Run away. We'll pursue, of course, and one day—one generation, perhaps—we'll run you to ground and destroy you. It's preordained." He motioned to General Allegria. "*We'd* prefer that you stay, of course, so we may have our battle. I've yearned for it all my life and nothing pleases God like the effusion of *heretic* blood!"

The sun had set and it was darkening quickly as Blair and Blas rode back toward the safety of their dragoons. Blas was actually surprised Allegria didn't send his Lancers after them, regardless. He had little to lose besides a few horse soldiers that would be of small use in the fight to come. "What a daamn waste o' time," she simmered, then shook herself like she felt fleas or lice in her pelt. "An' now, after just bein' around 'em, I waant a baath!"

"Why, Major Blas!" Blair mocked jokingly, "I know for a fact you bathed just two days ago, when we crossed that stream to the south!"

Blas chuckled, letting some of her tension flow away. "Yeah. Gettin' downright spoiled." She paused. "But whaat the hell did we learn?"

Blair's smile disappeared. She could hear it in his voice. "We learned that, unlike Nerino, Mayta isn't only slavishly loyal to Don Hernan, he's also a believer who doesn't care how many die. That . . . will be a problem. The most important thing we confirmed, however, is that he's smart." He waved a hand in the gloom. "I'm not talking about his blatant attempt to anger us, to make us do something rash—like launch our attack before Eleventh Corps arrives."

Eleventh Corps was only one of the missing pieces, still approaching from the southeast, but this time they *had* time to gather them all together. *Hopefully, we'll do it right,* Blas thought.

"I doubt he even thought it would work," Blair added.

It aalmost did, on me, Blas realized a little guiltily, *but Blair's right. It was pretty obvious. Oh, well. Who cares? I'm already maad.*

"And it may've actually backfired," Blair speculated thoughtfully. "At least with that bastard pup of Don Hernan's. If he retains a field command, it might be useful to discover his position in Mayta's defense. As for Mayta himself, we already suspected he was no fool, based on how he handled our respective commands and prepared for us here. But now we've met him. . . . Blast it, I'm convinced he really thinks he'll beat us. General Shinya and High Admiral Jenks need to know that, and they must discover why. In the meantime, we'd best be very careful."

"We learned somethin' else," Blas added, her mood already submerging beneath the lake of blood she knew would come, as she contemplated the implications of something else Mayta said. *How will the Vengadores—how will*

Sister Audry—*react to fighting civilians, even younglings, when it haappens*? "I think . . ." She paused. "I think we're gonna haafta kill 'em all."

Blair looked sharply at her. He couldn't see what she was blinking, of course, but her tone unsettled him a great deal.

/////// USS Fitzhugh Gray (CL-1)
At the mouth of the Zambezi River
Grik Africa
January 14, 1945

Captain Matthew Reddy, High Chief of the American Navy (and Marine) Clan, and Commander in Chief of All Allied Forces (CINCAF), collapsed exhausted on a chair in the wardroom of USS *Fitzhugh Gray* (CL-1), the first all-steel light cruiser and currently most powerful warship in the Allied fleets. Hopefully, the captured League superdreadnaught USS *Savoie* would usurp that status when her repairs were complete, a crew worked up, and her fire-control issues sorted out, but that could take a while. There'd soon be two more four-stacker destroyers as well, joining USS *James Ellis* (DD-21) and Matt's two surviving DDs from another world, USS *Walker* (DD-163) and USS *Mahan* (DD-102). Other "modern" warships were under construction at Baalkpan, the capital of the Grand Alliance, as well as Maa-ni-la, where more DDs and another (hopefully improved) Gray Class cruiser were rising. The Empire of the New Britain Isles was finishing their first steel-hulled warships, and even the Republic of Real People was making powerful "protected cruisers," as they called them.

The size of their guns and weight of armor made the Repub ships pretty impressive—on paper—but Matt was skeptical about the composite wood-and-steel design they'd adopted. He figured they'd be pretty rugged, since Grik BBs relied on armored wooden casemates and had become almost invulnerable to anything but torpedoes. Repeated close range doses of 4" and bigger armor-piercing shells could do them in eventually, and heavier, AP bombs were already available, but only the big, four-engine, PB-5D Clipper flying boats could carry them. They desperately needed better light bombers than the little Nancy floatplanes. But Matt's biggest concern about the Repub ships was that they might be just as slow as Grik BBs, and just as hard for damage-control parties to keep in action.

Still, for now, the bulk of the Allied fleets here and in the East were wooden-hulled sailing steamers, reminiscent of the mid-nineteenth century on the world he came from. They'd been a significant accomplishment, but were now outclassed even by the Grik. The Allies' greatest advantage at sea was its five aircraft carriers, but they were made of wood as well, and were huge, slow targets. The first had been *Salissa*, or *Big Sal*, originally an immense Lemurian seagoing Home. The rest were purpose built, getting progressively smaller and better, but they could still be amazingly vulnerable. The League of Tripoli—from a different 1939 than Matt remembered—had combined the modern warships, planes, and troops of a fascist France, Spain, Italy, and Germany to conquer British Egypt and the Suez Canal on that other world, and would make mincemeat of the Allies when they almost inevitably clashed. Likely the only reason they weren't already—openly—at war was because the League was still consolidating its hold on the Mediterranean. And the Suez Canal didn't exist here.

Matt rested his elbows on the green-topped table and rubbed his face with his hands. *Lord,* he thought. *We're scrambling to build a real navy as fast as we can, for a war we're not even in yet, while already fighting two wars that're bleeding us dry! And according to Walbert Fiedler, no matter what we do, it'll never be enough to match the League.* He took a breath. *First things first. For now, we have to focus on the Grik and Doms.*

Juan Marcos, self-appointed chief steward to the CIN-CAF, stumped into the compartment carrying a tray burdened with a coffeepot and several cups. He'd lost a leg fighting the Doms and walked on a wooden peg with a rolling, jerky gait. Somehow, awkward as he looked, the little Filipino never dropped such loads even in the roughest seas. "*Real* coffee, Cap-tan!" Juan proclaimed, setting a cup on the table and filling it.

Commander Toru Miyata, *Gray*'s CO, followed Juan in. "I know I'm early," Miyata apologized. "If you'd like more time alone before our visitors arrive, I understand."

Matt straightened, blinking tired eyes. Trying to coordinate the logistical nightmare of supplying, expanding, and protecting the Allied toehold in Grik Africa had taken a heavy toll and he hadn't been sleeping. "Of course not," he said. "Please be seated. This is your ship, after all."

Miyata smiled and sat beside him, accepting a cup, but remained rigidly erect. "No, Captain Reddy," he said quietly. "This ship—and I—are *yours*. It's my honor to command her and serve you."

Matt blinked discomfort in the Lemurian way. "Well, glad to hear it," he said awkwardly, genuinely appreciative but always uncomfortable with statements like that.

"The rest'll be here soon, anyway," Juan reminded, glancing at an Imperial watch he hauled from his pocket. He gestured at the pot. "I only brought a little real coffee aboard. Can't get those lazy Shee-ree on Madagascar to collect it while they're busy hunting all those stranded Grik. Got their priorities all mixed up." He ended with a grin, and Matt snorted. A large force of Grik had been sent to Madagascar to open a second front against the Allies, but couldn't be supplied across the Go Away Strait and were eventually abandoned. After being hunted by Grik for maybe thousands of years, the Shee-ree had gleefully turned the tables. "Drink up," Juan urged. "I don't have enough for everyone!"

Matt managed a real laugh. "You heard him, Toru. Command hath its privileges." He sobered. "Not very damn many. Certainly not enough to balance the weight of responsibility a *good* commander bears." He grinned and shrugged. "So let's not let this one slip by." He took a big gulp of the coffee he needed so badly.

Miyata allowed his small smile to broaden. "If you insist. If our guests never know there was real coffee here, they won't be disappointed when it's gone."

"Do I smell *coffee*?" a voice demanded in the passageway, and Matt rolled his eyes theatrically as General Pete Alden entered, followed by Admiral Keje-Fris-Ar and General Muln Rolak. Alden had been a wayward, wounded sergeant from USS *Houston*'s Marine contingent that *Walker* took aboard at Surabaya before coming to this world. Now he commanded all the land forces in this theater except for those of the Republic. Keje was one of the broadest Lemurians Matt knew, without being fat. Combined with rust-brown fur, his shape made him look more like a bear than a 'Cat. Still CINCWEST, and therefore Matt's deputy in the theater, Keje was also High Chief of USNRS (United States Naval Reserve Ship) *Salissa*, and Matt's oldest and closest Lemurian friend.

Rolak was a gray-furred, grizzled old 'Cat, originally Lord Protector of Aryaal. He was one of only a few Lemurians in the First Fleet AEF to lead his people in combat, on a *much* smaller scale, before the current war. His rough, scarred appearance contrasted with an urbane, thoughtful nature. He commanded I Corps and was Alden's second in command. Under Juan's disapproving stare, Matt poured coffee for them. Rolak grinned, blinking gratitude. One of the first converts to the ersatz coffee they'd subsisted on so long, he already craved the "new" stuff as fervently as anyone.

"That's it," Matt proclaimed mournfully, setting the pot on the tray. "Better open the portholes, Juan, to let the smell out. It'll be too hot to survive in here before long, anyway," he added glumly.

Juan motioned for one of *Gray*'s 'Cat stewards to help him, and they quickly ventilated the compartment. It was still cool outside, with the sun only now rising above the sea to the east, but it was summer here and would quickly get very hot indeed. Colonel Ben Mallory, in charge of the Army and Naval Air Corps, and Commander Steve "Sparks" Riggs, the Minister of Electrical Contrivances out from Baalkpan, arrived next. Riggs had brought a new level-crosslevel for *Savoie*, but was still waiting for the fire-control apparatus they'd cobbled up. When it came, he'd go back to Grik City on the north coast of Madagascar, where the big battleship lay at anchor, and help sort out all her electrical issues. After that . . . He was sick of riding out the war, safe in Baalkpan. Chairman Letts insisted he get his ass home as soon as he could, but Riggs begged Matt almost every day to put him to work out here. He and Ben accepted iced tea from Juan and sat sipping from their glasses, which were already condensing moisture in the humid air.

Last to come in were Colonel Chack-Sab-At and Chief Gunner's Mate Dennis Silva, escorting three humans: two former Leaguers and one Japanese. Chack was a brindled 'Cat, wearing the camo combat smock and blue kilt of a Marine. He'd started the war as a naive youngling, but now led the 1st Amalgamated Raiders or "Chack's Brigade," the most combat-hardened force in the western theater of war. Silva was a blond-haired and -bearded man-monster, born to war, and even if he seemed less psychologically affected by unrelenting combat, it had taken a physical toll. Most notable of his countless injuries was a ruined left eye, covered by a clean new black patch.

The Leaguers were off the German type XIB submarine, *U-112*, moored between *Gray* and *Walker* in the Zambezi River fan. Both men were bearded as well, dressed in dingy khakis. And they smelled. Everybody got pretty gamey at this latitude, and the foamy lather Lemurians secreted could get downright weird. Despite their long association, human odors probably surprised 'Cats just as much on occasion. And no matter how clean they got their clothes and bodies, the smells permeated the ships themselves and always lingered. The Germans brought something different; not new to anyone who'd ever visited or served aboard the lost *S-19*, but distinctly unique to submarines.

The redheaded Oberleuitnant Kurt Hoffman was the U-boat's skipper. Oberleuitnant Walbert Fiedler was dark blond and, ironically, not even a submariner. He was a pilot. More interesting still, he was known to Silva, Chack, and Matt. He'd been the first good source of information they had about the League, in fact, and they'd hoped he'd remain among them and slip them more intelligence when he could. Circumstances hadn't permitted that, but he was still their "expert."

The Japanese officer, Hideki Muriname, was another matter. He was thin and young but already balding, and wore small, round spectacles. Formerly General of the Sky for Hisashi Kurokawa, he, like Toru Miyata, had come to this world in *Amagi*. Instead of being a navigator, however, he'd been part of the ship's aviation division, flying a Type 95 floatplane. The more important difference was that he'd stayed with Kurokawa and served him to the last, developing fighters and light bombers, as well as the ubiquitous dirigibles the Grik never seemed to run out of. He'd come over with a handful of bombers and a couple fighters during the last Battle of the Zambezi, even as his XO tried to destroy him with the few fighters he took to the Grik. It had been a crazy mess. He swore he hated Kurokawa and the Grik, and would've switched sides before if he could.

The thing was, only a few people knew the "old" Muriname. Matt's pregnant wife, Minister of Medicine and Surgeon Commander Sandra Tucker Reddy; her companion/steward/bodyguard Diania; and Silva's pal, Gunnery Sergeant Arnold Horn, formerly of the 4th Marines, remembered him as their captor while they'd been in Kurokawa's hands. There was also Commander Miyata himself. He'd taken his chance to bolt Kurokawa long ago and served the Republic, then the United Homes, ever since. He hadn't known Muriname well, but was the only pre-Squall character witness. None of the Japanese they'd captured at Zanzibar were present, and their reliability must remain in question as well, for a while.

Sandra had told Matt what she thought of Muriname, and Horn and Diania had made their reports. Now they'd hear from Miyata and from Fiedler, who'd met him as a fellow aviator when he was on Zanzibar. Hopefully Matt could decide what to do with him and his flyers—two of which were Grik!—as well as sort out a number of other things they all had to worry about.

"Let's start with you, Lieutenant Muriname," Matt said, leveling his gaze at the Japanese officer. There was no way in hell he'd address him as General of the Sky, but he'd been a lieutenant before his leap in rank and that would suffice. "I appreciate the assistance you rendered during the last action and know you lost people, but it could be argued you only helped after the outcome was decided and you left the Grik to save your ass." He shrugged. "I'm not so sure about that, but I have to consider it. What do you say?"

Muriname adjusted his spectacles and frowned. "I can understand how that misconception might flourish," he conceded, "but in my defense, I'll cite what you just recounted: pilots loyal to my former executive officer, Lieutenant Mitsuo Ando, attacked and destroyed some of my planes while practically ignoring yours. If Ando survived, he's now most likely First General Esshk's new General of the Sky." He paused. "I must add that Ando's not a bad man. He's fiercely loyal and quite industrious, as a matter of fact, which may prove problematic. He did *not* tell Esshk I intended to defect and only attacked me when I helped you against his new lord." He looked down. "In a sense, he didn't turn on me so much as I failed *him*, by releasing him from his obligation to me. Without that, he considered himself honor-bound by his commitment to Esshk, through Kurokawa." He closed his eyes. "That madman continues to destroy the lives of *Amagi*'s crew, even after death."

He looked back at Matt. "Neither I nor any of my surviving aircrews feel the slightest urge to serve Esshk. We want to serve *you*, an honorable lord, and the clan you lead." He glanced at Fiedler. "As the Oberleuitnant might attest, by the time we met, my loyalty to Kurokawa had already been stretched to the breaking point." He straightened. "And even your wife must remember that I did my best to protect her and her companions from the worst of Kurokawa's madness."

Matt steepled his hands in front of his face, fixing green eyes on Muriname. "Captain Miyata?" he asked aside. Miyata shifted and cleared his throat, distinctly uncomfortable. He and Muriname had been equals in *Amagi*. Now he sat in judgement of the other man aboard a powerful ship he commanded for Muriname's former enemies. He sighed.

"Captain Reddy, as I've told you, I never knew this man well. I *saw* him, but we were both new to *Amagi* and I can't remember if we ever actually spoke." Miyata reached absently for his coffee cup but let it lie. "And honestly, I can't say for certain what I would've done if Kurokawa hadn't sent me to the Republic on what he must've thought was a suicide mission. I *hope* I would've found a way to escape and join you, and become what I am, but who knows if the opportunity would've ever come? Kurokawa might've eventually found some purpose that would've corrupted me as thoroughly as *some* of his other people." He pointedly didn't look at Muriname when he said that. "The only real difference between this man and myself could very well be that I was considered expendable at the time, and he wasn't."

"I suppose that's possible," Matt conceded, still looking at Muriname, "but we're defined by our actions, regardless of the circumstances. I actually believe most of what you said, and Fiedler corroborates your disaffection with Kurokawa. But you were pretty industrious yourself, designing zeps and planes that killed a lot of our people." He shrugged. "I get that. It was your talent, and the reason you weren't just thrown away like Captain Miyata. Considering the attrition among *Amagi*'s original crew, it's probably the only reason you're alive."

His eyes turned icy. "But don't you *dare* throw 'I helped your wife' at me! I'm just as sure as she is that you had personal, ulterior motives. And if you wanted out from under Kurokawa so bad, I'm sure his General of the Sky could've found some way to skip. Bringing out the hostages in a ship or plane before we had to come get them would've added credibility to your story and saved a lot of lives." He paused and took a breath. "To be honest, though, in spite of how my wife feels about you personally—that you're a slimy creep—she also thinks you had a rough time and really do want to redeem your honor. I left it up to her whether to use you or hang you, and you can thank your lucky stars she dumped it back on me."

He snorted. "On the other hand, I'm probably less objective and even more inclined to hang you than she was, so I passed the buck to Colonel Mallory." He gestured at

Ben, who nodded gravely back. "*He* wants you. You and your people won't fly for us, not for a while anyway, but you'll give him any assistance you can think of and answer every question he asks about your planes and the ones Ando wound up with. You'll draw pictures, re-create plans we didn't capture at Zanzibar, and tell him everything you think the Grik might know or Ando might tell them about. . . ." He shrugged. "Anything. Do I make myself clear?" His voice hardened. "You have *one* chance, Muriname. Screw it up, and I'll put the rope around your neck myself."

Muriname nodded. "I understand. And thank you."

Matt flicked his eyes at Silva and the big man grinned, stepping to the table from where he'd been leaning against the aft bulkhead with Juan, massive arms crossed over his chest. "C'mon, Jap," Silva said, not unkindly. "Let's leave the grown-ups to their business." He waved at Fiedler, whom he'd befriended at Grik City, and escorted Muriname from the compartment.

"I hope that was right," Matt murmured.

"Sure it was," Ben said. "I'll get to squeeze him, at the very least. He obviously knows his planes. His fighters aren't as good as ours, but their engines ain't bad. Not only did we capture a lot of the engines themselves, we got a lot of the machinery to make 'em. Still want to send all that stuff to Madras? They might use it in the Republic."

Steve Riggs coughed. "From what I've heard, the Repubs already have water-cooled engines as good as our stacked radials, from a power-to-weight standpoint, and they're working on better. With their production gearing up, we might just distract them. I say Madras."

Matt shrugged. "Up to you guys. What about the bombers?"

When it came to something that could carry a torpedo or the new, bigger bombs, all the Allies had were Clippers. They made decent high-altitude heavy bombers, but were way too big and slow to use in a torpedo attack. Even the Grik could shoot them down. After the Battle of Mahe, when Kurokawa's—and Muriname's—little bombers cost them so dearly, they'd started a crash program to come up with something, but they were flailing.

"They're okay," Ben granted, "but they're slow. And the best they can carry is that dinky short-range fish they used against us. Those were bad news, and a big surprise, but against anything with an armor belt"—he was clearly thinking about the League—"I'd rather have something that can carry more weight. Maybe even one of our Mark Sixes." An example of such a thing existed. A wrecked Bristol Beaufort from their own world (or one much like it) had been found in a Shee-ree village by the West Mangoro River on Madagascar. 'Cats had been flown down in Fiedler's old Ju-52, taken it apart, and ferried the pieces back to Grik City, where they were loaded in empty supply ships headed back for Baalkpan. The wood-and-fabric construction was familiar to them, but the engines and variable pitch props, as well as the overall design, would be very helpful. Clearly, Ben was dreaming of something like a Beaufort: big and powerful enough to carry a two-thousand-pound weapon and small enough to fly off a carrier. "Maybe Muriname can help us get our kinks straightened out."

"Maybe. Squeeze him hard," Matt stressed.

"You bet. My only question now is, Do we keep him here or send him to Baalkpan?"

Matt waved a hand. "Up to you."

"Yes, sir. Baalkpan, I think."

*M*att bit his lower lip, swirled the cold dregs of coffee in his cup, then turned to Oberleuitnant Kurt Hoffman. "I trust Fiedler. I'd like to say his word's good enough for me, but the stakes are too damn high. I *want* to trust you, and joining our cause with a submarine's a pretty impressive gesture of support—no matter how desperate you might've been."

Fiedler had described the circumstances that brought them *U-112*. The French Capitaine de Fregate Victor Gravois—a stone-cold, lying bastard in Matt's view—had been the head of French Naval Intelligence in matters concerning the Grand Alliance. He'd sent Fiedler across from *Leopardo* (*Dumped him,* Matt translated) when the big Italian destroyer left the Indian Ocean. Fiedler carried orders for *U-112* to linger and report on developments Gravois set in motion, specifically the outcome of the confrontation between Matt Reddy's First Fleet and Hisashi Kurokawa on Zanzibar. He'd obviously hoped they'd shred each other like fighting cocks. He'd very nearly been right.

Hoffman had already suspected *U-112* was being abandoned, however. His sub couldn't get home on its own, there'd been no provisions for replenishment, and their only base in the region was lost. With tensions between the League and Grand Alliance so high, only a strong force could come to their aid—sparking the very war Gravois's strategy was designed to delay. Hoffman and Fiedler both determined that *U-112* and its crew had been sacrificed, just like *Savoie*, to Gravois's ambition. But unlike the bulk of *Savoie*'s French crew, carried away in *Leopardo*, no effort would be made to rescue them. They were only Germans, after all, not numerous or powerful enough within the League to rate full membership in the ruling Triumvirate.

U-112's entire crew decided as far back as that that they'd probably have to seek asylum with the Allies. But Fiedler was adamant that Captain Reddy wouldn't grant it if they refused to fully cooperate. Even neutrality wasn't an option, and Fiedler had finally resigned himself to that as well. Initially reluctant to share information that might hurt the German contingent in the League, he was committed to opposing anyone, German or not, who'd defend what the League was becoming. Especially after it finalized an alliance with the Holy Dominion.

U-112 dutifully reported periscope observations that the Battle of Zanzibar had commenced and was apparently just as bloody as Gravois hoped, and then abruptly went silent. She hadn't made a peep since then, but she'd listened, and if anybody cared to wonder about them, they'd think the big German submarine was sunk by the Allies or one of the monstrous fishes cruising the sea on this terrible world. Possibly just as important, it might be a while before the League discovered that First Fleet had not only beaten Kurokawa and already landed in Grik Africa, but they'd also taken *Savoie* as a prize.

Matt chuckled lightly. "And to think how many times we tried to sink you, all while you were just trying to wave at us . . ."

"I assure you, Herr Kapitan," Hoffman interjected wryly, "it was not so amusing from our perspective. More than once, you nearly *did* sink us."

Matt nodded. "That would've been tough. Anyway, I'm sorry this is the first chance I've had to talk with you. I've been pretty busy at Tassanna's Toehold—the beachhead we established upriver—these past few weeks." His expression turned stony. "It's pure hell up there: trench warfare, nose to nose—exactly what we *didn't* want to get bogged down in." He shook his head, focusing back on Hoffman. "I haven't had a chance to tour your boat either, so why don't you give me a rundown on her condition and the state of your crew?"

"Of course, Herr Kapitan." Hoffman made a face. "As I'm sure you might expect, *U-112* is not in prime condition. She's been on station in these waters for almost five months and the crew hadn't been ashore since our last replenishment at Christmas Island, before you found our base. Thank you, by the way, for making a place for them here."

An old Grik fort and small town of sorts had stood at the mouth of the Zambezi. Pulverized by bombs, neither had been rebuilt, but now there was a city of hundreds of tents housing an ever-growing stockpile of war material, new arrivals, troops rotated back from the fighting, and many of the wounded they'd suffered. Officially, it was the Rest and Reorganization Area, but somebody'd started calling it Camp Simy, and it stuck. The whole thing surrounded a big new airstrip named Arracca Field, where hangars and workshops were going up and ramps were under construction down by the water. Soon, Jumbo Fisher's Pat-Squad 22 with its big Clipper flying boats, would move down from the Comoros Islands and double or triple the tempo of their heavy-bomber sorties over Sofesshk. Pertinent to the conversation, however, *U-112*'s crew had been billeted ashore, where they could breathe fresh air, sleep in tents, and feel dry land beneath their feet.

"I appreciate that," Hoffman said sincerely, "and so do my men." Matt nodded. "As to my command, you're familiar with her type?" Hoffman asked.

"Sure," Riggs piped up, then blinked apologetically at Matt in the Lemurian way. Matt motioned for him to continue. "You Krau—I mean, Germans had the same thing on the world we came from, though not many, if I recall."

Hoffman seemed a little taken aback by how informally Matt interacted with his subordinates. *And Courtney Bradford would be fascinated by how casually we all now accept that we come from different, divergent worlds, where history can be just a little changed, or a lot, depending on how far back things veered off track—from* our *perspective,* Matt amended to himself.

"On the other hand, they—and yours—are pretty impressive," Riggs continued. "Bigger than our newest Fleet boats back home." He chuckled grimly and glanced at a porthole, but *U-112* wasn't visible. "Hell, they're bigger than *Walker*. Nearly as big and well-armed as this *cruiser*."

"*Ja*, powerful," Hoffman grudged, "but not considered successful by our navy. Few were made, which makes them more difficult to maintain. And mine"—he also glanced at the porthole—"needs a great deal of maintenance."

"Like what, in addition to diesel, of course?" Riggs asked. They'd made diesel fuel at Baalkpan and Tarakaan for *S-19*, and the ICE houses—internal combustion engine plants—were working on diesels of their own. But there wasn't much fuel, and none was here.

"There's external damage, inflicted by some very large sea creatures"—Hoffman shuddered at a memory they could sympathize with—"as well as . . . more recent damage sustained when a few *vasserbombes* came uncomfortably close." He looked at Matt, almost apologetically. "Otherwise, much has been . . . How do you say?"

"Jury-rigged," Fiedler supplied, and Hoffman gave him an appreciative nod. "*U-112* is operational in the strictest sense of the word, but perhaps not reliably so."

Matt looked at Keje. "How are repairs coming to *Big Sal*?"

"Almost complete," Keje gruffed. "There's daam-age below the waterline thaat *Tarakaan Island* caan't get to, but it will keep for now." *Tarakaan Island* was a self-propelled floating dry dock, but wasn't big enough for something the size of *Big Sal*. Covered with cranes and full of parts, she could perform almost any other work, however.

"Very well," Matt said. "We'll put *U-112* in *Tara*'s repair bay. Do what we can for her. But I want her on her way to Baalkpan as fast as possible. A week at most. We can get her back in dry dock there, where our best people—some ex-submariners themselves—can help get her back in fighting trim." He looked at Fiedler and they shared a nod. "We're going to need her."

"I don't have fuel for a voyage all the way to Borneo," Hoffman protested.

"I know. She'll have to be towed. We'll use a couple of heavy haulers, heading back empty. It'll be a long trip, but save what fuel you have in case the weather turns bad."

"You mean . . . I'll be allowed to remain in command?" Hoffman asked tentatively. Obviously, that'd been much on his mind.

"Sure. For now, at least. You know your boat better than anyone, and can start teaching the prize crew how to operate her."

"Prize crew?" Hoffman asked dubiously. "You'll take my people from me?"

"Only some," Matt assured. They were down to it at last. "Look, like I said, I *want* to trust you, but to earn that trust and keep your boat, there's a few things you have to get used to. First, I'm going to have to keep my eye on you for a while, and I'll do that through the people with you." His expression hardened. "And almost all of them'll be 'Cats." He nodded at Keje, Rolak, Chack, then Juan's assistant. "I don't know about you, but Gravois—and the League in general—considers Lemurians 'ape folk,' and less than human. Well, they aren't human, but they're just as much people as anybody. Is that clear? This is your chance to get used to the idea, because where you're going, humans of all sorts are only about ten percent of the population. You'll be in a distinct minority, and, what's more, you come from a power that's done us a lot of harm. You might have to take—and roll with—some pretty hard feelings. If you make it through that, Chairman Letts'll have a better idea what you're made of, and my decision to let you keep your boat'll be based on his recommendation." He paused. "And chances are, you'll lose more of your old crew at Baalkpan because pig-boat sailors, their personal hygiene aside"—he grinned to soften the blow—"generally have more technical knowledge than other sailors. They have to." He gestured to Steve Riggs to continue.

"I've been ashore talking with them, and whether you know it or not, a lot of your guys, though admirably loyal to you, don't *want* back in your boat. Can you blame them? So we're sending some down to the Republic shipyards at Songze, maybe others in the west. They won't be prisoners," he hastened to add, "and I expect they'll be happy as clams. Lots of Repubs, human and 'Cat, speak German. Especially in the shipyards. Most of the engineering instructors and advanced tech they're working with came with a German ship that showed up in the last war."

"SMS *Amerika*," Fiedler supplied quietly. "Long story."

"And some'll stay at Baalkpan," Matt repeated, "be-

cause we need their expertise. I expect our snoops'll run
'em through the wringer," he confessed. "Most of the
Leaguers we took at Zanzibar weren't very cooperative.
But your people won't be mistreated—you have my word.
What all this boils down to, though, is that you can stay at
Baalkpan too, if you want, as an advisor to Chairman Letts
and Henry Stokes. That's what Fiedler plans to do. We can
use you there, and you won't have to directly fight your
countrymen. Think about it." Matt's eyes narrowed. "But
to keep your boat, you'll join our cause *and* the American
Navy Clan. That's the deal. What's more, you'll probably
have to take her out against the League someday, with a
crew that's mostly 'Cat. Can you handle that?"

"I . . . suppose I'll have to see," Hoffman promised
vaguely.

"Good enough for now." Matt looked at the others.
"So, the reason I wanted to get all this out of the way first,
even while our most pressing concern lies up that nasty
damn river to the west, is that we needed to get the sub
sorted out, and . . ." He paused and frowned at Pete
Alden. "It's possible you might lose some of your naval
support right when you need it most."

"Say *what*?" Pete snapped, then recovered himself. "Sir."

Chack and Rolak leaned forward, but Ben only nodded.
He was one of very few who'd known from the start. Keje
had now been told, as had "Spanky" McFarlane, Safir
Maraan, and Courtney Bradford. Possibly a dozen others
knew by now, including Letts, Stokes, and Riggs, of
course, as well as Kaiser Nig-Taak of the Republic of Real
People, and High Admiral Harvey Jenks and Governor-
Empress Rebecca Anne McDonald of the Empire of the
New Britain Isles. Each might've confided in a very few
others. But besides the obvious—that the League was now
allied to the Holy Dominion—information, largely supplied by Fiedler, regarding what military resources the
League could bring to such an alliance had been kept
mum. It was believed if news like that got out, it might
hammer morale. But with so many Leaguers now in custody, the facts would spill sooner or later, and might even
get exaggerated. Better to dish out the straight dope than
have it trickle out.

"We knew all along the League had a lot of power behind it," Matt temporized. "It consisted of most of a task force meant for a big job, after all. What we never dreamed was that it came here at anchor, in the port of Tripoli, and it brought a good-size chunk of the city itself along with it." He nodded at Fiedler to continue, and the man cleared his throat.

"It was . . . horrible. Everything—the ships, portions of the Tripoli *we* knew, the people ashore, thousands and thousands of tons of military equipment staged for our effort against the Englanders—just . . . fell out of the storm that swept across us. Few of the ships suffered significant damage, though a couple of them were grounded." He raised an eyebrow. "And by that I mean they landed *on*shore and were fit only for scrap." He rubbed his brow. "Worst of all was the city, of course, along with all its people, docks, warehouses, cranes . . ." He shuddered. "It all just crashed down atop what was apparently *another* city, already there, full of humans"—he nodded at the 'Cats—"some . . . different Lemurians, and other, ah, beings." He took a gulp of tea, clearly making an effort to push the nightmarish images from his mind.

"Besides the trauma of our arrival, on both sides—the carnage was indescribable—the indigenous folk were not glad to see us. They had a relatively robust civilization with various states surrounding the Mediterranean, all flavored by our own past in interesting ways." His lips twisted. "It never even occurred to our leaders to cooperate with them, as you have with the people here. Our first impulse was to conquer and subjugate. Thanks to the relatively primitive nature of the societies we encountered and the bounty of modern war material on our ships and salvaged ashore, conquest was brutally simple," he said bitterly, "though it's been tedious and time consuming. The problem from your—*our*—perspective is that pacification is nearly complete. The guiding force behind the League and its fascist ideology is conquest, and though even the Triumvirate must know it can never rule the entire world, certainly not for generations, the only thing that's held it together—much like the Grik Empire you now fight—is cooperation and expansion against external adversaries."

He looked at Matt and his eyes strayed to the others. "There are tribes of Grik in many places, as you've seen yourselves, though none known are as numerous and powerful as the ones infesting this continent."

"All the way past India, till we pushed 'em back," Pete growled.

"Indeed," Fiedler agreed, "and the League considered them a threat. Natural barriers and perhaps the climate are probably the only reasons these Grik and the League were not already in direct contact and conflict. Helping focus the Grik on you was part of Gravois's mission. The Dominion," he continued, "with its vast population and difficult terrain, was considered a threat for the future, as was the Empire of the New Britain Isles, the NUS in North America, and several others you do not know." He snorted ironically. "The Republic, much like the cultures in the Mediterranean in many ways, was considered a plum to be plucked!" Fiedler shook his head. "But you, Captain Reddy, gathered many of the most potent future threats and made them more pressing. Gravois's attempts to thwart you using Kurokawa and the Grik have weakened you and cost many lives, but"—he waved around at the new cruiser they were in—"they also made you more capable, not less. That's what drove the League to join with the vile Dominion, to seal the Pass of Fire and your access to the Atlantic from the west. Other efforts are underway to choke you out from around the cape of Africa, but the pass is deemed most critical. That's why they'll begin sending warships there. *Leopardo* is there already."

"Well, what *can* they send?" Pete Alden demanded.

Fiedler looked at him. "Little, at present," he confessed, "and therein lies some hope. Powerful as it is, much of the League's fleet is best suited to operations in the Med, not the World Ocean, and the maintenance of many long-range ships has been neglected. That oversight will be remedied, but it will take time. And they'll never send *all* they have against you, because they must maintain their grip at home. But"—he shrugged and spread his hands—"in six months, perhaps a bit more, you can expect the Dominion to have the aid of . . ." He considered.

"Perhaps three to five battleships, old and new, and at least that many light and heavy cruisers."

"Merciful Maker," Rolak murmured.

"Destroyers might be your greatest, earliest concern," Fiedler continued relentlessly, "because most of them, from all the navies in the League, were designed for the open ocean. They might send as many as twenty of those." Fiedler actually smiled at Pete's horrified expression. "With proper modifications, they *could* send more capital ships," he prodded lightly, but held up a hand. "I've neglected to point out your most important advantage, however." He looked back at Matt. "Gravois, in particular, and through him the Triumvirate, has always woefully underestimated *you*. I did myself," he confessed. "And paranoid as the Triumvirate is, that paranoia goes two ways. They fear the threat you pose, but will be reluctant to risk more of their irreplaceable naval might than they absolutely must. Unlike you, they only recently began preparing facilities to build more, and that's one reason it'll take so long to refurbish what they already have. Finally, and somewhat ironically, their arrogance will reinforce their caution. They won't think it will take that much to destroy you, so you might cut my estimate in half. And they'll likely keep their most modern Italian battleships to defend themselves. If you can get her operational, *Savoie* might even be a match for one of the more powerful ships they do send."

"*One* of," Pete groused.

Fiedler pursed his lips. "You'll have to make do." He looked back at Matt. "Contrary to what you may think, *Savoie wasn't* expendable. Not like *U-112*, which, as Oberleuitnant Hoffman pointed out, was difficult to maintain and filled with Germans. *Savoie* was the only long-range battleship fit for the mission she was given at the time, and Gravois squandered her for his own purposes. Given the circumstances, he may have thought he had little choice, and she was a small price to pay for destroying you, but she could be a very potent addition to whatever battle line you scrape together. Particularly if you can keep her a secret."

Matt frowned, doubting that. The League had left spies in the Republic, and even if most had been sniffed out, some must remain. And it was obvious the Doms had spies almost everywhere. If the Doms and League were in cahoots . . .

"What about air power?" Ben asked. "How bad will they outclass us there?"

Fiedler looked thoughtful. "You know about the Macchi-Messerschmitts and there are about sixty of those, all told. If they can prepare airfields and get them ashore, they'll be a problem. There are also dive bombers called Stuka. You're familiar with those? A few Italian torpedo bombers are available as well, but they've been used mainly as light bombers and there's been no torpedo training since they arrived. Again, perhaps the Triumvirate's arrogance will prevent them from brushing up. Other than that . . . there are several more Ju-52s, like I brought you. Little else."

"What can they carry at sea?" Ben asked.

"Nothing but scout planes on the cruisers and battle-ships, unless they convert a merchantman. Even then, there are no planes specifically designed to operate from a carrier."

"Okay, enough of this." Matt looked at Pete and Ro-lak. "All this means is we have to keep cranking out ships and training crews as fast as we can. Improve our planes and torpedoes . . ." He sighed. "And finish the Grik and take the Pass of Fire from the Doms." He barked a laugh. "Simple." That evoked nervous laughter.

"What's the score ashore?" Matt asked Pete for the benefit of the others.

"We keep scratching and clawing to expand our perim-eter and make room for Sixth Corps as it trickles in. Those pickup corps of Austraalans and volunteers from Baalkpan are still a ways off." XII Corps was composed of half-trained volunteers from Austraal, and XIV Corps was militia out of Baalkpan, Sular, and B'taava. All were armed with rifle muskets, taken out of storage.

"We'll take the Austraalans, but I'm sending the rest back," Matt said. "We need them back in the factories."

Pete nodded. "I guess so, but that'll leave us even more strapped."

"More will come from Austraal, now thaat they get training there and don't haave to go all the way to Baalk-pan for it," Keje consoled.

"In the meantime," Pete continued, "even as we push out, the Grik tighten up. We've got close to seventy thousand troops ashore, but we're up against all the Grik in the world. They've built proper trenches with overhead cover, and stuck more than a hundred thousand just in the first line surrounding us. They've got depth, and we don't have any."

"Not *all* the Grik are in front of us," Rolak reminded calmly. "Reconnaissance tells us maany thousaands are moving south to staand before the Army of the Republic." He blinked amusement. "It seems they're most ad-amaant thaat we not join forces with them."

"And they don't have *that* much depth," Matt corrected grimly. "Just seventy or eighty miles, back to Sofesshk. Hij Geerki's no expert on these new Grik troops, but he's still convinced that if we take their Palace of Vanished Gods, they'll fold. We've taken Grik *prisoners* now! We know they *can* surrender. Let's pray he's right."

"I'm prayin' hard every day," Pete said. "But prayin' won't do us any good by itself. We gotta *get* to Sofesshk first, and that means we have to have the river."

All the fighting in the river had left a myriad of wrecks, particularly stacked up at a narrow place named the Neckbone, which the Grik called the *nakkle* leg. Demolition teams ventured out night and day to blow the wrecks, but progress was slow. Wooden hulls could be blasted apart, their timbers released to sink or float downstream, but armored casemates and large machinery, like engines, were another matter. And there was so much of it, Silva had coined the term Iron Bottom Channel.

"We'll need naval gunfire to cover any push to break through toward Sofesshk," Pete continued, "and we need the navy to keep the Grik BBs from slaughtering us on the other side of the Neckbone." He paused. "Worse, we can't just sit here. As you say, Captain Reddy, we have to get this show on the road. If we wait too long and lose our naval support, we're stuck. And the longer we take, the thicker and harder the Grik defenses get too. Besides, we're all still kind of bunched up, and I can't believe the Grik aren't thinking about that. We control the air, so Grik zeps aren't a problem, and they haven't been able to move their rocket batteries into range. They're too obvious and vulnerable. But sooner or later they'll come up with some way to hammer the hell out of us!" He looked at Rolak. "I know we weren't really ready for this, the whole invasion got rushed and we chucked most of what we were working on to just get here. But we're here now, and we need a goddamn *plan* for what's next!"

Everyone nodded thoughtfully. All had ideas, Matt was sure. He did himself. But even if the overall strategy against the Grik was mostly his, he didn't feel qualified to influence the campaign ashore. He'd tried that before and didn't think he'd done as good a job as Pete and Rolak would. And he trusted them to get it right. *All the same...*

"Don't forget my Raiders," Chack said quietly, speaking for the first time. He'd been uncharacteristically quiet throughout the discussion, but then he didn't seem to talk much at all these days. His brigade was nearly shattered and he'd lost his sister and XO, Risa, coming to the relief of *Santa Catalina* and establishing the first toehold for the AEF to exploit. He'd had a little time with his mate, General Queen Safir Maraan, but her II Corps had rotated back to a reserve position behind the forward trenches. What was left of his Raiders were resting and refitting here. Matt was worried about Chack—everyone was. He'd been changed so much by the war that there seemed almost nothing left of the innocent, engaging, carefree young 'Cat they'd all first come to know.

"Your brigade's still healing and way understrength," Matt said.

"My brigade will never heal completely," Chack replied bleakly, then shook his head. "But thaat's true for us aall, isn't it? And we're not faar understrength. Replacements haave arrived, and maany of those wounded at Zaan-zi-bar haave returned. I'm paar-ticu-laarly glaad to have Major Jin-daal back." Alistair Jindal was an Imperial Marine from the Empire of the New Britain Isles, as were many of the Raiders. They were, in fact, the largest contingent of Impies fighting on this front and were highly motivated to repay the debt they owed the United Homes, largely composed of Lemurians, for all the blood it had shed on their behalf in the East. But Jindal had lost his left arm after Zanzibar and it had been touch and go for him. Chack blinked sadness mixed with relief. "He'll resume his post as my XO and commaander of the Twenty-First." He hurried on. "I'd appreciate it if you'd make Abel Cook's brevet raank of major permaa-nent. His wounds were superficial and he's much better. I'd like to give him official commaand of the First North Borno. The Khona-ashi trust and aad-mire him." He blinked genuine wonder. "I understaand Major I'joorka will live after all, despite his burns, but it'll be some time before he's fit for duty. In aany event, with Major Enrico Gaalay still commaanding the Seventh, the brigade leadership is intaact."

"Thaat's all good news," Rolak said, "and, rest aas-sured, we'll never forget your brigade. But whaat are you suggesting?"

"Only thaat you bear in mind, as you plaan, thaat the First Raider Brigade has proven time and again thaat it's capable of highly destructive, extremely distraacting, in-dependent operations." Chack's ears flicked vaguely in the direction of shore. "It's *not* good at sitting idle on its aass. And neither am I."

Matt nodded slowly, regretfully, his own cockeyed scheme taking firmer shape as another missing piece dropped in place.

CHAPTER 4

////// Forward Grik trench line
South bank of the Zambezi River
Grik Africa
January 20, 1945

W hat will they do next?" the Chooser asked anxiously, stretching his short, plump body and neck as far as he could to peer over the mounded-earth lip of the trench. His segmented, iron-strapped leather helmet made a comic jumble of his normally carefully coiffed crest, and the battle dress of an ordinary New Army soldier—gray leather armor with light iron plates over his vitals—looked stranger on him than his usual morbidly ornamented robes. Second General Ign practically gaped up at him from where he crouched in the trench, his own crest flaring instinctively to a position of disapproval. If the Chooser noticed, he made no sign. "First General Regent Champion Esshk—and the Celestial Mother," he hastily added, "require your observations at once!" The Chooser managed to stand even taller. "As do I," he continued. "After all . . ."

Ign snatched him down and threw him into the disgusting ooze filling the bottom of the position. It hadn't rained in weeks, but the warriors had to relieve themselves somewhere. The Chooser *splapp*ed and sputtered in shock—even as a flurry of heavy bullets struck just opposite from where he'd stood and started a small avalanche of loose dirt flowing down upon him. Still croaking indignantly, he tried to rise, *goosh*ing in the muck, but Ign caught him.

"You *touched* . . . You're *touching* . . ." the Chooser began querulously.

"Forgive me, Lord," Ign said, summoning his most respectful voice, "but I told you." He motioned with his snout at where the bullets hit. "You must be *very* careful here."

"I . . . Indeed," the Chooser agreed, still haughty, but he stayed down. "That might have hit me," he added wonderingly. "So far away? You said the closest enemy line is four hundred paces distant!"

"The closest we *know* of, Lord Chooser," Ign qualified. "They constantly push their trenches closer. You can hear them working at night when things are quieter. But even then, yes. Their garraks load from the back, not the front, and shoot much farther and straighter. Small, spiraling . . . grooves in the barrel spin the bullet, like fletching spins a crossbow bolt. Very dangerous."

"Our garraks can't do that?"

"No, Lord Chooser."

The Grik had painstakingly geared up to copy the best enemy weapons they'd captured on Ceylon, but no other samples had made it back to the heart of Grik empire and industry since. Like always, the enemy continually improved what they had, in small ways or great.

"Then . . . I will see what I can do," the Chooser promised, and Ign actually thought he might. The Chooser had taken increasing responsibility for selecting the best ideas to improve the lethality of their weapons. Since the primary purpose of his order—choosing which hatchlings went to the cookpots and which were allowed to live, or even be elevated—was currently suspended, it seemed an appropriate task. He'd been First General Esshk's closest advisor and confidante, but that relationship seemed strained of late. Ign suspected the Chooser had gotten too close to the Celestial Mother and allowed her tutors to instruct her along more traditional lines than Esshk preferred, telling her too much about what was, and less what Esshk would have her think.

Ign caught the scornful expressions of some of the

warriors nearby, Ker-noll Jash's Slashers, and he glared at them. The Chooser might've been fairly ridiculous, and even partially responsible for the situation they found themselves in, with enemies—*prey*—on their very shore for the first time ever, but it was Esshk who'd designed the battle and the war. Even Ign owned some of the blame. And since he still believed in Esshk and his reforms, he couldn't condone the freethinking in his ranks that condemned the Chooser. Besides, ultimately, it had been Regent Consort Tsalka who started the war and bungled its beginning so badly. Tsalka had suffered the traitor's death and would bear all the blame forever—if Ign could help it.

"What do you believe they'll do next?" the Chooser finally repeated, talking louder as the roar of big guns, 18 pdrs, sent dozens of exploding shells toward the enemy lines. They crackled and rumbled unseen in the distance, but Ign could easily imagine the bursts of smoke, scything fragments of iron, and erupting stalks of earth. Most of that fury would be wasted, he knew, but some wouldn't.

"They'll keep killing us, as we kill them. There's no end to it until we have sufficient forces to swarm them under. When might that be?"

"It depends on your definition of 'sufficient,' Second General. First General Esshk considers your swarm adequate now," the Chooser warned.

"This is no 'swarm'; it's an army," Ign retorted calmly, but inwardly he seethed. "It's all that stands between the enemy and our Celestial Mother and the Palace of Vanished Gods, our holiest, most ancient shrine. No mere swarm can do what it's done, and it mustn't be spent like one. It takes too long to make New Army troops. First General Esshk knows that better than anyone. He made *these*!"

The Chooser's battered crest fluttered, and Ign had to wonder if it was truly Esshk doing the prodding. Then again, Esshk was under tremendous strain. With the Chooser's full agreement, perhaps even urging—Ign wasn't sure—he'd culled the elite, soft Hij of Old Sofesshk, literally feeding them to his troops. That had removed resistance to his leadership and reforms within the principal regency, but word of his ruthlessness would undoubtedly spread to others, giving them pause as he demanded their support. The southern regencies, sparsely populated as they were, had already been lost under the advance of the long-discounted "other hunters" from the Republic of Real People. Now Sofesshk itself was in danger. In the perfect world Esshk's reforms would've made, with all the Gharrichk'k Empire literally as well as figuratively united behind the Celestial Mother, with Esshk behind *her*, time would've been their greatest asset, as warriors swiftly flowed to their aid from across the empire. But only a quick victory would sustain Esshk, the Chooser, *and* Ign now.

"And too many New Army troops are rushed south to reinforce Fifth General Akor," Ign complained, though he'd sent some of them himself. Akor needed a large force indeed, since he was engaged in a campaign of maneuver with the Army of the Republic in fairly open ground. If he dug in, the enemy would just go around him, and he had to stay between them and Sofesshk at all costs. "To attack decisively, I need more warriors, even of the old kind, from the far regencies."

"They're coming," the Chooser assured. "They *are*. The regents may have dragged their claws in the dirt for a time, possibly to weaken us before they commit," he confessed, confirming Ign's suspicions and adding another element to the internal battle Esshk was waging, "but they're on their way. Still, just supporting such movements is difficult. Warriors must be fed as they march, or they'll consume each other to the point of uselessness before they ever arrive. We have little experience maintaining armies that don't advance to feast on prey," he reminded darkly. After a tense silence, the Chooser gestured to the east, changing the subject. "In the meantime, however, how long can the prey remain content to just keep killing us, as you say?"

"For a while yet, I think," Ign snorted. "That's precisely what they came here for. To kill us all."

"But they can't do that just sitting there."

Ign considered. "No, but they gather their forces as well. Such takes longer for them, coming as far as they do. But they're better at maintaining armies, I think. They must be, since they don't feast on *us* and they do keep growing—and never seem to run low on ammunition." His last statement was punctuated by a reply to the Grik artillery, only it seemed to come from hundreds of cannon. They weren't as big; their preferred field pieces—here, at least—were 12 pdrs, but their shells were more reliable and far more lethal. Ign dragged the Chooser down to the bottom of the ditch again, and they remained in the stinking muck for quite a while as shards of iron whistled overhead or tore at screaming bodies.

"Terrible," the Chooser murmured. "It is terrible!"

"And it goes on day after day," Ign shouted back over the din of another blast almost overhead that sprayed iron slightly behind the line. Screams rose from the next trench back. "In all honesty," he continued, "I don't know what they'll do. Their flying machines can't see all our movements—we've grown better at concealment and misdirection—but they see far too much and shatter any force I try to amass against their lines. We, on the other hand, see nothing at all. No army can move on the north side of the river—it is far too rugged—and it *seems* we have them blocked here. But without a view from above I can't say whether *they* mass or not." He was silent a moment as the shells stopped exploding. "Tell First General Esshk I think it will continue like this for a time, but I can't know for certain. I must rely on him—and you—to tell me what the enemy does. With that information, I can counter their moves, but absent significant reinforcements, I can't force them to counter *me*. Do you understand?"

"Yes. I will tell him. And I'll do what I can to enlighten you. There may be a way. . . . Their flying machines are the biggest problem, are they not? And our hunter spies"—he lowered his voice—"our *Dorrighsti* Night Hunters know where they nest. Little can be done about the ships that carry them—as yet—but we may try something against their land nest soon."

"Anything would help," Ign understated, but the Chooser gave a diagonal nod of agreement.

"I must leave you now, but I'll see what I can do."

"Have care," Ign told him when the Chooser began creeping back the way he'd come.

Ker-noll Jash replaced the Chooser at Ign's side. He'd obviously waited for the other to leave. Jash had started as a Senior First of One Hundred, advanced to Ker-noll, or First of One Thousand, and though not yet a general, now commanded the remnant of the first division, or Ten Thousand, that had opposed the Allied landing. Ign considered him a prodigy, amazingly wise beyond his years. Unfortunately, he'd also grown remarkably cynical toward the Chooser and even First General Esshk.

"What will the enemy do indeed?" Jash asked mockingly.

"You'll choke that tone out of your throat before I do it for you," Ign snapped, his large crest rising through the gap in his helmet.

Jash looked down. "It won't happen again," he said, his words, if not his tone, penitent.

Ign studied him. His protégé was worn and battered after weeks of apparently futile, bloody battle. It was understandable if he'd taken a negative attitude. But young as Jash was, he was a respected leader now, looked to for inspiration by more than his own division. He must learn to control what he said and how he acted, or Ign would have to destroy him himself. For some reason, Ign could hardly bear the thought of that, but dared not think how corrosive Jash's example might otherwise be to the entire army. He felt his fury drain away. "It matters," he said softly so others couldn't hear. "You *must* not let it happen again. This army is different from any the Gharrichk'k ever made. It thinks, it feels, and when it starts to feel as you do—that all has been for nothing—I . . . fret that it may stop being an army." His tone lightened. "We approach that which I once promised you: the greatest battle that ever was, a battle that'll be remembered, as will our parts in it. Is that not some comfort? Something to look forward to?"

"Certainly," Jash said. "If we survive all the battles leading to the greater battle we crave."

Ign blinked, unsure if Jash was sincere or still sarcastic. If it was the latter, Ign knew it wasn't directed at him. It also meant Jash might've passed beyond the point where words alone could sway him. Or save him. "Well," he said brusquely, dismissing the thought, "we do have some time, and I don't think that great battle will be upon us for many days. Neither we nor the enemy is ready for it." He looked Jash up and down. "You've been with me here from the start, as have the troops under your command. The time has come to rest them, feed them properly, and re-equip. A moon spent sleeping somewhere other than this reeking pit will do them—and you—much good." He took a breath. "You'll arrange to pull your division from the line this very night and march for the hidden assembly area south of New Sofesshk. It's not as pleasant as the training ground beside Lake Nalak," Ign apologized, "but the forest conceals it from the air." He snorted. "One reason I'm surprised the enemy hasn't firebombed it. Perhaps they believe it's only filled with refugees from the city, but I won't begrudge any blessing."

"But, Second General . . ." Jash began to protest. He may have grown jaded toward First General Esshk, but remained devoted to Ign.

"Obey me," Ign commanded harshly. "I do not debate you." His tone softened. "And the main reason I'll send you only that far is so you'll be near enough to respond when I call." His eyes narrowed and his crest fluttered. "Or react to any . . . unforeseen crisis arising in Old Sofesshk," he murmured.

Ign was one of only a few aware of the campaign to eradicate opposition among the privileged Hij of the capital city. The original plan had been simple enough: dissenters were slaughtered by the garrison there, and their bodies sent to feed the army. Ign had actually been amused by the irony of that, but the culling had been more comprehensive than he expected or approved of (not that his approval was sought), and the population had dwindled to the point that much of the garrison had been withdrawn and sent north to protect critical industries. *The remaining Hij must be very afraid—and very resentful,* Ign mused. *Perhaps enough to cause problems at the palace.* Ign thought the purge misguided, particularly considering how indiscriminate it became, but he believed having gone so far, Esshk should've just finished the job.

He looked at Jash. "Commanding a division, you should be—deserve to be—a general, but I can't make you one. Only the Celestial Mother"—they both knew that meant First General Esshk—"can do that." Ign traced the tip of his lower jaw with a claw. "With this new way of reckoning rank, however, I do feel free to name you First Ker-noll, and place you above any other ker-noll you meet. That small thing may help you in times to come." He paused and considered, remembering how few New Army generals they had, and how resentful some older, longer-established generals commanding mere Uul warriors could be. "And if the occasion arises and you believe you must, you have permission to act in my name. I know you won't abuse that trust." He hissed a sigh. "If I call you early, you must come with whatever troops you can gather. That might require you to . . . supersede certain superiors. If that's the case, don't hesitate. At the same time, I'm . . . uneasy about affairs in Old Sofesshk. Never forget your first duty remains the protection of the Celestial Mother. No matter what."

Jash stirred, clearly conscious of the distinction Ign bestowed upon him, but his posture, narrowed eyes, and the position of his young crest betrayed he was troubled. "I'm to protect the Celestial Mother, no matter what," he repeated slowly, then added, "against *any* threat?"

Ign's eyes widened in surprise. He'd grown somewhat cynical too, and more than half suspected Esshk had deliberately left the Giver of Life in harm's way, vulnerable to enemy bombing and even insurrection. He couldn't imagine Esshk would take direct action against her, however. Apparently, Jash wasn't so sure. As much as he liked him, it made Ign uncomfortable that Jash was already *so* cynical and that he—a mere virtual hatchling—already saw through the intrigue that Esshk, the Chooser, and to a lesser degree Ign himself, had built. But none of that mattered now, did it? The real threat lay to the east and south. "Of course," he stated forcefully. "Go now—refresh yourself and your troops. I'll need you strong, rested"—he paused—"and more focused, very soon."

The Celestial Mother and Giver of Life to all the Gharrichk'k stood outside the Palace of Vanished Gods near the heart of Old Sofesshk, her fresh, young, coppery plumage dazzling in the morning sun. Her sister-guards, lethal protectors, moved around her in a loose ring as she began walking across the paving stones away from the arched western entrance to the palace. She gazed out upon the city. Old Sofesshk was ancient, older than could be imagined by one as young and recently elevated as she. Unlike the shapeless mud hovels across the river, often heaped five, six levels high, the buildings here were angular, geometric, and reminiscent of a time before memory when her people built more durably and in a way that still somehow pleased the eye. It had been the home of pampered, elite Hij, the Gharrichk'k ruling—and leisure—class. "Ruling" because their influence mattered to all previous regents, and "leisure" because, other than exerting influence, they had little else to do. Now somehow, for some reason, virtually all the Hij were gone, as were half or more of the troops left to protect them—and her—by her Regent Champion, First General Esshk. And the new city across the broad Zambezi, never built for durability anyway, was a smoke-blackened, rubble-strewn wasteland of death.

I'm very young, I know, she thought, *but none of this seems right. It doesn't* feel *right.* Nothing her tutors ever told her was consistent with what she saw. The Gharrichk'k were conquerors, ever-expanding graspers of distant lands and takers of prey. No species could stand against them, nor had it ever. Some had joined them in the Hunt from time to time, agreeing to the Offer, but only a handful of Japhs with no regency or lord were with them now. *I wonder whatever became of others in the past?* she asked herself again. Even her tutors hadn't known.

So great had been the power of the Vanished Gods, however, that their merest haunting thoughts and humors still resonated around the world, pushing the wind, making rain, even stirring storms, no matter how long ago they left. Occasionally, their moods and tempers converged fiercely enough to move the very earth or spew fire in the sky from cracks in the land or mountains heaped atop it. *These* things couldn't be conquered or opposed, even by Gharrichk'k. And it did no good to appeal to the

Gods, because they had, after all, vanished. There was no record of what they'd looked like, but legend said they became creatures of the sky, of air itself, and left for other worlds—leaving only their daughter to rule here in their stead.

But I'm their blood-daughter, she railed inside, *the legacy they left behind! Doesn't that make me something of a God myself? My tutors all said it was so. Therefore, if I think something isn't right—isn't how it should be— how then* can *it be?*

She stopped walking, her short feathery tail swishing behind her. "Because my lord Esshk tells me so; that I am wrong and all else is right," she said aloud, wonderingly. Her sister-guards didn't respond; it wasn't their place, and they'd only ever reply if directly spoken to by her. Esshk had never actually told her she was wrong, of course. Not in so many words. But he'd assured her that the tutors, all very grasping and self-interested Hij, he'd recently implied, were either mistaken or willfully misleading her. *And where are my tutors now?* she wondered. *I have no visitors anymore at all. Not even the Chooser!*

The Chooser was very strange, his presence disquieting. A lot of that stemmed from her understanding of his order's traditional role. She was indifferent to how it affected others, but she'd reached breeding age and would soon become a Giver of Life in fact as well as name. It was understood that Esshk would sire those first offspring, and she considered that only right. Not only because of his position, but also because he'd saved her and her surviving sisters. Saved her very *line.* But it bothered her that the Chooser could have the power to select which of her hatchlings might be preserved, regardless of her wishes. Didn't that also undermine her understanding of a God's gifted status?

A now-familiar drone, produced by the prey's huge, four-engine flying boats, rumbled far overhead. It sounded like there were dozens of the things, and no rockets rose to contest them. They didn't drop any bombs nearby this time. What was the point? They'd destroyed everything in view across the river—but they'd find *something* to wreck, somewhere. A profound frustration began to build, not only toward the Chooser and Esshk—despite her debt to both—but also with the realization that virtually *nothing* she wanted seemed to be coming to pass.

Her sister-guards' heads all turned to face the west, and she followed their gaze. Esshk himself was striding toward her, leaving a cluster of guards a short distance behind. He stopped a pace away and bowed deeply. Alone, of all the beings on Earth, Esshk didn't prostrate himself at her feet. His dingy brown, striated plumage wasn't remarkable, nor was his powerful body, for a warrior. But his sharp teeth gleamed bright in strong jaws, and the long, equally sharp ebony talons on his hands and feet had never seen hard use and were polished to a high sheen. Brilliant bronze armor glittered in the morning sunlight, as did his long red cloak, the emblem of the Regent Champion, dusting the ground behind him. Impressive as he was, Esshk was only about half her size, and she'd get larger still. Though tending toward plumpness, she'd probably never surrender to the gross obesity her mother had enjoyed. She'd seen for herself how that prevented her from escaping the Celestial Palace on Madagascar when the prey came there.

"You summoned me, Your Splendor?"

The Celestial Mother turned away, her own red cloak whirling behind her. "I did," she stated almost petulantly. "*Yesterday!* And only now you come before me?"

"Accept my most abject apologies," Esshk begged piously. "I came at once, but was too distant to arrive before now. Great things are happening! We develop new, wondrous weapons around the shores of Lake Galk northwest of here, where the flying machines of the prey have never ventured. And the battle against them is shaping exactly as I designed!" He reached up, grasping at the air with his claws. "Victory is not far distant!"

A far-off thumping noise reached them from the west, and the Celestial Mother recognized the sound of bombs exploding, probably ravaging the shipyards closer to Lake Nalak. She faced Esshk, gesturing toward the rumble of devastation. "Victory for whom?" she demanded. There, she'd said it, openly defying all his assurances for the first time.

Esshk blinked and took a half step back, but that was his only reaction. "For our race," he adamantly replied. "The enemy wastes its might against decoys now, mere lures." He waved at the thumping and the now-rising smoke. "They shatter such places daily, and we just as quickly rebuild them. General of the Sky Ando insists that will make the enemy even more certain the targets are important. So far, he's been right." He looked reflective. "Ando doesn't like us, but he and his followers are proving to be the most loyal, useful Japhs I've known." He snorted. "And compared to Kurokawa, even his honest dislike is reassuring."

"I'm glad you find it so," the Celestial Mother told him, scorn now rising in her voice, "but I'm not reassured at all. Despite your efforts to insulate me, I know the prey past the *nakkle* leg grows stronger every day. I know *another* army approaches from the south, and you're having difficulty securing warriors in the numbers you demanded from the far regencies, despite my commands that they obey you!" Her eyes narrowed. "And no, I won't tell you how I learned all this. My tutors are gone, the Chooser doesn't come, even many of my servants have disappeared. Whether my tutors were right about other things or not, I'm sure no Giver of Life has ever been so cloistered." She paused, thinking. "I remember little bits of my life, from before my elevation, something they told me was rare. Yet I know, even in her immobility and sequestration within the Celestial Palace, my predecessor had many advisors." Her eyes widened again. "I have only you now. You, who showers me with comforts, guarantees, and platitudes of triumph"—she waved across the river—"while all I see is the opposite. With no further counsel, I begin to believe my eyes more than my ears."

"You believe what you see here," Esshk placated, "while I tell you truthfully about things beyond your view. And you wonder why I keep those others, who fill your mind with doubts, away? The enemy *does* grow stronger past the *nakkle* leg. Let them! They're trapped, and when they feed the trap with all they have, it will close upon them! As for the army in the south, Fifth General

Akor leads it in circles, exhausting it, bleeding it, even as his own force grows." Esshk bared his teeth. "And any regency that denies me warriors—at your command—will *be* no regency when all is done. This I swear."

The Celestial Mother sighed, twin gusts whistling from her snout. "So again you tell me all is fine. . . ."

"I do, because it is," Esshk agreed.

"No!" the Celestial Mother snapped. "It's *not* fine. I want my tutors back, someone to talk to." She waved at the sky. "I want the prey's flying machines to stop. I want *all* the prey gone from these shores, and I want it *now*! I command it, First General Esshk, and you will obey!" Speaking to him only as the foremost warrior of the empire, she'd ignored his other title that allowed him to exercise guardianship over her. And by formally omitting it in such a way, combined with a command, she'd technically *terminated* it, declaring she no longer required a champion and was ready to assume all the authority of her exalted status. She'd just blurted it out without thinking, goaded by frustration, and would've immediately taken it back if she could. She had no illusions that she was ready to lead her race through the current crisis alone, much less prepared to command such as Esshk!

And she wasn't prepared for Esshk's reaction either. His crest flared in challenge and he snarled, snout wrinkling, teeth savagely bright. The Celestial Mother's sister-guards tightened around her, baring their own teeth and raising their claws. They were all bigger than Esshk and could kill him easily. Some would probably die, particularly if he reached his sword, but none would hesitate to strike. Still, Esshk didn't back down, nor did his crest even flutter with the slightest hint of submission. The Celestial Mother had never seen him so angry, and though she had no word for it, she was afraid.

Finally, Esshk spun away, striding toward his waiting guards. "I remain your Regent Champion," he called back through clenched teeth. "You're not ready to rule without guidance—nor may you ever be, if this is how you act with so much at stake. And as for what you 'want,' the sooner you learn you won't always get it, the better it will be for our race." He stopped and turned back, crest still high. "Your mother was a great Giver of Life, yet even she never recognized that few things can simply be wanted into existence. That's what killed her in the end. See that you don't similarly tempt the moods of the Vanished Gods."

CHAPTER 5

////// *Allied-Occupied Dulce*
SE of El Paso del Fuego
Holy Dominion
February 1, 1945

Fleet (Vice) Admiral Lelaa-Tal-Cleraan, 2nd
Lieutenant Orrin Reddy, and Flag Captain
Tex Sheider stepped ashore from one of the
motor launches off USS *Maaka-Kakja* (CV-4). This was
the first time any of them had been ashore at Dulce, a city
that had been, until recently, one of the most important
Pacific ports in the Holy Dominion. Lelaa wore her white,
high-collar tunic and sharply pleated white kilt over brindled fur, complete with one broad and two narrow gold
stripes under a star on each sleeve and three stars on gold
shoulder boards, marking her as the senior representative
of the American Navy Clan in this theater of war. Tex
Sheider was also in whites, though his short, fireplug form
seemed to stress all the seams across his shoulders and
sleeves. Orrin Reddy, looking like a younger version of
his cousin Matt, was incongruous in khaki shirt, trousers,
and the battered crush cap on his head. Even though he
was the commander of flight operations on "*Makky-Kat*,"
and therefore senior COFO in Second Fleet, he—like his
cousin—refused lofty promotions. He also still adamantly
maintained that he represented the *Army* Air Corps on
this world.

Waiting on the dock was a platoon of Saan-Kakja's personal guard detail, still wearing the black and gold livery of the High Chief of Maa-ni-la and all the Fil-pin Lands. Not only were Saan-Kakja's guards very good, but, being Lemurians, it was impossible for any rebellious Doms still in the city to infiltrate them. Of course, most Doms remained sure 'Cats were demons and preferred to avoid them anyway. That was just as well. Unlike in smaller ports and coastal towns to the south, people here had been "Doms to the bone" and the city only fell after a lengthy bombardment from the air and artillery in the hills around it, joined by an even more destructive shelling from the bay after Admiral Hibbs's battle line smashed past the harbor forts.

Even then, an infantry assault was required to overwhelm the small garrison General Mayta left behind. And the attack had been unexpectedly costly since just about every civilian inhabitant of Dulce anywhere close to military age joined the fight. They hadn't been very effective, but they'd inflicted enough casualties on the 'Cats and Impies that they'd actually grown reluctant to *risk* taking prisoners. Only at gunpoint, and apparently unwilling to martyr themselves, did the alcalde and his blood priests call a halt to active resistance. An uneasy peace ensued, but there were still occasional attacks, and no Allied personnel wandered the city alone.

"Good aafter-noon," greeted the captain in charge of Saan-Kakja's guards, saluting. "Please follow me," she beckoned, as black-and-gold-clad troops formed around them. "It's not faar."

Lelaa blinked consternation. "Is all this really necessaary?" she asked, taking in the scene around her for the first time. A surprising percentage of the city, far larger than Guayak, with more stone construction, had been reduced to rubble. People were working to clear the streets and shore up damaged buildings, and when she caught them looking her way, she was unnerved by their hostile stares. *We've been spoiled,* she realized, *by how maany Dom civvies greeted us as liberators, even joined us, in the paast. But these people see only conquerors, as destructive to their beliefs and way of life as they've always been to others.* She stiffened as she, Orrin, and Tex marched along with Saan-Kakja's guards. *Well,* she told herself, *we didn't staart this waar.* We're *not the baad guys. They're going to haave to get right with thaat or . . .* She considered, tail whipping back and forth behind her. *Or whaat?* she wondered.

It really wasn't far at all to the high, pyramidal temple appropriated for the forward-most Allied HQ on Dom soil. The building had been only slightly damaged by the shelling and stood alone on what had been a grassy court-yard crisscrossed with stone walkways. A few craters now dotted the lawn, and the grass—untended and trod on indiscriminately for weeks—was dry and brown. Arrayed around the temple were armed troops, facing outward, and Lelaa truly realized for the first time not only how sensitive and momentous this conference would be, but also, perhaps, how tentative was their hold on what they'd taken.

Their escort halted. "Please go inside. You'll be met. We must return to the haarbor and escort others here."

Lelaa nodded. She knew High Admiral Jenks was al-ready present, conferring with Saan-Kakja and the Governor-Empress Rebecca Anne McDonald, who'd both recently arrived from the front. General Shinya himself was supposed to be here, but Lelaa didn't know if he was. Hopefully, the enemy wouldn't know either, but she doubted it. That was another problem they faced on this campaign: it often seemed that for every dozen oppressed subjects of the Dominion flocking to their banners to throw off the blood-rite tyranny of their masters and the twisted faith they served, at least one or two were spies. Lelaa looked at the troops surrounding the temple again and realized with a twinge of relief that all were Lemuri-ans. *With the entire high commaand of Second Fleet and its Expedition-aary Force gaathered in one place, this must be a very tempting taarget.* She was glad the thought had occurred to someone else as well.

She looked up at the shape of the building once more before stepping through a narrow stone entrance, struck by how similar it was in general form to the "cowflops" of the Grik. She'd never seen those other places herself but had looked at drawings, even the wondrous new photo-graaphs. Grik palaces weren't nearly as artistic, being more chaotic, generally rounded, and, though unimaginably larger, squatter in proportion to their massive footprints. But just like the stepped pyramids of the Doms, Grik cowflops stood on squarish bases oriented to the four points of the compass. Some ascribed their rounded, weathered aspect to eons of actual erosion and proposed they were much older than the Dom structures. Regardless, they were just as sacred, just as central to the bloody culture venerating them, and she had to wonder if sometime, somehow, there'd been a common influence.

It was cool inside, but crowded and noisy. Voices echoing loudly around the stone chamber made an impenetrable din even her excellent hearing couldn't decipher. Chairs and stools had been arranged in the back third of the temple and a great, covered map hung low behind a hastily improvised lectern standing on a rough-hewn stage. There at last she saw High Admiral Jenks conferring animatedly with Shinya, Rebecca, and Saan-Kakja. She'd seen Jenks that very morning—*Maaka-Kakja* was his flagship, after all—as he went ashore in his new blue and white, gold-trimmed coat; black shako; and long, braided mustaches. His mild, honest face remained impassive under the growing harangue he was receiving from the hotly angry but still beautiful young Governor-Empress. Saan-Kakja was as radiant as always in her black fur, but her mesmerizing black and gold eyes were blinking deep concern. Tomatsu Shinya had grown a short, somewhat sparse beard and mustache since she saw him last, and he looked on as impassively as Jenks.

No one else seemed interested in approaching them, but Lelaa felt no such restraint and veered toward the argument. She acknowledged greetings from the other carrier skippers, nodded briefly at Admiral Hibbs, who rolled his eyes but wore a worried frown, and continued on, unaware if Orrin and Tex followed or not. They had, and all three converged on the two overall commanders and two heads of state.

"Paardon my interruption," Lelaa stated, with no apology in her voice, "but I understaand we're here to finaal-

ize plaans for the combined assault on the Paass of Fire."
She glanced at Rebecca. She had great affection and respect for the young ruler, but also recognized her impul-
sive, volcanic, and sometimes destructive temper. She
lowered her voice. "I beg you to consider the . . . chilling
effect this display might haave on the confidence of those
present."

Rebecca started to bark a retort, but her smoldering
eyes quickly cooled. Saan-Kakja looked relieved, Jenks
vindicated, and Shinya's expression didn't change at all.
Finally, Rebecca took a deep breath and spoke to Lelaa,
her tone low, urgent, still angry. "Your Captain high-and-
mighty Reddy has ordered—*ordered*!—Saan-Kakja and I
to 'remove ourselves' from this campaign!"

"That's not exactly . . ." Jenks began, but Rebecca interrupted him.

"As if our nations are his personal possessions, and we
his subjects to command!" She rounded on Jenks. "And
you, *my* high admiral, and subject of the empire *I* lead,
have taken *his* side! Some might call that treason," she
growled darkly.

Saan-Kakja's brilliant eyes flashed. "Thaat's *enough*,
my sister! You haave no subject more loy-aal thaan High
Ahd-mi-raal Jenks! You must aa-pologize at once!"

Rebecca bit her lip but looked stubborn, large eyes set
in her elfin face.

Orrin was shaking his head. "God knows Matt can get
pushy from time to time, but what the hell's this about?"

Jenks turned to him. "As the *agreed-upon* Commander in Chief of All Allied Forces"—he glanced at
Rebecca—"irrespective of whether those forces belong to
independent states or are members of the United Homes,
Captain Reddy appointed *me* CINCEAST, which means
I command all forces in this theater, on land and sea, unless and until he relieves me himself. Becoming increasingly concerned that we still have not one, but *two* heads
of state in constant proximity to combat operations"—he
spared a glare for Saan-Kakja—"one of whom *is* a member of the United Homes and has already ignored a direct
order from Chairman Letts to depart the theater." He
looked incredulously back at Orrin, his own voice rising

now. "Captain Reddy finally—wisely—*ordered* me to get them the hell off the front lines." His eyes turned back to Rebecca. "I'm merely attempting to comply with that order."

Rebecca started to speak, but Shinya interrupted this time. "High Admiral Jenks owes his ultimate loyalty to you, Your Highness. But in this you must obey *him*, since he can't be spared."

Rebecca blinked. "What on earth do you mean by that, General?"

"Simply that he can't serve two masters. In military matters, he's oath- and honor-bound to obey Captain Reddy. Yet you, his sovereign, would have him disregard that." Shinya shrugged. "If you persist, he'll have no choice but to resign as CINCEAST." He shook his head. "Is that what you want? Now? I certainly won't take the job." He looked at Lelaa.

"Me either," Lelaa said, blinking disapproval.

"Wait," Orrin said. "Let me get this straight. All this ruckus is because you and her"—he nodded at Rebecca and Saan-Kakja—"want to keep running around on the battlefield like a couple of kids when you ought to be running your countries? And you're mad that Matt and Jenks won't let you do it anymore?" He rubbed his eyes. "Wow. Hey, I'm not in your empire or Matt's Navy Clan either. The only oath I ever took was to the Army and the US Constitution. I'm just a volunteer, and figure I could technically come and go as I please like those AVG fellas in China." He grinned. "Easier, since I don't even have a contract." Only Tex, and maybe Shinya, got Orrin's reference to the American Volunteer Group, but his meaning was clear. "But while I'm here," he continued, "I follow Jenks's orders 'cause he's in charge, and I do what Lelaa tells me 'cause I respect her and I fly off her ship. But I'm not subject to anybody, even Matt, so I'll say what I like until somebody throws me out."

"And what is it you'd like to say, Lieutenant Reddy?" Rebecca asked through clenched teeth.

He glanced back and forth between her and Saan-Kakja. "Only that it seems to me, for two dames in charge of so much, with so much responsibility, whose people and industries are the only real support we have out here against the Doms, you're throwing the most childish fit I ever saw, at the worst possible time."

Rebecca looked furious, then stricken, and Saan-Kakja actually blinked regretful agreement. "He's right, my sister," she said solemnly. "Both my lord Meksnaak and your Sean Bates, whom we left as stewards in our stead, plead constaantly for our return. And not only out of concern for our safety, but so our people will be better motivated to provide whaat our troops need here."

Rebecca shook that off. "You're saying those we left safe at home need more encouragement than those who fight and die for us?" she demanded.

"Yes," Shinya answered abruptly for the Lemurian, and when he continued, his tone was uncharacteristically gentle. "Don't misunderstand; all Maa-ni-lo and Imperial troops in this theater are inspired by your presence, by your willingness to share their danger, but you've already shown that numerous times, and most would rather you were safely away."

"Hear him, please, Your Majesty," Jenks begged. "The Empire, the *new* Empire you made, remains a fragile thing. As is the Union Saan-Kakja's people joined. Their ideals aren't well enough established for our people to fight for them alone." He sighed. "Some would say our friends and allies still fight foremost for Captain Reddy in the west, but the same is true for the two of you here. What if you should fall?" he demanded harshly. Then he looked at Saan-Kakja. "Could your Lord Meksnaak keep the Fil-pin Lands in a war he's sometimes openly opposed? What will happen to the entire Union if he can't?" He turned to Rebecca. "Could Sean Bates finish the war and complete the reforms you began if you are lost? Think of it! I assure you that our troops and sailors do. You're the only symbol uniting the Empire against conspirators who'd turn it back to what it was—particularly without the stability of an heir for Bates to rally the people 'round." He shook his head. "There's no question in my mind that, without you, the Empire would shatter and all its component warring parts would be easy meat for resurgent Doms." He took a breath while that sank in.

"Therefore, your continued presence here is not only a distraction at home and a worry to the troops you care so much about, but also potentially cataclysmic to our allies, the cause, and our very nation. Don't you understand?"

Tears were falling down Rebecca's cheeks and she dashed them away. "Yes," she said softly, "I suppose I do at last. I've been selfish, haven't I? I tried to set an example, be the precedent that women in the Empire can be and do so much more than they've historically been allowed...."

"You accomplished that long ago, Your Majesty," Jenks insisted softly.

"Perhaps," Rebecca reluctantly allowed, then sighed. "Indeed, I suspect it's been more for my conscience than any other reason that I've remained so long. And that my interference has actually made things more difficult and costly at times has made my conscience even heavier." She took a shuddering breath. "I thought I could assuage it by keeping myself in harm's way, but I've finally really *heard* your arguments"—she glanced gratefully, but still somewhat accusingly, at Orrin—"after someone had the nerve to put my objections in perspective."

"Swell," said Orrin, a little uncomfortably. "Now we've got that settled, why don't we get on with it?" He tilted his head at the noisy, waiting throng. "We been gearin' up for this long enough. We're still getting stronger, but I'm not sure the enemy's getting weaker. There's stuff I'm worried about."

"I as well," Shinya agreed, obviously relieved that the command crisis seemed to have passed. "Our land forces are as ready as we can make them. They have been for some time, and await only the air and seaborne elements of the plan to assume their positions."

"But it's the fleet and its air power you're worried about," Jenks surmised.

Shinya frowned. "I've no doubt they'll do their duty, or that they'll destroy all the targets they're assigned...."

"But you worry about what we *don't* know about," Lelaa guessed.

"Of course," Shinya confessed. "Any rational commander would. There are always imponderables in battle, yet this time there's . . . something more."

"You're taalking about Gener-aal Blair and Major Blas's report," Saan-Kakja stated. Only those on the rough timber stage were privy to their account detailing the meeting between Blair, Blas, and the Dom commanders, as well as the commentaries accompanying it.

Shinya reluctantly nodded. "I've never fallen victim to fears before battle, or given much credence to feelings, but I've come to respect General Blair's opinion a great deal—and perhaps Major Blas's instincts more."

"As have I," Rebecca agreed, "and Blas has a *very* bad feeling about General Mayta."

Jenks was frowning. "But from my understanding, it stems mostly from the fact Mayta didn't seem afraid. Excuse me, but isn't that one of the elements of his perverted faith? That dying in agony will whisk him straightaway to his dark reward?"

"I think you misunderstood Blas *and* Blair's aassessment," Lelaa countered. "I didn't take it to mean only thaat he waasn't afraid, but thaat he's confident of victory. They also said he waas smaart, yet he let slip thaat he didn't think he waas outnumbered"—she blinked disgust—"even in the face of whaat we *know* his spies have told him."

There were simply so many spies, of varying degrees of skill and commitment, that quite a few were inevitably caught. The less committed quickly spilled what they'd passed—or attempted to—as well as what Mayta seemed most keen to know. From that, and what thcir own spies reported, it was easy to figure out what he was already aware of. He knew, for example, the composition of Hibbs's battle line, that the Allies now had *three* carriers and almost three hundred planes on land and sea. He could probably see that Shinya's X and XI Corps numbered more than sixty thousand troops—roughly equal to what Mayta had in El Corazon—but was also aware Second Fleet carried another entire corps of Impie Marines and would doubtless land them against him. With all that information, how could he be so confident?

"He's bluffing," Jenks stated. "Anyone in his position would."

"I don't think so," Shinya disagreed, "which means I must trust Blas's impression that he truly is eager for battle."

"So he's either anxious for the worm feast or really thinks he'll win," Orrin said.

"How can we know which?" Jenks asked him. "Have your reconnaissance flights revealed anything that, upon reflection, possesses greater significance than you might've thought at first?"

Uncertainly, Orrin scratched behind his ear. "Honestly? The only thing that really bothers me is how easy the runs've been. And I'm not complaining. But everybody knows I've been harping on that for a while."

Until recently, great flocks of Grikbirds (or dragons, as Impies called them) had ferociously defended the Pass of Fire—for the Doms—from any incursion. The things were about the size of a Grik, looked like them—except for their colorful plumage—and they flew. They were also at least intelligent enough to obey their Dom masters who raised, fed, and trained them. Other flying predators on this world moved in swarms but not cooperative packs, so the Doms had probably taught them their massed, "dash and slash" tactics as well, along with other ways to knock down planes. They'd even carry and drop small bombs. They weren't as fast as Allied planes but were a lot more maneuverable. They could be absolute hell on Nancy floatplanes, even when they were armed and their observer/copilots defended them with SMGs. When Orrin tirelessly begged for more and better planes and pilots, he never failed to point out that, savage as losses had been in the west, they'd lost more aircrews here, in air-to-air combat, than First Fleet had to the Grik, Japanese, and League combined. That was myopic and overlooked the hundreds of flyers and aircraft lost to ship and ground fire in the brutal fighting on the other side of the world, but his point was well taken.

The problem was, though recon flights still got bounced and Orrin's pilots still had to watch their comrades fall with shredded wings or tangled props—sometimes Grikbirds cooperated to dive in and pitch *nets* at unwary or preoccupied planes—attacks had grown less frequent and a lot more careful. Orrin was tempted to credit his pursuit pilots and their little P-1 Mosquito Hawks, or "Fleashooters," which were hell on Grikbirds, but even considering many of his Impie pilots were new and excitable, they hadn't claimed enough kills to account for the decreased numbers. Something was up.

Lelaa had proposed that the Doms pulled them out, unable to feed them. They were under blockade, after all. Nothing could reach El Corazon by land or sea from the west. But even though Nussie raiders were catching a lot of Dom merchies, the Pass of Fire wasn't closed from the east. And Dom cities on the north side of the pass had secure supply lines from local sources and were close enough to support plenty of Grikbirds. Besides, as they'd learned in the Enchanted Isles, if the Doms had trouble feeding their air power, they just gave them people to eat.

Jenks, perhaps overly optimistic, suggested the Doms knew they were licked and had pulled the Grikbirds back to defend their capital and the Templo de los Papas at New Granada. Or maybe most of those they'd already seen came from there originally and events had convinced the Doms they couldn't afford the losses anymore. That didn't add up either. During Orrin's occasional static-laced conversations with cousin Matt, they'd both agreed that Doms were basically human Grik and would never abandon territory uncontested. And even if they did pull out, they wouldn't leave any inhabitants behind. The experience of the NUS back in the 1840s, when the Doms razed a fair percentage of a continent because "heretics" had trod upon it and to create a barrier against their return, was an extreme example. But massacres of civilians ahead of the Allied army's advance—and the fight at Dulce itself—confirmed the mind-set persisted. Mayta knew he couldn't save Dulce but he'd wasted a token force—and a large chunk of the local population— *solely* to contest it. And to decimate any inhabitants who might be corrupted, of course.

"Honestly?" Orrin continued, "I think the Grikbirds're still around, somewhere. Maybe something else that'll bite us on the ass too."

"Like what?" Tex asked.

"No idea. But I'm with Shinya and Her Majesty, and I've got a bad feeling. If what I've seen in the air wasn't enough, I'd go with Blas's gut. Not only does she have a pretty good track record, she's got all those Vengadores and Ocelomeh in the Sister's Own to ask what they think."

"Which might be riddled with spies," Jenks murmured.

"No," Rebecca denied. "Certainly not as many as watch the rest of our army so casually. I'd wager half the local teamsters, sutlers, even scouts we rely on, are in league with the enemy. But the Vengadores are true believers in Sister Audry and her Benedictine Christianity. And the Jaguar Warriors in Blas's Second Marines all know each other. You can be sure they ruthlessly police their ranks."

"So let me be perfectly clear," Jenks said rather irritably, inclining his head toward the gathering of officers waiting for them to finish. "Are you suggesting we delay the assault on the Pass of Fire? *Again?*"

Orrin seemed to consider that but shook his head. "We really can't, can we? We've put it off and built up as much as we can. And unless Matt finally breaks things loose with the Grik in the west, we've pretty much reached the peak of what we're going to get. We have all the ships and planes and people that're available and they're all trained up for the job." He shook his head again. "Starting to lose their edge now. Especially the Impie Marines cooped up aboard ships or in camps at Manizales. Just as important, the Nussies are waiting—and getting edgy about what the League'll throw in, given time. We *have* to go now, no matter what the Doms are cooking up."

"Then whaat are you suggesting?" Lelaa asked.

Orrin shrugged. "Raids, I guess. Deep, destructive ones. Not just recon." He waved his hands. "We've got the planes: three carriers with full complements and the equivalent to more than four, with what we've got on AVDs and ashore. We've even—finally—got four PB-Five-Ds, configured as bombers. We've been holding all that back, but like you said, the Doms *know* we have 'em. Let's use 'em. Kick the hornet's nest and see what stirs up."

"We'd been counting heavily on the element of surprise," Jenks objected.

Orrin laughed. "What surprise? They know we're coming. And I'm not suggesting weeks of raids, only a few days, and that we don't focus on El Corazon. We knock 'em around all along the pass."

Lelaa was nodding. "And if the fuel and aammunition tenders from our friends in the Republic of Real People arrive in the Caar-ibbean quickly enough, we caan send planes on to them to resupply and hit the Doms from both sides at once."

That had seemed a dream at first. The NUS could manage light bombs with contact fuses, but though their ships burned oil, they didn't have gasoline. On the other hand, the Republic still hadn't completed their first oceangoing warships and was afraid to risk lightly armed vessels in seas where Dom warships, or even modern League vessels, might lurk. But the Republic was all in now, with more reason than most to oppose the League. Kaiser Nig-Taak and the NUS president had quickly realized how dependent they were on each other in preventing the League from gaining control of the entire Atlantic. If the League and Doms had the Pass of Fire, they could choke off all Allied assistance to the NUS from the west and it would be on its own. That would leave the Republic's Cape of Africa the only avenue for Allied support—a stormy, dangerous passage at best, on this other Earth—and a prime target for the League to focus all its attention upon. The NUS had finally dispatched some powerful steam frigates to protect the Republic tenders—from Doms, at least—and they were optimistically expected within weeks.

Months, more likely, Orrin suspected. "Swell," he said, "and Fred and Kari are over there to help 'em organize refueling, rearming, and basic repairs. And the Repubs'll have a few planes of their own." They'd come up with capable biplanes called Cantets, but also copied the Allies' Nancy floatplanes. Direct parts interchangeability probably wasn't an option, but they might completely re-engine an Allied plane if they had to. "Sounds like a plan. At least a little addition to the big plan everybody's here to go over. We'll tear shit up, raise some hell, and maybe make 'em show us what they've got up their sleeve."

Jenks looked troubled. "If you're right and they do have something, your raids might be dreadfully costly in planes and people," he warned.

"Could be, but we'll keep plenty back to cover your assault. And if we keep it *quiet*"—he looked significantly at them all—"we might still throw one surprise at Mayta and shake him up. If he takes the bait and shows his hand, it can't be as costly as whatever he's waiting to spring on us."

"All right," Jenks concluded, "we'll do it." He smiled vaguely. "Or, rather, you will, I suppose. I take it you're 'volunteering' for this as well?"

"In for a penny . . ."

"Very well." He straightened his coat. "Let's get on with this, shall we? There are a lot of people here with a great deal to do. Please, all of you remain beside me." He looked at Rebecca and Saan-Kakja, a sad smile forming beneath his mustaches. "I know how painful it will be for you, but after General Shinya and I are finished, with all still assembled, it might be an excellent time for you to say your farewells."

"Of course."

Jenks walked to the lectern and called for the great map to be displayed. A hush swept through the temple as everyone present recognized the features on the map and knew High Admiral Jenks was about to begin at last.

"All right," he said loudly. "This is what we've been waiting for. Pay close attention to what General Shinya and I have to say. The basic plan of attack isn't complicated; the enemy position is well prepared and leaves little opportunity for imaginative maneuvers. Still, in the interests of security, I'm afraid you'll have to commit a great deal to memory. You needn't memorize everything, however," he quickly assured them, "and individual assignments will be issued immediately prior to the operation. If, when this briefing concludes, you discover you've seen opportunities or concerns we failed to address, please feel free to bring them to our attention, but keep them to yourselves for now. I know many of you are used to speaking out at once"—he smiled at some of the Lemurian officers—"but I'll not have this briefing degenerate into a debate." He retrieved a long cane pointer from where it was leaned against the lectern and turned to the map. "General Shinya's Tenth and Eleventh Corps are here and here, enveloping the landward approach to El Corazon." He touched the map with the cane. "He will elaborate on their dispositions and that of the enemy momentarily." He moved the pointer southwest of the pass. "Here is where the fleet will assemble, and where the carrier battle groups will *remain* throughout the action," he stressed, "unless specifically ordered forward . . ."

CHAPTER 6

////// *NUS-Occupied Cuba*

I t's been a while since it was just the three of us," observed Captain Anson as he raised a clear glass filled with a minty drink in a mock toast. Lieutenants Fred Reynolds and Kari-Faask, both in fresh new whites made by a local tailor Anson suggested, raised their glasses as well. "Other than our brief flights across the isthmus," he qualified. "But those afforded few opportunities to socialize or reminisce." He emphasized his toast. "To our first meeting, and"—he smiled wryly—"a most interesting time together."

Times remained "interesting" and they weren't at all alone, sitting in the shade around an open-air table at a boardwalk café not far from Santiago's Government House. All the other tables were occupied by Nussie officers in uniforms ranging from white muslin, for the heat, to dark blue broadcloth, for appearances. Other than brightly colored branch-rank shoulder boards trimmed in gold and a lot of polished brass buttons, the uniforms had few decorations and nobody wore medals. There were different colored sashes under white leather sword and saber belts, but Fred and Kari didn't know what they signified.

It was easier to tell which branches the common soldiers belonged to, surging and jostling on the crushed coral street between the bright white, generally two-story shops and offices flanking it. They were from all over the

NUS, hurrying on their way or just gawking at the older, more ornate Dom buildings in the city. Some wore red stripes down the legs of sky blue trousers, others a kind of yellow orange. Most by far had no stripe at all, but their sky blue cotton jackets were trimmed in white. All wore dark blue wheel hats, but some of those boasted red or yellow-orange bands as well. Most surprising to Kari, all were men, and their faces ranged from almost blue-black to a white as bleached as the coral. Kari found that a little comforting, considering how varied Lemurian coloration could be. It was disconcerting to have so many stare at *her* as she watched them, however.

Fred fished the watch Captain Willis gave him out of a pocket and glanced at it. "Sure you can afford to be seen with us? Except for flying, you've avoided us like the measles."

"For security reasons only," Anson replied, clamping a long cigar between lips under a brushy mustache. He'd gone back to muttonchops after discovering beards were in style among the Impies. With a smile, he handed another cigar to Kari, who blinked appreciative pleasure while Fred rolled his eyes, and lit them both with a match that flared oddly bright and pungent. He blew out a cloud of smoke and sighed. "I'm a Ranger," he confessed, finally acknowledging what he was, if not exactly what he did. To their surprise, he actually elaborated. "Along with more traditional activities, Rangers have always been somewhat specialized soldiers paradoxically endowed with very diverse skills that allow them to operate and survive alone or in small groups in hostile territory. Alone, we're sometimes used as spies, even assassins," he conceded, "which is what the Doms consider us all. And in small groups we often take more ambitious direct action. With independent assignments like mine have been, we work directly for the president, under his orders alone."

"Wow," Kari said, blinking mild sarcasm. "I think we'd kinda figured mosta thaat, just not thaat whaat you did haad a title."

"Yeah, and that it's a real job," Fred added, chuckling.

"I'm sure," Anson replied with a raised brow. "And I'm equally sure enemy spies were aware as well. All the more reason to keep my distance from you, till now." He pointed his cigar at their uniforms. "And it's not as if you're inconspicuous."

"Lotsa folks here wearin' white," Kari objected.

"Not many have long, fluffy tails, my dear," Anson pointed out dryly.

"But not now?" Fred asked, glancing at his watch again. "No more creeping around?"

Anson smiled and redirected his cigar down the street, past the milling throng, at the narrow portion of the bay they could see. It was packed with ships of every description—masts; furled sails; tall, smoke-streaming funnels most readily apparent. "It's rather pointless to keep the secret now, particularly from my friends, though I still can't reveal my true name. I have a family, after all." He nodded at the bay. "But just *look* out there," he directed. "The entire NUS fleet has gathered here, from Port Isabel to Mobile. Even the Atlantic coastal squadrons stationed at the tip of Florida are here. There are transports sufficient to carry fifty thousand men, horses, and guns—which this island fairly shudders under even now—and enough warships to protect them from anything the Doms have retained in the Caribbean. That we know of," he added unhappily.

"In any event, it's the very cream of our armed forces and almost the entire fighting-age population of our country—at least that portion not actively devoted to supporting this force." He glanced at Kari. "Even women are fully engaged, if not necessarily in uniform. They fill the ranks of our industries, tend our crops, and ensure there'll be another generation at the end of all this. Do you honestly think the Doms don't already know our purpose? My only hope is that they remain unsure where we'll strike. *I* don't even know that, beyond the obvious, which is somewhere within the vast expanse of New Granada. I find some consolation in that." He grinned. "Rangers don't just monitor our *enemies*. In any event, my ignorance has rendered my person somewhat less prizeworthy in terms of information that might be pried from me. That's yet a further consolation, a profound relief, and why I feel comfortable meeting you socially at last."

Fred glanced at his watch again and Anson took an

exasperated breath. "Really, Lieutenant Reynolds. You do seem quite preoccupied with the time. Is my company truly so tedious?"

"It's a *gurrl*," Kari sneered. "A useless, helpless, empty-headed *gurrl*, who caan't fly, caan't shoot, an' don't know nothin' about nothin'."

"She's the daughter of Commodore Semmes," Fred defended, glaring at Kari. Then he looked at Anson. "*Kari* just doesn't like her because I spend a little time with her now and then. We have a date."

Anson chuckled. "Of course. Young Tabitha. Quite pretty too . . . if indeed somewhat empty-headed." He looked sternly at Kari. "If Lieutenant Reynolds has arranged a meeting with the young lady, he mustn't be late. She has many suitors, though I suspect most are more interested in gaining access to the commodore for their own purposes." He looked back at Fred. "Your . . . liaison might actually benefit our two nations—if it doesn't put us helplessly at odds." His chuckle turned to a laugh, and Fred's ears went beet red.

Kari pointed at them triumphantly. "Look at thaat! His ears is the same unnaatural color as the *fur* on her head! It ain't right. She's prob'ly gave him some naasty islaand jungle raash!"

"She may well have," Anson agreed good-naturedly.

Stony faced, Fred asked, "Why tell us all this stuff now? Don't you still need to lay low?"

Just then, the crowd in the street started peeling back, scrambling to find refuge on the boardwalk and get out of the way of a troop of horsemen cantering through. Carbines bounced and rattled, suspended by buff leather straps. The men were dressed like dragoons, in dark blue jackets and sky blue trousers, but their hair was long and wrapped in furs, and they wore what looked like the skins of furry Grik heads and faces for hats. These were decorated with lizardbird feathers and other colorful items. "Comanches," Anson said with admiration. "Even they are here. Finest cavalry in the world."

"Are they Nussies too?" Fred asked, just as amazed by their presence as how they might've gotten to this world in the first place.

"Yes, though they retain considerable independence on the Texas frontier. Many become great Rangers." If there was irony in his tone, Fred didn't catch it. "But you asked why I'm telling you all this," he continued when the Comanches were past, "and the answer's very simple. The Doms will certainly try to stop us wherever we land but can no longer do anything to prevent our coming. What happens next is in God's hands." He finished his drink and drew heavily on his cigar. "I'll soon be returning to the Ranger company I used to command. Once we land in New Granada, I'll be back to the more traditional and straightforward scouting, screening, and skirmishing role I've missed so much. You two, however, have been ordered to report aboard Captain Garrett's USS *Donaghey* once more, where you'll perform the same duties as my Rangers, from the air, on behalf of the fleet. Your plane has already been hoisted aboard."

He smiled a little sadly and glanced at his own watch. Looking surprised, he suddenly stood, dropping his cigar in his empty glass. Fred and Kari rose as well. "Wherever can the time have gone? I really must go as well," he murmured absently, then regarded Fred intently. "Go to your young lady, Lieutenant Reynolds. Enjoy yourself. There's little time left for that." Meeting Kari's gaze, he smiled. Extending his hand, he shook both of theirs. "Take care of each other. And if we never meet again, please know it's been one of the greatest honors of my life to call you friends. God bless."

"Cap-i-taan Aanson seem kinda low to you?" Kari asked as she and Fred threaded their way toward Government House. Fred was supposed to meet Tabitha Semmes there, and Kari meant to corral Captain Garrett and harangue him for messing with their plane without them around. And it *was* their plane. Garrett promised.

Fred looked thoughtful. "He never was a nonstop barrel of laughs, but yeah. Maybe more . . . serious than usual."

"I wonder whaat for. Maybe he's too used to runnin' around on the loose."

Fred shook his head. "I don't think that's it. He seemed happy to be back with his Rangers, back in the 'real army' again instead of sneaking around alone. I don't see how anybody could like that much."

Kari sighed. "We been on the loose enough ourselves to suit me," she agreed. "I'll be glaad to be baack in the Navy. *Wish* we waas baack aboard *Waa-kur*," she added quieter.

"Yeah. Well, I bet he's okay. Probably just worried about the operation because he doesn't know any more about it than we do, for once."

"Maybe," Kari agreed as they finally reached the steps in front of the big building at the end of the street. Guards stood on either side of the door and the redheaded Tabitha, slim and pretty in a cream-colored dress with a red sash around her waist and a matching ribbon holding the straw hat on her head, was waiting. She smiled radiantly and waved.

"Ain't naatural," Kari growled lowly, her tail hanging low. "An' red reminds me too much of Doms," she confessed, blurting it out.

Fred looked at her scarred fingers, where clawlike nails once were, and shuddered. He could certainly understand that. He had his own scars. "Well," he said lowly, "one thing Captain Anson, us, and everybody else knows: this next fight's gonna be a bear, and once we get tangled up in it there won't be any getting loose until it's done. And him so much as saying so long . . . I don't think he expects to make it, or doesn't think we will."

"Whaat do you think?" Kari asked. "Thaat's a buncha lizard shit, right?"

Fred hesitated only an instant before grinning and thumping his best friend on the back. "Of course." He snorted forcefully. "We've already been in worse jams than we're ever liable to see again. It stands to reason." He started to walk toward the waiting girl. "Wait for Captain Garrett, and don't go wandering around on your own." He waved at the mass of troops. "Who knows what some of them'll think of you? Double-check our plane when you get back to the ship."

"See you there later? When you're done with your *gurrl*?" Kari teased.

Fred rolled his eyes. "Sure." Then he took a step back

toward her, suddenly anxious. "Hey. You're not . . . jealous, are you?"

Kari looked genuinely shocked and her tail arched. "Jealous? Of *her*?" She laughed. "Even if you an' her got hitched someday, aafter all we been through, she'll ncvcr know you like I do. We're paals."

Leopardo
Puerto del Cielo
Holy Dominion

*D*on Hernan is *here*?" Capitaine de Fregate
Victor Gravois demanded incredulously as
soon as he stepped into the pilothouse of
the Italian Capitano Ciano's Leone-class "Exploratori"
destroyer, *Leopardo.* He'd been asleep and it showed as he
stood in rumpled shirtsleeves, peering anxiously through
puffy eyes out the pilothouse windows, searching for Don
Hernan's barge. His normally carefully combed hair stood
up in a comical wedge.

Ciano smirked inwardly. He had a careful respect for the
French Naval Intelligence officer and even tacitly supported
his schemes to make a stronger, bolder League. He suspected he'd go far if they turned out well. Of course, they'd
all be executed if they didn't, and that's why he hadn't
openly declared full agreement to some of the more outra-
geous things he suspected Gravois planned. Still, they
had an . . . understanding, and many mutually acknowledged frustrations, so the secret smirk had nothing to do
with contempt. It reflected only Ciano's vague amusement at seeing the almost pathologically dapper French
officer less than immaculately turned out for the very first
time. He frowned with a quickening anger when he remembered it wasn't the first. That had been when *Leop-*

ardo collected Gravois after his short stay among the
Allies—as Captain Reddy's "guest"—on Madagascar.
Ciano almost ached to meet Reddy and his dilapidated
old *Walker* with *Leopardo* someday, but still thought
Gravois had been lucky to get out of that alive and won-
dered why he had.

In any event, he couldn't blame Gravois for his appearance. There was little to do but sleep away the long, hot
days at anchor in the Dominion's principal East Caribbean port of Puerto del Cielo, where that OVRA *stronzo*
Oriani had effectively marooned *Leopardo*. They were
officially there to show the flag and maintain a presence,
reminding the Dominion of the League's support—and,
subliminally, the power and majesty of its modern ships
and weapons. They were also there as a floating embassy
and for Don Hernan's communications convenience. But
there was no liberty or any contact with the natives at all
except for the daily bumboats bringing fresh supplies like
meat, fruit, and a kind of tobacco.

Increasingly, they were also sneaking drugs aboard.
Ciano banned that of course, but couldn't have stopped
everything if he inspected every boat himself. He could
even sympathize with those of his crew who chewed the
strange leaves that made them drowsy and remote, since
most couldn't bear to look at the city for long and avoided
lingering on the landward side of the ship. Many slept
belowdecks regardless of the heat, often in a drug-induced
stupor, rather than risk seeing—or smelling—what went
on ashore at night.

What started as a disgusting evening ritual of fiery cru-
cifixions of a few "rebels" on the beach at the base of the
city's seawall had turned into a nightly orgy of dozens of
blood sacrifices and apparently senseless, flaming murder.
The effect on morale was obvious, as was the steep decline
in combat readiness—while the crew practically craved
combat. *Anything* to get away from here. They were in a
kind of hell while *Leopardo* and her ever-present ancient
oiler slowly rusted away, in more ways than one, under the
brutal tropical sun.

"Don Hernan's barge is approaching from astern, from
upriver," Ciano said. Gravois nodded as if to say "Of

course," and stepped out on the bridgewing to look aft toward the mouth of the River of Heaven. The Holy City of New Granada and the Templo de los Papas lay 320 kilometers up its broad, steamy course. An extraordinarily ornate bireme was churning toward them, its double ranks of oars flashing under the early-afternoon sun. Large red flags adorned with twisted golden crosses fluttered fitfully fore and aft, and people dressed in bright reds and yellows crowded the high poop under a broad awning.

"That's his barge," Gravois murmured irritably, "but why should he come all the way down here?" He stiffened. "And he's coming directly to us, not steering for the city." He managed a small, triumphant smile. "Perhaps we'll discover his purpose quickly, for once, without having to await a propitious day for his visit." Then his expression betrayed dismay. "I must refresh myself. Please do what you can to see he's properly received." Even Gravois was keenly aware of how *Leopardo*—and her crew's— appearance had declined since Don Hernan's last visit. He started for the hatch.

"One word, Capitaine," Ciano urged.

"Yes?"

"Please, for the ship's sake and our own, bear in mind our position. And the fact that Don Hernan could've easily sent word to summon us back to him." They knew the Dominion used what even Gravois considered flying Grik to carry important messages. "And he wouldn't have come 'all the way down here' without some urgency," Ciano finished. Gravois pursed his lips beneath his thin mustache and nodded.

"I'm astonished, Your Holiness, utterly astonished to see you here," Gravois said earnestly, leaning forward in his chair in *Leopardo*'s wardroom. The setting was exactly as when they last met, except this time Gravois and Don Hernan were entirely alone. The Blood Cardinal hadn't even brought his beautiful naked slave girls to pour his wine, and disconcert Gravois, of course. Other than that, the same electric fan labored to move the stifling air, and they were dressed the same as before: Don Hernan in his brilliant gold-trimmed red robes and ridiculous white hat, and Gravois in his meticulously brushed uniform and polished boots. They even had what probably really was Ciano's final bottle of Salice Salentino standing on the table between them. All this led to a sense that this was merely a continuation of their last conversation. In various ways, it was, but Gravois also sensed a carefully veiled new urgency in his visitor. "Pleased as well, of course," he continued, "and deeply honored. But surely there was some other essential purpose for you to make such an arduous trek? The voyage downriver must have taken *days*."

Gravois immediately regretted his sarcasm and admonished himself to swallow his resentment. Whatever Don Hernan was, Gravois—an atheist, who still wasn't exactly certain his visitor wasn't the devil himself—knew he was no fool.

Don Hernan merely smiled benignly and waved it away. "There are . . . incidental matters I must attend to in Puerto del Cielo, but my primary purpose was to visit you, my friend."

"I'm privileged indeed to be numbered among your friends."

For a moment, Don Hernan's face betrayed an uncharacteristically bleak expression. "Yes," he said, "I have very few." He snorted. "Precisely none, other than you. Particularly with whom I can share my passion for the vision of the future we discussed. The future we can build."

Gravois was more repelled than flattered by that admission, for what it was worth, but understood it implied vulnerability for the first time, and perhaps a willingness to engage in a truly frank discussion. "Your, ah, 'incidental' business . . . Might it involve the accelerated executions we've witnessed of late?" he tentatively pressed.

Don Hernan sighed. "I fear so. As you know, the heretic and demon hordes are poised to strike our final bastion on the west side of El Paso del Fuego, at El Corazon. They will fail," he stated flatly. "Unfortunately, though, word of their previous successes can't be entirely suppressed and has spread quite far"—he motioned vaguely off to port—"even here. The ungodly are encouraged to suppose the demons will aid them, and rise up against our benevolent rule. Those who do so must be *cleansed*!" he said forcefully.

Gravois pictured the nightly "cleansing" ashore in his mind and cleared his throat, dreading what further abomination Don Hernan might unleash. If things got too far out of hand he'd never be able to use the alliance with the Dominion to pursue his aims. Even the League, with plenty of blood on its own hands, could countenance only so much. "With respect, Your Holiness," he ventured, "we have some experience at suppressing uprisings in territory we've acquired. Reprisals are useful, but must be conducted with care. Most especially it should be seen that they specifically target individuals, groups, or acts they're designed to discipline. I might even go so far as to say that . . . chastening the family and associates of traitors, even their entire village, has merit on occasion, but the punishment is still *targeted*, don't you see? Once reprisals are perceived as utterly arbitrary and even the obviously innocent are punished, inducement to proper behavior is lost. Even more rebel who otherwise wouldn't, and opposition merely grows." He took a sip of wine. "Trying *too hard* to stamp out treason may only feed it in the end."

Don Hernan regarded him with wide, gentle eyes. "Indeed? What an interesting thought." He held up a finger and waved it back and forth. "There's a plant like that, a prickly, flowering, creeping vine that can choke a farmer's field in a single season. The harder the farmer hacks at it, the more insidious seeds it spreads." His expression turned hard. "That's why it must be cleansed with fire."

Gravois was close to despair, already picturing *hundreds* of barbaric executions, day and night, in full view of *Leopardo*.

"But people are not vines," Don Hernan reluctantly granted, "and there may be something to what you say. There'll be plenty of time to deal with *all* the traitors when the current crisis is behind us. For now I will experiment." He beamed. "Ha-ha! I'll burn the *executioners* for their impious and overzealous effusion of sacred, *perhaps* even innocent, blood!" His face turned sad. "Clearly they became intoxicated with blood—quite understandable—but inexcusable in those entrusted with its accumulation."

Gravois nodded sagely, while the flesh crawled across his arms. He suspected Don Hernan and the Dominion was probably *less* maniacal than various known human societies throughout history, even on this very continent, but that didn't make actually talking with someone who believed as he did any easier. He chose to change the subject back to the Pass of Fire. "You're quite sure you need no direct assistance at El Paso del Fuego? Perhaps you might"—Gravois smiled—"request that *Leopardo* go there to help ensure nothing unforeseen occurs?"

Don Hernan frowned. "In light of the fact your League remains unprepared to make a *full* commitment in this hemisphere," he began, already making Gravois fume. Whether he had any love for it or not, the League was trying to get ships sent out as quickly as it could. Things were difficult, however. The war to subjugate the Mediterranean had been long and taxing, and not only had many of the League's heavier, long-range fleet elements fallen into disrepair, facilities they'd built or appropriated had been focused on keeping ships better suited to the Med in action. That was changing now, but transitions took time—as he'd explained. The League was coming, there could be no doubt, but perhaps not soon enough to save the Pass of Fire. On the other hand, that might suit Gravois's plans even better. . . .

"I think we should leave El Paso in the capable hands of General Mayta," Don Hernan continued, lips creasing modestly. "*He* has the aid of one of my favorite sons, along with everything else we've lavished upon him. I'm quite confident El Paso is secure—and our loyal people need to know it was us alone who kept it that way."

He leaned toward Gravois, setting his wineglass aside. "Then again, I do have a request to make of you."

Gravois raised his eyebrows attentively.

"Our spies tell us los diablos del Norte"—Don Hernan grimaced—"the heretics in the pitiful, self-styled New United States, mean to land a large force somewhere upon the holy soil of Nuevo Granada itself, in cooperation with the offensive by the demon horde in the west.

We aren't exactly sure where it will come, and that presents a slight problem from a perspective of meeting it, but its ultimate goal is said to be the conquest of the Holy City and Templo de los Papas itself!" Don Hernan's eyes widened once more in furious astonishment. "Just imagine the hubris!" he exploded.

Gravois shifted uncomfortably in his chair. He'd been told, and it had always been his personal preference, to avoid initiating open hostilities with any Allied power—and, particularly now, the NUS—as long as possible. There'd *been* hostilities, of course, brought on by both sides—that the League destroyer *Atúnez* had been destroyed by a meager Allied sailing frigate and her Dom prize still infuriated him—but the League had started the shooting in every other instance. So far, however, there'd been no deadly encounters with the NUS. Like the Imperials, their sailing steam warships were equal to anything the Dominion possessed, but *Leopardo* could probably destroy everything they had all by herself. They couldn't possibly resist the exponentially greater resources the League was preparing to commit to the region. Yet avoiding confrontations and delaying large-scale active participation by the NUS in the war against the Doms had allowed everyone to focus on the greater threat from the west. Apparently that was all about to change.

Yet for diplomatic reasons, the League still needed to tread softly where the NUS was concerned. Taking *Leopardo* to the Pass of Fire was one thing. Her presence alone, implying a fait accompli, might continue to delay hostilities with the NUS and even *stop* them with the powers beyond. At least for a time. Attacking a NUS fleet was something else entirely. "Are you asking me to prevent their landing with *Leopardo*?"

Don Hernan shook his head. "No, my friend. Let them land. We've waited for the final confrontation with *them* for a century, and wouldn't stop them even if our own ships weren't already focused on the demon horde. Wherever they come ashore, we'll find them and meet them with our multitudes. The very land they desecrate with their heretic feet will devour them. And again it will be seen that it was *we* alone who defeated them at last," he stressed. "But our fleet being elsewhere, the favor I ask—the favor that will cement our bond forever, in this world and the next—is that you'll use your ship to destroy their fleet *after* they're in our embrace. Not only will that prevent the resupply of their troops, they won't be able to escape."

Gravois allowed a genuine smile to grow. That was something he *could* get away with, since it might even be argued in the NUS that he was only protecting an ally from *their* aggression. And the whole ridiculous, *wooden* NUS fleet would be at his mercy. There'd be little need to tread so softly after it was gone. Ciano would be pleased to get out of here and back to sea where he could turn his men into a crew again, and what a surprise it would be to Contrammiraglio Oriani when the men and ship he'd marooned saved the new alliance with the Dominion. He'd look like a fool and couldn't keep his command of *Ramb V* at Ascension Island. Perhaps Gravois would get the post? He'd probably be able to demand it, and the Triumvirate would have to agree. Then, coordinating all League naval operations in the Atlantic, he'd be in a perfect position to launch the rest of his great plan.

On second thought, however, why should he do *everything* Don Hernan requested? He needed Gravois and *Leopardo* now, but had grand ambitions of his own. Whatever happened, it was obvious he meant to take all the credit for himself. If Mayta successfully defended El Paso del Fuego without League assistance and *Leopardo* entirely crushed the NUS fleet and the Doms destroyed their army, Don Hernan would be free to pursue direct negotiations with Oriani or the Triumvirate itself at his leisure. Gravois had to keep Don Hernan indebted to the League through *him* and ensure he continued to require their protection. He thought he already knew how to manage that.

Still smiling, he raised his glass, and Don Hernan touched it with his own. "Tell me," Gravois asked, "how is His Supreme Holiness?"

"Poorly, I fear," Don Hernan replied with a face of pure regret. "He pines for the afterlife in the underworld." He smiled wistfully. "Or in the heavens above, as I understand your people believe? I'll try to get used to that." Strangely,

that statement probably surprised Gravois more than anything he'd ever heard the Blood Cardinal say, since it
showed how flexible the man who wanted to be Pope of the
League truly was in matters of faith. "Sadly," Don Hernan
went on, "I fear he can't resist the temptations of paradise
much longer. He'll never see the world you and I will make
while he inhabits flesh." He sorrowfully lowered his gaze.
"I'll always seek his guidance, of course. I'm sure he'll hear
my prayers."

CHAPTER 8

////// USS **Walker**
On the Zambezi River near the Neckbone
Grik Africa
February 8, 1945

*M*att Reddy was sitting in his captain's chair bolted to the forward bulkhead in the pilothouse of USS *Walker*, squinting to read the latest report on events and preparations in the East. The day was fading fast, however, and he finally blinked and gave up. *Later,* he told himself. Rubbing his eyes, he looked out past the number-one gun on the fo'c'sle and watched the work in the channel. The Seven Boat and two other PTs of Nat Hardee's MTB-Ron-1 were still dropping charges over the side. Each was essentially a depth charge fitted with a time fuse instead of a pressure-sensitive detonator. The explosive barrels splashed in the reeking, murky water and sank amid the wreckage choking the channel. A lot of junk had already been blasted out. *Walker* was standing by at battle stations to cover the operation against Grik armored cruisers that might try to rush through and pound the torpedo boats while they just sat there, laden with explosives and no torpedoes in their tubes. They'd be practically helpless if they couldn't get underway quickly enough.

"How're the kids doing?" asked Matt's XO, Brad "Spanky" McFarlane, suddenly appearing next to the chair, scratching the reddish hair poking out from under his hat. Even standing, Spanky was little taller than Matt sitting down, though, to be fair, the chair was elevated. Regardless, Spanky's presence had always been bigger than he was.

"Okay, so far. At least the lizards haven't thrown anything at them."

"Yeah? Good," Spanky said, still scratching. He stopped. "You know, maybe you ought not let Nat jump out front so much," he finally said.

Matt looked at him, surprised. "He's the CO, and it's his squadron. I can't tell him how to run it any more than I could tell Ben how to run the Air Corps, or Pete to run the army."

Spanky snorted. "That's a buncha bull . . . sir. You can tell *everybody* what to do. Why, you could get on the horn right now and say 'chicken' to Chairman Letts, and him and every member of the Union Assembly—except maybe the Sularans—would start runnin' around in circles, flappin' their arms fit to bust."

Matt stifled a laugh at the mental image but shook his head. "Even if that were true, it isn't how it's supposed to be and I'll never set that precedent. And I won't tell Nat how to run his MTBs either." He paused, looking intently at his XO. "What's this all about?"

Spanky rolled his eyes. "I know what you'll say before I even bring it up, but I'm gonna do it anyway." He pointed out at the darkening shapes a few hundred yards to the west. The boats were finally finished dropping their charges and had started their engines. Greenish-yellow phosphorescent water churned around their screws and at their bows. "Nat's just a *kid*, damn it," Spanky growled. "So's Abel Cook, who just lost his best friend at Zanzibar, nearly got killed here, and you just made a full-blown major. I doubt either of 'em's eighteen yet. They were just *little* kids when they came here in *S-19*. . . ."

"And they've been doing a man's job ever since," Matt interrupted. "Look, I know how you feel, but I bet we've got twenty thousand 'Cats aboard ships or under arms who aren't *fifteen*!"

"That's different," Spanky protested. "'Cats grow up quicker."

For the first time in quite a while, Matt reflected on his

own thirty-five years. Spanky had to be close to forty. He shook his head. "Maybe physically, but they've all grown up fast in every other way that matters, because they had to." He nodded out at the accelerating MTBs. "Just like Nat and Abel, and the even younger kids that came with them. Every one's a midshipman or nurse already." He barked a laugh. "Hell, Alan Letts is what, twenty-five? Twenty-six? He's the leader of the United Homes! Governor-Empress Rebecca McDonald is Abel's age and she's in charge of the whole damn Empire of the New Britain Isles! Saan-Kakja's probably less than twenty, leading the Filpin Lands." He frowned. "I don't think either Chack or General Queen Safir Maraan are over twenty-one, and do you know a deadlier pair?"

"Silva and Larry maybe, one on one," Spanky admitted reluctantly. "But that ain't my point—or yours either." He sighed. "It's just . . . Hell, I guess we're the old fogies in this war, the wobbly, white-haired 'brass' we always griped about. But I'll be damned if I'll turn *into* one o' those fossilized old bastards—an' I'll never quit worryin' about kids like Nat. Damn near his whole squadron got wiped out at Zanzibar and he's already at it again. Not many guys *our* age can do that, over and over."

"But we do," Matt said heavily. "We have. Everybody has to in this war."

"Yeah. But what's it costing us? And as far as the kids go, ours or the 'Cats', it's not so much about age as it is what they may think they have to prove *because* of their age, see? I guess that's what worries me most."

Matt chuckled darkly, quietly. "I doubt that bothers anybody as much as you think. As I said, it's a *very* young man's—and 'Cat's—war. I'd worry more whether fogies like us can keep up with them, if I were you." Louder he said, "Left full rudder. Starboard ahead full, port, full astern. Where's *Ellie*?"

"Left full rudder, ay!" cried the 'Cat at the big brass wheel. "Full ahead staar-board, full astern port, ay," answered the 'Cat at the EOT. *Walker* shuddered as the screws bit and she started to twist. "*James Ellis* is comin' up now," called the tiny 'Cat talker everybody called Minnie after a certain mouse, and because her voice was just as small as she was. "She'll take station as soon as we're outa the way."

Matt nodded. It was getting dark fast. With the night might come bombing zeppelins or rockets, even heavy artillery, if the Grik had managed to sneak any up in range on the rougher north shore. It would be hard, physically demanding work, but the same terrain that made moving large numbers of guns and troops nearly impossible made it easier for them to sneak in a few unobserved. They'd done it before. Regardless, the Allies had to keep a powerful picket in the river, and Matt's precious destroyers and Nat's MTBs were all they had for now. Even though the river here, short of the Neckbone, was more like a wide lake, the main channel was barely a mile wide and they couldn't risk *Gray* in such confined water. Not for this. She was surprisingly nimble for her size, able to turn almost as tightly as *Walker*, but her extra draft meant she had only half as much river to maneuver in.

It wasn't all bleak. No longer needed at Soala on the Ungee River to the South, two Republic Princeps-class monitors were supposed to be heading this way, creeping up the coast. With their shallow draft, heavy armor, and big breech-loading guns, they'd be perfect for this kind of duty. But they were never designed for the blue water they had to cross to get here and would have to proceed slowly, with great care. Who knew when they'd arrive? That left *Walker*, *Mahan*, and *James Ellis* to cover the MTBs. At least they were relatively small, agile targets.

Not like her, Matt thought grimly, gazing at the black silhouette of scorched and twisted wreckage that had been *Santa Catalina*, now off to port. *An awful lot of good people died in that old ship, especially after she was immobilized and became a sitting, half-sunk target. But my God, she went out with style!* "Rudder amidships," he said softly. "All ahead slow." *James Ellis* was just ahead now, steering to pass along *Walker*'s starboard side. They didn't dare steam so close in complete darkness because they couldn't show any lights and the bottom of the river truly was littered with an astonishing amount of hull-tearing wreckage. They had to stay strictly within the carefully marked channel and there was always danger of heavy floating debris.

The charges laid by the MTBs detonated behind them, throwing brightly glowing cataracts mixed with shattered timbers in the sky. *More debris'll wash downriver now,* Matt thought. *And more charges'll keep coming all night long. Sooner or later, the Grik'll have to try to stop us—if they haven't got something even nastier planned for after we force the passage. It's amazing how quickly imperatives change in war,* he mused on. Santa Catalina *died to jam this river, to protect us from the Grik. Now the blockage she made protects the Grik from us.*

"Wow," Spanky murmured, looking out past the bridgewing to starboard. A heavy Grik artillery barrage had opened up on the east side of the Allied defenses onshore. Long tongues of bright, yellow-orange fire stabbed the darkness in what seemed a continuous ripple of flashes. More flashes crackled on or behind the first Allied line as exploding shells popped and flayed the earth—and who knew how many people. *Not many, I hope,* Matt thought. *Most'll be under cover. The Grik do this every night now, sometimes several times. That's okay,* he added grimly to himself as Allied guns answered and the light show quickly intensified. *We do it back, and we're still better at it. And we bomb their asses wherever we want.*

"I wish *we'd* shoot at 'em," came Lieutenant Tab-At's voice as she joined them on the bridge. "Tabby" was a gray-furred Lemurian with a very female, very humanlike physique she'd once gloried in tormenting Spanky with when she was his understudy in engineering. Her reasons for doing so had been complex. At first she just did it for fun—until she realized she was crazy about him and wanted his attention. She'd grown since then, in many ways, and still loved him—hopelessly, she now realized—because he loved her in a different, fatherlike way. But she loved *Walker* too, and had risen to become her engineering officer in his stead. She'd absorbed everything he knew, and with the help of Chief Isak Reuben—possibly one of the best, if weirdest, snipes any navy ever had—Spanky was proud to acknowledge Tabby had probably become a better engineer than he'd ever been.

"I'd love to," Matt replied, "but we'd literally just be shooting in the dark. We'd kill some Grik, sure, but the army and Marines can do it as good or better, for now, and they have a lot more ammo. Ours is harder to make. And we *will* use plenty when we make our push, hammering the Grik on their river flank, but there's no sense reminding them we can every day."

"You don't really think they'll forget," Spanky said. It wasn't a question.

"No," Matt replied. "The Grik have finally wised up." He shook his head. "Some have, anyway. No sense educating the rest, though, or getting them used to us shooting at them. It ought to at least fluster them a bit when we do." He considered. "And we should have plenty of ammo when the time comes. We're still a little strapped, but supply will catch up."

"I hope so," Tabby said. "I wish the *Grik* haad more supply problems! How come they never run outa aammo? How come we ain't bombed out all the places they make powder?"

"That's a good question," Matt told her. "And I'm sure we've blasted a bunch, but I don't think they make powder the same way we do, in large-volume facilities. They had big, mass-production assembly lines for ships and such, and probably have the same sorts of places for small arms and cannon. Those upriver are mostly rubble now, but they've got a whole continent to draw on and hide stuff in. We haven't seen a speck of the joint. We've hit obvious factories around the lakes to the west and north, but don't have enough Clippers to hit everywhere. We never *will* have enough for *that*. So the Clippers raid around, or Nancys run around in daylight looking for smaller targets of opportunity, but they all still have to focus close, targeting stuff the Grik rebuild nearby, or hitting obvious supply runs on the land or river. It's like stomping ants. We might win—I think we can—but we'll never get 'em all, and there're a few things we'll never overcome. First, sticking to the ant analogy, there's just too damn many Grik we can't even see, doing stuff we don't know about. Second, while we're at the end of a very long supply line, we've pushed them back on top of theirs."

He shrugged. "And I'm sure they're running short of

stuff, maybe even powder. That's what they use for warheads *and* fuel for their rockets, and those've kind of quit around here. As fast and dirty as they were cranking them out, it has to make me wonder why. Is it a shortage of materials, labor, transportation, a place to make 'em? Or are they saving them back to smother us?" He took a long breath, still watching the artillery duel onshore.

"Well, how do you think they make powder?" Spanky pressed.

"Not me. Courtney Bradford," Matt replied. "A report he sent, which I got to read before it got dark, talked about all the cottage—or mud-hut—industries they turned up in the intact parts of Soala after they took it. The whole population of Uul laborers seemed in on it, making everything from leather armor to cartridge boxes, even the fins that stabilize rockets, which've never been seen in the south. It was all more or less unskilled labor, just cutting stuff out to a pattern, or sewing stuff together, but it fits in with the large-scale manufacturing we've seen them do, even on ships. One group works itself to death making one part, a certain frame assembly or something; another group makes something else. It all finally gets gathered in one place and assembled by some Hij overseer who knows the big picture."

"Sounds like BuOrd, in the old days," Spanky quipped, "only the Grik's stuff works."

Matt ignored him. "Anyway, seems somebody looking around for Courtney or Inquisitor Choon found a few places with stone crushers the size of tractor tires, screens, drying racks, and big clay pots full of all the stuff to make powder. Didn't find any stores of finished powder—that probably all got delivered as soon as it was done, which makes sense—but there was plenty of evidence on the crushers."

"And they had screens, which explains how they keep it consistent, if they mix it right," Spanky groused.

"Yeah. They probably use what's left for bursting charges, or rewet it and grind it again. The point is, Courtney's discovery is anecdotal, but if the Grik do that all over, they're probably not running out of powder or a lot of other things."

"So how do we beat them?" Tabby demanded. "You said you think we caan."

Matt nodded, finally ready to kick at least part of his scheme around with people he knew would keep it mum. "Hij Geerki's around all those Grik we took at Grik City every day. He's their mayor, for all intents and purposes." A small grin spread across his face at the thought. "He's seen how much they've changed as more and more of 'em live longer than they ever expected to, and they get a taste of a, well, less-oppressive life than they had before. Don't get me wrong, he works 'em pretty hard and none of 'em have it easy, but I guess that's a good enough description. The thing is, *all* the Grik are older now, even those in front of us. At least in the sense they're allowed to think a little." He glanced at Spanky. "All the same, don't forget, most of them are still basically kids too, and they've all been through a lot: total war that touches every one of 'em, blood and suffering, and crazy-fast changes to every part of their lives. And they can actually *see* change happening. I can't stress enough how new and disconcerting that must be for them. The only constant that remains is their new Celestial Mother, regardless of whether she has as much power as the old one did." There'd been a lot of speculation about that, and Muriname confirmed that Kurokawa had been sure that First General Esshk had usurped most of her authority.

"Frankly," Matt continued, "Geerki doesn't think they can take losing *another* Celestial Mother and still keep it together. I agree with him."

"So you sayin', aafter we been so careful not to blaast her aass, 'er even bomb Old Sofesshk too much, we gonna go aafter her in that cowflop paal-ace there?"

"Take out their queen," Spanky mused. He looked at Matt. "That's why we haven't plastered the joint all along. You've been cooking this up for a while and didn't want to chase her off."

"Maybe," Matt agreed. "Partly. I also didn't want to make a martyr of her and stir the Grik up even worse"—he glanced at Tabby—"like it did when that goofy Isak killed the old queen at Grik City and waved her head around on a pole."

Tabby snorted. "Good thing the baattle was pretty much over. I *don't* think he was expectin' the re-aaction he got!" She scratched her ear and blinked concern. "You think the new one's still in her paal-ace?"

"Sure. They've had no reason to move her, and her being there makes the Grik in front of Alden all the more determined. Just as significant," he added lower, "recon photos seem pretty conclusive. Something's happened to a lot of the Hij civvies in Old Sofesshk. There aren't near as many. Maybe they evacuated them, or sent them to the front. . . ."

"Or ate 'em," Spanky inserted.

Matt shrugged. "Who knows? But it also looks like they've dramatically reduced the number of troops there as well, from about ten thousand to only four or five."

"Then maybe they did move the queen," Tabby speculated.

"Henry Stokes's snoops with Pete don't think so, and neither does Geerki. Moving her would expose her to airstrikes, even random ones, and nothing our planes can drop can hurt her in that big stone cowflop. A lot of the warriors left in Sofesshk are scattered, probably keeping the remaining Hij in line, but most are in the vicinity of the palace. They're guarding *something* besides the silverware, probably from the Hij still hanging around." He cupped his chin in his hand, thinking. "Most significant of all, though, it looks like the four or five thousand Grik troops in Old Sofesshk are all there is inside one or two days' march of the place. Why keep more around, twiddling their thumbs in the rear, when they've got our beachhead and now the Repubs to worry about? And since the city's on a kind of peninsula, where two rivers join, if they can't reinforce from the north, they'd have to pull reserves from in front of Pete and take 'em across the water to get there."

"Sounds like a golden opportunity to rub her out, if we could get to her. But even if we could, we can't *kill* her, can we?" Spanky said, finally realizing where this was going.

Matt shook his head. "No. This time we have to *take* her."

Tabby blinked amazement, then rolled her eyes. "How

the hell we gonna do *thaat*? Even if she haad no guards at all, we still got all the Grik in the world between us an' her. An' somehow we get closer, they *will* move her!"

Matt slumped in his chair and looked straight ahead. Nat's PTs had passed them, heading for a tender to load more explosives. Three more of his squadron were already moving away, heading back toward the Neckbone. "Right," Matt agreed gloomily. "That's the part I can't figure out."

Spanky looked aft, eyes straying to the fighting now a couple of miles astern. It looked like small arms had joined in, as both sides went at each other hammer and tongs. The Grik had probably launched a probing attack, counting on the artillery barrage to keep I Corps' heads down. They didn't have any aerial recon right now, much less the detailed photographic maps the Allies had made of the enemy defenses, and throwing bodies into the grinder was the only way they could measure its strength. Mortars started falling, exploding in the no-man's-land between the lines, and some of the new parachute flares popped in the sky, illuminating the killing ground under sputtering orange stars. The small-arms fire intensified and a few machine guns joined in, bright tracers arcing out, bouncing into the sky.

Spanky's eyes suddenly went wide. "I think I just did. Figured it out, I mean," he said grimly, hesitantly, as if afraid to tell them. Matt and Tabby both looked at him and he took a deep breath. "Good God, I can't believe I'm gonna suggest this, but . . . You said Chack's doin' good, ready to get off his ass?"

Matt nodded, and Spanky pointed out at the flickering, drifting flares in the distance. Matt twisted in his chair to look past their wake as well.

"Parachutes," Spanky said at last.

Matt just stared for a moment, then stood. "You're right. Damn it, you're right." He was silent a long time, thinking. Finally, he took a long breath and rubbed his forehead. "I don't like it. *Nobody* will. But damned if I can think of anything else as fast and crazy and unexpected— or more likely to blow things open." He turned to Minnie and raised his voice. "Send to General Alden to try to speed up moving Sixth Corps into the line and pulling Second Corps' Third Division back to Camp Simy." He looked at Spanky and lowered his voice. "If we're gonna do this to Chack, he deserves the best backup we can give him. And that's Safir Maraan."

CHAPTER
9

W e're all gonna die!" Chief Gunner's Mate Dennis Silva proclaimed grandly, striding into Chack's tent without knocking on the pole by the flap. Lawrence, Silva's Grik-like Sa'aaran friend, stayed outside, placating Chack's orderly, who'd tried to stop the intrusion. Lawrence's strange-sounding voice was apologetic.

"Die!" screeched another familiar, annoying voice, from the small, colorful, tree-gliding reptile draped around Silva's taut, muscled neck.

"Ol' Petey's right for once," Silva agreed, pitching a cracker as if over his shoulder, but Petey caught it. The cracker exploded and crumbs rained down on the pile of paperwork on Chack's little folding table.

Chack was rapidly blinking gummy eyes at the big man and his lizard, silhouetted by the bright morning sunlight. He'd been in the trenches at the river beachhead toehold with Safir Maraan for several days while she coordinated the replacement of her corps by the Sixth. Movements like that were tedious and had to be made with care because the Grik were good at sensing weakness in the line. He hopped a ride downriver in *Walker*, the trip taking most of the night, and spent the time making plans with

Captain Reddy and Pete Alden. He hadn't slept until he came ashore.

Tossing off a light cottonlike blanket, he fumbled for his kilt and the Impie watch he kept in a pocket. "Whaat time is it?" he grated, irritated.

"Time to get yer lazy, stripey tail outa yer rack an' greet another hell-hot day in the luxurious liberty paradise o' Grikland!" Silva continued in his lofty sarcastic tone. "We got shit to do—if we're really gonna pull this latest turd beetle–crazy stunt." He shook his head in mock amazement. "An' it ain't even my fault for once. I didn't have nothin' to do with *this* goat-brained notion. Scuttlebutt says Spanky's to blame," he added darkly. He blinked thoughtfully and looked down. "Which makes sense, I guess . . ." His eye fastened back on Chack, who'd found his watch and groaned when he looked at it. Resignedly, he took the little key hanging from the same chain and started winding the piece. "But the skipper's on board, an' *he* ain't nuts," Silva continued, "which just proves he hates me after all, if he's willin' to go to such extremes to kill me off."

"Eat?" Petey screeched, and Silva tossed another cracker with similar results.

Chack eyed the accumulating mess on his table, then closed his eyes and shook his head. "Your logic is so twisted, how caan even you make sense of it? I've haad less thaan two hours sleep in . . ." He blinked confusion. "Days. And now you wake me up with this?" It took him a moment to figure out how Silva even knew about the plan. It wasn't out yet and Silva hadn't been part of making it. Then again, *Walker*'s crew, human and Lemurian, was as much family as the crew of any Home, and she was much smaller. Word got around fast. No enemy could've made Juan or the mess attendants in the wardroom talk, but they would've made sure Silva knew. Instead of pointlessly pursuing that, Chack simply said, "Nobody said you haave to come. Cap-i-taan Reddy might not even let you. I thought you were baack in the Naavy for good, your Maa-rine days over."

Silva scratched the short blond beard on his chin and glanced at his grimy fingernails to see if he'd captured anything. Cooties were becoming rampant in the trenches. "Sure, that's what I thought. But besides you, Gunny Horn was the only *real* Marine we had in our little band."

Chack was a bit taken aback by what was high praise from Silva on numerous levels, for him and Horn. Many of the same rivalries from the big destroyerman's old world were alive and well here, including traditional shipboard friction between deck-division "apes" and engineering "snipes," but so were those between the Army, Navy, Marines, Air Corps, even the various Allies. Rivalries were good for promoting competitive accomplishment, Chack knew, but sometimes hindered cooperation. Fortunately, so far, they always seemed to get tamped down before they got out of hand. But the point was, despite obligatory protestation to the contrary, Silva obviously admired *some* Marines, and his friendship with Gunnery Sergeant Arnold Horn predated either of their separate arrivals on this world.

"Arnie got shanghaied an' sent off to *Savoie* as her actin' *gunnery officer*, fer God's sake!" Silva began to rant. "All because he spent a little time on some old battlewagon in the old days an' learned to make the big guns shoot. Woop-te-do! How hard can it be? I heard Kurokawwy had *Griks* doin' it. But just imagine Arnie a goddamn officer. He'll hang hisself outa misery."

"Gunny Horn led a regiment, for all intents and purposes, when we went aashore upriver. So did you, for that maatter," Chack reminded.

Pctcy was leaning forward, eyeing the crumbs on the desk. Silva mashed him back down. "That ain't the same thing a'tall," he objected.

"Nevertheless," Chack continued, "while you might not"—he started to say "be fit," but stopped himself—"thrive as an officer, Horn might. And *Saa-voie* needs him."

"But they broke up the band!" Silva protested, then stopped. "Get in here, Larry. Quit sankoin' around out there." Lawrence joined them in the tent, hesitant, self-conscious. Silva might not acknowledge the vast gulf between his and Colonel Chack's authority, at least in "social" settings like he'd forced here, but Lawrence wasn't built that way. Lawrence wasn't Grik, though only his orange and brown coloration set him apart at a glance, but his birth culture—mostly wiped out and now changed forever—had been just as hierarchical. "Good 'orning, Colonel," he managed.

"Good morning, Laaw-rence. Would you like to sit?" Chack indicated a cushion on the grass floor. "I'd offer you coffee—or tea, if I had any," he added pointedly.

"You're gonna need me an' Larry," Silva forged ahead, "to fill Arnie's malingerin' shoes. Why, without Risa . . ." It was Silva's turn to catch himself. After an awkward moment, he exhaled noisily, but lowered his voice. "Yer gonna need us to keep yer head on straight," he finished.

"Oh, very well," Chack said severely, concealing his pain over Silva's mention of his sister, but also hiding pleasure as best he could. He hadn't even asked Captain Reddy for Silva. Everyone knew how much he'd been through, and, in reality, the entire fleet needed Silva's knowledge at least as much as Horn's. Horn knew the guts and gizmos in *Savoie*'s gunhouses, lifts, handling rooms, even her plot rooms and range finders better than anybody, but nobody knew general gunnery better than Silva. All the same, Chack knew Matt would give him Silva if he asked. Their mission was desperate, nearly suicidally so, and nobody had as much experience as Silva at getting things like that done. And this time all the marbles really were up for grabs.

"But we're *not* going to die," Chack continued adamantly. In the middle of the hellish bombardments upriver, Safir informed him there'd be a youngling between them. He was ecstatic—and agonized, knowing he'd have no more chance of getting her out of harm's way than Captain Reddy had of sending his pregnant wife, Lady Sandra, back to Baalkpan. Less, actually. Matt could *order* Sandra home, but Safir was a general, a queen, and a corps commander. He could spill her condition to Captain Reddy and *he* might pull her back, but Safir hadn't told anyone but Chack. She'd never forgive him and he'd lose her forever. And that was obviously why Captain Reddy didn't send his own much more pregnant mate away—though Chack was unsure how humans dissolved their matches. It didn't matter. Both females were devoted to their duty, Safir to the army and her people, Lady Sandra to the wounded. Chack and Matt would both have to endure their fear for the safety of their mates and younglings, and victory was the best, quickest way to protect them.

"Ha! Fat chance!" Silva laughed. "Did you miss the part about 'em throwin' us outa airplanes? Outa the god-damn *sky*, to plummet to our crunchy, spattery, agonizin' dooms, right in the middle of all the Grik in the world? Might as well take a bath with the flashies."

"Fat chance!" Petey echoed derisively.

Allied pilots had been issued tightly woven spidersilk parachutes for some time, though they were rarely used. Nobody was crazy enough to open one over the water or the Grik. Fish or Grik: take your pick, both would eat them alive. Scuttlebutt said pilots in the East had similar reservations about being taken by Doms. They probably wouldn't be eaten, but their deaths could be even worse. Parachutes were so rarely used, in fact, that a growing minority in the assembly, led by Sularaan representatives, wanted to halt their production to save money. That wouldn't happen because they *were* saving more aircrews all the time, mostly of crippled planes that made it back over friendly territory now that there was such a thing. But absolutely no one had ever imagined dropping armed troops behind enemy lines to fight. Not on this world.

"Cap-i-taan Reddy said the Ger-maans on your world attaacked the Dutch with paar-troopers. The Dutch were Con-raad Diebel's people, weren't they?"

Silva shrugged. "Who knows? I barcly knew the guy. Could'a been a Esky-mo for all o' me. Don't matter. Nobody here's ever done it. Nobody's even *thought* about it. Damn sure never practiced it! We'll have to cook up a way to do that, at least. Then, even if—somehow—a few of us make it down alive," Silva continued, "we won't have no artillery, hardly any ammo, food, or water, an' ever damn Grik in earshot o' the Salacious Mammy's screechy voice'll come a'runnin'."

"'Hat is 'salacious'?" Lawrence asked, always anxious to learn new words, but aware Silva often made up his own, or distorted real ones.

"Never mind," Dennis retorted, but cocked his head,

thinking. "Y'know? I ain't sure. I got called 'las-vicious' once. Don't know what that means neither, but I've heard both words aimed at the same folks from time to time."

Chack had taken the opportunity to pull on his kilt and stand. Now his tail was whipping back and forth behind him and he blinked impatience. "We *waant* the Celestial Mother to scream bloody murder—once she's secure and we've done all we caan to fortify our position in and around the Paal-ace of Vaanished Gods. Our presence will draaw a great deal of the enemy's attention, right when they'll be least prepared to spare it. At least thaat's the plaan."

"An' you know plans're for shit?"

Chack hesitated. "Often," he grudgingly admitted. "More often thaan not, in point of faact. It waasn't the case at Zaan-zi-bar, however."

"Maybe. Mostly. But, hell, I was makin' my part up as I went," Silva confessed.

"He all'ays do that," Lawrence complained lowly. "And *I* get shot!"

"I know, Dennis," Chack agreed, with a sympathetic blink at Lawrence. "You often use a great deal of initiaative. Your style caan be danger-ous," he qualified, "but is surprisingly effective. Thaat's one reason I'm glaad you're coming with me. You're always most useful when forced to be imaagin-ative. You and Cap-i-taan Reddy share few traits, but thaat's one."

"Yeah? Swell." Silva glared at Lawrence. "An' you don't *always* get shot, you fuzzy little salamander. Besides, ever'body else has got shot too. Why should you be special?" He looked back at Chack. "So what's the full dope? What's our little stunt supposed to accomplish, big picture, an' how do we get the fat lizard broad—an' our own asses—the hell out after we swipe her?"

Chack blinked at him, then laughed. "I guess the scuttlebutt misinterpreted what we meant by 'take.' You misunderstaand. We're not going to *swipe* the Celestial Mother from the Grik, we're going to secure possession of her at the paal-ace—and wait for the Grik to come for her."

Silva's right eye almost popped out. "Holy shit!"

Petey fluttered discontentedly on his shoulder. "Holy shit!" he cawed at Chack.

"You *are* talkin' suicide!" Silva objected. "I might as well go hang *myself.*"

"No. I told you we're not going to die and I meant it." *I must live, for my mate—and youngling now,* Chack thought. "If we secure the creature the Grik see as their Maker on Earth, they'll have no choice but to try to retrieve her—yet they'll be terrified of hurting her, or thaat we will. They'll go crazy, and think of the confusion! Thaat's when everything will break, and we'll get our chance to *wreck* the Grik!"

"Holy shit," Silva repeated. Then he looked at Lawrence. "Sorry, buddy. He didn't say nothin' about you. *You're* gonna buy it, sure." He thumped Petey on the head. "An' you ain't goin'."

USNRS Salissa (CV-1)

"So, Dennis Silva really *did* ask you to marry him!" Surgeon Commander Sandra Tucker Reddy asserted triumphantly as she, Surgeon Lieutenant Pam Cross, Diania, and several 'Cat and Impie SBAs completed their rounds among the men, 'Cats, and Grik-like Khonashi still collected on the aft third of *Big Sal*'s hangar deck. These had been some of the most seriously wounded during the fighting over *Santa Catalina* and Tassanna's Toehold onshore. Most still alive should remain so, but Sandra considered it too risky to move them. Keje agreed, and their presence hadn't caused any inconvenience. *Big Sal* had been receiving treatment of her own, from *Tarakaan Island*, and her air wing was operating from Arracca Field. New planes were coming aboard the hangar deck in crates, and Diania had caused a great sailcloth partition to be rigged between the work and the wounded. It was still noisy, but the space aft was spared the bustle and the dust.

"Yah, I guess. So?" Pam finally replied defiantly, her Brooklyn accent most pronounced when she was annoyed, and in sharp contrast to Sandra's softer Virginia inflection.

"I just think it's amazing, that's all," Sandra said. Rumors had swirled for weeks now, never confirmed by Silva or denied by Pam, and it was fascinating how many humans and 'Cats were caught up in the speculation. Then again, Silva, Pam, and Risa had never been bothered by such gossip in the past. Something had changed, and it wasn't just Risa's death. Still, truth be known, Sandra was enjoying her friend's discomfort a little. She couldn't help it. She knew her own discomfort, caused by a rough and unpleasantly adventurous pregnancy nearing eight months, had left her somewhat unkind at times; a propensity that appeared to increase in proportion to her own ungainliness. "What did you say?"

"I told him 'Hell, no!' That's what I said," Pam answered forcefully. "An' I wish everybody'd just lay off."

"But . . . I thought that's what ye wanted?" Diania said, utterly mystified. "Fer him tae ask ye, at long last!" If Pam and Sandra were small women, Diania was positively tiny. An "expat Impie gal," she'd been the first woman on this world to join the American Navy Clan, and among the first to escape the now-abolished system of female indenture in the Empire of the New Britain Isles. She was also exotically beautiful, despite the terrible damage to her left hand, mangled by a musket ball on Zanzibar. She couldn't do much with it and kept it wrapped, though she still had a thumb and two fingers. Sandra thought she'd eventually regain a lot of use from it, but knew it didn't matter a damn to Gunny Horn, who was nuts about the girl.

"Yah, well . . ." Pam hesitated. "It was as much how an' when he asked, as anything."

Sandra stopped short of their next patient, a Grik-like Khonashi with no legs, mercifully asleep. She knew they'd started doing wonders with prosthetics back home—'Cats were so imaginative when it came to things like that—but the Khonashi were relatively new, unexpected allies, and little thought had gone into helping them cope with such wounds. She'd spoken to this one before and he was proud of his service—and his wounds—but what kind of life could he have in the jungle of North Borno? The thought made her angry. "You were both in battle, fighting for your lives, and thought you'd probably die. What better time?" Sandra demanded impatiently.

"That's just it," Pam replied stubbornly. "He only asked when he thought we were done for. I want him to do it when he thinks we're gonna *live*!" She paused. "Besides, like I said, it was *how* he did it too. I'm not sure, under normal circumstances, it would even count as a proposal—an' I just *know* he did it that way on purpose so he could wiggle out later!"

Sandra frowned. "You know, there might not *be* much 'later' for any of us." She sighed and gestured around at the wounded. "Bad as it's been, I don't think we've seen anything yet." What they knew of the upcoming push was left unspoken. They'd been told to be prepared, but the scuttlebutt was running pretty dry on this one, and unprecedented effort was underway to keep it that way. Even the normally almost helplessly loquacious 'Cats in the know were keeping mum. The Grik were the least of their worries when it came to spying and counterintelligence, but they had Ando and a few of his people. And Ando obviously had at least one radio. Then there were the Doms and League, of course. Even if they weren't in contact with the Grik, if they learned too much about what was happening here, they could take advantage somewhere else. The Allies had been stung by slips too often, and even the 'Cats got that now.

"Yeah"—Pam had lowered her voice—"an' whatever's comin', Dennis'll be right in the middle of it," she said disgustedly. "No reason; he doesn't have to. He *wants* to. He doesn't give a damn how I feel."

Sandra started to say something to the effect that he was doing it for her, so she'd be safe. That he was doing it for the cause. All that might even be true, to a degree, but she knew Dennis Silva very well. Maybe better than Pam, in some ways. She knew what he was capable of when it came to protecting people he cared about, but that he *thrived* on chaos and calamity, mayhem and destruction. *Thank God we have him, because we need him, but sooner or later his number will be up. And Matt's the same*

way, sort of, she realized. *He doesn't love it, like Silva
does. He hates it. But when they 'loose the dogs,' his capacity for violence is just as great. Maybe more so because
he's so much more cold-blooded about it. Silva's all passion; he's hate and love, anger and obligation. He's vengeance unchained, all wrapped up in the joy of battle.
Matt becomes his ship; a steaming, deadly instrument of
destruction. And sooner or later, no matter how often
they've dodged it, he and USS* Walker *will both take the
big bullet. After so many have been shot at them, it's inevitable that the law of averages will eventually win.*

"*All* our numbers may be up soon," she murmured
softly, then glanced apologetically at her friends. "Our
men aren't the only ones in danger, you know. They could
lose *us.*" She glared at Pam. "And if you think that doesn't
make them crazy, you're nuts. I heard about what Silva
did on *Santy Cat* when he was out of his head. Didn't
think about anything but making sure *you* were safe." She
took a deep breath. "So. It's stupid to blame them for it
when they're in danger, and just as stupid for us not to
make the most of life with them when they're not."

"You . . . think I oughta said yes to Dennis?" Pam
asked slowly, and Sandra burst out laughing. She couldn't
help herself.

"Maybe, though it sounds like you should've gotten
witnesses and made him spell things out a little better."
She looked at Diania. "What about you and Gunny—I
mean Acting Lieutenant—Horn?"

Diania looked down but smiled. "We hae an . . . understandin'." Then she looked up, brows knitting. "But Arnold said we had tae hae a ring tae seal it—an' that before
we're even wed, mind." She blinked confusion in the Lemurian way. "Can ye tell me what that's aboot? I dinnae
understand. He wasnae sure how he'd *get* a ring, but 'twas
clearly important tae him."

Sandra and Pam both chuckled. Sandra and Matt had
been married in a huge ceremony on Respite Island, part
of the Empire of the New Britain Isles, and she proudly
wore the simple gold band he'd given her there. *One reason I guess I do owe Muriname,* she realized uncomfortably. *He could've taken it but he didn't.* Then she suddenly

remembered engagement rings weren't used in the Empire. With women practically being property until recently, why would they be? Briefly, she explained a little of that, then smiled. "Just roll with it, sweetheart. I'm so happy for you." She genuinely was. Diania had suffered as much as she had, right on the heels of her one great love being snuffed out. And Horn was a good man. He'd make her happy, if he lived. Sandra grinned mischievously. "And on a battleship, where will he find a suitable engagement ring, or something to make one from? It'll be a good test of his resourcefulness!"

She glanced at Pam and was surprised to see her suddenly looking very low.

"Dennis tried to give me a piece of a sling swivel he'd bent into a ring with some pliers. What a joke," Pam said quietly. "I threw it at him."

They continued on past the crippled Khonashi, and Sandra heard Pam muttering behind her. She was pretty sure she heard her say "What an idiot," but had no idea if she was talking about Dennis—or herself.

CHAPTER
10

*T*his don't look much like the flaat ground Courtney said this stretch of laand should be," groused Colonel (Legate) Bekiaa-Sab-At, staring out at the dusty, convoluted landscape beneath the hot afternoon sun as equally dusty, sun-faded troops of her own 23rd Legion marched past. Bekiaa commanded the newly designated 5th Division of the Army of the Republic, consisting of the 23rd, 1st, and 14th Legions. Each was "heavy," flush with replacements after the Battle of Soala. Counting support personnel, the new division designations resulted in somewhat larger forces than their counterparts in the Imperial and Union armies, numbering close to eight thousand men, 'Cats, and Gentaa. That would've made Bekiaa's force practically a corps, in the old way of thinking, but she knew Alden's I, III, and VI Corps on the Zambezi each had fifteen to twenty thousand now, and Safir Maraan's II Corps boasted thirty thousand or more.

Her XO, Prefect Bele, was the tallest human she'd ever known and as black as Safir Maraan's fur. Bekiaa sometimes wondered about that. The majority of humans in the Republic of Real People were generally kind of brown, like everywhere else, though some were just as pale as a few of the old destroyermen from *Walker* and *Mahan* who spent most of their time belowdecks. But there were a lot of darker-colored people in the Republic, and—she'd heard—in the NUS as well. She'd never seen any before she came here. *Maybe there aren't any on the world Cap-i-taan Reddy came from?* she speculated.

"It *is* relatively flat here . . . if one concentrates one's gaze solely on the distant mountains," Bele countered, amused, "and avoids looking at the eroded landscape. Washed out by runoff from those very mountains, I suspect." The flatland Courtney Bradford predicted might've looked that way at a cursory glance from the air, the general cover of scrubby, brushy acacia defying a proper appreciation for the contours, but on the ground it was anything but. The whole plain was crisscrossed and gouged by winding gullies, arroyos, even valleys. More detailed surveys and better maps had been made and those very features provided good cover from the Grik at points where the armies were in contact, as well as concealing avenues of advance and maneuver. Unfortunately, the Grik used the terrain as well, moving troops at night to avoid observation from the air, and probing for the flanks of the Republic advance—much like what Bekiaa and her division were trying to do. It made her nervous.

They *knew* large numbers of Grik were hurrying south to halt their advance. No restrictions remained on the exposure of Repub aircraft—the Grik knew they had them now—and swift, biplane Cantets combed the ground between their forces and the AEF almost at will. They'd even staged a couple of symbolic raids on the Grik trenches surrounding the AEF, firebombing positions across from their allies to boost their morale and prove they were drawing near. But every time massed reinforcements were reported heading south, they somehow dispersed, *vanished*, in the countless cracks and crevices, or under the insubstantial-looking ground cover, before airstrikes could be called against them. That told Bekiaa the terrain ahead must be working with Grik like maggots in meat. They just couldn't find them. Nor did they dare weaken their main force, now numbering close to eighty thousand troops, to look too far afield. Even heavy scouts like hers couldn't search too far and had to stay in constant contact with General Kim's HQ.

"But it's dry now, thaank the Maker," Bekiaa countered, "yet only dry at this time of year, most likely. If we caan't push through to join the First Fleet AEF at the Zaam-bezi before the rains come again, we could be cut off from them *and* our base at So-aala!"

"Possibly," Bele conceded, repositioning the sling of his rifle on his tired shoulder. Like those of their allies, all standard Repub rifles fired heavy black powder cartridges. They had more modern propellants feeding their Maxim-type machine guns, much like their allies used in their Browning-style .30s and .50s. But their infantry rifles, basically single-shot bolt-action copies of M-1871 Mausers, were little better suited to higher-pressure propellants than the Allin-Silva "trapdoor" rifles and carbines, though they were more adaptable to modifications for a magazine of some sort. That was one of many long-promised improvements.

All the Allies could've fielded better small arms by now, but the middle of a definitive campaign wasn't the time to make such profound changes and their industrial focus was on other things. Besides, not only did the Allin-Silva's .50-80, and Repub 11 x 60mm (.43 cal) kill Grik and Doms quite satisfactorily, they were also very accurate and still shot much faster than the enemy's smoothbore muzzle-loaders. Just as important, they were effective against some of the large, terrifying predators on this world.

Bekiaa adjusted her own sling, supporting the precious .30-06, 1903 Springfield that Colonel Billy Flynn gave her before he died. It might not be as effective against "big boogers" close up, but her '03 (and Courtney Bradford's Krag-Jorgensen, to a lesser extent) had the flatter trajectory required to hit anything she could see through its ingenious adjustable sight. And Flynn had replaced the front sight with a taller blade. That allowed precise point-of-aim shooting without the "foot below hold" prescribed in the 1940 copy of *The Bluejacket's Manual* he also gave her after incorporating the pertinent parts in his new manual for infantry tactics, used for the basic training of all Army and Marine recruits in the United Homes. Just as important to Bekiaa, her '03 and Courtney's Krag held five rounds. *I hope we get more rifles like them someday if we ever haave to go against the League,* she thought.

She and Bele resumed their march, near the head of the column. A shallow gorge lay before them, the object of their probe, and skirmishers had bailed over the edge to scout it. Bekiaa had no doubt there'd be Grik down there somewhere. The absence of other fleeing or attacking animals, already spooked out, was virtual proof of that. Still, she didn't expect too much yet; certainly not the enemy's extreme right flank, which was her personal pursuit.

A sultry breeze was their only relief from the oppressive dust and heat, and she paused again to take a sip from her canteen. Water butts on wagons drawn by suikaas traveled up and down the line of advance and Bekiaa encouraged her troops to send canteens with one member of each squad at every opportunity. She'd been desperately thirsty in battle before and couldn't imagine anything more miserable or easily preventable when they had the means. She'd spare her troops that experience if she could.

The dull crack of a rifle shot distracted her, and she put the stopper back in her canteen. Another shot followed the first, joined by a sudden flurry.

"Skirmishers probably found a few skulking Grik," Bele speculated.

"Prob-aably." Even as Bekiaa agreed, however, the firing steadily increased. They had two centuries of skirmishers ahead, about 160 troops, and within seconds she figured she'd heard that many shots, at least. "More thaan just a few skulkers," she decided, an ominous feeling rising in her chest. "I know it'll delay us, but let's deploy the legions to be safe."

Any sense such a measure might merely prove an overcautious inconvenience quickly dissipated as the now-frantic crackle of constant rifle fire was answered by the thump of Grik muskets. *Lots* of muskets.

"Bugler!" Bele called. "Sound column into line!" A

man, one of several horsemen and 'Cats riding slowly behind their commander, raised his bugle to his lips and blew a series of sharp notes. Only humans could handle bugles. 'Cats used whistles in other allied armies or aboard ships, able to mimic a bosun's pipe and its many calls by varying the force of the blow. High-pitched whistles could fall on ears deafened by the thunder of guns, however, while bugles might still be heard.

The long column of troops marching eight abreast hadn't been a pretty thing in the first place, due to the rough terrain, but it hadn't lost its cohesion. And all Bekiaa's legions knew her reputation and that something beyond mere excellence would always be expected. Their deployment wasn't pretty either, across such broken ground. It was noisy, a little confused, and accompanied by irate bellows of NCOs, but it was accomplished with a speed and efficiency any other division would have to envy. The 1st Legion spread out on the left, three ranks deep, troops hacking at the thorny acacia and stacking the brush in front of their line. That helped clear the line of fire and give them some defense. The ground was too hard to dig in. The 23rd was doing the same in the middle; the 14th on the right.

"Courier!" Bekiaa cried, staring downslope at what she'd decided must be an ancient, dry riverbed. A few skirmishers were moving back now, some wounded, others helping those who were, and the volume of musket fire had eclipsed the rifles. *There's a lot o' Grik down there,* she realized, *more thaan should'a been able to hide from our planes, based on the crummy maaps I haave. They show the thing as a shaallow, kinda narrow caan-yon—an' I guess it might look thaat way from the air. But how long is it? It could stretch for miles, an' we know the Grik been usin' such things to funnel troops in front of our advaance.* Her annoyance regarding their imperfect maps and recon evaporated. *An' I nearly led my whole division to its doom, most likely.*

"Your orders, Legate?" one of the mounted 'Cats prompted.

Bekiaa shook herself. "Bring up haaf the aartillery an' put it in the line. Just like we did at Gaughaala," she added resignedly. "Range is gonna be too short for the guns to fire over our heads, for the close-up work. We'll try the new caan-ister rounds, or set fuses for muzzle bursts. The rest of the aar-tillery'll stay baack an' fire long, into the vaalley for now. If there's as maany Grik down there as I think, maybe thaat'll chop 'em up too." More skirmishers were pulling back, some turning to fire as balls and the occasional crossbow bolt *vroop*ed past. Bekiaa still couldn't see the enemy, though a lot of dust and gunsmoke was rising beyond the canyon rim just a couple hundred yards ahead. "Take this mess-aage to the comm waagon," Bekiaa told another rider. "'Haave encountered a laarge force of Grik infantry in the defile across my paath. I don't know *how* laarge, but it seems prepared to press an aassault. I've deployed to meet it. Maybe we stumbled on an isolated brigade an' they're just chasin' our skirmishers, but it could be the main force lookin' for *our* flaank. Some air recon an' support would be aappreciated,'" she added dryly, then blinked concern.

"'If it *is* a sizable force, I'm not in the best position to stop it, due to the range of engagement. In aaddition to air, I might need indirect fire support. The aartillery observer haas our position. Please coordinate with him.'" She paused, considered, then shook her head. "Go," she told the rider. A last rush of thirty or forty skirmishers came in view, bolting for the safety of their lines. A hail of mostly ineffectual shots pursued them, but several spun and fell. Just as the first retreating men and 'Cats reached the brushy barricade, a solid mass of Grik appeared in their wake, panting from their sprint but wide-eyed with excitement. Their gray leather and iron armor and dun-colored plumage was chalky with dust, and tendrils of filmy drool streamed from open, toothy jaws. Bright musket barrels and bayonets gleamed and bloodred sword or sunburst and "meatball" devices glared garishly on stained pennants whipping above the leading edge of the charge. Apparently surprised to find 5th Division deployed and ready, the rush ground to an uncertain stop—just long enough for the last skirmishers to clear the front.

"Commence firing!" Bekiaa shouted, which was repeated by Bele, then her legion commanders. Staggered volleys, controlled by centurions, slashed at the hesitant Grik, and they reeled back down out of sight. When the smoke of that first rank of riflemen cleared, not a single standing Grik remained, though scores were down, dead or writhing and screeching on the ground.

"Maybe that was it," Bele speculated. "Must've been four or five hundred of them."

"Not it at all, Prefect, if ye'll pardon the intrusion," gasped Optio Jack Meek, hurrying up to join them. The young man looked as rough as the returning skirmishers, and his mustard-brown tunic was soaked in blood. He caught Bekiaa's concerned blinking and gestured at himself. "Not mine, Legate. One o' the lads took a ball an' I carried him out. Nearly didn't make it! Then I feared I'd be caught between them murderin' devils an' a volley!"

"Whaat the hell were you doin' out there?" Bekiaa demanded hotly. She glanced around. "And prob-aably without a rifle again, as usu-aal."

"I was scoutin'," Meek replied reasonably. "Don't need a rifle to scout."

"You're not a *scout*, Optio Meek!" Bekiaa almost shouted, blinking furiously. No one really believed Jack—son of Doocy Meek, the Republic's ambassador to the United Homes—was just an optio and Bekiaa's aide. "You're Inquisitor Choon's *spy*—on me," she continued lower.

Meek nodded, unashamed. "Aye, at first, but no more. I *am* your aide by choice an' Inquisitor Choon's command."

"Then that puts you under Legate Bekiaa's orders, not Choon's," Bele scolded. "Certainly not free to indulge your whims. If you wish to remain the Legate's aide you'll follow her orders to the letter, including those instructing you to arm yourself. Is that understood?"

"Aye," Meek readily agreed for once. "A rifle might've been of use back there." He nodded at the rim of the canyon, choked with Grik corpses. Other skirmishers had approached, waiting to report, and the troops in the line were nervous. Obviously, no one really thought this was over. "Make your report," Bekiaa ordered, but she wasn't looking at Meek. A man with a bloody scalp wound stood at attention and saluted.

"Centurion Honlee Fiske, Legate," Bele reminded, "commanding the Second Century of the Fourteenth Legion."

"Of course," Bekiaa said. "Whaat did you see?"

"Grik, Legate, thousands of them, packed as tight as could be back in yonder gulley as far as I could see. All moving this way. I . . ." He paused, uncertain if he should speculate.

"Go on."

"I think we've found that flank we groped for," he replied, "just as it was about to fall on ours."

Bekiaa studied Fiske a long moment, trying to find any doubt or exaggeration in his eyes. "Thaank you, Centurion. Thaat'll be all. See to your troops." She looked at Meek after the centurion left. "Was thaat your impression too?"

"Aye."

"Then I waant you to person-aally take this message to the comm caart: 'We haave repulsed a heavy enemy scouting force—fairly easily—but I suspect this truly is their extreme right flaank, positioning itself for a major attaack. We haave them in a bottle for now, but they'll soon deploy in the open and we'll haave to shift our line to meet them. A heavy aartillery baarrage now, coordinated with airstrikes, could cripple their entire offensive and leave the paath to Sofesshk open.'"

A tumult was rising in the depression ahead as more organized Grik forces pushed forward. Soon they'd crest the rim of the valley in their thousands, not hundreds, and start spreading out. Bekiaa put her hands on her hips like she'd seen Spanky McFarlane do so often. Bele imitated her unconsciously. Together they displayed as much unconcern as if suddenly confronted by an unexpected insect, not a seething, overwhelming horde of Grik. "Caarry on, Optio Meek," Bekiaa said. She looked at Bele. "In the meantime, let's see whaat we caan do. All our mortars and all three baatteries of Derby guns not moving into the line will staart putting as much fire as they caan down in that goddaamn hole in front of us."

"We should really move all the guns back," Bele objected. "They shoot too flat for this sort of thing."

Bekiaa considered. "No. Half on the line," she insisted. "I fear we'll need them there. And haave the rest send half their caanister forward. But leave them some infaantry protection. The Grik could pop out of any of these raa-vines now they know where we are."

General Kim, Courtney Bradford, Inquisitor Kon-Choon, and General Taal-Gaak stared down at a large map tacked to a rickety, collapsible table in General Kim's HQ tent. The map was bigger, but probably only slightly better than the ones Bekiaa referenced, and they'd all become painfully aware how poorly it depicted the convoluted local terrain. Artillery thundered constantly, targeting what they thought they'd identified as the largest concentration of Grik forces blocking their advance, massing about two miles away across yet another wide, thorny depression. General Kim had no choice but to deploy the bulk of his own army in a defensive posture until he had a better idea what the enemy intended.

With almost eighty Cantet biplanes now flying out of airstrips around Soala, he should've had sufficient aerial reconnaissance. And the planes were taking a grisly toll on the enemy with their firebombs. But in addition to the surprisingly troublesome terrain, the Grik had received hundreds of the ridiculously crude but disconcertingly effective antiair mortars they'd been using to good effect against the Allies for a couple of years. Basically just heavy pipes with rounded baseplates at the breech end to pivot against the earth, they required only a couple of Grik to carry them, quickly charge them with powder and handfuls of musket balls, and lean them in the general direction of slow, low-flying targets. They could be anywhere, and Kim had already lost a dozen planes and their two-man crews trying to get a closer look at things.

Ironically, the very presence of the mortars implied the Grik were trying to prevent observations over ground they protected, and that was another thing that had convinced Kim the force he'd deployed against and was expending so much ammunition on was the main enemy concentration. It still might be, but the report from Legate Bekiaa's division and General Taal's cavalry scouting to the east had thrown everything into doubt.

"So, in effect, you're telling me our pilots have told us only *exactly* what the Grik wanted them to," Kim growled at Choon.

The Lemurian spymaster blinked affirmative, lids flashing over large, pale blue eyes. "I fear that's the case. The *Fliegertruppen*," he said, using the Republic word for its army pilots, "have learned to equate ground fire with the presence of Grik. Where there's no fire, there are no Grik, and that's what they've reported." He blinked consternation, tail lashing. "I still find it difficult to believe the Grik could just crouch and hide from aircraft flying directly overhead. They've never displayed such discipline! But that's exactly what they must've done, if Legate Bekiaa's report is true—and I do not doubt her," he added fervently, glancing at General Taal, whom he considered his rival for Bekiaa's affection. "In fact, knowing Legate Bekiaa, I suspect her assessment that she faces a 'large force' is likely an understatement. We must move to reinforce her at once!"

"I agree," Taal said. "My cavalry has the farthest to go but can get there quickest."

Kim looked at him. "But you suspect equally large forces on our right!" He waved to the north. "And what of *that* force? We know it's large and has many guns firing into our forward defenses now. All indications suggest it's massing for an attack on this position, possibly as soon as tonight." He murmured aside to Courtney. "We've taught the Grik too much. Whether they like moving at night or not, they've learned to use darkness to close with us."

"Indeed," Courtney agreed absently, running his fingers through thinning white hair as he leaned over the map. His ever-present straw sombrero was tucked under his left arm. He traced the distance between them and 5th Division with his right index finger. "Will our artillery range that far?" he asked.

"The Derby guns and newest howitzers will. Not the mortars," Kim replied.

"Then I urge you to place all you can spare under the

direction of Legate Bekiaa's artillery observer at once."
He nodded at Choon. "And begin sending reinforcements as well." He looked at Kim. "I'm no military man;
never claimed to be. I used to consider myself a natural-
ist, though that . . . hobby no longer binds me as tightly as
it did. Perhaps someday . . ." He sighed. "But it did make
me a rather acute observer, if I say so myself, and I believe you'll admit I've scrutinized a deal more of Grik
strategy and tactics than anyone here." He pointed to the
map. "The Grik *have* learned from us and adapted their
tactics." He paused. "Yet I think I see a very ancient
strategy unfolding here, probably almost instinctive to
them, and they've used it successfully against us from
time to time."

Kim shouted orders to his signalman to have the field
artillery HQ stand by for fire commands from Bekiaa's
observer, via the wireless comm cart with her column.
Though wireless communication had been known in the
Republic, field communication of any kind was new to the
Army. Quickly grasped as essential after the Battle of
Gaughala, the strange Australian naturalist/ambassador
had arranged a gift of efficient, portable equipment from
the United Homes. He was still pointing at the map when
he had Kim's attention again. "You've only ever seen the
Grik do two things: full-frontal assault and defense. Neither was as successful as they would've hoped, I'm sure,
but let's quickly examine both events. At the Battle of
Gaughala they swarmed to the attack directly out of the
Teetgak Forest. It was a desperate bid to stop our
advance—which very nearly succeeded—but it had been
impossible for them to develop a more complicated, traditional assault within the dense confines of the woods.
Things might've turned out very differently if they had,"
he added ominously. "Then at Soala, Grik troops new to
the very concept of defense were faced by your carefully
laid plans and brilliantly executed attack. Frankly, I was
surprised they fought as well as they did."

"So what's their traditional strategy?" General Taal
asked impatiently.

Courtney looked at him and blinked. "It's very simple,
really. Not so different from what we did to them at Soala,

and one reason I was also surprised our plan worked so well against them."

"You talk in circles, Mr. Bradford," Choon complained.

"Yes I do, in point of fact," Courtney confessed, "but that's how Grik think. They encircle their prey. Think of war, in their minds, as an extension of the cooperative hunt. They fix the prey's attention in one direction while the killing blow falls elsewhere. It's been so almost every time they've launched a prepared attack against other members of the Grand Alliance. Always, there's a diversion at least, but the most carefully laid plans by their better generals—Hij Geerki calls them designs—embrace what they consider the dance of battle."

"Which involves?" Kim demanded.

"Fixing the prey's attention"—Courtney drove the idea home, pointing to the north; then his finger moved back to Bekiaa's position on the map—"so it won't see the killing blow. The attack you expect *will* come, General Kim, and though probably not exactly a feint—the Grik don't think like that and it'll come hard—the *main* attack"—he glanced at Taal—"or attacks will come from the flanks." He shrugged. "Only our luck we were looking about, trying to discover *their* flanks at the same time, and Bekiaa stumbled across this western envelopment force."

"By the Maker!" General Taal gasped. "All the more reason I should rush my cavalry there!"

"No," Kim said. "If Mr. Bradford is correct, that'll leave us utterly exposed to a heavy attack from the east. No," he repeated thoughtfully, staring at the map. "You may send a division, but the bulk of your cavalry corps, led by you," he stressed, "must block that attack alone, General Taal. Spoil it, delay it, bleed it dry, and remain ready to cover the withdrawal of the divisions I must leave here, their attention apparently 'fixed' on the enemy in front of us. They'll mount as spirited a defense as they can before I pull them out."

"Pull them out *where*, General Kim?" Choon asked.

Kim looked at him. "To the west, of course. The entire army will move to support Legate Bekiaa and utterly crush the force attacking her. If Mr. Bradford is correct, it's probably composed of at least a third of the Grik blocking our way, after all. Then we'll rush northeast as fast as we can, leaving the rest of the Grik in confusion and disarray."

"And standing right on top of our supply line," Choon interjected sourly.

Kim nodded. "True. We'll only have whatever food, water, even ammunition, we can carry. The closest supply convoys can try to join us, but the rest must turn back for Soala. And even with all our wagons and suikaas, we'll have to abandon a lot of equipment so we can focus on the essentials and move quickly." He sighed. "I know this is a great gamble, but worth the risk, I think." He looked at Courtney. "Please inform Captain Reddy of our intentions, and that I'll instruct our ships now moving supplies from Songze up the Ungee River to Soala to change course for the Zambezi. We'll desperately need those supplies when we link up with his expeditionary force." He frowned. "I know Captain Reddy is planning an audacious scheme of his own, though I have no idea what it is."

"No one does, General," Courtney consoled. "But I suspect he, like you, is preparing a great gamble and won't risk our enemies discovering what it is."

"Well then," Kim huffed, "I just hope he's able to spring his surprise as quickly as circumstances have forced us to commence ours." He smiled slightly. "Two mad ventures combined must surely be at least as confusing to the enemy as they will be to us."

Choon was staring at the usually so conservative Kim with openmouthed amazement. He recovered himself. "The Kaiser wouldn't approve," he warned.

Kim smiled even broader. "Oh, I think he would. He's more a gambler than you imagine. The *Senate* will wail after the fact, over the risk and expense if not the lives. Fortunately, it's not their decision, and by the time they vote on whether to replace all the ordnance and equipment this will cost, we will already have won." He blinked irony in the Lemurian way. "Or we'll all be dead and they'll have other things to worry about."

Grasping his hands behind his back, General Kim strode outside under the hot afternoon sun while Courtney dashed past the signal-'Cat and directly into the head-

quarters communications tent nearby. "Orderly!" Kim
cried. "All corps commanders to me in ten minutes. Any
not here will be replaced. Fetch me the supply train Dominus as well," he added, referring to the Gentaa logistics
supervisor. The 'Cat orderly blinked astonishment. "Except for divisions I specify, the army will prepare to
march in one hour," Kim continued, "including all support elements and their equipment. Whatever they can't
load in wagons, they'll accumulate here." He didn't add
that he'd leave orders for the rear guard divisions to burn
everything they left when they pulled out.

"But, Gen . . ." the orderly began, then saluted and
scampered off, tail high.

"By your leave, General Kim," General Taal said urgently. "I believe I've heard all I need to, and I have a
great deal to do!"

"Of course."

Taal bounded toward his horse, standing amid a squad
of his troopers, and hopped in the saddle. With a sharp
shout, they galloped off.

More quickly than Inquisitor Choon would've expected, Courtney rejoined him amid the rising confusion
as Kim continued barking orders. "That didn't take long,"
he observed.

"No," Courtney agreed. "We're relatively close"—he
gestured at the tall antennae telescoping upward from a
robust wagon with a wide footprint—"and have an excellent signal today." He shrugged. "And there was little to
add to my prepared message about our long-planned effort
to break through to our comrades in the AEF. I simply
instructed it be sent with the amendment that today's the
day, and any commotion they can add will be appreciated."

Choon chuckled, then blinked pensively. "Much rests
upon your observations, Mr. Bradford. One way or another, we've cast the die, as your people say."

Courtney nodded and smiled a bit wistfully, plopping
the sombrero on his head. "True, I suppose," he agreed.
"But I only told General Kim what Grik normally do. I
wonder what truly *is* normal for Grik these days? Still,
I'm amazed how quickly Kim acted. The responsibility's
ultimately his, and he shouldered it magnificently!"

"Nonsense," Choon denied. "You gave him what he's craved since the Battle of Gaughala: an excuse to run wild against the enemy, with a reasonable chance of success. If, that is, Captain Reddy's prepared to act as . . . precipitously."

Courtney snorted. "It's been my experience, sometimes to my extreme unease, that Captain Reddy's *always* prepared to act precipitously if lives, his ship, or his cause is at stake." He blinked reflectively. "And it does generally turn out for the best." He sobered and promptly began striding toward his own horse, a short-legged, potbellied thing, calm and docile as a lamb and utterly unfit for cavalry service. "But for now," he said louder, "I fear the greatest burden rests on our dear Legate Bekiaa-Sab-At and her brave division once more. I serve no further purpose fluttering about here, so I'll join my friend." His Lemurian orderly handed him his Krag. Slinging the rifle over his shoulder and across his back, he rose awkwardly in the saddle.

"Kim said an hour," Courtney called back to Choon, "but it'll be two or three at best before more than just the closest divisions reach the Fifth. If Bekiaa can't hold that long, the whole army'll get bogged down pushing through her straggling survivors and the rampaging horde behind. We could *lose* it all today."

Choon blinked, then straightened his colorful waistcoat and nodded. "I serve little purpose here either, now that General Kim has set his course," he decided aloud. "A horse for me as well!" he called.

A short distance to the rear of the command HQ, several guns barked, their projectiles shrieking away on high trajectories to the west. Minutes later, two more fired. *Finding the range,* Courtney guessed. *I hope they get it quickly!* His wish became reality when thirty guns, 3″ Derby guns and 4″ howitzers, all fired at once.

*P*our it in!" Bekiaa roared as volley after volley slashed out from her own 23rd, right in front of her. And regiment after regiment of Grik, carefully aligned, shoulder to shoulder as if on parade, seemed to magically appear in the dense cloud of smoke, marching steadily forward—only to wither under the incessant fire. Bekiaa was almost incredulous, but somewhat gleefully so. *They learned this from us too, these lineaar taactics,* she realized. *An' they worked—when we haad smoothbore muskets, like they do now. But they only haad spears an' crossbows then. We got breech-loading rifles!* And though in line, the best they could do without trenches, Bekiaa's three ranks of infantry were more spread out.

The first rank, lying prone, fired again at the shouted command. They immediately started reloading as the next rank, kneeling, fired over them. The rear rank stood, firing offhand, and taking most of the casualties when the approaching Grik clung to their composure long enough to return a volley. One did so now, and Bekiaa heard the meaty slap of musket balls hitting muscle and bone, or the hollow thumps when they hit torsos. Screams arose, but even so close, they just couldn't compete with the unending squeals of wounded Grik, the rattle and crash of rifles and muskets, and the ear-slamming pressure of Derby guns coughing canister as fast as their crews could slam shells in their breeches.

Above it all came the shriek of incoming shells. Bekiaa couldn't see where they burst, but runners raced back from several vantage points, heading for the comm cart.

One man sprawled on his face, a gaping red hole in his back. Minutes later, more shrieks filled the sky, joined by the first pair of Cantets swooping down to drop firebombs beyond her view. *Caantets look very sleek,* she thought, *almost like flying fishes. An' I hear their plywood bodies are stronger thaan our Mosquito Hawks an' Naancys. But thaat top wing makes 'em look kinda fraagile.* Black smoke roiled in the air, but one of the Cantets staggered as it climbed, streaming smoke.

So these Grik have aanti-air mortars after all, Bekiaa guessed dispassionately. *Sneaky baastards hid their force just by not shootin' at our planes. Smaart.* The wounded plane was trying to make it back over her line but it suddenly spun out of control and simply plunged straight down, adding its own impact to the new flurry of shells. Still more Cantets roared over, dropping bombs, even as what must've been half a hundred shells fell in the depression ahead. *Those pilots're all green as graass,* she realized, *an' the Maker help 'em if the Grik throw any of their Jaap planes against 'em. But they have plenty of guts, to fly right in with the big bullets!*

A long series of explosions erupted in the canyon, throwing smoke and dust plumes high in the air. She expected the Grik in front to react in some way, but they didn't waver. Either they had no idea what was happening behind, or were just that well-trained and disciplined. In spite of the afternoon heat, a chill went down her spine. *Whaat if we caan't break this aattack?* she wondered. *Gener-aal Kim thinks this could be a third of the whole Grik aarmy chasin' us. We're just one division—an' we're gonna run out of aammo faast.*

Prefect Bele joined her, striding briskly. He was pressing a bandage where a musket ball had torn a deep furrow in the flesh between his neck and shoulder, and his tunic was dark with blood. "As we feared, Legate," he began without preamble. "The enemy is deploying out of the canyon farther back"—he pointed—"pulling guns up on the flat and emplacing them to smash our left. Infantry is moving up behind them. I think you should order the First Legion to pull back slightly to face that threat more squarely."

Bekiaa blinked agreement. "Very well. The First can add little to the slaughter here. So far the Grik seem content to maarch straight against the Twenty-Third and Fourteenth. Perhaaps the grade's too steep elsewhere an' a slope funnels 'em to us?" She turned to a runner from the 1st Legion. "Did you hear?" she shouted over the roar of firing and the thunder of exploding shells. "Very well. My compliments to Col-nol Naaris, an' he's to move to refuse our flaank, his baattery an' best maarksmen to engage the enemy guns an' their crews. Under *no* circumstances will his right lose contaact with the Twenty-Third's left."

"Yes, Legate!"

A Grik ball ricocheted off Bekiaa's helmet, knocking it askew and leaving a deep gray dent. She dropped as if poleaxed.

"A true 'meeting engagement,'" Courtney Bradford shouted as he and Choon, their aides and guards, rode briskly to the sound of the guns. They'd passed a division already loping west at the double time and had been passed in turn by a hard-riding regiment of General Ta-al's cavalry that Kim had allowed him to send. It was a good thing. They were a little higher than the developing battle and could see how it was shaping better than Bekiaa could. So could the cavalry, and they spurred their mounts from a canter to a gallop and veered left. A female Lemurian optio trotted back and saluted Choon and Bradford.

"My centurion asks if you'll remain here to direct the infantry to the left as it arrives," she said. As always, Courtney was a little surprised by the Repub 'Cat's enunciation. Of course, Lemurians in the Republic had been speaking human languages longer than anyone.

"We're heading down to join Legate Bekiaa," Courtney replied impatiently.

"Of course," Choon told the optio, blinking admonishment at his companion. "I want to be with the Legate as much as you, Mr. Bradford, but we came to support her. Can we do that better by directing troops where they're most needed, or adding our own few weapons to her firing line?"

"The former, of course," Courtney replied, then grinned. "Which you can do without me." He nodded toward the rising smoke and dust of battle. "I'll go on—and send back word if the Legate has a different idea about what support she needs. Sometimes the big picture isn't as critical as the small. She may need direct reinforcement, for example. I'm sure she needs more ammunition by now."

Choon blinked rapidly, a combination of anger, frustration, and agreement. No doubt he wished he'd thought of that first and it was he, not Courtney, who'd continue on.

"Let's go, mates!" Courtney called, kicking his plump mount with his heels, his sombrero falling back, suspended by the stampede string around his neck. His aide and several guards followed.

"Blast that preposterous, irrepressible, brilliant . . . buffoon," Choon fumed. "I'll never forgive him. *Particularly* if he's killed!"

"Mr. Bradford!"

Courtney somehow heard the familiar voice of Optio Meek over the tumult of battle, yet he spun his horse and looked around in vain. The Grik were *right there*, their thickening ranks surging just sixty yards in front of Beki-aa's thinning lines, doggedly, manically trading volleys at ranges even smoothbores could hardly miss. And the space behind the line was choked with wounded, corps-'Cats treating or carrying them, and runners dashing back and forth. The noise was stunning, all encompassing, and it was no longer possible to separate the sounds of small arms, mortars, artillery, or planes flying overhead. Courtney was sure the bombs and artillery must be doing terrible work, but their gunners were still inexperienced with the new art of precision, indirect fire. They simply wouldn't risk firing too close to their own people. Courtney understood that, but the very effectiveness of the barrage falling on the bulk of the enemy might be pushing the leading edge more determinedly on.

His horse squealed in anguish and spun faster. He tried to hold on but the saddle had no horn or anything else to grab. He fell and hit awkwardly, trying to roll as best he could with the Krag on his back. The bolt handle gouged his side over his short rib and he gasped, but he looked in time to see his poor horse stop, shudder, and fall to the ground, nearly pinning his legs. He scrambled back until he came up against a corpse, and his aide and Optio Meek were beside him at once. "Are ye all right?" Meek demanded.

"Ah . . . yes. I believe so. Just a few bumps, I'm sure. I fall off horses quite often, you know," Courtney assured, trying to stand and frowning unhappily at this latest horse to be shot out from under him. "Poor fellow," he murmured. He managed to straighten, with Meek's assistance, and immediately looked around. "Where's Legate Bekiaa?"

"Down," Meek stated flatly. Then seeing Courtney's expression, he hastened to add, "But not badly wounded. Knocked on the head an' just a bit addled, but in no shape for this at the moment." Meek nodded around. "Prefect Bele's taken charge. That'd be well enough, but Colonel Naaris o' the First is senior an' he's arguin' with Bele that we must retreat!"

"Where?" Courtney demanded. "Take me at once!"

It wasn't far, but even if Naaris's verbal assault on Bele was almost as violent as the Grik's, it couldn't be heard more than half a dozen paces away. And Bele stood, arms crossed, taking the abuse as unshakably as the 23rd and 14th had withstood the Grik so far.

"You're disobeying a direct order from a superior officer in the face of the enemy!" Naaris ranted. Courtney actually had to stifle a laugh at the sight of the small Lemurian Naaris yelling up at the towering, immovable Bele. "And I can't withdraw the First unless the Twenty-Third and Fourteenth fall back in concert. We'd all be overwhelmed piecemeal." He gestured at the relentless Grik, shrouded in musket smoke, balls whizzing past. "Yet if we stay, we'll be overwhelmed together. We *must* retreat!"

Courtney formed a disparaging retort but stifled it. Naaris was no coward; he was merely reacting to what he saw from his limited perspective. With the pressure mounted by the Grik, it seemed impossible the 5th Division could stall them much longer—*Yet they must,* Courtney knew.

"Legate Bekiaa is *our* commanding officer," Bele replied respectfully, "and her orders are to hold."

"She's incapacitated!" Naaris spat, blinking furiously.

"She is . . . vertiginous," Bele conceded, "but in no other way impaired."

"That alone is sufficient impairment for me to assume command," Naaris shouted. "And I order you, once more, to prepare to fall back!"

"No!" Courtney interjected. "You must hold this position at all costs!"

Naaris looked at him, probably noticing him for the first time, and blinked incredulously. "With all respect, Mr. *Ambassador*, you've no place in the chain of command and no authority here."

"I bear the authority of Inquisitor Choon, awaiting my report less than a kilometer away," Courtney shouted, gesturing back the way he came, "and the trust of General Kim and Kaiser Nig-Taak. I know more about your battle than you, and have seen it with better eyes." *Not better* literally, Courtney amended to himself, *but hopefully Naaris will get my point.* "I really haven't time to explain, but the fate of the entire army, probably the war, truly depends on the Fifth Division holding here."

Bele nodded. He'd suspected as much, and Bekiaa somehow *knew.* She'd told him so herself. Even Naaris suddenly deflated, apparently convinced by Courtney's intensity.

"Yet bayonets and worn and bloody flesh alone can only do so much," Bele said. "We're almost out of ammunition."

Courtney turned to his aide, staring in awe at the interesting but often absent-minded man he'd only recently been assigned to serve. He'd never suspected the strength of will lurking below the surface, that could so quickly dominate a monolith like Bele, or subdue a veteran like Naaris.

"Gallop back to Inquisitor Choon at once!" Courtney ordered. "Tell him, as I predicted, we need ammunition and direct reinforcement immediately, or all is lost!" He looked at Naaris. "Your legion's hardly in contact at all. Shift it to the right, behind the others." He looked at Bele. "How can that best be done?"

"Have them form two more ranks behind those already on the line. Leave your artillery, but bring what canister there might be."

"But what of the enemy massing on the left, around their guns?" Naaris objected.

"They'll be dealt with," Courtney assured. "More infantry and some cavalry are already moving to strike them on the flank! We must hold here until further reinforcements arrive." He glanced furtively to the rear, hoping to see those promised troops now. He saw only the little cluster of horsemen surrounding Inquisitor Choon. But was that dust rising beyond, perhaps stirred by thousands of feet? He prayed so.

With a final measuring glance at Courtney, Colonel Naaris trotted to the left, to coordinate the movement of his legion. It would still take time, and the pressure in front was unbelievable. Yet Courtney's heart swelled with pride. These Repubs were not the same men and 'Cats who'd faced the Grik at Gaughala for the first time. Then he did a double take, realizing that several guns, their crews slaughtered, were being served by Gentaa! He knew the creatures—resembling a cross between humans and Lemurians—trained with weapons, but he'd never actually seen them fight. Even when things got desperate before, they'd always remained aloof, highly protective of their role as dedicated support personnel, somehow above the direct butchery their countrymen engaged in. That had somehow changed, and Courtney even saw a fair number of Gentaa right in the firing line, loading and shooting rifles—and dying as well.

Bele must've guessed what astonished him so. "I was amazed myself," he said. "But when Legate Bekiaa fell, they all just pitched in. It was a wonder to see." He cleared his throat. "Are reinforcements truly coming?" he asked pointedly.

"Yes," Courtney replied, unslinging the Krag from his shoulder. The first scattering of troops from the 1st Legion were starting to rush past. They'd be welcome when they were in place, but the Grik could see the movement and were sure to push even harder. "I'd recommend, however, that you order your troops to affix their bayonets."

"How many?" Bele pressed, growing somewhat suspicious. "If they're sending a division to deal with the Grik on the left, what are they sending us? A couple of legions?" He paused. "How much of the Army of the Republic can we really expect to join us?" he demanded.

"Honestly?" Courtney asked, then smiled. "All of it, Prefect Bele. The whole bloody thing. We're going to smash through this mob in front of us and push straight on to Sofesshk without looking back. How does that sound to you?"

The Grik fired another whickering volley, and several 'Cat and human troops very close went down. They were only about ten yards behind the third rank. Courtney blinked and reached down to pick up his sombrero. The stampede string had been cut.

"Back to work!" Bele shouted, then nodded at Courtney's Krag. "Do you mean to use that or merely pose with it?"

"I've used it quite a lot before," Courtney replied gamely, opening the side loading gate to ensure there were cartridges inside.

Bele grinned but the expression quickly faded. "Are you sure we're the ones who'll be doing the smashing?"

"Absolutely," Courtney assured, grinning back, but his eyes said nothing.

F iery arcs of sparkling, molten metal showered
down to die amid squeaking spurts of steam
on the wet deck of the repair bay aboard USS
Tarakaan Island. Matt Reddy, Spanky McFarlane, Lieutenant Tab-At, and Dennis Silva (with Petey wrapped
around his neck, of course) all stared up at the hasty
modifications being made to USS *Walker*, and all wore
identical frowns. Tabby's may not have *looked* precisely
the same, with her cleft upper lip, but the sentiment was
the same.

"Ugliest thing I ever saw," Spanky grumped, squirting
a yellowish stream of Aryaalan tobacco juice at a lingering, glowing hunk of slag. He missed, and Silva immediately ejected a thicker stream that spattered and quenched
the target.

"I guess that's why you're a chief gunner's mate,"
Spanky observed dryly. "Gotta be something somebody
as stupid-nuts as you can do."

"Just applyin' my basic understandin' o' ballistics,"
Silva replied piously. "Calculatin' proper windage an' elevation in local control—combined with a heavier charge
under a bigger pro-jec-tile."

Matt snorted, and Tabby's frown vanished as she burst

into a kind of clucking giggle. "You two, spittin' thaat yellow yuck, look like a pair o' lizardbirds in a shittin' maatch!"

Dennis laughed. "Yeah, maybe." Then he pointed up. "But Spanky's right. That's about the most dis-gustin' thing I ever laid my eye on, an' it was your idea."

Aided by half a dozen 'Cats on a scaffold high above, Chief Isak Reuben was welding another piece of what looked like a giant bird cage to the bottom of the old destroyer's port propeller guard. Only a few pieces were left to add, and when they were finished, the contraption should provide some protection for the ship's screws against heavy floating timbers and other debris still choking the upper Zambezi. Isak wasn't any happier about it than anyone, but insisted on doing it himself, saying, "If anybody's gonna weld that abdob-mition to my hull, it's gonna be me. One o' them welds goes, an' the whole wad o' spaghetti'll get wound around my screws, seize my engines, an' pop ever' valve an' seal in my firerooms!" Now he stood on the scaffold, staring through dark goggles with deathly intent while the 'Cats held the piece in place and averted their gaze.

"Gotta do somethin'," Tabby countered, "if we're gonna do . . ." She paused and looked around. "Whaat the skipper waants to do."

"Oh, knock it off," Spanky groused. "Comm and operational security's one thing, but any idiot on *Tara* can see what we're up to—and what it means." He rubbed the reddish whiskers on his cheek, and Matt noticed those on his chin seemed whiter every day. *Much like mine would be,* he conceded, *if I let my beard grow.* The hair at his temples was already white.

"True," Matt agreed, "but even if the Grik are spying on us, there aren't any on *Tara,* and nobody outside her can see what we're doing." He scratched his own chin. There *had* been Grik spies, and guards and scouts had killed more than a dozen skulking in the reeds along the shoreline. Some had even attempted to get close to Arracca Field and Camp Simy. "I don't think they'll notice the difference to *Ellie*, *Gray*, and *Mahan,* now they're back in the water." *U-112* was already bound for Baalkpan, and they'd modified *Gray* first, then each destroyer rotated back from the Neckbone. It would take a careful and knowledgeable eye even to note a difference in their wakes since there'd been no reason for any of the ships to steam very fast. But that was something else. Nobody knew how well the contraptions would hold up under speed, especially if they hit something. The result might be worse than if they'd done nothing at all. But doing nothing only invited disaster, and they couldn't afford to let any of their modern ships get incapacitated in the operation ahead. Thinking of that, Matt turned to Silva. "What about our old sailing steamers?"

All but one of the surviving sail/steam frigates (DDs) remaining in First Fleet had been radically altered, their topmasts and spars removed, leaving only the most rudimentary auxiliary sail capacity. Their heavy guns had been shifted ashore and added to the impressive firepower assembling at the front. In their place, USS *Bowles*, *Saak-Fas*, *Clark*, *Kas-Ra-Ar*, and *Ramic-Sa-Ar* had each been equipped with a pair of Baalkpan Arsenal DP 4"-50s, mounted fore and aft, on heavily reinforced decks. Their sides had been as thickly armored as they could manage with armor plate captured at Grik City, and it was hoped they'd fare better against armored Grik cruisers in a close-range fight. Their fewer guns were far more accurate and faster shooting, and equipped with armor-piercing projectiles.

Only the newest "old-style" DD, USS *Revenge*, had been spared the change for her speed, and because she carried the same anti–mountain fish (and -submarine) equipment the new steel-hulled four-stackers were getting. She'd been sent to escort the deadheading heavy haulers towing *U-112* and carrying Muriname, his people, and their disassembled aircraft.

"All done," Silva said. "But that work was carried out alongside. Grik spies'll have seen it, sure." No one had any illusions they'd stopped all observers.

"Nothing for it. We can't take them by surprise with everything we do," Matt added significantly. Silva nodded a little uneasily, and Matt wondered again if he was asking too much of the big man and Chack's Brigade this time. *Of course I am,* he scolded himself. *And I've done it over and over. Silva only came out to help tie in the fire control for the converted DDs. He should still be training with Chack. Then again,* he consoled himself, *I doubt he's missing much. He always seems able to adapt to anything, and do new, crazy stuff almost instinctively.* He frowned. *But this is different. . . .*

"How much longer?" Spanky shouted up at Isak. Instead of answering, the scrawny little man stopped, turned, and raised the goggles from his eyes. Sweat streaks left bright, spiderweblike lines in the dark grime on his face and neck.

"It'll take as long as it goddamn takes . . . sir," he snapped back in his reedy voice.

"God*damn!*" squawked Petey, rising on Silva's shoulder and flapping the membranes between his front and back legs as if just as surprised by Isak's outburst as anyone.

"Hey!" Spanky began, but stopped, flustered. Isak hadn't really intended any disrespect, and his already bizarre personality was just as plagued by frustration and stress as the rest of them. Ranting at him now would only make him more sullen than usual and slow him down. "Just hurry up. We gotta get her out of here tonight, and I ain't real happy about the weather." He waved off toward the northeast. A dark line had been building all day. Reports from Grik City on the northern tip of Madagascar said it had been raining hard, the wind whipping up. None of the Sky Priest "weather weenies" were predicting one of the unusually violent cyclones called strakka, at least not yet, but they were confident one was likely coming soon. Matt hadn't told anyone, but he was actually counting on it, intently conferring with the Sky Priests and Keje as often as he could.

"I can go faster," Isak groused, "an' burn a buncha holes in these cornflake-thin plates. Some o' these back here were riveted on at the Fore River Shipyard back in 1919. I bet they've rusted down to a quarter inch thick." He raised his voice. "Don't worry, I'll get it done—but I wanna be back up here torchin' these doohickeys off again as soon as we get the hell outa this Grik sewer river!"

"That goes without saying, Chief Reuben," Matt assured, though of course he couldn't really guarantee *Walker* would ever leave the Zambezi, or Isak would live to do the work. He'd always worried about such things, but as his "old hands" became fewer and fewer, he caught himself brooding on the possibility *none* of them would survive this terrible war. *I need to see Sandra,* he decided. *Get away to* Big Sal *for the night. Spend some time with my wife.*

He suddenly noticed the unexpected face of Corporal Neely peering down from beside the depth charge rack. He was the only citizen of the Empire of the New Britain Isles aboard USS *Walker*, and unlike most of the few other humans left in the ship, he didn't wear a beard. That, and the fine, long mustache flowing from his upper lip, stylish in his country, made him quite distinctive. He was an Imperial Marine, lent to *Walker* for his talent with a bugle, but also, Matt believed, so the Empire would have *some* representative aboard the flagship, such as she was, of all the Allied fleets. He seemed a decent young man and practiced diligently with the ship's reduced Marine contingent. He'd also been learning ship handling as well as signals. Welcome as a proper bugler was, particularly after the final demise of *Walker*'s long-tormented general quarters alarm, that couldn't be his only duty.

"Captain Reddy," Neely called down.

"Yes, Corporal?"

Neely waved a message form. "Word from Mr. Bradford, with the Army of the Republic."

Matt's eyes narrowed. "Did Mr. Palmer make you bring that?" Lieutenant Ed Palmer was *Walker*'s signal officer, and it was no secret he'd started to think Matt hated the very sight of him for all the bad news he'd brought. That was ridiculous, of course, though Matt did dread seeing him rush up, waving a message form with a worried look on his boyish face.

Neely shook his head. "No, sir. He's aboard *Mahan*, helpin' sort out some issues with her comm gear. I was on watch meself, but Minnie—I mean, Ensign Min-Sakir—decoded it an' sent me ta find ye." With that, he folded the form and clenched it in his teeth, grabbed a line trailing over the side, and slid down to join them. "Sorry fer the bite marks, sir," he apologized, handing the message over. Matt unfolded it and read. Sighing, he looked up.

"Bad?" Spanky asked. His tone sounded certain it was.

Matt cocked his head and wrinkled his brow. "I don't know, to be honest." He glanced at Silva, then back at the work being performed. "Damned inconvenient, but we might cope."

"What's the dope we gotta cope with, Skipper?" Silva asked.

"Dope!" Petey insisted.

"There aren't a lot of details, but it seems our Bekiaa— and Courtney Bradford—managed to stop a major flanking maneuver against the Army of the Republic. General Kim counterattacked and not only smashed the Grik right, but a good chunk of the middle. Maybe half the Grik army facing him is either shattered or in disarray, and now he's racing, hell for leather, straight for us." Matt smiled slightly, almost sadly, perhaps nostalgic for a time when he would've been stunned by Courtney's high-level participation in a major military campaign. They'd all changed so much, and Matt hoped Courtney's somewhat frustrating but still endearing enthusiasm for the wonders of this world wasn't gone forever.

"But what about the rest of the Grik?" Spanky asked. "Half of what they had is still bigger than Kim's whole army."

Matt nodded. "Yeah, but it's out of position, confused, and playing catchup. It'll cut Kim's supply line," he conceded, "but Kim's got the Grik cut off too. In the meantime, the Repub supply effort's been diverted here. When it starts coming in, we'll send their ammo forward with ours. That'll complicate the hell out of our own logistics, but Kim won't do us any good if he shows up without ammunition."

"Damn chancy," Silva reflected, but he obviously approved of the bold move. *He* would, of course . . .

"Yeah, an' those Grik Kim bypassed'll get their shit in the sock sooner or later. They'll chase after him and catch him up against the bigger army surrounding our beachhead," Spanky growled.

"Right, but with Kim roaring up their skirt, they can't ignore him either. They'll have to redeploy to watch two directions."

"An' that's what your plan's all about," Silva murmured, nodding. "Whip-sawin' the lizards back an' forth so fast, in so many directions, they just lose their whole damn sock." He looked at his captain. "Kim's move should help with that, but what's it mean for us?"

Matt shrugged, pasting a false, carefree grin in his face. "Nothing particularly unusual. Only that instead of maybe another month we thought we had to get ready for our big push, we've got weeks. Maybe days."

CHAPTER 13

////// *Over El Paso del Fuego*
Holy Dominion
0420
February 26, 1945

It was eerily, almost metallically bright under a full moon hovering over the western entrance to the Pass of Fire. Even the stars seemed kind of washed out by the luminous mercury glow above. Making the night feel even more surreal to 2nd Lieutenant Orrin Reddy were the ruddy rivulets of lava streaming from various vents on the towering flanks of the great volcano to the north. It wasn't alone. There were volcanoes everywhere around here, but most were just big, broken-looking mountains. That one, the biggest he'd seen, was always doing something. *Damn thing oozes fire like festering sores,* he thought uncomfortably, *but the story from the locals is that's normal. It's only when it* quits *that folks have to worry.* He wasn't so sure about that, and didn't even remember what they called the volcano. But standing considerably higher than the six thousand feet he and his raiding force were flying, it was without a doubt the true, fiery heart of the pass, and he figured the dully lit city of El Corazon to the south was named after it.

It was actually kind of cold, and he nestled farther down behind the windscreen in the cockpit of the brand-new PB-1F Nancy he'd swiped from USS *Raan-Goon*'s

7th Naval Air Wing, along with half its 18th Bomb Squadron. The exhaust flares of nine more engines added bluish stars to the firmament angling away to the left. If he looked hard, he'd see more. He'd taken half squadrons from each carrier as well as the entire 7th Pursuit Squadron off *Maaka-Kakja* under Ez "Easy" Shiaa. They'd be joined at dawn—his fingers were crossed—by two entire bomb squadrons and another pursuit squadron operating off a protected bay by the recently, rather easily, occupied Dom city of Nicoya, and a new grass strip nearby.

Two of their precious PB5-D Clippers had gone in earlier, alone, for a predawn strike against a known Dom concentration on the other side of the pass at Boco Caribe. It was hoped, like the hype around the B-17 Flying Fortress of their old world, the array of defensive weapons Clippers carried would protect them. Particularly during the safer darkness. Like ordinary Grik, Grikbirds didn't see as well at night. If things went well, the Clippers would join Orrin's retiring strike and they'd all head back to the barn together in layered defensive formations. In any event, with seventy Nancys, forty Fleashooters, and two heavy bombers, this first deep raid on the Pass of Fire should make a helluva splash. *Not literally, I hope,* Orrin added mentally as he calculated that all those planes carried almost two hundred men and 'Cats.

"What do you think of her?" he shouted in the voice tube beside his face over the roar of wind and engine, referring to the plane.

"Is okaay," came Sergeant Kuaar-Ran-Taak's, or "Seepy's" tinny, noncommittal voice. Seepy had been Orrin's backseater from the start. They weren't really friends— Orrin had finally figured out that Seepy resented him because he wouldn't take the oath to his cousin's Navy Clan—and Orrin gave him every opportunity to bail, but Seepy always stuck with him. "I think they gone as faar wit' this aar-frame as they caan, though."

Orrin was inclined to agree. Nancys were amazing little planes. Pretty good to start with, various improvements had made them better and better and they'd been the backbone of Allied aviation throughout the war. First of all, they were seaplanes, which meant their aircrews

weren't automatically doomed to feed the voracious predators in this world's seas if they crapped out over water.
Second, they were tough and had a big wing with a lot of
lift. Combined with the surface area of their hull and
their just-forward-of-center CG, they could slam on the
brakes in a hurry, in a dive, and that made them pretty
decent dive-bombers and ground-support aircraft. The
problem was, as improved enemy antiaircraft weapons,
Jap/Grik fighters, and League fighters began to appear,
not to mention Grikbirds, which were always a menace, it
was increasingly clear the time had come to move on. Unfortunately, the middle of an existential war, being fought
on a shoestring with limited production capacity, is an
awkward time to halt an assembly line producing lots of
"good" and gear it up to make "better" that may not come
in time.

But production had improved and new ships were in the
works. Light bombers to replace Nancys and medium
bombers based on that crashed Bristol Beaufort were
coming, and new pursuit planes were being experimented
with in more innovative facilities while the old ones kept
running. And even those weren't just turning out the same
old thing. This F model Nancy, for instance—probably the
first example of something new making its way east before
Matt got it in the west—had the improved 10-cylinder,
410-hp radial engine they were putting in the latest C
model Fleashooters, and it was faired in to reduce drag.
On top of that, it had the Allies' first variable-pitch prop
with wooden blades set in spring-loaded cammed steel
sockets. The thing was a Lemurian design and kind of
glitchy, relying on another small spring-mounted plate
under the propeller hub, activated by a Goldbergian crank
shaft with several (failure-prone) U-joints to bypass the
engine crankcase, but they'd have better when they had a
good look at the Beaufort's props. Still, not only did the
new prop and engine add almost fifty mph to the ship's
max speed while actually using less fuel, they also allowed
a heavier bomb load and two .30-caliber machine guns in
blisters on either side of the cockpit.

Orrin liked them even if they were still slower than he'd
prefer and were pretty damn touchy on the controls. Only

experienced Nancy pilots got them. That was one of the reasons for his converging attack. All the F models were with him, flying straight up the pass, while the Bs would meet them after a more leisurely cross-country run.

"Yeah," he agreed with Seepy, "I guess the war's passed these Nancys by. 'F' model probably stands for 'Final.' Maybe I'll get one for myself when it's all over, though. Fly around. See the sights."

"You think it'll ever *be* over?" came the skeptical response.

Orrin hesitated. "Sure," he said. *One way or another.*

A little more than an hour later, they'd descended to five thousand feet. Just as the sun was creeping over the horizon to glare in their eyes and they got their first glimpse of their target—an anchorage called La Calma within a wide bay *inside* the Pass of Fire—the first Grikbirds tried to bounce them.

"Grikbirds, Grikbirds!" came a human shout over the radio. "Ten o'clock high!"

Orrin looked up and slightly left. The sunrise on his flat glass goggles found that really bad angle and briefly blinded him. He swore, mostly at his own stupidity—the problem with the goggles wasn't new—and quickly got past the glare.

"I see 'em!" Seepy shouted. So did Orrin then, as the bright afterimage of the sun started to fade. The Grikbirds were close, half a dozen or so, arrowing in with talons extended, wingclaws ready, for one of their trademark slashing runs.

Orrin looked ahead. He'd only penetrated as far as La Calma once before, and it was a weird place. There wasn't much of a city, but the bay served as a critical stopping place for ships that couldn't make it all the way through the pass on one tidal race and the brief slack that followed. A steamer might still make it if it beat the full force of the opposing tide, but that was chancy. A sailing ship had no hope at all, and the shattered debris of ground-up wrecks was always washing to and fro. Thus, La Calma, reported to have some wicked swirling currents, maybe the most extreme daily sea level fluctuations in the world but a good, clean, rocky bottom a stout anchor could grab, would probably always have a few ships taking refuge there. There'd been six or seven steam transports the first time Orrin came this far several weeks ago. Today, however, as he'd kind of suspected, the place looked packed. "Bombers hold steady. Prepare for defensive fire," he ordered over the radio, flipping the switch to transmit.

Seepy shifted in his aft cockpit behind the spinning prop, readying his Blitzerbug SMG. Coming in like they were, he wouldn't get a shot until the Grikbirds actually hit them or blew past, and it was a tense few moments of waiting for that. Maneuvering wouldn't help. Scattering the formation to spoil their attack, dilute their defensive fire, and make them easier to hunt down one by one was exactly what the Grikbirds wanted. Besides, most of these Grikbirds were already doomed and Orrin wondered if they were smart enough to know it.

P1-Bs were the oldest Fleashooters still in service. They were smaller, slower, and less heavily armed than the newer C variant, but were plenty fast, deadly, and even maneuverable enough to absolutely slaughter Grikbirds committed to tight attack formations. And that was the quandary Grikbirds faced in the diminished numbers they'd been seeing; lone or scattered attackers could be driven off or killed by a Nancy's defensive fire, but attacks like this were terribly vulnerable to pursuit ships. This was demonstrated yet again as smoky tracers started arcing through them, shredding wings in clouds of bright feathers, starting vaporous red streamers of blood, or simply crumpling the ferociously stooping predators like starlings slamming panes of glass. One wounded Grikbird landed a glancing, tearing blow on a Nancy's wing as it tumbled past. A couple escaped, tucking tighter and abandoning their prey, but the rest were already falling lifeless to Earth even as three pairs of Fleashooters roared over Orrin's formation and pulled up to resume their protective overwatch.

"Who's hit?" Orrin called out to his bombers. He could see blue-painted fabric fluttering behind a Nancy to his right.

"Akka Five, over," came the quick response from one

of the experienced Lemurians in the mostly human squadron. The 'Cat's voice sounded strained but calm.

"You need to head back, Akka Five? Over." Any lone, damaged Nancy that had to abort wouldn't stand a chance and would cost them a pursuit ship to protect it.

"Neg-aa-tive. We caan make it through the strike, over," came the response.

"Okay, if you're sure. Good job, Sabers," Orrin called to Easy's pursuit pilots. There were a lot of Impie replacements in the 7th and this was their first action. He was proud of them. A little envious too, since he'd been a pursuit pilot himself. *A pretty good one,* he thought, having bagged several Zeroes in a P-40 over the Philippines. But that was a world—and what seemed a lifetime—away. Sometimes he longed for one of the four or so P-40Es they still had on this world, but at the rate they'd squandered them he doubted he'd ever lay eyes on one again.

"Thaank you, sur," Ez said.

"Strike Lead, Strike Lead, this is Gri-maax Lead." That was Colonel Fao-Nuaak, bringing the fighters and bombers in from Nicoya. "We're at six thousaand feet, coming in high on your staar-board quarter. Over."

Orrin wrenched his head around, saw the large, stacked formations of planes approaching. "I see you, Gri-maax Lead. Any trouble? Over."

"A few Grikbirds," came the dismissive response. Orrin nodded but frowned. It was early yet, but he'd still expected a little more resistance, even in the dark, with the moon they'd had. He looked back down at La Calma, getting closer, and felt a chill. There were at least twenty large ships at anchor, maybe half that many smaller ones, and that looked like about as many as the bay would hold. Most of the heavies had the high-sided, blockier outlines of steam-powered Dom ships of the line, and there were more here than remained to protect El Corazon. He wondered if they'd stripped the Caribbean entirely. But they couldn't have, could they? The Nussies would've warned them.

"The target is rich," he announced. "We'll go first and take them from the south. You follow us in, Gri-maax Lead. Over."

"Roger thaat, Strike Lead."

Orrin banked slightly south, studying the layout of the ships and making assignments while his strike force followed, then he turned sharply north, the world pinwheeling below. "All Akkas, tallyho. Don't forget: focus on the heavies. Drop two eggs each and we'll come around and follow Gri-maax flight's attack for another run." Pushing the stick forward, Orrin led his Nancys in.

Throughout the war in the east, the Doms had struggled to come up with effective antiaircraft measures and hadn't managed much more than massed musket volleys and swivel guns. The Grik, with Kurokawa's aid, of course, had done better. And Allied ships had been badly plagued by Grikbirds until recently, when more automatic weapons became available. It looked to Orrin as he dove that the Doms were still stuck with swivel guns. They were dangerous, of course, and there were lots of them lining the bulwarks of the ships and in the fighting tops. More than he'd ever seen. But he didn't intend to get close enough for their little clouds of canister to be tremendously effective. The trouble was, whether the League gave them the idea or there'd been contact between the Doms and Grik—or Kurokawa—they'd never been aware of, or the Doms simply came up with a similar notion all their own, the heavy swivel-gun volleys vomiting up from the targets weren't composed of short-range spreads of musket balls; they spat hundreds of little shells the size of baseballs that carried much farther—before exploding right among the diving planes like clouds of hand grenades.

"Shit!" Orrin roared through the popping smoke and blizzard of balls the size of buckshot laced with small fragments of iron that shuddered his Nancy and sleeted through its wood and fabric. A few pieces stung his forearms and legs as well, but everything still worked, so the cuts must've been small or shallow. He refocused on his target, straightening his dive at the smoke-shrouded ship. "You okay?" he shouted at Seepy.

"I don't know. I hope so."

"Stand by." Orrin reached for one of the two bomb-release levers and wrenched it back, even as he pulled back on the stick. To his relief, the Nancy slowed and swooped obediently, and he could finally spare an instant to look around. Nearly all the ships on the south side of the bay were wreathed in smoke from their protective fire, and more than just a few of his planes weren't pulling up. Most of those crashed into the sea, blasting up tall columns of spray. One smashed directly into the ship that shot it down, all its bombs going off, and the ship exploded under a rising plume of burning airplane fuel. A few bombs hit other ships, but most exploded alongside their targets.

"We hit *our* taarget," Seepy reported. Orrin was so sickly engrossed in watching the disaster unfold, he hadn't even looked. "One hit the deck, blew the hell outa the fo'c'sle. The other hit the side an' blew, but didn't look to hurt it. I think they've aarmored 'em up!"

Orrin figured Seepy was right. Greg Garrett had reported he suspected as much after his prize ship, *Matarife*, tangled with some Doms on the other side of the pass. He hadn't been there to fight, though, and hadn't had the luxury of staying to confirm his hunch.

Orrin flipped his Talk switch. "Gri-maax Lead, Gri-maax Lead, begin your attack *now*." Only a few of Fao's older Nancys carried even a single .30-caliber machine gun, so they couldn't go in firing to keep the gunners down—as Orrin *should've* directed his strike to do. . . . "Take some Fleashooters with you to shoot 'em up and focus on the ships that already fired. But get a move on. Don't give 'em time to reload!"

"Roger, Strike Lead," replied Commander Fao. "Staarting our run now. . . . But whaat'll we do about the others?"

"We lost six planes," Seepy was saying. "Some others is daamaged." That left maybe twenty Orrin could use. He'd've liked to bring more Fleashooters down to cover them, but his pursuit pilot's instincts kept screaming that there *would* be more Grikbirds and he couldn't thin their top cover too much.

"We'll take care of those, Gri-maax Lead, following our own guns in this time," he added bitterly. He was supposed to be the experienced commander, and had even developed that tactic here in the East against ground targets, but they hadn't fought ships in a while and he'd still been thinking in terms of old defenses. Of *course* the Doms adapted! "This is Strike Lead. Sorry, guys. My screwup. All Akkas, follow me. We'll attack the ships in the north bay this time, east to wcst. You all saw about how far out their swivel bombs went off. This time we'll chase our tracers in."

And that's how it went, at first. Despite how effective the Dom's initial aerial broadside was, the enemy had been taken by surprise and was still rattled. The land-based squadrons hammered hard at the now-near-helpless ships closer to the main channel, and several erupted in flames. Masts and stacks were blown down amid towering jets of white water that inundated ships with spray. Mixed with the gleeful chatter, however, came increasing reports that if bombs hit decks, the ships got blasted bad, but if they hit the sides, they had little noticeable effect.

Orrin's squadrons were in position now, aiming at un-scathed ships closer to shore, swooping down in staggered lines, starting to angle toward distinct targets.

"Grikbirds!" came several shouts at once. "Maany Grikbirds!" punctuated the 7th's Ez Shiraa.

"What's happening, Easy?" Orrin demanded tensely, aligning the nose of his plane on another Dom liner. This one, like others on the inside, looked squatter, lower in the water, and had only rudimentary auxiliary masts. Its paddleboxes looked bulkier than others Orrin had seen as well. More disconcerting, he wasn't seeing a bright wood deck with people running to their weapons or to get under cover. That's when it dawned on him that people were *already* under an armored cover. Or were they people? Even as he watched, Grikbirds started boiling *out of the ship*, fore and aft.

"Goddamn!" Orrin shouted over the radio. "They're *carriers. Grikbird* carriers, and they're scrambling! Get down here, Sabers, or they'll eat us alive."

"There's Grikbirds up here too," came Ez Shiraa's strained voice. It was clear he was maneuvering hard. "They comin' from ever-where!"

Orrin felt another chill but managed to blot out the rising fluttery feeling in his chest. "Okay, Akkas," he said lowly instead. "Looks like we surprised 'em—while they were getting ready to mousetrap us. We're even now. Pick your targets and just flow through the flying lizards. Chase your tracers, like I said. Those carriers are bad news and we have to get them."

Twenty-one PB-1F Nancys of the 3rd, 6th, and 7th Air Wings barreled down into the swirling maelstrom, smoky tracers lancing out. Grikbirds swarmed out of six of the ships like bats from a cave at dusk, rising to meet them, flapping their wings, instinctively making high-pitched, challenging shrieks. Twin .30 cals in each plane, then the observer/copilot's .45 ACP Blitzers, swatted at them, scythed them down, made a twinkling fog of blood spray and colorful spinning feathers in the early-morning light—but there were already more than a hundred Grikbirds in the air, wheeling, pouncing, slashing at what they no doubt thought were other creatures not unlike them, attacking their nest.

Somehow, through all this, Orrin and his Nancy pilots scored hits on all six carriers, and even though all they had were high-explosive incendiaries—just the thing for wooden ships—the topside armor, at least, wasn't very thick, and two of the new Dom ships went up quite spectacularly. Four didn't seem hurt at all. After Orrin dropped his bombs, all he could do was fly, jinking through the savage, swirling Grikbirds, firing bursts from his guns at any coming at him from the front, and relying on Seepy to keep them off his back. One hooked his rudder with its teeth, nearly swinging the plane out of control, but Seepy stitched it—probably shooting a few holes in the tail himself—and it fell away. Immediately, he shouted, "Whaat the hell's *thaat*? Three o'clock low!" and Orrin risked a glance at one of the burning carriers. He thought he saw a Grikbird—or something that *looked* like one, only it was three times as big—fly out of the forward part of the ship. It furiously beat its huge wings at first and then soared toward shore, low over the water, and directly into the tall trees beyond the beach.

"Don't know," Orrin replied, gritting his teeth and trying to keep the plane under control. It wasn't easy, fighting against the savaged rudder, and he still needed more

speed before he could climb. Banking right, he followed . . . whatever it was, and pushed the throttle to its
stop. Nothing was chasing them at the moment, but the
sky seemed full of falling Grikbirds and staggering
planes. A lot of those looked like they'd never make it
back, and his gut twisted with dread. Pilots on this raid
were supposed to bail out and let their damaged planes
crash, preferably in the water if they could arrange it, and
if it looked like their chutes would carry them to shore.
Then their real nightmare would start. Doms might not
eat prisoners, but they did torture them and didn't keep
them, and sometimes they fed them to other things. Few
would let themselves be taken alive, and *very* few downed
pilots had ever walked out from behind enemy lines.

"All bombers, this is Strike Lead. Get up high and into
formation as quick as you can. Pursuit ships will protect.
Do *not* chase Grikbirds."

"Then whaat're *you* doing, Strike Lead?" came Gri-
maax Lead's familiar voice.

What am *I doing?* Orrin asked himself, realizing he'd
been scanning for the strange, huge Grikbird, flying low
over the little town of La Calma now. There were a few
shots below, and musket balls warbled past. He noticed
there were some new warehouses and wished they'd
thought to bomb them too. He also noticed one of the
land-based Fleashooters that joined Gri-maax's attack
had come up alongside and he wasn't just risking himself
and Seepy anymore. "Just getting some speed," he said,
reluctantly pulling up and back to the west. Behind him
to the left, great columns of smoke stood over La Calma
Bay, and Grikbirds still swirled around, carefully avoiding the smoke—they didn't like it—but looking almost as
dense as bees around huge gray hives. Troubled, he kept
climbing.

Reaching the rallying strike at six thousand feet, he
found only nine of the initial thirty members of Akka
Flight, which meant he'd lost twenty Nancys and forty
people out of the force he led directly. The 7th Pursuit
Squadron lost four planes. Another nine Fleashooters and
Nancys from Nicoya had fallen. Ironically, the two PB-5D
Clippers joining them shortly after, returning from their

predawn strike against Boca Caribe, hadn't even seen a Grikbird until they skirted the hornet's nest over La Calma. The few that challenged the huge planes there had seemed intimidated by their size and approached tentatively. They were easily driven off with machine-gun fire.

But all together now, heading west, the formation started coming under almost constant attacks, and despite how many Grikbirds they shot down, a lot of planes were taking damage. Several were lost to slashing attacks that darted in and ripped away control surfaces or flipped planes out of control. One of the Clippers completely lost an engine when it collided with a Grikbird, and the whole skin behind the engine tore away as well. Leaking fuel streamed from punctured copper tanks. Orrin turned the Sabers loose to chase the Grikbirds for a while, and they got several, but a Fleashooter was mobbed out of the sky when the pilot's wingman couldn't shoot the creatures that snatched on to the plane. More Grikbirds got through gaps the Sabers left and shredded a couple more Nancys. It was incredibly frustrating, and Orrin finally called the pursuit planes back, and they all fought on together.

At last, around midday, as what remained of the strike finally passed between El Corazon and the massive, smoldering mountain, the last Grikbirds broke off. More planes were coming to escort them in, from Nicoya and the carriers. The Fleashooters out of Nicoya were particularly low on fuel. Except for his painfully sore ass on the parachute/cushion he was sitting on and the exhausting battle with his bucking rudder pedals, Orrin no longer had to think about the actual flight and was free to ponder its implications. Recovery operations when they reached the ship, in daylight, would be routine.

The mass Grikbird attacks might've been a spontaneous reaction to such a large Allied intrusion by various flocks on the prowl, or maybe the Grikbirds themselves quickly carried dispatches describing the raid far and wide. It was known they were often used like giant, vicious carrier pigeons. In the latter case, maybe somebody in command finally just said "To hell with it" and turned big reserves of the creatures they'd been hoarding loose. Regardless, the myth that they'd run the Grikbirds off was broken, and that alone was valuable information. They'd learned quite a lot, in fact; things the Doms couldn't have wanted them to know, like about the carriers, and that they still had loads of Grikbirds, of course. In addition, they'd confirmed that whether the Dom warships still around El Corazon were armored now or not, the ones coming through the pass sure were. *Good* information; exactly the sort of thing Orrin had pushed for the raid to find out.

On top of that, they'd done some damage, more than they expected since there'd been more targets. But the raid had been costly as hell and raised as many questions as answers. What the *hell* had he and Seepy seen? What kind of threat did it represent? Did anyone else see it? Were there more? Instead of waiting for a mission debrief, he asked around now and got a few hesitant affirmations from pilots who hadn't been sure what they saw. In his mind, that confirmed it.

Still contemplating bizarre creatures, Orrin looked down at the sea. As usual, the approach to the Pass of Fire was thick with what looked from above like small moving islands. They weren't islands, though—they were animals: mountain or island fish to Lemurians, and leviathans to Impies. Dwarfing blue whales on the world Orrin came from, they were the largest living things on this one. Normally, in other seas, they were solitary and highly territorial monsters that, though somewhat passive feeders (they could swallow anything that came along, including their own young up *to* the size of a large whale), their aggressive territoriality, ability to sprint short distances at stunning speeds, near invulnerability, and occasional extravagant hunger, made them dangerous to passing ships of any size. Only here, where the violent tidal races through the pass provided a constant, abundant food source, did they apparently gather from all over the world to mate and calve, as well as eventually die—though no one knew how long they lived—in the shallow Sea of Bones to the north where the Sea of Cortes should be. But because there was such a bounty here, not only were their newborns safe, so were passing ships. For the most part.

Orrin was scared of the damn things and was thankful

they were so acoustically sensitive. That's how the Allies warded them off: with active sonar or depth charges if they got too close. Heavy cannon fire was known to discourage them as well, and he wondered how they'd react to the inevitable naval battle off El Corazon, right in the middle of their breeding-ground buffet. Something about that tickled the edge of his tired brain, as it had before, but he just couldn't put his finger on it.

He shook his head and looked off to the southwest, where he finally saw the mottled purple shapes of the distant carriers under high, bright clouds. They'd be home soon, and he could rest. Belatedly, he ordered the least-damaged Fleashooters and worst-damaged Nancys to land first, then sent Seepy crawling down in the hull to count holes. He knew there'd be some, and it was up to Seepy to calculate how long they could float before they were recovered by the cranes lining the sides of the carriers.

"We'll float long enough," Seepy reported in a surly tone.

"What's the matter with you?" Orrin shouted back. "Sure, it was a tough run, but I guess we did what we set out to."

"Yeah, stir shit up," Seepy snapped. "We done thaat fine, an' I'm still bleedin' for it."

Orrin started guiltily, remembering his own superficial wounds. They still stung but they'd stopped bleeding long ago. The new Dom antiair bombs weren't very powerful, but they didn't have to be to tear up fragile planes and flight crews. They'd have to adjust their tactics. "Well, damn it. You spent so long *not* griping about anything, I thought you must be okay. Are you?" he asked.

"Yah," Seepy grudged. "Not too baad, I guess. Jus' would'a been nice if you aask earlier."

"I *did*," Orrin countered, but remembered guiltily that he hadn't followed up on the initial ambiguous reply.

"Well . . . you could'a aask agaain," Seepy groused. "You gonna tell Ahd-mi-raal Jenks we need to hold off? See more whaat's whaat?"

"No," Orrin said, somewhat surprised by how em-

phatic he was. "I think we need more raids," he temporized, "to keep the pressure on and learn more, but I
really think we've held off long enough as it is."

"*More* raids? Like *this*?" Seepy asked mournfully.

"Maybe *too* long," Orrin continued, as if Seepy hadn't
spoken. "Appears to me, more time just lets 'em cook up
deadlier stuff to shoot at us, and more surprises to spring.
I think we need to start beating the hell out of them as
fast as we can, before they kick *our* asses."

////// **USS Maaka-Kakja (CV-4)**
Off El Paso del Fuego
Holy Dominion
March 5, 1945

W hat the hell was it? Are you sure you even saw it?" demanded Captain Tex Sheider. Orrin could only spread his hands in frustration and let them drop against the stained coveralls he wore. They'd been through this several times over the past week or so. "Like I told you the *first* time, I would'a figured I imagined it if some other fellas hadn't seen it, or some others like it, too." He shrugged. "Some kinda big-assed Grikbird."

He and Seepy, dressed the same and just as filthy, were talking to Tex and Admiral Lelaa-Tal-Cleraan near one of the open bays on *Maaka-Kakja*'s hangar deck. The white-capped purple sea churned noisily below and between that, the wind, and the general bawling babble of ground crews racing to keep as many planes airworthy as possible, they practically had to shout at one another. USS *New Dublin* (CV-6) was steaming relatively close alongside, and Orrin saw the tall masts of one of Admiral Hibbs's ships of the line jutting up beyond the other carrier. The big ship also blocked his view of the brooding shore of the Holy Dominion on the horizon. That was fine by him. He'd seen enough of it.

"But nobody's spotted one since," Tex pointed out. His tone wasn't as much challenging as perplexed. They'd flown several more deep raids, each costlier and more vigorously opposed than the last. The Doms had apparently given up trying to hide their reserve of Grikbirds. That led them to try a night raid, like had been so successful for Matt in the west, but it turned out even worse. Not only did the inexperience of some of their newer pilots cause too many casualties due to accidents, a couple might've even just wandered off course in the dark, never to be seen again. Worse, they'd lost two precious Clippers and their crews to "dash and slash" attacks. It turned out Grikbirds didn't have to see as well in the dark since a plane's exhaust flare was more visible than its attackers, and aircrews couldn't shoot at what *they* couldn't see. It infuriated Orrin that there'd been little choice but to concede the night sky to the enemy.

The only good thing was, Nancys and Fleashooters both had the legs on Grikbirds, and the Doms couldn't get at Second Fleet this far out unless they used their new carriers, which the pickets should warn them about. Or if these mysterious new giant Grikbirds posed some unknown threat, of course.

"Damn near didn't see the first ones," Orrin objected. "The one me and Seepy saw bolted from the carrier we hit. Other fellas said the same." He shrugged. "Maybe they're just females, bigger than the rest."

"Possibly," Lelaa conceded. "But why keep them on ships? To lay eggs? I don't believe it. Intelligence reports it takes a year or more just to train baby Grikbirds to behave. Longer to teach them to obey commaands." She shook her head and her tail twitched as she blinked frustration. "I must always guard against crediting Doms with behavior *we'd* consider raational, but I caan't imagine they'd take whaat amount to flying Griklets out to sea. They'd be unmanaage-aable." She paused. "That leads me to contemplate other possibilities."

"Such as?" Tex asked.

"Well, just as the enemy haas always referred to Grikbirds as 'lesser draagons,' there've long been rumors of 'greater' ones. We thought they must be the enormous superlizards they used in the attaack on Fort Defiaance, but local myths describe laarger *flying* draagons, big enough to caarry a maan."

Orrin was taken aback. "I hadn't heard that." He looked uncertain. "But that's impossible, right?" He glanced at Seepy. "I mean, we saw something, sure, and Greg Garrett even reported lizardbirds as big as a Nancy on some island in the Indian Ocean. Not sure I really believed that till now," he confessed. "But what I mean is, seems something that big could barely heave its own ass up in the air. How could it carry something as heavy as a man?"

"Ordinaary Grikbirds caan caarry at least twenty-five or thirty pounds," Lelaa pointed out. Some had dropped cannonballs and even exploding shells on ships. "Cap-i-taan Gaarrett's lizaardbirds are surf predaators, hunting fish as laarge as flaashies, which caan reach a hundred and thirty pounds or more. They obviously don't eat them in the waater, so they must caarry them elsewhere." She waved it away. "I'm no engineer, physicist, or naatur-aal philoso-pher like Mr. Braadford, so I caan't speak to whether it's possible or not. I caan say something *like* them does exist. The question is, if the enemy haas them, how will they use them—and whaat caan we do about it?"

Orrin ran his hands through sweaty hair. He and Seepy had been working on planes as hard as anyone. "You're the admiral, and I know you and Jenks've al-ready considered the probability Doms have contact fuses for their bombs by now, which'll make Grikbirds tossing them around even more of a nuisance. But I'd figure, if what you say is right, these things can carry heavier bombs, and that's what they'll have 'em do. The only an-swer I can think of is to make sure our most vulnerable ships, like carriers and transports, stay as far from shore as possible at night when my pursuit ships can't protect them as well. During daylight, I bet a Fleashooter could knock one down even easier than a regular Grikbird."

Tex frowned. "We'll have to keep back a heavier com-bat air patrol to protect our ships when the operation kicks off."

"Which means less protection for our planes and pilots devoted to the attack," Lelaa said, staring hard at Orrin.

He sighed and nodded irritably. The grand, coordinated assault they'd planned against El Corazon might be tough enough as it was, because they weren't sure what defenses they'd meet. So far, all their raids had gone deep and hadn't so much as scratched the primary objective or the modest but respectable fleet offshore. The reasoning was that no attack could come as a complete surprise, so they had to do their best to achieve confusion. The best way to do that, even Orrin agreed, was to lull the defenders at El Corazon as best they could—then drop an avalanche on them out of the blue. Hopefully, the shock inspired by the sheer ferocity of the attack would substitute for surprise.

The trouble was, now it seemed the enemy might have a weapon in the overgrown Grikbirds that could prevent them from closing the shore under cover of darkness. That would necessitate drawn-out, fully observable daylight maneuvering for the naval, ground, and amphibious assault—if they were all still supposed to happen at once. And Orrin's Nancys would have less protection from already alerted Grikbirds. It could be a nightmare in the making.

"Not really a good answer for this mess, is there?" Orrin asked absently, staring at the men and 'Cats working around them to repair or replace engines, patch torn fabric on wings and fuselages, and replace broken support struts. The pungent smells of gasoline, oil, sweat, and the various nitrate dopes sometimes came at him separately, swirling in the hangar deck, and sometimes hit him all at once. The rubberized dope they put on Nancy hulls under the blue and white paint really stank. "Can't we go in and smash their fleet and harbor defenses first?" he suggested. "Just my planes and Hibbs's battle line. We can cover the transports with the same CAP I'll have to leave over the carriers, and all my pilots'll have to worry about is hitting their targets and watching their asses."

It was Lelaa's turn to sigh. "Gener-aal Shinya and I both aargued exactly thaat with High Ahd-mi-raal Jenks and Ahd-mi-raal Hibbs. I suspect thaat, still, neither of them thinks quite as much in terms of air power as you or me." She blinked that away. "Actually, thaat's not true. After whaat happened to TF Eleven, I think they appreciate it perhaaps too much and fear it more. Especially since none of our new-construction ships are here yet and their old baattle line's as vulnerable from the air as the Doms'. They lean toward the single, mass, coordinated attaack, hoping it'll still be strong enough to create the confusion they desire."

"You're pullin' my tail," Seepy objected disgustedly. "Ah, Ahd-mi-raal," he added quickly, blinking contrition. "But, Jeez! First we give 'em months to get ready for us, then give up surprise for shock, shock for confusion, now confusion for whaat? We aimin' to staartle 'em now? They see us comin' on top of ever'thing, we'll be lucky if they're surprised we're so stupid!" He cut his eyes at Orrin. "That aact-uaally might confuse 'em some, thinkin' we caan't be thaat dumb."

Lelaa looked as though she agreed but blinked denial. "No, Sergeant," she said. "No maatter whaat we do now, the cost will be high, but I'm sure we'll do faar more thaan staartle the enemy."

Orrin looked down, then nodded slowly as his gaze turned to Seepy. "She's got a point. Where I came from, in our Philippines, we heard about the Japs hitting Pearl Harbor at about oh four hundred and *knew* we were next. We all ran out and jumped in our planes, waiting for the word to go after 'em, our bomber guys itching to hit Formosa. What we didn't know was that everybody in charge was running around like . . . akka birds with their heads cut off. *Damn* MacArthur," he swore bitterly. "Anyway, time went by, the sun came up, and we sat there, all morning long, cooking in our cockpits. A few planes took off chasing ghosts, but most of us finally climbed down and took naps in the shade under our wings. *That's* when the Japs hit us, right in the middle of the day, and you can't imagine a more tragic, screwed-up mess."

Tex was nodding grimly, but then he got Lelaa's attention and showed her his watch. She nodded too. "Very well, caarry on," she told them. "But if you think of a way to confirm the presence of laarge numbers of these greater draagons, or come up with a counter for them, please let me know."

"Ay, ay," Seepy said.

"Yes, ma'am," replied Orrin.

When Lelaa and Tex were gone, Orrin let out a disgusted burst of air. "Me and my big mouth. Should've just kept quiet about those things from the start. Even if they're as dangerous as Lelaa thinks, there can't be many of 'em, can there? We only saw one bolt out of a ship full of ordinary Grikbirds. Some of the other fellas might've seen the same one, so there couldn't've been more than two or three."

Seepy looked thoughtful. "Yah, but if they're only legends here, then they musta come from somewhere else. Maybe the Dom Pope's private birdcage, off to the southeast where their big temple is. They'd haafta bring 'em here—an' they mighta brung a bunch already." He shook his head, tail drooped in resignation. "Nope. Jenks may be right, I guess. If we're gonna run into somethin' weird, it's prob-aably best to do it in daylight so we caan see it." He shrugged. "Maybe the Jaaps thought thaat about you? 'Sides, if we get croaked then, the Maker'll see it an' we'll get claassier digs in the Heavens—unless you croak us stupid, by runnin' us into a mountain or somethin'."

Orrin just looked at him and blinked until he remembered that wherever Seepy was from, he clung to the Aryaalan belief that the sun *was* the Maker. They'd had a hard enough time getting those who thought like that to fight at night at all.

"Well, at least we can shoot 'em if we see 'em," he agreed at last, "but it's gonna be hell for Hibbs's battle line, and worse than hell for the Army and Marines. We'll do our part," he added grimly. "But I wouldn't trade places with any of *them*, or give a wooden nickel for their chances." He nodded at some 'Cats working on a Fleashooter with all its jugs off and dripping pistons sticking out at odd angles. "Let's give those guys a hand, then see if the dope on our plane's dry enough for paint yet," he suggested. "We'll get some chow after that."

Even as he worked and talked cheerfully, his mood darkened. Sure, he'd avoided taking the oath to Matt's Navy Clan, but that was as much because, though he liked and admired his cousin, he was glad to be out from under his thumb. Besides, he'd never even seen a Grik, not counting Lawrence and the few Grik prisoners in Baalk-pan and Maa-ni-la, and would've just been another pilot in First Fleet; probably already dead like most of Ben Mallory's 3rd Pursuiters. Here he was the *Fleet* COFO, the fight against the Doms had become his own, and Second Fleet's flyers were *his* pilots. Still, he had to think Matt would've come up with something better than a day-light frontal assault, and for maybe the first time—other than the simple fact he was family, and sometimes Orrin *really* missed his family—he caught himself wishing Matt would hurry up and finish with the Grik so he could come take charge out here.

"Hey," he said, wiping his oily forearm across his brows. They'd pulled the engine entirely and he'd stuck his hand down in the back of the crankcase to feel for metal shards while the whole thing gently swayed under the hoist. "Gimme a rag, wilya? I got stuff in my eye."

CHAPTER 15

Operation Whipsaw

////// Camp Simy
At the mouth of the Zambezi River
Grik Africa
March 14, 1945

W e *are* all gonna die, y'know," Dennis
Silva stated casually, stepping from the
improvised dock directly through the
large hatch forward of the observer/gunner's open window in the portside fuselage of the big four-engine PB5-D
Clipper. The thing was huge, with an even deeper fuselage than the old PBY Catalina they'd found on this world
and Ben Mallory'd flown to death. The wing area was
about the same, Silva judged, but all four of the new
stacked radials together barely exceeded the 1,200 horsepower each of the PBY's Pratt & Whitney Twin Wasps
could summon. It worked out, Silva supposed, since the
Clipper's lighter construction meant they weighed only
about a quarter of what a PBY did.

And Clippers were damned impressive, capable of
hauling six crew, eight passengers, five .30-caliber machine guns, and 2,500 lbs of ordnance at 145 miles per
hour. Perhaps even more than the new steel-hulled warships, Clippers represented how far the Allies had come

since *Walker* and *Mahan* first steamed into this bizarre world. They made good long-range reconnaissance birds, transports, even bombers. Fifteen would be bombing Old Sofesshk tonight, targeting it specifically for the very first time. Fifteen more, the entire remaining complement of Walt "Jumbo" Fisher's Pat-Squad 22, would—hopefully—add another role to the Clippers' list of capabilities. With only a pilot and copilot, fuel tanks half full, and all their guns removed, they carried no ordnance. Instead, each would be packed with forty of Chack's Raiders and all the combat gear they could carry.

"We're *not* going to die," Lawrence hissed, clambering aboard behind Silva, his voice a little odd. Silva looked back, his one eye wide. More troops filed aboard, heavily loaded with weapons and ammunition. Even more weight was represented by the three or four water bottles each had slung over their shoulders. The veterans in Chack's Brigade had been very thirsty in their last action.

"Why, Larry! You ain't *skeered*, are ya?"

"Yes," Lawrence replied simply.

Taken aback, Silva dropped it. If Lawrence wouldn't rise to the banter bait, he must really be on edge. *Understandable too,* Silva realized, *bein' a tad uneasy myself. Not about fightin', o' course,* he amended, *an' I know that ain't what's botherin' Larry. Nobody's keen on the way they're takin' us to* this *scrap.*

The fifteen bombers were the pathfinders, meant to sow confusion on the ground and light the way. The transports, carrying a combined total of six hundred Raiders, would make as many runs as it took to drop the entire brigade—or as much of it as circumstances allowed. After the bombers' initial task was complete, they'd be loaded with supplies to be dropped to the troops.

Choosing a different tack, Silva nodded and glanced at the other Raiders, cramming themselves on benches lining the interior of the plane, even squatting on the deck. There weren't any Grik-like Khonashi aboard; all except Lawrence and Silva were Lemurians. Each was blinking rapidly, unconsciously, a combination of fear—even terror—mixed with determination. "Ain't natural,"

Silva continued loudly. "Takin' us up in a airplane an' throwin' us out to fight. Why, I bet won't one in ten of us live long enough *to* fight!"

"An' you won't be one of 'em," snapped a familiar voice. Silva couldn't see the speaker well in the gloom inside the plane but knew the voice belonged to a grizzled old Lemurian NCO he'd known a long time.

"Well, whaddaya know? It's ol' Moe!"

"*First Sergeant* Moe," the 'Cat corrected.

"In the First North Borno," Silva agreed. "Why ain't you with your lizardy Khonashi pals? They kick you out as too damn old?"

"No. Col-nol Chack asked for NCO volunteers to ride with you." Moe snorted. "I *got* volunteered 'cause nobody would."

Silva feigned a hurt expression. "But why?" he asked, the picture of innocence.

"Cause you crazy!" Moe snapped. "You maybe save the baattle, but you get ever-body 'round you dead." A lot of the 'Cats blinked even faster.

"I bet I've fought alongside plenty o' these other fellas before," Silva pointed out. "An' look at Larry! He's been in more fights with me than I recall an' he ain't even *half* dead yet!"

"He haas been—an' he's just as crazy as you."

Silva nodded philosophically. "Can't argue that. But what makes you think I'm done for?"

Moe hacked a laugh. "You chute!" he said. "Ain't no way you gonna laand soft enough to live, big as you are an' as much junk you caarry!"

Lemurian parachutes worked very well—they were simple enough after all—but that very simplicity made them difficult to control. Those who used them were pretty much at the mercy of the wind. More to the point, however, like 'Cats, they were fairly small. They'd save a normal-size man, which was close to what the 'Cats now weighed with all their gear, but Dennis Silva was . . . a little bigger. And as usual, he carried quite an arsenal. In addition to the Thompson SMG slung low across his front so it wouldn't interfere with his parachute, he wore his signature weapons belt with braces. It was loaded down with a .45, 1917 cutlass, '03 Springfield bayonet, and lots of ammo pouches. In fact, he'd forgone his usual canteen for a couple of water bottles with shoulder straps so he could carry more ammo on his belt. In addition to all that was a new holster he'd made for Captain Reddy's single-action Colt .44-40, which the skipper insisted he keep for now. Over and above everything else was his very favorite weapon of all, his Doom Stomper. It looked like the standard Allin-Silva breechloaders only it was much larger, having been made around a turned-down 25 mm Japanese antiaircraft gun barrel. It fired a 1-inch slug from a straight brass case that looked like a 10-gauge shell. The Doom Stomper didn't weigh much more than the fully loaded Thompson, but it was long, bulky, and very abusive to shoot.

"Then it's a good thing for all you little kitties that Colonel Mallory gave me a man-size parachute; one o' the extras they had for the two P-Fortys we got left out here!" Out of twenty-odd P-40Es they'd long ago salvaged out of the old *Santa Catalina*, only four remained in flying condition. One, Ben Mallory's personal M plane, was only marginally so. His and Shirley's, the last of the old 3rd Pursuit Squadron, were still aboard *Big Sal* and wouldn't see action in this fight. They and two others still in Baalkpan must be saved in case of desperate need against the League.

"*Five* chutes won't take you down safe," Moe scoffed.

"I just got the one, an' you better hope it will," Silva said with a smile. "Yer gonna need me—an' all the junk I carry. Guaranteed."

It was getting darker outside, and bare feet rumbled above them as 'Cats propped the engines. All four quickly coughed to life and Silva saw the 'Cats hop down on the dock. He turned back to Moe, genuinely curious. "I don't know why you've took such a set against me," he shouted over the noise. "I thought we was pals. Had some fun times, chasin' rhino pigs, rompin' across Borno, an' fightin' Japs together. You never even got hurt, as I recall. But you been skittish o' me ever since."

Moe's voice changed, and Silva would've bet that if he could see him, the ancient 'Cat was blinking embarrassment. "I *am* old," he finally admitted, "but I got a new mate baack in Baalkpan."

Silva gaped. "Why, you ol' scudder! I always thought you was joshin' us. You really did buy some sweet young thing with all that prize money you got outa that ol' Jap bomber!"

"I got money," Moe confessed, "but I not buy mate. You no buy people!"

Silva waved it away. "Figure o' speech."

Moe ignored him, continuing. "My mate is old an' ugly, like me. Still, she knows old ways—like Kho-naashi, but for 'Caats—an' say she 'sees' my time to come, in dreams. She always say I come home, the waar over . . . unless I fight with you." Moe's dark form looked at the 'Cats around him. They were listening intently. "She say you get me killed an' I never see the end o' this waar."

Silva snapped his fingers. "So *that's* what you're worried about! Gettin' home to your mate!"

Moe suddenly grinned, showing his few teeth in the darkness. "I don't care about thaat. I got no use for homes or mates. Never much did." He sobered. "But I waant to see the waar over."

Silva conjured a bantering retort but let it pass. "Well," he said as low as his voice would carry over the engines. The plane was wallowing now, moving away from the dock. Another would take its place. "I never knew you was so damn superstitious." He waved his arms. "Guess I am too, a little. That's why I always say 'We're all gonna die.' I'm just funnin' an' ain't nothin' to it. Kinda like knockin' on wood." He was met by uncomprehending stares. "Like predictin' somethin' so it *won't* happen, see?" he urged, then looked at Lawrence. "You get it, don't you?"

"No." Lawrence turned to the others and raised his voice. "Yet I ha' seen hany 'attles hith Dennis Sil'a. He *does* all-'ays say it, and I not dead."

"Sure. See?" Silva rolled his eye. "Here, Larry, hold my Doom Stomper. I'm goin' forward an' see who's flyin' this crate." Handing off the big weapon, he squirmed through the tightly packed compartment until he reached the elevated flight deck. Stepping up, he stood behind the flight crew, busily maneuvering the floundering beast into the

lane between the ships that had been cleared for their operations. To his surprise, he saw several Clippers already
waddling through the choppy water ahead. Even more
unexpectedly, he recognized the pilot of their plane. "Hey,
Jumbo. What're you doin' here?"

Walt "Jumbo" Fisher was almost as big as Silva, which
made him a very unlikely fighter pilot in the world they'd
left behind. What had been barely possible in the P-40s
he'd loved, however, hadn't been remotely so in something as small as a P-1 Mosquito Hawk Fleashooter. Too
good a leader and pilot to waste, he'd been given Pat-
Squad 22. He might miss the performance of a pursuit
plane but fit more comfortably in the bigger aircraft. "I'm
about to *fly*, you dimwit," he responded sarcastically to
Silva's question.

"Well . . . yeah, I can see that. But I figgered—you com-
mandin' this flock o' geese an' all—that you spent mosta
yer time sittin' on a porch in a rockin' chair somewhere,
drinkin' mint jaloops."

Jumbo barked a laugh. "Ha! Yeah, you caught me.
That's my usual pastime. But knowing what you're going
to do, I wanted to take you to this party personally."

"Bullshit," Silva said. "No way you'd know I'd be in
your plane."

Jumbo shrugged. "I'm in charge. I know everything."
He grinned back at Silva. "Now I get to watch your crazy
ass fall out of the sky!"

Still unconvinced, Silva watched the first of the planes
ahead start their takeoff runs. The sunset glared in the
spray they made like rainbow rooster tails. "How long
after we're airborne before we drop?" he asked.

"About two hours. We'll have to gather my geese, as
you say, and stay as tight as we can. And we'll have to do
it over the target too, if you don't want to wind up in the
river, or on the other side of it. That would be tough.
Bombers coming down from the Comoros Isles should hit
the joint half an hour before we get there, if the wind
doesn't slow 'em down. It's picking up out in the strait
again," he added with a tinge of concern. "Another storm
brewing out there. Sky Priests say this one might be a
strakka." He shook his head. "Won't stir things up much

tonight," he reassured, "and with any luck, us showing up right after the bombers'll make the lizards hunker down, expecting more fireworks." He glanced back at Silva again. "Imagine their surprise when *you* show up!"

"I expect they'll be a touch flustered," Silva agreed, "if enough of us land close enough together to actually accomplish anything," he countered gloomily.

"You will." Jumbo shrugged. "Look, none of us has done anything like this, but the whole formation will circle the target. You'll probably be scattered fairly widely over the city, but you'll be *in* the city. I guarantee you'll see the palace, even in the dark. Shouldn't be hard to gather up there."

"Circle," Silva said with a frown. "All while they're shootin' them damn rockets at us."

"Well, yeah," Jumbo conceded. "Probably. And that isn't any fun. But they have a hard enough time hitting us in daylight. Dark is harder. And they'll set their fuses too long, to burst way above us, since we've never bombed from as low as we'll be dropping you."

"Right. About fifteen hundred feet," Silva agreed, remembering the briefing.

"That's the plan." Jumbo nodded ahead. "Now shut up and go sit down. We're next." He glanced back once more. "Your job is to get everybody out, as fast as you can, as soon as I say."

"I know," Silva confirmed. "That's my *first* job."

"Good. And as for the rest . . . Good luck."

Silva went back and joined Lawrence leaning against the aft bulkhead while the ungainly plane labored into the sky. There'd been no way to shift enough 'Cats to cram his butt on a bench, and Lawrence wasn't built to sit like that. Silva wondered how they managed it on planes carrying Khonashi. *Probably had 'em all lay down, spoonin' on the deck,* he mused. When the Clipper was airborne, he lurched forward and clung to the heavy bamboo frame supporting Jumbo's wicker seat and talked to the pilot some more, learning about Jumbo's adventures during the Battle of Mahe. Silva and Chack's—and Lawrence's—exploits at the time, on the Western Mangoro River, were well known. Sooner than Silva would've expected, he could see gun flashes below, forming a surprisingly large, blinking semicircle, delineating the respective positions of the forces around Tassanna's Toehold near the Neckbone. He'd heard the mutual bombardment was nearly continuous, if desultory. Both positions were strong and well protected by now. Grik guns fired to harass, provoking Allied guns to try to destroy them. A brighter, sputtering series of flashes showed that at least one Grik gun or its caisson or limber had been hit. More strobes of light started flickering far to the northwest.

"That's our bombers hitting Old Sofesshk," Jumbo confirmed. "A little early. You've got about forty-five minutes, so you better go on back and get your guys ready." Without a word, Silva squeezed Jumbo's shoulder and went to stand among what he was starting to think of as his platoon. The large hatch cover had never been clamped in place and the opening gaped before him. There'd be no moon at all that night, but the stars made it lighter outside. That didn't dispel the sense of void beyond the opening, in reality and metaphor. They'd all soon be jumping into the unknown, in more ways than one.

After a while, Lawrence moved to stand on the other side of the hatch, still holding the Doom Stomper. "I go hirst," he said simply, low enough that only Silva could hear. "Hut . . . you got to throw I out."

Silva's eye widened, but he nodded. "You bet, buddy. I may have to do the same with some o' these other rascals. I'll crack jokes about it later, o' course, when recountin' the hee-roic tale o' the first-ever airborne assault in the history o' this goofed-up world, but"—he grinned—"I kinda wish somebody'd throw *my* ass out!"

Squinting in the darkness, he noticed some dull red lights for the first time, pacing them, and realized they were the wingtip navigation lights of other planes. Smaller aircraft didn't have them, relying on each other's exhaust flares to prevent collisions in the dark, but even though Clippers had exhaust as well, their size and need to maintain tight formations made such lights essential. He figured they must be shielded from below since he'd never seen them before.

Another light, impossibly bright, suddenly streaked

past, clawing straight up into the sky atop a column of flame and sparks. "Whoa!" he shouted, recoiling involuntarily. To his dazzled eye, the thing could've been right there, or a quarter mile away. Another one shot past, then another. "Goddamn!" he yelled. "We must be gettin' close for sure. They're shootin' rockets at us!"

The Grik had been gifted simple rockets, and many other unpleasant things, by the Japanese under Hisashi Kurokawa. According to Muriname, none of these benefactors besides Ando's pilots remained. *An' Kuro-kawwy got his final reward,* Silva reflected with satisfaction. But the technology his people unleashed was still plaguing the Allies. Grik rockets were ridiculously crude, their engines merely a solid column of black powder. Ignited at the tail, a jet was directed through a simple conical nozzle. At first they'd been little more than projectiles with light, contact-fused bursting charges, more dangerous to their operators and their own people on the ground than to their targets. But more and more Grik, as they came of age (artificially, by Grik reckoning), were apparently contributing intuitive improvements to what the Japanese gave them. The rockets kept getting bigger and more capable, tipped with heavier warheads that detonated on a time fuse set to explode and spray shrapnel in all directions at calculated altitudes. They still couldn't be aimed very well, and certainly not guided, and the vast majority still missed their aerial targets. But "vast majority" wasn't the same as "all," and as the weapons and their operators improved, they were taking an increasing toll. Just as bad, the Grik had finally figured out that rockets were pretty effective against ground targets. The only good thing was, the bigger they got, the easier they were to spot from the air, and Ben Mallory's Army and Naval Air Corps hunted them with a passion.

Another rocket screeched by, likely exploding far overhead—Silva didn't see—and on reflection, Silva thought there really didn't seem to be that many, compared to earlier accounts he'd heard from Mark Leedom, Tikker, even Jumbo himself. *An' they don't shoot 'em off where they might come down on Old Sofesshk at all,* Silva remembered with relief, *so we shouldn't be in the barrel long. . . .*

A rising lance of fire slammed into the belly of the Clipper flying off their port wing. The plane didn't stop the rocket and it blew out the top of the fuselage at a distorted angle. Unfortunately, the cutting-torch heat of the jet ignited everything in its path and the body of the plane aft of the cockpit burst into flames. The nose dropped, the control cables to the tail probably cut, and the Clipper started to fall with forty troops and two pilots. Silva caught a last brief glimpse of burning, writhing bodies leaping out the hatch or side windows just before the fuel tanks caught and the big plane shattered into a cloud of plummeting meteors.

A damn unlucky shot, for us, Silva knew, but he suddenly sensed that the dread he'd felt—and felt around him—had turned. He and his platoon still weren't looking forward to what they had to do, but they were ready for anything that got them out of the plane and on the ground where they could fight. They might still die, but they wouldn't be helpless targets, sitting on their butts.

Even after the plane banked sharply to port, the signal they were turning into the target area, more rockets kept flashing skyward. "They're still shootin'," Silva shouted at Lawrence, catching his first glimpse of Old Sofesshk below. Quite a few fires were still burning, the result of the raid that preceded them. "That's prob'ly why," he continued, pointing. "Either they're too fixed on keepin' us from hittin' their holy city again, or they're mad enough they don't give a shit if they rain a little shrapnel on it."

A rocket exploded nearby and he either felt the overpressure or something hit the plane. "Now!" shouted the Lemurian copilot in that penetrating way 'Cats had. Silva turned to grab Lawrence as he'd asked, but his friend was already gone. A 'Cat instantly bolted after him without giving Silva the chance to check if his left hand was clutching his ripcord. "Jump free, count to three, jump free, count to three," he shouted as each 'Cat went by. He had to grab one's shaking hand and slap it against the ripcord handle, but didn't have to throw anyone out. In barely a minute he was the last, and with a final look around, he shook his head. "Shit," he said, "that damn

Larry still has my Doom Stomper!" Grasping the wooden T handle on his own ripcord, he jumped.

The trip down was actually sort of fun, once the big white parachute opened. Well, after he was nearly jerked apart, that is. He'd been so busy worrying about the others, he'd forgotten to tighten his Thompson sling, and everything else seemed to have come a little loose as well. It all wanted to keep falling after the chute brought him up short. He cursed. After that, though, there wasn't much to do but look around. He'd studied the aerial pictures of Old Sofesshk as well as he could, but the fires and all the rocket glares made a hash of his sense of direction. It was kind of pretty, though. Other chutes were drifting down around him, reflecting the fires and flashes. He thought he caught a quick glimpse of the cowflop palace in the distance, lit by another rocket, but something made him glance down. "Shit!"

He'd momentarily forgotten how low they'd dropped, and this wasn't a sightseeing trip. Inordinately pleased he wasn't about to land in the water—or a fire—he just had time to prepare to . . . *Crash!* The ground had been closer than it looked. In fact, he didn't hit the ground at all, but a roof covered with strangely shaped ceramic tiles. Fortunately, the structure beneath—he got the impression of ancient, musty straw and light timbers as it all joined his descent—wasn't all that substantial. He landed on his ass in the dark on what felt like more tile, and shrugged out of his chute as quickly as he could untangle the debris. In that moment, unable to bring any weapon to bear, he felt extremely uncomfortable. Nothing lunged at him, however, and he finally stood, Thompson in one hand, Zippo in the other. He flipped the lighter open and spun the wheel.

That's when the Grik came at him. There were three, and they'd all been clustered together by a wall. *Maybe they thought I was a bomb,* Silva thought as he swung the Thompson, flipped the safety off, and squeezed the trigger. Downy fur exploded amid the ear-numbing *Braaaap!* of a long, corkscrewing burst, and blood sprayed him in the face. One Grik actually slammed into him and he spun away, expecting the slash of teeth or claws, but it merely tumbled to the floor, already dead. One was writhing, shrieking, the sound incredibly loud in the close quarters. He put the muzzle of the Thompson near its head and fired the last two shots in the twenty-round magazine.

Somehow, he still held the flickering Zippo. "That was a neat trick," he murmured, stooping to inspect the closest corpse. "Damn, look like civvy lizards, dressed fancier than I ever seen," he thought aloud, quickly examining the others. They all wore robes of some sort, the color indefinite in the gloom, but of a finer material than even the Hij of Grik City had possessed. "Sure weren't warriors—no swords or nothin', not that it matters. They're born with more weapons than any honest critter."

He straightened and swiftly circled the chamber, the lighter getting hot in his hand, and found a low, narrow wooden door. There was no latch, just a leather thong with a hole in it looped over a peg. Clapping the Zippo shut, he stuffed it in his pocket, inserted another magazine in his Thompson, then lifted the thong and eased the door open. A rifle bullet struck the doorjamb and blew splinters at him.

"Hey, goddammit!" he shouted. "Hold yer fire!" He wasn't so deaf that he couldn't tell the *crack* of an Allin-Silva from the *boom* of a Grik musket. When no more shots were forthcoming, he stepped slowly outside, squinting in the direction the shot came from. Five forms were trotting toward him, and he almost killed them. They *looked* like Grik. Only when the flare and flash of a rocket washed the scene in light did he realize they were Khonashi, wearing white bandannas to distinguish them from the enemy. "Watch who yer shootin' at from now on, you fuzzy little geela monsters!"

"Chee Sil'a?" came a questioning, startled voice.

"Pokey?" Silva replied, equally surprised. "Is that you?" Pokey was a *real* Grik, taken long ago, who'd somehow survived what they'd always believed was the captured warrior's imperative toward self-destruction. Almost all those early prisoners just . . . died. A few, caught after wandering around alone for a while, seemed able to function, even cooperate, but Pokey and some others practically *vol-*

unteered when given a choice. Looking back on it, especially after recent experiences, his behavior made sense.
He'd been confined for a time of course, but in his mind he
wasn't a captive; he'd joined the Hunt of the Allies.

Silva hadn't been much impressed by Pokey's intelligence during their first association, and the little Grik had
just been a bearer and brass picker on the expedition across
Borno where they met and befriended the Grik-like—and
human—Khonashi. Pokey stayed with them. And every
time Silva saw him, Pokey seemed a little sharper.

"*Sergeant* Koky," the Grik stressed, substituting a k for
the p he couldn't form.

"Yeah, whatever." Silva gestured at the four Khonashi.
"This all you could round up?"

"As yet." Pokey's eyes narrowed. "'Ore than you."

"Yeah, well, I had a little chat with some locals." He
cocked his head. The rockets had stopped and the drone
of engines was fading, but the crackle of rifles and stutter
of Blitzerbug SMGs was starting to rise. A small group of
'Cats scampered out of an alley not far away, firing behind them and taking cover. "Let's go get with them."

They joined the 'Cats just as about a dozen Grik warriors rushed into the open. A fusillade of rifle and SMG
bullets mowed them down before they could even fire.

"Break their muskets, then let's go," ordered a 'Cat
who then turned to Silva. "I'm *glaad* to see you," he confessed.

"Me too, Chackie," Silva replied without a hint of sarcasm or irony. He waved around. "What a goose pull.
We're scattered everywhere!"

"We expected thaat," Chack agreed, blinking regret.
Then he nodded to the west. "At least we haave an obvious raally point." Silva followed his gaze. From here he
could clearly see the Palace of Vanished Gods, illuminated by a growing fire in the city around it. As he'd suspected from the glimpse he got, it looked about three
miles away. "Not much resist-aance so faar," Chack continued as his troops and the Khonashi swung the Grik
muskets down hard against the baked brick pavement and
shattered their stocks. "The enemy is prob-aably as scaat-
tered as we are, keeping order in the city." He paused.

"Though there seem to be few civilian Hij to control. I hope they haaven't taken their Celestial Mother away aafter all."

"Yeah." Silva knew if that was the case, they were probably all as good as dead. "There's *some* civvies here—or there was," he amended. "The ones I came across decided to join the fight."

Chack nodded, needing no details. "As maay others, once they determine our objective." All the Grik muskets had been rendered useless. "Which lies thaat way." He pointed. "Let's go."

CHAPTER 16

////// *Palace of Vanished Gods*
Old Sofesshk
Grik Africa

The Celestial Mother stood on the smooth paving stones at the entrance to the Palace of Vanished Gods and stared out, uncomprehending, at the glowing fires scattered throughout Old Sofesshk. Never had the prey dared target the ancient city itself, and First General Esshk and the Chooser had sworn they never would. A few errant bombs must be expected from time to time, the Chooser had soothed, blaming the wind. But not even this prey, their "enemy" (the Celestial Mother still had trouble understanding a distinction General Esshk and the Chooser now seemed to take for granted), could ever be mad enough to rain destruction on a place so important to the Vanished Gods, where they must know she herself resided. Yet that was clearly what they'd done that night. As far as she could tell, not a single bomb had fallen across the river, or even upriver, where the bulk of their nearby industries still lingered. A dozen or more of the huge flying machines had deliberately, maliciously, dropped their entire loads on the very heart of Gharrichk'k civilization—on *her*!—and at least one bomb, perhaps more, actually struck the palace itself! There'd been no damage—the dark granite of the prehistoric structure was proof against everything but age and the elements—but that was beside the point.

The rest of the city was not so invulnerable and sections, all older than any living memory and some possibly ancient enough to have been inhabited by the Vanished Gods themselves, crumbled under blistering pyres. The Celestial Mother was overwrought with anguish.

"Why? *How* could they do such a thing?" she demanded aloud, her voice small.

"I cannot say," replied her Senior Sister. "I beg you," she added hastily, "return to the safety of the palace at once. This wicked prey showed long ago they were capable of unthinkable acts when they slew she who gave life to us all. Now this. There seems no limit to their capacity for evil." She hesitated. "Come inside. We can't protect you from fire bursts that fall blindly from the sky. If you die without issue . . . If we *all* fall, the bloodline of the Gods will be extinguished forever."

"There is no danger," the Celestial Mother countered more harshly than usual. "Not to me," she stressed, "or us. Not now. The flying machines have gone." She paused. "And I must view—and think about—this thing my champion and chief advisor promised could never happen."

"As you wish," the Senior Sister conceded.

For some time they merely stood, watching the flames slowly diminish and breathing the faint smoke that lingered near the ground. Fortunately, unlike New Sofesshk across the river, largely built of mud dried on frameworks of wood and woven prairie grass, only the roofs of the older city were backed by flammable material, and it was protected by tile. Unless the breeze strengthened sharply, the fires shouldn't spread. Still, the Celestial Mother imagined the reduced garrison would be hard-pressed to fight them. *And what about the Hij population?* she wondered. It had inexplicably diminished as well. Esshk told her most had gone to directly supervise the various industries they were responsible for, but that struck her as absurd, even at the time. They may have been like regents for those endeavors, but few actually knew anything about them. Now that Old Sofesshk had been bombed, contrary to everything she'd been assured with such certainty, she wondered again what became of the Hij in the city.

A bright arc of fire flashed skyward from downriver,

followed by another, then a small cluster clawed upward, diverging as they flew. She quickly recognized them as the rockets used against enemy flying machines. *But why use them now, after the bombers have gone?*

"Giver of Life," her Senior Sister urged. "We must go inside! The prey returns with more fire bursts."

The Celestial Mother hesitated, finally hearing the telltale drone of engines. It must be true, yet she wanted to see, to *remember.* Regent Champion or not, First General Esshk would have a lot to answer for. "Just under the archway, then," she agreed. "We'll be safe enough there unless a bomb strikes right on us. If such ill chance befalls us, it must be a sign it's time for our bloodline to end."

The guards ushered her back, reluctantly allowing her to view the bombing. Whereas they'd been astonished before when the bombs fell, they were now equally amazed when the flying machines just seemed to circle for a time and no explosions shook the ground. Explosions lit the sky, however, as rockets reached the height they were fused for, and there was danger they might be struck by falling fragments, but the big machines seemed to do nothing harmful. The Celestial Mother, slowly easing out from under the arch with her sisters to gain a better view, was perplexed.

The rockets tapered off, someone probably realizing they were firing over the city, but one final burst silhouetted dozens, *hundreds*, of what looked like big white balls floating slowly down.

"What can it mean?" asked one of the sisters who shouldn't have said anything unsolicited. The Senior Sister was so distracted she didn't admonish her.

"I don't know," replied the Celestial Mother, equally diverted. "Those can't be bombs . . . Can they? Surely they're much too large. And the flash above shone *through* them. Nothing so insubstantial can be harmful . . . Can it?"

A carriage clattered toward them on the baked brick road by the river, drawn by forty warriors at the run. It practically skidded to a halt nearby on the slicker paving stones around the palace. The door swung open and the Chooser's short, paunchy form hopped to the ground and waddled toward them at what, for him, was a sprint.

Gasping, he flung himself down at the Celestial Mother's feet.

"I'm here to fetch you, Giver of Life!" the Chooser cried urgently, squirming like an alligator nailed to the ground with a spear.

"Do get up, Lord Chooser," the Celestial Mother commanded. "And what's the meaning of this? How came you to be so near? I thought you were with General Esshk at Lake Galk." Her coppery eyes narrowed. "And *you* do not fetch me like a stick of wood for a cookfire! Particularly not as I watch all your promises wither in the flames of my city!"

The Chooser stood, but it was clear he would've preferred to continue grinding himself into the paving stones.

"I was here," he replied, evading her question, "and well that I was. The world is undone!" he wailed. "The Other Hunter prey to the south has smashed past the force sent to stop it. Even now they rush north to join the enemy beyond the *nakkle* leg! In the absence of First General Esshk, I commanded Second General Ign to respond as he sees fit, yet I must assume all our enemies will soon drive northwest together, putting your holy person in jeopardy. I came to take you to safety!"

In spite of the bombing, the Celestial Mother wasn't that shaken. "Surely it can't be as bad as you say. We still outnumber the prey by a very large margin, not so?"

"That *is* so," the Chooser agreed, "but . . ." He suddenly cocked his head to one side, his own eyes narrowing. Then they widened in horror. "There is shooting! In the city! Listen . . ."

It was true. The Celestial Mother hadn't heard the sound of small-arms fire since before her elevation, but like an unusual number of other things, she remembered.

"The enemy is *here*!" the Chooser almost squealed. If he hadn't kept his crest erect by artificial means, it would've lain flat against the top of his head. "I don't know how, but they are. We must go at once!"

"Can their warriors fall from the sky inside clear whitish balls?" the Celestial Mother asked herself as much as the Chooser.

The Chooser was taken aback by what he must have thought was an utterly random, fanciful question. "What?"

"Their flying machines circled above and dropped such things. That must be how they came!"

The Chooser shook his head. "It doesn't matter *how* they're here, only that they *are*. We must flee."

"Never!" the Celestial Mother snapped, sharp teeth clacking in her jaws. "We are Gharrichk'k! We do not flee from prey." Her voice hardened further as she raised it to the warriors pulling the carriage. "Use that to block the entrance to the palace." The sound of firing was growing, mostly to the southeast. Some was fairly close. Grik warriors, other than the hundred or so always near, began arriving from the closer billets where they'd been stationed. Unsure what was happening but sensing a close threat to their Celestial Mother, they immediately began dragging carts and rail fencing up to add to a natural breastwork formed by the low wall surrounding the palace and the avenue of trees bordering the riverside road. No buildings stood closer than a couple of hundred yards or so, and they went about clearing the best killing ground they could.

"But . . ." the Chooser chirped.

"We'll make our stand in the Palace of Vanished Gods," the Celestial Mother decreed. "All our warriors must do is hold the one entrance. Nothing can harm us inside. Send runners with news of our predicament across the river and spread the word to First General Esshk and Second General Ign." Her eyes narrowed again. "With so few Hij in the city, there are plenty of small boats along the docks"—she eyed the Chooser—"something else you might now better explain to me." Abruptly, she turned back toward the archway, her cloak whirling behind her. "I expect General Esshk will relieve us as soon as he hears," she called back over her shoulder. "He better."

"But . . ." the Chooser yipped once more.

"Attend me, Lord Chooser," the Celestial Mother commanded.

Watching his warriors disperse into defensive positions while the gunfire in the city continued to mount and his carriage began moving to block the entrance under the archway, the Chooser could only obey.

The Streets of Old Sofesshk

Little clusters of Raiders and members of the 1st North Borno, wildly mixed together, gathered to Chack and Silva like iron filings to a magnet as they fought their way closer to the palace. But Chack had been right and the resistance they met tightened commensurately, turning their initial rush into a bloody, ammo-gulping slog, fighting from one weird Grik house to another.

The architecture was different from anything they'd ever seen Grik build. If anything, it looked a little like some of the stone ruins they'd run across in Indiaa, but few had time to contemplate that. At least it was substantial enough to provide some cover, which helped them more than the Grik. The enemy seemed fresh and well equipped but not seasoned. Leaderless packs attacked them on sight, probably reverting to instinct. Larger, more disciplined groups tried to block their advance by forming firing lines in the streets. Those were quickly shredded by fire from protected vantage points.

And the closer they worked to the towering Cowflop, the more worried about Lawrence, Moe, and the rest of his platoon Silva became. Two or three had joined them but had no more idea about the rest than he. Trying to envision where most should've landed, considering the bearing of the plane, and backtracking in his mind from where he'd jumped and wound up was impossible. Everything was too confused, and even the little maps everyone carried didn't help much. The streets were laid out more geometrically than in any other Grik city, but the only real landmarks were the river and the palace itself. All Silva could do was hope Lawrence, in particular, wasn't alone. He looked way too much like a Grik for his own good, especially in the dark, and could easily get shot by some trigger-happy Raider.

After what seemed like half the night but was probably less than two hours, Chack and Silva's force, more than a hundred now, had fought to within just a couple hundred yards of the dark, towering palace. Most of the closest Grik seemed to have pulled back into a defensive perimeter behind low walls and ornamental trees and shrubs. It was the first time Silva ever saw evidence the Grik engaged in any kind of decorative landscaping. *Oh, well, we'll do a touch o' landscapin' ourselves, before this is done,* he told himself. More Raiders had already assembled there, spreading out and concealing themselves around the enemy perimeter. They sniped at Grik inside and any they spotted trying to join them. The mixed company Chack and Silva brought increased the attackers' strength to nearly three hundred. They were still heavily outnumbered by those they'd surrounded, but the enemy couldn't know that. *They gotta be more confused than we are,* Silva reasoned. *'Specially since we can put out more fire than them. Probl'y think there's five thousand of us. That won't last after sunup, though, when they can see better.*

A small, two-story structure bordering the brick-paved road approaching the palace entrance from the west had been seized for Chack's HQ—when he arrived—and he and Silva were directed there by relieved troopers guarding it. *Come daylight, it'll give a good view of the palace, the river, an' New Sofesshk beyond,* Silva surmised. "Fancy digs," he appraised, stepping inside. The lamp-lit interior was full of 'Cats and Khonashi, and a battered wooden table had been moved to the center of the room. Another table already supported a comm-'Cat's heavy radio pack, the wires for the aerial trailing up rough-cut stairs. Another comm-'Cat was sitting in front of a collapsible tripod-mounted generator, spinning the handles on each side. "Practically a mansion, for Grik," he added, as Chack returned salutes. There was little more floor space than in the two-story shack Silva grew up in, but the place was well maintained (discounting the bullet holes in the walls and drying blood on the tile floor). It stank of Grik, but not so bad that the smell of sweaty 'Cats and Impie humans hadn't almost covered it.

"Took you long enou' to get here," came a familiar voice that filled Silva with relief. "I thought you is dead," Lawrence told him. The Sa'aaran was in a corner, an Impie corpsman wrapping his arm while Moe tried to arrange a sling. That was always awkward for Grik-like beings, since their shoulders weren't very broad.

"*There* you are!" Silva exclaimed when he saw his friends. "Where's my Doom Stomper?"

"O'er there," Lawrence exclaimed angrily, nodding his snout at a corner of the room. Moe grunted at him to hold still.

"Whaat haappened to you?" Chack asked, concerned.

Lawrence looked accusingly at Silva. "His dan gun. He ne'er took it, so I did. Didn't sling it though, and it nearly tore this arn out. I such a dun-ass," he said, shaking his head. "Should'a go hithout it, then should'a let go 'hen it yanked I arn." He closed his eyes. "Hut nooo, I a dun-ass."

"Is it broken?" Chack asked the corpsman.

"No. Overextended, maybe torn muscles. Don't know how he hung on."

"Good thing he did," Silva grumped, moving to the big rifle and examining it. "Prob'ly his most important contribution to the whole damn war."

"You're an asshole," Lawrence stated.

Chack nodded, blinking at Silva with something like surprise. "Yes, he is," he said. Then he looked at the comm-'Cat. "You've made contaact? Staatus report," he demanded.

"Two Clippers didn't make it baack. Nobody seen whaat got the other one. Thirteen haas loaded an' took off wit' most o' the second haaff o' Major Jindal's Twenty-First Regiment. He's wit' 'em."

"Good," Chack breathed.

"The next run'll bring Major Cook an' more Khona-aashis. Thaat'll complete the command element. Following flights'll bring us up to strength . . . hopefully."

"What about supplies?"

"Bombers loaded 'em an' turned around just before the traansports." The comm-'Cat blinked skepticism. "Course, they'll drop stuff all over the place, just like they did us. We'll haafta go find ever-ting. Colonel Maallory aasks caan we secure the supplies quickly."

Chack snorted. "It took almost two hours to secure

ourselves, and only a little more thaan haaf our force haas
fought its way here so faar." He blinked annoyed acceptance. "The rest of the Raiders'll haave to do the same,
bringing whaat supplies they find in with them."

"That's about what we figgered," Silva put in, satisfied
with his huge rifle. "We knew it was gonna be a circus
from the start."

"Grik!" somebody shouted outside, and they funneled
out the door, ducking behind a low wall.

"Hold your fire!" Chack hissed loudly when he saw
twenty or thirty Grik-like forms double-timing up the street.
"Bandaannas," he explained. "First North Borno, over
here!" he called. The trotting troops veered toward them,
and NCOs directed them forward. Grik muskets thumped
and flashed in the darkness, shooting at movement.

"Stupid," Silva growled. "Never should'a brung Khonashi
to fight Griks. They look too much like 'em. Should'a sent
'em east to kill Doms." He chuckled. "Them Doms would'a
wet theirselfs."

"And got whaat in return?" Chack countered. "Jindaal's
regiment's the only orgaanized force of Imperiaals in this
theater. Do you think they would've sent more in exchange? They haave their own problems."

"Still," Silva grumped, glancing back at the door to the
HQ. "Havin' just one lizardy-lookin' pal to watch over is
nerve-rackin' enough." Chack nodded, realizing—again—
that Silva wasn't as big an asshole as he pretended to be.
He'd probably transferred all his concern for Lawrence
onto his Doom Stomper to avoid embarrassment for them
both. And he'd been doing more and more of that, Chack
realized, since they lost Risa. *She was my sister,* he thought,
*but her death tore Silvaa's soul as deeply as mine. If not for
my beloved Safir, I don't know whaat I would've done. Yet
Silva haas no similaar source of solace. Paam could be, but
often tears him even more, in her way.* He didn't have an
answer.

Rockets flared, reaching for more droning engines. It
looked to Silva like they were still shooting high, the
bursting charges exploding above the planes. Somebody
must've gotten wise, however, because a cluster of rockets
suddenly erupted all around a couple of Clippers. One

caught fire and fell away, beginning to spin. It impacted in the rubble of New Sofesshk with a roiling gout of flame, followed by an extended sputter of secondary explosions as its cargo of munitions went up.

A couple of armored Grik battleships anchored downriver, pinpointed on the maps but forgotten till then, opened up with antiair mortars emplaced on top of their high, sloping casemates. The spherical case shot they lofted could reach two thousand feet—barely—but all detonated well behind their targets.

"Wonder what them Grik sailors think is goin' on?" Silva said.

"Who knows?" Chack replied. "But right now they're only adding to the confusion. The longer thaat persists, the better. Each of those ships haave sufficient crews to overwhelm us if the notion struck their commaanders to put them aashore."

"Not so easy," countered Moe, to Silva's surprise. The old 'Cat usually wasn't one for offering opinions in combat situations. "The waater by the docks on this side o' the river is too shaallow for 'em, I bet. An' no Grik waarship *ever* haave lifeboats. Whaat for? Griks is just Griks. They make more. They ships only ever caarry a couple o' boats to tote they officers aa-roun'." He shook his head. "They haafta *raam* theyselfs haard aground to laand they crews." He hacked a gristly laugh. "Be a while before thaat occurs to anybody, an' they maybe won't even suggest it. Daamn sure won't *do* it widdout permission—which'll take even longer to get." He blinked amusement at them. "*You'd* do it, no aaskin', if you thought you should. You both been runnin' aroun' doin' whaat you waant so long, you never even ask youselfs if the higher-ups'll baack you. Thaat don't work for me, so it daamn sure don't work for Griks." He nodded out where the battleships lay, invisible now that they weren't firing. "They may give us fits later, but don't waste your thinkin' on Griks surprisin' us—while we're still surprisin' them."

"You're a philosophyzer, Moe," Silva said admiringly. "I've always said so. Just stay the hell away from me. If your broad really conjured up some sweet fantasy o' you croakin' 'cause you're fightin' with me, let's stay split up. Better for us both. You might take me with ya."

The Clippers were almost overhead now, parachutes silhouetted once again against the flashing rockets. Another volley of the weapons, maybe directed by the same commander as before, shattered another of the big planes. A wing fluttered away amid a smear of fire, and the burning wreckage fell on Old Sofesshk barely a mile away. A rising toadstool of orange flame marked the death of another brave crew. "Been a rough night for Pat-Squad Twenty-Two," Silva muttered grimly.

"Yes," Chack agreed. "But the next wave of reinforcements will approach from a different direction."

"Maybe should'a had 'em keep comin' as they have," Silva countered. "Griks're gettin' better with their rockets, sure, but they ain't got as many as they did. Might've used up mosta the ones they had on that flight path."

Chack shook his head. "Not my caall, thaank the Maker. I haave enough to worry about. Imaagine how Cap-i-taan Reddy must feel at times, at the top of the heap, as you say. All caalls are his, whether he makes them or not, since his plaan required others to."

"Yeah."

Several of the supply parachutes fell within sight and details went to get them. This initiated more musket fire from the Grik, shooting at shadows, but Chack spread the word for the Raiders to hold their fire. Supply drops or not, they were liable to run very low on ammunition. Best not to waste it.

Apparently, Colonel Mallory's decision to vary the direction of approach was correct, because no more Clippers fell that night. Fighting dropped off in the city, and with excruciating slowness Chack's entire brigade was drawn to the position encircling the Palace of Vanished Gods. Major Jindal reported, armed only with a naked sword in his right hand. "Can't use a rifle, and can't reload a pistol," he explained cheerfully, "but I'm honored to be back in it with you fellows at last!" Major Cook finally arrived as well, surrounded by almost an entire company of Khonashi loaded down with crates of mortar bombs. Nearly everyone coming in after the first wave carried something; machine guns, ammunition, mortar tubes, food. The stuff wasn't hard to find, still attached to parachutes fluttering fitfully in the streets. The chutes were all wadded up so others wouldn't risk their lives to retrieve something already claimed.

"We all leaped from the planes so quickly, we nearly became entangled on the way down!" Cook excitedly exclaimed and grinned. "I must confess, I've never been so terrified—and exhilarated—in my life!"

A helluva thing for him to say, Silva thought, *considerin' how young he is—an' how much exhilaratin' shit he's done already.* "I'm glad you enjoyed yerself, Mr. Cook," he said aloud. Major in the 1st North Borno or not, Cook was still a lieutenant (jg) in the American Navy Clan.

"As am I," Chack agreed dryly. "I'm sure I can aarrange for you to leap from aircraft more often. Now please move to the left. Most of your commaand haas already been deployed on the northeast side of the palaace."

Cook's boyish face fell. "I'd hoped the First North Borno would have the honor of storming the entrance. The Grik-like appearance of some of my troops might cause confusion."

"Not as much as they once did," Silva countered. "I figger the enemy got a fine look at 'em on the ol' *Santy Cat* an' when we took the beachhead." He nodded toward the palace in the humid gloom. "An' we ain't gonna storm the *outside* o' that joint till we have to," he added cryptically. "For now, we're still just tryin' to keep more Griks out."

The rest of the night passed in relative quiet. Occasional furious fighting erupted on the perimeter as more Grik did indeed attempt to join their comrades, but the rest of the city grew eerily still and silent. Raiders crept in, some that were injured in the drop, and details still searched for packets of supplies, but all reported that the city had become like a tomb. Fires burned out of control in several sections, the worst centered where the Clipper augured in, but nobody fought them. No doubt many Hij were still in hiding, but there appeared to be no more Grik combatants beyond the perimeter they'd established around the palace. It was surreal. Gradually, the sky in the east took on the slightest hint of a cloudy dawn. Their long, eventful night would soon be over and Chack's Brigade's mission could begin in earnest.

CHAPTER 17

Battle of the Pass

////// El Corazon
Holy Dominion
March 14, 1945

I t was mid-morning under a sharp, bright sky that crisply illuminated the dormant volcanoes flanking the brilliant white city of El Corazon. There were no clouds, and the only imperfection in the clear blue above was the distant, dark, ever-present smudge rising at a slant from the live volcano across the mouth of El Paso del Fuego. The Sister's Own Division was arrayed for battle on the plain seven hundred yards to the south of the city wall, near the very center of General James Blair's X Corps. The massed ranks of more than thirty thousand men and Lemurians ranged from the flanks of one tall mountain on the coast to a smaller one roughly three miles east. Angling from there northward to the pass itself was XI Corps, under General Ansik-Talaa, with another thirty thousand Imperial Marines and Maa-ni-lo Filpin Scouts. They were also poised to assault the city, as well as prevent the arrival of any unexpected enemy reinforcements from the east. The formations weren't particularly tight—shoulder-to-shoulder tactics had disappeared with the smoothbore musket—but they were impressively deep.

The Sister's Own was composed of Major Blas-Ma-Ar's

2nd Battalion; 2nd (Lemurian) Marines, which included the human Ocelomeh, or Jaguar Warriors; and Colonel Arano Garcia's Vengadores de Dios. The Ocelomeh with Blas had taken the Navy Clan oath and were armed, equipped, and trained as the Marines they'd become. On paper, Blas's 2nd of the 2nd was still just a battalion, but it had swollen to the size of a brigade. The same was even more true for Garcia's Vengadores, now almost a division by itself. It could've been one, in fact, but not only was Garcia keenly conscious that his core regiment once fought for the other side before coming to the light, he was also canny enough to understand, regardless of their record, many Imperials would deeply resent his Vengadores if they became independent of Blas. It didn't matter. Garcia knew how passionately loyal his men were to Colonel Sister Audry.

At least the Vengadores finally had breechloading Allin-Silvas. And somewhat ironically, theirs came from a brand-new factory established on the main island of the Empire of the New Britain Isles. All "regular" troops in the Second Fleet Allied Expeditionary Force had the new weapons now, finally replacing the mishmash of Imperial and captured Dom smoothbores and Union rifle-muskets. Not only did that make them more lethal, it also relieved the logistical strain of supplying such a variety of small arms, despite the flood of ammunition the faster-firing breechloaders consumed. The only Allied force still carrying muzzle-loading muskets was a single large division of indigenous volunteers from as close as the outskirts of Dulce and as far as Guayak in the south.

This auxiliary division, called the Pegadores, styled itself after Garcia's Vengadores, but was largely composed of his castoffs: poorly trained (and somewhat suspect) new arrivals, and even a sprinkling of regular Dom deserters. Blas figured most were sincere because, unless they were actual spies, their membership in the Pegadores would mark them for death. She was uncomfortable around their leadership, though. Garcia and his officers wanted to save their people from Dom rule. The Pegadores seemed more focused on punishing the Doms, and boasted they'd take no prisoners.

Blas tightened the straps on the stained and worn leather rhino-pig armor over her smock, sighed, and stepped closer to the division's standard bearers. Popping briskly in the warm breeze was Sister Audry's flag of the Vengadores, a busy white banner with a guy named Saint Benedict painted on it. He was holding a cross different from the one the Doms revered in one hand, and a book of some sort in the other. He was also surrounded by phrases painted in English, so the Impies could read them too. Blas had learned to read English herself, but rarely paid much attention to the fading letters on the flag anymore. Still, a couple of phrases caught her eye as she neared. The first was "May he protect us in the hour of our death." She could certainly identify with that. She'd gotten over her "don't care if I live or die" phase, whether anybody believed it or not. But another phrase said "Your hate shall be vanquished by our love," and she grunted, sincerely doubting love was going to kill any Doms that day. At the same time, she figured the sentiment probably set the Vengadores apart from the Pegadores more than anything.

Still, the flag that drew her closest attention and the one she loved the best was the Stars and Stripes of the Amer-i-caan Navy Clan and her own Second Marines. It was shot-torn and ragged and the colors had faded some, but the gold-embroidered letters on the red and white stripes recorded all the actions they'd been in and took her back a long way indeed.

"It won't be long now," came a soft voice beside her, and Blas turned to look into Sister Audry's sad but shining eyes. The Dutch nun was dressed for battle, wearing a helmet, camouflage smock, even a sword and pistol belt—though they both knew she'd never use either weapon. She wore them only because Arano Garcia insisted. Her hair had grown out and swished around her young face in the breeze like a straw-colored mop. Blas nodded at her and looked back at the glaring, twenty-foot-high walls of El Corazon. There were a couple of gates in it, about two hundred yards apart, that once opened into a larger city sprawling as far as Blas now stood. That section of El Corazon had been even more thoroughly erased than when she and Blair noted it before, and she could hardly tell it was ever there. Both gates were large and heavily reinforced, but the one to the west looked bigger. Twenty-eight heavy guns—naval 24 pdrs by the look of them—poked through high embrasures on this southern wall alone, and they glimpsed uncountable infantry moving busily atop the parapet. Blinking angrily, Blas glared at the open ground again. *Ground we haave to* cross, she told herself. *In broad daylight.*

Looking to the sides at the seemingly endless ranks of Allied troops and remembering the enemy had basically ceded the heights to them, heights they'd quickly crowded with artillery of their own, made her feel a little better—but not much. "This is stupid," she growled low so her XO, the Ocelomeh Captain Ixtli, wouldn't hear. "You say 'It won't be long,' but it's already too late—or too early. We should staart the aassault under cover of daarkness." She pointed at the plain in front of her. "Cross thaat when they caan't see us so well."

"Have faith," Audry chided her. "High Admiral Jenks won't fail us. I'm sure there'll be suitable distractions soon."

There already had been one. Even they could see that Admiral Hibbs's battle line was coming in fast, screening the transports full of Impie Marines. The warship's paddle wheels were churning hard, funnels streaming smoke within full sets of sails. Hibbs himself would be aboard the lead ship, HIMS *Mars*, closely followed by *Centurion*, *Mithra*, and *Hermes*—all veteran ships with veteran crews—and joined by the more recently arrived *Diana*, *Ananke*, *Feronia*, *Poena*, and *Nesoi*. They were attended by an equal number of Imperial steam frigates based on the Union Scott class. Far across the mouth of the pass, USS *Destroyer* and USS *Sword*, with six frigates of their own, protected more transports taking Impie Marines to occupy a small town at the base of the great volcano. Little resistance was expected there, and *Destroyer* and *Sword* probably weren't needed. Powerful as they were, however, both ships were Dom prizes, slower than Hibbs's main battle line. He'd feared they couldn't keep up and might open gaps in his line the enemy could exploit.

Sailing out to meet the closer ships were ten Dom liners and as many frigates, all under their garish red flags. They were the last enemy warships believed to be on this side of the pass—the survivors at La Calma hadn't joined and couldn't now, before the tide turned in several hours. In any event, the shaping naval battle was bound to bc drawing some of the defenders' attention, and Blas's sharp eyes saw a small cloud of dots racing in from the western horizon. More would be coming from the south, and the Army and Naval Air Corps would soon be making their presence felt as well.

There was a stirring in the ranks behind her and Blas looked to see armed men moving up between the files of her own troops. "Whaat the hell?" she murmured, recognizing one of the officers of the Pegadores shouldering his way through. His eyes met hers with a satisfied smirk as he passed, his flag bearer supporting his division's black banner edged in gold. His men, most wearing Allied combat smocks and cartridge boxes, but without any uniform head- or footwear, streamed through to the front of the line, in *front* of the 2nd Marines and Vengadores. There they stepped off another dozen paces or so and began the awkward process of forming close to four thousand poorly trained men into some semblance of order.

"What the *hell*!" Blas raged, shaking off Audry's restraining hand and marching into the gap. Audry, Garcia, their Lemurian Sergeant Major Koratin, Captain Ixtli, and First Sergeant "Spook" followed. They were immediately met by a short column of Imperial Dragoons galloping up, led by General Shinya himself. He looked somewhat out of place atop a tall spotted horse, but General Blair, Colonel Dao Iverson of the 6th Imperial Marines, and Captain Faal-Pel with the 1st of the 8th Maa-ni-la were with him. The 8th Maa-ni-la was deployed to the left of the 2nd Marines, and Faal was perhaps better known as "Stumpy" after losing part of his tail in *Walker* long ago. The officers deliberately edged their horses between Blas and the Pegadores before the dragoons could do it for them.

"Whaat's this about?" Blas demanded.

"What does it look like, Major?" Shinya asked in return. "The Pegadores have been given the honor of making the first assault on El Corazon and are deploying to do so."

"You promised that honor to *us*," Garcia stated, just as hot as Blas. "Have we not earned it? Has the blood we've shed not sufficiently proven our loyalty and worth?"

"Of course you have," General Blair replied more softly, holding out his hands in a calming gesture.

Garcia waved at the Pegadores. "Then what's the meaning of this?"

Shinya sighed and stepped down from his horse. Blair and Stumpy joined him. Stumpy looked a little upset too, and blinked rapidly. "I never said you'd make the first *assault*, Colonel Garcia," Shinya explained, then glanced at Blas. "I only promised you'd be the first of all our troops to *enter* El Corazon."

Blas was taken aback, but Audry leaned forward. "That doesn't make sense, General. You know the order of battle isn't nearly as important to me as the outcome, but honor and promises mean a great deal to the men"— she glanced at Blas—"and females of the Vengadores and Second Marines, not to mention the Ocelomeh Marines among the latter. Please make yourself clear."

"Very well," Shinya stated matter-of-factly. "I'm as opposed to the nature of this assault as anyone, but it wasn't my decision." He very pointedly didn't remind them whose decision it had been, but they knew. "That said, I understand the logic behind it. All we can do is hope it's sound." He gestured behind him. "Regardless, there's no escaping the fact that the first troops to cross that space will be *slaughtered*, and there's nothing I can do about it." His expression turned intent. "The Sister's Own Division may well be the finest in this entire army. Do you suppose I'd waste it so indiscriminately here, with so much fighting left to do and the greatest prize—the Dom capital itself— still so far away?" He shook his head. "I may be many things, but I don't think I'm a fool. If circumstances allowed it and I hadn't already made that unfortunate promise *my* honor demands I keep, I'd hold your division back from this fight entirely." He sighed. "As it is, I'm quite certain you'll still be the first troops *in* the city, if you're not all killed in the attempt, but you'll need protection to reach the walls." He glanced at the Pegadores. "Thus . . ."

Blas was stunned, but Sister Audry was aghast. "You mean you placed those men in front of us as *shields*, to soak up enemy shot for *us*?" she stormed.

"Makes perfect sense to me," Koratin said philosophically, and Audry glared at him. Koratin had been an Aryaalan lord and could sometimes be excessively pragmatic, particularly about his own failings. That's why he wouldn't accept a commission or any other official status that might feed higher ambition. His prime imperatives now were his passion for Christ, as Sister Audry's very first Lemurian convert, and destroying anyone—Grik or Dom—who threatened the children and younglings of the world. His devotion to younglings had been the one redeeming constant, as he saw it, of his life. Senior NCO in the Vengadores—still as a Navy Clan Marine and Sister Audry's chief protector—was sufficient rank for him.

Now under Audry's searing stare himself, Koratin waved defensively at the Pegadores. "This is their laand. *We* daamn sure don't waant it. If they're going to make something of it and build a nation of people we don't haave to kill to make them leave us alone, they haave to fight for it."

"My sentiments exactly, Sergeant Major," Shinya agreed.

"But it's our country too," Garcia reminded through clenched teeth.

"For which you've already fought and bled many times, Colonel," Shinya reminded tersely, losing patience, "at greater cumulative cost than the Pegadores will likely endure today. It's their *turn*," he added simply.

Seemingly as an afterthought, Shinya stepped up to Blas and urgently whispered something in her ear. Her eyes went wide. "Do you understand?" he demanded. Blas hesitated a moment, then blinked dreadful acceptance. Turning abruptly, Shinya remounted and stood high in his stirrups, shading his eyes and staring northwest. The fleets were about to meet and the planes were getting close. "Signal the artillery to commence firing," he called back to his dragoon escort. Nodding at Stumpy, he urged his mount forward and galloped to the right, Iverson and the dragoons, their standard bearer now waving a black-edged red swallowtail high overhead, close behind. Blair paused long enough to render a salute and call, "God bless."

That left only Stumpy, who'd be returning to the left. He rolled his eyes at Blas. "Did he tell you?" he asked. Blas nodded. "Yeah," Stumpy went on, "Gener-aal Shin-yaa ain't in a good mood. Ain't haappy about this at all. But, like you, I remember when he waas just 'thaat Jaap,' an' I never figured he haad so much . . . ruthless in him." He looked thoughtful. "But he cares about the cause, an' he cares about us—all us 'oldies' from the early days who took him as a friend even when he *waas* just 'thaat Jaap.'" He shook his head, as if that was more than he cared to think about, then grinned and waved. "So long!"

"There may be something to that," Audry murmured as they resumed their place in the line. "And perhaps he learned his 'protect those who matter to him, first and foremost' attitude from Mr. Silva." She frowned. "Only General Shinya has been given a much broader brush and a deeper pail of blood with which to paint *his* canvas."

Blas looked at her curiously. "I got my own reasons to be grateful to Sil-vaa, but do you still think he's some kinda tool for the Maker?"

Audry actually chuckled. "Yes, indeed—unless he's changed a great deal since I saw him last." She hesitated, then asked, "What did General Shinya say?"

Blas immediately told her, and Audry's eyes went wide. "The *entire* second wave?" she demanded. Blas nodded, and Audry sighed. "Given the tragedy already set in motion, it makes perfect sense—as Sergeant Major Koratin would say—in the most calculating, cold-blooded fashion." She tilted her head in the direction Shinya went. "He does God's work as well, I suppose," she murmured with regret, "and not for his own sake. But he *has* changed, and his brush is *much* broader. Sometimes I fear more for his soul than Silva's."

A great, thunderous roar punctuated her comment as seven full batteries—forty-two guns—fired almost simul-taneously from their positions partway up the flanks of the mountain to their right. Their primary targets were the great gates, and solid shot shrieked down to strike all around them, scattering splinters and shattered shards of masonry in great clouds. Isolated cheers rose up in approval of the long-range marksmanship of the cannoneers, but most remained silently thoughtful and the cheers died away. If their cannon could do so well at eleven or twelve hundred tails, what could the Doms' do at seven—or closer?

The 12 pdrs on the mountainside would keep at it until the infantry got too close to continue; then they'd switch to case shot and fire longer. Ten more batteries opened fire on the heights to the left, and a full one hundred guns, firing by batteries, bellowed behind them, sending smoke-jetting case shot high overhead. Even before the first shell burst over the city, there was a deeper booming in the mouth of the pass as the two fleets came to grips, and four great Vs of six three-ship Vs of Nancys dropped their bombs on El Corazon. "I will pray for all our souls," Audry shouted through streaming tears as bombs and shells exploded and the city was wreathed in smoke and flame. "And those of the enemy, who forced us to this."

CHAPTER 18

HIMS Mars
El Paso del Fuego

Admiral E. B. Hibbs was a pious man but not much given to praying. He figured the Lord had more important things to do than listen to his pitiful pleas. On the other hand, this was quickly getting very serious by anyone's estimation, and prayer might be his only recourse. Another deafening forty-gun broadside of 20 and 30 pdrs roared out from *Mars*'s high, tumblehome sides, the armored paddleboxes amidships marking the only gap in the jetting flames and smoke. All his ships but *Nesoi* and *Ananke*, still bringing up the rear, were fully engaged now, pounding the Dom liners from less than three hundred yards. The frigates had formed their own battle lines farther out and were having at each other in similar fashion. Yet except for the damage they'd done to the enemy's masts and rigging— their sails weren't set—Hibbs couldn't tell that his fire was doing much at all to the enemy's hulls. The Doms, on the other hand, firing slightly fewer 24 pdrs than he'd expected, were tearing his ships apart.

"They've armored their entire hulls, stem to stern," exclaimed an astonished Captain Resiah Karki, standing on the open quarterdeck by Hibbs. "I can see the rust streaks on the iron!" A large roundshot shrieked close enough between them that the air pressure of its passage nearly knocked them down. Feigning disregard, Karki collapsed his telescope. "Even our heaviest shot is deflecting!"

"Of course," Hibbs snapped. "They sacrificed their lighter guns for armor, while we kept ours and only bolted light armor over our paddleboxes and engineering spaces!" He shook his head mournfully. "What a terrible age we've lived to see when noble ships like this, hardly five years old, are rendered obsolete overnight."

Another broadside rippled down both sides of the ship, the starboard guns blasting great white clouds of stone and rubble from the northwest bastion of the city fort barely half a mile away. An instant later, the base of *Mars*'s foremast exploded in a streak of splinters, scything down men along the starboard fo'c'sle rail. The mast teetered and crashed down forward, taking the main topgallant with it and smashing off the bowsprit.

"All stop!" roared the captain, hoping to stall the spinning paddles before they got jammed or shattered by the ship's own wreckage as she steamed over it. "Cut away!" he added, shouting forward through his speaking trumpet. "Chop those lines loose. Fend off that debris!" More enemy shot pounded the hull, from sea and shore.

"A foot in the well, an' risin'!" cried the third lieutenant, bringing the report from the carpenter.

"Very well. Return to your guns, if you please."

Hibbs glanced astern, fearing *Centurion* might run them down, but she was already veering toward the Doms. *Mithra* was following suit, but *Hermes* was entirely dismasted and burning aft. "Damn!" Hibbs exclaimed, pounding his hand with his fist. A few Nancys were stooping on the Doms and one of their ships was bracketed by bombs. Another was hit and staggered under a satisfactory explosion, but all were shooting swivel guns at the planes and little explosions crackled in the air. A plane tumbled down and pancaked on the sea on its back. There were dragons too, suddenly quite a lot of them, swarming among the masts and snatching at sailors trying to furl the sails or cut away entangling lines. Marines shot muskets at them—few shipboard Marines had the new rifles—and one slammed into the spar deck by the longboat. The bomb it was clutching exploded, throwing two men over the side and chopping others down. More dragons threw bombs at *Mars*. One went off close aboard and another detonated against the port paddlebox, leaving a large dent in the thin armor. The other ships were getting it too. A huge, ear-splitting *crack* sounded aft, and Hibbs turned again to see that *Hermes* had exploded. "My God," he murmured. "Five hundred men . . ."

Suddenly, he stabbed a finger at *Centurion*. Almost alongside a Dom liner now, she was firing furiously and no dragons were near. Either they were avoiding their own ship or the dense gunsmoke was keeping them away. "I think her captain has the right idea," he shouted at Captain Karki. "Signal all ships to engage the enemy more closely!"

"But, Admiral!" Karki objected. "What of the transports? We can't abandon them."

Hibbs regarded the ships full of Marines closing on the rocky shore. Large shot from the city bastion threw up cataracts of spray around them. "We're all taking fire from the fort. They're closer and pose a greater threat. Signal our planes to focus on the shore batteries, but the transports must try to dash in under the guns. We'll do our best to keep the enemy fleet occupied." He turned back to Karki. "To do that we must get close, and out from under these damnable dragons! Signal the transports to go straight in, ground their ships if they must, but get those Marines ashore!"

"But . . ."

"Do it, Captain Karki! And bring us alongside those bloody Doms, hull to hull. Our guns *must* hurt them at that range." He paused, looking aft. *Mithra* had lost her mizzen; *Hermes* was a flaming wreck. He couldn't tell much about the rest, but all were closing with the Doms independently, their captains already realizing what must be done. "But the bitter truth is simply this," he continued. "We may lose our entire battle line today. We'll take as many of the enemy with us as we can, if we have to board them and fight them with our teeth. But when all is done, El Corazon is the key to controlling this side of the pass—and taking it is more important than you, I, or our entire outmoded fleet. Am I clear?" He looked away. "It'll require newer ships and aircraft, God help us," he added a little bitterly, "to hold this pass forever, but they can only do it with El Corazon in their grasp." He looked back at Karki. "These *old* ships of ours will make that possible."

With the foremast and attendant debris cut away and paddle wheels churning again, *Mars* pounded in, wreathed in smoke beneath swirling monsters and a hail of fire, to strike a last defiant blow for her kind.

CHAPTER 19

////// *El Corazon*

General Anselmo Mayta and General Allegria stood impassively on the parapet facing south, near the bastion on the corner of the eastern wall extending to the sea. A stunning number of exploding shells were bursting nearby, but they seemed chiefly focused on the ramparts over the two eastern and two southern gates. Solid shot was pounding the gates themselves.

"Their artillery practice is disconcertingly professional," General Mayta observed loudly, but his manner made it seem as if he'd mentioned it only in passing.

"Perhaps," General Allegria grudgingly agreed, pulling the red facings on his coat closer together. "But at least the long wait is over and they're coming at last." His tone mixed nervousness and eagerness in equal measure.

"Nonsense," General Mayta countered, waving a recently arrived messenger away to rest. "Just as their fleet attempted to bombard us from the sea"—he nodded toward the runner looking for a place to shelter from the hail of iron in the air—"and has been stalled by our gallant navy, the heretics will bombard us here and to the east for some considerable time. Perhaps days." A shell burst high above in a ragged puff of gray smoke, and several men fell screaming from the parapet nearby, savaged by chunks of case or iron balls. Mayta continued blithely.

"I've studied these people and their campaigns, you know. Almost invariably, they've established strong defenses on our holy soil and waited for us to attack. Here, the circumstances are reversed. And though they have generally better weapons, ours are improved. And wc have other advantages they can't yet imagine." He flicked his eyes toward the sky. "We won't have to endure their bothersome flying machines much longer, for example." He looked back at Allegria. "And as for their army, it simply hasn't the will to openly assault so strong a place as this in daylight."

"But they *have* attacked strongpoints to the south. Dulce, for one," Allegria argued, "then Nicoya quickly afterward."

Mayta dismissed that with a smirk. "I'd hardly call either place strong." His expression hardened with bitterness. "And treacherous Nicoya fell with hardly a whimper. Yet Dulce—which did resist—proves my point. The heretic infantry only struck after a lengthy bombardment, and even then they came with the dawn." He pointed out at the distant ranks of men and 'Cats impressively arrayed to the east and south. "That is but a show designed to intimidate us and bolster the courage of their own troops while we endure their battering."

Several more shells exploded behind them in the narrow streets, right amidst a company of regulars rushing to stiffen the southwest gate. Whitewashed stone walls reflected the lethal shell fragments down the alley, mulching men in smoky sprays of blood. Mayta continued without pause. "I do wonder where their Major Blas might be," he confessed. "I know she's but an animal, but she clearly has talent of a sort and is most tenacious. Perhaps the latter is inspired by her animalistic characteristics? A fascinating notion, worthy of study." Solid shot drummed against the wall around the closest gate, jolting the parapet beneath their feet. Mayta leaned casually out to gaze at the damage and saw great splinters whirling away.

"The gates will fail," Allegria noted, then squinted through the blowing smoke to the south and saw sudden movement. "Ah, General . . ." he said, voice rising.

"I'm sure they already have," Mayta agreed, oblivious,

"but don't concern yourself. Naturally, they'll focus their assault on the damaged gates, but we'll have already created impenetrable barriers behind them." His lips formed a smile of self-satisfaction. "All part of my plan. Besides, I doubt they'll ever get past our massed infantry on the parapets or the great guns mounted in the walls." He sighed. "These tiresome festivities will bore us for some time, I suspect. I may even retire to my forward quarters until nightfall." He grimaced. "The accommodations aren't what I'm used to but they're in a durable structure, secure from this irksome shelling."

"General Mayta," Allegria insisted, pointing south. "You might want to remain a little longer."

Horns sounded and the Pegadores lurched forward uncertainly, their four-hundred-yard front bowing slightly at once. They were joined on the right by Dao Iverson's far more disciplined 6th Imperial Marine Division, however, advancing under an Imperial flag edged in green. Most of the 6th hailed from New Ireland and Iverson had requested the "privilege" of participating in the first assault (and bolstering the Pegadores) on their behalf. Like the Vengadores, New Irelanders thought they had something to prove, and 6th Division hadn't had as many opportunities.

So it was that seven thousand men, nearly a quarter of Blair's corps, set out at the quick time across the scorched and barren killing ground the Doms had prepared, headed toward the easternmost gate still receiving the most attention from the artillery. A couple of guns on the high walls finally fired, their big roundshot blasting through the volunteers, spattering whole files of men before bounding on through the Vengadores. Screams clawed at Blas's heart. More enemy fire came, and though the relentless Allied bombardment was helping keep the enemy down, increasing numbers of mulched and steaming gaps ripped through the Pegadores and the 6th. By the time they'd made two hundred long paces, some locals were already trying to bolt to the rear. They were met by file closers supplied by Iverson. Just as fearsome and more certain than the enemy, they roughly shoved reluctant Pegadores back in the ranks.

Sister Audry gently stroked Blas's arm and nodded at her. "I told the others about General Shinya's . . . revisions." She paused. "It's time, I'm afraid." Blas nodded back, blinking affection. As Sister Audry and Arano Garcia both knew, it was also time for Blas to take charge again. "Cap-i-taan Ixtli, Cap-i-taan Bustos," she shouted at hers and Garcia's XOs, "the Sister's Own will prepare to advance." The two men repeated her command, and bugles and whistles replied. The same sounds rose from other regiments and divisions nearby, along with a few screeching bagpipes. Sergeant Major Koratin's and First Sergeant Spook's loud Lemurian voices thundered over all, shouting, "Lose your bedrolls! Toss everything but waater an' aammo! Two more aammo haulers to each mortar team! Laadder bearers, take your places!" Hopefully, they wouldn't need ladders, but they had to bring them. It would've been nice to have some of the new portable LMGs, like the First Fleet AEF, but the few .30 cals they'd received were either in planes or on frigates and transports, to defend against Grikbirds or suppress enemy fire from shore. There were a lot of Blitzerbug SMGs now, though, and they'd be handy in the tight confines of the city—if they made it past the wall.

Blas took a last look around as she unslung her Allin-Silva and checked the breech. "Fix bayonets!" she cried. She was answered by a defiant roar and the rippling, clattering *click-clack* of socket bayonets locking on rifle muzzles. She looked to the rear of the initial advance, now halfway to the wall. It was taking a terrible beating as it moved in range of Dom canister. Only the looser formations they'd adopted prevented twice the casualties.

"Sister's Own!" she roared. "At the double time . . . Maarch!" Her division and three more falling in behind immediately set out at a lope, covering ground fast, Arano Garcia's Captain Jasso—and his bugle—close by her side. The smoke and fiery fury consuming the Pegadores and the 6th must've hidden them for a time, because they got nearly halfway across themselves, to where the dead and wounded really started piling up, before facing much more than bounding roundshot aimed at their predecessors. That didn't last. Case shot—that they'd *known* the

Doms must have by now—started bursting overhead, flailing them with smoking shards of hot iron. Men and 'Cats screamed and fell, their places taken by those behind—who fell in turn beneath the rousing storm.

Blas lost track of Audry and Koratin—who'd be sticking to Audry like glue—and couldn't locate Colonel Garcia anymore either. She did see Lieutenant Anaar-Taar of her own C Company killed while directing a mortar team, "Set up here, right here! Range, three hundreds. Drop 'em right over the waall!" They had to get the mortars in tight to drop their bombs so close, but that left them terribly exposed—and those were the last words Anaar ever said. An instant later a shard of iron the size of a jagged saucer tore into his chest beneath his throat. He went down without a sound. Blas saw *so many* fall like that, and to the canister sweeping away dozens at a time. More canister or musket balls tugged and slapped at her leather armor and smock, or kicked up stalks of dust all around. Jasso stumbled, but Blas and Spook carried him along while he kept protesting "*Estoy bien.*"

At two hundred tails the second wave started firing its rifles independently at the top of the wall. Blas could barely see anything through the smoke, and the world seemed carpeted with bodies. She did observe what remained of the Pegadores and 6th Marines huddled at the base of the wall, under the guns, but now being savaged by massed musket fire from above. And the top of the wall *teemed* with Doms, apparently drawn from everywhere to join the massacre. This was mostly evident by the sheer volume of muzzle flashes darting through the smoke, but also consistent with what Shinya predicted—and told her to do about it.

A few Pegadores and New Irelanders were doggedly shooting back, the latter doing the most good with their breechloaders, and Blas wondered if they'd actually breached the shattered gate. A few ladders had gone up against the wall but there wasn't anyone on them so maybe they had. It didn't matter. They were a broken force and would now only get in the way if the second wave joined them—as Shinya also foresaw—and this was confirmed by the tearful relief on their faces, gazing longingly at their "reinforcements." That made what she was about to do feel like she herself was betraying them.

"Sound your bugle, Cap-i-taan Jasso," she gasped. She was tired from helping carry him and could hardly breathe through the dense white smoke.

Jasso tried, but gasped. "*Agua!*" he pleaded.

"No time! Do it!"

The bugle *brapp*ed dryly, then sharp, clear notes rose above the tumult—and the shot-torn Sister's Own, as well as the three divisions stacked up behind it, suddenly veered sharply left into an oblique charge aimed at the other, larger gate to the west.

General Mayta was badly rattled by how mistaken he'd been about the enemy's intentions. He'd been so *sure*, and this was so uncharacteristic! He actually ducked down when the first volleys slashed against the top of the parapet, flinging tightly packed Dom troops back from their firing positions where they'd been enjoying a free-for-all—till now.

With great effort, he willed himself to regain his composure. Regardless of the error, no regular officer could openly concede it to someone like General Allegria—or any Blood Drinker—if he wished to retain command. And situations like this required professionals to deal with them. "Just as I told you to expect, General Allegria," Mayta shouted over the firing, coughing dust and smoke and looking disappointedly at his damaged uniform; it cost more than most Dominion citizens made in a lifetime. "They've stopped to shoot. They *always* do that!"

"The first ones didn't."

Mayta waved it away. "Undisciplined rabble, seeking the safety of our walls under the guns. The infantry we summoned will destroy them—and the rest that so foolishly follow the first assault so closely."

"The heretics still have significant reserves. Won't they exploit the other gate? I fear we've drawn too many troops from there."

"They were the closest. All they had to do was run here along the parapet. They can return quickly enough

if something unforeseen develops. Certainly before another wave can sweep across such a distance," Mayta replied confidently, pointing at the Allied divisions still
arrayed to the right, their ranks rising on the lower flank
of the dead volcano by the sea. Then he stared, stunned,
as what seemed to be the entire follow-on force suddenly
surged, en masse, to his right.

"You were saying, General Mayta?" Allegria demanded bitterly.

Mayta shook himself. "Go!" he cried. "But forget the
wall. They'll likely get through before you can take sufficient forces to stop them. You must meet them in the city
itself!"

Allegria waited a heartbeat. "Have I your *permission*,"
he asked, the word dripping sarcasm as all subordination
fled, "to meet them with whatever I deem appropriate?"

"Yes! Yes, of course! Just go at once."

Allegria saluted, a strange, almost joyful expression
on his face, and trotted off, collecting messengers as he
went.

Captain Jasso was dead. He'd probably been mostly dead
when he sounded his last bugle call with a gaping hole in
his chest. *At least he made it inside,* Blas told herself,
watching a pair of Vengadores gently lay his corpse to the
side of the shattered gate, out of the way of the troops
surging in. She snorted. *Like thaat makes any difference.*
She quickly reconsidered. *Maybe it did, to him. It would
to me.*

Even with so many defenders drawn to counter the
first push against the east gate, the Sister's Own and the
divisions behind had been savaged by the heavy guns on
the walls. But these were all veterans who knew hesitation
was death and they stormed forward relentlessly through
the hail of iron and crashed through the shattered gate
left practically undefended. A lot of debris had already
been heaped behind the breach—heavy timbers, over-
turned carts and wagons, stony rubble, even horse
carcasses—but these didn't slow Blas's Marines, who
quickly spread out to cover the Vengadores and slaughtered the shell-shocked Dom brigade rushing to fill the

gap. They all pushed deeper while the 4th, 9th, and 21st Imperial Marine Divisions crowded through to join them. The 9th would deploy here, to keep the back door open and stop the Doms from cutting in behind them.

"Gotta keep 'em off our flaanks too," Blas murmured to herself and Captain Ixtli as they surveyed the respectably broad avenue ahead. Ixtli had spent his whole life in the forest and an occasional village. He was noticeably uncomfortable in these confines. Maps made from aerial photographs showed four main thoroughfares, two running north and south, two east and west. This one reached all the way past the main temple at the center of the city to the harbor, but was connected to every other by hundreds of side streets, all lined with two- and three-story stone buildings with flat roofs. Most had balconies and nearly every window was curtained by a red flag with a twisted gold cross that snipers could hide behind.

"What was that, Major Blas?" Sister Audry asked, Colonel Garcia and Sergeant Major Koratin at her side. Audry was still breathing hard from the final push, and from personally helping move debris from around the gate. Blas thought that was stupid until she saw the near-worshipful stares her Vengadores aimed at her. *Course, they already worship her. Why's she gotta keep that silly shit up in the middle of a fight?* she asked herself cynically. Then it dawned on her. It was because Audry *couldn't* fight. She had to be "one of her men" in other ways.

"It's obvious, Santa Madre," Garcia answered for Blas. Audry only winced slightly at the term she'd forbidden. Now wasn't the time to bring it up again. "This main road is intersected by countless narrower ones, each capable of sheltering packed ranks of men with the buildings themselves securing their flanks. We must spread out quickly, to get more depth to maneuver in."

The brief lull in nearby firing was broken by shots down the street, and Blas was sure she saw movement on the rooftops inside the perimeter they'd already established.

"We're gonna haave to move faast," she confirmed, "spread out as quick an' faar as we caan. But we also gotta clear these daamn buildings behind us." A pair of paalkas strained past them, mooing discontentedly as they pulled a 12 pdr gun and limber. Another gun followed with men straining at a harness they'd probably cut off their dead animals. "Get those guns forwaard," Blas called. She turned to Ixtli. "Signaal Gener-aal Shinyaa for more. We'll advaance behind them at every street."

More musket balls spalled the walls beside them, spattering them with stinging rock and lead fragments. "Goddaamn Doms're gettin' sorted out faaster thaan I hoped," she observed, idly touching a broken musket at her feet with the toes protruding from her sandals. "Look at thaat too," she said. "Idiots finaally caught on an' made socket baay-o-nets instead of plug types. Spread the word: they caan shoot you and stick you at the same time now."

A Blitzerbug rattled in a nearby alley and rifle fire backed it up. Another Blitzer lit up a room behind one of the hanging flags. "Tell our guys to rip those flaags down outa every joint we clear."

"Won't the enemy caatch on to thaat an' tear flaags down themselves?" Koratin asked. A musket ball blew up a dust cloud at his feet, but the gunsmoke betrayed the shooter and a dozen bullets flailed the edge of a nearby rooftop.

"Maybe. But whaat else caan we do?" Her eye caught a battery of much smaller guns rattling past, hooked to smaller limbers, all pulled by crews of six to eight 'Cats. "Cap-i-taan Aakon," Blas called to the Lemurian officer in charge as she quickly strode over. He didn't salute, of course. Not here.

"Hold up!" Aakon shouted at his battery then turned to Blas. "Ay, sur?"

Blas waved around. "Those little mountain howitzers," she began, but when Aakon started to bristle, she grinned. Cannoneers on the little guns were ribbed unmercifully by "real" artillerymen and gun-'Cats. Blas raised a calming hand. "Maay just save our aasses," she continued, watching Aakon's rising resentment subside. She waved around again, particularly at the rooftops. "You caan get them up *there*, caan't you?"

A returning grin split Aakon's white-and-tan-striped face. "Ay, sur. Two guys pull the tube, three get the aaxle an' trail, one each carries a wheel."

"Aammo?"

"I'll need more guys—for thaat, an' to cover us." Aakon had already figured out exactly what Blas wanted and knew his gunners' carbines would be useless if they got jumped with their hands full.

"You got 'em. Graab whoever you need." Blas turned back to the others just as a line of infantry in white and yellow—regulars—rushed out of an alley to try to form a line across the main avenue a couple of hundred yards ahead. They were right on top of the farthest advance of the 2nd Marines and Allin-Silvas started tearing into them before they could even dress their ranks. It was a slaughter. Still, it was only a taste of the bloodbath to come, and it wouldn't be long before every step was contested.

"Every little gun we get goes up on the roofs." She looked at Ixtli. "Ask Shinyaa for all of them." She faced Audry and Garcia. "We'll leapfrog them along as we secure the buildings. Get mortar teams above as well, where they caan see stuff. We'll still haave to slog through the streets, but maybe thaat'll keep the snipers down. An' the guns an' mortars can help clear streets ahead of us too." She glanced at the sky. "'Specially since there ain't near as much air support as I hoped. Wonder whaat's up with thaat?"

CHAPTER
20

////// Above El Corazon

rrin Reddy felt sick to his stomach. Not because of the wild acrobatics the Grikbirds forced him and his five Nancys from *Maaka-Kakja*'s 12th Bomb Squadron to perform, but because of what looked for all the world to be a disaster in the making. This was his second sortie of the day—his first leading elements of the 12th—and his and Seepy's Nancy carried four incendiaries, basically egg-shaped drums with stabilizing fins, filled with a mixture of gasoline and gimpra sap. But what had started to appear a little troubling on his first run looked positively awful now. Despite a heavier artillery barrage than anything Orrin had witnessed on this world, the ground assault against the south wall of the city was being churned to pulp. Worse, it looked like Shinya was just throwing *more* troops at the same meat grinder. He didn't get that. Shinya could be an asshole, but he wasn't an idiot.

On the water, Hibbs's battle line had disintegrated and not a single one of his ships of the line remained underway. A couple were burning. The only consolation was they were burning *alongside* Dom liners and appeared to be grappled tight. *Those Doms might be ironclads,* Orrin thought, *but there's wood underneath. They'll still burn.* All of Hibbs's liners seemed to have latched on to an enemy ship, in fact, pretty much taking them out of the fight one way or another. Only one Dom liner was still maneuvering and it seemed more concerned with dodging Nancys than anything else.

But the Nancys were busy dodging Grikbirds. Fleashooters were killing the hell out of them, running interference, but there were just so many. And they'd lost a lot of Fleashooters too.

"Two on your tail, Daakr," Orrin shouted in his mic at *Raan-Goon*'s COFO, who'd just nailed a Grikbird with his Fleashooter and was starting to pull up. His wingman was nowhere in sight. "They're dropping on you out of the sun! Break left!" It was too late. The flying reptiles had the angle and nobody'd seen them in time. Daakr made a heroic effort to twist away, but a stooping Grikbird snagged his starboard aileron and tore the whole thing off. The plane went into a corkscrew spin and Orrin watched it all the way down until a greasy ball of flame rolled up near a stepped pyramid at the center of El Corazon.

"You lousy sons of bitches!" Orrin seethed at a flock of half a dozen Grikbirds that suddenly appeared in front of his flight, swanning along like their only concern was avoiding the rising smoke. "Let's get 'em, Twelfth!" he shouted on his flight's frequency. Pointing his plane at the Grikbirds, he unleashed his pair of .30 cals, chasing tracers with his stick. Four of the things, flying in a line, were torn apart in a chaotic explosion of feathers and flailing wings before the others got the hint and peeled away. One took late hits from another plane and tumbled out of the sky.

"Okaay, you haad your fun. Now whaat we gonna bomb?" Seepy demanded testily. Orrin looked around. There were more Grikbirds and he was tempted to go after them, but Nancys weren't pursuit ships and plenty of people on the ground needed their bombs right now. The trouble was, he wasn't sure who needed them most. And as he got a better grasp of the overall situation, he realized it wasn't all bad.

Not only did Hibbs have the Dom liners in a death grip, the frigates out in the middle of the pass were holding their own. Even Jenks's old *Achilles*, now commanded by Captain Grimsley and probably the oldest frigate in the fleet, was tearing the hell out of an opponent. Apparently, the Doms hadn't armored their lighter ships. Looking east, Orrin saw XI Corps hitting El Corazon hard from that direction, its artillery fire and a blizzard of mortars setting much of that side of the city alight even as the assault was grinding against the wall. And some XI Corps troops were lapping around the southeast bastion to join Shinya's stalled spearhead.

On the northwest corner of the city, where it touched a dormant volcano and the sea, he saw that the heavy guns in the fort had sunk one transport a couple of hundred yards offshore, its masts sticking up, but the rest of the ships had made it in—sort of. All appeared damaged to varying degrees and Grikbirds still plagued them, but they were now hard aground in the gravelly shallows. That made them easy targets for serious punishment, but most of the Marines of XV Corps were streaming ashore, either wading (which gave Orrin the creeps) or motoring in aboard shoals of stackable dories. They were taking withering fire, but hundreds were already at the seaward wall, fighting through some rubbly breaches Hibbs's liners must've blasted with their heavy guns. Best of all, as far as he could see, all those things had drawn a lot of Doms from *another* attack already through a different section of the south wall. "Didn't *think* Shinya was stupid," he told himself out loud.

"Whaat?" Seepy shouted.

"I said 'Don't be stupid,'" he yelled back. "I haven't had any *fun* since the early hours of December seventh—eighth, where I was—1941!" He flipped the Mic switch. "Twelfth, we're gonna lay all our bombs on those Doms converging opposite the breach in the wall where the Marines from the transports are trying to get in. Follow me!" Orrin banked hard left and kicked the rudder over, starting a sharp, turning dive.

The ground came up fast, the brilliant white coastal city now charred and battered, writhing under exploding shells that left some sections smoldering and others burning out of control. Smoke was everywhere, piling high in the air and leaning toward the east, but that left his target—and the tiny yellow-coated specks converging on it—easy to spot. He felt a twinge, knowing there were civilians down there too: women, old folks, even little kids. . . . He shook his head violently. By all accounts, not just what Blas and Blair reported, there were no noncombatants. He didn't believe that, but what could they do? Gritting his teeth, he stared through the same crosshair sight that aimed his guns, centering it a little beyond where he wanted his bombs to go. Caressing the release at his side, he waited until he could almost see the horror on the upturned faces, then he pulled the lever. The plane bounced in the air as bombs fell away, and he immediately pulled back on the stick. Blasting through the tower of smoke in front of him, he started a climbing turn that would take him east to west over the water, paralleling the city docks facing the pass. Rising up through two thousand feet he saw mighty orange and black toadstools climbing over his target, reinforced every few seconds by more sprouting beside them.

"Maker!" Seepy snapped, and Orrin thought he was reacting to what they'd done. But the 'Cat quickly shouted, "Look up, two o'clock high, 'bout five thousaands!" Orrin did—and couldn't believe what he saw. There, at last, were the "greater dragons" they'd been worried about, and "dragons" was the only word for them. There were probably twenty-five or thirty, easily as big as his Nancy, their great wings flapping almost leisurely but propelling them swiftly west. Another twenty or thirty Grikbirds swarmed around them. Orrin doubted the little escorts could make it all the way to the carriers and back, but suspected the big dragons could—and that was clearly where they were headed. Bitterly, he realized that if they were going out now, range had never been a problem for them, day or night, and a lot of guys on the ground were probably dying for nothing. No, they probably could've attacked at any time and only waited till the height of the Allied assault— thinking all their planes would be here and their carriers helpless.

Well, if that's the case, they're gonna be in for a helluva surprise, Orrin consoled himself, twisting the knob by his Talk switch and opening the frequency direct to *Maaka-Kakja. As long as our guys aren't too surprised by* them, he added to himself. "*Makky-Kat, Makky-Kat*, this is COFO Reddy, over." He took a breath as he plowed through smoke rising from the sea battle below and started to cough.

"COFO Reddy, this is *Maaka-Kakja*, over," came the quick reply, but just as they cleared the smoke and Orrin took a deep, clean breath, he heard Seepy screech, "Grikbirds! Grikbirds! Right daamn *there*!" The Lemurian's Blitzerbug stuttered for an instant, and something slammed hard into the plane.

There was a terrible, tearing, crunching sound, then a jolting *whack! whack!* that made the engine skip a beat and somehow sprayed blood all over Orrin. It completely coated his goggles and made his suddenly frantic battle to keep the plane out of a flat spin seem even more impossible. Heart pounding, he tore his goggles off and threw them away, centered the stick, and jammed the throttle to the stop. The engine roared with a terrible new vibration— and it didn't make any difference. No matter what he did with the stick or rudder, the wounded Nancy slid into spin like a flung saucer, out of control, skidding toward the city. He thought he saw the Grikbird that hit them, plummeting to Earth, but also saw more coming. "We may have to jump for it, Seepy!" he shouted. If the 'Cat responded, he didn't hear, and he wasn't sure they *should* bail out over a Dom city in the middle of a battle. The voracious flashies in the sea might've given them a kinder end, but that wasn't an option now. *Probably better just to ride the wreck down . . .*

Increasingly desperate and still moving the stick in all directions as the altimeter spun down under a thousand feet, he fought against the forces pinning him to the left side of the cockpit and tried idling the engine. The vibration lessened, but nothing else.

Orrin was just a pilot, not an aeronautical engineer like Ben Mallory, but he thought the physics that essentially nullified control surfaces in a flat spin had still been mostly theoretical, even after the problem got more attention due to rumored issues with Bell's Airacobras. But Orrin never flew one of those, and honestly hadn't much kept up with how the theories were working out. His instructors had basically always just taught him to "try everything" if ever faced with the dreaded situation. He thought he had.

"Shit! I can't stop it," he confessed. "Jump or not, Seepy, it's your . . ." Another Grikbird hit them, tearing the port wingfloat off and flipping them into a crazy, nose-down barrel roll. Suddenly, though, with rising exhilaration, Orrin felt the stick stiffen and he arrested their roll. They were falling fairly straight. Whooping, he opened the throttle and pulled back on the stick. The engine bellowed and the vibration returned, but they were flying again—just as Doms on the ground started shooting muskets at them. "Hang on, Seepy! I'm heading back over the water. That last Grikbird must've stabilized us, tryin' to kill us." He paused. The vibration was getting worse. "What happened? We lose part of the prop?" Still no answer. Worried, he wrenched himself around to look aft.

Seepy was gone. Orrin's first suspicion was that his observer-copilot jumped after all, until he saw the bloody, shredded, fluttering fabric all around the aft cockpit.

"Oh, Jeez, Seepy," he murmured sadly, "I'm so sorry."

Turning back out to sea, he nursed his Nancy higher—head constantly in motion, watching for more attackers—while trying to get *Maaka-Kakja* back on the horn. It was no use; the antenna aerial stretching from both wingtips to the vertical stabilizer was gone and his radio was out. Just as bad, by the time three other Nancys from the 12th Bomb Squadron found him and clustered protectively around, the frightening flight of dragons had disappeared in the west. He couldn't even point them out to his comrades. Hopefully, *somebody* else saw the damn things. Suddenly inspired, he caught the eye of the closest pilot, a human Impie staring with amazement at his battered plane, and gestured in the direction of the carriers. He also pointed to his eyes, made the hand signal for Grikbirds (they didn't have a signal for "giant dragons"), and made a slashing gesture toward the carriers again. Finally, he shook his mic. The other pilot made an exaggerated nod.

Realizing he'd done all he could and really starting to feel Seepy's loss, Orrin concentrated on keeping his savaged, rattling Nancy in the air. About halfway back to *Maaka-Kakja*, about when he should glimpse the ships on the horizon, he noticed two dark gray columns of smoke rising in the sky. *No way the dragons I saw could've gotten there already,* he protested to himself, and that's when he knew, with a twisting gut, he must've only seen part of the attack force. More dragons had gotten past them, or taken off from somewhere else.

He glanced down at the water, surprised to see a *much* larger concentration of mountain fish basking below than they'd ever noted this far out. The gathering looked like a tight pod of whales, only *these* whales were the size of cruisers, even battleships, and they stretched for miles to the north and south. *Things probably got too noisy for 'em up close to the pass,* he supposed, then looked bleakly back at the distant smoke. *Wonder if there'll be any carriers left to set this heap down beside? Boy, what a mess this has turned out to be!*

CHAPTER 21

////// *El Corazon*

*G*oddaamn *draagons*, big ones, hit the fleet
and tore up our caarriers," Blas grouched at
Sister Audry and Arano Garcia after jump-
ing down behind some blasted rubble to join them. Musket
balls kicked up dust and ricocheted, warbling away down
the street or *whock*ing against something solid. A little
howitzer thumped a case shot through a top-story balcony
doorway to the front, and the whole floor blew out and
collapsed, making and stifling a chorus of screams. "Just
got the word from the Ninth Impies baack at the gate," Blas
continued. "They got the raadio up." She blinked quizzi-
cally at Garcia. "You ever hear of draagons—Grikbirds—
big as a plane?"

Garcia looked uncomfortable. "Rumors only. Legends.
Tales to frighten children. I never believed them."

"Well, they're real," Blas stated flatly, taking a gulp
from her water bottle, "an' they're baad news. Thaank the
Maker they ain't got enough to pester *us* with." She looked
at the billowing smoke overhead. "Or maybe they don't
like smoke any more thaan regular Grikbirds." She blinked
disgust. "Anywaay, thaat explains what happened to our
air support. Whaat's left'll be runnin' baack an' forth all
the way to Nicoya, an' poundin' Doms in front o' Fifteenth
Corps thaat way." She nodded north. "They're in, by the
way, an' headin' for us. We're s'posed to link up at the

temple. We'll haave haaf the city then, if we make it." Her tail whipped behind her. "'Leventh Corps still ain't in to the east, though they got a foot in the gate the Pegaa-dores died for. Don't know whaat good thaat does."

"It keeps more enemies away from us, Major Blas," Sister Audry chided gently. "Many men are dying elsewhere so we can continue our advance."

Blas took another gulp of water, knowing Audry was right. They were waiting, hunkered down, while elements of 12th Division moved up on several narrower parallel streets, clearing buildings as they went. The fighting was intense and there was a constant rattle of rifle and musket fire, punctuated by grenades and frequent blasts of canister scything down alleys. Mortars and mountain howitzers on the rooftops were doing terrible destruction as well, sometimes close, sometimes pretty far when they caught sight of tempting targets. The rubble they used for cover now had once been a three-story shop of some sort until a case shot went in a window and blew the whole thing down in a gust of shattered rock, roiling dust, and gobbets of flesh. Apparently, the Doms had been using it as an armory or reserve magazine.

In any event, when 12th Division caught up, they'd all push toward the temple together. And the top third of the temple itself was finally visible, barely a mile away, its oddly dark, stepped slopes rising the equivalent of only six or seven stories. Blas reflected again that it seemed fairly small for such a large city, particularly compared to others they'd heard of. She wondered why.

"More Doms!" somebody cried, and Blas peered over the rubble to see a solid block of yellow-coated troops surging into the avenue ahead. Many went sprawling under rifle fire even as they ran, and Blas shouted out to the section chief of the two full-size 12 pdrs positioned in the street to stand by. He nodded briskly and brought his guns to the ready, crews stretching lanyards.

Blas's eyes narrowed when she noted that the facings on the enemy uniforms were red. "Blood Drinkers," she snarled, and Sister Audry and Sergeant Major Koratin rose to look for themselves. Even Audry now understood there was no redemption for Blood Drinkers, but absolutely no

one could've expected what happened next. A sudden
stream of smaller figures started running out in the street
in front of the Doms, doubling their ranks about forty
yards across every few moments. A couple fell to reactive
shots, one kicking violently as it flailed on the ground, most
of its head blown away, but other forms raced past, unheed-
ing, to join the thickening line.

"My God!" Sister Audry wailed, and the nearby shooting swiftly dwindled to a feeble patter. Furious firing
continued on the parallel streets, howitzers still barked
on rooftops, and mortars fell beyond their view, but their
crews couldn't see what they now saw. Standing in front
of the Blood Drinkers still deploying behind them, grimly
holding pikes aloft that were far too big for most to handle, were more than a hundred small children, and more
rushing to join them. Blas stood. Sister Audry rose beside
her, but it looked like Arano Garcia had to keep her
steady. As if in a trance, Sergeant Major Koratin strode
slowly out to the middle of the street beside the guns.

The children stirred in the center of their line and a
young man in the attire of a Blood Drinker general stepped
out between them. Blas hissed.

"You know him?" Captain Ixtli asked, rushing up to
her.

"Yes," Blas ground out. "Thaat's Gener-aal Allegriaa,
Maytaa's XO—and a son of Don Hernaan's!"

"Of course he is," Garcia seethed. "Only he and his
wicked offspring are capable of such depravity!"

"I doubt it," Blas replied dully.

"Ah!" Allegria shouted cheerfully, seeing her. "It is
you, Major Blas! I'd *so* hoped to meet you today. Yours
has been a laudable effort indeed. General Mayta told me
so himself. He admires you tremendously, you know."
The voice turned harsh. "For an animal." He gestured
around, and his expression became cheerful again. "What
do you think of my militia? They're not really ready for
the firing line, I fear. Too small for modern weapons. But
they're quite committed, I assure you, and each has given
his or her life to His Supreme Holiness! Just look at them,
staring you down, pikes at the ready! Even the little girls
are a credit to the Holy Dominion!" He feigned thought-

fulness. "But perhaps it is they who have halted your advance! Are you all cowards, afraid of children, or merely sentimental? If the latter, I suppose it was somewhat impolite of me to insert such an awkward moment into our otherwise deliciously straightforward battle."

His eyes radiated astonishment. "I've heard animals have been known to demonstrate sentiment toward their young. Even the young of other species. Quite surprising, actually. Tell me, Major Blas, does my militia give you pause? Do they fill you with fear, or pity? Should I send them away, for the sake of fair play"—his voice lowered—"or order them to attack?" He chuckled, knowing he was succeeding in buying the time he desperately needed, while simultaneously tearing the inertia out of the attack and the hearts out of everyone watching. He obviously didn't feel the horror he inspired but knew it was real, and probably more effective than he'd ever dreamed.

Blas didn't respond to Allegria's taunts and every fiber in her being was screaming at her to order the cannons to fire, to end this farce and sweep the unimaginable, unreal ghastliness of such evil, vile *things* hiding behind younglings from her sight. But those *were* younglings over there, and the guns would kill them too. There'd been a time when she'd have done it without thinking, before her wounded inner self had a chance to mend a little. Still . . . Sister Audry couldn't possibly give the order, and Garcia probably wouldn't. Ixtli might, but it wasn't his job. Blas wasn't sure even Silva would do it if he were here. It all fell down to her, again, and her soul cried out in torment because at that moment, with more and more Blood Drinkers clogging their path to victory and the battle— perhaps the entire war in the East—in the balance, somebody had to do it *now* and she just . . . couldn't.

"General Mayta believes you deserve study, Major Blas, and I agree," Allegria shouted. "I think we simply *must* find out how capable of sentiment you are. *Mis hijos*," he called around him in a kindly, gentle voice, "attack the heretics. Kill them all." He said the last in English so all the Allies would hear, but the children understood. With what looked like perfect determination, the children— almost two hundred now—lowered their pikes with a shrill shout. Most had to hold the weapons toward the middle to balance their weight. With a louder but still obscenely soothing voice, Allegria called out again and the children marched forward.

Sister Audry was standing on top of the rubble now, holding her hands out. "No! No! For God's sake, children, please! Save yourselves, move aside. We mean you no harm!"

Her plea had no effect and the nightmare marched closer with every step. General Allegria began to laugh.

Blas stared longingly at the twin 12 pdrs in the street, aimed and stoked with canister, practically begging to be unleashed. But their crews were just as horrified as anyone, helplessly watching their own destruction play out before them in their minds. Blas saw Sergeant Major Koratin then—Lord Koratin he'd once been—who'd turned to simple soldiering and away from corrupt intrigues because of his deep and genuine love for younglings. He usually hid it well, beneath his gruff facade, but his blinking now betrayed an anguish even deeper than Blas could fathom. She saw him look at Sister Audry, now screaming hysterically for the children to stop, disperse—even as those same children started chanting "*Matarlos*! *Matarlos*!" with every step. Koratin's blinking came so fast, Blas caught only impressions of tenderness, appreciation, even sympathy. Then Koratin looked at her and very distinctly blinked protective love—from a doomed spirit that would never touch the heavens.

Abruptly, before Blas could move or even shout, Koratin turned and snatched the lanyard from a stunned cannoneer and pulled it hard. The gun roared and leaped back, the muzzle dropping away from the jet of fire, yellowish smoke, and the sheeting canister that screeched downrange to be enveloped in high-pitched squeals of pain.

Without a word or the slightest hesitation, Koratin stepped through the smoke around the blackened muzzle of the first gun, snatched the lanyard of the second, and pulled it too. Another deafening blast thundered down the lane amid more choking smoke and piercing screams. Koratin pulled his pistol. Blas first thought he'd shoot himself, but he ran forward all alone, roaring forth the torment of a shattered soul. He disappeared in the smoke. A moment later there was a quick *pop! pop-pop!* of a 1911 copy, then a ragged musket volley. A number of balls whined by. There was also the wrenching sound of crying, hurt, and terrified younglings, diminishing now as many—*most*, Blas prayed—fled back down the narrow street they came from.

Blas shook herself, clearing eyes that had gone opaque with tears, then bellowed as loud as she could, "Up! Aat 'em! Spare the younglings if you caan dodge 'em, knock 'em aside if you must, but *kill those goddaamn Doms!*"

Hundreds of men and 'Cats, utterly immobilized moments before, leaped out from behind what cover they'd taken and charged after Koratin. The smoke was still dense and it got even thicker as rifles and muskets fired. Then came a roaring crash of steel on steel and men—*Adults, at least,* Blas bitterly corrected herself—began to scream. She knew her people were dying too, but their maddened fury would carry them through anything right now. Startled, battered Doms, who'd just taken the bitter remainder of a double dose of canister, certainly couldn't stop them. Blas moved back to Sister Audry, who was sobbing and supported now by Ixtli and Garcia. She noted Garcia's wretched expression and knew he was torn as much by what happened as by Sister Audry's reaction. "Go," Blas snapped. "Lcad your men. You too, Cap-i-tan Ixtli. I'll be along directly. First Sergeant Spook, waater for the Col-nol."

Garcia and Ixtli hesitated, then trotted away to join the growing fight. Blas helped Audry steady Spook's canteen as she took a sip. Finally, Audry managed to speak. "He's dead, isn't he? S-Sergeant Koratin."

"I expect so," Blas replied. "An' just as well for him. He never could'a lived with whaat he did. I couldn't, you couldn't, but it haad to be done. He took it off us. Did it for us."

"*Died* for us," Audry whispered low.

"Yeah."

"Why don't I take the Col-nol back to the gate," Spook

suggested awkwardly. "Lotsa wounded baack there'll be glaad to see her."

"No!" Audry snapped, suddenly forceful. "Sergeant Major Koratin took all our sins upon himself—a *far* better Christian than I, at that moment! I *will* see his work completed!" She looked at Blas. "We go *forward*, Major Blas. Together."

CHAPTER 22

////// *USS* **Maaka-Kakja**
Off El Paso del Fuego

What're we doing?" Orrin Reddy hotly asked Admiral Lelaa-Tal-Cleraan, stepping briskly onto *Maaka-Kakja*'s broad starboard bridgewing over the flight deck. He looked terrible, still spattered with Seepy's or the Grikbird's blood, and his eyes were red from the wind and hollow with exhaustion. He was too keyed up to notice how confrontational his exhaustion and frustration had made him. A harried Tex Sheider glanced up from where he was conferring with damage-control personnel. Even the thin, squirrely Chief Gilbert Yeager was there, though there was nothing wrong with his engines. Like his half brother Isak, still on *Walker*, the weird little guy was a whiz at coming up with unlikely fixes for things, and a lot of stuff was coming apart right now. High Admiral Jenks stood apart from them all, watching *Raan-Goon* burn. Her whole forward flight deck was afire and she'd turned downwind. Several escorts were alongside, their hoses helping fight her flames.

"We haave to withdraaw *Maaka-Kakja* and *New Dublin*," Lelaa replied bitterly. "No choice. Our flight decks are too daamaged to launch and recover fighters, so we've lost our combaat air paatrol." She nodded at *Raan-Goon*. "Our CAP—and luck—are the only things thaat kept us all from winding up like her. But the fighters were low on fuel and I haad to send them to Nicoyaa. If the Doms have *more* of those greater draagons, we've haad it."

The big dragons, some of which actually did carry pilots—or handlers; who knew what?—*had* been seen by another flight of returning Nancys that got off a message just before the escorting Grikbirds mauled them. Most of the surviving Grikbirds then dashed back to shore. Regardless, there hadn't been much warning—the one Orrin's flight tried to relay hadn't made much sense and came too late—and the dragon's appearance was a big surprise. Even then, the fighter CAP butchered them, chopping up the big flying lizards almost as easily as it would be to strafe running paalkas. Orrin had been right; though the greater dragons were faster than Grikbirds, they couldn't turn as tightly. Particularly carrying a man, or a pair of hundred-pound bombs. And large as they were, either they couldn't soak up as much damage as one would think or they were smart enough to choose not to. A fair number dove down to the wave tops and turned back for land when they saw what was happening to the others.

There'd been a lot of them, though, too many for such short notice. Enough got through to damage the flight deck of every carrier, to varying degrees. Their bombs were pretty big compared to what Grikbirds could carry, but not very powerful; basically just contact-fused iron casings full of gunpowder. Alone, they might destroy a smaller ship or badly splinter the tough wooden flight deck of a carrier, but they couldn't penetrate the heavy timbers to the hangar deck below. They *could* destroy and ignite assembled planes waiting to take off, however, and burning fuel and exploding ordnance could do a lot of damage indeed.

Raan-Goon was the worst hit, with nearly her entire wing preparing to sortie. Almost all her fighters and many of her Nancys—and their pilots—were gone, along with the forward half of her flight deck. *New Dublin* was hit hard as well, but didn't have as many planes aboard and her fires were nearly out. *Maaka-Kakja* was luckiest. She'd been waiting to recover planes and only had a couple P-1s on catapults when the dragons struck. Despite a ferocious antiair defense with her dual purpose 4.7"s salvaged from *Amagi*, the ship still took five bombs. She couldn't recover fighters until they chopped out the splintered timbers, added reinforcing, and pounded temporary plates over the wounds. Work was proceeding feverishly, but Tex and Gilbert thought it would take at least two hours before *Maaka-Kakja* could resume operations.

"What about *Raan-Goon*? What about our people ashore? We have to support them!" Orrin insisted. "I know you can't see it from here, but Tenth, Eleventh, and Fifteenth Corps, not to mention the rest of this fleet, are in a helluva fight over there," he added sarcastically, pointing east.

Lelaa blinked acceptance. She knew what Orrin had been through: his battered plane sank right under him as he was hauled aboard. "*Raan-Goon* will haave to take her chaances. She's disabled and probably sustained more daamage thaan the Doms ever dreamed to inflict. I suspect they'll be content with thaat. They caan't do her much more haarm, in any event." Her voice hardened and she blinked determination. "As for the baattle onshore, I'm quite aware how desperate it is and how baadly our troops need support from the air. No doubt you saw how busily this ship is refueling and re-aarming Naancys from all three caarriers." Orrin had, and most of it was being done at great risk to the ground crews as well, without even hoisting the planes aboard. "We'll continue to tend as maany as we caan, even aafter we move faarther from shore. Most, however, including all airborne pursuit planes, will haave to divert to Nicoyaa as well."

"That's too far," Orrin objected.

"I agree," Lelaa said. "Not only will faa-cilities at Nicoyaa be overtaaxed, but it'll take longer to turn the planes around, reduce the number of sorties, and further limit how long they caan linger over the taarget. Paarticularly the fighters." She glanced at Jenks, who'd finally turned to look at them, face ashen. *He thinks he screwed up,* Orrin realized. *And maybe he did—it's too early to say—but the decision was his. It's his responsibility and things ain't looking so hot.* Lelaa cast her eyes down at the flight deck. "But until we caan operate fighters again, it's the best we caan do."

"Surs," said *Maaka-Kakja*'s second lieutenant, striding out to join them. Like all the ship's officers, the Lemurian wore whites and they contrasted sharply with her brown-and-black-striped fur. "A mess-aage from General Shin-yaa, from his position on the southwest heights overlooking the city."

Jenks roused himself and took the message form. After looking at it a moment, his features brightened. "General Shinya says elements of Tenth Corps, led by the Sister's Own"—they all knew that meant Blas—"have forced their way into the city. Fifteenth Corps' Marines have broken in as well. Both face fierce resistance but are trying to link up." He managed a tentative smile that barely twitched his mustaches. "That's good news, at least." Glancing back down at the message, his brows furrowed and the smile became a frown. "On the other hand, the Clipper we sent to observe the pass reports that the tide has turned. We expected that, of course," he added absently, then looked intently at everyone. "But all the ships from La Calma, plus others that must've joined them, are riding the tide and will arrive shortly." He shook his head, at a loss. "I knew they'd get word of our attack fairly quickly, but never dreamed they'd respond so fast." He stiffened. "Unless they were ready and specifically waiting for us."

Orrin blinked surprise in the Lemurian fashion. "Well, of course they were! I *told* you that's what it looked like to me. But let me get this straight; you sent a *Clipper* up there? In *daylight*? With all these damn dragons and Grikbirds flocking around?"

"They weren't at first, if you'll recall," Jenks snapped, but he sounded a little defensive. "And the Clipper is well escorted by a full squadron of pursuit planes from Nicoya."

"A squadron we won't have to cover my Nancys," Orrin retorted hotly. "God knows we don't have anything else left to hit this new fleet with when it gets here! Hibbs may've stopped the Dom liners around El Corazon, but he's finished. I *saw* it. And you can bet the Doms'll have more liners coming, screening those Grikbird carriers— which I can't even guarantee we can take out from the air.

Like I told you, they got armor on top too." He looked at Lelaa. "Them an' their swarms of Grikbirds'll be coming for *you*. They ain't near as big, but I bet they're just as fast as this fat tub."

"We still have USS *Destroyer* and USS *Sword* on the north side of the pass," Tex defended. "They haven't even been engaged, besides scattering a little Dom garrison before putting their Marines ashore."

Orrin was thinking feverishly, grasping for an unformed notion hovering around the periphery of his mind. "That won't do any good," he murmured. "They've got lots of guns, like Hibbs, but little or no armor either. They'll get creamed. No," he added, voice warming, rising, "what we really need is to get all our ships the hell *out* of there. Evacuate the west approach to the pass completely, as fast as we can!"

Jenks just stared, incredulous, but Orrin was turning almost giddy from the crazy scheme bubbling up inside him. "I've got an idea," he said. "A way to maybe stop all the Dom ships before they add their weight to El Corazon or get out to sea. It's gonna take all our Nancys and probably DDs too, and our guys fighting in the city'll be on their own for a while. Probably little or no air cover at all."

"What do you have in mind?" High Admiral Jenks demanded, glancing from Orrin to Lelaa as if wondering if this was something they'd discussed before. Lelaa only blinked surprise, but her swishing tail betrayed her interest.

"Just something Seepy and I talked about a long time ago, and might've been simmering in my skull ever since." He shrugged. "Who knows? Maybe it'll even work."

////// *El Corazon*

The push to the temple dissolved into a chaotic, house-to-house brawl. In a way, it was some of the most nerve-racking fighting Blas ever participated in. She and Sister Audry never caught up with Garcia, Ixtli, or the bulk of the division, and were mainly forced to battle over the very same ground against Doms it bypassed or missed and who continually swept in through side streets. C Company of the 2nd of the 2nd Marines, about half Lemurian and half human Ocelomeh, a few of Audry's Vengadore guards, and an increasing number of 9th Division Impie Marines became Blas's entire direct command. The 4th and 21st Divisions were still slogging forward to the right, but that was probably pushing even more Doms in front of them. Only their breechloading Allin-Silvas and Blitzerbugs—and a profligate expenditure of ammunition—gave them a chance. For the first time in this war, Doms could still shoot with bayonets fixed and the Allies had lost an edge they'd taken for granted.

They shot and stabbed their way into buildings, following grenades until they ran out. A lot of Marines died doing that, since these Doms were mostly Blood Drinkers and were always ready for them, waiting at the door. All but four of Sister Audry's little group of Vengadores were killed. The survivors quickly divided the ammunition of the slain and continued on. The street fighting was more one-sided. Allied weapons weren't just breechloaders; they were rifles, far more accurate than smoothbore muskets. Every time Blas's men and 'Cats saw Doms trying to get in positions to oppose them in the open, they shot them down with almost contemptuous ease. It got really nasty only when they had to bust down doors and go face-to-face with Blood Drinkers.

Blas rushed through another shot-up doorway, whipping her rifle up horizontally in front of her and slamming into a pair of Doms loading muskets they'd just used to kill an Ocelomeh Marine. Blas wouldn't give them time. Both men tumbled back and Blas bayonetted one to the floor. Twisting her weapon, oblivious to the screams, she pulled it out and shot the other man in the jaw. His head whipped back and he fell flat, the gory wreckage of his head bouncing with a sickening crunch. First Sergeant Spook ran in behind her and hosed a couple more Doms with his Blitzer. They fell kicking on the floor. A six-man squad raced past and up a stairway where there was more shooting. Blas opened the breech of her Allin-Silva, ejecting a smoky cartridge, and inserted another. Sister Audry and her guards dashed in next, the guards almost shoving Audry in a corner and forming a semicircle around her.

"Clear!" came the shout down the stairs, and Spook called outside. Moments later, amid a flurry of musket shots from across the street—answered by the booming crack of Allin-Silvas—Captain Aakon's 'Cat gunners ran inside and up the stairs, carrying the pieces of two mountain howitzers. It was his last section. The rest of his people had been killed, wounded, or swept along with the bulk of the division. Impie Marines from the 9th thundered after them with crates of ammunition, followed quickly by a Lemurian artillery lieutenant Blas vaguely recognized. More balls smacked against the stone walls or whizzed through broken window shutters, and one of Sister Audry's guards went down, crying out.

"I got two more Naa-po-leons comin' up!" cried the lieutenant, stumbling slightly on a jumble of shattered chairs. The two guns Koratin fired had advanced with the first charge.

"Good," Blas gasped, "but much as I'd love to, we caan't shoot 'em down the street. Don't know how close our people are."

"If they were thaat close, they'd turn an' clear the Doms in front o' us, wouldn't they?" Spook demanded through teeth clenched in pain and blinking frustration. He'd taken a wafer of lead from a flattened ball in his side, under his armpit, two or three—or ten?—buildings back. He was starting to feel it.

"They may not realize the situation," Sister Audry said, pushing through her guards. "They advanced rather . . . ardently, and may now be isolated themselves. Obviously, no messengers can get through."

"Daamn! I wish we haad raadios! Field telephones are swell, but only work when you're wired up," Blas griped.

"At least we still got comm back to the gate," Spook consoled. "Ninth Div spread out along the south waall, killin' crews an' spikin' Dom guns. Met some 'Leventh Corps guys comin' from the other waay, doin' the same. South waall's quiet now, an' Shin-yaa's bringin' the whole aarmy in."

"Old news, from an hour ago," Blas snapped back skeptically. "Either waay, we still gotta link baack up with our division and reach the temple. I'll be *daamned* if those Fifteenth Corps newies beat us to it!"

"But . . . then whaat can I do with my caannon?" the gun-'Cat asked almost plaintively. "We went through hell gettin' 'em here."

Blas laughed. "We *all* been through hell gettin' here, Lieuten-aant! Join the club!"

"You can't just blast canister down the street," Sister Audry agreed thoughtfully. "But dangerous as Doms in the open are, the buildings pose the greatest threat and provide the most cover. Captain Aakon can only do so much on the rooftops with a single section, and all the nearby mortar teams have either been killed or stayed up with Colonel Garcia as well. Some may have advanced far enough on the flanks to join Twenty-First Division." She looked at the lieutenant. "Do your best to destroy the buildings along the main roadway," she instructed. "Give special attention to those on side street corners. Collapse them *into* the streets, if you can."

Blas grinned. "Yeah!"

The lieutenant looked concerned. "How do I know there aren't any of our guys in 'em?"

"If there's a Dom flaag haangin' in a window or doorway, put a shell through it," Blas instructed grimly. "An' keep it up till the building drops!"

"Ay, ay, Major Blas."

Blas looked at the others and made for the door. "Let's get movin'."

Methodically, systematically, the two guns in the street started blasting the buildings on the main western north-south avenue. A lot of their crew members were cut down by frantic musket shots and replaced by more cannoneers, even infantry. All while the remainder of Blas's small force took careful aim from behind cover and killed anything they saw wearing yellow. Two more guns clattered up and unlimbered beside the first pair, brought by a full regiment of the 9th Division that fanned out to join Blas's Marines. Both gun sections, almost hub to hub, continued blasting that part of El Corazon into dust- and smoke-choked heaps of shattered stone and timber rubble. The rooftop howitzers were working on buildings in the side streets themselves. Men might still pick their way through debris, but they couldn't approach in organized units anymore; the only way regular Dom infantry was trained to fight. Blas started seeing yellow-coated figures jump out from behind mountains of debris and vanish in the smoke. More astonishing—Blas had seen regular Dom soldiers flee before, but only once witnessed them surrender—some even started tossing their muskets away.

"C'mon!" she roared. "After 'em! If regulaars'll surrender, let 'em. *No Blood Drinker prisoners!*" A thunderous roar answered her, and troops—mostly the fresh ones—stampeded past. Some even paused to help push the guns forward though they'd be lucky to get them past the wreckage they'd made. "Single 'em up!" she shouted. "Try to take 'em through one at a time." She started to join the charge, Spook still at her side, and nearly didn't hear her name called from behind.

"Major Blas," the voice repeated. "A word, if I may."

Turning, Blas saw General Shinya, General Blair, and several other officers, all mounted, surrounded by a company of dragoons. Sister Audry was already with them. The sight was so unexpected and incongruous amidst all the devastation, she could only stare. Spook poked her.

"Okaay," Blas replied, tail whipping rapidly, dissipating nervous energy.

"Perhaps you'd like to join us," Shinya said, indicating one of several riderless horses. There was blood on the saddle. His party had apparently taken some casualties of its own getting here.

"An' go where?"

Shinya smiled and pointed ahead.

Blas laughed. It had a brittle sound. "Gener-aal Shin-yaa, case you ain't aware, there's a *helluva* lotta Doms thaat way."

"I'm quite aware. More than even you imagine, I suspect," he said. "But listen."

Blas did. The charge she'd just unleashed was shooting and there was still sharp fighting to the east, but beyond that, in the square around the temple, where most of her division should be by now, there was almost quiet. "I don't hear whaat I thought I would," she confessed.

"Understandable. It's been somewhat noisy here. And since we were already coming this way, it seemed expedient to bring you the latest reports ourselves."

"What's goin' on?" She looked at Audry and blinked anxiously. "Is our division in one piece?"

"Not complete without its principal commanders, of course, but largely intact," Blair told her dryly.

"An' the linkup with Fifteenth Corps?"

"Already happening," Shinya responded. "It's through Fifteenth Corps that I have my most recent information, in fact. It remained more cohesive than Tenth Corps and maintained better comm with its forward units—though yours *did* apparently reach the temple first."

Blas saw a wistful smile appear on Sister Audry's face. "Col-nol Garcia?" she pressed.

"Alive," Shinya confirmed, "and currently stalling, as a matter of fact."

"Stalling?" Sister Audry asked, surprised. "What for?"

"You," Shinya said simply. He sighed. "Right now, there is a very large number of people, perhaps a quarter of the civilian population of this city, waiting to hear what you have to say. Colonel Garcia is the messenger, but word of you has spread even here, it seems. In any event, a large percentage of those people are armed, skeptical, and very afraid." He glanced at Blair, then down at Blas's ragged, filthy, blood-spattered form. "And despite recommendations to the contrary, I don't *want* to 'kill them all.' " He looked back at Sister Audry. "We're still fighting half this city. If we can get the other half on our side, we might finish this before nightfall." He paused. "If not, we could still lose. Just as bad, we'll be fighting here for days or weeks and it'll all be like . . ." He waved back behind them, at the devastation and misery of the battle they'd endured so far. "Let's avoid that if we can."

"What do I have to do?" Sister Audry asked.

"I don't really know," Shinya confessed a little awkwardly. "Go to the temple, talk to the people. Tell them what you once told Arano Garcia. It's certainly their only hope, and might be ours."

Sister Audry nodded then, and without another word put her left foot in a dangling stirrup and swung into the saddle. She was ready.

Blas took off her helmet and scratched at the drying, foamy sweat in the fur around her ears. "Wait a minute. Still lots of Doms thaat way," she warned. "Prob'ly snipers."

Shinya smiled. "Possibly. But listen again; even the charge you just ordered has stopped fighting." There was occasional firing but not much. "They'll be clearing the buildings. You're really not far away at all."

It was true. For the first time in quite a while, Blas looked toward the temple and saw how close it was. They'd almost made it on their own.

Shinya was nodding ruefully. "I actually tried to get here in time to stop you. It might've upset everything if you kept fighting right into the square around the temple. As it is, I'm sure Garcia halted your troops, and even the civilians must understand you had to clear the Blood Drinkers out." His expression hardened. "I heard what they did with the children, from wounded heading back. I expect Colonel Garcia told the people as well. If they're capable of being swayed by anything Sister Audry says, that should push them over the edge." He glanced at his watch. "Come along, Major Blas. We really must hurry. Colonel Garcia can only stall so long. Besides, I'm told the Navy has planned something extraordinary. I'd like to see it, and the temple might be the best vantage point."

CHAPTER 24

////// *Above El Paso del Fuego*

*U*SS *Destroyer* and USS *Sword* were called back and ordered to proceed north at full steam along the coast as soon as they cleared the mouth of the pass. All the frigates accompanying them, or that had survived their fight with the Doms, were told to avoid the dense archipelago of mountain fish as best they could and make for a point about eight miles out from the Pass of Fire. Every other escort or auxiliary armed with depth charges, no matter how fresh or battered, would converge there as well, in a north-south line. The carriers, including *Raan-Goon*, got underway, pulling farther back from El Paso, though *Raan-Goon* had to creep along with her engines reversed. Her fires were finally under control but weren't out.

The Clipper was still aloft, still reporting the progress of the enemy fleet, though its escort had been severely depleted. By 1700 hours that afternoon, when the slack tide began to turn again, twenty-eight Dom liners and armored Grikbird carriers had already swept into the wide, baylike mouth of El Paso del Fuego. They quickly formed into two distinct battle groups and pressed on. The smaller of these, composed of ten ships of the line, proceeded toward the tangled, smoldering wreckage of the earlier naval battle near the convulsing city. The larger force of nine Grikbird carriers and nine liners steamed for the open sea.

All that seemed to oppose them were twenty-six much smaller ships. Some were frigates, a few—including the old *Achilles*—already severely damaged. Most were older AVDs, basically "scout frigates" or seaplane tenders. They retained a few guns but were no longer fit for serious combat. Their primary roles were escort duty, reconnaissance with the single Nancy each carried, and refueling and repairing other Nancys that set down beside them. None carried airplanes now, but like the frigates and assorted other armed auxiliaries, all had depth-charge racks at the stern and launchers on either beam.

Gathered in the space between the still-somewhat-distant forces, however, was the most important element of Orrin Reddy's harebrained scheme. It was difficult to credit, viewed from the surface, but from five thousand feet, where Orrin now led every plane they could scrape up, it was easy to see *hundreds* of giant mountain fish, the tightest concentration of the massive monsters anyone ever heard of, rolling, basking, even awkwardly mating under the bright afternoon sun. Pushed from the mouth of the pass by all the annoying noise, they wallowed in strikingly companionable accord, waiting for things to settle down so they could return to the endless smorgasbord furnished by the pass.

There was no way to know how they'd react to what was about to happen, and every Allied skipper about to execute his or her orders probably suspected, whether the plan worked out or not, they were screwed. But there was nothing for it, and their Impie and Lemurian crews were as closely tied together and intimately committed as their comrades fighting so desperately in the city onshore. They knew this stunt, cooked up by an *aviator*, had quite literally been thrown together on the fly, and they were taking a desperate gamble. But it was all they had left to try, and they would do their duty.

Orrin toggled the microphone in his new Nancy while looking out at the nearly two hundred planes around him, the ships below, the awe-inspiring herd of gigantic sea creatures, and the Dom fleet beyond. The nearest enemy had formed no line this time, content to gaggle forward in an unpracticed approximation of an Allied battle group, their liners deployed protectively around the carriers. On the south side of the pass, the battle for El Corazon seemed to have intensified, the afternoon sun glaring at the towering smoke, thick enough to cast a dark shadow on the mountains beyond.

Though not as large or impressive as the enemy's, the Allied ships five thousand feet below were more ascetically deployed, arrayed in a roughly concave line about four and a half nautical miles long and 350 to 400 yards apart. A few smaller mountain fish, relatively slender and only two or three hundred feet long, actually swam among them. Orrin was concerned about that, but the youngsters weren't as aggressive as the great bulls. He looked at his planes again. Thrown together as they'd been, there wasn't time for careful flight assignments. They'd do their part as wings. *Raan-Goon*'s depleted wing combined with *New Dublin*'s. Taking a last deep breath, he spoke.

"*Makky-Kat, Makky-Kat*, this is COFO Reddy, over."

"COFO Reddy, this is *Makky-Kat*. How's it look? Over," came Tex Sheider's voice in Orrin's earphones.

"I don't know," Orrin confessed. "About as good as it's going to, I guess. Recommend you give the signal for your guys to shove off. As soon as they've had their fun, we'll jump in. Over."

"All right, Orrin," Tex replied, abandoning radio protocol. "I'll pass the word. Godspeed. From me, Lelaa, Jenks—everybody."

"God *help* us," Orrin replied forcefully, watching a cloud of Grikbirds start spewing up from the distant Dom carriers. "Grikbirds, Grikbirds," he called out. "Nicoya Pursuit, stand by to intercept. Everybody else, assume defensive formations and stack 'em up until I give the word. Over."

A line of flashes and wisping white smoke caught his eye from below as each Allied ship in the long line flung pairs of depth charges forward at 45-degree angles to their line of advance. Fifty-odd splashes marred the sea, and shortly before the ships drew abreast of them, the purple-blue water spalled white. An instant later, bril-

liant white stalks gushed up, generating sun-washed rain-
bows with their spray. Orrin couldn't hear the blasts. He
was too high and the engine too loud, but the sound waves
and possibly water pressure they produced seemed to visibly jolt the nearest islands of blubbery flesh. He was later
told the mountain fish even vocalized a kind of anguished,
low-frequency groan nobody had ever heard before. At
present, however, Orrin observed a great turmoil of monstrous flukes whipping the closest beasts directly away
from the sonic assault, propelling them toward the denser
concentration, also beginning to react to the painful
pummeling to their sensitive auditory organs.

Many of the great fish dove out of sight but some heaved
themselves up, as if actually trying to launch themselves
from the water. Virtually every one, however, performed
stunningly rapid turns, cyclonic in their intensity, and the
majority of the herd—pod; whatever the proper term was—
began a ponderous, if tumultuous retreat back toward the
Pass of Fire.

"I think it's working," Orrin shouted to his new backseater, an Impie Marine sergeant named Humphrey.

"Aye, sir, they're movin'."

But Orrin's plan didn't envision the mountain fish leisurely repositioning themselves, and the DDs, AVDs, and
other Allied ships pressed on, relentlessly launching more
depth charges and rolling others from their stern racks. The
continued onslaught sent the mountain fish into a frenzy.
Even some truly enormous old bulls, wearing islandlike
ecosystems on their backs, were swept along with the herd.
They'd been Orrin's biggest concern because they normally
attacked the *source* of whatever aggravated them. But the
pain they were enduring and the herd instinct—in this
place, at least—was overpowering. The impossibly dense
cluster of rampaging islands roared on toward the pass.

There were a few exceptions, of course. A number of the
great beasts, disoriented and separated or maddened by
pain, rounded on a Scott class Impie frigate and demolished it as effortlessly as a man might smash a crate of eggs.
An AVD was flung on her beam ends, probably by accident, when a fleeing mountain fish scraped her keel with its

back. The ship filled quickly and her boiler burst, spewing
what looked like smoldering matchsticks all around.

"*Makky-Kat*, *Makky-Kat*, this is COFO Reddy, over,"
Orrin shouted in his microphone. "Call the cowboys off."
He glanced at the escalating melee between Fleashooters
and Grikbirds. Numerous flying reptiles and a couple of
planes were already plummeting to the sea. "The stampede's underway, and we'll keep poking it in the ass. Tell
Jenks to get your ships back, Tex."

He looked around. "Stand by, Third Bomb Wing," he
called. "Remember, when we go in, dump your bombs as
close behind the pushers as you can. Don't hit 'em if you
can help it. We don't want cripples; we want 'em all running up the mouth of the pass." He didn't add that he
personally saw no reason to needlessly harm any of the
amazing creatures. Dangerous, destructive rogues sometimes had to be killed, but that was different. They weren't
evil and they weren't the enemy, and except for a couple
of unfortunate instances, they were allies today. "And for
God's sake," he added, "don't waste bombs on the goddamn Doms. If there's any left when this is done, we'll
deal with them then." He mentally crossed his fingers and
glanced from side to side as the remaining Nancys from
Maaka-Kakja and a number of the AVDs joined him in
a line. "Let's go!" he shouted, pushing the stick forward,
aiming at the momentous tsunami of flesh that only
seemed to grow as the entrance to the pass narrowed and
the bottom of the sea came up.

CHAPTER 25

////// *El Corazon*

General Tomatsu Shinya and his party did get shot at on their way to the temple, but the muskets missed their mark, and men and 'Cats with Blitzerbugs converged on whatever place just spouted a gust of white smoke. After everything Blas had been through, the danger hardly registered. She just watched appreciatively, professionally detached, as the culprits were hunted down and killed. She was utterly unprepared for what she saw in the vast plaza surrounding the great temple of El Corazon, however.

Twenty thousand—maybe more—men and women were gathered there, and like Shinya warned, most were armed. Very few had muskets, probably taken from dead or retreating Dom troops, but some of the better dressed carried well-made fouling pieces. Most had pikes, like the children before, which probably meant General Mayta or somebody actually issued them, expecting everyone to fight to the last. A few even carried wooden pitchforks or clubs. Few swords or long blades were seen.

Blas was probably most surprised by how festive their simple yet colorful attire appeared, especially after she'd slogged through the bleached-white city, the only other colors being yellow uniforms and the red and gold of the hateful Dom flags. And the blood, of course. Men almost universally wore long-tailed shirts and kilts, though a few had trousers of a sort. Women were just as uniformly covered in wraparound dresses that showed their faces, if little else. But the colors were striking, with purples, reds, yellows, and oranges predominant, though they varied immensely with lighter and darker shades. Everyone wore what looked like straw sandals on their feet. Interestingly, possibly because of what had happened or because these people truly were prepared to fight and hoped to protect them, she saw no younglings at all. Then another horrible thought intruded: *maybe their younglings haave already been taken, to be . . . used again.*

Shinya slowly led them through a passage cleared by Impie Marines with leveled bayonets and they rode to the lower steps of the temple. High on her horse, Blas saw the Sister's Own and substantial elements of the 4th and 21st divisions arrayed on the south side of the plaza, twenty-odd cannon facing inward. The 4th and 21st must've brought their own guns. A fair-size chunk of XV Corps was to the north, and if they didn't have cannon, they seemed to have brought every machine gun they could carry off the grounded transports. It struck her that despite continued fighting elsewhere, the Allied troops might actually outnumber the civilians here. If they chose to start something, all would die. But she and the others were moving to their center, well away from aid, and they'd be just as screwed if things turned sour.

She noticed for the first time that a lot of people were staring at her with open hostility. *Probably should've stayed out of this,* she thought. *I'm a* demon, *faar as they're concerned. But maybe Shinyaa brung me to prove I'm not. Who knows? He caan be so weird.* She looked up at the temple and saw Garcia and Ixtli standing alone beneath the flag of the Vengadores. Both held colorfully painted speaking trumpets in their hands and looked *very* relieved to see them. Dismounting from their horses, Shinya, Blair, Audry, and Blas walked up the temple steps to join their friends. From there they could see the entire plaza, the columns of smoke to the east, the sea to the north, and the great volcano on the other side of the pass. It was smoking more heavily than usual too, and Blas wondered if that was a good or bad omen.

Probably desensitized to such things by now, Blas
didn't pick up on many other details as quickly as Sister
Audry did. She was first to notice the scorched crosses
arranged around the temple, the black-stained, sharpened
poles set firmly in the ground at regular intervals, and that
the darkened steps they stood on were deeply stained with
blood. She caught Blas's attention and pointed those
things out. Blood sacrifice, implements of fiery crucifix-
ion, and impaling poles. No matter how civilized and devoted to festive garments these people might be in some
ways, they'd existed with, if not condoned—*Who knew?*—
unimaginable atrocities for a very long time.

Smiling tightly, Sister Audry took the speaking trumpet from Captain Ixtli. "Please interpret for me if I falter,
Colonel Garcia," she asked, but she didn't really need
him. She'd had a lot of time to learn the odd Spanish mix
of her Vengadores and she'd made the most of it.

Waay more than me, Blas thought, though she picked
up the gist of what Audry said next.

"We didn't come here as conquerors. We wouldn't
have come at all if we weren't driven to, in self-defense,"
she shouted at the assembly, her words echoing off surrounding buildings, quieting the disturbed, curious, and
frightened murmuring of the crowd. "But *in* our defense,
and yours as we've come to know you, we came through
battle and blood with a simple message." She took a deep
breath. "Your God is the same as ours, the same Maker
of All Things, but He's *not* a God of pain and suffering,
demanding that your children shield His cowardly warriors. He's a God of *love!*"

She waved at Garcia, shouting louder over the confused, angry rumble. "And this is not some new, heretical
interpretation; it's the ancient *truth* your masters have distorted. That profound understanding is what persuaded
Colonel Garcia's men to fight so bravely to liberate you
from your tormentors!" She paused a moment in deathly
silence before beginning again. "The details of this new/
old faith will come in time, if you allow me to witness them
to you, but first and foremost is the lesson of love we fought
so hard to bring."

Blas had no love for these people, and talking about

love here, now, while bitter fighting still raged, struck her as bizarre. Not so Sister Audry, who gestured at the flag behind her.

"That banner says a great deal by itself. Saint Benedict was a holy servant of Jesus Christ on another world, devoted to teaching people to live together in peace and love and work for the common good, while celebrating individual merit." Sister Audry paused, recognizing that was a somewhat controversial interpretation, but this was no time for semantics. Instead, she read off some of the most pertinent phrases: "'The drink you offer is evil. Drink it yourself!'" she cried, then pointed up at Grikbirds swirling high overhead. "'Let not the dragon be my guide!'" She looked back down. "And perhaps most relevant here, 'May the holy cross light my way'—but not with *fire*," she stressed, gesturing at one of the charred crosses nearby, "but as a symbol of the Lord Jesus Christ, who suffered and died on one."

She shook her head. "You're taught that suffering is the path to grace, the toll to a 'paradise' of subservience like you already endure each day. *That's just not so!*" She took a deep breath. "Jesus didn't suffer for *His* grace, but to bestow it upon all of us. He suffered on the cross in our place, so we wouldn't have to, and took our sins upon Himself!"

Blas saw tears on Sister Audry's face and wondered if she was thinking about Koratin.

"That's the ultimate perversion of His teachings on this world, that blood and suffering, not love of God, is the key to salvation and everlasting life." She hesitated, then continued harshly, waving at the bloodstained stones. "And what God, what afterlife, could be *worth* suffering for if this is the price? The blood of Jesus Christ made all this unnecessary!" she practically screamed. "All the bloodshed, all the lives you've tossed away . . . all the *children* your masters have slain today and down the ages, haven't been for the glory of *God*, but for themselves, to keep you fearful, willing tools for their ambitions! God loves you," she added simply. "He loves us all. Each of us was born in the light of His love, and He wouldn't have us kill one another to earn it, or feed it with innocent blood!"

She turned grimly toward the east, where the fighting

remained fiercest. "God will still love you whether you join us now or not. He'll even still love you if you fight us," she conceded, drawing a concerned glance from General Blair. She waved around once more, taking in the crosses, impaling poles, and finally the dark stain on the temple again. "But can you feel *worthy* of His love—or truly love yourselves—if you don't finally rise against unholy men who wallow in your children's blood to perpetuate their ungodly rule?" Her voice gone hoarse, she stabbed a finger back down at the blood-soaked steps. "Or is *this* what you'll fight for, the kind of 'faith' you'll embrace forever? Because this will be your only chance to throw it off!"

"No!" screeched a nearby woman, face wet with tears of her own. Blas wondered if Koratin had killed one of her children.

"No!" came a louder shout, from hundreds. But many seemed unconvinced, looking furtively at the armed men and 'Cats surrounding them. Some started shouting something about demons, and still more were too deeply entrenched in generations of hard beliefs for a short, simple sermon by an invader to sway them. Pushing, yelling, and shoving broke out, and there were a couple of muffled shots.

No way to reason with 'em—they're Doms! Blas thought bleakly. *If more haad muskets, we'd be dead already. How're we gonna get off this stupid temple an' baack in the fight?*

That's when Shinya quietly said, "Look," and pointed northwest, out to sea. Everyone else followed his gaze, and Colonel Garcia raised his speaking trumpet. "Look!" he roared, gaining the crowd's attention. Thousands of heads turned, but few could see past the buildings and the throng.

"Get some of them up here now," Shinya directed the Marines who'd followed them in and ringed the base of the temple. The people they chose resisted at first. They weren't allowed on the temple from day to day, and those who did ascend it usually came down in pieces, following their bouncing heads. Very quickly, though, thirty or forty men and women, all disarmed, were dragged up to watch what was happening in the mouth of El Paso del Fuego. They cried out in alarm.

"Maker!" Blas breathed.

"My God," Sister Audry murmured.

"Pretty slick," said Spook.

It looked like a giant, frothing tsunami approaching the pass from the west, but nothing about it seemed natural. It was too tumultuous, too chaotic, the leading edge too frenzied by far. And almost immediately in its path was a fleet of eighteen Dom vessels, shaped and rigged like ships of the line, though Shinya knew some were Grikbird carriers. And quite a few Grikbirds kited above them as if unsure what to do. They'd been brought out to attack Allied ships, but now their own ships, and only source of rest and support far from land, had made a panicky turn to flee a mountain range of foam. Dark smoke gushed from tall funnels, paddle wheels spun furiously, but there was no protection from what was coming, and the Grikbirds somehow understood.

Shinya raised his Impie telescope and saw some Nancys now, distant, distinctive silhouettes, swooping behind the great wave. Waterspouts raised by bombs they dropped, prodding the mountain fish onward, were invisible beyond the closer turmoil but were undoubtedly having the desired effect. "I wonder if we'll be safe from the bow wave even here?" Shinya speculated aloud. "I expect so," he answered himself immediately. "The wave itself is mostly froth and the mass behind it can't come ashore."

"This is whaat you wanted to see?" Blas demanded. "You knew?"

"Oh yes."

"They're mountain fish," Blas stated, shocked. She and Spook could see what Shinya, Blair, and now Garcia needed their Impie telescopes to view, and were able to pick out individual beasts as they smashed through the first enemy ship, grinding it under half a dozen bodies.

"The fastest, at the leading edge, must be the smaller ones," Shinya murmured somewhat distractedly.

Blas could only stare. One by one, the Dom ships were consumed by the living tide of flesh and each was shattered, splintered, ripped apart. One was simply stampeded over by a larger fish and it scorched its killer with a scalding gust of steam. Maddened, the fish went berserk and crushed another Dom liner with its mighty flukes. A couple ships even tried firing cannon at the elemental force, but if the shots dissuaded their targets, there were just too many more. It took less than two minutes for all eighteen ships and eight to ten thousand men to die.

The seething wave churned on, still tormented from the air, though Nancys started falling now, tangled with the Grikbirds. The ten Dom liners that went to finish Hibbs and bombard XV Corps' disembarked Marines had more time to prepare themselves, but there was nothing they could do. One or two turned for shore, trying to run aground, but the mouth of the pass was narrowing now, concentrating the monstrous fish, and all were caught and smashed. One seemed charmed for a moment; bashed back and forth, its masts tumbling over the side, it stayed afloat like a stick in a maelstrom, and Blas even caught herself rooting for it to live. It couldn't be. A great old bull struck it directly amidships and it folded around the nose of the beast, shedding timbers, guns, and bodies.

"Ahd-mi-raal Hibbs," Blas suddenly said. "They're killin' our people too!" she accused.

Shinya looked at her. "Admiral Hibbs was killed this morning, I'm sorry to say, and most of his ships were finished. One or two were still fighting," he conceded, "and I wish we could've informed their people. But all knew they were fighting now only to take more Doms with them. We granted their wish."

"You bastaard," Blas spat, amazed, shaking her head.

"Actually, it was High Admiral Jenks's decision, but I endorsed it fully." Shinya's expression turned harsh. "Come now, Major. We both know what the Doms do to prisoners, and we certainly weren't in a position to rescue them."

The main surge of mountain fish had passed them by, and they discovered later that their wave did indeed gush through the wall and inundate several shoreside streets. Most of the beached transports were briefly refloated and destroyed, though one was deposited high and dry and another washed out to sea, where it sank two days later. Blocked by the Pass of Fire itself, however, the stampede of mountain fish started stacking up. The race from the west was beginning, but either they were simply too big to make the passage or instinctual urges stopped them and they'd go no farther. That's when the ecological consequences of Orrin Reddy's scheme fully manifested themselves. Even in this "neutral ground," mountain fish couldn't abide such tight confines with their own kind and turned on one another in a titanic, writhing, furious mass of flesh. To Shinya it looked like a colossal pod of cannibalistic elephant seals trying to slam ashore on a rocky coast without a beach. Some began to fight, and it was astounding to see creatures so enormous heave a third of their bodies out of the sea to crash down on another, often splitting the blubbery hides of both. The water of El Paso del Fuego churned red with blood as mountain fishes started to die.

Considerably later, after dark and unnoticed by people otherwise engaged, the hideous contest in the pass subsided and the battered, stunned, exhausted survivors painfully swam away. Not even the smallest fishing boat remained afloat among the gigantic, wallowing dead, and a stunning flurry of carrion seekers of every imaginable sort—including most of the Grikbirds, by then—swept in to join the unprecedented feast.

"Do you see?" Arano Garcia now roared at the confused, frightened, and growing crowd through his speaking trumpet. More civilians had packed into the plaza, probably fleeing the waterfront area behind XV Corps. That was a nervous moment for the Impie Marines, who found themselves surrounded, but word of what happened in the pass was spreading fast. "God is on our side!" Garcia loudly proclaimed. "The Blood Drinkers have *offended* God with their depravity, and He has caused the monsters in the water to destroy them on the sea. *We* must annihilate the child killers in the city, and wash the streets with their blood!"

The crowd surged, roaring angry agreement. There was no question something amazing had occurred, something as supernatural as anything they'd ever heard of—and profoundly unfavorable to the Holy Dominion. The people of El Corazon were still very afraid, probably more so than before, but they were also on their side at last.

"I'm sorry, Santa Madre," Garcia told Sister Audry, genuinely contrite. "Your fine words touched *me* as deeply as ever. And they'll touch others soon, when they'll be heard with open hearts. But remember how long it took you to bring me and your Vengadores to the light. For now we must rely on God's vengeance." He motioned at the mob, perhaps thirty thousand now, beginning to press eastward in a roaring babble of their own exhortations. "Vengeance is all they understand at present, and they needed a sign."

"The city is lost, my general," Coronel Urco sadly proclaimed, turning away from another breathless messenger. General Mayta merely nodded, unseeing. The smoke was so dense that it was already dark, in any event, even though the sun remained slightly over the horizon in the west. The heretics had broken in everywhere, and Mayta and his command corps had retreated time and again, until it was pressed against the northeast bastion of the great wall. The enemy's XI Corps had bashed its way in at last, fanning out through the city; XV Corps had linked up with X Corps at the temple; and Mayta had watched with his own disbelieving eyes as the leviathans of the deep obliterated his carefully hoarded fleet, and his dragons—lesser and greater—dispersed. Now even the populace was against him!

"It's all General Allegria's fault," Urco snapped savagely, apparently reading Mayta's mind. That wasn't entirely true, of course; Mayta had underestimated his foe—particularly the demons such as that horrible Major Blas; no mere "animal" *she*, after all—based on his small successes against them. He'd opted for a static defense like that which had served their General Shinya so well at Guayak and Fort Defiance, but that was a terrible mistake because it allowed the enemy to focus all its might, from land, sea, and air, upon him. Even so, he was confident he would've prevailed if not for the leviathans. And General Allegria, of course. So, ultimately, Urco was right.

"All the people, even the children, *would* have fought them, my general," Urco continued, "if Allegria used them together to attack, and not just the children as *shields* for his Blood Drinkers!" He spat the name. Ordinary service rivalry aside, regular soldiers didn't like Blood Drinkers any more than the general populace, for the same reasons. Chief among those was fear. Disputes between regulars and Blood Drinkers, even off duty in a cantina, always resulted in the regulars suffering brutal consequences. Blood Drinkers were unquestionably the best troops in the Dominion, but they lorded it over everyone. Even the alcalde of a city as prominent as El Corazon had reason to fear the wrath of junior Blood Drinker officers unless he had high, secure connections. Any accusation by one of them was tantamount to conviction. Therefore, after the way Allegria used the children—the word spread like lightning—as far as the people of El Corazon were concerned, it was he and his Blood Drinkers who murdered them as surely as if he'd fired the enemy cannons himself.

"I suppose you're right, Coronel Urco," Mayta finally agreed, "but it makes no difference now."

"It *does*, my general!" Urco pleaded, physically pushing Mayta toward a small courtyard behind the corner bastion tower. Three greater dragons fitted with saddles for their riders—couriers in this case—waited, milling waspishly. The scent of blood was heavy in the air but so was the smoke they hated, and they were growing irritable and hard to manage. Two already had riders; short, small men in heavy coats with carbines hooked to broad straps slung diagonally across their torsos. The dragon wearing an empty saddle swung its head toward Mayta and snapped at him, red eyes glowing malevolently. Mayta drew back. He instinctively feared dragons—any sane man would—even as he admired their lethal beauty. They were a bit more than just oversize lesser dragons; equally colorful in their plumage, but smarter by far. And though they were more delicate, pound for pound, their teeth and claws were proportionately longer and sharper and they used them with greater cunning. Most important of all, they'd grudgingly accept riders and understood more complex commands.

"You must fly to the east," Urco insisted, "prepare our defenses there. Only *you* fully appreciate how the heretics fight!"

Mayta snorted. "Even if that's true, I doubt His Holiness, Don Hernan, will forgive me the loss of El Corazon, El Paso del Fuego, and therefore virtually everything to the *north*, which will now be isolated. Not to mention one of his favorite, if stupidest, sons. He won't appoint me to command anything above the scavengers he gives me to. I suspect they won't obey me," he added darkly.

"Then *take* charge!" Urco pressed. "*You* remain supreme commander beyond the city of Nuevo Granada and the Holy Temple itself! Everything we had was placed at your disposal. At present, it remains so. Once you begin to truly exercise that command, even Don Hernan must hesitate to remove you." Urco gestured around at the calamity surrounding them. "Only you can stop the heretics now, and Los Diablos del Norte will certainly take advantage of this. His *Supreme* Holiness in El Templo de los Papas will need you more than ever."

Mayta took a deep breath of acrid air and finally nodded. "Very well. I've never ridden a dragon," he added a bit nervously, "but my duty to the Holy Dominion is clear. You're wise, Coronel Urco," he blurted in a tone of genuine affection. "I wish you could come with me."

Urco shook his head. "No, my general. I'm flattered, but someone with your vision must remain. The city may be lost, but the battle continues. I'll ensure that all those loyal to the Holy Dominion fight to the last."

Eyes damp, Mayta allowed a man to dress him in a heavy coat and help him up on the back of the restive dragon. The man, probably the creature's usual rider, made sure Mayta was securely fastened in place, then retreated to stand by Coronel Urco. Mayta's expression contorted with earnest emotion and he saluted them. Then, following the other two, Mayta's mount abruptly leaped into the sky and furiously beat its wings until it cleared the wall. Staying low under the smoke, all three dragons swiftly accelerated eastward toward the mountains bordering the south shore of the Pass of Fire.

Sighing, Coronel Urco rubbed his smoke-tortured eyes and visibly deflated. "Teniente Tucli," he called, "you may proceed. Spread the word as quickly as you can: all regular army units will immediately cease firing at civilians, even if they keep fighting us. Pull our men back as far as you must. Capitaine Xamirez? Your men are most pressed by the hereti—" He paused and took another breath. "The *enemy* forces of their Eleventh Corps. Do whatever you can to stop the fighting. Break contact and retreat if that's your only choice, but try to speak to their commander. If successful, inform him we're aware they treat their prisoners generously." That information was suppressed, but most officers knew it. What were the Vengadores, after all, but former soldiers of the Dominion?

"Tell him we'll surrender under a single condition," Urco continued, holding up a restraining hand. "We won't disarm until we've purged this city of every Blood Drinker we can find." He considered. "They're more than welcome to help with that."

Urco, Tucli, Xamirez, and many more had been loyal servants of the Dominion, but they were native to El Corazon and all had families—and children—there.

"Why did you let Mayta go?" Tucli demanded.

Urco frowned. "Several reasons. First, we're all traitors now, and our families depend on the enemy's success for survival. Mayta left with the last greater dragons and will think, for a time, that all of us are dead. He'll expect the enemy to learn a great deal from prisoners, but not what *we* will willingly tell them. Second, though he's a zealot, Mayta isn't necessarily a *bad* man. Not like Allegria or Don Hernan. And while he may survive to fight again east of El Paso, his presence could cause considerable confusion and disarray, particularly in regard to army relations with Don Hernan."

"You'd ignite a civil war?" Xamirez demanded, astonished.

"No," Urco denied. "I hope not. Not between our people, at least. There's been enough of that already. Here, and through the ages," he added lower. "But between Mayta and Don Hernan?" He almost smiled. "That might be interesting. Either way, if Mayta lives," he qualified again, "at the very least he won't work well with Blood Drinkers. Particularly after his experience here."

CHAPTER 26

**Operation Whipsaw
Second Day**

*////// Second General Ign's HQ
South Bank of the Zambezi River
Grik Africa
March 15, 1945*

Second General Ign was conferring with generals from around the perimeter in the flickering light of oil lamps when his aide, a First of One Hundred new to the forward trenches, rushed into the underground bunker. Flinging himself to the dank dirt floor, the aide squirmed vigorously, implying he brought important news. Ign sighed inwardly at the antics, doubtless performed for the benefit of the other generals. He never required such things, particularly in urgent circumstances.

"Yes, what is it?" he demanded impatiently.

"Lord General!" the aide cried, still twisting. "A message from the watchposts along the river!"

"Is the enemy fleet moving?" Ign demanded. All the Allies' metal warships, even the newest, biggest one, had assembled in the wide place in the river downstream of the *nakkle* leg, doubtless preparing to provide gunfire support for the attack Ign expected. The aide raised his head to look up at him. "No, Lord. The message comes from upriver, across from Old Sofesshk." He hesitated as if for dramatic effect.

"Indeed?" inquired a general responsible for the sector to Ign's right. "What did the pennants say?" Grik had always made limited use of signal flags at sea, but only used horns on land. Inspired by the seemingly instantaneous communications the enemy enjoyed and no longer possessing the luxury of passing messages by airship in an environment where the enemy could destroy them at will, Ign himself had created a system employing signal pennants, or fires and mirrors at night, to send information across vast distances via relays along the line of sight. The crude semaphore remained in its infancy and its operators were imperfect. Many mistakes were made. It was better than nothing, however, and as with all new things, the system would improve with time. Everyone present appreciated its potential, or Ign would've replaced them long ago.

The aide's eyes widened in horror. "The prey has attacked the Holy City itself, my lords!" he cried.

Ign straightened to stand as tall as his forward-hunched frame would allow and gusted a sigh. "It was inevitable they'd bomb it eventually," he grumbled. "Just as well most of the Hij have already been"—he hesitated—"taken elsewhere. Otherwise they may have demonstrated in some fashion. As it stands, I'm sure the Giver of Life is quite safe within the palace," he quickly assured.

The aide was shaking his head, his snout whipping from side to side. "No, Lord, no!" he practically shouted. "I mean, yes, their large flying machines did drop bombs, but then the enemy *attacked* as well, on the *ground*!"

Ign was stunned. "Impossible!" he countered. "The only way there is through us, or upriver through our warships!"

"It's another mistake of the pennants," one general stated confidently.

"No, Lord," the aide objected, flinching slightly to contradict such a lofty being. "I waited until the message was confirmed by one of the greatships anchored there. Still suspecting a misunderstanding, I demanded further details. The initial message was confirmed. . . . And observations added of fighting in the city."

All the generals looked stunned now, their crests lying flat, and Ign finally understood his aide's behavior. *He* would've groveled when bringing such a report to First General Esshk.

"Could they have marched there on the north side of the river after all?" one general breathed skeptically, but Ign shook his head impatiently. Neither side was much interested in the terrain on the north bank of the Zambezi, particularly upriver of the *nakkle* leg. It was wild, steep, and rocky, full of small river gashes, virtually trackless, and clotted by impenetrable forests. It would take far too long for a force of any size to negotiate the region. And between the small garrisons and shore batteries (supplied from the river) that Ign had established along its length all the way back to Sofesshk, and the various bands of hunter Uul that eked out a living there, they'd have had some warning if anyone tried. *No*, Ign decided, *the enemy would sooner sprout wings and fly*. "When did the attack begin?" he demanded. "How long has it gone on? Does the commander of the greatship know how the enemy got there? What did he see?" The questions came fast, spilling over one another.

"Fighting was observed soon after the bombing," the aide replied, "and may continue yet. The day begins outside," he reminded the generals who'd been sequestered underground for hours. "As for how . . ." The aide hesitated. "After the bombing, many flying machines still came throughout the night, but no more bombs fell. The greatship's commander thought he observed . . . *things*, drifting down from the sky, however."

Ign's crest jerked erect. "*White* things? Like balls?" he demanded, razor claws twisting in his guts. *Perhaps they* did *fly*, he thought with dread.

The aide touched the floor with his snout. "I do not know. He didn't say, and I . . . didn't know to ask."

Ign looked at the others. "It's possible," he stated flatly, "though I never imagined . . ." He shook his head. "I—many of us here—have seen the flyers of damaged machines leap away as to their deaths, only to be suspended by white balls of fabric that lower them gently to the ground. None have ever done this over ground we control, so we've never seen exactly how it works. Yet we know it does." He turned to stare at the white lines painted on the earthen wall of the headquarters, a map depicting the region, their deployments, and what they knew of the enemy's. "Somehow they dropped troops, perhaps a great many, into Old Sofesshk from the sky!" he said with certainty, the slightest hint of admiration joining the horror in his voice.

"What shall we do?" one of the generals almost wailed.

Ign stabbed the wall to the south with a claw, and dirt and white paint crumbled away. "The Other Hunters from the Republic have smashed past Fifth General Akor." He made a diagonal nod across at the general responsible for containing the Allied beachhead to the south. "Your reserves moved to counter them, as have others I've sent. Your line is thin but you needn't concern yourself. The enemy must break through *here*"—he pointed at the section of the line where they now were, close to the river—"where they can use their powerful ships. Here is where their greatest force assembles, and here we've put our strongest defense." He looked at the other generals.

"And I must take *more* troops from you all, since I'm now convinced the enemy attack is imminent. It *must* be if they mean to take advantage of the confusion they've sown with this attack on Old Sofesshk." He stepped back.

There were nods. It seemed obvious. "I'll begin shifting forces to bolster yours at once, Second General," agreed the commander of Ten Thousands defending the southwest portion of the line. "But what of Sofesshk? What if they . . . *destroy* the Celestial Mother?" he added, voicing all their fears.

"They won't. They *can't*," Ign stated confidently. "But I'm sure the enemy's attack there was executed precisely so we'd think so, and to throw us into disarray." His crest flared. "It shall not be. It's nothing but a sacrificial thrust against our *minds*, and it won't strike home." He pointed northwest at the area of concern. "I'll have all available forces attack across the river at once, but with the air in the enemy's claws that may not accomplish much," he conceded. "Yet you all know the quality of First Ker-noll Jash. He's near there, and I have no doubt he'll plan a more . . . deliberate rescue of the ancient city and Celestial Mother. He will succeed, and destroy these strange, flying warriors."

The other generals nodded, apparently satisfied. Some resented Jash's meteoric rise in the ranks but all acknowledged his ability. "Where is First General Esshk?" one asked. "And the Chooser?" he added as an afterthought.

"I have no idea where the Chooser is," Ign said dismissively, "but Esshk is in the north again, at Lake Galk, inspecting the new wonder weapons General of the Sky Ando labors to complete."

"They'll have to be told."

"Yes," Ign answered. "I actually suspect the Chooser is in Old Sofesshk now, and knows more than we already. First General Esshk is quite far, however, and it'll take time for word to reach him, even with the pennants. The mountains require a much greater number of signal stations and each relay still tends to compound errors. . . ." He paused, considering. "I'll risk my airship," he said decisively. One of Esshk's black zeppelins was maintained ten miles back in a great, camouflaged pit that had once been a cavern, its roof blasted away. Exposing it was chancy, but now was better than later. He looked back at the aide. "I'll prepare a report and ensure the airship's crew has the latest news you brought us." He raised his gaze to the officers around him. "As for you, begin the redeployments we discussed at once. Have a care for enemy flying machines, however. They mustn't suspect we've guessed their plan. I *want* them to come to me here with everything they have!"

Lake Galk

"Most impressive, General of the Sky Ando. Most impressive indeed," First General Esshk almost gushed, looking out at the lake and the fat, drifting pall of smoke standing over the sinking carcass of an unfinished ironclad greatship of battle. A wispy, dissipating tendril of white smoke still connected the settling wreck to another greatship on the horizon to the north. Esshk's entourage included the local regent and numerous influential Hij of the relatively thinly populated province surrounding Lake Galk. At least it had been thinly populated before the war. Now the formerly pastoral mountain shores around the long, deep lake, resembling a ragged crack in the earth filled with water, teemed with Uul laborers, new industry, and shipyards. The forests on the nearby mountains were rapidly being denuded for their timber. "An expensive demonstration," Esshk chided gently, "but effective."

"Thank you, Lord," Ando replied, less effusive. Like Muriname before him, he hated and feared the Grik. Who wouldn't? With their tightly packed teeth, tearing claws, and reptilian shape, they horrified him. And their feathery fur added to his sense that he was surrounded by vicious, flightless birds of prey. The fact that Esshk and the senior officials accompanying him were dressed in ornate, if macabre, finery only underscored their barbarity. But Esshk was Ando's lord now, and he'd sworn to serve him. He'd do it despite his inner fear, but couldn't pretend to like it.

Esshk didn't care. If he noted Ando's lack of zeal, he more than made up for it himself at present, and Ando was relieved. A happy Esshk had been a rarity during their association, and was less likely to allow Ando and his few comrades to be eaten. Movement caught Ando's eye and he glanced to the south, spying one of the big Grik airships approaching in the distance. Its shape and dingy black coloration disturbed Ando on a primal level, reminding him of a painting of *Namazu* he'd seen as a child. But this giant catfish wasn't a mythical beast, and it could fly.

He looked back at Esshk. "And not that costly. The old-style all-gun ironclad battleships are doomed. Though powerful and well protected, they're excruciatingly slow. Only longer-range weapons can keep them relevant. Yet even if we had time to strengthen and rifle their guns, we'd never improve them enough to counter the still-greater range advantage of the enemy guns on their new iron steamers. Certainly not in time to influence the current situation." He waved out at a shipyard across the lake to the west. "Though only one conversion is yet complete, we have more than sufficient unfinished hulls to make a formidable *fleet* of flying bomb carriers. And the fact they're unfinished actually makes conversion simpler. You'll have half a dozen of them in just a few months, and that should more than meet your most pressing need: to drive the enemy from your shores. When you can focus on rebuilding your offensive capability, we'll start an entirely new class; smaller, faster, more difficult to see or hit, that can perform the same task as their lumbering predecessors. Obviously, since they are smaller and require less labor and materials, we can make more of them."

"Obviously," Esshk agreed, noticing the airship now himself. It was aiming for a mooring mast near the once-scenic lodge where he was staying barely a mile away.

"In fact," Ando continued, "the greatest cost of this demonstration was the trained pilot. The only drawback to this system is the time it takes to train skilled operators who can only perform a single mission."

"Perhaps," Esshk agreed, "but there's no shortage of trainees. Those you use now were doing little but helping guard Old Sofesshk. The need for that is past," he added cryptically and with evident satisfaction. "And once you've sufficiently trained the trainers, the program will become self-sustaining and you can develop other weapons."

Ando bowed. "Of course, Lord." He gestured aside. "Would you care to examine one of the flying bombs more closely, while the ship that launches them approaches? Sadly, the ship's no faster than others of her kind, even with fewer guns. We'll have time for refreshments before it arrives."

"Excellent," Esshk said, clearly enjoying himself. It'd been so long since he had good news! He and his entourage walked in the direction Ando indicated and stopped to stare. Lying on its side in the soft green grass by the lake shore was an ungainly cylinder about three feet in diameter and twenty feet long, with three fins at the back. Attached to the other end was a second, pointed cylinder of the same diameter but only half the length. It had two

broad, stubby wings near the center, with an opening
fronted by a small wind screen above them. Three stabi-
lizers, two horizontal and one vertical, were just forward
of the joint with the longer section.

"Now that I've seen your flying machines up close," Esshk said, referring to the five Muriname-designed AJ1M1c
fighters Ando had left, "I understand better what I'm looking at. But please explain the similarities and differences."

"Of course," Ando replied. "The launch section is
merely an enlarged version of the highest-reaching antiair
rockets you've used . . . to some effect . . . against the enemy bombers. The engine is identical in concept, merely
a solid mass of gunpowder dissolved in alcohol and
poured into a heavily reinforced form and dried." He
arched his eyebrows. "The form becomes the engine casing and, as you can imagine, accelerating a uniform drying process using external heat and a forced draft is one
of the most complicated and dangerous aspects of the
process. When complete, however, the solid gunpowder
fuel burns as vigorously as granulated powder, but more
slowly, so instead of exploding, it jets the gas and flame
through a narrow opening, creating thrust. Imagine the
recoil of the great guns, only much prolonged"—Ando
smiled—"and the 'gun' is considerably lighter."

"Yes, yes," Esshk said impatiently. "As you say, the
principle is the same as the rockets I'm familiar with. Do
not condescend to me," he warned.

"Never," Ando assured, though he realized he'd been
doing just that. *Careful,* he admonished himself. *The
Grik are barbaric monsters, but those such as Esshk
aren't stupid.* "I merely thought a brief explanation might
be helpful to others here," he lied. "In any event, the size
of the engine was what required the greatest care to develop. Even to my surprise, increased size doesn't necessarily mean a linear, proportionate increase in pressure.
Pressure can rise alarmingly, exponentially."

Esshk nodded, though Ando doubted he understood
that. They'd blown up a lot of engines before they got it
right, and quality control remained so poor, particularly
when it came to ensuring there were no voids or bubbles
in the gunpowder, Ando suspected there was still a 25 to

30 percent chance any given weapon would explode when launched. He'd warned Esshk of that, and he'd seemed unconcerned. He *was* unconcerned about casualties, and Ando suspected he would be one himself if the nearing battleship launcher blew up.

The Grik zeppelin had finally secured itself to the mooring mast against a gustier wind than they felt down low, and figures were snaking down lines dropped from the forward gondola. *They must've brought dispatches of some importance to hurry so,* Ando mused.

"Very well, good. But tell me about the bomb," Esshk insisted. "It looks different from those we once dropped from airships."

"It had to be, to mate up to the launch section and withstand the thrust. Those earlier models only had to fall and glide."

"But once launched, they'll perform the same? Their controllers can aim themselves at their targets?"

"Yes. And since they'll be going much faster, they'll have better control and range."

"How far?" Esshk demanded greedily.

"Fifteen miles, perhaps more. Much depends on the initial launch angle, but you'll note there's another small engine behind the pilot. It's ignited by a final burst of flame from the launch section when it's consumed, also causing the two to separate. This occurs at about three miles, again depending on the launch angle," Ando cautioned. "But by then the piloted bomb has reached a truly astonishing velocity." He chuckled slightly in spite of himself. "Our one surviving test pilot who flew without a warhead was so enthusiastic about the experience that he wanted to do it again. Needless to say, his request was denied and he's become our primary instructor."

"The bomb," Esshk repeated, focusing on what was most important to him.

Ando pointed at the long nose forward of the tiny cockpit. "Five hundred pounds of superfine gunpowder, detonated by a contact fuse. An iron casing would've been best, but we had to use wood to save weight. There's little inherent armor-piercing capability, but as you've seen"—he waved at the dissipating smoke cloud drifting away from where the nearly eight-hundred-foot-long target had finally gone to the bottom of the lake—"the charge, combined with the velocity of the impact, perhaps even the forward-facing force of the initial detonation, is sufficient to destroy heavily timbered, even lightly armored targets. The . . . directed force is a concept I'm not fully familiar with and it came to me through a half-remembered conversation with Commander Riku, an old comrade of mine."

"A bomb that can sink the enemy from the horizon!" Esshk breathed, almost giddy with calculation. "I wish we could deploy them on land!"

"An agreeable ambition," Ando allowed, "but impossible as long as the enemy controls the air. The launching apparatus is too large and vulnerable to move except by ship." He nodded at the approaching greatship. It was close enough now for them to see that while its sloping casemate was still armored down the sides, the frontal armor and structure backing it had been removed and replaced with what looked like folding shutters sufficient to protect only from the weather. And the rear of the casemate had been similarly opened to vent the back blast.

Esshk turned to gaze benevolently at Ando, a disconcerting expression the Japanese flyer had never seen. "You've done very well," he said. "With these ships we can turn the tide back against the enemy. Tell me, though: I know I gave you leave to name your weapon. What did you choose?"

"Yanone. It means 'arrowhead,'" Ando replied, frowning. Two figures from the airship were literally galloping toward them now, rapidly closing the distance.

If Esshk noticed, he made no sign. "Appropriate. Most appropriate," he agreed, then paused. "Why do you make that . . . down mouth moving, so much like Kurokawa always wore?"

"Because even Yanone can't win the war alone. In fact, the ships carrying them must *never* be sent alone to battle and must always be protected because they can't protect themselves."

"But what protection do they need if they can destroy the enemy so far away?"

"They must be defended from the sky, for one. The enemy *had* few bombs that could destroy armored ships from the air, but that may have changed. And the Yanone carriers have openings in their armor. Secondly, torpedoes remain a threat, both from their swift destroyers—which will be very difficult for Yanone to hit while underway—and their torpedo boats, which will be next to impossible to destroy. All Yanone carriers must have a defensive screen." He frowned even more deeply. "Finally, you must recognize that Yanone have limitations. While their long-range capability will be formidable, particularly against enemy aircraft carriers and other big ships, you should keep them near their maximum range, not only for the safety of the ships firing them, but because the Yanone themselves will be more effective. Regrettably, their pilots can't control them while the launch engine burns. Their controls must, in fact, be locked during that phase. Any attempt at radical maneuvers near the nose at that point will almost surely send them out of control and destroy them. I therefore strongly urge you never to use them against targets less than five miles away."

The two running Grik arrived, gasping, and flung themselves to the ground, the grass in front of their muzzles blowing back and forth with their gusting breath. The rest of the entourage had clearly noticed them now, but took their cue from Esshk, who still ignored them, grunting thoughtfully. "There are always disadvantages, it seems. Why must I always be given weapons more powerful than anything the enemy has, only to be told I can only use them under the most perfect conditions?"

"That's not necessarily the case," Ando denied. "Use them as they're intended; destroy the enemy from a distance and all will be well."

Esshk considered that a moment longer, then sighed, finally glaring down at the prostrated messengers. "Oh, what is it?" he demanded. "I've viewed a fascinating weapon in the company of fine companions, there's food"— he dipped his snout to the host regent—"and a female in estrus at the lodge." The female in question was actually from the regent's own small harem of "mates," semielevated offspring of Hij that could actually talk. Keeping such was rare in the older, more congested parts of the empire, though less uncommon in secluded or pastoral regencies and on the frontiers. "I should've known I couldn't enjoy a single pleasant day without some befuddled underling demanding my attention to a matter easily addressed by the lowliest Uul!" Esshk concluded snappishly.

Both messengers were senior firsts, so whatever they had to report would probably be both coherent and important. A sense of dread quickened Ando's pulse, even as he noted the black and red slash marks painted on their gray leather armor and wondered again what the significance was. He increasingly saw the device on Grik close to Esshk.

One of the messengers tentatively raised his snout but kept his gaze averted. "Old Sofesshk—and the Palace of Vanished Gods—have been bombed," he blurted, then quickly added, "and possibly heavily assaulted by enemy *warriors*. That has been confirmed by messengers sent across the river from the palace."

"What?" demanded Esshk, glancing quickly at the regent beside him. "How can this be? Prey warriors loose in Old Sofesshk!" he scoffed. "Ridiculous!"

"Yes, Lord, but true," the other messenger ventured. "It's not known precisely how they did it, but Second General Ign believes they *fell* upon the city. From the sky!"

Esshk whirled to face Ando. "Is this possible?" he demanded.

Shaken and considering the implications, Ando nodded. "I . . . Yes, Lord, I believe it is, using parachutes. But I didn't know the enemy had them on this world. We didn't on Zanzibar."

"And you didn't share knowledge of this parachute device with me?" Esshk growled menacingly.

"They're primarily used to escape damaged flying machines, my lord," Ando stated, his voice stiffening with defiance. "All our operations were conducted over water and no sane . . . being could wish to escape a quick, clean death in his plane, only to endure a worse one in the terrible sea! I honestly never gave parachutes any thought, and I'm surprised the enemy did."

"The enemy has operated more and more over land of late," Esshk snarled, looking back at the messengers. "When?" he demanded.

"Last night, Lord. We came as quickly as we could, risking flight to outrace the pennants."

"Perhaps it was just a raid," Ando suggested. "I can't imagine they have enough parachutes for a large force."

The first messenger spoke again. "But there have been no further reports from the city, even by pennant. That strongly implies the garrison, at least, has been overwhelmed." All this seemed to come out in one breath, and the messenger hastily took another. "Second General Ign suspects the enemy force may be formidable enough to *hold* great Sofesshk, if not the palace itself, in their claws."

"Lord First General," the regent began, but Esshk held up a hand, claws extended.

"Silence!" he snapped. "There's nothing you can say that I'm not already thinking. If Old Sofesshk *has* fallen, we must reclaim it at once! Our sacred Giver of Life is in peril!" Esshk had no real concern for the welfare of the increasingly headstrong and rebellious Celestial Mother, and had finally decided to do away with her after she'd made sufficient hatchlings—*his* hatchlings—to continue her line. And since she so rarely appeared in public, it might be years before he even had to acknowledge her passing. But for now, his authority as Regent Champion, to rule all the Gharrichk'k in her stead, was given legitimacy solely by his guardianship of the young Celestial Mother. He'd easily squelched the fact she'd tried to throw him off, but it was impossible to hide that she was threatened. He briefly toyed with the thought of killing the messengers and everyone present, even Ando, but that would accomplish nothing. His whole army in the south might be aware of the situation by now.

"Second General Ign will divert whatever resources he must to secure our Giver of Life," Esshk told the messengers.

"It is already being done, Lord. And several Ten Thousands encamped around New Sofesshk under Eighth General Alk should have begun their attack even as we left."

Esshk made a noncommittal sound in his throat and

Ando got the impression he didn't have a high opinion of Alk.

"There's one further concern Second General Ign instructed us to convey, Lord," the first messenger ventured.

"And that is?"

"Regardless of what it accomplishes, the force that descended on Great Sofesshk could have only one real objective: distraction. With Republic hunters rampant in the south and forces necessarily dispatched to block them, the bulk of the enemy fleet massed beyond the *nakkle* leg on the Zambezi, now this . . . He's certain the enemy is poised to strike out of his lair with all his might. He's confident he's divined the thrust of their plan and will stop them, but believes his long-predicted 'greatest battle that ever was' is at hand, and craves your presence."

Esshk nodded brusquely. "Of course. I will come at once." He turned to face Ando. "With you."

Ando gaped, speechless.

"The new flying bomb carrier will be your flagship, and I will accompany you. There are a few armored cruisers here and more can be added as we steam downriver. Such a shame your remaining flying machines have so little fuel and ammunition," he reflected, "or we could take them too."

"But, Lord!" Ando finally managed, fleetingly relieved Esshk hadn't ordered his planes to come regardless. But he had to make him see the even greater error. "Only that *one* flying bomb carrier is ready for action, armed with just six weapons! I told you from the start they'd only prove decisive if used en masse!"

"What possible good is *any* weapon I can't use when I need it?" Esshk almost bellowed, crest rising. Then, inexplicably, his crest fell and his voice softened. "What good is General Halik, still months away to the north?" he asked rhetorically. "I won't have the one I counted on most when I need him either, it seems." He cocked his head at Ando. "One is a 'mass' compared to none," he stated simply, "and you also said their *first* use would be most decisive of all." Esshk hesitated, and for an instant, all his hauteur, arrogance, even his formidable physical menace, seemed to gush away. "I trust Second General Ign above all others, but the enemy has chosen a place we must defend to fight. He's chosen the time as well, most certainly not convenient for us, and that's difficult enough for me to grasp. Always in the past it was our race—it was *I*—who chose the time for battle."

Ando thought Esshk would've shrugged if he could. "So the time comes sooner than we'd prefer, and we must make do with what we have." Esshk stared intently at Ando. "Our enemy has faced such predicaments over and over yet still prevailed. We must do the same." His voice hardened. "The decision is thrust upon us, General of the Sky," he said, glancing around at his entourage almost contemptuously, "and we must make it."

"Then I implore you to *decide* to delay," Ando said. "You say you trust General Ign, so trust him with the battle. We can't materially affect the outcome with only six weapons. And win or lose, we'll absolutely *waste* them if we use them now. Worse, we'll never make more, because the secret will be out and even if he's defeated, the enemy won't be *gone*. He'll bomb here next." He waved his arms in frustration. "There's no place else left to do what we're doing here!" He took a breath and tried to calm himself. "Finally, Ign believes the battle's imminent. Have you forgotten the locks?"

A series of amazing locks, possibly as ancient as the Palace of Vanished Gods itself, were the only things that made Lake Galk possible, not to mention moving ships from there to the lower river. The things were massive and leaked horribly, but their construction was so robust that Ando expected they'd last another thousand years. Whoever built them had been exceptional engineers. If it was the Grik, they'd fallen far indeed.

"It'll take too long to get there, an entire day for each lock alone," Ando pressed, "and then several more to complete the passage. Everything might be over by the time we arrive. You'd likely squander your only flying bomb carrier just to appear in time to find the battle already won—or lost." He sighed. "I applaud your courage," he said, and realized with surprise he meant it. "You're a worthy lord. But I beg you to let Ign fight his battle. If he wins, we'll continue our work and eventually win the war." He paused. "If he loses, this work will be even more important because it's all you'll have left to stop the enemy on the water."

Esshk looked away, surprised by his feelings. He wanted to kill Ando for his impertinence, but at the same time he was grateful for sound counsel. He fluffed his crest and let it drop before letting out a breath. "Very well, General of the Sky. It will be as you say. And whatever happens, you too have earned my trust." He gazed off to the south. "It's hard to imagine that the last great battles are about to begin, battles that will ultimately bring the end to our enemy or our race. It amazes me," he added, a trace of wonder creeping into his voice, "that all could finally be balanced so precariously, with such momentous consequences on the scale."

He looked down at the two messengers. "Return and inform Second General Ign he has my utmost confidence and the battle is his to fight. You'll also remind all the other *Dorrighsti* you encounter that the Celestial Mother must *not*, under any circumstances, fall into the claws of the enemy, and they'll do whatever they must to prevent it."

"Yes, Lord, of course," the messengers chorused. Probably grateful to be alive, they jumped up and bounded back in the direction of the airship.

Ando pondered what Esshk said about the Celestial Mother. It sounded straightforward enough, but also struck him as vaguely ominous. And what were *Dorrighsti*? He'd never heard the word before, but he got the impression it had something to do with the painted slash marks.

CHAPTER 27

////// *Palace of Vanished Gods*

C hack studied the ruins of New Sofesshk across the river through his Imperial telescope, squinting against the bright sunlight lancing over the low clouds to the east and glaring in the glass. Once a vast, nightmarish warren of chaotic adobe, resembling something vomited together by flying, stinging insects called *yits*, which Silva likened to "mud dobbers," the months-long bombing had left a wasteland of fire-blacked mounds of red clay clods and scorched timbers.

The Grik had tried to move into position to cross the river that morning, a gaggle of galleys gathering to carry them, but the galleys were ridiculously exposed and there was nothing to conceal the troops advancing through the rubble. A swarm of P-1C Mosquito Hawks from Arracca Field bombed and strafed the galleys to shreds, and the Grik troops were immolated by firebombs dropped by successive waves of Nancys from the carriers. Now new columns of dark smoke rose over the devastated south-bank city with little more than corpses left to feed the fires.

It had been a massacre, in spite of the numerous portable antiair mortars that knocked a few planes down. Obviously, some antiair rocket batteries still lingered in the vicinity, lining the river approach where they could be supplied at night, but they were ineffective against low-flying planes and extremely vulnerable to them. They'd clearly chosen to hunker down and hide during the day. The two fat ironclad battlewagons lying at anchor hadn't been molested, but neither could they contribute. None of the planes came close enough for them to engage, and they seemed reluctant to fire on Chack's Brigade, so close to the Celestial Mother's guard troops.

Thaat could change at any time, Chack realized. *The Grik commaanders must've gotten some kind of waarning thaat we're here, but they caan't know whaat's going on. The heavy probe, just wiped out, is proof they're concerned. Now they'll get even more worried—and confused. Exaactly what Cap-i-taan Reddy waanted.* Chack adjusted the focal length and watched a few Nancys still swooping, far away. The bulk of the aircraft devoted to Chack's support would soon have another task. *The Grik caan't even effectively stage an aassault near the city. Not in daylight. There're mountains to the west and north of Old Sofesshk, but little more than forest, rolling hills, and graass-laand prairie due south of the ravaged newer city. Still, they must do something.*

He closed the telescope and dropped it back in the leather tube hanging from his neck. "They'll come again tonight," he predicted aloud to the gathering around him. Most of the brigade's senior officers had joined him by the river, concealed from the Grik around the palace by a retaining wall running alongside the road. If they had enough troops and some artillery, they could focus on the docks and make a landing very costly. But they didn't have either of those things and that wasn't the plan. "As overloaded by unexpected threats as they must be, from all directions, their greatest difficulty will be arranging river traansport on such short notice."

"Indeed," Major Jindal agreed, "and it'll be *most* interesting to see how many troops they devote to the endeavor. If they come at all, they'll need a sizable force. They can't know how few we are and they've already discovered our air alone will make it costly for them."

"Yet if our next objective goes as planned, we may not know how large their effort truly is," Abel Cook observed with a troubled frown.

"I'm sure we'll get some idea," Jindal assured wryly, but

then laughed out loud. The others looked at him questioningly. "My apologies," he said. "It just now struck me that this may be the only time in history any force has deliberately put itself in a position to be overwhelmingly surrounded and utterly cut off, then actually hoped it would happen!"

Silva scratched his beard. "I reckon the skipper knows a few times it's been done to lure a enemy to slaughter, but prob'ly not *exactly* like this. The way you put it, it does sound kinda nuts."

"No," Chack disagreed. "Don't forget our true purpose. The greater the enemy response to us, the greater will be our proof that Esshk, or whoever commands them, is so focused on our various distractions that the final element of Cap-i-taan Reddy's plaan will take him completely by surprise." He shrugged. "Even if it doesn't, he'll be weakened." He grinned, showing bright canines. "And the plaans within the plaan should dumbfound him as well. At least at first."

"Swell," Silva said, growing impatient with all the talk. "We're just chippin' paint here. Ever'body knows this shit. Let's quit bumpin' our gums an' get on with it."

Jindal laughed again, looking fondly at the big man. "Tactfully eloquent as always, I see. I've missed you."

Silva grinned back at the one-armed Impie. "Same here. Try to get through this ruckus without stringin' any more parts o' yerself around, wilya?"

"Indeed I shall."

Ker-noll Jash and his Slashers had been camped several miles from New Sofesshk, in the safety of the forest. They'd seen the shocking night raid over the Old City and been furious, but also baffled by its latter stages. Then came even stranger reports of signals received, and Jash formed his division at once, even before it was entirely clear that somehow the enemy had actually put *troops* in Old Sofesshk. With the dawn, he practically whipped his Slashers through the dense forest and emerged at its edge bordering the ruins of New Sofesshk—just as Eighth General Alk began his moronic daylight assault across the city.

Alk obviously hoped to reach the river and cross it on

a few hastily gathered galleys and attack the mysterious enemy force in Old Sofesshk—a force of utterly unknown strength and disposition. The move was under concentrated air attack from the start and it only got worse as it proceeded. Warriors were slaughtered in droves as they swarmed through the debris of the broken city, but the worst by far came while they waited, bunched up in the open, to board galleys that were shredded before them. Jash had seen battles of all sorts now, but this senseless disaster was born of nothing short of abject incompetence and that nameless feeling that invaded one's being, just short of turning a warrior into prey. And like cornered prey, Alk was just lashing out, sensing that doing nothing would be worse. *Better that he'd simply turned prey entirely and run shrieking into the woods,* Jash thought bitterly. Even as the shattered survivors were still dribbling back to the forest, Jash took charge.

The first thing he did was round up Alk's remaining shell-shocked troops, feed them (mostly with the bodies of their comrades, of course), and see that the lightly wounded were tended by his healers. Counting those with fight left in them brought his own strength to nearly thirteen thousand. He then sent runners to contact every other ker-noll in the area, discovering three, along with twenty-two thousand more mixed troops. Roughly half were New Army; the rest were Uul. Proclaiming himself in command, in the name of Second General Ign, he summoned them to join him.

"Trouble," Ker-noll Naxa growled under his breath, pointing to the west with his snout.

Eighth General Alk was stalking toward them, followed by a large entourage.

"What's the meaning of this?" Alk snarled, stopping in front of Jash. "Who do you think you are? How *dare* you proclaim yourself commander here?" He'd watched his assault under the shade of the trees, as he believed all good generals should, but the only sensible order Jash observed was when he sent foraging parties into the smoldering abattoir to claim the "rations" his attack became. Jash turned to regard him with a quiet calm, the burned-meat aroma of Alk's genius filling his flaring nostrils.

"It's quite simple, Lord General," Jash stated. "I'm First Ker-noll Jash and I bear a direct commission from Second General Ign to defend the Celestial Mother at any cost, against any threat. Having seen that you're incapable of doing so, I'm assuming command."

"Seize this jumped-up hatchling!" Alk roared incredulously, and Jash swept his sword from the scabbard at his side and opened Alk's belly from pubic bone to throat in one swift stroke. The general only stared, stunned, as coils of his intestines dropped to the ground at his feet. Then *he* dropped, screaming, trying to stuff his guts back in the bloody gash. Ker-noll Naxa stepped forward without a word and drove his bayonet into Alk's eye, nailing his head to the ground.

"Now," Jash continued casually, glancing at the sky as if nothing had happened, "I'm told we can expect a storm. That may give us a respite from the flying machines, but the weather can't help before nightfall at the earliest. As you've seen, another daylight crossing would be madness, so storm or not, we make our next attempt tonight. That leaves us all the rest of the day to prepare. We'll gather every warrior"—he glanced contemptuously at Alk's corpse—"that's left, and stage as much transport nearby as we can." He blinked at Alk's stunned entourage. "Will that be a problem?"

"Ahh . . . no," replied one of the Firsts of One Hundred. Most of the others seemed just as willing to please, but three, wearing red and black slash mark devices Jash hadn't seen before on their iron and leather armor, stood a little apart. "The gathering will commence at once," the First assured, his voice gaining strength, "but transport will be even more difficult now."

"We have those," Jash said, pointing at the dark hulks of the greatships still moored in the river. Only the tops of their casemates and tall, smoking funnels could be seen beyond the rubble of the city. "And there may be more upriver at Lake Nalak. Send inquiries at once, by pennant. Whether there are or not, we can bring these inshore after dark and board."

"They draw too much water to dock across the river, ah, Lord First Ker-noll, and the docks here are too congested with wrecks," another of Alk's former staff members informed him.

"Then the transports will ferry our warriors to the greatships, and some to shore, under cover of darkness and the greatship's guns. We'll count a great deal on those guns, in fact."

The staff officer hesitated. "How many warriors do you mean to take?"

"Possibly thirty thousand."

There were gasps and the staff officer's eyes went wide. "It will be most difficult to pack that many on two ships even as large as those, particularly if you desire them to participate with their guns," he objected.

Jash snorted impatiently. "I said 'ferry.' Did you not hear? There will only be a few thousand on them at any given time."

"You also said 'some' warriors, Lord First Ker-noll," stated another, far older ker-noll, who'd nevertheless accepted Jash's leadership.

Jash nodded. "Yes," he agreed cryptically. "Many will cross from the greatships to shore . . . by other means." He looked around. "Now, is there an airship nearby— anything I might use to send a more reliable, detailed message than pennants are capable of?"

Another of Alk's staff flattened his crest. "Two of First General Esshk's black airships usually lie concealed in the forest a few miles away, but one was with Second General Ign. The pennants report he already sent it to First General Esshk to inform him of events unfolding here. I . . . strongly urge you not to reveal the other in daylight."

"So Second General Ign already knows," Jash mused.

"By pennant," the staff officer reminded unnecessarily.

Jash huffed and looked at Naxa. "You'll stand by to take the last airship to General Ign at my command. That may be tonight . . . or later," he added vaguely. "If there is a storm, your mission may be hazardous, but pennants and mirrored lights will be useless. You'll carry the latest intelligence we gather and acquire any more you can along the way. Ign may have great need of it by then." He nodded across the river. "I suspect this is only the first of many inconveniences the enemy has planned for us."

"I have no doubt," one of the warriors wearing the slash device agreed, lingering after the rest scattered to perform the tasks Jash assigned.

"Who are you?" Jash asked, and pointed his snout at the slashes. "What is that? It's nonstandard. A new device?"

There'd been no standard badges of rank, or even official flags, in all the Gharrichk'k Empire until recently. Still, Jash thought he'd learned all the accepted emblems.

"'First Ker-noll' is also new," the warrior replied. "I'm First of One Hundred Sagat, in service to Lord Regent Champion First General Esshk." His tone was touched with the slightest hint of insolence and he drew a claw across the painted slashes. "These mean I'm *Dorrighsti*, and belong directly to Esshk."

"As do we all," Jash snapped, "and through him, the Giver of Life." He paused. "Ah, I see. You're in the garrison across the river, part of Esshk's personal guard."

"I am, and I brought word of the invasion." Much older than Jash, with a tall, broad crest, Sagat looked appraisingly at the younger warrior. "You've taken much upon yourself, First Ker-noll."

"That may be," Jash agreed coldly, "but you already failed *your* duty."

Sagat seemed to accept that and the insolence vanished. He spoke earnestly instead. "The Giver of Life must *not* fall into the claws of the prey!"

"I've sworn to protect her."

"And I'm sure you'll do your best. But what if she's taken?"

Jash looked at Sagat and blinked, bewildered. "Then I'll take her back." His eyes narrowed, suspicion forming. "*I* will do my duty," he snapped, then turned and stalked away, shouting for runners.

"As will I," Sagat murmured, and went to join his two comrades waiting for him by the trees.

CHAPTER 28

////// *Palace of Vanished Gods*

*D*uring the hour after all Chack's officers and Silva returned to the HQ, some went on to their units and discreetly started pulling them back from their covering positions around the palace. Only snipers remained to keep Grik heads down and cover the movement. This was aided by a methodical but frugal mortar barrage. Chack had hoped to capture a few Grik cannon, but there weren't any in Old Sofesshk. If there ever had been, they must've been moved to the front. And the only cannon of any sort they'd brought with them was a pair of mountain howitzers, their main parts—tube, carriage, and wheels—disassembled and dropped separately. All had been found, as well as most of their ammunition, but they had another, specific purpose.

As soon as it was confirmed that the fallback had begun, Chack merely nodded and turned to the comm-'Cat. "Send 'Execute Claam Bake,'" he said. Then he, Silva, Lawrence, and several others—Moe and Silva's "platoon" was gone now, reabsorbed by their units—went outside to watch the show.

It took almost another hour. The storm building off the east coast had remained stationary—fine for now, but slow storms often become strong ones—and the sky in that direction had taken a dark, purplish tinge. The sky overhead remained a bright, hot yellow blue, however, and eventually dark little dots began to fleck it, coming from the southeast. Lots of dots.

"Must be every Nancy we have," Silva observed, squinting his one eye.

"Almost," Chack confirmed. "And a few Fleashooters. The rest stay on alert. We know the Grik still haave a few of Muri-naame's planes."

"I guess," Silva reflected, "but what about fuel? They can't burn the same shit Grik zeps do. Not good, anyway. An' they can't have many bullets left. Prob'ly savin' 'em up for some surprise o' their own. Hopefully, we'll make 'em use 'em stupid."

"Hopefully."

Silva grunted, looking at Lawrence. The Sa'aaran's left arm remained in a sling but he held a Baalkpan Arsenal copy of a 1911 Colt in his right hand. He could move his injured arm enough to reload it. "I sure wish ol' Gunny Horn was here," Silva muttered wistfully. Unspoken was a collective wish that Risa, Simy Gutfeld, I'joorka—too many to list—were along as well. "He'll be sorry he missed this."

"No he 'on't," Lawrence denied adamantly. "*He's* not a dun-ass. And he's doing a crucial task in *Sa'oie*, training crews to her great guns." He eyed Silva. "As *you* should too. Lots greater things you should do than this."

Silva rolled a layer of sweaty grime off his wrists and frowned. "Nah," he said. "Maybe you're right about Arnie, but I reckon I'm doin' what I'm best at. An' killin' Griks is about the most important thing I can do—for me."

"Whaat'll you do if you ever haave to stop?" Chack asked, genuinely curious.

Silva looked skeptical and waved that away. "There'll *always* be Griks that need killin'," he predicted, "but even if there ain't, I can kill Doms. That's pretty fun too, if you recall."

Chack blinked distaste. "I didn't enjoy thaat. Some Doms are baad as Grik, maybe worse, but some are just people. I *don't* enjoy killing people."

"An' then there's them damn Leaguers," Silva continued, ignoring Chack and warming to his subject. "*Lots* o' them need killin'." He shrugged. "Look, maybe I'd be useful in *Savoie*, or trainin' gunners for *Walker*'s new sisters." He nodded at the Allin-Silva rifles held by some of the troops around them. "Hell, I'm pretty good at comin' up with stuff to kill things with. But I'm at my very best"—he hesitated uncertainly—"my . . . *safest*, when I'm killin' whoever Captain Reddy points me at. Let him figger out if they need it or not." He looked at Chack. "Ever'body hates this war, an' I get it. I hate like hell what it does to people I care about. But . . ." He shrugged helplessly. "It's kinda like Mr. Cook said about jumpin' out o' the plane. It's like that fer me ever' time I go in a fight, an' honest to God, I never had so much fun in my life." He looked down. "Never been on the right *side* so much or done so much good . . . Just by doin' what comes natural," he added more softly, then took a long breath. "I *ain't* a good guy, Chackie. Not by nature. But as long as there's this here war, an' the skipper shows me the way, I *can* be, see?"

The flight of Nancys was diving now, a long string of them aiming directly at the palace.

"Don't know *what* I'll do if the war ever ends," Silva continued distractedly, watching. "Go off by myself an' kill boogers for a livin', I guess. Won't be fit to be around decent folk, an' that's a fact," he added gloomily.

Pairs of large bombs, the biggest Nancys could carry, dropped from each little floatplane as it pulled up and away. The first impacted on the palace itself, exploding with a bright orange ball of flame that gushed down the massive structure. The other hit in front of the entrance, washing fire across dozens of Grik. Many jumped up and danced in the flames, the macabre movements punctuated by hideous shrieks. But that was only the start. Bomb after bomb fell remorselessly to build the conflagration into a live thing that convulsed and swirled and consumed all other life beneath it. It seemed impossible anything could survive, even inside the palace, but there'd been underground tunnels and vents beneath the Celestial Palace on Madagascar. They could only hope the same applied here. It made sense. The Grik didn't always get along with each other, and they'd always used fire in war as well. So those inside *should* be protected and have provisions for ventilation. At least that was the theory. If the new Celestial Mother got cooked, they'd deal with that when the time came. It might eliminate a few options, but wouldn't materially affect their plan—in the short term.

The last bombs fell among flames already dying. The gasoline and gimpra sap that filled them would set fire to just about anything flammable but was quickly consumed when dispersed. Within the perimeter established around the palace, there was little other than bodies to burn. Smoldering Grik rolled on the ground, wailed and reeled drunkenly, or staggered through the desolation. Small whumps were heard and bubbles of white smoke appeared when cartridge boxes cooked off. Chack was blinking horror at the scene, as were many others, yet he waited only a short while before he stood. 'Cats, Impies, and Khonashi all tied moistened bandannas around their faces. Those enclosing the long, toothy snouts of the Grik-like Khonashi looked like feed bags for horses.

"Attack!" Chack roared. His order carried around the perimeter, repeated by yells and whistles.

Silva stood and helped Lawrence to his feet. "Hope you been polishin' your Grikish!" he shouted with a grin. "Might hafta do some talkin'!"

"Let's go," Chack urged them impatiently as his Raiders started vaulting the low wall and began their sprint. Silva adjusted the Doom Stomper slung across his back, glanced at his Thompson to make sure the bolt was back, then nodded. Lawrence released the slide on his .45, chambering a round. Together with the troops around them, they dashed into hell.

Nothing could prepare them for the scene they beheld as they met the enemy breastworks, and certainly not for how many Grik, scorched and in agony, still managed to fight. Charred, smoking apparitions rose up and met the Raiders' charge with a ragged volley and fixed bayonets. Most were almost helpless—eyes blind and streaming, chests heaving as they gasped or coughed uncontrollably— but many had somehow escaped serious injury and fought like maniacs.

A couple dozen Raiders fell to that first, ill-aimed volley, but the Grik had no time to reload. Allin-Silvas crack-

led, their big slugs blowing Grik back, and Blitzerbug
SMGs stuttered continuously, sweeping all before them.
Across the breastworks they poured, slackening rifle fire
replaced by bayonets. Blitzers, pistols, and Silva's Thompson still clattered in short bursts, but otherwise the fighting turned to steel on steel.

And the smell! Hot smoke scorched Silva's lungs, even
through his bandanna, but the stench of burned fuel,
cooked flesh, crisped feathery fur, and voided bowels
nearly made him retch. He deflected a weakly thrust bayonet with the barrel of his Thompson and fired three rounds
into the Grik that aimed it. "Larry!" he croaked, "to your
right!" Lawrence spun and shot at a healthy but unarmed
Grik, leaping at him with teeth and claws. Its head jerked
twice in midair and it collapsed at his feet. Chack was using
the bayonet on his Krag, the trusty rifle already empty.
Lawrence's pistol popped twice more; then he paused to
eject the empty magazine and insert the next, ready in his
left hand. Two Grik went for him while he was distracted.
Silva killed one, but then the Thompson was empty. He
swung the heavy weapon against the side of the other
Grik's head, knocking it aside with a crunch of breaking
jaw. Lawrence dropped the slide on his fresh mag and shot
the reeling, smoldering Grik.

"Goddamn!" Silva roared as razor-sharp claws raked
down the back of his left shoulder. He spun to swing the
Thompson like a club again, but Chack was already driving his long bayonet into the enemy's chest. It squalled
hoarsely until blood spewed from its mouth. Silva nodded
thanks at his friend and reloaded his weapon. "Need my
cutlass an' pistol for this," he shouted, but he wasn't about
to drop the Thompson. With the Doom Stomper already
slung, trying to do the same with the heavy SMG would
leave him too clumsy to fight with anything.

"Should'a not take that stu'id Doon Stonker to this,"
Lawrence scolded, emptying his own pistol again. "Is useless!"

"You brung *that*," Silva shouted back, nodding at the
long-barreled flintlock pistol bouncing from its hook on
Lawrence's belt. Of all Silva's weapons, that one had
really been more a trophy than anything, and he'd finally

discarded it. Yet Lawrence, who'd never been sentimental about "things," retrieved and kept it for some reason. Silva doubted it was even loaded. "An' you never know," he continued, loosing a burst at a group of Grik that had some of their guys at a disadvantage. "We may be here awhile. The ol' Doom Stomper's come in mighty handy before." He peered through the drifting tendrils of white and black smoke, eyes burning and fuzzy with tears. "Heads up!" he bellowed. "Fresh lizards comin' outa the chute!"

Uninjured Grik were rushing from the arched palace entrance. All were yelling their own defiant cries. "God-*damn*!" Silva exclaimed, almost admiringly, emptying his Thompson again, firing into the pack. "They're fightin' like fiends!"

"Of course they are!" Chack replied. The new Grik were dressed and armored more richly than the others, but carried only spears. "I bet those're paalace guards. But all these Grik've been protecting their Celestial Mother! Their living *Maker* on this world!"

Enough Raiders with Blitzerbugs had gathered near the opening that the initial fearless charge quickly collapsed under a fusillade of lead. But more came, deliberately or accidentally late, bolting out while their enemies reloaded. Their spears found a few victims, but then they turned into spinning, rolling, leaping machines of death, teeth and claws combined with astonishingly acrobatic moves reminiscent of demonstrations Silva once saw in China. They too were soon shot down, but not before killing or crippling three times their number.

"Sonovabitch," Silva gasped, reloading his Thompson again and pointing it at a few Grik squirming on the charred, blood-spattered paving stones. Abruptly, there were no more dangerous Grik nearby and the firing around the palace had diminished to an intermittent patter. "Thank God *all* Griks don't fight like that!"

"Indeed," Major Jindal agreed, suddenly joining them in the smoke. His eyes were running, like the rest of theirs, and his sword looked dark and lumpy with drying blood. "Ghastly! Utterly ghastly!" he exclaimed, gazing at the corpses all around. More than a thousand Grik had probably died just in the six or seven acres inside the breastworks on this side of the palace. Who knew how many more surrounded it? Most had been burned alive. A couple hundred Raiders also lay dead or wounded, and the cries of the latter tore his heart. Corps-'Cats were already busy, scattering and helping those they could.

Abel Cook approached with First Sergeant Moe, Sergeant Pokey trailing behind. Abel was walking slow and staring around, eyes haunted. Silva suddenly remembered the kid had been the one in charge of the giant flamethrowers on *Santy Cat.* Cook had lost his helmet and blood coated the side of his face, streaming from a cut near his hairline. He didn't even notice it as he watched a Grik trying to drag itself away, breaths rasping short and rapid, laced with pain. With its plumage burned off, its tail naked, it really did look like a crawling lizard.

"Perhaps . . ." Cook began. "Perhaps we should put them out of their misery."

Silva spat a stream of yellowish tobacco juice on the living corpse. "What for?" he snapped coldly. "They're just Griks."

Abel stiffened before him. "They're living things in pain, that look a great deal like some of my Khonashi," he retorted. "They're certainly related." He turned to Chack. "Do you want any member of our force to see their cousins treated so callously, particularly after Major I'joorka suffered such similar wounds?"

"Khonashi may look like Grik, but they ain't Grik," Silva countered, looking appraisingly at Pokey as if wondering where he fit in. He shook his head, frustrated, then blurted, "An' they didn't kill Risa."

Chack blinked sudden understanding. Despite everything Silva said earlier, he wasn't an indiscriminate killer. He needed to hate those he slew to "enjoy" it. He'd always hated the Grik and their other enemies before for what they'd done, but Risa's death made his hatred more personal—and darker. He'd heard the hint of admiration in his voice for how hard the Grik were fighting, but that came in the heat of battle when his feelings were more normal, for him, and less complicated. With a moment to reflect, the Grik had reverted to vermin in his heart.

"Detail a compaany to baayonet the enemy wounded," Chack ordered Abel, "but be quick about it. The rest of your regiment'll staart clearing bodies and reinforcing the breastworks. Make them as strong as possible." He tried to see across the rivcr through the smoke but it was impossible. With Allied air roving at will, there wasn't much chance of a counterattack now, but that would change after dark. "We've secured the perimeter around the paalace, but once the Grik react with sufficient force, we may not be able to hold it any better thaan the enemy did. We must secure the paalace itself." He nodded at the dead guards that had spilled out. "Clearly, some haave survived inside. So caan we. And we must hurry or our 'prize' might still escape through hidden tunnels."

Abel Cook stepped in front of Chack. "The First North Borno was the least resisted and suffered the fewest casu-alties in the attack," he stated. "I request the honor of leading my regiment into the palace."

Chack blinked compassion at him, then gestured at the arch. "Your request does you honor, but I fear you'll find none in there. Not only do I need the steadfaast courage of your Khon-aashi outside, to guard against the unexpected— there *must* still be Grik in the city—but our objective now is to secure a certain Grik *female*," he reminded delicately. "Even the Khon-aashi segregate their youngest mating-age females until they learn to control the . . . smells and signals they caan send. We know Grik females have the same pow-ers over males." He blinked at Lawrence. "*He* withstood the presence of the old Celestial Mother, but he's also al-most as different from these Grik as you are from me. The Khon-aashi are closer 'cousins,' as you put it. Never haav-ing haad the opportunity to expose them to the caaptive Grik female on Mada-gaas-gar, we caan't predict how they'll reaact."

Abel Cook pursed his lips, but nodded understanding. Chack turned to Silva. "You'll lead the way. Maany of us haave been in the Celestial Paalace on Mada-gaas-gar, but you and Laaw-rence are the only ones who know how they defended it. Your experience will be our guide. Laaw-rence, our only Grik speaker, must stay a bit baack, however."

"I talk Grik," Pokey reminded.

Chack started to object that Pokey would be more affected by Grik females than anyone, but Silva interrupted. "Might be handy to have the brass-pickin' skink along, like a canary in a coal mine. He starts actin' squirrely, we know we're gettin' close. An' there's only one o' him. Should be able to keep him from hurtin' himself or anybody else."

Chack blinked uncertainty—he had no idea what a canary was—but nodded. "Very well, but he must also stay back. Laaw-rence can keep an eye on him."

Silva raised a brow at Lawrence. "I'll miss the little gecko by my side."

"Don't worry," Chack said. "He won't be faar." He blinked irony. "And you'll haave me."

CHAPTER
29

G ettin' pretty ripe around here," General
Pete Alden grumbled with a frown, waving
at the flies buzzing around his face. He was
standing in one of the forward trenches near the river,
staring across the ragged no-man's-land between the Allied line and the closest Grik position a quarter of a mile
away. The oppressive sun was nearing the distant mountains far to the west, but the storm brewing offshore behind him was beginning to spread chaotic wind gusts that
carried the stench of the congested Allied beachhead
past him. "And it ain't all just because we're surrounded
by Grik," he added a little sheepishly.

The Lemurian troops nearby were members of General Taa-leen's "Triple I," or the 1st Battalion, 1st Marine
Regiment, 1st (Galla) Division. They could've added a
fourth I, since they were attached to I Corps under General Muln Rolak. As they had from the very start, some
of the 1st of the 1st's NCOs still carried Krags. They
watched Alden apprehensively because *everyone* was a
little scared of the force of nature they perceived him to
be, but also for what his visit to Taa-Leen—joined by Rolak and XI Corps' General Grisa—implied. Everyone
knew the curtain was about to go up, and they were ready,

but Alden wouldn't be here if the Triple I wasn't going to have a starring role in the show.

"But it is, in a sense," General Muln Rolak denied, his tone almost cheerful. "We haave almost *five corps* ashore, clustered more tightly thaan when we haad fewer troops around Flynn's Lake. One caan haardly take a step outside the works without faalling in a laa-trine. And the relaa-tively dry heat we 'enjoy' here, as opposed to the sodden heat in Indiaa, only intensifies the eff-luv-ium."

"Effluvium." Pete chuckled. "Right. Whatever that means, it sounds appropriate."

Rolak grinned back. "I do miss Mr. Braad-furd and his unusual words. Perhaaps we'll soon be reunited." He gestured almost benignly at the cloud of flies around them, multiplied to an insane degree by the waste and proximity of so many Grik corpses between the lines. Their density had actually driven a few troops mad, but most had gotten used to them. "Ready or not, we couldn't stay here much longer before the aarmy was decimated by disease. Thaat the Aarmy of the Republic haas aaccel-erated our plaanned offensive is prob-aably for the best."

"True," Pete agreed, "but a helluva lot'll have to go right for us to see Courtney." A little trepidation crept into his gruff voice. "We've put it all on the line. The whole Army of the Republic's running loose, without supply. Chack's Brigade jumped right down the Super Lizard's throat, and now we've got to do exactly what we *hope* the Grik are expecting, and try to bash through the thickest part of their line. This ain't gonna be a cakewalk," he warned.

"It will likely be . . . unpleasant," Rolak agreed, gazing out at the river, the glare of the setting sun further distorting the dazzle-painted shapes of USS *James Ellis*, USS *Mahan*, and USS *Fitzhugh Gray*. USS *Walker* was still a dingy, rust-streaked light gray, and the newly—finally— arrived Republic monitors, RRPS *Ancus* and *Servius,* were a rusty off-white, with fanciful sea serpents painted along their waterlines and around their round, boxy turrets. They looked a little ridiculous to Pete, but were tough customers with big guns. Des-Ron 10, composed of USS

Bowles, *Saak-Fas*, *Clark*, *Kas-Ra-Ar*, and *Ramic-Sa-Ar*, all with their new guns and armor, completed the naval-bombardment element.

The only things Pete really missed on the water were the two additional brand-new tin cans, diverted from their sea trials but still in the Java Sea, and *Savoie*, of course. *Savoie* could steam, and even without fully integrated fire control for her main battery, she'd still be a monster firing in local control. But Matt was reluctant to deplete her magazines or risk her and her extremely inexperienced crew. Besides, things were suddenly happening much too fast to wait for her—or anything else.

Pete took a deep breath. "Let's just hope General Faan can do his part in the south, and for Chack's sake, Safir can do hers," he groused.

"General Faan will aaccomplish his mission," General Grisa assured. He was a mild-mannered Lemurian, most recently under Safir Maraan's command, but now he had VI Corps after its Sularan commander was sacked for basically goofing off in Indiaa. There was suspicion he'd been up to a great deal more of benefit to his fractious island Home—and himself—at the expense of the new Union. "Nor should you worry about General Queen Safir Maraan aaccomplishing hers," he added loyally.

Rolak blinked concern mixed with frustration. "No," he agreed, "and I do not. My queen—for thaat's whaat all Aryaalans now consider her—will complete her aassignment if she reaches her objective. I haave no doubt. My only reservations concern the safety of her traansports, and"—he paused, tail swishing—"thaat in the heat of baattle she might press *beyond* her goal. She's done thaat before, you may recaall," he added wryly.

Pete stuck a PIG-cig in his mouth and lit it, sucking the acrid smoke. He'd heard there was real tobacco in the NUS, but who knew when he'd taste any? And this stuff didn't even make him cough anymore. "Yeah, well, this time it might be okay if Safir *does* run a little wild," he said thoughtfully. He looked at Taa-Leen. "Everything ready on your end?"

Taa-Leen nodded and absently stroked the facial fur he'd cultivated into something like the braided mustaches

Imperial officers wore. He'd become friends with General James Blair back when they were both untested lieutenants, and besides the mustache, he'd taken on a few of the Imperial's mannerisms as well. "Of course, Gener-aal," Taa-Leen said. "Some squaads are aarmed entirely with Blitzerbug sub-maa-chine guns, but each haas at least one Blitzer and one shotgun. And every *Maa-reen* com-paany haas one of the wondrous maa-chine guns on the new wheeled carts." *His emphasis on "Maa-reen" makes it clear he considers that unfair,* Pete thought. *Tough. We ain't got enough to go around.* "And every comp-aany haas its own mortar section," Taa-Leen continued. "Finaally, as you ordered, each soldier and Maa-reen in the Galla Division haas three days' raations and three hundred rounds of aammunition." Taa-Leen paused, blinking curiosity. "They're to carry *nothing* else?" He glanced significantly to the east. "Not even blaankets or rain gear? No tents?"

"They can take a poncho," Pete relented, "so long as I don't see anybody hunkered down under one, or flapping around while they're trying to fight. They won't need blankets or tents. If the rain comes, it'll ruin the Grik's ammo but won't hurt ours and we'll push even faster and harder. Either way, everybody'll be too busy for pitching tents and sacking out for the next few days." He frowned. "They better be," he growled.

Nodding, Taa-Leen passed the revised order to an orderly, who scampered away.

The sun finally touched the distant mountains and the gloom gathered fast. A squadron of Nancys flew over from the east, then banked south, swooping low over the thinning Grik in front of III and XII Corps. "Gotta bomb there too, from time to time," Pete explained. "Their general's too sharp. If we hit 'em in the south too hard, he might get to thinking, but if we leave 'em completely alone, he'll be sure we got something headed that way. Can't have that," he added softly. "We need to drag as much as he can move over here in front of us"—he nodded out at the water—"and under Captain Reddy's guns."

"Not to mention in front of *them*," Rolak said, looking behind them. Long after the Nancys' engines faded, other engines could still be heard. To cover them, Nat Hardee had brought three of his MTBs close to shore, revving their own loud, twin six-cylinder motors as if daring Grik artillery to shoot at them. One gun did, missing badly, its roundshot skating far out over the water, and the MTBs popped a few light mortars back, just as ineffectively, from tubes erected in front of the MGs on their fo'c'sles. What they were really doing, however, was covering the advance of eight lumbering iron monsters, creeping up a sunken road prepared specifically for them. Ten more did the same, a little farther up the line.

"Yeah," Pete agreed. "Chack's gonna hate that he missed this." Chack had taken the Alliance's first four "tanks" into battle on Zanzibar. They'd been little more than armored boxes protecting what reminded Pete of the engine, drive train, and tracks of the first bulldozer he ever saw, except the tracks were bigger and the engine was in back. The armor had been riveted together in such a way that the things looked like turtles with a pair of small sponsons for machine guns slightly inset in the "shell" above the tracks. Two had survived the attack on Zanzibar and were actually here, but they were too slow to keep up with this newer model, which was supposed to be able to make a whopping eight to ten miles an hour. The older pair were assigned to General Faan. "I don't know how Chairman Letts got 'em built and shipped so fast, especially after they got canceled, but Chack's report must've helped."

Rolak coughed. "Don't be ridiculous, Gener-aal Aalden! It's obvious Chair-maan Letts never stopped their development, 'caan-celled' or not, for not only are they here sooner thaan would otherwise be possible, they're better thaan the prototypes in every way!"

They'd immediately noticed improvements in the first few additions that arrived even before the invasion, and more kept coming on the heavy-hauler transports, one or two at a time. The new machines were still only about sixteen feet long and ten feet wide, and used the same big water-cooled 6-cylinder engine as their predecessors and MTBs. They *looked* pretty much identical, in fact. But their suspension and tracks had been improved in various ways and they were a couple of feet taller and carried slightly heavier armor. More significantly, they could get up and move their approximately seven tons twice as fast. Lemurians' burgeoning understanding of geared-head engine lathes and advancements in reduction-gear technology required by the new steam-turbine ship engines allowed them to bless these machines with a transmission, clutch, three forward gears, and one reverse. For the first time, they could finally harness more of the abundant—for their size—horsepower the engines were capable of. Just as important, they were expected to be more reliable and they were better armed.

The Mk-II *Grikoshai* or "Grik Smusher" required a crew of four, though five Lemurians were small enough to squeeze inside. That made them the ideal operators, since an extra 'Cat could help keep all the weapons loaded and serve as a relief driver. (Scuttlebutt had it that driving a Smusher was physically exhausting.) At a glance, they kind of reminded Pete of the interwar British Mk-II, and maybe a little of the US M-3, except the now-welded armor was more sloped in places and should—hopefully—better deflect Grik shot. There was no cannon yet, something Chack suggested, because the new 25 mm guns—loosely based on the Japanese Type 96—were still in development and there wasn't enough room inside for anything larger. But in addition to the two .30-cal machine guns on either side of the crew compartment, mounted in smaller, cleverer sponsons that weren't only more recessed, but allowed a wider arc of fire, the commander now had a small round turret on top. It mounted a *.50-cal* machine gun, slightly offset, so the commander could squeeze down the hatch between it and its big ammo can. The turret itself was pretty light, supposedly only proof against a square hit from a Grik 9 pdr, but it rode on roller bearings, with angle lips to keep it from being knocked *off* by a Grik 9 pdr, and was easy to manually traverse.

"Well," Pete replied, "I'm glad for it, if he did." The engines started cutting off, 'Cat commanders shouting down below over the din. Pete was somewhat grateful for the strong odor of rich exhaust washing over him, momentarily covering the reek of the beachhead.

"Indeed," Rolak agreed. "Chaar-maan Letts waas never the greatest soldier or sailor, though to his great credit, he served his time. But he's been the indispensaable person when it comes to meeting the needs of our forces."

"Damn straight." Pete nodded. He glanced at his watch, the hands barely visible in the deepening gloom. "About an hour yet," he murmured. "Lizards'll be surprised by that, at least. They don't like to fight at night."

"No," Taa-Leen said, "but they're better at it thaan they were. And why should they be surprised? We almost always attaack in the daark."

"Yeah, but in the dark before the *dawn*." Pete snorted. "That's gotten to be almost as universal on this world as it was on my old one, so hittin' 'em all-out, right after dusk, ought to add to their confusion."

"Hopefully enough to counter-aact our own," Rolak observed dryly, then waved to the northwest. "And I fear whoever they send against Chack may think the same. Reconai-saance confirms another contingent of unknown size aassembling at the edge of the great forest bordering the city, south of the river."

"When did you hear that?" Pete asked.

"On my waay to join you here," Rolak answered. "They'll be bombed, of course, but most of our air power will soon be focused on other things. Or grounded," he added gloomily, flicking his eyes to the east. "The enemy doesn't know thaat yet, but obviously knows he caan only cross the river in the daark."

"Chack knows too," Pete said with certainty in his voice, but blinking worry in the Lemurian way.

"And haas been reminded by raadio, I aassure you," Rolak stated mildly. "He won't be taken unaware."

"Little guy's been through a lot," Pete reflected, then snorted. "So's Silva, whether he knows it or not. Things're bound to be heaping up on both of them."

Rolak blinked agreement, tail now swishing more sedately. "True." He looked at Pete, now blinking irony. "In . . . a few smaall ways, those two often remind me of younger versions of you and I. *Much* younger, in my case," he added, blinking amusement. "Yet though I doubt they could do whaat you and I haave done with such laarge forces at our disposal, I also doubt either of us could've prevailed in vaarious situations they've found themselves in."

He unexpectedly raised his voice so even the Marines around them could hear. "All will be well with them," he declared, "as all will be well with us. Reconai-saance also reports more Grik shifting from the south to face us here." He chuckled at the nervous blinking, then added, "Which might ordinaarily be caause for concern."

Uneasy laughter followed his understatement, but Rolak's voice rose higher, harsher. "In this case, however, the more Grik we summon to die before us, the greater will be our share of glory!"

Pete blinked. Whether he personally still believed in it or not, Muln Rolak was probably the only Lemurian alive who could stir his troops with promises of something like glory.

"And we will *slaaughter* them, my brothers and sisters!" Rolak proclaimed with utter conviction, eyes bright and tail lashing. He waved around. "Even in this time of profound change, we cling to the faamily of claans. Thaat's good. And thaat those claans grow ever laarger is better still. You Maa-reens belong to the Amer-i-caan Navy Claan. Others belong to the Homes, the 'States' of Aryaal, Baalkpan, B'mbaado—maany others—but all are now joined together in the *Union Claan* of the United Homes or within the Graand Alliaance. We're *all* claan brothers and sisters," he roared, "and all here upon this field shaall be remembered as such until the final setting of the sun!" He waved at the Grik. "They know nothing of the force that binds us, drives us, and caan't *imaagine* whaat they've brought upon themselves."

Barks and yips of approval threatened to drown him out and Rolak raised both hands. "The will of the Maker of All Things shaall be done tonight and in the days to come," he bellowed, "and forlorn with shame will be aany you know who waasn't among us to see it through!"

The intensity of the answering cheer made Pete a little uneasy. *Then again,* he realized, *the Grik know we're coming—and we're about to make a lot more noise.*

"That sounded kinda familiar," Pete shouted with a

grin, even as Rolak's words were repeated and waves of cheering thundered along the trench line, taken up by thousands of throats.

"It should," Rolak yelled back. "The inspiration came from a book from your world. Readings Courtney Braadfurd once suggested from *Waa-kur*'s library. The essence of it seemed appropriate now."

Pete remembered the book, from long-dead Doc Stevens's collection. "You ought to run for chairman someday. Everybody here'll remember this as long as they live."

Rolak shook his head and blinked disinterest. "I already hold the only civiliaan office I desire: Protector to Queen Safir Maraan. I doubt I'll live thaat long, in any case. You forget," he reminded, without the slightest hint of regret, "I owe my life to Cap-i-taan Reddy, and suspect he'll still need it before all is done." He nodded back at the cheering troops. "No, I'll be fortune-aate if aany remember my name one day, but the flavor of the words I borrowed are timeless and unbounded by worlds. If they remember *them*, I'll be content."

CHAPTER
30

C ap-i-taan on the bridge!" Minnie called loudly.
"As you were," Matt hastily responded,
walking to his chair. He'd been gone only a
moment, to the head. "Must be something I ate," he
added under his breath, but if anyone heard they made no
sign. *Strain, more likely,* he confessed honestly to himself.
Worry, tension, anxiety, fear . . . He took a deep breath.
Fear? Hell, it's terror, he conceded. "Has Commander
Miyata returned to his ship?" he asked.

"Aye, sir," Chief Quartermaster Paddy Rosen answered,
looking resentfully out at the normally sparkling white
whaleboat hooking on alongside USS *Fitzhugh Gray.* In the
low light, the boat looked more like a capering gray silver-
fish trying to climb some kind of freak, geometrically blem-
ished sea monster. "Can't believe that Jap bastard thought
you'd leave *Walker* for *his* fat tub," Rosen ventured. But he
quickly added, "Sorry, sir. That was out of line."

He was right, but Matt was tempted to let it slide. Old
feelings died hard and lingered longer when somebody
else tried to beat them to death. Matt knew Rosen—most
of the old hands—actually trusted and respected Toru
Miyata, but even many 'Cats hadn't been excited to see a
former enemy given their new cruiser.

Still, Matt suspected Rosen's outrage had more to do

with Miyata's perfectly reasonable suggestion that Matt shift his flag to *Gray* during the operation, than with the fact he was Japanese. The cruiser was bigger, more powerful, and better protected after all. But she didn't have any better comm gear than *Walker*, and that's what really mattered. There'd never been any danger Matt would go anywhere other than where he belonged, and Rosen should've known. Besides, this would be Miyata's first action commanding his new ship. He'd be nervous enough without the Commander in Chief of All Allied Forces hanging over his shoulder.

"Put yourself on report at the end of your watch," Matt ordered sternly. As quartermaster, recording such things in the log was Rosen's duty, but he was also *Walker*'s best helmsman. In these restricted waters, in the dark, it might be a while before he was relieved. "That 'Jap' is not only an officer in the American Navy Clan; he's also your superior!" Matt continued relentlessly. "You'll show him the respect he's due or I'll transfer you off this ship so fast, your head'll spin smooth off. Is that absolutely clear?"

"Aye, aye, Captain. Won't happen again," Rosen promised sincerely, straightening behind the big brass wheel. Discreet chitters came from some of the 'Cats, loudest on the port bridgewing around the torpedo director, but Matt figured he'd made his point.

He leaned back in his chair, outwardly satisfied, but his insides roiled tight once more. *Sure Miyata's nervous,* he almost laughed to himself, *but I've never been this scared in my life,* he realized. *Not even when Kurokawa had Sandra—or I faced that crazy damn* professional assassin *with a* sword *on the imperial dueling grounds!*

The first came the closest, but even then his fear for his wife and unborn child had been slightly tempered, pushed back, by how busy he'd made himself directly preparing the operation, then by the frenzy of the action itself. And, frankly, he'd somewhat steeled himself to discover Sandra already dead, perhaps even killed in bombings he'd ordered. So there'd been a distracting measure of hot, furious anticipation over the prospect of finally, specifically, *personally* going after Kurokawa, once and for all.

The dueling ground was another matter. He'd been

physically afraid then, at least at first. That was notable because it was one of the few times he'd ever been more than fleetingly gripped by such a . . . selfish fear. *Probably all the pomp leading up to it,* he suspected, *and it passed as soon as the fight got started, like fear always seems to.* But that had still been a very personal contest and it haunted him on occasion. Much more than his own life had been at stake, but things probably would've turned out about the same for his people and friends in the long run, even if he died. *So, third in line to this,* he accepted, *even if it's a* distant *third. But now . . .*

He felt sick, and tried to distract himself with all that was right and ready. *Sandra's safe on* Big Sal. *Five entire corps, almost* eighty thousand *combat troops,* he realized with a little awe, *are as prepared as we can make them. Maybe seventy-five thousand Repubs are pushing north to join us. What's maybe half a million Grik—give or take a quarter million,* he added sardonically—*compared to that?*

General Grisa's got Sixth Corps now. The troops are green but Grisa isn't, and he'll back Rolak's First Corps in the main push west. And talk about experience! First Corps has the longest-serving units in the Allied Expeditionary Force. Pete's big hammer'll have plenty of muscle swinging it. As for the rest, Faan-Ma-Maar has never been in the spotlight, but he and his Third Corps might be the most quietly competent troops we've got. And I'm sure he'll get the best out of Twelfth Corps and its untested Austraalans, despite their having only rifle-muskets. He smiled slightly. *Faan'll have Colonel Saachic's First Cavalry Brigade as well. These Grik may've heard of Repub horse cavalry in the south, but I'd love to watch their reaction to a bunch of wild-ass Maa-ni-los swooping down on top of me-naaks!*

He frowned. *Safir wasn't happy with splitting Second Corps, and that's understandable, but we just can't move it all—and we need backup for Rolak's and Faan's assaults. Besides, regardless of its size, Second Corps is still beat-up. Except for Safir's Third Division—which she'll lead herself, of course,* he thought with concerned irritation, *Second Corps is the obvious choice for a reserve.*

Staring out at the darkness, he sighed heavily, racking

his brain for any last-minute detail he might add to save lives and increase the chances of success. Nothing came to him, and he blinked dissatisfaction. *So, why am I so apprehensive?*

"Got the jitters?" Spanky asked lowly, stepping up and standing by Matt's chair. "I know I do," he admitted.

Matt snorted. "Why do I find that hard to believe? Next to maybe Chief Gray, you're the most levelheaded human I ever knew." He cocked his head. "Well, Silva's up there, I guess, though I don't think 'levelheaded's' the right description."

Spanky barked a laugh. "No. Neither is 'cool under fire,' 'cause he burns hotter than a cuttin' torch. I'd say 'focused,' but that ain't right either. Sometimes that maniac has the attention span of a three-year-old. Maybe he's just too stupid to be afraid."

Matt shook his head. "You know better than that. He just doesn't worry about the big stuff—because he's got us to do it for him."

"Maybe," Spanky granted, "but what's got me is, well . . ." He paused and shrugged. "Talk about 'big stuff,' this is *it*. We're goin' for all the marbles this time." He shook his head in frustration. "Which is fine—we have to—but it eats me that with everything goin' on, here *we* sit, wallowin' on our asses, nothin' more than glorified artillery support while the whole damn war gets decided over there." He tipped his helmet toward shore. Matt hadn't ordered general quarters yet, but everyone was ready.

"We'll be in it soon," Matt countered. "The Grik still have a lot of ships past the Neckbone." He pursed his lips, then confessed, "But I know what you mean." He wasn't confiding any secrets to Spanky; his XO knew him too well. "I once kind of promised myself I'd stay out of planning Pete's battles, for good reason, but here I went and did it anyway for what might be the biggest battle we'll ever fight in the west."

"Now, wait a minute," Spanky objected, "you may've drawn the big picture, but it was Pete an' Safir an' ol' Rolak who colored it. It's their plan as much as yours."

Matt shook his head. "No, not the way it matters." His philosophy had always been that responsibility rolled uphill, not down. "And if it all goes in the crapper this time"—he waved out at the darkened shore—"just *think* how many of those kids out there'll die because of me," he added miserably. "Not to mention we'll probably lose it all," he continued. "No way we'll ever be this strong compared to the Grik again. Oh, we'll have a few years," he said bitterly, "but it'll all be a retreat, a rear-guard action, doomed to fail in the end—unless I do finally dump that killer kudzu on the Grik, and risk spreading it all over Africa. Wouldn't that be a helluva thing!"

"Stuff might not even thrive here," Spanky reminded. "Courtney ain't sure it will."

"But it might. And I *will* use it if I have to. But that's beside the point. We'll still have lost too much."

Spanky's voice, low enough that he hoped he couldn't be overheard, turned angry and took on a new intensity. "Quit this shit, sir. You got no right."

Matt looked at him, surprised.

"So what if it is your plan? Pete went for it, and he wouldn't have if he thought it was boneheaded." He shrugged. "Maybe he didn't *like* it. Hell, nobody could. It's a helluva risk! But him and Rolak are the experts, and didn't come up with anything better, so here we are. And it's a damn good thing we were almost ready or the Repubs'd get smashed for sure. As it is, we have a chance. Probably the only one we'll ever have," he agreed, "but we wouldn't have it at all if you hadn't stuck your neck out." He snorted. "We would'a all been dead within days of windin' up on this screwy world if you weren't the man you are, with the courage to make the plans you do an' then carry 'em out!" he hissed forcefully. "So, cut this crap, an' be more like that dope Silva for a change." He managed a grin. "The big plan's already rollin', no matter who cooked it up. Nothin' anybody can do about it now—except our jobs—an' all you have to do is fight your ships."

Matt nodded ruefully. "Thanks for the pep talk, Spanky." Then he chuckled. "You sounded just like Sandra, except for your ugly voice."

"Wasn't a pep talk, Skipper. It was a chewin' out."

Matt laughed out loud. "So even more like what Sandra would've done."

"Well," Spanky muttered, a little uncomfortably now, "somebody had to do it, and you needed it." He lowered his voice to a whisper once more. "And I'm scared enough for both of us."

Matt glanced at his watch in the dim red light in the pilothouse. "Sound general quarters," he ordered. "Time to assume our positions." Corporal Neely, standing by Minnie, waited for her to open the shipwide circuit, then blew the familiar notes on his bugle. Almost immediately the reports started rolling in, and Minnie quickly announced, "All stations maanned an' ready!"

"Very well. Call the anchor detail and stand by to get underway." Outside, Chief Bosun Jeek rushed out on the fo'c'sle, blowing his bosun's pipe. Just a couple of hundred yards away, the Republic monitors were already moving, their ungainly low-slung forms following a pair of MTBs closer to the Neckbone. The monitors wore the heaviest armor of any ship in the little fleet and carried the biggest guns—eight inchers—but those guns were twenty years old, based on technology from an even earlier generation, and had the shortest range. They'd fire at their highest elevation to drop shells on the southernmost Grik defenses about four miles away, while comm-'Cats acted as spotters for the rest of the ships.

"All ahead slow, right standard rudder," Matt called when the anchor rattled aboard and was secured to the billboard. *Gray*, *Ellie*, *Mahan*, *Bowles*, *Saak-Fas*, *Clark*, *Kas-Ra-Ar*, and *Ramic-Sa-Ar* fell in behind *Walker* as she followed two more MTBs in a circle to starboard, retreating as far as they could in the river. They couldn't gain enough distance for plunging fire, but even slightly higher trajectories would help a little. Once they took their pre-calculated positions and anchored again against the steady river flow that stabilized their orientation, the six guard MTBs accelerated east, roaring toward the Neckbone. They'd been posted near hazardous underwater wrecks—*Santa Catalina*'s mangled corpse remained obvious and was marked with smudge pots—but now they'd sweep beyond the treacherous river bend to warn against approaching Grik warships. Tiny targets in the dark, each bearing a pair of Baalkpan Armory MK-6 torpedoes, they'd also engage their much-larger opponents if any drew near. They couldn't risk the Neckbone getting blocked again.

The thundering drone of engines, many engines, soon became apparent over the wheeze of the blower behind the pilothouse, and Matt looked back at his watch. "Good old Ben and Walt," he said. "Right on time."

"The Clippers," Spanky observed. "Every last one we've got, all with a full load of bombs. Ground crews've sure been earnin' their pay. I heard Cecil Dixon is ops officer for all the Army-Navy Air Corps in the west now. Guy was wasted just wrenching for the Third Pursuit, and Ben still had to practically hold him down and cram a commission down his throat." He stood quietly and listened for a moment. "They're flyin' lower than usual," he fretted, "but high enough the antiair mortars shouldn't get 'em. Can't hit the forward Grik trenches, though."

"No, but they'll raise hell behind them and light the way for the Fleashooters and Nancys."

"And as soon as they're clear, *we'll* light things up." Spanky nodded.

There was no warning; they heard no wail of falling bombs, but bright, greedy balls of flame started marching across the Grik positions in front of I and VI Corps on the south side of the Zambezi. On and on it went, as the incendiaries—some as large as five hundred pounds—roiled skyward in greasy orange toadstools, blowing Grik and their works apart and splashing gushing, roaring, burning fuel in thc trenches. They could barely hear the *whump*ing bursts—they weren't particularly loud—but Matt imagined he could hear the teakettle screech of hundreds or thousands of burning Grik. He could only be thankful that, in air power at least, the Allies had always enjoyed an advantage and now seemed virtually unopposed.

"We damn sure learned our lesson after Pearl, Cavite, and all the hell after, Skipper," Spanky said quietly, apparently mirroring his thoughts. The nightmarish helplessness they'd felt in that old war on another world when their enemy controlled the sky still haunted those left to remember. But that very experience was why Matt pushed so hard, so early, to get his new people in the air. It had paid off all along, but maybe never better than now. "*Jeez,*" Spanky continued, "if we could do that to the whole Grik line all night, instead of just in front of Pete, we'd burn every damn Grik over there!"

It certainly looked that way, but Matt knew better. "Well, we can't, and it wouldn't anyway. But focusing our attack where they expect it should bring more of them running. Either way though, our people will still have to go and kill them."

Their loads expended, the big Clippers rumbled away, and ten or fifteen minutes passed while the leaping flames they left continued their work, detonating magazines and ammunition chests, and searing Grik. Yet even as the flames finally began to subside and the first stunned Grik probably started raising their heads, the Nancys of the 1st, 8th, and reconstituted 5th Naval Air Wings stooped on their prey. This attack combined common bombs with incendiaries, to "plow the earth and burn the chaff," as Mark Leedom put it, though only about half the planes hit the same area as before. The rest split off to attack all around the perimeter and the flashes they made were smaller, their placement more dispersed, as pilots sought specifically appointed targets. This went on for quite a while and the Grik managed to knock a few planes down with antiair mortars, but there was little real response until the air attack began to wane.

That's when Grik cannon started firing. Chances were they hadn't even been ordered to open up; they just did. Not even the best-trained Grik could sit idly for long under the hell they'd just endured without trying to hit back. What started with a few scattered shots built into a general bombardment all around the Grik line, and exploding shells crackled indiscriminately across the Allied position.

"See?" Matt said simply. "One thing those Grik've learned is how to dig in tighter than a tick. Maybe they don't have an air force to speak of anymore, but they've moved up a helluva lot of guns and protected them well." He turned around in his chair and looked at Minnie. "Send to all ships: Stand by to engage assigned targets. Load and hold."

"Ay, ay, Cap-i-taan. Comm-aander Tikker sends 'All planes're clear.'"

"Very well. Acknowledge." He turned back to watch the number-one gun on the fo'c'sle train out slightly to port, muzzle rising as 'Cats on the "bicycle" seats on either side spun their wheels to match pointers with the solution sent by the gun director above the pilothouse. They'd ranged the enemy trenches very carefully over the past few weeks. "Mr. Caam-peti reports, 'On taarget!'" Minnie cried.

"What's the status of the rest of our ships?" Matt asked impatiently.

"All but *Graay* and *Bowles* report they on taarget!"

That was to be expected. The cruiser's crew was still inexperienced and probably overexcited. As for *Bowles*, Matt was surprised she was the only converted DD to lag. Their crews were still adjusting to firing much more sophisticated weapons. And their primary mission was protecting the heavy haulers assembling behind them during the second phase of the operation.

Hundreds of tongues of flame suddenly blasted outward from the Allied position onshore as 'Cat, human, and Khonashi artillerymen also got the word the sky was clear. Pete had assembled almost four hundred guns, including quite a few older 6 pdrs scraped up from as far away as Madraas. And he had a fair number of heavier naval guns off the converted DDs as well. Still, the vast majority were 12 pdr "Napoleons," which had been the best standard field piece the Allies had until the Repubs joined the fight, being relatively light and mobile and sufficiently accurate for the ranges at which they usually engaged the Grik. And their case shot reigned supreme, until the Grik caught on and made their own. Matt had hoped they'd get some of the Repub's breechloading Derby guns, similar to the French 75, or they'd be able to field their own light breechloader by now, but there'd been other priorities and things came to a head too fast. Regardless of their obsolescence, the 12 pdrs were still good guns, and their crews remained better than their Grik counterparts. More importantly, they were well protected from the Grik iron flailing for them in the night and they'd amassed an impressive ammunition reserve. The return bombardment they unleashed—joined by hundreds of mortars—would've dwarfed the Grik fire even before the air attack mauled and rattled the enemy.

"All ships now report 'On taarget,'" Minnie finally amended.

"Very well. Stand by." Matt looked at his watch one last time and suddenly realized he wasn't afraid anymore. He took a deep breath. "Execute," he said firmly. "Commence firing."

Within seconds of each other, twenty-one 4"-50s, six 5.5"s, and eight 8" guns stabbed their sharp jets of flame at the night, and thunder and overpressure—particularly from *Gray*, close astern of *Walker*—was like something barely remembered. It took Matt's breath away. The bright jets quickly turned to yellow balls, rapidly fading to brown, but unprotected eyes would keep afterimages of the nearly instantaneous event for quite a while. Shells shrieked downrange, flaring tracer compounds drawing orange-red arcing lines to their targets. Stuttering flashes, brighter, bigger than the snapping case shot of the field guns, lit the Grik positions. Earth vomited into the air, silhouetted by lingering fires started by the bombing.

"On target, on target!" Matt heard Sonny Campeti shouting above. "Rapid salvo fire! Commence firing!" The salvo alarm, silent the first time, dully rang somewhat guiltily against the aft bulkhead. *Wham! Wham! Wham!*

"*Mahan*'s really puttin' 'em out," Spanky observed with respect, looking aft. Like Miyata's, this was *Mahan*'s young female Lemurian skipper's first action in command. "So's *Ellie*," Spanky continued. "Wow! *Gray*'s slower to load her bag guns, but damn, does she light up!" He spun to watch the fall of her shot. The effect was twice that of *Walker*'s, and the dispersion was tight. Matt was pleased. They'd all feared *Fitzhugh Gray* had been a waste of time and resources. Maybe not.

Wham! Walker jolted again, and Matt watched her latest salvo streak away. He leaned forward in his chair, expectant, content. His old ship had joined the fight again and his fear had turned to something else—that sometimes worried him later.

CHAPTER 31

Palace of Vanished Gods

reathlessly, Major Jindal and a platoon of Impie Marines joined Chack and Silva's company of Raiders where they were taking a moment to rest and tend the wounded in a large, blood-splashed chamber only one level up from the entryway. The space was dank and gloomy, lit by guttering, reeking, fish-oil lamps set in alcoves in the walls, but it was large enough to serve as an auditorium. Maybe it did, or had. And just like in the Celestial Palace on Madagascar, there weren't any decorations; no sculptures, tapestries, or panoplies like one might expect in a similarly large chamber used by any of the Allies. Even the Khonashi decorated their strange living abodes with imaginative limb weaving. Here, except for the occasional rusty bracket that might've once supported something, there was nothing but naked, dripping stone.

And though not quite as massive as its counterpart at Grik City, the Palace of Vanished Gods was still immense. Its external shape implied internal solidity—like the cowflop it actually vaguely resembled—but hid a vast interior honeycombed with confusing passageways and odd chambers, large and small. Grik corpses littered the stone floor in this one, as did a number of 'Cats', the latter being covered with their oilcloth ponchos and arranged along one wall. Obviously, not all the specially trained

Grik guards had sortied earlier, and the fight here had been as brutal as it was somewhat unexpected.

"We've got the lower level, and access to the tunnels," Jindal gasped. "Quite a maze down there. I sent squads down each tunnel to discover the exits and a means of blocking them. We must assume the enemy knows where they are."

"Find any poodledragons?" Silva asked, holding his left arm out while a corps-'Cat wrapped a bandage around a jagged claw slash extending from elbow to wrist.

Jindal grimaced, remembering the bizarre, frightening predators the Grik unleashed in the Celestial Palace. "No, thank God. Perhaps they're native to Madagascar. Can't imagine trying to transport one!" He coughed. "I say, it's damned close in here. And what little air can be had is . . . quite unpleasant!"

"That's Jindal-ese for 'The joint stinks to high heaven,'" Silva explained to the corps-'Cat. He looked back at the Impie. "Yer just outa shape, is all. Spent too much time m'lingerin' in the hospital an' lost yer wind." He inhaled deeply. "Smells like flowery clover in here!"

Some of the troops muttered, the consensus favoring Jindal's assessment.

"It smells like shit and blood and death," Chack retorted, not in the mood for Silva just then. Not with dead comrades on the floor. "We must press on. This haas already taken longer thaan expected, and it's getting daark outside. We must secure this place and prepare to defend it."

"I saw they'd already torn most of the wall down and contracted the breastworks to defend only the west side of the palace," Jindal supplied. "Took a quick peek outside on my way here," he explained.

"Good," Chack said. "Mr. Cook's been busy. It was foolish of the Grik to defend more than thaat. The paalace can't be scaled by anyone encumbered with weapons. It's too steep and slick. I don't think we need worry about whaat the Grik do behind us."

Silva started to point out that Grik *always* had the weapons they were born with, but Chack was aware.

"Oh, by the way," Jindal added, "Mr. Cook emplaced the howitzers as well, but so far there's been no enemy interest in us. Even their battleships seem content to brood at anchor."

"Thaat'll change tonight," Chack insisted.

"No doubt."

"Take chaarge here, Major," Chack instructed. "This'll be the raally point for any reinforcements we require and the collection point for wounded. See thaat ammunition and supplies remaining outside are assembled here as well." He pointed back the way Jindal came. "There's only one way in from the lower levels"—he nodded at the dark stairway at the opposite end of the chamber—"and one from above. There may be other paassages between the upper and lower levels, but only two we must defend here. This'll be our fall-baack strongpoint."

"Aye, aye, Colonel," Jindal agreed.

Chack looked at Silva, the corps-'Cat's bandaging complete. "Are you ready?"

Silva unslung the heavy Doom Stomper and handed it to one of Jindal's Impie troopers, along with the bandolier of huge shells it fired. "Take care o' thaat," he instructed. "Gentle, like a broad. Don't get no blood er goo on it either."

Wide-eyed, the Impie looked at Jindal, obviously afraid of the responsibility and the possibility of incurring Silva's wrath. Under the circumstances, Jindal was amused and somewhat heartened that the trooper was more afraid of Silva than their situation. He smiled and nodded back. "Your weapon will be well cared for," he assured.

"Then I'm ready," Silva said, patting the refilled magazine pouches on his belt. "Let's go a-huntin'."

Chack checked his Krag. "Laaw-rence, you and Sergeant Pokey are with me. Blitzers and shotguns to the front. Do *not* use grenades in the stairwell," he reminded, and managed a faint remnant of one of his trademark, carefree grins of old at Silva. "Aafter you."

The first stairway was a narrow, switchback affair, barely wide enough to take three abreast, and the ancient steps were smooth, rounded, and very slick. Nothing met them in the near-total darkness at first, but then a flurry of crossbow bolts whickered past, their iron points striking sparks off the stone walls. A 'Cat beside Silva screamed and fell back against others pressing behind and the advance was thrown into confusion. Silva fired a burst from his Thompson, and another 'Cat's Blitzer stuttered. Bullets clattered up the passageway, ricocheting off rock and striking flesh amid howls and shrieks of invisible Grik. "At 'em, fellas!" Silva roared and the column surged forward, upward.

"A light!" someone called.

"No light!" Chack instantly countered, blinded enough by the muzzle flashes. Torches would only make it worse, and make them better targets besides.

"Empty!" Silva shouted, letting 'Cats wriggle past and keep firing while he and the first rank reloaded. They turned another corner into more crossbow bolts, falling 'Cats lit by bursts of fire going wild. More Raiders rushed around the corner and fired up the stairs, Blitzers punctuated by the dull, smoky boom of an Allin-Silva shotgun. Desperate shrieks echoed down the passageway and Grik bodies followed, tumbling down the stairs and crashing into the attackers. A couple weren't dead, and lashed out wildly with swords and claws.

Silva pushed forward again, but a claw hooked his calf above his leggings. "Jesus!" he snarled, instinctively firing a short burst down at the dark, grasping shape, hoping he wouldn't shoot himself in the foot or bounce a bullet into somebody. The form thrashed and lay still, only to be trampled by following Raiders that carried Silva along, starting to yell with rage and mounting frustration toward the seemingly endless confines they fought in. At another switchback, Silva slipped on something slick and spongy and fell to his knees. Pressure from behind pushed him down on another reeking Grik, its belly torn open by several hits, his free hand sinking down, down, until he felt ribs. "Shit!" he bellowed. "Gimme a break! Ease up back there or you'll trample me an' half our own guys to death!"

The Raiders ignored him, surging past against another torrent of crossbow bolts, and then meeting a charge of sword- and spear-whirling Grik. The advance dissolved into flash-lit kaleidoscopic images of shooting, stabbing, slashing shapes. If Lemurians shared one genuine phobia as a species, it was of tight, enclosed spaces, and while Chack's Raiders would never run from a fight, this was turning into a special nightmare and they'd go forward against any threat or obstacle to clear this tangled, hellish passageway. A crossbow bolt *thunk*ed into the stock of Silva's Thompson. He was trying to hold it up and away from the gore he wallowed in, and the bolt hit with almost enough force to wrench the weapon from his grasp. Off balance, he dropped full length into the heap of offal.

"Yick! Dammit! I'm gonna kick somebody's ass!" he thundered when sandaled feet ran across his back, pushing him farther into the congealing slush. Suddenly, strong hands grabbed him, helping him up.

"This is no place for a naap," Chack chastised, his voice falsely cheerful and edged with the same nervousness growing in the cries of his troops.

"Yah, well, tell that to your Raiders. Little bastards ran me down. Never seen anybody so panicked to run *to* a fight!"

Blitzers rattled ahead, around another turn, followed by the stuttering crash of several grenades. At the same time, Silva realized he could see slightly better. There must finally be another lighted chamber ahead.

"So'thing stinks," Lawrence declared, snout rising, questing.

"No shit. I'm covered with Grik guts," Silva snapped at his Sa'aaran friend.

"No," Lawrence denied. "Stinks . . . di'rent."

"I think the scent is . . . good," Pokey murmured dreamily, eyes unfocused, and Silva glared at him.

"Right. I think the canary just croaked. Time to get his ass outa here." Without warning, Pokey lunged forward. "Whoa! Somebody grab him!" Several Raiders tried, but Pokey struggled loose, actually slashing one with his claws. Leaping over some wounded 'Cats, he bolted up the stairs.

"Stop Sergeant Pokey!" Chack ordered as they raced after the friendly Grik. "Don't hurt him if you caan help it, but stop him!"

Turning the corner and topping the stairs, they saw there was indeed another large chamber, full of struggling forms. The floor was littered with bodies, probably killed by grenades, but more Grik were pouring in through a passage at the far end. And these were "special" Grik like they'd fought under the entrance arch. They came on, fighting wildly and well, oblivious to losses. And they'd closed so rapidly and ferociously, nobody could shoot without hitting a friend.

"Shit!" Silva groaned, dropping his Thompson and whipping out his cutlass just in time to slam the heavy blade crossways into a gaping mouth about to close on his face. The blade sank deep, severing the bottom jaw and stopping in the muscle behind the neckbone. The Grik dropped, and Silva yanked the cutlass free. Chack was fighting with his Krag, bashing swords and spears aside and thrusting with the bayonet. Lawrence dropped his cutlass in favor of his 1911. With only one good arm he couldn't use both, and he started judiciously shooting when only enemies were behind his target. *Good idea,* Silva grudged. Hacking down another Grik, he pulled his own .45 and fired two shots, as fast as he could, at a Grik trying to spear him low. Another leaped high, a sword in each hand, but a Blitzer from the stairway caught him in midair and he crashed on top of Chack, taking him down in a tangle. Three Grik went after Chack while he tried to heave the body off and reclaim his rifle. Silva took them from behind, shooting one in the back of the head and severing the spine of another with a backhand chop. The last raised its spear to pin Chack, and Silva slammed into it, taking it to the floor, his cutlass already protruding from its chest. Gurgling and blowing blood, it reached around and slashed his left arm again even as he jammed his pistol against the side of its head and blew its brains out its right eye socket.

"Look out!" Lawrence screeched.

Silva rolled—too late—and a Grik pinned him to the corpse with a sword.

Even through the searing pain, Silva knew the hit wasn't too bad, only piercing the flesh along his ribs. He pointed his pistol but it was empty, the slide locked back. His cutlass was still jammed in the pincushion Grik that held him transfixed like a bug, and there was no time to draw Captain Reddy's Colt or the '03 bayonet. Lawrence couldn't shoot without hitting him too, and Chack was fumbling for his own 1911. He'd never get it out either.

Somehow, the Grik sensed it had all the time in the world—an entire second, maybe two—and instead of simply jerking its sword free and stabbing quickly down again, it twisted the blade. Grinding his teeth together, Silva rolled violently to his left. With searing agony, the flesh parted, and the Grik's head exploded when Lawrence's pistol went *Pop! Pop! Pop!*

"*Lawsy*, that smarts," Silva hissed through clenched teeth as he stood, jamming his hand against his side. The fighting had surged toward the far opening and several Raiders were suddenly around them, helping Chack up and looking at them. "Right on time, you buncha dopes," Silva snapped sarcastically. "One o' you, fish my sticker outa that lizard, wilya?" He glanced at Lawrence, who was awkwardly reloading his pistol with shaking hands. Instead of the crack that first came to mind, similar to what he'd said to the 'Cats, he managed a grin. "Thanks, little buddy. Save my ass five, six hundred more times, we'll be even."

"Us e'en now," Lawrence replied, his voice shaky as well, "counting tines you nearly get I killed."

"I'd thaank you both," Chack said, blinking rapidly at the red stain spreading down Silva's side, "but we're beyond the necessity of saying such things now, I think." He blinked more rapidly as the blood started pooling by Silva's boondocker. "Go baack where we left Major Jindaal. Get paatched up."

Silva shook his head and raised his eyebrow at Lawrence. "Not this time, Chackie. I never made it to the Sequesteral Mammy's digs at Grik City, an' only Larry an' that goat wit Isak lived ta tell the tale. This time I'm goin' all the way, so you might as well get a corps-'Cat to plug my leak. I've had worse than this from Pam."

"You two fight too much," Chack scolded.

Silva's grin turned beatific. "Who said anything about fightin'? Gal's got sharp fingernails!" He looked around, really noticing their surroundings for the first time, and realized they'd finally discovered a room with decorations, of a sort. "I'll be derned. Look at that!" There were tapestries on the walls, actually woven of metal. Probably the only reason they'd survived, since they looked absolutely ancient. A corps-'Cat cut Silva's shirt off even as the three friends moved to study one of the wall coverings in the low yellow light.

Some of the thread was gold, obviously, since it hadn't tarnished, but there was black and green thread as well, probably corroded silver and copper. It was impossible to tell what kind of scene or design might've been depicted, since the gold had been used to accent shapes, not form them, but the quality of the weave was finer than they expected of Grik, even though their textiles had never been lacking. Courtney once proposed that they must've had looms for millennia. And they'd seen decorative—if garish—objects made by Grik, so some artistic talent existed among them. It just never occurred to anybody they'd find something like this.

More expected, appropriate to the setting, and certainly contributing to the bizarre nature of the find, was the addition of hundreds of skulls crudely hooked into the tapestries, obscuring them even further. Skulls as decoration they'd seen before, but these represented such a wild variety of creatures—large, small, recent, ancient, vaguely familiar, and utterly unknown—that they almost had to be a catalog of some kind, a collection or index of known species. That some were arranged by likeness seemed to confirm that. Still, though many of the skulls were very old, even yellowed with age, none rivaled the age of the tapestry damaged to mount them, and Chack couldn't shake the feeling they'd desecrated it—whatever it was—in some way. "Courtney would be amazed," he breathed, blinking amazement of his own. Then he shook his head. "Will be, someday. Now we have work to finish."

He looked at Silva. The corps-'Cat had quickly stitched his wound, smeared it with the curative polta paste, and bound an absorbent bandage to his torso with strips of clean linen. "Are you ready?" he asked.

"Rarin' ta go."

With nods of acceptance for whatever was to come, the three friends retrieved and checked their weapons and followed in the wake of the battle.

They hadn't gone far up the steeply ascending passage-way when they heard the fighting reach a crescendo—then silence. Moving faster, they were met by a huffing 'Cat, who stopped in front of them and saluted Chack. "Sur, we got . . . a sitty-ay-shin."

"Well, Corpor-aal?"

"We found it—her—I mean, the Grik high chief!" the Raider gushed, blinking with pride.

"Where?"

"A couple chambers baack. As ordered, we din't kill her, but we ain't actually *got* her yet. She haas guards bigger'n any Grik I ever saaw!"

"Her sisters," Lawrence stated.

The Raider blinked questioningly at him, then lashed his tail and shrugged. "Whaatever. They's holed up wit nowhere to go, but my lieuten-aant says get you. Don't see how we gonna get her wit'out maybe killin' her. All the regu-laar Griks is dead, but those laast guards is *big*," he repeated, "an' look ready to keep fightin'."

"Did you catch Sergeant Pokey?" Silva asked. The 'Cat blinked annoyance. "Ay, but he's goin' nuts! Haard to hold wit'out hurtin' him. He scraatched up some o' my paals pretty baad."

Chack looked at Lawrence. "How do *you* feel?" he asked.

"Kinda odd," Lawrence conceded, "'ut okay. I not going nuts," he snorted.

"I wonder why all them Griks we killed defendin' the joint didn't lose it?" Silva suddenly speculated. "I mean, they ain't no whole different breed like you, Larry. Dif-ferenter than a Peekin-ese from a coonhound. We'll say you're the coonhound," he granted graciously aside to Lawrence, to everyone's confusion. "But these're just regu-lar lizards to look at. Maybe scarier than average fighters, but nothin' else. Why didn't *they* go nuts like Pokey?"

"Perhaaps we'll learn thaat at our destination," Chack replied impatiently. "Lead on, Corpor-aal."

CHAPTER 32

////// *Tassanna's Toehold*
South bank of the Zambezi River

G eneral of the Armies and Marines Pete Alden had never seen anything like the barrage that flailed the Grik positions. The effect of four hundred field guns and the Lord knew how many mortars was impressive enough, but add in the naval bombardment, and the land across the space between the two armies seemed to buck and thrash to the fireworks-inspired gyrations of a miles-long Chinese dragon. Regardless of Pete's position, and in spite of all the action he'd seen on this world, he'd never been in anything beyond a few brushfire scraps before he came here. And the closest things to this he'd seen was the fighting around Flynn's Lake and the Rocky Gap in Indiaa—yet those actions paled in terms of scale. He imagined Billy Flynn had seen something like this in France, in the Great War, but Flynn was dead and nobody else on this world probably ever had.

And the Grik return fire had been terrifying and damaging as well, at first. They had almost as many guns, most even bigger, but no matter how much their gunners improved, they still weren't up to the standards of Pete's veterans and those they trained. Hundreds of shells exploded in and over his trenches, heaving dirt, bodies, and supporting timbers in the air. Limber chests and some small "ready" magazines they'd scattered and protected as best they could detonated here and there, blowing craters in the earth or scything gun's crews down. Hundreds, maybe many more, were surely killed back behind the line, but the Grik reply to the stupendous pounding Pete and Captain Reddy unleashed—in the wake of the Air Corps' concentrated attack—was relatively short and increasingly sporadic.

Part of the reason was a lucky wind. It remained confused, blowing harder, but for now it betrayed the Grik. Their gun flashes were clearly distinct from the case shot exploding over them, and sometimes whole Allied batteries brought a single gun under fire, hammering its crew and the area around it until the gun was wrecked and nothing nearby could live. Then they engaged another. Slowly, surely, the return fire ebbed. And still the bombardment continued.

Pete looked at his watch, the explosions reflecting off the clouds like lightning to reveal the face. "Five minutes!" he yelled, the words rushing outward in the packed forward trenches while he turned to look at the tankers standing in the open hatches of their vehicles. He energetically waved them forward. They'd restarted their engines shortly before, the raucous, unmuffled exhaust overwhelmed by the bombardment, but now they roared louder as gears clashed and the first Smushers lurched ahead. Pete, Rolak, Taa-leen, and the staff surrounding them stepped back and saluted the female commander of the first metal monster, and the 'Cat crisply returned the gesture. One after another, the Smushers clanked, rattled, and roared past the commanders of the First Fleet AEF; climbed the earthen ramp prepared for them; and thundered into the wasteland beyond, noisily accelerating and spreading out.

"Ain't it wonderful?" Pete asked emotionally, raising his binoculars to gaze south where the other half of their latest tanks were joining the assault. The bombardment had reached a crescendo, and the mighty crescent of Grik works erupted under the planned final flurry of shells. "The guns and mortars closest to the line'll keep pounding, reaching farther as long as they can," he said, though the plan was fully understood by those around him. "And

Captain Reddy's naval support'll parallel our advance for a time." He looked at the sky, a growing, frenetic drizzle spritzing his face under his helmet. "But the weather's going downhill fast." Strangely, the gloomy words didn't affect his cheerful tone. "I'm afraid we're gonna lose our air support quicker than the Sky Priests said."

"Most likely," Rolak agreed. "But if we move quickly enough, it may not matter. Mud will hinder the enemy as much as we, and rain will be our ally, rendering the enemy's weapons less effective."

"But the chaos of fighting in a strakka . . ." Taa-leen began, blinking concern.

Rolak flashed a predatory grin. "Is whaat Gener-aal Aalden and I haave been praying for," he stated definitively. "The Grik haave built a proper aarmy of real soldiers," he conceded, "yet they've writhed in the fires of Chik-aash already. They'll be hurt, demoralized, and afraid, and haave no idea whaat's coming. More important, they still laack the essential elements to make them *proper* soldiers, equal to ours."

Taa-leen blinked questioningly.

"Experience and motivation," Rolak said. "Our troops are used to chaotic baattles, they know their objectives, *and*," he stressed, "they know why they fight. Some of those Grik haave tasted the first, but their only real 'cause is survi-vaal. Fear not, all will be well."

Pete hoped Rolak was right. "If we break through," he cautioned, glancing irritably at a tardy Smusher—their last—just starting to climb the berm. The rest, all seventeen, were roaring full-out across the rough, putrid, corpse-strewn ground. At ten miles per hour, they'd already crossed a third of the distance to the enemy line and it seemed nobody had even noticed them yet. *The shelling's pushing back, though, and that won't last.* Even as Pete thought that, a Grik cannon snapped and a shell slammed against a Smusher, ricocheting up to explode high in the air. Another fired, then a third. All were shooting case shot, probably what they'd been loaded with, and it shouldn't do much more than ring his tankers' bells. No doubt they'd see how Smushers stood up to solid shot soon enough. Of course, cannon couldn't shoot solid shot and canister at the same time. . . . Pete glanced at his watch and saw almost six minutes had passed, but no matter. The time was now. "Sound general advance!" he shouted.

Talkers yelled in the mouthpieces of their field telephones, whistles shrilled, even drums—still traditional in some units—rattled insistently. With a momentous roar, the thickly packed trenches seemed to convulse as every combatant in First Corps along a two-mile front scrambled up and out in the open, advancing with long, ground-eating strides that would take them across fairly quickly but not leave them exhausted. They knew what to do. These were 1st and 2nd Divisions, flying the proud regimental flags of the 1st and 2nd Maa-ni-la; 5th, 6th, 7th, and 10th Baalkpan; 4th, 6th, and 7th Aryaal; and the Stars and Stripes of the 1st Marines. All were Lemurians and many were veterans. Some had been with their regiments since they were formed and had fought and bled through the most desperate battles of the war. And this night, this battle, was why. They'd have their payoff or die trying.

General Rin-Taaka-Ar had the far left, and General Taa-leen was preparing to lead the right, following his own Triple I as it cleared the trench. There were twenty thousand 'Cats in that first wave, and Pete knew Rolak was right. Every heart and mind among them knew exactly what they were about—as did those who'd follow. Even as the forward trenches emptied, elements of VI Corps started filling it back up, awaiting their turn.

Pete Alden was suddenly distracted from the grim, beautiful purpose of the moment when the Smusher on the berm jerked and died. He supposed it was inevitable they'd have breakdowns and was actually surprised all the other tanks were still going, but his gut told him this wasn't a mechanical failure. Trotting to the tank, he climbed the rungs welded to the back and stepped on the sloping deck over the engine compartment. *It's hot as hell up here,* he realized, watching raindrops sizzle on the steel. He jumped closer to the hatch on the low turret and slapped the commander, who was shouting down below, on his padded leather helmet. It reminded Pete of a tight-fitting football helmet, except the ear holes were higher—and bigger—so ears could actually protrude. The 'Cat spun with a snarl, but blinked terror when he saw who was standing over him.

"What's the problem?" Pete demanded. "Pop the clutch?"

"Aah, ay, sur. We don't get to praac-tice much, aan my driver, she's . . . could be not the best."

Pete heard the distant clatter of machine guns and looked up. The first Smushers were firing on the Grik line now and not a single one had stopped, despite the growing fusillade of musket fire and the attention of a *lot* more heavy guns than Pete hoped would survive the bombardment. He raised his binoculars and saw the dark shadow of I Corps surging like the tide. Some of those troops were already dying, but they weren't shooting yet, and most of the Grik might not even see them. They had a closer, more terrifying concern. "Get this thing started. The war's *that* way," he pointed.

"I *do*!" the tank commander practically wailed, nodding behind them. All the tanks' support crews had followed the column, and a pair of Khonashi had already unclamped the crank and were about to turn the engine over.

"Is your radio up?" he demanded of the 'Cat below him.

"Not with the engine off," the Lemurian replied, careful to avoid sounding like he would've added "idiot" if he was speaking to anyone else. *Next thing we really need to focus on, for everything, is electric starters,* Pete grumbled to himself. *And better batteries, of course. Always better batteries!*

The engine roared to life and the Khonashi hastened to clamp the crank back in place, but Pete was watching the assault again and didn't move. Most of the enemy fire was still directed at the tanks, but more and more was pecking at I Corps. Pete glanced down, impatient with something ill-defined in his mind, and realized Rolak and his staff, even General Taa-leen, who should've already gone with his troops, were staring at him.

"What're you lookin' at?" he demanded over the loudly idling engine.

Rolak made a very human, almost Gallic shrug. "You, Gener-aal," he shouted in reply. "I wonder whaat your intentions are."

Pete was confused, then realized Rolak had known his mind before he did. He grinned and shrugged as well. "Oh, I don't know. Guess maybe I'll tag along this time. Tired of sitting on my ass, watching everyone else fight."

"This aarmy needs its gener-aal," Rolak admonished. "How often haave you told *me* thaat?"

"Pretty often," Pete agreed, "but the army's got you— and you aren't going anywhere." Pete pointed at the light show and leaping earth under the barrage creeping ever onward. First Corps was taking a lot of fire now, but it and the Smushers were dishing it back. "I'll be careful," he promised, "but I have to go—I have to *see*." Suddenly he sounded almost like he was pleading for Rolak's understanding. And with himself.

"It would be silly of you to just walk out there with your rifle," Rolak stated matter-of-factly, and Pete wondered if the old warrior would physically try to stop him if he tried. He patted the turret in front of him. "I'm not walking anywhere. You, what's your name?" he asked the tanker.

"Aah, Sergeant Kaalo!"

"You a better driver than your driver?"

"Yes, sur."

"Then throw her out and take her place." He looked down. "Get up here, Taa-leen! You're a division commander *and* tank commander now! We're goin' into battle in style."

General Taa-leen blinked amazement mixed with horror. His tail dropped limp. "I don't haave the first idea . . ."

"You can shoot a machine gun, can't you?"

"I've been . . . faa-miliarized with one."

"Good. Then get up here. I'll give you a refresher." Pete pointed in the hatch Kaalo just vacated. "You don't think *I'll* fit in there, do you?"

"Whaat *are* you going to do?" Rolak asked, sounding less severe than before.

Pete unslung his Springfield and opened the bolt to check his magazine while Taa-leen scampered onto the tank. Patting his ammo pouches and shaking his canteen, Pete grinned down at Rolak. "I'm gonna hide behind this turret and shoot Grik. I'll meet you at the rally point!"

The rally point was ten miles away, beyond the last Grik strongpoint for the forward defenses, and was considered an ambitious objective for the night's assault. But that was as far as the tanks could go and was where fuel and ammunition would be waiting—if Captain Reddy made it that far upriver.

Taa-leen squeezed down into the turret behind the gun, and the normally stoic 'Cat suddenly grinned back up at Pete like a youngling. "Let's go!"

"Right," Pete shouted down past him. "Let's go, Sergeant Kaalo! I'm all dressed up, the music's playin', an' I wanna cut a rug!" The engine roared and the Smusher rumbled up the berm and into the fight.

"Gener-aal!" cried one of Muln Rolak's aides, pointing. "How caan you let him go? Exposed up there on thaat great, slow taarget, he will surely die!"

"Perhaaps," Rolak agreed, "but it's his choice and he out-raanks me. And he's right: the baattle will go as plaanned or not. If not, there are other plaans I will resort to. I know which ones he would waant."

"But . . . whaat if he's killed?" the aide persisted.

Rolak blinked sternly at him. "Then Gener-aal Aalden will die as a fighting Maa-rine." He paused before continuing, as if to himself. "He's been a good gener-aal of the Army and Maa-rines, though he never waanted the job, any more than Cap-i-taan Reddy waanted *his* responsibilities. But someone haad to do it and no others could at first." Rolak straightened. "Thaat's changed, on laand at least, and Gener-aal Aalden knows it." He blinked extreme weariness and regret, and the dampness around his eyes was only partly due to the rain whipping harder. "This waar will soon end in defeat or glory." He blinked wistfulness and his tail slashed. "So we'll all be dead, or, as Gener-aal Aalden says himself, must 'endure our glory behind a desk for the rest of our lives.'"

"So he'll throw himself away?" the aide demanded hotly.

Rolak blinked admonition. "Of course not! His aact isn't suicidaal, and it's only paartly selfish. He merely . . . senses—as do I," Rolak confessed, "thaat he'll be needed more out there thaan here." He gave the aide a benevolent pat. "Don't worry," he added wryly. "I expect we'll *all* be out there before this is done." He turned away, but called over his shoulder, "And if he lives, I won't let him do it again." *Because it'll be my turn then,* Rolak promised himself. He raised his voice. "Sixth Corps! Prepare to ad-vaance!"

Batteries and springs, Pete thought, adding to the mental list of things the new tanks needed, as he hung on to the handholds welded to the low turret and bounced on the hot deck over the engine compartment. Smushers had big, fat leaf springs under the road-wheel axles, but large spring technology was still new to Lemurians. They were good at the small springs they made thousands of, for firearms, for example, but tended to overdo the big stuff they had less experience with. So Smushers needed *better* springs that wouldn't shake the teeth out of the crew. *And this is over fairly level ground,* Pete thought with growing concern. Up ahead, past the backs of the advancing troops, he saw the first tank about to reach the enemy trench.

"Go! Go! Go!" he urged. Then, to his horror, he watched it slow down. Its gunner/commander was still firing, but the tank was just creeping ahead. "What the hell? No! Gun it!" Pete shouted.

Aerial photographs had shown the Grik trenches weren't very wide in most places. Where they were, mostly around gun emplacements, there were ramps behind them to ease ammo delivery and allow shells landing around them to bound onward, exploding well behind. That probably even worked when the ground was dry and hard. But they'd calculated that their tanks needed to take the trenches at speed. They couldn't jump them, obviously, but needed their tractorlike treads to get a solid bite on the far wall and let their inertia—hopefully—help them crash and gouge their way along. It would be rough as hell, probably even dangerous for those inside the tanks, and those who *did* cross at gun positions might drop three or more bone-jarring feet before crawling up the other side—if they and their machines were able. But what Pete watched now was exactly what they'd all agreed the tankers must *not* do.

It would've been comical if it weren't so tragic. Like a blind armadillo nosing along, the first tank tentatively felt its way to the trench while musket balls *whang*ed off it and a roundshot boomed against its front slope and whistled away. Then, like a diving duck, the nose pitched down and slammed into the bottom of the trench. Grik swarmed it immediately, but another roundshot punched through the deck over the engine, just like where Pete was standing, and probably shattered the carburetor, spewing fuel everywhere. With a wind- and battle-muffled *whump*, the hot engine compartment caught fire. The fuel tanks quickly followed, throwing a red-orange mushroom in the air, and burning Grik fell away.

"Gimme your headset!" Pete roared at Taa-Leen. All the tanks were on the same frequency. The 'Cat fumbled with the unfamiliar device and handed it over. "This is General Alden," Pete shouted into the microphone. "All Smushers, take the trenches at speed! No screwin' around! You can't just dip your toes in 'em. *Charge* over the trenches!" He handed the headset back. "Confirm everybody got that."

Rain or not, the firing was constant now and I Corps troops fell in windrows. They were shooting back but they were in the open, catching absolute hell. These Grik were proper soldiers, no matter what Rolak said. Pete had no idea what they thought they were fighting for, but they damn sure knew how. And unlike the Grik on Zanzibar, the tanks didn't panic them. They drew a lot of fire—they had to be frightening—and somebody over there surely knew what it would mean if they bashed through the line, but the infantry didn't break and run as they'd all hoped.

"Oh, well," Pete muttered to himself. "There's a difference between 'hoped' and 'expected,' and I never figured they'd run."

A Smusher charged through, as ordered, and slammed across the trench. It nearly stalled on the other side, most likely while the driver shook off the blow, but the engine roared and it climbed up and on. Its machine guns spewed tracers down the trench line.

"Yes!" Pete shouted. Another tank bashed its way across. Almost immediately however, a large cannon fired directly into its side from about fifty feet away, dense smoke washing over it. Tracers sparkled around the crew that turned the gun and they all went down, but the tank stopped dead. It didn't explode—there was nothing in the crew compartment that would blow—but it started to burn.

A solid shot banged against the front of Pete's tank and *vroom*ed up, right over his head. Taa-Leen was still standing in the turret and he ducked instinctively. "Stay down there," Pete commanded.

"Whaat about you?" Taa-Leen shouted back.

"I'm fine—right where I wanted to be," Pete replied with rueful sarcasm. "Just tell your machine gunners to spray the flanks when you cross the ditch."

Musket balls spattered against the armor, sharp fragments of lead cutting Pete's face, but he was watching I Corps now. It had been battered and bloodied, particularly as it crossed the last hundred yards or so, entering effective smoothbore range. But nearby cannon were still preoccupied with the tanks, muskets were starting to get wet, and those still shooting fired ill-aimed and poorly coordinated volleys. Only a tithe had been taken from the wave of Lemurians sweeping out of the growing storm behind the mechanical beasts. And nothing could deter or blunt I Corps' deadly purpose as it spilled into the Grik trench.

Pete held on, rocking to and fro as the charge went in. He was fully exposed and couldn't have cared less. What he saw at that moment filled him with so many emotions, he couldn't have described them all. His army was smashing a prepared position full of its most ancient enemy that had dispossessed, harried, and eaten them for longer than their history recalled. And they were doing it with the remorseless, relentless efficiency of a well-oiled machine. Volleys slashed down in the trenches from the front ranks of whole regiments that arrived as close to their preassigned sectors as made no difference. The following ranks threw hundreds of grenades, and Grik were blasted apart by a thundering wave of sleeting iron. Those ranks hurried forward to deliver their own rapid volleys right in the faces of stunned, wounded, shell-shocked Grik. Stabbing fire and sleeting lead mowed defenders down. Machine guns on wheeled carriages clattered and clawed at Grik beyond trying to flee or join their comrades.

Then, with bayonets fixed and a roar full of grim resolve and primal expectation, I Corps waded into the slaughter.

Many were dying, Pete was sadly certain, but it was like the pent-up rage of countless generations had been unleashed and, proper soldiers or not, the Grik had finally goaded their age-old prey into a savagery even they couldn't counter. Pete was overwhelmed with sadness that it had come to this, that his people—as he considered them—had found such brutality within themselves. Yet at the same time he felt a roaring torrent of love and pride, almost a reverence for the army he'd helped make and which was now vindicating all his expectations.

His tank was nearing the trench now, late to the fight, and his gunners had stopped firing because the Triple I was right in front, already shooting and stabbing in the trench. Pete fixed the long bayonet on his '03 Springfield and pounded Taa-Leen to get his attention. "This is my stop," he shouted over the rain and gunfire.

"You must not leave the taank!" Taa-Leen objected.

"You'll *bounce* me off when you cross the trench," Pete replied reasonably. "I'd be lucky to live through it." He pounded on Taa-Leen's shoulder again. "You got this. Keep up the scare and keep the Smushers moving. Don't stop for anything, but don't get too far out in front of your infantry either. You need 'em to keep the Grik off your backs."

"But whaat about you?"

Pete grinned. "I'm borrowin' the First Marines off you for a while. You'll get 'em back."

"Slow down," Taa-Leen called down to Sergeant Kaalo.

"No! Keep goin'." With that, Pete dropped to his butt, slid across the scalding deck over the engine compartment, and hopped to the ground. He meant to absorb the impact with his knees and roll, but landed on a dead 'Cat the left tread had pulped and he slipped, landing hard on his back. The impact smacked his helmet against the back of his neck, but he figured he was luckier than the dead Lemurian. Rising, he jogged toward the trench. His tank had just bashed its way across, almost flopping Taa-Leen out the commander's hatch, but the Lemurian general quickly gathered himself and started plying his machine gun.

"My turn," Pete muttered, and jumped into the nightmare.

The bottom of the trench was layered with torn and shredded bodies, two or three deep in places, tangled with their shattered weapons, implements, and other debris. Moving through it was like wading in brambles growing out of tapioca pudding. 'Cats and Grik were all around, bashing, shoving, stabbing with bayonets, and clubbing with their buttstocks. Teeth slashed and claws raked and rifles boomed and flashed. There was the occasional stutter of a Blitzer. Pete was a spectator for a fortunate instant while he found his footing, but then a cluster of Grik were in front of him, reaching for his torso with their bayonets. He shot one and deftly deflected another's weapon before stabbing with his own. He was rewarded with a squeal, and he kicked the body off his blade. 'Cats to either side shot and stabbed more Grik away, and some started crawling up the back side of the trench, making for the rear at last. None Pete saw had dropped their weapon, however. On the other hand, these particular Grik wouldn't be a problem again, because Taa-Leen's tank had lingered—Pete hoped Kaalo hadn't popped the clutch himself or bashed his brains out crossing the trench—and two machine guns chopped the Grik down. The tracers moved on, probing in short bursts. Roaring and spewing exhaust, the tank lurched on.

Suddenly, there were only a few Grik left, unwilling to flee and fighting like fiends. 'Cats pressed them from the left and they staggered through the mush toward Pete—and the other 'Cats who'd joined him. "Let's get 'em," Pete roared, and promptly slipped on a string of steaming guts, going down in front of the desperate Grik. He tried to bring his rifle up, but the sling snagged on a protruding bone. Something struck his helmet and drove him down, face-to-face with a dying Grik, blood bubbling and streaming from its feebly working jaws. Weapons crashed together right above him. 'Cats and Grik bellowed and screamed.

Finally getting his feet under him, Pete managed to stand—but there were no more Grik. Instead he saw a very large, heavily muscled 'Cat with a vaguely familiar face. Grinning teeth flashed in the dark fur surrounding them. "Is thaat how you 'fight like a Maa-reen'?" the Lemurian asked in a joking, mocking way. "You once told me you were a 'mud treader,' but I find you now like a graawfish grubbing in swaamp slime!"

Pete grinned back, wiping goo from his beard. "I remember you from the parade ground at Baalkpan, back in 'forty-two. You were off *Fristar* Home with a bunch of toughs, shoving the city folk around. Had to kick some of your buddies' asses. Now you're a Marine."

"I *been* a Maa-reen since then," the 'Cat replied, grin fading. "An' those buddies are all dead. All who left *Fristar* with me to fight for you," he amended.

"I'm sorry," Pete snapped, suddenly angry, "but if they were fighting for me, they were idiots."

The big 'Cat's tail whipped behind him, then paused. "Yes," he finally agreed. "If thaat was why. There are better reasons."

"No shit." Pete pointed west. "And right now, they're getting away. No sense letting 'em catch their breath. And if we keep after 'em, *they'll* break the next trench for us!"

The trench was emptying fast, most of I Corps already pressing. Sixth Corps would be on its way. The big 'Cat grinned again. "Then let us fight like Maa-reens together, Gener-aal!"

"You bet, Sergeant . . . whatever your name is. That's why I'm here."

"He's no saar-gent!" someone protested. "He stays in too much trouble!"

"He is one now," Pete countered. "It's a night for troublemakers, so let's go raise some hell!"

Back where he truly belonged at last, surrounded by a cheering company of Marines in the Triple I, General Pete Alden climbed back into the growing musket fire from the next trench and rushed onward.

CHAPTER
33

////// *USS* **Walker**
Zambezi River

Jeez!" Commander Spanky McFarlane shouted over the pounding guns. He was standing in *Walker*'s pilothouse with Captain Reddy, staring at the hellacious battle to port. They'd gotten underway at last and were creeping past the Neckbone. Major obstructions were marked by MTBs and five more scouted ahead, following Nat Hardee's Seven Boat. The rest of the ships proceeded upriver in a long battle line led by *Walker*.

Their fire support wasn't as close as Matt would like; it couldn't be. Their only spotters were fast-moving troops on the ground whose relayed requests might already be out of date by the time the rounds were on the way. And there was no aerial observation. The storm was building fast, especially on the coast where the carriers and Arracca Field were. The Sky Priests in the weather division on *Big Sal* couldn't agree what the storm would do, and Matt couldn't blame them. The Shee-ree had experience with strakkas on Madagascar, mostly flailing the island from the southeast, but nobody had a clue what the vicious storms did to the coast of Africa, running up the strait. Ben Mallory and Keje had reluctantly grounded their planes.

"Now we've got the commander of the whole damn AEF romping through mud and guts on the back of a tank, driven by a division commander!" Spanky continued, slapping the report they'd just received from Rolak against Matt's empty chair.

"What the hell does Pete think he's doing?" Matt fumed. "You'd think he'd know better than to lead attacks himself, at this stage."

Minnie and some of the 'Cats on the bridge had trouble stifling ironic snorts, and Spanky just looked at Matt and shook his head. "You would, wouldn't you? Like you're one to talk!"

Matt dropped in his Captain's chair, shifting uncomfortably despite the embroidered cushion that just appeared there one day. "This is different," he deflected, and Spanky rolled his eyes.

"Contaact!" Minnie cried, mashing one of the headphones to her ear under her helmet. "Seven Boat reports, 'Sur-faace taar-gets, dead ahead.'" She was listening through the TBS receiver, its frequency reserved for task-force chatter. Ed Palmer and his assistants were un-hashing all the radio and CW traffic in the comm shack below. "Three Grik BBs," Minnie said. "They's raisin' aanchor an' gettin' underway! Lieuten-aant Haardee requests permission to make a torpedo attaack!"

"Very well," Matt agreed, "as long as he remains undetected." *He might be able to, with this wind and rain,* he thought. *The river's even starting to whitecap.* It would be a while before the river rose, however, or its flow increased. And then only if the storm pressed inland. "But he'll break off if he's discovered or takes any fire," Matt qualified. "We'll deal with the BBs then. We can't risk Nat's boats. We're running up an unfamiliar river, in the dark, in a storm. His MTBs are the only eyes we have!"

Minnie spoke into her microphone, then said, "Order's received an' understood."

Walker steamed on at five knots, three guns still firing to port, one to starboard. Most of the ships had similarly dispersed their fire, starboard guns hammering shore batteries on the rugged north shore. *Fitzhugh Gray*'s 5.5"s and the Repub monitors' 8" guns remained focused in the vicinity of the third and fourth Grik trench lines, however. They held mostly reserve troops and supplies, but were probably filling with those retreating or rushing to reinforce. *Hitting them now should increase the confusion,* Matt hoped.

Something bumped the hull, bouncing along it as *Walker* passed. Matt assumed it was debris stirred loose from the wrecks in the Neckbone. He steeled himself for the pounding shudder of a screw striking whatever it was, but it didn't happen. He smiled. Perhaps Isak's weird propeller guards had saved them.

"We're through!" came a cry from the lookout on the starboard bridgewing.

"Confirm," Spanky barked.

'Cats had been scurrying back and forth between the bridgewings and the chart table, examining both, but now there came the flash of a Morse lamp on one of the MTBs.

"We're through," Matt breathed before the final word was passed. The river would veer northwest now, broadening and straightening for twenty-five or thirty miles before swinging sharply east, then north and west again. They had a stop to make, but then they'd steam on as fast as they could, for Sofesshk itself.

"Recommend course three four zero," Paddy said. He knew the chart by heart.

"Very well. Make your course three four zero. Maintain speed for now."

"Aye, aye," Paddy replied, staring at the compass binnacle instead of through the rain-lashed windows. "Making my course three four zero."

"Turns for fi' knots," stated the 'Cat at the repeater.

Matt turned to Minnie. "Inform Colonel Will that his division'll land as planned after we get past a few little obstacles first."

"Ay, ay, Cap-i-taan," Minnie said.

Colonel Will commanded a consolidated division of Maroons and Shee-ree. Maroons were descended from human ancestors they had in common with the people of the Empire of the New Britain Isles, and the Shee-ree were a tribe of Lemurians that never fled the Grik. Both had been found in the incredibly hostile wilds of Madagascar where they'd suffered under the occupation of the Grik as semicaptive "sport" prey for bored Grik generals.

They were highly motivated, and their job tonight might be the most dangerous of the entire operation: landing and guarding supplies behind the Grik front lines. That would make them *all* "Maroons," in a sense, and they'd proudly adopted that name for their division after volunteering for the mission.

A flash lit the water off the port bow, then another. Both in turn illuminated rising waterspouts alongside huge, dark forms.

Score one for Nat, Matt thought.

"Three surface targets, designated Grik BBs, bearing three four five. Speed: two knots. Range: four thousand yards!" came Sonny Campeti's voice, shouted down from the fire-control platform above the pilothouse.

Matt glanced briefly at the land battle raging to port and took an anxious breath. *Pete—or Rolak—he snorted—is on his own now. He knows what to do.* It was time for the bombardment element, except for the two Repub monitors, to become Task Force Pile Driver—with its own fight, its own objective.

"Very well," Matt said. "Send this," he told Minnie. "'As soon as all elements are through the Neckbone, the guard MTBs will follow. Task Force Pile Driver will execute a turn to zero three zero in succession and engage the enemy.'" They'd planned very carefully how to fight in the river, maneuvering to get as many ships and guns on target as they could where the river widened. Things might get pricklier in the narrows.

"What's the distance to the northeast shore?" Matt demanded, and the 'Cat at the chart table instantly replied.

"Nine hundreds an' increasing," she barked.

"Helm, commence your turn," Matt told Paddy. "Zero three zero." He looked at Spanky. "Get aft, where you belong."

"Aye, aye, sir," Spanky and Paddy chorused, and Paddy continued, "Making my course zero three zero."

"Six more sur-faace taar-gets!" Minnie reported loudly. "Prob-aable Grik croosers!"

"Acknowledge," Matt shouted back. The torpedoed Grik battlewagon was burning fiercely, listing hard to starboard, but another had bloomed massive fiery flowers as its huge forward guns sent a pair of four-hundred-pound roundshot shrieking toward *Walker*. There was no telling where they went, or if the Grik even saw the old destroyer after she turned and her guns ceased firing, but Matt was quickly reminded that just one of those big balls in the right place could shatter his ship. And TF–Pile Driver faced maybe fifteen more Grik BBs and an equal number of cruisers, according to recon, on the deadly, winding path to its destination.

"Torpedoes, Captain?" Bernard Sandison asked hopefully from the port bridgewing. After all this time, Bernie still sounded like a kid when there was a prospect of firing his beloved fish.

"Not yet. With this crummy visibility, I'd want to be closer than I really want to get, if you know what I mean. And we might need 'em later." He raised his voice. "Have Mr. Campeti commence firing at the Grik BB that shot at us. All other ships'll commence firing at targets they identify as their guns bear!"

Matt spent a final glance on the battle ashore. It looked terrible. He could only hope it was terrible enough to entirely focus the attention of whoever commanded over there. Was it Second General Ign, as Muriname predicted? Or Esshk himself? Whoever it was, Operation Whipsaw ought to be giving him an awful lot to think about just now, and one of the biggest surprises was yet to come.

Sonny Campeti had already been tracking his target. As soon as he got the order to open fire, the salvo buzzer rang and Matt's own focus contracted back down to fighting his task force and his ship.

Gasping, Second General Ign practically collapsed and fell into the third trench line. There were already bodies heaped at the bottom, from the bombing and shelling, and he struggled to rise amid the yielding corpses and soupy slurry of bloody mud beginning to run. He was still strong despite his nearly thirty years, but hadn't actually had to *run* anywhere in more than twenty. It nearly killed him. Of course, he'd already be dead if he hadn't fled the secondary trench and his primary HQ. And he wasn't alone. When the first trench fell, the second quickly filled with those escaping. Somewhat to his surprise, especially considering the speed and ferocity of the enemy attack—on the heels of the terrible bombardment—very few warriors actually turned prey and kept on running. But he'd felt something rising, something similar to mindless panic building among his troops. Still, given time and the aid of unflustered underlings, he thought he could've held his second line together. But there hadn't been time. To his shock—though he didn't know *why* he was shocked—the enemy just kept coming! Of course they did. His troops may not've *been* prey yet, but they'd fled like it in front of an enemy just as much the predator as they were, now. And any predator will chase when its enemy shows its back.

What made things incalculably worse was that the enemy hit the second disorganized and reeling trench just as hard as the first. More of Ign's troops ran immediately, not even waiting for the blow to fall, not even trying to fight. He had no choice but to order a second withdrawal, hoping distance would give him time to stabilize the situation. He hadn't counted on it taking him, personally, so long to reach the third trench, however. Any time he might've gained was lost. *I should've had warriors carry me,* he fumed, peering back the way he'd come and trying to catch his breath. He looked around.

The trench was packed to overflowing and chaos reigned. Shells and mortar bombs still exploded around him, tossing clouds of earth or gobbets of shattered flesh into the sky. "Control yourselves!" he roared. "Stand fast! They're only prey!" He knew it was a lie. So did his troops.

"What *are* those things, Lord Second General?" cried a young ker-noll standing by, gasping as well. He was looking through the lashing rain across the corpse-scattered space at one of the seemingly impervious iron monsters lumbering toward them, spitting bullets from two or more fast-shooters as it came.

Ign glanced at the officer, wishing it were Jash. Young as Jash was, Ign had come to rely on him more heavily than he'd known to help him adapt to the new and unexpected. *But even Jash would be at a loss now,* Ign expected. *I must make do.* "Armored machines," he shouted back. Lightning ripped the sky and thunder boomed heavily. "Like our greatships of battle," he continued, "only these are smaller, of course, and move across the land. I don't know how." He considered. "They're very loud, like flying-machine engines. . . . So the engines in these must spin the wheels that turn the . . . belts they ride on." More thunder cracked, followed by the blasts of mortar bombs.

"But how do we stop them?" the ker-noll wailed.

"With resolve—and cannon," Ign roared scornfully. "Very close. Command all cannon crews to load solid shot but do not fire until the machines are nearly upon them." The aide only stared. "Go!" Ign bellowed. "Send runners; go yourself. We *must* hold this line!" Ign would never survive another retreat like the last, and his army would probably just keep on going, the Giver of Life knew where. . . .

That's when it finally hit him: the sheer disastrous scope of all Esshk had done, and he'd been a party to. *The Giver of Life* wouldn't *know,* he realized, *because she knows nothing. If she yet lives, she may know she's attacked—and hopefully Jash has preserved her—but she* can't *know more because Esshk denied her wisdom, kept from her the powers of Sight that come with a full, independent consciousness!* He wondered briefly if Esshk somehow knew, having usurped her powers, but he thought not.

Several members of his staff found him then, possibly even hearing his bellowing over the racket. They were just as harried as he, watching as another and another of the iron monsters advanced, followed by the roaring ranks of thousands of enemy troops that had already demonstrated their murderous equality—at least—to any Gharrichk'k. *Now I know how our enemies have felt all this time, when we fell upon them,* Ign thought. *And not just this enemy, but all we've conquered through time. Our new weapons are wet and will not work, our defenses are crumbling, our cannons are ineffective against a new and terrible thing, and our warriors have run away! They* will *continue to do so if* . . . He snarled. *I've* never *understood this new way of war. It's unnatural to me, for us. Perhaps that's the problem?* he thought bleakly, gazing around at his *own* thousands, some frantically trying to fire soggy muskets, but most just waiting, bayonets fixed, flinching under the shells exploding overhead or debris raining down. *Perhaps I must allow them to fight once more as they were shaped to, as they always have. As their* instincts *drive them. Is attack all that now remains?*

He actually started to give the order that would send all around him into the storm of rain and lead and iron. He knew it would be a cyclone of death, but a rising thrill beguiled him with instinctive urges of his own despite his rational expectations of what would happen.

"Lord General!" cried one of his aides who'd been in this line from the start, battering his way through the press to join him. "Lord General, I bear news!" he shouted frantically.

Ign whirled to face him. Bullets struck and spattered him with mud. *The mud is getting bad,* he thought. *The rain hurts us, but can the mud help?* He doubted it. Mud would only make things equally inconvenient for both sides. "What?" he demanded.

For an instant, the aide stood transfixed, staring at the approaching horde and the iron beasts it herded. He visibly forced himself to focus. "As you commanded, troops in the south trenches are shifting here as fast as they can. Tenth General Kuaka is massing for a flank attack on the advancing prey! The attack will strike like a thunderbolt—"

"If it's not too late," Ign growled.

"Indeed," the aide had to agree. He waved a hand at the foe. "Such warriors! And only prey! They fight like nothing we have seen!"

"What of our troops farther to the south, facing the Other Hunters, the Republic forces?" Ign demanded.

"I know only that the Republic hunters renewed their assault at the same time this attack came. They must be trying to keep us from shifting more troops to stop the main attack."

Ign grunted. It made sense . . . *if* this was the main attack. He shook his head to clear it. It must be. *The enemy could never have amassed sufficient strength to strike* everywhere *this hard! If only I had some means of rapid communication with Kuaka, I'd have him drive straight at the enemy line instead; it must be nearly empty now. But signal flags are useless in the dark, flashing lights indistinguishable from fire and storm. Horns—if they are even heard—are incapable of relaying what I want so specifically. And with Kuaka's movement already begun . . . No, by the time runners reached him, any change would only confuse his troops as badly as mine and there'd be chaos everywhere.*

"What of the enemy fleet?" Ign suddenly asked. "Its heavy guns no longer bear on us."

The aide blinked. "It has left," he said simply. "Gone past the *nakkle* leg. Even now it fights our greatships waiting there."

Ign glared north. He was still close to the river but could see nothing but rapid orange flashes on the water. Something erupted flames and he suspected darkly that it was a greatship. "The enemy fleet makes for Sofesshk," he stated with utter certainty, "to support whatever force they landed there. If our fleet can't stop them, our holiest city and the Celestial Mother herself will be in their claws!"

"What can we do?" one of his staff squealed in dismay.

"Nothing!" Ign snapped. "Except stop them here." He glanced back at the river. "Ships can savage Ker-noll Jash and whatever force he assembles to secure Sofesshk, but they can't take the city." He expelled a decisive breath. "Nor can the enemy think so! Captain Reddy pushes here while trying to pull us there!" He waved at the tortured sky. "Yet without his flying machines, he can't know Kuaka marches to our aid." He nodded at the closest tank, now taking hits from roundshot almost continually. The enemy infantry was loading and firing as they came, rifles, Blitzers, and machine guns stitching the berm in front of the trench and pitching Grik back. A heavy shot hit the front of the foremost iron monster hard but still didn't penetrate. The ball caromed up, tearing away the barrel of the forward-firing fast shooter. The rest of its weapons seemed out of action as well, but after a short pause, the machine kept coming.

"We won't oblige him by doing what he wants," Ign shouted loudly, his crest rising. "We *will* relieve Sofesshk—after we smash the enemy here."

"*If* Kuaka attacks in time," the aide qualified, just before a bullet punched through the iron scales on his leather helmet. His eyes bulged and pulpy, bloody brains spewed from his snout as he dropped to the bottom of the trench.

"Indeed," Ign said distractedly, unconsciously echoing the dead aide.

The enemy infantry was closing now, not as quickly as before, but fast enough. *They have to be tiring,* Ign thought, *but the volleys will soon come, then the grenades.* He looked at the warriors lining the trench, eyes flashing in lightning and fire. Some stood, teeth clenched in determination, claws tight around their muskets. Many more stood with tongues lolling, eyes wide, glancing to the rear. They were choosing their path, looking for safety, for life. *My warriors will break with the volleys,* Ign knew. *My whole army, prey or not, will run.*

Attack really was all he had left. He had to hold until Kuaka struck, and there was only one way.

"Sound the horns!" he bellowed harshly at the aides and officers gathered round. "Sound them at once! Blow the single ancient note of doom!" Several just stood and stared at him, but the rest rushed to comply. Moments later, the first horn blared, deep and rumbling, the tone carrying like the thunder. Other horns joined the rising drone that stirred the instincts of the Grik and almost stalled the charging Lemurians with equally strong feelings of dread.

"Up, my warriors!" Ign roared. "I am your Lord General Ign! Hear the horns of death and fight as your ancestors did!" He drew his long, sickle-shaped sword and brandished it overhead. "Out of the trench and charge them! Attack and save the Giver of Life! Kill them all; feast on their flesh. They are only prey!"

CHAPTER
34

////// *Tassanna's Toehold—South*
South bank of the Zambezi River

General Faan-Ma-Mar normally had light tan fur, fading to white on his face, and was short even for a Lemurian, standing barely four and a half feet tall. He was also somewhat plump, equally unusual in a lean, hard-fighting army. And unlike his longtime fellow corps commanders from the traditionally warlike land Homes of Aryaal and B'mbaado, Faan had been a Baalkpan fisherman before the war. He'd made a good living with a large, swift felucca capable of catching and rendering the biggest gri-kakka farther out than most of his peers would go. As was customary, his crew had been his family. Most were dead now.

Like nearly everyone from Baalkpan in his trade, he'd been active fishing, scouting, and carrying freight and provisions for the fledgling Alliance when it first opposed the Grik. A terrible strakka had slammed the Allies' first expeditionary force to Aryaal, however, and he'd lost his ship and all but a niece and his mate's brother when they were driven aground on the north coast of B'mbaado. He probably should've joined the new navy that was building, but it was a chaotic time, and he'd defended Baalkpan as a common soldier when the Grik came there.

To no one's surprise who knew him, he'd distinguished himself, exhibiting quiet courage and leadership in some of the harshest fighting along the Baalkpan waterfront. He'd become a disciple of Pete Alden's and then Billy Flynn's, and quickly risen to command a regiment. He was given a division after the Battle of Sinaa-Pore, and finally III Corps for the Allied invasion of Indiaa. Ever so slowly, III Corps had filled some of the void in his heart left by the loss of his family, and he thought of it like a huge, extended family, to a large degree. That didn't keep him from using it for the greater purpose of winning the war, however—the war that indirectly cost him those he'd loved the most.

Yet despite avoiding the notoriety (and horrific casualties) endured by Muln Rolak's and Safir Maraan's I and II Corps, General Faan and his III Corps had fought well and reliably ever since it was formed. Their biggest test came in Indiaa, where they'd pretty much saved the rest of the army through brisk marching, hard fighting, and quiet, unassuming competence. Now Faan, with his fur dark and slick with rain under a tortured sky, his corps crouching miserably in muddy, flooding trenches, enduring the dreadful anticipation of battle—if not the hellish return fire pounding their comrades closer to the river— prepared to do it again.

"It must be almost time," Colonel Saachic said eagerly, leaning in his saddle to shout in Faan's ear over the roaring storm. Both were mounted on me-naaks, and though the vicious beasts seemed oblivious to the furious battle to the northwest and the silent gun flashes of artillery amid the low hills to the southwest where the Army of the Republic clashed with the Grik blocking force, they were somewhat sullen and grumpy. None of the me-naaks in Saachic's 1st Cavalry Brigade had been fed before they were assembled, and they didn't like rain at all.

"So it must," Faan agreed dispassionately, with a glance at General Loi-Ta-Saa, also mounted. She commanded 9th Division, consisting of the 2nd and 3rd Maa-ni-la and 8th Baalkpan. Eleventh Division, composed of the 7th and 8th Maa-ni-la and 10th Aryaal, was under General Priaa-Ka, also female, far to the right. Fann briefly contemplated what it was about this war that advanced so many females to lead everything from infantry squads to states in the Union, even to other nations, in the case of Rebecca Anne McDonald. Though it wasn't considered unusual if they did, relatively few females controlled ships and Homes—land or sea—before the war. Most seemed content to support their mates who did those things and raise their younglings. *Perhaaps they will again, someday,* Faan thought doubtfully, looking closer at Loi's unblinking, determined face. *Even if they will—or even should—they must fight this enemy,* he suddenly realized, *because with only males to do it, we would've lost long ago. And thaat the Grik threaten all younglings everywhere seems to make them fiercer, even more unwavering thaan the males. Thus, naturaally, they rise in the raanks.*

Faan's tail thumped his side as it swished like a sodden, dripping rope, and he remembered why he looked at Loi. She already knew. Her HQ and comm shack were closest, near the very center of the line. "Nothing yet, Gener-aal Faan," she said gruffly, "though Gener-aal Mu-Tai complains again about the rain."

Faan nodded. "Understaandable, considering his entire Twelfth Corps of Austraalans is new to baattle and only aarmed with muzzle-loading rifle-muskets. He fears their wet weapons will perform poorly, and he's right. Reports from Gener-aal Rolak confirm the enemy is similarly aafflicted." Faan blinked uncertainty, one of the few times anyone had seen him do so. "But Mu-Tai's Corps haas only one major chore tonight: to break whaat *should* be a single thin line of Grik. I'll be pleased if they caan still press on, but surely each raank caan manaage one volley before their weapons drown—if they were loaded properly," he added darkly. "And they haave as maany grenades as anyone. Beyond thaat, courage and their baayonets should suffice."

"I think he worries most thaat they won't haave the preparaa-tory bombaardment lavished on the Grik in front of First Corps," Saachic proposed.

"Also understandable," Faan agreed, "but the fury and sacrifice of First Corps' assault has presented us a greater gift: surprise." He looked at the two thousand menaak-mounted cavalry arrayed behind the line, and lightning showed him the backs of some of 9th Division's

Maa-ni-los massed in the trench ahead. Soon they'd advance with almost thirty thousand troops against a position that should've been heavily robbed by now. The storm made it impossible to know how heavily, but Faan was sure his III Corps could've broken through even what was there before.

It would've wrecked my corps, however, he thought with a stab of anguish, *as surely as thaat other strakka wrecked my ship and faamily. And it could never haave continued on to accomplish the rest of its mission. That's why Twelfth Corps has to go first and has to perform. A great deal rests on the "greenest" troops in the aarmy.* "But we were all 'green' once, were we not?" he asked aloud. Those who heard him understood.

A comm-'Cat raced up, splashing through wind-whipped puddles starting to run like little rivers. "Gener-aals!" he cried. "Gener-aal Rolak sends that First Corps has baashed through to the third Grik trench. Only one remains behind it. The Grik haave come out of their trenches, however, and counterattaacked! And the left flaank of his assault reports *maany* Grik maassing to strike." The comm-'Cat straightened, rain gushing from the rim of his helmet, soaking his smock. He looked somewhat pitiful, but was apparently conscious of the momentous orders he carried, perhaps even his own small place in history. "The time is now," he said loudly, tail slashing with excitement, "and Gener-aal Rolak requests thaat you will begin your attaack!"

"Very well. Paass the word to Gener-aal Mu-Tai to move immediately. No whistles, no drums—nothing to alert the enemy." Faan was sure *something* would happen—somebody would fire a weapon or lightning would illuminate the assault—but they were only about three hundred yards from the Grik trench here and if the Grik were as surprised as he hoped, a little warning shouldn't matter.

"Whaat of our taanks?" Saachic asked, waving at the machines behind them, still silent. They'd been attached to his cavalry.

"You may staart them, but we'll leave them for now unless they're needed. If all goes well, they'll be too slow to help us. If not . . ." Faan shrugged. "We'll know soon enough."

Where they sat on their miserable, dripping me-naaks, they never heard or saw XII Corps begin its attack. By some miracle of the Maker, nobody accidentally fired a weapon, and nothing occurred to alert the Grik. The first they saw, under a searing bolt of lightning lacing the heavy clouds, was an eerily silent mass of troops cutting across their front in an oblique approach toward the opposite position. Twelve thousand Austraalans churned through the mud, keeping a creditable line of advance without a sound they could hear.

"Gener-aal Loi, remind me to compliment Gener-aal Mu-Tai and his Austraalans. Untested or not, I doubt your Ninth Division could maaneuver better under the circumstaances." Faan wished he could see, and unconsciously reached for the Impie telescope in its leather tube. His hand drifted away. Even if it wasn't so dark, the glass would be fogged to uselessness. It didn't matter. More lightning revealed that XII Corps was almost halfway across. "I believe the time haas come, Gener-aal Loi," Faan said. Loi nodded, actually blinking gratitude, and dashed forward, shouting at the comm-'Cats in the trench. In seconds, dozens of field telephones up and down the line started sounding a distinctive *whoop, whoop, whoop!* repeated over and over. Muffled shouts reached them, and 9th Division clambered out of its trench and paused to dress its ranks and await its comrades to the right. The entire corps started across just as the first panicked Grik cannon opened up. A shell burst behind Faan, Saachic, and his cavalry, shattering empty tents. The wind took scraps of canvas and carried them away. Me-naaks shifted sullenly, a few glaring about. They were used to this and ready to go. Besides, they were hungry.

"Didn't even take time to aim!" Saachic cried with satisfaction.

"Maany will," Faan countered, to cool his enthusiasm. He looked at the young cavalry officer. "I wish I could send the entire corps behind you aafter we break through, but Twelfth Corps may be crippled by then. If so, it will certainly need the experience of Ninth Division to bolster it. Eleventh Division will follow you as closely as it caan. Leave a sufficient screen," he reminded fussily.

"Of course." Saachic grinned.

"And with the Maker's help, the rest of us won't be *too* faar behind," Faan shouted, as several more case shot exploded nearby, still long, where there was nobody left to hurt.

"With the Maker's help," Saachic agreed, then grinned again. "Sure you don't waant some of my caaval-ry to accompany you?"

Faan patted his impatient mount. "You'll need them," he said grimly, then surprised Saachic with a chuckle. "I fear the few me-naaks we *must* take will cause problems enough! I understaand Repubs haave fine caaval-ry, but ride something caalled 'horses.' Haave you ever seen a horse? I hear they're very faast, but may not bear the presence of me-naaks. It would be a terrible thing if our caaval-ry chased theirs away!" He paused, staring ahead. Cannon thundered along the line, now clawing hard at XII Corps as it neared the enemy trench, but there was even less musket fire than he'd expected. *Surely the Grik caan count on at least one shot from their weapons as well?* he thought. Twelfth Corps' front rank poured its first volley, ragged but fierce in comparison to the enemy's. Grenades thumped, barely audible under another pounding band of rain. The second-rank volley flashed, the roar lost in thunder. Then, to Faan's amazement, he heard . . . cheering.

"Advaance your caaval-ry *now*, Col-nol Saachic!" he ordered tensely, blinking concentration. "I'll come with you."

It was just as well he did. By the time the 1st Maa-ni-la Cavalry Brigade thundered up to the enemy trench, the fighting was all but over and the gleeful confusion of victory was almost as bad as a defeat, from an organizational standpoint. Both corps had stopped and intermingled to a shocking degree in and around a practically empty trench. Apparently, only the guns had been fully manned, and the troops, expecting a bloody melee, were stunned by their insignificant losses and perhaps just the fact they were alive. Saachic's brigade kept a tight rein on their rebellious mounts, extremely upset they weren't allowed to feast on Grik, and General Faan rode forward, bellowing for officers to control their units. "This isn't over!" he roared. "Whaat's the maatter with you?" He pointed to the northwest. "Your brothers and sisters are dying there, and here you caper like younglings! Gener-aal Loi!" he shouted, seeing 9th Division's commander at last. "Form your troops! Where's Gener-aal Mu-Tai?"

A crack of lightning briefly illuminated a burly older Lemurian, bawling at troops in a strange accent. "There you are!" Faan cried. "We must push on! I thaank the Maker for this easy crossing, but if the enemy isn't here, he's there." He pointed northwest again. "First Corps will suffer accordingly," he added bleakly. "*Your* war is thaat way, however!" He pointed south. "Lead your troops; reform them on the maarch. There'll be more Grik, I promise!" He hesitated very slightly, making a decision on the fly. "I'll find you directly."

He whirled his mount back to face Loi, but looked to Saachic instead. "Send a runner baack to your taanks. Haave them and all our reserves drive due west and strike the enemy that left this position in the flaank." He turned back to Loi. "As for you, find Gener-aal Priaa. *All* of Third Corps will now follow Col-nol Saachic and strike the Grik attacking First Corps in the rear. *You* command Third Corps now, and there's not a moment to lose!"

"But . . . whaat about you, Gener-aal?" Loi asked between shouted orders to junior officers trying to untangle their troops. Faan was glad to see she wasn't intimidated, only confused, by the greater responsibility he'd cast upon her.

"You're senior to Priaa and with Saachic's help caan easily get Third Corps moving without me!" he shouted back. "You haave disciplined troops with plenty of experience. Twelfth Corps is . . . less experienced, and Gener-aal Mu-Tai may need me to see opportunities and hazaards the Grik might present." Mu-Tai could be fully capable of independent movement, but that was still unproven. His troops were obviously game, but XII Corps would have to smash past the Grik in front of the Repubs without 9th Division now. Faan himself must bolster it.

He grinned at Loi. "Besides, as agreed, it would still be best if I were there when we meet the Repubs at laast!"

The Third Trench
South bank of the Zambezi River

General Taa-Leen had taken to his new, unexpected command of all the Smushers with a gusto he hadn't anticipated. His machine, designated Number 4, he discovered, radiated unbearable heat, ruined his hearing even with the headphones Sergeant Kaalo gave him, and his position in the turret was painfully cramped. The spattering lead of Grik musket balls had forced him lower in the turret, and he could only see through narrow slits. Worse, everything around him was hard and sharp, and he suspected he hadn't taken a worse beating in the old shield walls they used to fight in. That was saying something. And if it weren't for the excitement, he might've gone mad in the tight confinement. Roundshot banged off the dented armor carapace of the Smusher with a stunning, mind-numbing regularity, and just the motion of the vehicle bruised and cut him and jarred his bones.

But Taa-Leen was killing Grik with an impunity he'd never imagined. He fired the hot machine gun, sweeping tracers through a raging mass of Grik, using controlled bursts as he'd been taught. His only disappointment came when the big gun was empty and he had to wait while the overworked youngling loader quickly brought more ammunition. *Thaat poor loader haas the worst job of all,* he thought, *squirming around, taking aammunition to each weapon as the gunner shouts for it. He haas nothing to brace himself with against unexpected jolting, and caan't even see outside!* But Taa-leen could see, and he gloried in the slaughter he was wreaking.

"All Smushers, spread out! You're bunching up too much!" he called into the big round microphone in front of his face. "Smushers on the left, be on guard. The dope on the horn is thaat all the Grik in the south trenches are heading this way." The mic was supported by a thin strap of leather-bound brass attached to the earphones, in turn supported by two more straps across the top and back of his head. He didn't have one of the padded leather helmets, and uncomfortably wore the one he'd been issued over it all.

Another roundshot banged off the portside sponson, smashing the water jacket on the MG and sending the gunner screaming to the hard, bouncing deck. Taa-Leen glanced down and saw a spreading pool of blood that the loader was trying to staunch. *The breech probably claapped him as haard as the caannon-ball,* he thought grimly. A bright flare erupted to his right and he saw a Smusher engulfed in flames. Troops crowded around, trying to pull the crew out. He sighed, realizing he had only nine Smushers left. Two had been destroyed at the first trench, three at the second, and three more had gotten stuck or otherwise disabled. The one on the right was the first to die as they neared the third trench, but they were taking heavier fire than ever. *Still, the Grik are running,* he thought with satisfaction. *Break this line and I doubt they'll stop at the next.* He fired his gun, shredding the top of the berm in front of him, sending bodies jerking back, making a fine spray of blood that glowed orange under the stabbing lightning. Then he blinked.

He couldn't hear the Grik horns over the roar of the engine, but saw the infantry jogging alongside the tank begin to slow. That's when the Grik ahead came out of their trench and he was taken back in time. They carried muskets with bayonets instead of spears and swords and crossbows, but they were coming as they had the first time he faced them. A bomb of terror went off in his guts and he hesitated for an instant before he knew what to do. He may have been playing tanker, but he was still an infantryman. "Turn left to bring the right gun to bear and stop," he shouted down at Sergeant Kaalo. Without question, the iron beast slewed left in a shower of mud thrown up by the starboard track. It lurched to a stop.

Taa-Leen stood in his turret and saw the troops around him beginning to waver. They had plenty of courage but hadn't expected this. Their initial reaction was just like his, but he had to rally them—if he could be heard. He squeezed the Press-to-Talk switch on the braided wire to his headset, so the other tankers could hear him too. They'd repeat what he said if they were able.

"Staand!" he roared down at the troops. "Re-form your raanks, three deep. Staand steady and we'll slaughter them!"

He felt as much as heard a pounding behind him and was amazed to see Pete Alden rejoin him on the tank. He was splashed with mud and blood and his beard was a tangled, matted mess. A gaggle of Marines were with him, some dragging a comm cart, one of the heavy radios, complete with batteries, enclosed in a box on a wooden carriage. Pete was holding his rifle and a long, thin staff with wires trailing behind. "Call half your tanks back on the left to form a line at a right angle to yours," he hollered, voice hoarse. "I've already got Sixth Corps doing the same. Gotta refuse our flank. Half the Grik left in the world are about to hit us there." He pointed south. Lightning bloomed behind him. "Rolak's bringing the Second Corps reserves and everything we've got left," he continued, "and General Laan's sending *his* reserves to hit *their* flank!" Pete grinned, and his teeth glared bright in the muzzle flash of a Grik gun. "What a glorious, screwed-up mess!"

Taa-Leen didn't understand.

"General Laan got bogged down a bit, but sent his whole corps to kick the Grik in the ass," Pete went on. "All we hafta do now is hold and bleed the bastards." Taa-Leen blinked, and Pete finally realized he didn't get it. They could all hear the Grik horns now, and tens of thousands of them were charging, drawing close. The first hastily formed rank, staggered and wavy, but at least half a mile long, began delivering company-, then regiment-size volleys that sent hundreds of Grik facedown in the mud. Machine guns on tanks were still stuttering, and a few small mortars were lofting bombs into the enemy rear.

Pete laughed. "Don't worry, Taa-Leen! So what if the plan went in the shitter an' the whole Grik army's about to hit us like a steel strakka straight outa hell? Look on the bright side: now we don't have to chase 'em anymore!"

Taa-Leen just blinked again, then shook his head. "You better move, Gener-aal. I gotta staart shooting."

"Sure, sure," Pete agreed, but jammed the staff supporting the antenna in the turret. "You can still shoot with that in there," he shouted dismissively. Hefting his rifle, he jumped down and was gone. *Baack to playing Maa-reen,* Taa-Leen predicted sourly, trying to avoid the antenna as he realigned his sights on the charging Grik. "Then again, whaat else caan any of us do now?" he asked himself aloud.

First and VI Corps' volleys were continuous, their smoke swirling and gushing away as rank after rank presented their rifles and fired into the Grik army that had become a rampaging horde again. And volleys lashed southward now as well, as the first Grik summoned from the rest of the line began to appear. Seeing what was happening and with no further orders to guide them, they charged directly into the attack. Some groped for the eastern flank of VI Corps' line, running up the abandoned trenches only to be met by Rolak and his reserve. Taa-Leen knew little of that, though the chatter of excited, panicky tankers filled his ears. More than once, their voices were cut off by screams. Tank Number 4's engine still rumbled, but it had become a stationary fort. With nothing else to do, Kaalo was helping the overwrought loader. The portside gunner was dead, and the one to starboard soon joined him when an unlikely musket ball slipped through his viewing slit and hit him in the side of the head. The compartment below was filled with a furry, nauseating mist and the sound of retching. But Kaalo took the starboard gun and joined the fight.

Taa-Leen was aware of all this but couldn't even spare a moment to look. The Grik wave was breaking against them, the front rank of riflemen resorting to their bayonets. Taa-Leen's gun jetted steam from the water jacket, the fitting from the reservoir loose with heat, and all he could do was kill—and hope they didn't run out of ammunition. Thunder wracked the heavens, grenades exploded, Blitzers rattled, and tracers probed the driving rain and fleeting fog banks, hacking at bodies, shattering bones and weapons, and adding bloody rivers to the flooding night. 'Cats and Grik screamed and screeched, and all there was was noise.

CHAPTER 35

////// *Palace of Vanished Gods*

The anteroom to what was apparently the final, uppermost chamber in the palace, where the desperate Grik guards made their last, furious stand, was an abattoir. The dark stone walls were splashed with blood, spalled by hundreds of gray bullet strikes, and almost seemed to be growing fur from all the downy, feathery Grik fur stuck to the blood. Weapons, entrails, severed limbs, even an extraordinary number of broken teeth were scattered all over the floor, and the pile of bodies heaped in front of the inner chamber almost blocked the entrance. Chack realized sickly that there were more Lemurian dead than Grik. As always, his Raiders had lost all caution when their objective was near. Dazed wounded were being helped or carried past them, and tired, blood-spattered Raiders were dragging corpses aside from the pile, blinking nervously at the opening as if expecting attack from within at any moment.

Pokey was writhing on the floor, jaws bound shut, secured by six resentful, battered-looking 'Cats. His eyes bulged, questing spastically, and he made a dismal keening sound. Blood bubbled and sprayed from his snout with every heavy breath, and Chack suspected at least some of the broken teeth they'd seen were his.

"Poor little fella," Silva said solicitously.

"Him?" a 'Cat retorted indignantly. "He nearly killed

us! He fought them other Griks too, but you tole us to caatch him." Pokey suddenly thrashed, trying to break loose, and his captors pressed down harder. "Well, we caatched him," the 'Cat gasped. "Now whaat?"

"Bind him and take him below," Chack decided. "He's no use like this. He should recover when he's away from here." He blinked anxiously at Lawrence. "Are you sure you're all right?"

Lawrence jerked a nod. "I a coonhound."

Silva nodded at the arched entry. "Then sidle over an' yammer some o' that Grikish gibberish at 'em. Get 'em to roll over on their backs an' wave their arms an' legs in the air er somethin'. You an' Pokey's the only ones ever got fightin' Griks to surrender before."

Lawrence hissed at him, then looked at Chack. "I'll try. 'Ut these aren't Uul 'arriors or sailors," he added skeptically. Moving to the wall, with Silva backing him with his Thompson, he slowly eased his head around to peer into the gloomy space. Abruptly, he jerked back just as a spear whipped past his snout and sailed down the passageway, clattering on the stones. It was amazing it didn't hit anyone.

"That's it," Silva said definitively, plucking a grenade from his web belt. "I don't talk to nobody who tries to poke *my* coonhound in the nose!" He squinted his eye at Chack. "We tried. Now let's blast 'em!"

"No!" came a shrill cry from the chamber beyond, and Silva almost dropped the grenade in surprise.

"Who the hell's that?"

Rapid clicking-gurgling Grik syllables instantly replied, followed by an even higher-pitched "No kill!"

Lawrence was blinking at them now, the pattern easily recognizable to Lemurians as astonishment. "They're in there, all right," he said. "The Celestial Nother, her guards—and the Chooser. *The* Chooser," he stressed. "It's he who cried out not to kill they." He looked significantly at Silva. "He understands English, just can't talk it nutch." Lawrence opened his jaws slightly in what for him was a kind of grin. "I don't think he hants to die."

"Throw down your aarms and you'll live!" Chack yelled. Immediately, muffled shouting filled the room, some plaintive, some apparently adamant. Nobody but Lawrence could really tell. "The Chooser hants too," Lawrence whispered. "The guards don't. Say they can hold. The Celestial Nother say nothing."

"You caan't hold," Chack shouted angrily, "and in ten seconds we'll throw a dozen grenades in there and you'll all die, including your Giver of Life! We're the same waarriors who slew her mother," he added harshly, "so don't try us."

There came what sounded like panicky squalling.

"What now?" Silva asked.

"He hants to know 'hat a grenade is."

"Hand bombs that'll blow you all into a hundred gobbets o' goo!" Silva shouted gleefully.

The arguing grew more intense, then came another querulous question. Chack looked at Lawrence.

"He doesn't know how long a 'second' is."

"Two heartbeats," Chack shouted, blinking increased impatience.

More squalling.

"He asks, 'Two heart'neats or two *tens* o' heart'neats?'"

"Shit," Silva spat disgustedly. "Time's up. Here come the grenades!" he shouted.

Pokey went first. His guards had been distracted by the bizarre negotiations and he broke loose, leaping up and bounding over the bodies and into the chamber of the Celestial Mother.

"*Shit*!" Silva roared, and without thinking pushed Lawrence aside and chased the little Grik. Chack and Lawrence went because he did—along with the half dozen 'Cats close and quick enough to follow.

Even before he had a chance to note that this chamber was different again from all the others, covered from floor to ceiling with strange, flowering ivies, the first thing Silva saw was a huge stone table, tipped on its side. It must've been at least six feet wide and twelve feet long. And rushing out from behind it was an absolutely massive, naked female Grik. Six or seven more followed her—they couldn't all have hidden behind the table even if they wanted to—and they quickly fanned out. The closest monster opened its jaws and spread its talon-studded hands as it came. Silva fired. Bloody holes marched across a creamy dun-colored chest in a rising diagonal, but the thing kept coming. Holding the trigger down, Silva allowed the recoil to raise the muzzle of his Thompson, then controlled it long enough to empty the magazine in the gaping maw. The monstrous Grik seemed to lose focus and lumbered past him as he dove aside, crashing into the wall behind him.

But there were more. Chack shot one twice, working the slick bolt of his Krag with lightning speed, then drove his long bayonet into its throat. Blood sprayed like a broken water main, but the dying guard collapsed with Chack's Krag beneath it. There was no way to retrieve the weapon; these sisters of the Celestial Mother—for that's what they had to be, if what they'd heard was true—looked like they must weigh six hundred pounds.

Instantly, Chack had his cutlass and .45 in his hands, wading forward, shooting and slashing, Lawrence at his side. A 'Cat Raider blew one down with a single shot from her Allin-Silva, the big bullet crashing deep to shatter the spine. Leaping the corpse, she bayonetted another, but was batted effortlessly aside. Two more 'Cats fired at another guard with their Blitzers, but it slashed both their throats as it charged them, then crushed a third as it fell. Even lying there, it lashed at a 'Cat running past, clamping its jaws on the Raider's leg. With a twist of its head and a Lemurian shriek, it tore the leg off at the knee. More blood fountained, spraying the Raiders behind, even as they shot the thing some more.

Silva had dropped the empty Thompson again and pulled his own cutlass and Captain Reddy's Colt, the cutlass slashing and revolver roaring. The Colt was loaded with "full-house rifle loads" and bucked heavily as fire and smoke spat bullets slightly lighter than his 1911, but flying much faster. Subconsciously, he figured the damage it inflicted at this range probably evened out, but the revolver went off more dramatically. If nothing else, it might give the enemy pause. Maybe it did, or it might've simply been that, big and powerful as the sister-guards were, they didn't have the agility, weaponry, or, frankly, veteran killing skill of the smaller intruders swarming into the chamber. Blitzerbugs clattered, 1911s popped rapidly, and Allin-Silvas boomed, deafening everyone and filling the room with floating fuzz and a smoky red mist.

Finally, all the sister-guards who'd exposed themselves were down, but another suddenly stood from behind the slablike table, holding a wriggling, clawing Pokey in her grasp. Silva had scooped his Thompson off the leafy floor and inserted another magazine. Now he aimed, but couldn't get a good shot without risking Pokey. Besides, he was a little stunned. Pokey had entirely lost his mind and was convulsing wildly in what struck Silva as a decidedly obscene fashion. Lawrence was yelling something in Grik, pointing the long-barreled flintlock pistol, of all things, and Chack and several 'Cats were hurrying to reload as well. Silva could only assume the Celestial Mother and Chooser were still behind the massive table.

With a defiant snarl directed at Lawrence, whom the last sister-guard apparently understood, she suddenly drove the claws of her left hand into Pokey's chest, those of the right into his neck under his jaw. With little visible effort, she simply tore his head off his body. Silva fired, and she flung the head at him. The trembling body was cast toward Chack and his Raiders. All avoided the blood-spewing projectiles, but for a moment only Lawrence remained undistracted. Standing in what was probably accidentally the most perfect dueling stance his form could replicate, he pulled the trigger of the large-bore pistol Silva once liberated from an assassin named Linus Truelove. With a spectacularly loud *ker-KRAK*, a one-ounce ball spattered the monster's left eye and crashed into her brain, dropping her to the floor in a kicking heap that sent leaves and flowers flying.

"Goddamn!" Silva hooted. "How much powder'd you put in that thing?" Lawrence was looking at the smoking pistol as if checking to see if the barrel had burst. He tapped a claw about halfway to the muzzle. "Idiot!" Silva snapped. "Lucky you didn't get pieces of it up your damn stupid nose!"

For a moment then, as soon as Pokey and the guard finished thrashing, all was silent except for the metallic sounds of breechblocks closing on fresh cartridges or bolts being drawn back and slides snapping shut.

"No kill!" came a small, trembling voice from behind the barricade. "No kill!"

With a darkening glance at what had been Pokey, Silva's face lost all expression and he took the grenade from where he'd hung it back with others on his belt. He casually tossed it in the air, catching it. "Scram, fellas," he said conversationally, but Chack knew the deceptively mild tone came only from Silva's most murderous mood.

"No," he said harshly. "Chief Sil-vaa, put thaat away." Without waiting to see if he was obeyed, Chack turned to Lawrence. "Tell whoever's behind thaat baarricade to staand and surrender at once. There'll be no time to decide, no seconds to contemplate." He raised his voice. "Surrender now or die."

Jerkily but almost instantly, a rather short, rotund Grik stood from behind the table. He was dressed in a bizarre, stained, and dusty cloak festooned with tiny bones like polished ivory sequins. His crest stood erect but somewhat . . . bent, and his big eyes darted about from within a face covered with strangely smudged and oddly colored fur. "No kill?" he almost pleaded.

"Where's your Giver of Life?" Chack demanded. The strange Grik glanced down and jabbered rapidly in his own tongue.

"She's there," Lawrence confirmed. "Not hurt." He snorted. "The Chooser 'shielded' her." He cocked his head to the side. "He acts like it's critical to us that he did."

"Perhaaps it is," Chack said, looking hard at Silva. At least the big man had put the grenade away. "Staand her up," he told the Chooser.

Gently but urgently, the Chooser spoke as if to the floor. Finally, another very large, almost obese Grik tentatively stood from behind the cover. Large she might've been, compared to other Grik, and certainly compared to Lawrence, but she was also probably the most magnificent specimen of her species alive. The coat under her long red robe was very fine, almost the color of a new penny, and it shone to even greater effect against the dark, leafy background under the flickering lamplight. Her teeth gleamed brighter than the Chooser's macabre decorations, and her claws resembled polished ebony.

With a voice that seemed small for her size, she spoke directly to Lawrence for several moments, while all anyone else could do was stand and gape. At last, with a growing air of confidence and satisfaction, she completed her monologue and glared at everyone else, including the Chooser at her side.

"What did the fat lizard prattle on about?" Silva ground out, eye straying back to Pokey. "She wanna eat our pal?"

"She's not . . . as you say," Lawrence replied, a slight trace of Pokey's earlier dreaminess in his voice. "She's ideal."

"Maybe to *you*," Silva began, then looked alarmed. "Whoa! She's gettin' to *you* now. What the hell?" He aimed the Thompson again.

"Hold your fire!" Chack roared. "Lawrence?" he asked lower, voice tense.

Lawrence shook his head and his eyes seemed to focus. "I . . . I okay. Her scent is *strong* and it . . . does things. I'll tell you things I think, and all else she said."

Quickly he explained that, like Khonashi and Sa'aaran females of mating age, elevated Grik females—of which there were very few and they may've just killed all but one—had considerable control over their fertility. What's more, they could express scents from certain glands in their legs at will to signal their readiness to mate. They'd expected that, of course, though the single-mindedness of Pokey's reaction came as a surprise. Apparently, almost any normal Grik male would behave the same, losing all thought of anything but the mating imperative. That made it even more amazing Pokey hadn't killed anyone to get to the Celestial Mother. His own natural elevation and all the time he'd spent with his new friends had clearly given him admirable control over the all-powerful urge.

"But you're . . . yourself?" Chack demanded.

Lawrence managed to look a little embarrassed but answered firmly, "Yes."

Silva shook his head. "Poor little guy," he murmured, looking back at Pokey's head, but he might've been talking about Lawrence. He turned to eye his friend. "Relations 'mongst your folk ain't often allowed, are they? Rare enough that even talkin' about it's kinda taboo?" He'd seen Lawrence's reaction to lewd suggestions before, par-

ticularly concerning the captured female secluded at Grik
City. "Sure it is," Silva continued, warming to his subject.
"An' you'd flip out bad as Pokey if that"—he jerked his
head toward the Celestial Mother—"was a Sa'aaran dame.
But *your* broads *hafta* keep their pixilation under wraps
'cause you come from a island that'd get overrun in no
time otherwise. Same goes for Khonashi an' other North
Borno tribes with small territories. They were always
fightin' little border wars, anyway. Their populations puff
up, an' it starts a breedin' race that not only kicks off real
wars, but wipes out all the local resources!" He considered. "Explains why unelevated Grik broads, their broodmares, few as they are, are always locked up. They might
light off their boilers at any time. Probably ain't safe to be
around 'cept when they're layin' eggs er somethin'!"

"I think you haave it," Chack agreed, blinking surprise. "Mr. Braad-furd would be proud of you."

Lawrence was nodding, reluctantly it seemed. "'Ut it
ne'er is a nuisance to Sa'aarans, Tagranesi, or Khonashi,
'cause us is . . . ci'ilized," he snapped out, glaring at the
Celestial Mother. "*Our* gals that are old enoug' know not
to stir us to go nuts! They not *e'er* use their sex to hurt!
They don't ha' to get locked a'ay!"

"So how'd that work?" Silva asked, jerking his head
back the way they came. "How come her squeezin's just
made her guards fight harder?"

"Aggression's part of their mating," Chack speculated,
"and some are conditioned somehow to chaannel their
urges to defend their Giver of Life from"—he smiled
mirthlessly—"advaances of any sort. Mating or attaack."

"Or maybe they're all geldings," Silva quipped, arch-
ing an eyebrow at the Chooser, standing anxiously by the
Celestial Mother. "Maybe *he* is too. That, or he's the first
Grik *coward* I ever saw."

"I not a co'ard!" the Chooser denied, somewhat feebly.

"Damn! He does understand us!" Silva regarded the
strange Grik. "Tell that lizardy bitch to shut off the love-
potion spigot right damn now." He nodded at Lawrence.
"It only affects him enough that he'll know if she don't."

"Yes, do," Chack declared, but looked intently at Lawrence. "What did she say to you?"

Lawrence looked even more embarrassed somehow. "She thinks I in charge; I your general." He was truly mortified to report that the Celestial Mother was certain he somehow led the entire war effort against her race, unnaturally enlisting prey animals to aid him. In her insularity, she still likened the war to the common conflicts between various regencies and had no concept of its scope. She was very astute for one so young, Lawrence reported, but also extremely naive. Even now, surrounded by the blood and gore of her guards, she believed she wielded the ultimate power here. Lawrence finally added, almost inaudibly, that since he was so obviously superior to First General Esshk—at least when it came to designing battles—she was tempted to name him her new Regent Champion, despite the fact he was so small and ugly. *If*, that is, First General Esshk didn't ultimately prevail.

Silva laughed out loud. "Now, don't that just beat all! King Larry the First! Ha!"

"I'll tell her I *not* a general, I *not* in charge!" Lawrence smoldered, the skin on his neck beneath thinner fur turning pink.

"Not yet," Chack countered, glancing down the passageway. He could hear running boots and sandals, accompanied by a growing commotion. "Don't lie to her—thaat might be importaant later—but if she continues to aassume you commaand, let her. For now."

A squad of 'Cats and Impies rushed into the room, followed by Major Jindal. He was breathing hard again. All paused for a moment to take in the scene. Finally, Jindal spoke to Chack. "We have problems outside. Everything's on schedule back at the Neckbone; the barrage hammered the Grik and General Alden's begun his push, but our pickets along the river are vigorously pressed. Seems the Grik are coming ashore."

"How did they aassemble enough boats so quickly?" Chack asked, surprised.

"They didn't. At least not to bring them all the way. One of the Grik BBs has moved closer and perhaps they ferry troops to it, but from there they're *swimming*!" Jindal seemed stunned even to hear himself say it, but

Chack only nodded. He'd seen indications *some* Grik knew how to swim, during the hellish battle around *Santa Catalina*. Most had doubtless been eaten by the high concentration of predators the battle summoned, but water monsters couldn't always be everywhere in such numbers. The Grik knew that too.

"Then they caan't be heavily aarmed. No way to keep their smaall aarms dry. They must be trying to force our pickets baack and gain control of the docks." He looked at Lawrence. "You stay here, my friend—with a sufficient guard, of course." He blinked at the Celestial Mother. "Within the guidelines I gave you, try to explain to her about the real world and why we're aact-ually here. Correct aany notion she may haave thaat the world can remain as she imaagines it or haas been told it is. We're here to *destroy* her murderous culture, not just tweak who's in chaarge of whaat. She caan help with thaat, to save her race from extinction—and possibly even a measure of her authority." He shrugged.

"Or else?" the Chooser suddenly asked, surprising them all again. He'd clearly had a *lot* of contact with humans.

"She won't be haarmed," Chack assured, "but she and a haandful of your race'll be all we preserve for study." He grinned wickedly, displaying bright, sharp teeth. "We haave a friend who'll waant to exaamine these glaands of hers, to discover any differences from other races. I doubt she'll enjoy the experience, but she won't be injured. Of course," he added offhand, "her glaands will serve no purpose then, since we'll save no males at all." He turned to Silva and Jindal. "Let's go."

"Right. Gotta go meet the new neighbors." Silva lowered his voice. "You never have been one to brag, Chackie, but you pulled it off pretty well. I just hope she believes it."

"Why not?" Chack countered. "She clearly haas little graasp of reaality. And in the end, as faar as she knows, we've conquered our way to her very bedchamber and Esshk couldn't stop it. Thaat'll help her to believe we caan do as I said." He blinked thoughtfully as they stepped briskly back down the passageway that had cost so much blood. "And perhaaps the Chooser'll help convince her. Muri-naame reported thaat he's . . . opportunistic."

Silva chuckled. "An' you didn't include *him* in your list o' specimens."

"No."

It took them almost half an hour to wind their way back down to the palace entrance, and Major Abel Cook met them there. Rifles flashed in the distance, all along the waterfront, as men and 'Cats shot swimming Grik in the water. Blood was probably drawing predators, and there were shrill screams as water monsters snatched top water morsels.

"I tried to call a strike on the battleships," Cook reported. "Sink them, and the Grik should stop. They can't possibly swim all the way across. Certainly not if they intend to fight when they arrive." A frown creased his young face. "But all our planes are grounded. The storm in the strait is growing into a strakka. The battle to the southeast is being fought in the rain already. The consensus of the weather division on *Salissa* is that the storm will soon reach us." He glanced at the arch. "Did you secure the objective?"

"Yes," Chack responded. "Hopefully, it'll be of use."

"They got poor ol' Pokey," Silva told Cook, his voice uncharacteristically somber, and the boy looked down. Pokey had accompanied them all the way across the vicious wilds of Borno, and stayed with Cook and his Khonashi ever since.

"How?" Abel asked quietly, looking up to meet his eye.

Silva squinted and looked uncomfortable, clearly trying to soften the blow. Abel Cook had seen more in his short life than he ever should have, yet Silva couldn't help thinking of him as a gangly kid, full of wonder, shadowing Courtney Bradford. "Well," he finally began thoughtfully, "let's just say he went down hard."

Chack snorted and blinked reproach. "Sergeant Pokey was . . . overwhelmed by the enemy," he assured. "Let thaat be the end of it. Now, tell me more about whaat we face out here."

With a suspicious look at Silva, Abel Cook led them to the breastworks. A lot of effort had gone into it while they were in the palace, and just about every loose stone, beam or timber, door, table, fallen tree, even Grik body within a quarter mile had been added to a roughly 450-yard, semicircular barricade beneath the western face of the structure. Chack hoped they wouldn't be stuck there long enough for the reeking corpses to become more of a problem than they already were. Paving stones had been torn up behind the breastworks and trenches begun. Six water-cooled .30-caliber machine guns were dug in, as were the two light howitzers. Manning the defense was all of Cook's 1st North Borno and most of Jindal's and Galay's regiments as well, totaling around two thousand troops.

It was a pretty stout position and should hold against anything but artillery or a *much* larger force willing to take a hell of a beating. On the one hand, everybody knew these Grik were soldiers, not a mob. Their tactics might be a little dated, but they actually *used* tactics and were increasingly—disturbingly—clever. The days of mindless flock attacks seemed over. On the other hand, if there was anything on Earth that could still inspire the Grik to that degree of sacrificial fanaticism, it was in the palace behind them.

The crackle and flash of rifles along the waterfront was nearly continuous, and swirling, fitful breezes whipped acrid gunsmoke back in their faces. Chack rubbed his tired eyes and looked at the sky. High-level clouds were reaching across the flickering stars, racing from north to south, even as the humid surface winds remained confused. "A storm is certainly brewing," he said grimly. He sighed. "Major Gaa-lay," he called to the Filipino officer who'd just joined them. "Pull your skirmishers in." They were nearly all Impies, members of the 1st Battalion of the 11th Imperial Marines, and part of Galay's 7th Allied Regiment.

Galay frowned. "They're really murdering the bastards, literally like shooting fish in a barrel. Sure you want to call it off?"

"An' they'll get the docks," Silva warned. "Thought we wanted to stop that."

Chack nodded but pointed. "There's heavy firing the length of the line, but the shore—and other docks—extend beyond it. Grik crossing faarther upriver must swim a greater distaance but have less to fear from water monsters. I expect they're already ashore beyond your defense, Major Gaa-lay, possibly in force. And the more distaant companies risk attaack from the rear. Besides, to *really* kill them, we need them to concentrate. The only place they'll do thaat is here. Pull your men baack, Major. It's going to be a very long night."

"Aye, aye, sir," Galay replied. "Bring them in," he told the comm-'Cat standing nearby. "All companies will fall back to the strongpoint in succession, starting with those farthest out."

Suddenly, the great Grik ironclad battleship closest to their position lit with twelve stuttering flashes amid ballooning white balls of smoke. Blind in the darkness after watching the muzzle flashes of rifles for several minutes, Chack hadn't noticed the thing, close to five hundred yards or less. Maybe nobody had. A dozen hundred-pound case shot reached them shortly before the roar of the guns. Most went long and burst in Old Sofesshk and a few impacted the south side of the palace, but two exploded with terrific thunderclaps and sheeted white-hot iron fragments down on Chack's Raiders. Screams erupted at the far side of the perimeter and close to the arch. Silva stood—they'd all hit the dirt—and squinted through the smoky haze.

"Damn. I guess they figgered they can't hurt the Cowflop, just like we did, but they can clobber anybody around it. Now we're in the same shit the lizards were, and I reckon it's gonna fly fast an' hot." He shook his fist at the Grik battlewagon, which was doubtless already reloading. "An' there ain't a damn thing we can do about it!"

"We can dig," Abel Cook shouted grimly. He stood as well. "Finish the trenches!" he roared. "Dig for your lives!"

Silva glared at Galay. "Well? Gimme a goddamn shovel!" Every member of Chack's Raiders carried a short, T-handled entrenching tool strapped to their pack.

"Where's yours?"

Silva scoffed. "I brung guns."

"So now you want to trade one for a shovel?" Galay barked sarcastically.

The BB lit up again and they all dove for the dirt. "I might," Silva ground out as more shells exploded overhead.

His otherwise unquestioned, even reckless courage aside, it was well known Silva really hated being on the receiving end of artillery. Everyone did, of course, but Chack suspected the sense of helplessness that came with the arbitrary, impersonal nature of the peril bothered Silva even more than most. He'd stood stoically by *Walker*'s number-one gun many times while more and bigger shells fell around him, but then he'd been moving—and shooting back. "Which gun do you want?" Silva added louder, but more screams and cries of anguish drowned him out. His eye met Abel Cook's. "Looks like we're gonna get another taste o' what we been givin' the Griks since this war kicked off," he shouted, "an' I don't like it one damn bit."

There was a brief lull, and Cook rose on his knees. "Dig!" he roared, unstrapping his own entrenching tool. Someone tossed another to Silva and he started hammering at the hard dirt where paving stones had already been pried up.

"What about my Marines?" Galay insisted.

Chack reached over and dragged the cowering comm-'Cat closer. "Haave the Eleventh pull back to the temporary HQ we set up laast night—this morning, whichever. They'll dig in there until recaalled. No sense paacking more troops under this." Several more shells exploded overhead and one on the ground, heaving bodies, stones, and timbers in the air. Most still went long, exploding in the city, and a few buildings were already flickering with flames. Apparently, the other Grik BB had joined the bombardment. "Everyone elsc, except those holding the line, will move inside the paalace and take cover there." He blinked apology at Cook. "No nonhumaan Khonashi yet, I'm sorry. Not until we know it's safer for them inside than out. There are . . . smells in there thaat might drive them maad," he tried to explain.

Unsurprisingly, Cook understood. He'd spent more time around Khonashi than anyone left alive. That didn't mean he liked the situation. "Sergeant Moe," he called. "Take a detail of human Khonashi and guard the arch. Don't admit any but humans and Lemurians, even those bearing wounded. It's for their own good," he added bitterly.

"Ay, sur," came the reply, and the ancient 'Cat stood

and walked briskly toward the palace, not even flinching under the heavy detonations.

"Dumb-ass," Silva gasped, flinging dirt in the air in great arcs. "An' he's afraid bein' close to *me'll* get his scrawny ass killed!" He glared at Chack. "You better get under cover too. Galay's boys're out there, an' Mister Cook's're here. We got this. You get blown to pieces, we're all screwed."

"Major Jindaal's more than capable of taking my place," Chack retorted, blinking at the one-armed Imperial sitting upright in a shallow trench behind one of the MGs.

"No he ain't!" Silva snapped, waving his shovel at Chack. "Jindal's a swell fella, but this ain't his brigade. *You're* who holds it together an' keeps it fightin'." He pointed the shovel down toward the river's edge. "An' there'll be plenty o' hard fightin' when they're done poundin' on us, so git!"

"With respect, sir, he's right," Jindal agreed. "We have the finest brigade in the Alliance, but only because you command." He grinned and glanced at his empty sleeve. "And since I missed so much of that affair on Zanzibar, it's my honor to do my part now." His grin faded. "You might even say the honor of the Empire of the New Britain Isles is at stake, since we've such a small presence in the west. So many of your people have died fighting the bloody Doms, I fear the future of the Grand Alliance relies on it being remembered there were Imperials in this fight as well—even if only by our names on the graves."

Chack blinked something too complex to follow in the gloom, but nodded. "Very well. I'll see whaat progress Laaw-rence is making. But send word at once when the baar-rage lifts. I expect a heavy aassault will follow." He blinked irony. "It's whaat we did."

He hunkered down with the rest while the next salvo swept the open ground with sizzling iron, then jumped up and trotted toward the arch.

"You better not be *plannin'* on gettin' yer name on a slab," Silva grumbled sourly at Jindal. "If you are, I'm takin' Moe's advice an' gettin' the hell away from you. I *ain't* fallin' off the twig in *this* shithole."

"Never fear, Chief Silva," Jindal chuckled. "I don't . . ." A large iron ball, roughly ten inches in diameter, slammed down heavily in the shallow trench Jindal shared with several 'Cats. Silva had the slightest impression of a flame-jetting wooden fuse. Jindal glanced down, then back at Silva, eyes wide with surprise—and maybe a touch of amusement—just before the shell went off. The trench vomited earth, debris, shattered paving stones, and other things, and a vast, rising cone of fire and smoke. Silva was protected from the initial fragments but was blown back by the blast. Rolling into a ball, he tried to make himself as small as he could under his helmet, but that did little good. Dirt, rocks, and other debris showered down, some slamming hard on his naked shoulders and back. More shells exploded nearby, mostly airbursts, but Silva immediately uncoiled and crawled to where he'd seen Cook. "Major Galay!" he called at the same time.

"Over here!" replied a strong but strained voice. "Where's Cook?"

Silva heaved a shattered timber aside and pulled a weakly thrashing form out from under the rubble. "Found him," he shouted back. "You okay, Mr. Cook?" he asked, raising the helmet that had dropped across the boy's face.

"Perfectly fine," came the gasping reply. 'Cats and Khonashi were already rushing to join them. A couple pulled a body from behind the closest machine gun and started checking the weapon for damage.

"Good," Silva grunted, grimacing at the trench where Jindal had been. Fortunately, all he could see was a crumbly-looking crater and parts of a shattered rifle. "'Cause you may be in charge out here. Corps-'Cat!" he shouted. "Take a look at Mr. Cook!" He patted the boy's cheek. "I'm gonna check Galay."

"I heard him . . ." Abel Cook murmured.

"Me too," Silva assured, crawling quickly toward where Galay had been. Others were there already, and as he'd suspected, Galay was wounded. An Impie was fumbling with a field dressing, and Galay was gritting his teeth and pressing hard against a gash above his hip. Flashing explosions revealed a lot of blood welling past his fingers.

"Shit," Silva swore. "Corps-'Cat!"

CHAPTER 36

////// *Palace of Vanished Gods*

What's that?" the Celestial Mother asked, looking at the trembling ivies surrounding them. Tiny leaves and little blooms quivered in conjunction with muffled cracking sounds, like a sledgehammer pounding a massive stone. The fur that floated so freely before had finally settled, but now there was a haze of falling dust and occasional leaves. Troops had righted the huge table, and the Celestial Mother assumed her place on a rather modest saddlelike "throne" behind it. At least it was modest compared to the one Lawrence remembered in her mother's palace at Grik City. Also unlike that other encounter, Lawrence was learning that this creature's apparent arrogance had been more a conditioned facade. She *didn't* presume she knew everything—or that what she didn't know had no importance. She was also beginning to grasp that she might not be immune to consequences.

Lawrence would strive to educate her further. "That's one of the many sounds of war, Your Highness," he declared in her tongue. "One it makes when it's trying to kill you." He blinked irony in the Lemurian way. "We're safe here, for now. Unless whatever arrangement that allows sunlight for your ornamentation"—he gestured around—"is vulnerable."

"It is not," snapped the Chooser. There were guards

outside, but only Lawrence remained in the chamber, and the Chooser had recovered considerably. He didn't feel as intimidated by a single enemy even smaller than he. "And it's past time that *someone* removed these"—he gestured imperiously at the corpses of the sister-guards still lying where they fell, though all the Lemurian dead, and Pokey, had been carried away—"from the Celestial Presence!"

Lawrence had suspected as much about the light. He'd seen the same indoor flora on Ceylon and Madagascar, lit by a complex series of polished silver mirrors arranged in tight, convoluted passageways. Air could get in, as could poison gas, he supposed, but it might've gotten only a little smoky inside after the firebombing. As for the corpses . . .

Lawrence looked at the Chooser. "No. Her Highness hears war, but needs to see and smell what her war does."

"It's not *my* . . ." the Celestial Mother began to object, but the Chooser actually interrupted her.

"You'll address her as Giver of Life!" he snapped.

"But she *isn't* and I *won't*!" Lawrence suddenly snarled, crest bristling high, eyes narrowing to furious slits. "She leads here, or is supposed to, so I call her Highness, but it *is* her war, fought in her name, and her people, race . . . tribe . . ."

Lawrence shook his snout and snapped his jaws in frustration. Distinctions between those things had begun to blur in his mind. They had little meaning in the United Homes anymore. Khonashi, humans, Mi-Anakka, even his own Sa'aarans, were all part of the same "tribe" now, the same Union. It included diverse individuals, to be sure, who in their own self-interest generally worked together toward a common goal. But how better to achieve it? Of course, there'd always be some who were corrosive to the whole, but he firmly believed the whole was . . . good.

"The Gharrichk'k *culture*," he stressed at last, finally recognizing the real culprit, the primary difference between good and evil as he saw it—represented by the Doms and League as surely as the Grik! The epiphany came like one of the shuddering impacts outside, and he barely paused. "The Grik," he continued, emphasizing the Allied pronunciation, "give life to nothing, and bring only death to all they touch. That's all they've ever done, or will do, unless they—*you*—are stopped! I can't count how many of my people, my *friends*, have been lost!" He glared at the Chooser. "Now she, they, *you* bring death and destruction upon yourselves!"

"You insolent hatchling," the Chooser began, taking a step toward Lawrence, but the Sa'aaran didn't retreat. He seemed to welcome attack, in fact, and the Chooser hesitated.

"I'm no hatchling for you to discard, Chooser," Lawrence hissed. "I'm full grown and as elevated as you. My people are smaller," he conceded, but even as he did, the long claws of his left hand flared menacingly, even though the arm was strapped against him once more. "But *these* have probably killed nearly as many Grik as you have— even if you only slew hatchlings that couldn't fight back." He raised the long pistol in his right hand. One of the 'Cats had reloaded it, with a lighter charge, for him. "I don't even need this to finish you," he said matter-of-factly. "I can do it with the hand that holds it, and *it* doesn't even have claws!"

The Chooser bristled, still confident, and took another step.

"Enough," the Celestial Mother told him. "Do you doubt he can do as he says?" she demanded. "And if not him, then the guards outside? For one so celebrated for divination, Lord Chooser, in war, or the characteristics hatchlings may acquire," she added with open skepticism, "you're remarkably shortsighted at present." She glanced at her dead sisters. "Perhaps under the circumstances you only *feel* the present and only *see* a single enemy." She looked back at Lawrence and her tone turned mocking. "But even if you killed him, others who slew my sisters— and sent you to hide—would return."

The Chooser bowed his head, but the artificially stiff-ened crest couldn't lie flat in submission. "His unruliness and disrespect—in your presence—renders my fury near uncontrollable," he said, "but I'll do my best."

Lawrence was already laughing. It came out as a snort-ing, *kakk*ing sound, and the Chooser and Celestial Mother had never heard anything exactly like it, but rec-ognized it as amusement at their expense. "Unruliness!"

Lawrence managed. "I'll tell you a story of unruliness, Your Highness, as it was told to me by your former General of the Sky Hideki Muriname, and confirmed by our observations and prisoners we've taken. Yes," he added swiftly, "we take prisoners, and they're well treated. Especially when they tell us so much about what General Esshk and the Chooser"—he glared at the Grik—"have been up to." Returning his gaze to the Celestial Mother, he continued. "It's a long story, but"—he gestured at the shuddering ivies—"since we can't stop the battle, we have plenty of time. I doubt you'll be bored, but you may be amazed to what extent Esshk and the Chooser have undermined your authority, squandered your armies and the treasure of your empire, and provoked the destruction of your cities and countless numbers of your subjects. All for their own aggrandizement and acquisition of power. I doubt you care how much destruction they heaped on us, but they left us no choice but to come and destroy them and all they have made."

Lawrence waved his pistol almost negligently at the Chooser, who appeared to be coiling to strike once more. "*Your* fate's incidental to that now, Your Highness, but you do control it. Probably an unusual experience. Have you ever made a single decision regarding the war or even the conduct of your empire?"

"Yes," the Celestial Mother affirmed with certainty. "I commanded First General Esshk to finish the war!"

Lawrence laughed again. "And he obeyed?"

The Celestial Mother's jaws clamped shut. Then she spoke again, looking at the Chooser. "I wondered about that," she confessed, "and even . . . implied I no longer needed his protection. That I'd henceforth be Giver of Life in all respects!"

"How did that work out?"

She looked uncertain. "He . . . I . . . But First General Esshk and the Chooser saved me! They elevated me!" she defended.

"They *used* you," Lawrence spat bitterly, "to seize power. We've long suspected they kept you in the dark about how astonishingly unruly they've been, and how that finally brought us to this point."

The Chooser appeared on the verge of lunging then, eyes darting back and forth, but to Lawrence's surprise, he suddenly hurled himself to the floor, snout pushing the ivies aside as he groveled. "No! No! Not I. Never I! I only ever had your protection in sight! I cooperated with Esshk at first—he was the rightful Regent Champion of your choosing—but . . . the more power he tasted, the deeper he drank from the spring." His eyes rolled up at Lawrence. "It has ever been our way to crush our prey, but Esshk grew reckless, more desperate, more reliant on his New Army generals to design his battles so he could disavow their failures. Yet more than one failure was his alone!" he quickly blurted at the Celestial Mother, casting all cautionary allegiance to Esshk aside. "I hinted as much to you as often as I dared. Suspicious, Esshk sent me from you!"

Lawrence could tell by the Celestial Mother's reaction that the last, at least, was true, but even she had to doubt he'd done it solely for her benefit. "*That* led to this," the Chooser almost wailed. "My counsel went unheeded, the distant regents delayed their full support for the Great Hunt—seeking their own advantage, no doubt—and protection was stripped from the palace. Everything"—he hesitated—"even the Hij of Old Sofesshk, went to feed the armies!"

So that's where everyone went, Lawrence thought dispassionately, even as the Celestial Mother's eyes went wide. "Truth, of a sort, at last." Lawrence sneered at the Chooser, then looked at the monarch of all the Grik. "It seems Esshk misbehaved even worse than we thought."

"The hatchlings of the Ancient Ones! Even they?" The Celestial Mother seemed stunned, more at a loss than at any time before. "The Hij of Old Sofesshk have always been the constant of our race!" She looked at Lawrence. "The foundation of our culture. If any ruled from the shadow of the palace before my mother's time, it was they. How can *I* rule without the wisdom of their moods?"

"You can't," Lawrence replied simply. He looked thoughtful. "Or maybe you can still rule, as implied earlier, but in a different way. There *are* other ways." He took a long breath. "That choice lies with you, Your Highness.

Maybe the biggest choice any Giver of Life has ever made. Your culture will end; it must. But there *can* be peace, and you might even truly lead what's left of your empire for the first time."

"This is madness!" the Chooser practically stuttered. "You can't seriously consider joining *their* hunt—for that's what is proposed! Not on the meager basis of what they've attacked with here. I don't know how they came, but they couldn't be many! Second General Ign still blocks the bulk of their might beyond the *nakkle* leg, and in the south, First General Esshk might *still* win. . . ."

"Silence!" the Celestial Mother snapped, her gaze never leaving Lawrence. "And in the event of war between the reluctant regents, Esshk might *lose*, so you strive to remain tolerable to them, Esshk, and me as well!" She narrowed her eyes. "Much has not been right. Nothing has been as my tutors—who were taken from me," she inserted with a quick glare at the Chooser, "gave me to expect regarding my position and those who serve me."

"*I* didn't take them," the Chooser appealed obsequiously.

"No," the Celestial Mother agreed, "but they *were* taken, even as what they taught tasted more . . . genuine than anything I've heard from you or First General Esshk. I *will* learn the truth," she declared. "I'm sure our enemies have their own version," she allowed, "but perhaps it is *a* truth, and much is borne out by what you revealed about the Hij of Old Sofesshk." She still looked stunned by that. "Without the hatchlings of the Ancient Ones, what's *left* of our culture to preserve?" she asked rhetorically. "I would hear more of how unruly my closest advisors and protectors have been." She glowered down at the Chooser. "One, at least, may speak in his defense, but *I* will decide which truth to believe."

CHAPTER 37

////// *Southwest of Tassanna's Toehold*

To General Faan-Ma-Mar's surprise, General Mu-Tai not only whipped XII Corps back into marching order, but he did it fairly quickly. The junior officers and NCOs did the gri-maax's share of the job, of course, but that still reflected well on Mu-Tai's leadership and the training and example he'd provided. Both of them rode me-naaks now, one of their scout's remounts provided to Mu-Tai. The Austraalan hadn't ridden one of the fearsome beasts before and approached the prospect with caution. There were similar creatures on the Great South Isle, but they were even larger, equally vicious, and no one had ever been ridiculous enough to try to train one. They had other animals, though, like paalkas, so at least he knew vaguely how to ride. In the end, he got to know his me-naak on the move and had few problems, since neither had much time to think about it.

The long, fat column snaked southwest toward the flashing guns, splashing through deepening, watery mud among hills remarkably vacant of Grik. Apparently incapable of imagining such a breakout behind them, the Grik facing the Republic advance left no pickets in their rear. Maps compiled from aerial photos would've kept XII Corps on course in any event, but the lightning of cannon reflected against the storm clouds left General Faan no doubt about their heading. Then, suddenly, they could *hear* the guns over the booming thunder and raging wind and knew they were getting close. A stutter of shots flared in a gap ahead, shapes backlit by heavy gun flashes and jetting vents. Faan and Mu-Tai galloped to the front of the column, mud splattering hurrying troops, and a pair of scouts on huffing me-naaks quickly met them.

"The Grik aartillery is there!" cried an excited 'Cat, pointing behind him.

"You were seen," Mu-Tai observed. It wasn't a criticism; merely a statement of fact.

"Aammunition haandlers," the scout agreed. "Waarning will spread, but in the noise of the guns, few likely noticed the shots."

"We must attaack at once," Faan shouted. "Make our signaal to the Repubs to cease firing their aartillery!"

Mu-Tai blinked full acceptance and whirled to one of the division commanders close behind.

This may have been XII Corps' first battle, but lacking arms to train with for so long, it had spent a great deal of time rehearsing maneuvers and evolutions on the drill field. Faan watched with approval as soggy, tired troops responded to the shrill eruption of whistles and swiftly shifted from the column into three division lines with the fluidity of the rain-swollen streams coursing down the hills. Troops spilled into their ranks, four deep and tighter than was now the norm, but perfect for the relatively narrow gap ahead. Especially with no one shooting back— yet. Me-naak-mounted couriers splashed back to the center of the line from the wings, reporting they'd shaken out in good order.

Thus the corps waited, poised in the rain, expectant, tense. A rocket soared into the sky a short distance behind, riding a glare of fire and a pillar of smoke. It burst high overhead, glowing bright red even through the rain, and was quickly swept away downwind under its tiny parachute. Another rocket rose. Then another.

"I hope our friends caan see them," Laan shouted to Mu-Tai, "but regaardless, we caan't wait." He raised his voice as loud as he could. Even his peculiar Lemurian volume wouldn't carry far in the storm, but his words would be repeated. And somehow it seemed appropriate, at this moment, to roar. "Twelfth Corps! At the double time! Forwaard!"

Legate Bekiaa-Sab-At was so numbed by exhaustion, eyes so thick with the bloody goo of fatigue and another scalp wound, and so desensitized to the continuous orange flashes of Grik guns that she hardly noticed the first dim glare to the north. Only the color and the fact it lingered so long as it darted west on the wind, like a meteor under the clouds, finally registered. Then a second and third meteor chased the first, and she knew she'd finally seen the signal rockets she'd been praying for.

Her first reaction was surprise they'd actually come, since nothing else had gone as they'd hoped. Her life had become as much a battle against fatigue, chaos, the elements, and despair as it had against the enemy. Despite its horrendous losses, Bekiaa's 5th Division—including the 1st, 14th, and 23rd Legions—was actually somewhat over strength, having absorbed the shattered remnants of two other legions she couldn't even name. More battered but intact legions had coalesced into another division and—surprisingly—Courtney Bradford was given responsibility for this Provisional Corps. Still reeling from its breakout battle, the Corps had been technically in reserve, refitting and reorganizing on the march, but when the 4th Legion made first contact with the blocking Grik and was virtually annihilated, General Kim threw the Provisional out to his right, with every gun he could spare, to face a new Grik line.

All they were supposed to do was hold, fixing these Grik in place while a quarter of the army guarded the rear from those they already smashed aside, and the rest, under Kim himself, kept marching northwest. But Kim was stalled now as well, just as exhausted and depleted, grinding against a heavier force while his energy and ammunition dwindled. Recognizing the importance of Bradford's position on the flank, however, and still hoping their allies could break through, Kim kept sending bedraggled fragments of other shattered legions until Bradford's Provisional Corps became the second-biggest chunk of the army.

To Prefect Bele's surprise in particular, almost all the

Gentaa had armed themselves once again and joined the ranks. There'd been no request that they do so, or permission asked. They just did. When Bele, grateful but just as mystified as when they'd done it before, finally requested an explanation for this previously unprecedented behavior, the Dominus—the Gentaa supervisor of all the engineers and teamsters with the pack train—merely blinked at him. "My people have supported yours throughout your history on this world. *Supported*," the Dominus stressed, "not led, not served, though at times it may have seemed we did both. Yet always we remained apart." He shook his head, his hard leather hat slinging droplets from the lighter, earlier rain. "Many of us believe that must end. This war will either define us as a people or end us all." For the first time in his life, Bele actually saw a Gentaa grin. "What better time for the Gentaa to fully join the Republic than when you need us most?"

General Kim told them he didn't expect the Provisional Corps to advance anywhere, but with all the additional troops—and Gentaa, of course—it should be able to hold. Little else mattered. If General Alden's plan failed, the Army of the Republic was doomed. Bekiaa knew Alden's assault had begun; she'd seen the distant strobing lightning of battle to the north before the heavy rains came, but remained darkly skeptical of Alden's overall strategy and its reliance on two isolated and vastly outnumbered forces rescuing each other. She knew Pete had "pulled mir-aacles out of his aass" before, and though she hadn't been there at the end whcn he did it around Lake Flynn, she'd seen what little he had to work with. But this was *so* different. . . . Wasn't it?

The last inkling that her—or Courtney's—force remained part of a bigger scheme came with a series of airstrikes against the Grik in front of her, though she didn't know if the planes had been Nancys or Cantets. It was too dark by then to tell. And then came the full fury of the storm and she knew nothing more of what transpired elsewhere—until the signal rockets popped.

"Did ye see?" asked Optio Meek. He hadn't left her side since her injury and had grown more protective than ever.

Bekiaa shook her head and blinked, dispelling the random thoughts clouding her tired mind. "Yes. Send runners. Ensure thaat . . . Mr. Braadford is aware"—Courtney flatly refused to be addressed as "general"—"as well as Col-nol Naaris and Prefect Bele." Bekiaa had direct command of the 14th and 23rd Legions, Naaris still had the 1st, and Bele had organized the "orphans" as best he could. His was actually the largest force, but also the most difficult to control. If anyone could do it, Bele was the man. "Another runner will haave the aartillery cease firing," Bekiaa continued. They had few rounds left for their batteries of Derby guns, and they'd been focusing on the enemy artillery. If the rockets were to be believed, that position would soon be swarming with friendly troops.

Bekiaa removed her helmet and turned her face to the pouring rain, trying to wash out her eyes and rejuvenate herself. "Sound 'Staand To,'" she said at last, "and spread the word we may soon haave friendlies to our front." She took a long breath. "Or running Grik." She hacked and spat, then managed an ironic grin. "Or both! Most importaant, however, we must be ready to attaack, if Mr. Braadford commaands. With the bayonet alone, if necessaary."

"The bayonet's all most of us have left," Meek grumbled.

Though their artillery remained active, the Grik breastworks across the muddy, rocky field had been largely quiet since the rain began, the Grik squatting miserably in flooding trenches with drowned muskets, no doubt. And there were only a few shots now as XII Corps quickly overran the enemy artillery line and surged forward to slam the Grik defenses from behind. All Bekiaa could tell, from a rain-drenched quarter mile, was that the Grik cannon in the center went abruptly silent.

There were other noises, however. Even over the roaring wind and sluicing rain, she heard a rising turmoil. It brought back memories of when she'd fought behind a shield and thousands of shields and swords and spears had slammed together. Rising above it all was the unmistakable tenor of fury and agony mixed with terror.

"Marvelous!" shouted Courtney Bradford, suddenly behind Bekiaa. He wore an ordinary combat smock, his usual straw sombrero replaced by a glistening, dripping helmet. In his hands was his trusty old Krag. White teeth flashed in the white beard surrounding them, and his eyes glowed with an inner light. "Bloody marvelous. We should hit them now!"

"Ay," Bekiaa agreed, "but whaat're you doin'?"

Courtney looked at her, and his expression softened with the love he felt for her. "I told you, my dear, at Soala. I've as much right to fight this war as anyone, and my days as a spectator are done. Now let's get on with it, shall we?" He chuckled ruefully at the disarray of their own defensive line. "Not much point in finesse, I suppose." He raised a speaking trumpet hanging from the cartridge belt around his waist and roared into it.

"We'll attack!" he bellowed, the tinny sound carrying. "Attack them now! Our *chance* is now, a gift to *us* after all we've endured, to smash the filthy buggers!"

Bekiaa could hear nothing over the new thunder of near-perfect accord that followed, nor could she do anything but shout "Gener-aal advaance!" to her orderlies as she was swept along at Courtney's side. *Whaat's happened to this maan, once so mild and alive for . . . life?* she wondered, but she already knew. Courtney's war had become a holy crusade against the extinguisher of life, personified by the Grik. Only by destroying them could the man he'd been return, and Bekiaa knew that feeling well. She only hoped it was so. For them both.

Roughly forty thousand Grik—crack troops of Esshk's New Army—had fortified the stone and brush breastworks thrown up to halt the right flank of the Republic advance. They thought they'd succeeded and were content to wait, letting their artillery batter the exhausted foe. Twelfth Corps slammed into their "secure" rear somewhat haltingly at first, disorganized by the fighting for the guns and the serried obstacles they presented. But the lightning lit the Grik infantry from behind, and XII Corps saw the surprise and terror with which they reacted to the unexpected threat. The inexperienced Austraalans swept on, casting their own terror aside. The Grik buckled under the blow, rear ranks recoiling against the front—which now perceived the eighteen to twenty thousand (no one would ever know how many Gentaa and "orphans" accompanied the Provisional Corps), sprinting across a field they'd also believed secure. For the very first time, despite their breeding, training, "modern" weapons, and superior leadership, New Army Grik broke, en masse.

Only the flanks were open and they surged east and west, trampling one another in their haste to escape. Hundreds, maybe thousands died, crushed or savaged under the thundering weight of tens of thousands and the razorsharp claws on their feet. Those flowing east, away from the fight, were forgotten. Those fleeing west were pursued with a relentless, murderous vigor. General Laan's menaak-mounted scouts and the guards surrounding him—fewer than a hundred—pursued as well, smashing through any groups that tried to reorganize, hacking Grik from behind with cutlasses or shooting them with carbines. It was a slaughter. And though far more escaped than died, they became terrified fugitives, lost or hiding in the storm.

"There you are at last, General Laan!" Courtney gasped, leaning over to support himself with his knees, hands still grasping the Krag he hadn't even fired. Several Gentaa stood around him, weapons raised, eyes questing for threats. Laan and Mu-Tai had reined their animals and stared, neither speaking, not recognizing the aged, muddy warrior confronting them. Even Laan, who knew Courtney well, could be forgiven that. The Australian's beard would be new to him, as would the setting. Chack and Silva had seen Courtney fight, but only those in the Army of the Republic had ever seen him on a battlefield. He smiled and stood. "Well done! Well done indeed!" He peered at the me-naak Laan rode. It was munching a Grik, limbs dangling from its jaws. An arm fell to the ground and splashed in the mud as it chewed distractedly, seeming to regard Courtney as a potential second serving. Courtney didn't care. "Such a lovely mount you have," he praised. "I've always admired me-naaks." He blinked as the beast swallowed, then nosed the mud for the dropped morsel. "I doubt our departed opponents can say the same," he added gleefully, glancing at the rider by Laan's side. "And you must be General Mu-Tai!

I applaud you, sir, and your Austraalans. I'm from your land myself, you see—on another world, of course—but have a . . . nostalgic fondness for you and your troops regardless. Especially now!"

"Courtney Braadford!" Laan suddenly blurted as recognition struck.

"*Gener-aal* Braadford," Bekiaa stressed a little haughtily, striding through the corpses to stand at his side. Optio Meek and two more Gentaa followed. It seemed protecting leaders they respected was part of the new role Gentaa had taken upon themselves. "He commaands this Provisional Corps of the Aarmy of the Republic. An' he's still Aambaassador to Kaiser Nig-Taak."

"Really?" Mu-Tai replied, blinking an elevated appraisal. "We've not met, Gener-aal Braadford, but your reputation in other pursuits precedes you. I haadn't expected to meet you here, like this."

"Nor I," agreed Laan.

Courtney smiled fondly at Bekiaa. "I'm no general," he replied, looking back at Laan. "If there is one here, it's her," he proclaimed, patting Bekiaa's shoulder. She hid a wince. They'd suffered amazingly few casualties in the assault, though many were probably now so exhausted they might as well have been badly wounded. On the other hand, she'd taken a painful jab from a bayonet in the back of her shoulder, by someone charging behind her! She wondered how many were seriously hurt or killed by accidents like that. Courtney regarded the two generals once more and his expression turned earnest. "What ncws?"

"All goes as close to the plaan as maay be expected, except Gener-aal Aalden's advaance haas staalled." Laan shrugged and flicked his tail. "I feared as much, since his primary objective was to draaw so maany Grik away from us onto himself. I've dispatched Third Corps and all my caav-alry to strike the enemy reinforcements from behind, even as they attempt to hit First and Sixth Corps on the flaank." He shook his head. "I fear it won't be enough. We *all* must turn to join Third Corps!"

Bekiaa was speechless, and Bradford could only shake his head. "General Kim's heavily engaged to the west"—he gestured vaguely around—"and I fear this force is spent. It's entirely exhausted, sir, and virtually out of ammunition. It must rest and resupply or half'll drop before they even see another Grik."

"Aammunition for your rifles and aartillery haas been maassing at our beachhead and is coming behind us in paalka-drawn waagons. There's plenty for those you have left, fit to fight. The unfit and wounded caan guard this position and the enemy aartillery we captured."

"There's a point to this?" Prefect Bele asked, moving up to join them. He alone looked like he could march another twenty miles and fight a battle at the end, but he spoke for troops who'd been marching and fighting nonstop. "A *reason* to push these legions past endurance? We can't catch Third Corps before it attacks."

"More thaan likely not," Laan agreed. "And it, like First and Sixth Corps, may be overwhelmed. But the point is, even if thaat's so, we'll then attaack those that shaattered *them*. We caan hold nothing baack for later. If we don't destroy all enemy forces in front of Aalden entirely, tonight, 'later' will haave no importance!"

That seemed to satisfy Bele, and he looked to Bekiaa.

"But . . . what of Gener-aal Kim?" Bekiaa asked. "We caan't just leave, expose *his* flaank!"

Courtney was stroking his soggy beard. "What's left to threaten it, my dear?" he asked. She started to respond, then stopped.

"Send . . ." Laan paused and took an impatient breath. "I *aask* thaat you'll send couriers to Gener-aal Kim. Tell him aammunition's on its way, and all he needs do now is hold the enemy in front of him. If he caan spare any legions to join us as we maarch paast his baattle, they may turn the tide." Laan blinked determination and his voice hardened. "And one way or another, the tide *is* turning." He blinked regret at them all. "I know you're tired. We all are. But there caan be no rest until this baattle's done. We caan rest forever when we're dead."

Courtney nodded slowly, resignedly, eyes taking in the reeling mob drawing around, many supporting others, to hear what lay in store. But Courtney saw only the physical: the wounded and bone-weary standing among the dead. "You're right, of course," he told Laan, then raised his voice. "The wounded and those who simply can't go on will remain here. Colonel Naaris will organize you and take command. The rest . . ." He smiled sadly.

"No," Bekiaa said sternly, shaking her head, and Courtney looked at her with surprise. "Only the wounded and enough to protect them stay. Col-nol Naaris will provide a number and he will choose." She glanced at Bele. Unlike Courtney, she and Bele had the experience to see beyond the physical and knew their legions had the heart for more. He nodded back. Optio Meek was looking at Bekiaa and saw her sigh. "Gener-aal Laan's right," she growled. "However haard it is, we must go on. We caan smaash the Grik tonight—or they'll smaash us all tomorrow."

CHAPTER
38

Git yerself inside this instant, ye hear?" Diania scolded Sandra Reddy harshly, calling through a doorway in the side of USNRS *Salissa*'s vast Admiral's Suite at the base of the huge Home-turned-carrier's island superstructure. Diania's tone wasn't natural to her, especially when addressing Sandra, but was born of angry disbelief when she saw her very pregnant friend standing out in the violent, wind-whipped rain. She wasn't utterly exposed, only a couple of steps out by the starboard rail, and would've ordinarily been protected by the deck above where a couple of *Salissa*'s DP 4"-50s were mounted, but this wasn't an ordinary rain. She'd been out there only several minutes and was already soaked to the bone.

"I'm fine, sweetheart," Sandra protested mildly, staring upriver at . . . nothing; near-utter blackness except for the harsh, rippling lightning probing inexorably inland. Closer by, more lightning lit *Salissa*'s escorts, bounding at their long anchor chains and cables in the rough shallows. A couple of heavy haulers had even moored themselves to *Big Sal*'s and *Madras*'s comparatively immovable forms when their anchors wouldn't hold on the silty bottom. A few lights flickered onshore to the south, lamps burning in the big new hangars and other structures they'd raised around Arracca Field, but the lightning also showed them whipping canvas and the flying apparitions of entire shelters. The tent city of Camp Simy would be scattered for miles by dawn.

A lot of planes were taking a beating as well. *Big Sal* and *Madras* had recovered as many as they could after their last sortie, but it grew too windy. Fully half their Mosquito Hawks were out there on the field, secured to long spikes driven in the ground by spiderwebs of padded ropes. A few Nancys had been pulled ashore and secured in similar fashion, but less could be done for others moored to the docks. Diania expected many would beat themselves to pieces.

She also knew Sandra saw none of that, however. She was watching something entirely different in her mind. Almost everyone she cared about was fighting for his or her life out there: Courtney Bradford and Bekiaa-Sab-At with the Repubs, Pete, Rolak, and so many more pushing out of the perimeter. Then there were Chack, Silva, Lawrence, Galay, and all of Chack's Brigade, cut off at Old Sofesshk. And of course there was the fleet, and Second Corps, and Safir Maraan . . . and Matthew Reddy. Sandra had been part of so many desperate battles, often at her husband's side, she knew exactly what was happening, what they were all going through amid the roaring gunsmoke, blood, and fear. It terrified her as much as anyone, of course, but the torture of not being there now was worse.

Ignoring Sandra's protests, Diania ushered her back inside the starboard fraction of what was once Admiral Keje-Fris-Ar's Great Hall. What remained was still big enough to accommodate comfortable apartments for Keje's high-ranking visitors and personal guests, with plenty of space left for a large, ornately carved and painted conference room. That's what Sandra had wandered out from, unnoticed in the chaotic bustle inside, and the door had been lashed open so the Sky Priests consulting with Keje and his officers could "feel" the storm.

Keje himself broke away from the others, calling for blankets and hot tea. Taking a blanket from an orderly, he draped it around Sandra's shoulders. Almost instantly, Petey launched himself across the compartment and landed on Sandra's shoulder. He started to settle in, but looked accusingly at her soggy hair. "Wet!" he screeched. "Goddamn! Eat!" he demanded, as if she owed him food for disordering his favorite perch.

"Whaat's this nonsense?" Keje demanded softly, ignoring the colorful, feathery reptile. "You caan do no one any good if you don't take care of yourself." He blinked significantly at her distended belly. "And your youngling."

Sandra suddenly hugged the barrel-chested Lemurian, dampening his white tunic. "I know. I just feel so damned . . . useless!"

Keje patted her. "As do we all." He raised her chin so she would look into his large, rust-colored eyes. "But you've proven time and again you're *not* useless. Far from it." He nodded at the storm outside. "And *we* won't be much longer. Unlikely as it seems, this is only the periphery of a relaa-tively mild strakka, and the Sky Priests agree it's not only picking up speed at laast, but the center—the eye—will stay in the Go Away Strait. It may laand to the north, which will necessitate Col-nol Maallory and Jumbo Fisher moving their Clippers again"—they'd already pulled them baack to the Comoros Islands—"or it may even circle baack around and hit Grik City on Maada-gaas-gar, but it shouldn't trouble us here paast tomorrow. *Then* we'll haave something to do again," he added firmly.

"*You* will," Sandra grumped, turning back toward the outside doorway, clutching her abdomen with both hands and wincing.

"Are ye all right?" Diania asked, concerned.

Sandra's brow furrowed. With so much going on, it was pointless and selfish to go on about how the tension was killing her and how miserable she felt—especially when the absolute worst thing was that she felt like she needed to pee all the time and couldn't. "I'm fine," she replied, forcing a smile. "Just really tired." She gazed out through the doorway toward Arracca Field, seeing little but the racing blasts of blue-white lightning. Suddenly, though, there was an *orange* flash near the airstrip, followed quickly by another. Her first thought was that lightning had hit some planes, and it was clearly planes that exploded: burning wings and other debris scattering quickly downwind. Then she gasped as a third plane went up, and a fourth. "Keje!" she cried, just as half a dozen more fighters around the airfield exploded almost simultaneously.

"Shit!" Petey agreed, equally surprised.

The First of One Hundred commanding the troop of First General Esshk's *Dorrighsti,* or Dark Hunters, didn't have a name. He'd never earned one. Leading the hundred Grik infiltrators around the large herbivores (and beasts that hunted them), through the tall grass prairie surrounding the place where the prey's flying machines roosted, was his very first assignment. Armed only with traditional spears and swords—they'd never been taught to fire garraks and couldn't have used the loud, attention-drawing muskets anyway—they'd hidden in gullies during the day, pulling grasses over them, and traveled only at night, as they'd been trained. Still, for them, the storm must've been sent by the Vanished Gods themselves, because not only was the roost normally heavily guarded, day and night, but the flying machines themselves might spot them in the sunlight, even concealed. They'd been forced to watch from a distance as time crawled by, subsisting on muddy water in near-dry creeks, whatever creatures they could catch at night, and eventually, two of their own party the First chose at random. Their primary burdens would be carried by others.

Then the storm came and the First knew their chance was at hand. *I will* have *a name after this,* he exulted, *perhaps bestowed by First General Esshk himself!* Idly, he touched the black and red slash marks painted on his armor. The *Dorrighsti* were as Esshk's own hatchlings—he'd told them so himself—created to obey him alone. The majority resided in Old Sofesshk, posing as garrison troops, and had been commanded not to distinguish themselves from other New Army soldiers. But the slash marks identified them to each other, showing them who they could *really* trust and work with, and all knew who their lord *truly* was.

Even so, from the perspective of his deliberately limited worldview, the First rather looked down on those relegated to garrison duty. They'd been given more tedious instruction in other things and invariably looked down on *his* hundred, but as far as he was concerned, they were merely guarders of things, not really hunters. More specifically, most were safe in Old Sofesshk, doing absolutely nothing that he knew of, while he was here with his hundred—ninety-eight, now—about to earn his name.

Carefully, he raised his head above the whipping, stinging grass, eyes blinking constantly to clear the rain. A healthy respect for the vision of their prey had been lashed into them, as had a need for stealth beyond anything most hunters were taught anymore. But the storm had made everything almost ridiculously easy, and they'd crept closer and closer to the lightning-illuminated sharpened stakes forming a loose barricade around the perimeter of the roost. The stakes were intended only to discourage large animals and the First's troops could easily pass between them two abreast. More important now, however, the lightning also revealed that the storm must've driven most of the guarders of this place under the shelter of some low-slung shacks placed at widely spaced intervals. The First could see only a couple, trudging dejectedly through the rain, tails low, garraks slung muzzle down, probably staring at the muddy ground in front of their feet. A primal exhilaration seized him.

Rising slightly higher, knowing all eyes were on him, the First lunged ahead for several quick strides before ducking back down in the grass and scrambling forward on hands and feet. It was the sign, probably as old as time, for the pack to follow and join the hunt. He practically galloped between the stakes, hands and feet splashing in the standing water, unheard even by him under the thunder. Focused as he was on covering ground, he almost slammed into a prey warrior standing on the short grass where the open space the flying machines preferred began.

The creature shouted something, lost in the wind, bringing its garrak up. The First rose on his hind legs, still running, and raked his handclaws across the prey's throat without even breaking stride. Other *Dorrighsti* were around him now, sprinting across the mushy, close-cropped field, starting to spread out toward the strange machines crouching under their lacework of lines in front of several large structures. *There are so many!* the First thought, unsure he had enough troops to get them all— especially when he heard the first muffled thumps of garraks. *No,* he thought. *We have surprised them completely. They can't stop us now! Even if we can't get them all, we'll get most!*

His troops were most vulnerable when they bounded up on a plane and fumbled with the leather packs strapped to their backs. Someone had come up with the bright idea—*Probably a* garrison *Dorrighsti,* the First thought darkly—that the fuse had to be protected from accidental activation during day-to-day activities, but that made it hard to use when the time came. Crouching for a moment, searching for a suitable target of his own, he felt a sick sense of failure when a hail of bullets sent several Night Hunters tumbling off their planes. Then one exploded! And another! On the far end of the field, planes started going up in quick succession. He whirled to look where most of the shots were coming from and saw prey of two different kinds rushing out of one of the big structures. For an instant, the First got a glimpse inside and his heart thundered to match the heavens. The building was *full* of flying machines!

Pulling off his own pack so he wouldn't have to fumble with it, he bit through a leather strap securing a flap and exposed a little wooden handle with a thick string tied around the middle. Looking up, he saw a pause in the stream of prey exiting the structure and bolted for the door. One of the prey with a tail met him there, but he bowled it aside and raced in among the dimly lit machines. *There must be two tens of them!* he crowed to himself, firmly grasping the pack in one hand and the handle in the other. He pulled.

One consequence of such a limited, focused consciousness that the First never appreciated was that armed with one of the wondrous new friction primers being developed for artillery and any number of other useful things, the fuses on his troops' explosives were—ideally—instantaneous. Therefore, of course, if he performed his duty properly, as First General Esshk hoped and expected, he'd never actually *need* a name.

*   *   *

"My God," Sandra moaned as one of the new long hangars erupted in a quickly swelling ball of flame, and an entire squadron of Mark Leedom's P-1C Mosquito Hawks, already fueled and armed with the heaviest bombs the little planes could carry, blew the place apart. Whether by accident—perhaps the wind showered it with flaming debris—or design, one of the tank batteries full of fuel went next.

Keje's conference room erupted in uproar, Lemurians and a few men shouting over the distant blasts, but Sandra knew their outbursts were fueled more by surprise and shock than anything. And frustration, of course, that they couldn't do anything to help. Petey jumped off Sandra's shoulder, squalling, "Goddamn! Goddamn!" and coasted to a corner of the room, wide eyes flicking back and forth.

"Silence!" Keje roared, echoed by Commander Sandy Newman. "Sound 'Gener-aal Quaarters,'" Keje told Newman. "We don't know whaat happened, and the fleet may be in danger." He spun to one of the signal-'Cats. "Try to contaact Col-nol Leedom. Find out whaat's haappening. Whaat's the nature of the attaack? Is there anything we caan do?" He turned to Captain Jis-Tikkar, COFO of *Salissa*'s 1st Naval Air Wing. The young 'Cat was better known as Tikker, and was absently fingering a polished 7.7 mm cartridge case thrust through a hole in his ear while he watched the disaster ashore. He did that sometimes, in stressful situations, and probably didn't even realize it. Knowing he was next, however, his eyes fastened on Keje. "Aassume we just lost *all* our laand-based air," Keje rumbled darkly. That was almost half of what they had in theater, and only the possibility they'd be needed elsewhere had kept their last two operational P-40Es this side of Baalkpan aboard *Salissa*. "Get with *Madraas*'s COFO and generate strike plaans based on thaat, and as maany contingencies as you caan imaa-gine!"

"Ay, ay, Ahd-mi-raal," Tikker replied, and rushed from the room.

The noise started to rise again. "The rest of you!" Keje roared. "There's a mighty baattle out there tonight—more thaan one! Caalm yourselves and focus!"

Just as the chaos began to fade and 'Cats started moving and talking with a purpose again, Diania suddenly looked down at Sandra's feet and covered her mouth with her scarred left hand. Sandra followed her gaze. "I'll be," she murmured distractedly. There was far more water on the deck than her damp clothes would account for. Petey had crept carefully forward and was standing by it, staring. Experimentally, he touched it with his long, thin tongue.

"No, you little monster!" Sandra cried. "Oh, I'm *so* sorry," she told Keje, in the face of his astonished blinking.

"There's nothing to be . . ."

Diania grabbed Sandra's arm.

"Wait!" Sandra objected. "Where are we going?"

"Tae the infirm'ry, ye madwoman!"

Sandra hesitated. "But I actually feel a little better now," she insisted.

"I've nae had a child meself," Diania snorted, "but I've seen it done. *Ye've* seen it! I'll warrant ye won't feel better fer long, so come now, an' gi' me nae more guff."

"Go, my dear," Keje commanded sensibly. "I'll send a Sky Priest to attend. Haave you a preference?"

"Sky Priest?" Sandra asked, confused. She was *very* confused about a lot all of a sudden.

Keje blinked. "For the rites . . ."

Sandra vaguely remembered something Adar once told her about that. Abruptly, one thing stood out crystal clear. "Sure, swell. Send whoever." She looked around and recognized a Sky Priest named T'nis who'd been one of Adar's acolytcs. "Send him." Her expression hardened with determination. "But whatever you do, don't tell Matt," she ordered fiercely.

Keje blinked surprise. "Why not? Surely it caan only give him joy at a time he maay need it most."

"It might also distract him, right when he needs to concentrate on fighting a battle and staying alive," Sandra countered sternly. "*Promise* you won't tell him, or I swear I'll stay and have this kid right here!"

CHAPTER 39

Operation Whipsaw
The Third Day

////// The Third Trench
South bank of the Zambezi River
0422
March 16, 1945

K eep firing! Pour it in!" General Pete Alden rasped, voice nearly gone, as he trudged through ankle-deep mud behind the Triple I's decimated line. The rain had stopped—for now—but the wind had actually increased as the huge east-west, north-south backward-L-shaped line formed by I and VI Corps was slowly pushed back toward the river. Rolak had extended the east-west line with all their reserves, including cooks, clerks, supply personnel, and transport sailors. Even La-laanti stevedores, who'd never touched weapons like those they were handed, retrieved from the dead, joined the battle.

"I'm almost out of aammo!" a 'Cat in front of Alden called back as the Grik surged against the line once more and were met by furious fire and the clash of steel.

"More's coming! Ammo's on the way!" Pete shouted back, hoping it was true. They still held the line all the way back to the perimeter and now back down to the river, but the perimeter itself was virtually empty now.

Who'd bring the ammo? Pete trusted Rolak. The old Lemurian warrior knew as well as anyone what battles required. He'd find a way to provide.

The pressure was mounting everywhere as fresh Grik kept coming to fling themselves against them. *Maybe my plan worked* too *well,* Pete thought sheepishly, but he did know III and XII Corps had broken through to the south and doubted the Grik here did. The momentous question still remained: What would Esshk or Ign—whoever was here—do when he found out? Would he peel back and try to reestablish his blocking line to the west? Would he turn on Laan and try to shatter his strung-out divisions in the southeast? Pete doubted that. His own communications were so confused, he could barely control what was in front of him. It was wholly unrealistic to expect he could rush Laan and Mu-Tai, or coordinate their arrival with anything he could do. *They know the fix we're in,* he consoled himself. He could keep them apprised of that. *And they'll do what they can.*

For the second or third time, Pete glimpsed a large, impressive-looking Grik general pacing behind his attacking warriors, bloodied bronze armor glaring red in the muzzle flashes and under the streaking lightning. Pete whipped the Springfield to his shoulder to take a shot but the opportunity passed. He fired at an ordinary Grik instead, blowing the top of his head, including the iron-scaled leather helmet, completely off. For an instant, he saw the Grik general again, glaring directly back. He worked the bolt, chambering another round, but the target was gone. *No,* Pete realized. *He has even less control than I do, knows even less about what's happening elsewhere. He's totally focused on me—just like I wanted,* he added ruefully. *All he can do is fight what he sees, and he'll keep coming until he smashes us back to the river and kills us all.*

For a fleeting instant, Pete almost wished that was Halik over there and he could call a truce and talk. *Tell* him he was outflanked, and Captain Reddy would have Sofesshk before he could stop it. But maybe it was just as well it wasn't. Halik was too sharp. He'd honor the truce and they'd have their talk, but then he'd find a way to redeploy his force to counter Laan and still smash Pete.

And he'd probably come up with something to stall Captain Reddy too.

"Gener-aal!" cried a 'Cat runner, splashing up to him, his mud-plastered tail hanging limp. "Gener-aal Rin-Taaka-Ar is dead and the Second Maa-ni-la is buckling. . . ."

"The Seventh Aryaal'll have to stretch left, back 'em up."

"Gener-aal Grisa already ordered thaat, but the Ary-aalans are haard-pressed as well." The 'Cat's voice rose to a near-hysterical pitch. "We haave no more reserves and the aammunition is gone!"

"Calm down, young fella," Pete said absently, scanning the Triple I. It was near the corner, at the bottom of the L, and seemed to be holding well enough. When *its* ammunition was entirely gone, however . . . Things were beginning to crack. "All right, lead on. Take me to Grisa."

They found him sitting on a crate. He was wounded again, in the upper chest this time, and Pete realized the very competent Lemurian commander seemed to get hurt, somehow, in every fight he participated in. He was directly behind the 6th Aryaal and the whole division was bulging back, getting closer to where he sat. There was little firing, the Grik weapons useless as anything other than spears, but on equal footing with empty Allin-Silvas. Bodies lay everywhere: 'Cats, as well as Grik that had broken through and been slain. One of these had slashed Grisa deeply with its footclaws as he shot it down with his pistol. Even now, the teeming horde of snarling Grik was only yards away, checked by a thinning, bloody line of exhausted 'Cats, superior training, experience, and resolve their only advantage. Grisa didn't seem to care.

"What can I do, General?" Pete shouted over the roar of battle. Grisa looked up.

"Whaat caan anyone do?" he asked dejectedly, shaking his head. A corps-'Cat was trying to bandage the wound but a lot of blood was spilling out.

"Just a little longer," Pete shouted, hoping the confidence in his voice would reach the Aryaalans fighting nearby—and didn't sound too artificial.

"Just a little longer left, you mean," Grisa murmured. He looked at Pete. "I favored this plaan, as you know, but considered my Queen Safir Maraan's part in it too aambitious for her and dangerous for us." He looked around, blinking bleakly. "If all of Second Corps waas here . . . Just another division . . ."

"There'll be two more *corps* before much longer," Pete assured.

Grisa smiled. "Too long for us," he said. "Too long for me."

Several Grik broke through and came charging at them. Pete shot one and drove his bayonet into another, slamming it onto its back. It screeched and bloody froth spewed in his face. The couriers who'd followed him slashed and hacked at others with their bayonets and cutlasses. Pistols popped. For just an instant, everything seemed to hang in the balance. Aryaalans were trying to seal the gap, but Grik were fighting just as hard to widen it. Pete knew if the Aryaalans broke now, all was lost. The troops to the right would recoil into a square—they'd have to—and those to the left would have no choice but to withdraw back to the second Grik line, at least. There'd be no chance to reinforce or resupply those who were cut off.

Pete pulled his bloody bayonet from the flopping Grik and shot another—just as a rising roar reached him from the left. His first thought was that the Grik had broken through elsewhere, and Grisa's despair gripped him as well. Then, to his amazement, he saw a tight knot of *La-laantis*, of all people, the scales of their fish-skin kilts wet and glistening in the stuttering light. They gouged more Grik aside, fighting without art but with brutal competence. Some rushed into the gap while more raced ahead. And behind them came a stream of moose-shaped paalkas. Eyes rolling in terror but harnessed to the weight of limbers and guns, they charged as fast as they could. Rooster tails of muddy water kicked up by the wheels made their advance even more dramatic. Gun-'Cats rode the animals and limbers, bashing Grik with their implements as they passed, and more than one Grik was run down and crushed by a paalka or gun. More gun-'Cats trotted alongside, armed with carbines they'd been issued or weapons they'd picked up.

That's when Pete realized that Rolak had dipped into their *final* "reserve," and it made perfect sense. More

than five thousand artillerymen had been left behind
in the perimeter, but even if they could range on targets
now, they couldn't see them. And their guns! Smoothbore
12 pdr "Napoleons" couldn't compete with the Republic's
Derby guns at range, but were still brutally lethal up
close. Particularly with canister. Even as Pete watched,
one paalka veered away, gun crew leaping from its back
and off the limber. And they loaded the gun even as they
heaved it forward in the mud, its gunmetal snout nosing
for the gap the La-laantis just filled. Screeched warnings
shoved the La-laantis aside, and the great gun took their
place. Even as the trail splashed down in the mud, the
gunner stretched his lanyard and a vast gout of smoke and
flame exploded in the face of the foe.

Scores of Grik went down in a broadening swath and
dozens more were pelted by shards of bone, fragments of
shattered weapons, and gobbets of flesh. The La-laantis
immediately resumed a spirited if somewhat awkward
fire, covering for the gunners as they reloaded. Another
cannon blast churned the Grik, off to the right, as more
guns rapidly came on line. Soon the fire was continuous
and it began to rain once more.

"You should've taken guns from the staart," a familiar
voice scolded Pete, and he turned to see Muln Rolak himself slide down from atop another paalka. This one drew
only a sled but it was heaped with ammunition crates.
'Cats swarmed them like flashies, bashing the crates open
with their rifle butts or prying off the lids with bayonets.
Snatching handfuls of oilcloth-wrapped packages of fifty
rounds, they raced back to the firing line with an energy
most probably thought they'd lost forever. They were
keen to get back to the killing.

"What're you doing here?" Pete growled.

Rolak blinked false remorse. "You protest? Perhaaps
I should not haa—" He stopped and looked at the ground
behind his friend. Pete turned. There, beside the crate
he'd been sitting on and cradled by the corps-'Cat, lay
General Grisa. Eyes open, jaw slack, he was dead. "Perhaaps I should not haave waited so long," Rolak continued bitterly. "But I waanted to make sure of Third Corps'
arrival first. Generals Loi and Priaa . . . blundered about

somewhaat before making contaact on my left. Perhaaps they were waiting for their taanks." He shook his head.

"Where's Laan?" Pete demanded.

"With Twelfth Corps. It broke through to the Repubs and they come. I doubt they'll arrive in time, but perhaaps we won't need them." He nodded at the seething mass of Grik. They'd been thrown into confusion by the point-blank barrage and renewed rifle fire. Rolak pointed southwest. "And Third Corps is attaacking there now. The enemy will feel it soon." He managed a small, satisfied smile. "Just as decisive, I think, will be Colonel Saachic's arrival in the enemy rear with two thousand hungry me-naaks. Even Gener-aal Haalik disliked our me-naaks, and these Grik haave never seen them. I expect even greater disaarray thaan the taanks wrought—and Colonel Saachic haas always haad a taalent for choosing his moment well." Rolak glanced back at Grisa, smile fading. "Unlike me."

"Shut up," Pete growled. "He was finished. At least maybe he saw you and knew the rest of us aren't."

Cannon snapped and recoiled back, digging deep trenches with their wheels and trails. Torrents of rain were shaken from the pregnant clouds. The roar of battle had intensified, but there was also a roar of triumph as Grik, now practically helpless, were slaughtered with near impunity. Still, Pete's fury rose, his bloodlust spiked. *Those . . . animals brought this on themselves; they* drove *us to this*. . . . A gust of wind revealed the Grik general once again, standing defiantly, virtually alone for an instant before new guards could replace others that had fallen. Rolak saw him too. With a snarl, Pete raised his Springfield.

"No," Rolak said.

"Why the hell not?" Pete demanded, still aiming, finger taking up the slack in the trigger.

"Because he's beaten," Rolak replied. "He may already know thaat, but if he doesn't, he will soon enough."

"So?"

"So, if you kill him, who will lead the survivors of his aarmy—or the next one they raise against us? It may not be as good as this, but they haave the numbers."

"All the more reason to wipe the good ones out!" Pete snapped, still aiming. The Grik general just stared.

Rolak actually chuckled. "Oh no, my friend. We *spare* the smaart ones, remember? The ones who know how baadly we beat them. And if the mission upriver succeeds . . ."

Reluctantly, skeptically, Pete lowered his rifle. The Grik general stared a moment longer, then whirled away. Seconds later, a gust of smoke and canister whirred across the space, chopping more Grik down. Pete felt vaguely cheated. "If those redleg gun-kitties got him after you made me let him go, I'll bust you back to private!"

"Please do," Rolak said.

"He could have slain me twice, I think," Second General Ign gasped as his guards swept him away, practically carrying him to the trench. A hundred more warriors crowded around, led by a ker-noll that must've just arrived from somewhere else. His gray armor was soaking wet, some of the dye running from the leather, but he wasn't splashed with blood and mud. "Why not?" Ign demanded. "I'm sure that was their General Alden, and I've no doubt he knew *me*. At least as his counterpart. Yet he didn't even do me the . . . the *courtesy* of killing me when he could!" The last came as a bitter roar. "I would've slain him without thought," he added, as if that made him more virtuous. Suddenly, just as they reached the trench, he seized a musket from one of the guards and hurled it into the mud. "To the smelting fires with these useless garraks—and this whole new way of war!"

"Crossbows would've been equally ineffective in this weather, Lord General," the ker-noll objected as reasonably as he could. "The strings—"

"And you are?" Ign snapped.

"Ker-noll Naxa. I was raised by and second to First Ker-noll Jash. He sent me here himself."

Ign thought he remembered Naxa, not as the calm, collected ker-noll he now appeared to be, but as a capricious First of Fifty, then One Hundred, who'd once denied Jash and even rebelled against him. But Jash was . . . extraordinary, and Naxa had apparently recognized it as well, as he matured. Ign grunted, returning his attention to the present disaster. "Rain did not affect *their* weapons. *They* only stop when they kill enough of us that they can't feed them anymore!" He turned to view the field he'd left but still could hardly see. What was apparent was that the force he'd led into the charge, and that which swept up from the south, was almost entirely ringed in fire. Cannon roared all around it, and rifle and fast-shooter fire stuttered and flashed with an irresistible frenzy. The small hand bombs the enemy had used to such effect clearing the trenches were cracking again, throwing mangled bodies aside and spewing smoking mud. *They must've gotten more of those,* he realized darkly. *Like everything else.* Even the iron monsters were moving again, firing as they went. One stalled, spinning the belts around its wheels, the ground too slick with mud or corpses, and Ign felt a sudden thrill when his warriors swarmed it under, prying out its crew and hacking them apart. But it was only a tiny, momentary victory, and all the warriors atop the machine were blotted out by the fast-shooter fire of another.

"Lord General, there's little time," Ker-noll Naxa suddenly insisted. "Runners arrived here while you . . . fought out there." The pause implied Naxa thought Ign had been foolish to join the charge himself. He pointed southeast. "As you no doubt began to feel, an enemy force with more death machines is rolling up your rightmost flank. Worse, the enemy has broken through to the south as well, joined with the Other Hunters—Republic forces—and rounds on us as we speak. Yet *another* enemy force landed from the river as their fleet passed, and quickly fortified a clawhold behind you. I saw that with my own eyes as I hurried here. It's not a large force," he conceded, "but it would take an organized, purposeful effort to destroy it." He gestured helplessly around, and Ign took his meaning that any such effort now was impossible.

"I suggest you ignore it," Naxa continued. "It can do nothing and is probably yet another distraction." Obviously, like Ign, Naxa understood that Alden—or whoever designed the enemy plan—built the whole thing upon distraction, misdirection, and diversion. And it had been so simple! So uncomplicated! All the enemy had to do was show Ign the part of the plan he most expected, then take advantage of how he so predictably reacted. Over and over again. He felt like a fool and, truth be told, was so spooked that even now he doubted he'd seen the full extent of the enemy design unfold.

"In addition . . ." Naxa continued.

"There's *more*?" Ign snapped sarcastically.

"Regrettably. That small clawhold is not all that's behind us. Besides the mysterious assault on Old Sofesshk itself, which I know you haven't forgotten, there are rumors that thousands of large, ferocious beasts, like *rinooks*, but bearing enemy warriors, have utterly routed your reserves to the southwest and may be drawing near."

Ign blinked. "Rumors. Dream fancies of warriors turned prey," he speculated, though at this point he'd dismiss nothing.

"Perhaps," Naxa agreed, "but there's no doubt the enemy fleet has bashed upriver behind us. Our fleet may hold it yet," he suggested doubtfully, "or stall it with their sunken hulks as at the *nakkle* leg. But if it reaches Sofesshk before Ker-noll Jash retakes the city and secures the Celestial Mother . . ."

"All is lost," Ign practically moaned. "*All.* Better that you'd left me out there"—he pointed at the battle with his snout—"to die with my army!"

"No, Lord General! Only you can save what remains. But you must disengage and march northwest. The enemy fleet will meet resistance, and must creep north through the winding narrows before turning west again. You can still get there first and cross the river to Jash's aid!"

Ign snorted. "There'll be no disengaging here. And even if I could, I'd never march—no, *run*—these exhausted troops sixty, seventy miles through a storm. To a battle? Impossible!"

Naxa gestured at the fighting. The Grik still hadn't broken and many were surging against the enemy lines, dying in hundreds, but fighting nonetheless. "Not *those* troops, Lord General. Don't forget: you have just as many strung out on the march from here to the city."

Ign hesitated, glaring out at the slaughter. "We couldn't hold the city long," he objected, though tacitly acknowledging Naxa's point. "But we might buy time for Esshk to come. Or secure the Celestial Mother and take her away to him." He remembered his earlier effort to gain time by quitting the second trench before he absolutely had to. It failed, but the principle was sound. He jerked a nod. "Very well. We'll sacrifice the portion of the army now engaged—it can't withdraw in order and will only turn prey if it tries." It would turn prey soon enough in any event, he was sure. "Send runners!" he bellowed. "Nothing else comes here. Any troops not already engaged will turn and rush to the ruins of New Sofesshk. The entire swarm will rally there."

He glared at Ker-noll Naxa, suddenly suspicious. "How did *you* get here so quickly?"

"I was already on my way, in one of First General Esshk's black airships. I'm sure, under the circumstances, he won't object. As you can imagine, however, I was forced to set down when the storm grew too extreme." He gestured at the hundred warriors he'd arrived with. "They pulled a carriage the rest of the way, at the run. They and others can take us back the same way. Or perhaps the Vanished Gods will pause the storm long enough that we can make it partway in the airship once more. Regardless, you and I can be at New Sofesshk by midday tomorrow, but we must go now."

"Can you arrange sufficient transport to get the army across the river? That of it which we save, of course," he added bitterly.

For the first time, Naxa seemed less self-assured and his answer wasn't definitive. "Preparations of a sort were already underway when I departed. All that can be done will be. Ker-noll Jash is most resourceful and entirely committed."

CHAPTER 40

////// *USS* **Walker**
Zambezi River

Surfaace taagit, dead ahead!" screeched the port bridgewing lookout. Matt raced to the starboard bridgewing, shouldering Bernie Sandison and the 'Cats by the torpedo director aside. He didn't even raise his wet and fogged binoculars, and didn't need them to see the wind-whipped sparks gushing from the single stack of the fat Grik cruiser lying squarely athwart their path. Otherwise, the ship was darker than the night because the sky was alive with lightning, and the steep forested banks on either side flashed with still more light shore batteries. Those seemed concentrated in the narrows and were slowly beating First Fleet to death. Matt briefly wondered why the lookout in the crow's nest—or Nat's MTBs, for that matter—hadn't reported the enemy ship. The damn thing was barely two hundred yards away.

"All astern full! Rudder amidships." Matt glanced back in at Minnie. "Tell *Gray*—Signal *all* ships to back the hell up! Commence firing!" he shouted at Campeti, who was leaning over the rail above to look down at him.

Almost instantly, the number-one gun barked and recoiled back, the tracer just the briefest flash before the shell detonated against the enemy ship—which fired a broadside of seven 50-pound roundshot in reply. Most missed, but one gouged a deep dent in *Walker*'s rebuilt bow and splashed close alongside, showering reeking spume down on the amidships deckhouse. Another shot slammed into the bridge structure directly beneath Matt's feet—right where his new cabin was—and almost sent him sprawling. The torpedo director saved him, but anyone on the bridge without something to cling to went down. The number-one gun fired again and again, blasting the cruiser ahead with high-explosive shells even as *Walker* drew inexorably closer, screws slashing the river to slow her. Two machine guns on the fire-control platform yammered, spraying the areas around the enemy gunports to delay their loading.

"All stop!" Matt roared, almost *feeling* USS *Fitzhugh Gray*'s substantially larger form looming up behind him. "All ahead, slow!"

"Commaander Spaanky reports *Graay*'s about to run right up our aass!" Minnie cried. Matt knew. Even if Miyata reacted instantly to the warning, *Gray* weighed five times what *Walker* did. It would take much longer to stop her. "Direct the searchlight off the starboard bow!" Matt barked reluctantly, hating to give the enemy such a fine aiming point, but he had to see where to steer to avoid a collision. Suddenly, disconcertingly, since Matt had been expecting the pure white glare of the searchlight, the Grik cruiser— barely a hundred yards distant now—glowed orange between its timbers and plates and erupted into the sky.

"Take cover!" somebody yelled, and the crew around the number-one gun dove under the light splinter shield just as debris started to fall. Most was small, clattering on the steel deck of the fo'c'sle, but one heavy shattered beam smacked the edge of the spray shield in front of Paddy Rosen and crushed one of the ready lockers below. Another heavy blow against the pilothouse windows in front of the lee helm cracked the glass and left the panes painted with blood.

The harsh searchlight beam on the foremast lit up and exposed the scene for an instant—the cloud of smoke and falling, smoldering timbers—before swinging right. It paused for an instant on the speeding form of Nat Hardee's Seven Boat, peeling away from the sinking wreck, then quickly veered farther to starboard. There was open water. "Right full rudder!" Matt called in at Paddy, watching the Morse lamp on the Seven Boat flashing. Round-shot from shore threw more spume up close aboard, and several drummed against the hull. "Searchlight off," Matt ordered. "Damage report!"

"Mister Haardee's sayin' . . . " one of the signal-'Cats started to report.

"I know," Matt cut him off, reading the signal himself. Scouting ahead, MTB-Ron-1 had simply missed the darkened cruiser nestled against the shore, and it moved to oppose TF–Pile Driver after the torpedo boats were past. Nat *did* see this but couldn't warn them—he'd discovered his radio set was soaked and shorted out—so he turned and sped back to do the only thing he could. He ended the message by apologizing for expending his last torpedo.

Matt snorted and walked to the port bridgewing and watched the burning, sinking cruiser slide by. There were Grik in the water, clinging to floating wreckage, but they wouldn't last long. "Rudder amidships," he called. "All ahead one third. Get us past that thing." The flames were silhouetting *Walker* and marking her for even more attention from shore. A loud bang came from aft, and Matt wondered what his poor ship would look like in daylight. Few of the light Grik shot could punch through the old destroyer's plates at the range they were firing, but some could, and all left dents and opened seams. "All guns return to local control and concentrate on those damn shore batteries."

For the first time since the port lookout shouted, Matt felt the tension ease in his chest. It wasn't anybody's fault, not even the highest lookout. Everyone was tired after fighting their way past—he'd lost count of how many—Grik ships, with *Walker* and *Gray* alternating in the lead when they could. Only the crummy conditions *he'd* chosen were to blame, and everyone was doing their best. "Send to the Seven Boat: 'Well done.' And ask if Lieutenant Hardee can repair his radio equipment."

"He says no," the signal-'Cat replied. "They already gone through all their spare tubes." He paused. "The Seven Boat's set is one of the older ones, Skipper, first meant for planes. It ain't well per-tected from waater, an' it's been wet before." He hesitated again. "Should I haave Lieuten-aant Haar-dee motor aaft an' seek spares from the fleet?"

Matt considered. MTB-Ron-1 was Nat's and he had to be able to command it, but they didn't have time for that. "Negative," he said. "He won't like it, but have Mr. Hardee transfer to another boat. The Seven Boat'll take the place of one of those marking the channel as we progress. And keep 'em closer," he added. "We couldn't see any of their running lights in the rain, and the river only gets tighter from here. If any of us runs aground . . ." He shook his head and didn't finish. The signal-'Cat knew, and so did Nat.

"Cap-i-taan," Minnie called, "Com-aander Toos make his report." Commander Toos-Ay-Chil was a burly, middle-aged 'Cat from the Baalkpan shipyards who'd found his way to *Walker* via one of their first floating dry docks, then *Mahan*. Not only had he built *Mahan*'s new bow, but he'd also designed lasting repairs to *Walker*'s. Matt had essentially swiped him to fill the long-vacant First Officer/Damage-Control Officer slots, which Spanky, Tabby, and Chief Jeek had been dividing among them. The only drawback was that Toos had a long way to go as a bridge officer. He'd built ships all his life but never handled them. He was making progress, but in the meantime, *Walker* had never been as well maintained on this world.

"What's he got?" Matt asked, afraid of the answer.

"Few dents an' dings on the fo'c'sle"—Minnie blinked disgust—"along wit whaat looks like parts o' half thaat crooser's crew. There's no leaks from the strike for-aard," Minnie proclaimed triumphantly. She hesitated. "But your stateroom's wrecked. The shot punched through both sides an' slaammed into the gaalley. Raang Earl Laanier's bell. Surgeon Lieu-ten-aant Cross is exhaa-mine him, but says he's okaay. No other caa-sul-tees on *Waa-kur*." She blinked. "Gener-aal Safir Maraan reports one trooper on her traans-port went overboard when it got taangled wit another. Recovery efforts failed. Somethin' . . . gotteem."

Of course *something got him,* Matt reflected bitterly. No water on this world was safe.

"Only other thing waas *Mahaan* brushed *Gray*'s faan-tail an' bent her jaackstaaff," Minnie continued in a positive tone. "Could'a been a lot worse, Skipper," she reminded.

That was true. But it *would* get worse. It had taken longer to land the Maroons than Matt expected since, with reports of such chaos ashore streaming in, Safir suggested they needed a larger force for their depot beachhead. Matt agreed, and they'd landed another nine hundred troops from her 6th Division—the 5th B'mbaado—to reinforce Colonel Will. Even so, all the Maroons and the 5th had to protect them until the skies cleared or I Corps arrived— something that was looking increasingly doubtful—was RRPS *Ancus* and *Servius*, and the few guns on the transports they'd left standing by. It had been tough to leave them like that.

The added delay meant TF–Pile Driver started out behind schedule and was only losing time as it crept so slowly up the unfamiliar river, while Chack's Brigade and the 1st North Borno were hanging on to Sofesshk by their teeth and tails. Who knew what the Grik were gathering to oppose TF–Pile Driver—or throw at Chack? *On the other hand,* Matt consoled himself, *the Grik are still reacting to us. If we're having a hard time dealing with the situation, just imagine how confusing it must be for them.* He'd stopped underestimating the Grik a long time ago, and that had certainly made him better at what he did. But even in light of the enemy's improvements, he'd begun to realize he couldn't fall into the opposite trap and *overestimate* them either. That way lay only paralysis— and defeat.

Walker's, *Gray*'s, and *Mahan*'s guns went silent after all the shore batteries were hit—or quit—leaving no targets for *Ellie* and the DDs of Des-Ron 10. Matt went back to his chair and sat, trying to peer through the wavy, rain-washed glass. Juan Marcos stumped up on the bridge with a pot of coffee—only "monkey joe," unfortunately, Matt could tell by the smell—and a platter covered with a towel. Juan looked like a drowned rat, but when he removed the towel he revealed a heap of dry, thickly-packed sandwiches pinned together with toothpicks. Matt took one before the tray was passed around, and Juan poured him a cup of the ersatz coffee.

"A little more excitement," the Filipino said.

"A little more," Matt agreed, taking a bite of the big sandwich. He liked the pumpkiny bread, and the pulled rhino pig between the slices—fresh from the freezer and not a salted cask—tasted like fine pork barbeque. He chewed and swallowed. "Thanks for this," he said. "I probably won't get down to the wardroom tonight."

"Or your stateroom either," Juan agreed. "I hear it has been ventilated. Not necessarily a bad thing, ordinarily, but in this weather?" He shook his head with a smile. "I already had your important things moved down to your wife's room—your old quarters." Matt smiled as well, knowing Juan's definition of "important" was probably Matt's dress uniform. "Perhaps you might briefly visit there, for some sleep," Juan suggested, knowing it was hopeless, but his words sent Matt's thoughts winging back to Sandra.

I bet this storm's even bucking Big Sal *around,* he mused, *blowing harder on the coast. But at least she's safe. She and the baby.* He rarely let himself think about the baby, and what life might be like after it was born. He knew it was impossible that it would be born in peace—but maybe he could at least finish *part* of the damn war first!

He smiled sadly. "Afraid not, Juan. That last cruiser just jumped up out of nowhere. It was an easy kill, but the whole column nearly stacked up like a train wreck. Damn rain! I'd string the ships farther apart if we could see each other better!"

"But the damn rain is part of what will make our victory possible," Juan reminded.

Reluctantly, Matt nodded, and changed the subject. "How's Earl?"

Juan chuckled. "He'll be fine. He was sleeping, reclined against the bulkhead, when the shot struck it. Two feet lower and it might've knocked his brains out. Small loss. Even so, it threw him across the compartment against the stove. Burned his arm a little. The only permanent casualty was his favorite chair. It was utterly destroyed, I fear." Matt remembered the poor thing, wood framed with a wicker seat and painted a disreputable orange and blue, it was never intended to support something the size of Earl. Particularly leaned back on two legs. . . .

"Maybe we can arrange a suitable ceremony," he joked, but saw Juan frowning.

"What is it? Spill."

"I fear that Surgeon Lieutenant Pam Cross is *not* fine."

Matt took a breath and nodded. "Worried about Silva?"

"Against all reason," he agreed, "she loves him."

Matt frowned too. "Well, she's right to worry about her heart if she's given it to that maniac to play with. But to worry about his safety?" He laughed and waved around. "She might as well worry about this storm. Silva's a force of nature. When all this is over and Mr. Bradford's back to writing his book, Silva's liable to be the only one of us left for him to quote."

Juan chuckled ruefully but shook his head. "I rarely disagree with you, Cap-tan Reddy," he said, "and I'm not really now. You already know no man—or Lemurian—is immortal. Dennis Silva isn't, and neither are Lawrence and Chack or Mr. Cook." He topped off Matt's cup and retrieved the empty tray. This time he threw the towel over his head before starting aft toward the ladder and the storm. He paused. "Nor are *you* immortal, Cap-tan," he called back, "or this fine crew and this old, worn-out ship we love so much. All will die for the cause we serve, if we must, because it's right. But there's no shame in fearing for our friends, our ship, our cause—or ourselves. I do, just as much as Lieutenant Cross. But I have faith in God, our cause, and you as well." With that, he turned and stumped back down the ladder in the rain.

"Wow," Paddy Rosen muttered, breaking the spell of silence that filled the bridge. "Juan's a great guy and makes swell sammitches, but sometimes I wish he'd save his moralizing for Earl an' the snipes in the firerooms. Damn snipes need all the deep thoughts he can throw at 'em, little as they get out."

"And *you* don't need a different viewpoint now and then?" chided Bernie Sandison in a playful tone. "Your whole world is the bow of the ship, a brass wheel, and a compass. Maybe you ought to try reading a book sometime. Juan's an educated man! Why, I bet he's read every book ol' Doc Stevens had aboard."

"Nah," Rosen denied, "I've looked at 'em. Not enough pictures. They'd just make me grumpy as him."

Matt shook his head. "Juan's not grumpy, just realistic. Doc Stevens wasn't immortal either." Realizing he'd ruined the effort to thaw the chill in the pilothouse—and calm the nervous blinking of the 'Cats—he forced a grin. "But we're not going to die. Not tonight. We've finally got the Grik by the tail, and when we get to Sofesshk, we'll find Silva, Chack, Larry, and all the rest waiting for us. They'll bitch because we took so long but they'll be there, sitting on the Grik capital and their big, fat Celestial Mother! It'll be better than Grik City, because we won't just *have* a city. We'll have a hostage they can't ignore."

There were growls of approval, and Lemurian feet tramped on the wooden strakes in the pilothouse in acclamation.

"Cap-i-taan," Minnie said urgently. "The Twenty-One Boat, scoutin' out front, reports a laarge surfaace taagit, probaable BB, about four miles ahead, just before the river veers nort'-east."

Matt leaned back in his chair. "Very well. What's the river width here?"

"Six hundreds to staar-board, eleven hundreds to port. Is gettin' wider again before it naarrows."

"Good. Have *Gray* come up along our port side. We'll take this one together. With *warning*," he stressed to the rest of the bridgewatch, "and it'll be a cinch."

USS *Fitzhugh Gray* avoided the wreck herself, then surged up alongside her smaller consort. Together, the old DD and new CL led the rest of TF–Pile Driver toward the next action they must win on their long, winding river "road" to Old Sofesshk.

CHAPTER
41

/////// *Palace of Vanished Gods*

*T*he large chamber just inside the arch was packed with Khonashi wounded, and quite a few others had finally been allowed to join them there. Apparently, the broad entrance ventilated the space well enough to minimize the effect of the strange smells deeper in the palace. The human and 'Cat casualties were mostly in the auditorium the next level up.

Thaat waas a crummy decision to haave to maake, Chack thought, peering from the archway into the gloomy, stormy dawn. *But I couldn't risk nearly half my brigade going nuts.* The terrible bombardment had finally ceased, and he gazed out at the fits of sheeting rain, the wildly whipping wind driving the raindrops like stinging projectiles. *A* baad *decision,* he now knew, *thaat probably killed a third of the troops I waas trying to save!*

Lieutenant Isaa-Kaas of the 1st Battalion, 9th Maa-ni-la came running up, sliding on the shell-blasted paving stones and almost tripping over a corpse. Finding Chack, she was nearly startled into saluting but stopped herself. She looked punchy and half drowned. "Beg ta report: Cap-i-taan McIntyre says there's movement in the city," she said, pointing to Chack's right. McIntyre, of the 2nd Battalion, 1st Respite, commanded Jindal's regiment now. Chack looked north. Despite the rain, great swaths of Old Sofesshk were burning fiercely, destroyed by the

Grik themselves. "Major Cook figgers the Grik creeped in around us, like you said," Isaa continued, "an' wit' the shellin' stopped, they'll be comin'."

"Anything from the Eleventh Maa-rines?" Chack asked. The shelling had chopped up almost all their comm wires and most of their field telephones. They still had a radio inside, wired to an aerial on the north side of the palace where it had been protected from the cannonade. That left them in contact with TF–Pile Driver and the Expeditionary Force, but reduced to using runners for internal communications. At least until they could roll new wires.

"Their laand-line's still cut, but somebody over there risked a Morse laamp. They seen the movement first an' reported it."

"Whaat does Major Gaa-lay think?" Galay had been wounded again, in the arm this time, but refused to leave his regiment on the line—or his Marines flapping in the breeze. Chack couldn't blame him, but couldn't spare him either. Especially not with Jindal gone.

"Thaat the first thing the Griks'll do is drive a wedge 'tween us an' the Eleventh," Isaa said.

Chack was nodding. "Right. We haave to pull them in."

"But if the Griks hit 'em while they're on the move . . ."

"They'll be cut to pieces. I know. Sound 'Recaall' with whistles."

"Whaat if they caan't hear 'em over the wind?" Isaa asked doubtfully.

"Major Gaa-lay'll haave to use a Morse lamp himself." The Grik knew exactly what those were now, and the flashing lights often marked their source for a lot of unwelcome attention. Chack blinked distractedly. "Does anyone know where Chief Sil-vaa is?" Chack had briefly glimpsed the big man a few hours before, when the barrage was at its hottest and most effective, and wounded were pouring in the palace. Without a word, Silva had simply drifted in like a bloody wraith, the bandages around his torso ragged and filthy. Grinning and shaking his head at Chack as if to say "What the hell?" he'd scooped up his Doom Stomper and bandolier of massive cartridges and stepped back out in the flashing, booming night.

Isaa shook her head. "Not for sure. Major Cook thinks

he went over to the Eleventh durin' the shellin', when we lost contaact. Thinks he's the one sent the signal. Said it was too sloppy for anyone else."

Chack grunted, hoping Cook was right. He knew even Silva wasn't indestructible, but he was as close as they came. And he just couldn't imagine him dead out there under the cracking shells and flailing iron. He was up to something for a reason that seemed good to him—which usually meant it was a pretty good reason—and he could take care of himself.

"I'm *tellin'* ya, we gotta get the hell back over there," Silva growled hotly, blowing out the oil lamp in the blinker lantern and setting it down, then pointing at the dark shape of the palace a quarter mile away. Somewhat to his surprise, they hadn't taken any fire during the signal, but the Grik probably took note of where it came from. He was talking to an Impie Marine captain named Milke, who was huddled behind a low stone wall under an eve beside the same building Silva first arrived at with his scratch company two nights before. Sheltering with them from the intermittent deluge was a squad of 11th Marines, some who'd been with him then and were glad to have him back.

Milke pursed his lips. They'd all caught glimpses of Grik massing inshore among the shattered buildings, and it was obvious Silva was right. But Milke was new; a replacement from New Ireland, via the Maa-ni-la ATC, where the tactics and military discipline he'd learned only reinforced the stiff, hierarchical, upper-class Impie restraint he'd been raised to exhibit. In other words, he was unused to the freewheeling initiative often required of junior officers in this war, and was determined to do things "right." Silva wasn't sure how he'd made captain, but actually liked him and thought he'd make a good officer—if he ever pulled the six-foot broomstick out of his ass.

"Our orders from Major Galay were to fortify this position and hold until recalled," Milke stated pedantically.

Silva rolled his eye. "An' I'm tellin' ya—again—Galay's wounded; might not even be over there. An' Chackie—

Colonel Chack to you—will expect us to have the spiz-zerinctum ta jump up an' do what needs doin'. If we don't move *right damn now*, you'll have seven hundred guys plumb surrounded by the whole Grik army an' cut off from the rest of the brigade. Not only will we get rubbed out, but Chackie'll lose damn near a third o' what he needs to defend that stupid dump." He nodded at the palace again. It was more visible now that the day was brightening and the latest band of rain was starting to taper off. "The Griks've quit shellin'. We *seen* 'em, an' they're comin'," he stressed.

"'Hold until recalled,' Chief Silva," Milke quoted, affecting calm, though his voice was an octave higher than usual.

"Which meant until the shellin' stops!" Silva snapped at the Impie. "I've known Galay a long time. I was there when he gave the order. I *know* what he meant!"

Milke waved at the Morse lamp. "Then light that again and clarify his intent *for me*. I haven't the ability to read my commander's mind." His tone turned disapproving. "I don't know you, Chief Silva, but I know your reputation. I'd never dispute your courage or . . . flamboyant supplementary contributions to certain tactical aspects of several campaigns, but I take issue with your methods. *Imperial Marines* don't simply run about, doing as they please." His voice hardened. "And I won't disregard a direct order."

Silva mashed at his soggy eyepatch in frustration and grimy water trickled down his face. He stood. "Well, sonny, *I* ain't under *nobody's* orders but Cap'n Reddy's . . . an' Colonel Chack's, when it suits me. *They're* the ones who turn me loose to 'run about,' an' I've always snatched up whoever I wanted along the way an' never heard shit about it." His growing grin was disconcerting to those who didn't know him, and might terrify those who did because they knew what it meant. "So I'm fixin' to *commandeer* the First Battalion of the Eleventh Imperial Marines to save its ass. Take a guess which one o' us winds up polishin' grenades or guardin' coast watchers from swamp lizards at Chill-Chaap."

"Cap'n Milke! Listen!" interrupted one of the Marines.

"It's whistles!" another agreed excitedly. "I hear 'em too. It's the recall!"

Milke listened intently for several moments, the piercing, warbling notes coming and going through capricious gusts. Finally, he stood as well. "It seems all your bluster has been for nothing, Chief Silva," he said, self-satisfied. "Now we can . . ."

A great moaning roar swept down upon them, its lower frequency carrying clearer than the shrill whistles mocked by the wind. On and on it went, building in intensity until it seemed the whole city reverberated and more rain was shaken from the heavens.

"Well, shit," Silva said disgustedly, squatting back behind the wall. Slinging his Thompson, he slid the heavy Doom Stomper up over the stones. "Too damn late." Veteran Marines were imitating his preparations all along the low wall they'd been scrunched up behind all night. Quite a few who'd been surreptitiously sheltering from the storm splashed through puddles, back to their places. Some just found thin spots in the line and took positions there.

"Very well," Milke told his aide hovering near. "Form the men and we'll move to the breastworks around the palace at the quick march!"

The aide, a veteran, just stared, eyes wide.

"Are you out o' your goddamn gourd?" Silva shouted, pointing north at the nearest ruins. *"Here they come!"*

Milke's eyes followed Silva's finger and he paled. Grik were *pouring* out of the rubbled city about two hundred yards away, rushing directly toward the gap between the 11th and the palace. A soggy volley clattered from the flanks of the assault, sending chunks of lead and damp shards of stone spraying around them. Milke dropped behind the wall. "Prepare to commence firing!" he yelled. "Pass the word to the machine gun on the left to suppress the enemy fire. You," he shouted at the machine-gun crew on the weapon slightly to their right. "Fire into the mass of the enemy charge, but don't traverse to the right beyond those trees to the left of the palace." He raised his voice again, as loud as it would go. "Eleventh Marines! Open fire!"

Silva nodded to himself and aimed his huge rifle at the

mass as Allin-Silvas started crackling around him and a
few Blitzers opened up. The .45 ACP SMGs wouldn't kill
many Grik at this range, but they'd wound. "Least he
knows what to do when a goddamn battle drops in his lap,"
he muttered. The Doom Stomper roared, shoving him
back. As usual, he had to shake his head to clear his vision.
The two .30-cal MGs opened up, tracers sizzling into the
smoke-puffing ruins or the surging Grik, peeling them
away in a welter of blood. The single 3″ mortar section
they had started lofting shells as high and fast as the two
tubes could fire them, and explosions blasted Grik apart
behind the line they'd established to cover their push.
Silva fired again, and a Grik musket ball blew the forward
hand guard of his weapon apart as the barrel recoiled up.
"Ahhhsh!" he hissed, pulling splinters from his left hand
with his teeth. Quickly looking at the rifle, he saw the barrel was fine and the stock was sound behind the first barrel
band. He slammed another big cartridge in the breech and
cocked the hammer. *Wham!* He couldn't tell, but each 1″
slug slamming through such a mass ought to be tearing
through five or six Grik, maybe more.

Yet the tide of Grik seemed unstoppable. None of
those charging were even shooting, but bayonets bristled
from the tightly packed, running phalanx. Machine-gun
and rifle fire scraped away rank after rank, and still it
came, not even slowing. A man next to Silva pitched back,
his skull a crater and his helmet flying, and Silva remembered there *were* still Grik firing muskets in support. The
range was too long for their smoothbores to be accurate,
but the big balls were still lethal and the volume of fire
was impressive. *Some must've managed to dry their weapons after their swim,* he thought, loading the Doom Stomper again. *Or towed a bunch, an' all their ammo in boats.
Maybe more boats crossed after we quit lookin'. But the
rain and wet'll slow or stop just about any muzzle-loader
eventually, while it won't hurt our fixed ammo.* Still, something was nagging him.

He fired again, then laid his damaged Doom Stomper
aside and unslung the Thompson. The Grik were getting
close and the leading edge of the wedge had already
passed the point he could shoot without stray bullets fall-

ing among his friends. But the Grik were fanning out now,
attacking both directions with bayonets leveled. The firing
redoubled, concentrating on the nearest targets, and even
more Grik went sprawling. Bullets blew through them,
weapons were shattered, adding their jagged parts to the
hail of projectiles. The sodden air took on a reddish haze.

The charge that finally hit the low stone wall was a bit
thinner, due as much to dispersion as attrition, and had
lost a lot of punch. Rifle fire tapered off as bayonet met
bayonet, but Blitzers and MGs still rattled. *They came to
this fight for this,* Silva realized as he sprayed a full
twenty-round magazine at a tighter group. *Most of 'em
swam a goddamn river to get at us with empty muskets, to
use their bayonets, claws, teeth....* They were acting just
like "old" Grik, but he didn't believe they *were* for a
second. They'd timed this too well, and the Grik at the
wall were using their bayonets like pros. *They* swam *a
goddamn river*, he repeated to himself with a different
emphasis, and icy mercury gushed down his back. "To fix
our attention!" he roared out loud, blasting away with his
Thompson again. Whirling, he looked at the river. It was
raining again, the wind whipping harder, and whitecaps
lashed the gray water—as well as the scores of Grik wearing gray leather armor surging up out of it to join hundreds more already forming on the flat below the retaining
wall beyond the road.

"They're *behind* us, goddammit! Form squares by companies!" he bellowed, but his voice was lost in the crashing
tumult of fire and wind.

Milke was shooting a pistol, taking deliberate aim between shots. Silva grabbed him by the arm and the pistol
whipped around toward his face. Instantly, Milke lowered
it. "What?" he shouted, rain sluicing down from his helmet.

Silva pointed. "Form. Squares. By. Companies!" he
yelled, carefully enunciating each word. And Milke saw.
For an instant, he looked lost, helpless, but then grasped
the whistle hanging around his neck and blew a series of
blasts meant to translate his command to the battlefield.
Few heard him at first and the battle thundered on, but
his aide took it up, then his first sergeant. Soon the call

was repeating all around the perimeter, joined by a bugler, and Marines started fighting even harder to disengage and cut their way into formation. Grik began leaking through.

With a roar of fury and regret, Silva snatched up his Doom Stomper and slammed it against the rock wall with all his strength. The buttstock shattered through the lock, and the breechblock broke off at the hinge and whirled away. Satisfied he'd sufficiently "spiked" his big gun, he slung his Thompson and grabbed a heavy ammo crate for the MG as its crew wheeled the weapon away from the wall and took off with it. He ran after them. *Dumb-ass Milky,* he seethed. *Wouldn't'a had to bust my favorite gun if he'd got a move on.* But he couldn't carry it in the fight he expected, and wouldn't leave it in one piece.

He watched the MG in front of him, wheels bouncing on rubble. *Those new carriages're kinda shoddy,* he reflected irrelevantly, *cobbled up in* Tara's *workshops. But the idea's pretty bright. Lightweight, with tall, spoked wheels make 'em easy to move, an' guys can pull the wheels to shoot 'em from behind lower cover. Even easier to tip 'em up an' drop the wheels back on the axles an' go, than waggin' the heavy gun an' tripod around, puttin' 'em together an' takin' 'em apart. . . .*

He was wondering why he never thought of it himself when a Grik loomed in front of him, jabbing with its bayonet. Silva used the crate as a shield and the bayonet drove into the wood. Rushing forward, he bowled the Grik over with the crate and slammed it down on the thing's head. He felt a crunch, and then another bayonet slid through his right triceps and he saw the narrow triangular blade just . . . appear in front of him, barely missing his chest. There wasn't any pain at first and he rolled away, off the blade, but then there *was* pain, *lots* of it. He tried to block it out, flipping open the flap holster protecting Captain Reddy's Colt, but then there was Milke, smoking pistol in hand, dragging him back to the crate. Together, they picked it up and rushed, gasping, past the flashing muzzles of a growing mass of men jockeying to form a ragged rectangle.

Whistles still trilled and another bugle joined the first,

but many of the defenders would never make it. Quite a few never even heard the calls and were swarmed under alone or in small groups because the attacking Grik didn't let up. They just hopped the wall and came on, hot on the heels of fleeing Marines, and only the quickly stiffening defensive formation was able to blast or stab the closest down at last, finally stalling those behind. The three "company squares" never happened, nor would independent squares have been wise. Some of the new training at the ATCs had value after all. So instead of disorganized, panicked prey, the Grik suddenly faced a tight, disciplined, bayonet-bristling hollow rectangle—not unlike the wedge they'd initially charged with. Most were momentarily taken aback. Just in time, too, because the Grik on the shoreline below the retaining wall chose that moment to swarm over it and attack. Instead of the distracted backs of their foes, they were met by a withering fire that blew them back down into the river.

For a breathless moment, while Marines reloaded, there was almost silence—except for the thunder of the wind and sheeting rain, and the continued droning of Grik horns, of course. That's when Silva was graphically reminded that whether Grik were willing to swim it or not, the river truly only belonged to other things. A lot of Grik still hadn't reached the shore and many never would. Dark, scaly bodies rolled in the current, tearing swimmers apart. Enormous crocodiles lunged out of the water and snatched struggling, shrieking morsels from thicker ranks forming below the wall. And then something else, like Silva had never seen, *reached* out of the water and grabbed a Grik with a huge clawed paw and swept it into gaping jaws that barely appeared above the water. Just as quickly, it was gone.

"*Did you see that?*" Milke demanded in horrified wonder.

"Yep," Silva agreed, the pain in his arm reminding him to check the wound. It didn't look too bad. Straight in and out. Since he wasn't wearing a shirt, he ripped the soggy sleeve of a combat smock off a startled Marine in front of him. Instead of complaining, the Marine tied it around his upper arm. "Damnedest thing," Silva continued. "'Member me mentionin' swamp lizards a minute ago? They said the boogers had a big queen, or somethin', mighta been kinda like that. Damn. And *these* Griks *know* there's shit like that out there! Almost gotta admire their guts." He shook his head. "Respect 'em or not, though, more're pilin' in around us. An' them by the river *gotta* come again, as much to get at us as away from the water."

Milke nodded. "Battalion!" he shouted, beginning the parade ground commands for the maneuver he planned. "Wounded to the center. Outer ranks, level bayonets. Inner ranks will fire at will at my command." Whistles and bugles repeated the orders, as did hoarse-voiced NCOs. "Without interval," Milke continued, meaning the rectangle would *not* revert to squares, "at the quickstep." *Damn risky,* thought Silva, but he approved. "March!"

The short, fat, ragged column lurched into motion like a cross between a centipede and a porcupine, and the Grik jumped back at first, surprised. They'd known taking down the survivors of the 11th would require hard fighting, but even as well trained as they were compared to previous Grik armies, they'd never expected this. Belatedly, they pressed in.

"Commence firing!" Milke roared, and the "porcupinipede" exploded in a flash of fire and smoke and spitting lead. Silva started to laugh, rain washing down his face.

"What amuses you so?" Milke demanded hotly.

"You left out part of the order!" Silva shouted gleefully. "You didn't tell 'em where to *go*! Wait'll I tell Major Galay!"

Milke frowned, then actually managed a small smile of his own. "I should've thought the *direction* would be obvious," he retorted.

"'Zactly!" Silva crowed, unslinging his Thompson again. He missed his Doom Stomper, but it would've only hindered him now—and there were still a couple more Stompers nobody else wanted. "You're gonna do fine from here on, Cap'n Milky, 'cause you already learned one o' the biggest lessons there is: they don't fight wars on parade grounds, an' sometimes shit just *is*, see? You gotta do what's obvious, no matter what somebody who ain't there told you. Maybe they see somethin' you can't from time to time, but usually you see shit they don't." He waved the muzzle of his Thompson around above the heads of those surrounding them. "These guys knew which direction you meant 'cause there ain't but one way to go, even if there's more Grik that way than the other. Nine times outa ten, with good troops, it's as simple as that."

Grik slammed into the rectangle from three sides, bowing it in with a clash of steel and a flurry of shots. Blitzers snarled and MGs paused to spray the flank of their advance, but the column slowed to a walk. Silva looked ahead at the swirling mass blocking their way. They'd made it seventy or eighty yards before the Grik tightened up, but even as he watched, the mass began to solidify into a solid, defiant formation. His first thought was to lead with the MGs, but they couldn't shoot that direction, just as their friends couldn't shoot this way. They'd have to cut their way through with bayonets and blades. *Well, there's plenty Griks on our flanks,* he thought. "'Scuse me, Cap'n Milky," he said lowly, unaware if he was heard or not. "It's obvious to *me* we got a heap more killin' to do." Squeezing into the sidestepping ranks where men fired their rifles or plied their bayonets straight out or overhead like spears—and far too many were falling to Grik that did the same—he started firing controlled bursts. *Good thing there's only three, three fifty yards to go,* he tried to cheer himself. He glanced ahead again as he reloaded and frowned. *Might as well be miles.*

CHAPTER
42

////// *Palace of Vanished Gods*

O ut! Out!" Chack bellowed back inside the palace. "Everybody out! The First North Borno will reinforce the right. Everyone else, form up to the left!"

"Whaat's up, Col-nol?" Moe asked. He'd just reported on Lawrence's progress upstairs, but things outside were changing rapidly. Chack's eyes whipped back and forth, surveying the scene. He'd shifted the leftmost mountain howitzer to the right, where it joined the other, coughing gouts of canister into the charging Grik. The Khonashi already on the line were savaging the enemy with slashing rifle fire, two MGs were suppressing fire from the closest ruins, and two more clawed at the enemy sweeping down. "We *should* hold," he murmured aloud. *Those outside all night haave been through hell, but the fresh troops'll stem the tide,* he tried to reassure himself.

His gaze shifted to the left, where his greatest fear had been realized. The Grik had caught the 11th trying to rejoin and had it completely surrounded. *At least whoever's in chaarge over there haad the wits to maass an' try to baash their way through. . . .* But now the fighting rectangle had stalled under the sheer weight of the relentless onslaught and was withering as he watched.

"Those men'll never reach us, Sergeant Moe," Chack shouted, the wind suddenly gusting so hard, he had to practically scream in the old 'Cat's ear. Men of the 1st Respite and Lemurians in the 9th Maa-ni-la and 19th Baalkpan were rushing past them now, running into the rain, gathering with their mates on the left side of the line.

"And it's aall my fault," Chack berated himself aloud. "I left the Eleventh out there to spare it from the bombaardment, and now it's doomed unless I expose *more* of my brigade beyond the breastworks to bring it in." He looked at Moe and blinked fury at himself. "Even if we're successful, we'll likely lose more troops in total thaan if I do nothing."

"You caan't do nothing," Moe observed simply. "The First Raider Brigade doesn't abaandon its people."

If Chack had pondered it, he would've realized Moe's statement was the most carefully enunciated thing he'd ever heard him say.

"No," Chack agreed grimly. "Maker help me, we haave to go for them." He nodded to the right. "Inform Major Cook he's in chaarge of the defense. If he caan spare anyone, send them to me. I'll lead the relief sortie myself."

Moe jerked a nod. "Ay, ay, Col-nol." He was gone.

The rush of troops from inside the palace became a flood, and Chack moved to join it.

"Col-nol," came a cry from behind, and he whirled to see a female comm-'Cat. "Cap-i-taan Reddy's on the horn!"

Chack shook his head. "I caan't taalk. Tell him our situation. He'll understaand." He started to race out into the wind and rain but caught himself. "Aask him to hurry!" he added.

There was little fighting in front of the line on the left side of the breastworks. The Grik that veered against it had been repulsed, and with neither side able to shoot at the other, for different reasons, the Grik dribbled away, by what appeared to be squads and companies, to join the slaughter of the 11th Marines. That left a space in front of the breastworks closest to the river. Chack and Major Galay, arm in a sling, jogged back and forth, shouting at NCOs, and rushed to organize as solid a phalanx of their own as they could. Nothing like what they wanted— basically a massive square that would transform into a wedge on the move—had ever been contemplated at the

Advanced Training Centers. Those at the point of the forming wedge would have to advance without firing, even as their front decreased in size. They'd be replaced or reinforced by fresh troops as they pressed forward, and the idea was to project a firing line out at a right angle to the breastworks. Hopefully they'd extend it far enough to reach the 11th, which—again, hopefully—could manage to fight its way a little closer. The right side of the forming line was free to fire on the enemy and should keep them far enough back that they wouldn't get cut off themselves. If the line ultimately had to detach from the breastworks, their fire and that of those remaining under cover *might* be sufficient to keep the enemy from exploiting the new gap.

The rain had eased a bit by the time all this was ready, and a stray ray of sunshine even briefly lanced down before it was swallowed by more dark clouds, but the battle still raged, and the 11th was still fighting. "You should stay here," Chack told Galay as he moved toward where the first point of contact would be.

"Fine. I'll stay in the middle," the Filipino responded.

"I meant you should remain behind."

"Like hell," Galay snapped back. "Those're *my* men over there." He raised the arm in the soggy gray sling. "I won't be walking on my hands. Let's go."

Blinking exasperation at one of his female signal-'Cats, Chack merely nodded. "You heard him. Let's go."

The 'Cat's whistle, quickly joined by a dozen more, signaled the advance and the leading edge of what Chack was thinking of as his "flying square into a wedge" formation surged over the barricade. Tight defensive formations were still practiced, but with the more open field tactics their better weapons allowed them to employ, nobody thought they'd have to resort to such bloody, brute-force offensive tactics again. So even if an instructor ever dreamed something like this up, it was never taught. Chack hoped it would be a one-time thing.

There was almost no resistance at first, but the Grik heard the whistles too and started turning to face them. Chack saw what had to be Grik NCOs roaring sharply at warriors around them, desperately flinging a defensive line together. The first was ground under as Chack's wedge began to develop and slammed into it like a battering ram, bayonets and even a few cutlasses slashing, stabbing, hacking the enemy down.

"There's lizaards on the riverbaank!" somebody shouted, and those at what was becoming the bottom of the wedge started shooting down at Grik, strung out at the base of the retaining wall. There weren't very many—yet—and most looked like damp, bedraggled stragglers from the fight ahead, wary of the water and unwilling to climb the wall. Crackling shots mowed them down. More and more Grik rounded on them, though, slamming into the point of the wedge with fierce resolve, bashing with muskets, stabbing with bayonets, slashing with teeth, their jaws agape. The trickle of wounded moving to the rear became a flood, and the wedge rushed on over a growing number of dead.

Nearing the point of contact himself, Chack finally unslung the long Krag-Jorgensen from his shoulder. Beads of water formed on the dull gray blade of his bayonet and were whipped away by the wind. A Grik bashed through the narrow line ahead, taking a hacking blow from a cutlass and two bayonets, but more Grik used its sacrifice to force their own wedge into the press. Chack stabbed one in the throat just under the jaw. Blood spewed back, carried by the wind. Another tried to duck under his rifle, but a Respitan crushed its skull with the butt of his rifle. Then *he* went down, a bayonet slammed through his chest, hands grasping the musket barrel. The Grik released the weapon and flailed about with long claws on its left hand. *Just like Laaw-rence and the Khonaashi filed them off their right haands long ago so they could haandle caartridges and weapons better, these Grik haave done the same,* Chack noted. But men and 'Cats screamed as the remaining claws tore flesh. More bayonets quickly finished the creature.

So odd, Chack reflected. *For this kind of fighting, the Grik would've been better off with swords and spears—and us with shields. But only the weather makes it so. If the Grik muskets weren't soaked, the Eleventh would already be dead and we'd be taking even more casualties, still behind the breastworks.*

Such thoughts evaporated as *he* suddenly became the point of the wedge and all he could do was jab, parry, and thrust in a whirl of muscle-memory responses. It was simply impossible to think as fast as he had to fight. He could hardly breathe in the sodden air, and each gasp was almost a shout. Painful blows fell on his helmet and rhinopig armor, but none disabled him, so they must not've been serious. He knew men and 'Cats were still around him; he could hear them shouting, *feel* their presence, but it was easy to sense that he was entirely alone against the ravening mass of Grik. His vision began to blur with rain and blood and tears, and everything turned into a surrealistic smear of motion accompanied by howls, shrieks, the clash of steel, bellowing cries, and the thunder of the storm. Then even the sounds merged into a thudding, booming, indistinguishable roar.

An instant of near panic seized him, and he felt almost like he had that day so long ago, at the base of *Salissa's* forward wing. He'd never intentionally harmed anyone before, yet the Grik had come, he was expected to fight them, and he was afraid. That's when he'd seen his sister Risa wounded and he'd become a killer. The path between what he'd been and what he was had been long and bloody, but he'd learned to follow it in his sleep. And just as Risa, who'd been the warrior then, had lost her heart for fighting at the end, he'd come to love it in a way, for the satisfaction it gave him to kill those who hurt so many he cared about—had come to love—and had finally taken even Risa herself. He was a machine of death, uncontrolled, that only death could still.

"Whoa there, Chackie!" shouted a voice, only vaguely familiar in the state he was in. A big, blood-blurry shape redirected the equally bloody bayonet and muzzle of his Krag up and away. "*Hold it,* goddammit!" the shape insisted, dodging the butt of the rifle that Chack tried to slam into his head. "It's *me*, Chackie! Dennis! What're you so mad at *me* for?"

Chack suddenly felt like all his tendons had been slashed and burned, and he slumped against supporting hands. He blinked rapidly and shakily tried to wipe his eyes, but the rain, foamy sweat, and blood-soaked fur on his arm only made it worse. For the first time in longer than he recalled, the cacophony of battle drifted back to his consciousness. It sounded even fiercer than he remembered, with more shooting, but there was also cheering now; damp, dull, exhausted, but real. Someone had produced a field dressing and was wiping his face while Silva held him and his Krag. He knew it was Silva by the distinctive smell of his battle sweat.

"My God, Chackie!" Silva exclaimed in admiration. "You was a fightin' *fiend*, tearin' into them lizards like a goddamn push mower an' spewin' out Griks like grass clippin's. What a sight! Why, I thought you was gonna get *me* for a second!"

Chack nodded, managing to stand on his own and grasp his weapon. He realized with a sick feeling he nearly *had* gotten Silva. Blinking and looking around, he first realized Moe was the one who'd been wiping his eyes, and he started to say he doubted Cook had been willing to spare him, but thought better of it. Next he realized his wedge had become a stable firing line, behind which the exhausted, battered survivors of the 11th were staggering back toward the breastworks. There weren't as many as he'd hoped.

Silva knew exactly what he was thinking. "'Bout four hundred left," he shouted over the shooting and the wind, which was whipping even harder, scouring their smoke away. "Maybe half that fit for duty," he continued.

"Beg to report," said a young man Chack didn't know, bringing up the rear of the Marines. He looked as bad as the rest and his hoarse voice was hard to hear. "Captain Randal Milke, Company B, First Battalion, Eleventh Marines," Milke supplied. "I'm new to the Seventh Regiment," he added superfluously. "But I must report that none of us would be alive if not for Chief Silva—and your timely arrival, of course. My own inexperience . . ."

"Oh, belay that shit, Milky," Silva shouted with a trace of irritation. "You did fine." He looked at Chack. "He did fine!" he yelled over a heavy gust. "Now let's all get the hell outa here." He pointed. The Grik had fallen back, some even taking cover behind the low stone wall. Many still fell to fire from the line and the breastworks, but more were shooting back as well. Musket balls whizzed around them and there was an occasional *thwack* and scream. "They're startin' to wad up again, back in the city. Good thing they couldn't send more than they did, or they'd'a got us all no matter what. But they still got the numbers an' we got nothin' but a dinky line o' sticks an' rocks to hunker down behind. They'll *all* be comin' soon."

"I expect so," Chack agreed, gulping from a water bottle someone handed him, and watching to make sure most of the 11th was finally secure. "And now it's time for the rest of us to skee-daaddle as you say, baack behind cover. But I believe we may soon haave more thaan our in-aadequate breastworks to protect us," he added cryptically. Silva arched the brow over his good eye, but Chack just shook his head. Tail whipping behind him, he raised his voice. "Relief detail! By the right flaank, at the double time, maarch!"

First Ker-noll Jash, surrounded by several officers and twenty guards—all Slashers—as well as the ever-present trio of "garrison" troops left by First General Esshk, raced through the ruins between the main part of Old Sofesshk and the battered buildings fronting the road along the riverside retaining wall. A number of buildings there, where the fighting had been fiercest, were relatively intact. The greatships hadn't hammered them, and Jash didn't have artillery. Gasping, they ducked behind a stone wall with bodies heaped on both sides and crawled through the ragged, bullet-pocked entrance to an abandoned dwelling. Jash paused to peer at the battle a moment longer, even as his new "executive officer," Ker-noll Shelg, tried to tug him inside.

He shook off the hand; he'd been restrained long enough. He understood, as a commander, he must protect himself, but his earlier experiences had taught him that even if a commander can't lead from the very front, he must be able to *see* it. Not only to direct the battle, but so his troops could see him do it. He was convinced it made a difference. Throughout this fight, however, he'd been held back in the city at the insistence of Esshk's enigmatic guards who somehow radiated more authority than their rank suggested. And besides, Jash could see fairly well from where he'd been. The assault—the whole operation, down to the costly but audacious crossing—had seemed to go according to the plan he'd designed. He'd been content, confident of victory, even if it looked like the enemy had already taken the palace. That revelation drove the garrison guards to distraction, and Jash assumed it was because they realized how miserably they'd failed their own duties. But he suspected the Celestial Mother *should* be safe. The enemy wouldn't actually *harm* her. . . . Would they? He'd get her back.

Then, of course, as most plans do, his began to fall apart. Having fixed the one force in place along the waterfront, he'd moved to isolate and chop it up, coordinating his great assault with what should be the utterly unexpected lighter attack from the river. To his consternation, both had failed. He'd seen the enemy overrun and engulfed, but then been amazed to see the dense, protective formation begin to emerge from within its own annihilation. He couldn't imagine how they did it. No degree of discipline or ferocity could possibly overcome what he'd sent against them.

For the slightest instant, even from the distance at which he viewed the battle, he was sure he caught a glimpse of the light-haired giant he'd first seen at the land battle near the *nakkle* leg, hacking and stabbing all around with a broad blade no longer than those the Gharrichk'k used. It seemed too small for him, but he plied it with artful dexterity and savage force. Jash was seized by the conflicting impressions of rage and admiration, and felt safe indulging the latter, since the giant's force was still clearly doomed. Then another shooting, bayonet-bristling column churned outward from the breastworks around the palace, along the riverbank, and fought its way into contact with the force that should've already been destroyed! He'd never seen anything like it. And even as his frustration mounted, so did his respect.

"I must get closer," he'd pronounced brusquely. "Sound the call to halt the attack, but send runners to direct our troops into the forward fortifications abandoned by the enemy. All other forces, wherever they've landed, will advance to join them there." He had no idea how many warriors he'd lost in battle and the crossing. Perhaps a whole division. But he'd started with thirty thousands, less than half yet committed to the fight. And most of what he'd lost in the water, at least at first, were only Uul. He could *see* what the enemy had left, barely three thousands behind their breastworks or recoiling back to them, and many would be exhausted, wounded, perhaps ready to turn prey—though he'd never actually seen the enemy do that.

Better, though the wind still howled and the air was thick with moisture, the rain had finally stopped entirely. Judging by the midday sky, it could even begin to clear. That might bring enemy flying machines, of course, but he should have time to pause the battle and allow his troops to clean and dry their weapons at last. His final assault would be overwhelming, and even if flying machines appeared, they couldn't attack the point of decision without slaughtering their own.

He couldn't know it, but he was watching his troops draw back from the doorway of the same HQ building that had served his enemy. Warriors already under cover were frantically swabbing their weapons with hunks of dry, absorbent fibers, passed out by Firsts of Ten and twisted onto the ends of their rammers. Iron rods methodically pumped, driving water from breeches and wiping greasy black fouling from garraks that had managed to fire. The same Firsts of Ten, with no finger claws at all, rapidly plied their specialized tools, unscrewing the cones threaded into thc backs of barrels, clearing them or just replacing those they dropped from bulging pouches on their belts. Jash ordered that dry caps and ammunition be distributed.

For a time, except for the wind and the occasional long-range shot that invariably dropped one of the Firsts of Ten the enemy must've identified as important, there was almost silence. Jash was free to contemplate the light-haired giant again. *Such a massive creature—so strong!* he thought, unable to help wondering if he could defeat him alone. *And the battle thus far, despite its unfortunate beginning, from my perspective, had been such a good fight,* he grudged. *A . . . wholesome fight, with warriors standing on the ground, on their own two legs. Not at all like the battles in the galleys against* Santa Catalina. He'd absolutely hated that, though it helped form him. He regretted his losses, particularly among his Slashers, but was generally pleased, considering his first battle as a general— in all but name—essentially won. *Whatever happens now,* he thought, *I will be remembered.* He turned and entered the dwelling at last, moving to a battered table. A hide with a crude sketch of his and his enemy's dispositions was already tacked to the uneven surface, and he began to design his final assault.

A runner lunged through the entrance and hurled himself to the floor with a muddy *splap.* Ker-noll Shelg attended him, while Jash continued to concentrate on the map.

"Lord First Ker-noll," Shelg spoke excitedly, getting his attention. "There's word from across the river, from Ker-noll Naxa!"

Jash regarded him, wondering how such specific word could come. Signal pennants would be almost impossible to read in this wind, across the mile of river. "How?" he asked.

"This one brought it," Shelg replied, nodding at the now-upright warrior, "in a small boat at the height of the latest fighting." Despite the rain, little had fallen far enough inland to quicken the river. It remained rough from the wind, but sluggish.

"Tell me," Jash insisted.

Naxa—and Second General Ign—had raced all night by carriage and would soon arrive in the woods beyond New Sofesshk. Just as important, they were bringing sixty thousand troops, turning them around as they marched to the battle in the east. More would join them as "the direction their duty lay was made increasingly clear."

"That is *exactly* what was said?" Jash demanded, troubled, and the courier jerked a diagonal nod.

"The very words of Second General Ign himself. He also cautions you to hold in place if you can, and wait for him to join you. Above all, defend the Celestial Mother."

"Then . . . the battle at the *nakkle* leg is over. Ign must have won." Jash looked down, then raised his head. "But Ign can't know the palace—and probably the Giver of

Life—is already in the claws of the enemy, and he can't cross to join us now. The enemy's flying machines will slaughter his warriors as easily as General Alk's." He paused. "We remain on our own, and our forces are quite sufficient." Inwardly, he was relieved he couldn't think of a way for Ign to come to his aid. This battle—and the victory—would still be his.

"Yes!" First of One Hundred Sagat snapped urgently. "The palace must be secured *now*." He stopped and regarded Jash with the utmost seriousness. "Even at the cost of the Giver of Life herself," he stated flatly. "This is the command of Regent Champion First General Esshk."

"What? Nonsense!" Jash exclaimed, stunned. "Her life is what we fight for!"

"You forget yourself," Sagat sneered. "We fight for the Race—and *Esshk*! *He* has decreed that the Celestial Mother not be taken or defiled by prey. If she has been, she cannot live."

"You forget *yourself*," Jash snarled back. "Regardless of the patron you *claim* and airs you assume, *I* command *under Second General Ign's* authority, and Esshk is not here. I'll hear no more of this, and only the possibility you speak for Esshk has preserved your miserable life!"

Ker-noll Shelg cleared his throat. "Should we signal the greatships of battle to resume their bombardment?" he asked diplomatically. "Now that all the enemy is massed near the palace once more?"

Jash stepped back outside and crouched by a broken lamp he knew the enemy used to pass signals of their own. Beside it was the remains of a very large garrak of some kind, shattered, and partially covered by a dead Grik. Nearly everyone else followed him, also crouched low. Jash's eyes left the broken weapon and he peered over the wall at the palace, considering Shelg's suggestion. The troops around him appeared ready, and their weapons were clean and loaded. More were moving in behind, their Firsts shouting for them to tend their garraks as well. *A bombardment would be wise,* he thought. *These are good troops and have suffered much already.* He glanced at the sky and saw tiny smears of blue peeking through. *But a bombardment will take time to order, pre-*

pare, and have its effect; time the enemy flying machines may not give us. Besides, he almost snorted, *much as I appreciate artillery, it is so impersonal. Don't the foes we face—have already faced today—deserve better than indiscriminate slaughter? If there ever was such a thing as worthy prey, capable of becoming other hunters in the way things once were reckoned, this enemy would certainly qualify.* He shook his head. *What a strange thought! My very existence, and that of the New Army itself, proves this war has left such ideas behind!*

"Yes," he said abruptly, gazing at the brooding battleships on the river, then back at the enemy breastworks. "Signal the greatships to resume their bombardment. Admonish them to hurry, however, and make their fire as destructive as they can. We can't wait long." He gauged the wind direction by the smoke from the city, now boiling away to the northeast. "The pennants will signal them to cease firing when we begin our assault."

He'd started to step back into the building when he unexpectedly heard the great, thumping roar of one of the greatships opening fire. Mere moments had passed and his command couldn't possibly have been relayed. He whirled to see. The more distant greatship had certainly fired, and had either raised or loosed its anchor to get underway and turn somewhat to ripple its heavy broadside downriver. Jash's fury turned to bafflement. The ship would never fire at *nothing,* and the Palace obscured his view of any possible target. Apparently, his troops closer to the water could see, however, and a rumbling moan of dismay rose among them. The monstrous forward guns on the closer greatship vomited fire and smoke—also downriver—just as something exploded against its forward armor, throwing shattered plates far in the air, and a tight pattern of tall splashes erupted alongside it.

Jash jerked his head up to the sky but saw no flying machines. *What could . . . ?* More explosions hammered the farther greatship amid still more tall, tightly concentrated splashes. A funnel toppled in a rush of smoke and sparks, and iron plates were blasted away—just as two monstrous columns of water jetted high in the sky alongside, heaving the huge ship over. A great gulp of steam joined the spume, then the three remaining funnels twirled away as the top of the iron-plated casemate erupted like a volcanic ridgeline. Fire and smoke roiled high and away downwind past the palace, further obscuring this new threat from Jash's eyes. The same apparently wasn't true for whatever was shooting at the greatships, because the impacts against the closest one and the splashes rising around it only intensified.

"First Ker-noll Jash!" shouted a First of One Hundred, running up from the riverside, disdainful of the bullets suddenly whizzing around him. He finally crouched down under cover, and a hail of jagged lead and rock fragments pattered around him.

"What is it?" Jash demanded. "What have you seen?"

"The enemy fleet is here!" the warrior practically screeched, eyes bulging. He was bleeding from a bullet gouge across the top of his snout.

"Impossible," Jash snarled—even as he knew it wasn't. He'd seen what the enemy warships were capable of and had firsthand experience with how devastating their deceptively small guns could be. He'd also seen how fast their small, narrow ships were when they raced in to turn the tide of the first battle at the *nakkle* leg. And only their strange fast-swimming bombs could so quickly and thoroughly destroy a greatship—as he'd just seen occur. That ship was already sinking, lying on its side, flames and steam roaring from its gun ports. And the closest ship had clearly slipped its own cable and was *backing away*, the whole forward casemate a smoking ruin. He realized almost vaguely that it was out of control, backing toward his shore with growing speed. The intent of the likely dead hand on the wheel might've been to unmask the undamaged guns along its side, but it would smash aground, curving in to strike near the palace. If it made it that far. Accurate enemy fire still punished it relentlessly.

In any event, it was dreadfully evident the enemy fleet *had* arrived. He simply couldn't grasp how it did it so quickly in the face of all that must've stood against it: shore batteries, rockets, their own fleet. . . . *Surely* someone had thought to block the narrows in the same way the enemy's *Santa Catalina* had done?

He stiffened. *But why do I assume that?* he asked himself. *Only because it's what I—and probably Ign—would've done? But neither of us was there. Ign likely knew the enemy fleet was coming, but couldn't have gotten word to all ships' masters to sacrifice their vessels to block a narrow channel if they must. And no Gharrichk'k ship's master would make such a momentous decision on his own. Esshk—wherever he is—should've commanded every ship they had to prepare to do that very thing,* Jash thought bitterly, *but this wouldn't be the first time Esshk was found wanting in foresight.*

Jash saw the enemy ships now through a brief gap in the smoke, furtive sunlight dashing down to illuminate them against the dark backdrop of high, wooded hills a dozen miles downriver. He glanced again at the wreckage of the greatships and saw the closest grind to a halt sixty or seventy yards from shore. *The enemy's closer than the hills, of course, only two or three miles. But they did all this from that far!* He suspected the enemy fleet must be fairly large, but all he could see was four sleek shapes, one larger than the others, advancing into this wider part of the river. A couple of smaller ships, actually very fast boats, were closer.

Jash noticed something else. Not only had the enemy all but stopped shooting at the grounded greatship, but they were also taking fire themselves. Shore batteries and antiair rockets flailed at them from the south bank of the river, mostly churning water, but they had to be doing *some* damage. *And the cumulative damage of their long passage might be severe,* Jash hoped. But when he saw how furiously the four lead ships pummeled every gun, every rocket emplacement that revealed itself, a suspicion formed that quickly became a certainty.

"They're clearing a path for more vulnerable ships behind them!" he cried at Shelg.

"*Troop* ships," Shelg guessed with horror, and Jash nodded.

"It must be so." He looked across at New Sofesshk and knew Ign could never reinforce them now, and the enemy would only get stronger. "We must attack *at once*," he decided. "Carry the breastworks in one great rush, secure the Celestial Mother, and retreat to the north!"

"There'll be no time to carry her away," one of Esshk's garrison troops with Sagat snarled. "She must be destroyed!"

Without a word, and just as quickly as he'd dispatched General Alk, Jash drew his sword and slashed the blade across the warrior's throat, its sharp edge gliding against the neckbone. The body leaped back in a spray of blood, convulsively kicking at the troops gathered round. Jash glared at Sagat. "Have I made myself clear?" he demanded. Raising his voice, he shouted as loud as he could. "The enemy approaches, and we must save the Giver of Life! Sound the horns! General attack! Hold nothing back!"

////// Palace of Vanished Gods

Chack, Silva, Galay, Milke, and Moe had stood gasping behind the breastworks as troops quickly scattered to take their places again, or help wounded up toward the arched entrance to the shell-pocked Cowflop. The rain had stopped and isolated flickers of sunlight cooked steam out of the ground wherever they touched. Somewhat to their astonishment, they'd also watched the Grik pull back and go to ground as best they could.

"Gatherin' for a *really* big push," Silva guessed.

"Yeah," Galay agreed. All of them were covered with mud and washed in blood and at least lightly wounded, but Galay looked like he could barely stand. The comm-'Cat who'd tried to get Chack's attention before the sortie now literally grabbed his sodden sleeve. Just as he began to shout into his ear, one of the Grik BBs on the water opened up. They cringed as they looked at it, but quickly realized it wasn't shooting at them. "What the hell?" Galay shouted over the din. Then they saw the shells start tearing into it.

"That's the style!" Silva roared gleefully. "Take *that*, you lizardy bastards! The skipper's here, an' you're *really* gonna get it now!"

Deafening explosions rolled across the water, shaking more raindrops out of the sodden air.

"Go!" Chack shouted at Moe. No one but Chack heard what the comm-'Cat said or what Chack told the old Lemurian hunter. "And take Major Gaa-lay inside for treatment." His amber eyes fastened on the Filipino who was clearly about to object. "I think Cap-i-taan Milke haas proven he caan lead your Maa-reens for the present, and you're of no use to your men if you're dead."

The deep, rumbling drone of the all-too-familiar Grik horns started booming across the bloody, corpse-strewn space around the palace, and Chack turned to Silva, smiling slightly but blinking sad resignation. "I think we're all going to get it now."

The surrounding Grik swarmed up out of their positions like a vast gray wave, relentless as the tide. "Here they come!" came a dozen shouts at once.

"Commence firing!" Chack roared.

There'd been little said inside the Celestial Mother's chamber for some time, and Lawrence had moved into the anteroom where a constant stream of messengers kept him apprised of developments outside. Because of the labyrinthine passageways runners had to negotiate, however, reports were often half an hour out of date. He understood radio transmissions would never reach him through all the surrounding stone, but wished somebody had thought to give him a comm section and run wires to a field telephone. *No doubt they're all in use,* he thought. But the most recent report described a very desperate situation, with the Grik massing for a final, all-out assault. He wondered if Silva was still alive, and his gut ached with a flash of fury that his friend might've been killed while he was stuck here, doing nothing.

"Better news," called a familiar, creaky voice from the passageway, and Lawrence saw Sergeant Moe. The old Lemurian looked terrible. His eyes were puffy and his mouth was bloody enough that he might've lost his few remaining teeth. The rhino-pig armor over his combat smock was gouged and stained and washed in rain-thinned blood. His scruffy fur was slick and dripping pink. Despite all that, the ancient 'Cat didn't seem seriously injured, and moved with an ease that belied his age. He also managed a hideous grin. "Caap'n Reddy's fought his way upriver at laast—there was less Grik ships 'tween him an' us thaan we thought"—he paused and blinked concern—"or some pulled baack paast us in the daark, to one o' them big lakes." Certain now, he added, "I *thought* the shellin' waas too heavy for jus' two BBs." He flipped his tail as if that didn't concern him. "Either way, he's here wit' Second Corps. The traansports is slaammin' aashore east o' the pal-aace, an' Gener-aal Queen Safir Maraan's un-aassin' now. Col-nol Chack says now's the time to use the Grik broad to stop the fightin', if we caan."

"How?" Lawrence asked, but Moe only shrugged. "Is Chee' Sil'a . . . not dead?" he ventured.

Moe shrugged again. "Not when I lef' 'em, but I try ta stay away from *his* crazy aass!"

Lawrence nodded. "Rest. I'll send an an-ser 'ith an-other."

"No," Moe said. "I go baack out. Whaat you say?"

Lawrence took a deep breath. "I'll try." Striding directly into the Celestial Mother's chamber, he returned to her language, reflecting how odd it was that it came easier than the English he now considered his own. "You have lost," he said without preamble. "Our fleet is here, with reinforcements."

Lounging on her throne, the Celestial Mother glared at the Chooser on the far side of the chamber, then looked back and bowed her head. "You expect me to take your word?"

"No need," Lawrence replied, "though you'll probably agree I've told you nothing but the truth. Still, you could step outside and see for yourself. I warn you, however, if that's your choice, I can't answer for your safety."

"Your warriors will kill me?" she demanded hotly, and even still a little doubtfully.

Lawrence considered. "No. Much as many might want to, they'll obey their orders. But the battle still rages, and battles are very dangerous. Other than that, I suspect the greatest threat may come from others."

The Celestial Mother clearly didn't understand.

The Chooser sighed deeply and stepped closer. He looked as ragged as Moe, in his way, and had apparently been fighting a battle of his own, with himself. "Giver of Life, if I may?" he asked. For the first time, his voice was devoid of any affectation and he only sounded . . . drained.

"Speak."

He took another long breath. "It's . . . possible you're in greater danger from your own troops than the enemy." The Celestial Mother went rigid. "The New Army is beholden to Ign and Esshk *before* you," the Chooser added miserably. "Why do you think, virtually banished as I was from your presence, I came here when I did? I came to take you away myself." He pointed his snout at Lawrence. "Not from him—whom I couldn't know was coming—but from Esshk. I had motives of my own," he stipulated, "but foremost in my mind was to take you to another regency, still strongly loyal to you, while this one collapsed in fire." He faced Lawrence. "I take it you have no word of First General Esshk?" He turned back to the Celestial Mother. "He's been"—he shot a glance at Lawrence—"elsewhere, and will doubtless attempt to continue the war. It's the only way he can preserve the power he craves! And how much more difficult might that be if you're in the claws of the enemy?"

The Celestial Mother was genuinely astounded. "He'd . . . have me *slain*? He could *do* that?"

"I consider it likely there are those in the New Army with orders to do whatever they must"—he inclined his head at Lawrence—"to keep you from their grasp."

"And my former *Regent Champion* is *capable* of issuing such a command?" the Celestial Mother breathed aloud.

"Don't forget the Hij of Old Sofesshk," the Chooser reminded, slowly lowering himself to the leafy floor. Lawrence noted he made no mention of the part he played in the purge, but decided the Chooser had realized his own survival depended on how useful he might be in gaining the Celestial Mother's cooperation. He was certainly right about that. "I've failed you in many ways," the Chooser pronounced loudly, his face in the ivies again, "but I beg you'll hear my counsel once more. My life is yours and I would rededicate it to your service!"

To Lawrence's amazement, the Celestial Mother actually rolled her eyes and glanced at him as if sharing some secret joke. He bristled. There was no joke here. Nothing about this was amusing, and his friends were dying outside! Sensing something new, however, he restrained a furious outburst and observed.

"Will you destroy yourself, Lord Chooser?" she demanded.

After a long pause, the Chooser finally replied in a small voice. "If you so command."

"Very well. I do not—yet. Speak your counsel."

The Chooser visibly breathed a sigh of relief. "In that case, I believe you must . . ." He caught himself. "*Should* accept the offer the invaders make. Join *their* hunt against First General Esshk! When he's defeated, all will be as it was before. As it should be."

"*Not* as before," Lawrence snapped harshly. "I already told you your old ways are dead. You'll accept this if you wish to save even a portion of your empire."

The Celestial Mother looked at him. "Must indeed. From you." She looked away. "I'm very young and haven't even learned all the old ways yet. How can I balance them against what you offer?"

Lawrence considered his next words with care. "There is no balance to contemplate, and it's only because you *are* young that I can make any offer at all. Unlike your mother, perhaps you're young enough to learn new, better ways, *instead* of the old ones that brought us to this."

"Will you teach me?" the Celestial Mother asked, and suddenly Lawrence again caught a whiff of the scent that drove Pokey mad. So close, it had a noticeable effect, and his thoughts turned hazy. Even the Chooser began to squirm.

"Stop that at once," he said sternly. "Using that . . . weapon is one of the *first* things you must change."

Apparently disappointed, the Celestial Mother relaxed slightly on her throne and the smell began to dissipate.

"I . . . and others . . . will see that you're taught," Lawrence hedged. "But first we must end the fighting. There must be a way without exposing yourself to danger. Many are dying on both sides as we speak, and the second lesson you must learn is that *all* lives are precious and not to be wasted."

"An easy lesson to learn with my mind," the Celestial Mother said doubtfully, "but so different from everything I've already been taught, it may be difficult to *feel* as truth." Her eyes narrowed and she regarded Lawrence deeply, as if he were the only other being in existence. He fidgeted. "There *is* a way to call those outside the palace to attention," she finally confessed, pointing a clawed toe at the Chooser. "He can direct the operation of the device and speak to your general. I would . . . speak more with you here."

Lawrence gulped. "No others remain with our force who can speak your tongue," he said quickly, then nodded at the Chooser himself. "And I don't trust him to say only what he's told."

"Very well," the Celestial Mother agreed, eyes still intent, jaws and even posture forming an expression he'd never seen. Of course, his experience with females of any race resembling his own was nil. "But I expect you to return as soon as the fighting's done and begin my . . . education."

Lawrence gulped again but managed to jerk a nod. It was then he noticed that the Celestial Mother's expression had changed back from . . . whatever it had been. "The first thing I'd *like* to know is how you came to command prey."

He hesitated, conscious of Chack's admonition not to lie, but uncertain how to proceed. "Come, Chooser," he snapped instead, "we must hurry. There'll be time for such discussions later." The Chooser stood, and Lawrence motioned two 'Cats inside to escort him. Instead of following immediately, however, he paused and turned back. "I don't command prey," he stated simply, "and that's the third thing you must learn. There is no prey in this fight, except that which we make of each other." He nodded at the Lemurians. "They rescued my people, and I found my place among them—and others—by choice. They're all my people now, and are far nobler than yours have ever been allowed to be." He turned to follow the Chooser but called out behind him. "Prepare yourself. For all our sakes, I hope you're the one to change that."

CHAPTER 44

////// *Palace of Vanished Gods*

C ommence firing!" Chack bellowed again, setting off for the breastworks at a run, Dennis Silva at his side. Six machine guns were already chattering, peeling deep layers off the charge, and the two mountain howitzers coughed their sprays of canister. Mortars popped and rifles crackled in earnest. But the swarm was only slowed by the ranks the fire melted away, and thousands more replaced them. Chack's Raider Brigade braced for the seething horde swarming down.

Of all the regimental commanders that began the operation, only young Abel Cook remained. Jindal's place had been taken by Captain McIntyre, and Randal Milke stood for Enrico Galay. Perhaps Jindal had been right and it was appropriate that here, now, both original Raider regiments be led by Imperials. *Symbolism's importaant,* Chack reflected as he and Silva, puffing, took their places close to McIntyre near the center of the line. *And if my brigade's destroyed and the palaace retaken before Safir aassembles enough of her corps aashore to save us, it* will *be importaant to the survivaal of the Graand Alliaance that Imperiaals were here.*

Runners were racing back and forth from the entrance to the palace, bringing ammunition. There wasn't much left. Silva snatched a satchel of grenades from one as she rushed past, and Chack managed a genuine grin for his big friend. "Your favorite toys."

Silva grinned back. "Not my *very* favorites," he denied, "but they're pretty fun. Never got to play with 'em much in the old days. Spanky wouldn't let me. Remember when I had to actually getteem ta write a *note*, sayin' it was okay? An' then he took it back!"

The leading edge of the Grik tide erupted in smoke and musket balls. Too many found targets, with metallic clanks or hollow thumps. 'Cats, men, and Grik-like Khonashi fell back from the barricade or dropped to the ground, screaming and thrashing. Chack and Silva both crouched instinctively, but Captain McIntyre stood entirely erect, apparently unconcerned, nothing but his sword in his hand.

"Get *down*, Cap-i-taan," Chack shouted at him. "And get a rifle. The chaarge is still a hundred tails out! Precious seconds remain to kill more Grik before you need a sword!"

McIntyre blinked at him, and Chack recognized his own hypocrisy. Somewhat sheepishly, he unslung his Krag and slid it up over a jagged timber in front of him. He spared a glare for Silva, who shrugged, thumping his battered Thompson down as well. "Just waitin' on you, little buddy. An' mine's better for up close." He squinted his eye. "Course, they're *gettin'* pretty close." Without another word, he hunkered behind the weapon and started throwing long bursts at the enemy. Chack fired as well, and it seemed Silva was changing magazines almost as fast as Chack could work the Krag's smooth bolt.

The firing intensified all around them, driven by the controlled, experienced terror that felt so much like panic, but couldn't be more different from a practical standpoint. Instead of causing those afflicted to rise and flee, this kind of terror, infused with a rising dose of desperate rage, only turned the veterans of Chack's Brigade into a more focused, lethal, single entity, with one thought in its collective consciousness: kill Grik. It became a unified organism dedicated to destruction. And even as its component parts—like fingers, toes, and tails, then hands and eyes—started to fall away, it fought more urgently to destroy the thing attacking it.

Blitzers crackled unceasingly as the Grik charge neared the barricade. Nearly everyone had one now, whether they'd brought their own or not. Blitzers once belonging to the fallen still fought to avenge them as Raiders laid their powerful single-shot rifles aside in momentary favor of rapid fire. Grenades arced out in streams, thrown as fast as their pins were pulled, and Grik were shredded or blown into the air, knocking even the unhurt down. Silva did the same, lobbing grenades forty, then thirty yards, just past the leading edge of the assault, blasting those in front down from behind and leaving smoking gaps in the charge. That furious final convulsion of destruction was enough to slow the onslaught ever so slightly, so when it finally drove home against the breastworks, the defense was bristling with bayonets on retrieved rifles once more, each held by a man or 'Cat or Khonashi who'd learned to use it well. And the sound of the impact—the shooting, booming, crashing, screaming roar of it all—must've been something like the cataclysmic noise a sinking ship makes when it smashes into the bottom of the sea.

These Grik soldiers might've been the best in the world, led by a commander they respected and fighting to recover their holiest shrine and the "mother" of their species. Chack's Brigade was the most experienced, deadliest cream of all the Allied armies—and it was better. But Jash's Slashers, revealed by attrition and among the first to bash into the breastworks, had experience of their own, backed by an overwhelming quantity of respectable quality.

Even as they suddenly fought for their lives—and each other's—Chack and Silva realized how different this was, even from the fighting earlier that day, and that they'd been engulfed in the fiercest, wildest, most animalistic struggle either had ever known. Silva was battered and nipped by countless jabs and blows in that first great collision and managed to empty his Thompson twice more, spraying blood, bone, and brains away, practically at the muzzle. There was no time or opportunity to reload after that. He couldn't even sling the weapon and had to drop it again. He instantly reverted to his weapons of choice in such intimate situations: his 1917 Navy cutlass and 1911 Colt .45.

Chack's Krag, with its '03 Springfield bayonet, became a glorified spear again, with a razor-sharp blade on one end and a heavy, steel-shod club on the other. And it was wielded by a 'Cat who'd become an artist at killing with that combination. But this was tighter, more vicious even than the whirlwind at the point of the wedge, and Chack's beloved old Krag, battered by Grik muskets, its stock cracked by the very skulls it crushed, slowly came apart in his hands. He finally let its shattered remains fall in the mud of a shell crater behind the breastworks, and drew his own pistol and cutlass.

And so Chack and Silva fought, side by side, trying to cover each other while they loaded pistols or strained to free cutlasses jammed in Grik ribs. They hewed limbs, necks, heads; hacked away hands and fingers clutching bayonet-tipped muskets that probed for them; and blasted bloody holes in chests and open, ravening jaws. Bodies heaped before them. Yet ever so slowly, they—and the entire diminishing but still unbroken line—were pushed inexorably back from the breastworks, through the muddy trenches and shell holes, and onto the rain- and blood-slicked paving stones before the arched entrance to the Palace of Vanished Gods.

This came with an unexpected advantage, however, since as the brigade contracted, its line thickened and the Grik numbers began to count for less, because fewer could come into contact. Maybe four machine guns still stuttered on the flanks by the palace, preventing the Grik from cutting them off, but two MGs had been overrun; their crews killed before they could retreat. And who knew how long the ammo would hold? 'Cats and Khonashi with Blitzers hosed down Grik trying to scale the slick sides of the palace itself and drop in behind them. Both light, stubby howitzers were still with them, pulling back, belching clouds of canister, but there couldn't be many rounds left for them either.

"We may haave to pull baack into the palaace," Chack gasped, shouldering inside the reach of a Grik musket and hacking the wielder's head half off, severing the

spine. The Grik dropped like a stone, bright blood foun-
taining up under a sky still clearing, but dimmed by the
low-hanging smoke and haze. Even the capricious wind
had dropped almost to nothing, but it might've just shifted
again and only been still in the lee of the palace. McIntyre
was covering Silva's left while he jammed another magazine in his mud- and blood-caked 1911, and Silva had to
admit he was impressed with the Impie's swordsmanship,
weaving like a cobra to avoid thrusts or shots and jabbing
deep in the press with the point of his blade, taking Grik
in the chest, throat, or eyes.

Silva was damn good with his cutlass; hacking, primarily, which was what it was best for, but he suspected he
wouldn't last a minute against McIntyre. He grinned. *Unless I cheated.* Dropping the slide, he pointed the 1911 at
a Grik about to skewer Chack with a bayonet and blew the
top of its head off. Two more shots killed more Grik beyond it. "We go in that hole, the battle's over," he warned.
"Fine for us, 'cause even cut down as we are, I don't think
they can pry us out." He paused to shoot more Grik and
reloaded again. "They can *burn* us out. Smoke us out, any-
how," he amended, "if they don't care about the Sequesteral Fat Broad anymore." He paused to hack down on a
Grik musket barrel, and clawed fingers flew. He kicked the
weapon aside and shot the Grik down the gullet even as
its terrifying jaws snapped inches from his face. It coughed
blood all over him and fell. "They *must*, though," he continued, shooting another Grik climbing over the body,
"'cause they seem pretty fixed on gettin' in. Long as we
keep fightin', they stay glued to that. Sure, we'll get a rest
if we go in an' hunker down, but we'll be turnin' these
Grik loose to redeploy to the sides o' the Cowflop an'
stand against Second Corps when it comes up!"

They knew II Corps was behind them, east of the palace, offloading from the transports and shaking out as
fast as it could. And nobody would speed that up faster
than Safir Maraan. Maybe the Grik knew they were there
too now, but were staying as packed up in front of Chack's
Brigade as they could, whether they could come to grips
or not. Silva didn't get it.

Another musket barrel slammed down, glancing off

his helmet. He caught it on his left forearm, pushed up, then stabbed the Grik that swung it in the chest. The clipped point of the cutlass avoided bone, like it did so well, and protruded from the Grik's back for an instant before Silva jerked it out. *Thing's pretty good for pokin' too,* Silva conceded, *but sometimes it gets stuck an' you feel a weird kind o'* . . . quiverin' *in it when it does.* . . . He spun and fired two shots into a Grik about to club McIntyre, and his slide locked back. That had been his last magazine. Deliberately, he shoved the filthy, smoking pistol in its holster and drew Captain Reddy's nickel-plated Colt. *Thing's so pretty, I hate to use it in a mess like this,* he lamented. *But this is what it's for, why the skipper made me keep it.*

That's when he happened to glance at the river beyond the heaving mass of Grik that had pushed in between him and it. He blinked his good eye to clear the bloody, sweaty goo. It helped only a little, but there was no questioning what he saw. "Good God a'mighty!" he thundered. "*There she is!* Look, Chackie, just yonder!" He pointed his cutlass south.

"I'm a little busy," Chack shouted back, sarcasm thick even under his exhaustion.

"Well finish up an' *look*!" Silva demanded.

Like a dreamed-for apparition under the haze-filtered sun, USS *Walker*'s battered gray shape was gliding into view. She was scorched and scraped and carried many new dents and scars. There were even a number of new holes here and there, but those were mostly in her thin funnels, as far as Silva could tell. But she, the big "163" standing tall and proud on her bow above the small wake she was making, and the huge Stars and Stripes battle flag whipping incongruously forward from her foremast, remained the most beautiful things in Silva's world. Her machine guns and 25 mms aft of her torpedo tubes flickered unheard over the roar of battle, their tracers chopping at the Grik farthest away. Then, together, her numbers one, three, and four guns fired a salvo, and a tight trio of explosions erupted among the Grik mass. That *was* heard over the battle, and almost immediately Silva felt a shift in the press before him. He had to quit his gawking because the Grik were still fighting, pushing even harder, it seemed, but he could sense a subtle pressure to the right, and the Grik felt it too.

"It's Second Corps!" came a jubilant Lemurian yell, and Chack grabbed Silva hard with his left hand, his tired eyes suddenly wide and alight. "Safir has come! Attaacking on our right between the palaace and the city!"

"Swell!" Silva shouted back, blasting a Grik with the shiny Colt. "Stay focused, Chackie. We ain't done yet!"

He was right. The enemy *had* known reinforcements were coming, had seen the powerful ships drawing near, and obviously expected Allied aircraft to appear at any time. That's why they continued to fight so fiercely to stay so close. Besides their objective to secure their Celestial Mother, the remains of Chack's Brigade was their *protection* from the water and the air. Unfortunately for them, they'd done their job too well and forced their imagined safeguard into too tight a knot, while underestimating the accuracy of the mighty guns on the water. All the warships on the river, besides the elements of Des-Ron 10 still covering the transports, slowly steamed past in a stately procession. *Walker* was first, followed by the similar-looking but comparatively huge USS *Fitzhugh Gray*. Then came USS *James Ellis* and the truncated USS *Mahan*. All looked battered by their journey up the Zambezi, the new dazzle paint schemes on all but *Walker* kind of smudged together now, making them look even worse. But their guns still worked and their rapid salvoes swept away great swaths of the Grik rear, firing so close on flat trajectories that the HE shells ripped through dozens of bodies before exploding and scouring scores more away in vast cones of destruction.

The Grik pressed tighter against Chack's Brigade, trying to escape the slaughter, and the fighting briefly became even more frantic, if that was possible. Once more, Silva and Chack were unable to even think about anything other than staying alive. The shiny Colt was empty. Too slow to reload right now, it was back in its holster. Silva had replaced it with the '03 bayonet he always carried and fought now with a blade in each hand. He was uncomfortably aware that the last time he'd been forced to such extremes, he'd nearly bought it. Chack fought the same, with his cutlass and, somewhat awkwardly, a Grik blade he'd seized. But the roar of battle, of *shooting*, which had all but stopped around the palace arch, was growing, competing now even with the roar of guns on the water. And that was when another roar commenced that seemed to shake their very bones.

It came from behind them, obviously, from somewhere in the palace, but it *felt* like it came from the sky as well and even the ground beneath their feet. The frequency was so low, so loud, that the sudden, booming drone almost overpowered the crack of *Gray*'s 5.5″ rifles and could probably be heard for miles. Clearly, it was a Grik horn of some kind, like they'd all heard on many battlefields, powered by bellows pressing air through pipes. But this noise had to come from a horn so immense that the bellows alone would probably fill one of *Walker*'s firerooms. Chack and Silva didn't even try to talk, but they exchanged anxious looks. Grik horns had a purpose—other than just annoying or unnerving their opponents—and different tones represented distinct commands. The variety and complexity of those commands had increased as the war progressed, and new, more elaborate horns were made to convey them. And the meanings *changed* from time to time, like codes, after the Allies once used captured devices to sow confusion. But what did *this* all-encompassing tone mean, from a horn never meant for the battlefield? It had to be something very basic, very ancient, like the oldest Grik battle horns that only blew three notes, two of which commanded different methods of attack.

To Chack's and Silva's utter amazement, the Grik in front of them, pressed so rabidly close only moments before, suddenly just . . . stopped. That resulted in a brief flurry of killing, of course, as Chack's beleaguered troops merely continued what they'd been doing without thought for so long. But sooner than one might imagine, even without orders they couldn't have heard if Chack thought to give them, even the most crazed, battle-mad 'Cats, men, and Khonashi began to halt their slaughter of Grik that only stood there, unresisting. Most would surely—

happily—still flip any switch that would wipe out every Grik on Earth, but regardless of what they'd been through and how they'd suffered, they just didn't have it in them to keep killing helpless Grik face-to-face. They hadn't sunk that low.

Silva turned back to Chack, his blood-smeared face slack with fatigue and incomprehension as he mouthed the words, "What the *shit*?"

Chack could only shake his head and stumble against the big man as all his strength seemed to drain away. Silva, McIntyre, and Abel Cook—*Where did he come from? He should be on the faar right. Of course, the right isn't very faar now*—were suddenly holding him up. All else he could focus on was that Safir was here, and Lawrence must've accomplished . . . something, inside the palace.

First Ker-noll Jash watched helplessly as his entire force halted in place and the battle ground to a halt. He'd already suspected his cause was doomed when the enemy reinforcements slammed into his unprotected left and the terrible ships on the water started their nightmare shelling. The enemy flying machines hadn't even appeared yet, and his whole army was dying. But just as the enemy was trying to hold the palace, if he could just get *in* and hold it himself, Second General Ign might eventually drive the weakened enemy away, reinforcements or not. It was his only hope. And then the Great Attention Horn sounded, and everything fell apart.

He'd heard attention horns before, of course, preceding most commands on the battlefield. And warriors usually stopped what they were doing to hear what came next, but that didn't mean they should stop *fighting* if they were so closely engaged. Yet he'd never heard the *Great* Horn, from the Palace of Vanished Gods, in his life. He doubted any in his army had. But just like his troops, he instinctively, furiously, helplessly stopped and stared and waited—because *this* was a command from the Celestial Mother herself.

Gradually, the ships on the water ceased firing and the killing around the palace eased as well. Finally, the terrible drone of the horn—like the roar of the Vanished

Gods returned—faded away, and the only sounds came from the wind and wounded, the latter sweeping across Jash in a rising, suffused gust of misery. The individual shrieks and moans were indistinguishable, having commingled into a dreadful drone all their own. Jash had heard similar sounds before, at the front with Ign after a particularly heavy bombardment, but they were extinguished as the badly wounded were hastily dispatched and their bodies sent back to the cookpots. And he'd heard the same sounds, muted, from wounded left on the field after an unsuccessful attack. Those could go on for quite some time. He'd even heard worse, in a way, on the river when the galleys battled *Santa Catalina* and cries of pain turned to the high-pitched squeals of terror that always accompanied death in the water. But those sounds dwindled quickly as warriors were eaten or simply disappeared.

Jash had always been able to separate himself somewhat from the desolate cries of those they left in front of the enemy on land. He couldn't see the individuals making them, and it only intensified his anger that *the enemy* let them linger so long in pain—until he came to understand their adversaries didn't eat the dead. They'd risk much to recover their own wounded, however, to heal them if they could, and that only made Jash vaguely angrier, though he remained unsure at what—or whom—and suspected that had contributed to his decline into cynicism.

But this was the first time he'd ever been there, *on* a battlefield after the fighting stopped, to hear and see the anguish all around on such a scale. He'd probably lost half the troops he brought across the river, and the scope of the slaughter might be as great as that which occurred during the galley fights. Yet these wounded, these mangled dead, hadn't sunk conveniently out of sight; he stood among them and knew he'd remember the dreadful sights, sounds, and nauseating smells until the day he too was slain.

Another Great Horn sounded within the Palace of Vanished Gods, and Jash almost snorted with a kind of sick amusement. He'd heard this tone before, used for "officer's call" in the New Army, but originally reserved for summoning the Hij of Old Sofesshk to hear decrees. The irony was, he suspected few such Hij remained, and none would venture onto a battlefield. The horn could have only one purpose.

"The enemy reinforcements are pushing our troops aside, moving to support the knot of warriors still guarding the palace arch!" Ker-noll Shelg cried indignantly, as if their opponents were somehow cheating. *In a way, they are,* Jash admitted to himself, *and they probably know it. But what can we do?*

"We must resume our attack at once!" snarled Sagat, and again Jash glared at him, wondering what authority Esshk had given him to make him presume to speak so freely around his betters.

"No," he snapped. "The ships will only open fire once more, and we'll be slaughtered to no purpose." He gestured at the entrance arch with his snout and his young crest drooped. "Upon reflection, I suspect we never had a chance of forcing our way inside. The enemy grasped the advantage of strength of arms and position from the start—with that brief exception—and used those advantages with daring and determination."

"You *admire* them!" Shelg accused.

"I *hate* them," Jash countered harshly, "but yes. I do admire them as well. I understand that in another time, in other conflicts, now is when we'd offer them the opportunity to join the Great Hunt," he hissed derisively. "I'm quite sure, under the circumstances, they'd decline," he added, watching as more and more enemy troops, led by a small but energetic specimen with black fur and cape and silver armor, rushed to fill the bewildered, widening gap between Jash's army and the palace. Unlike the light-furred giant, Jash had never seen this leader before, but immediately recognized a confident commander of the fresh warriors it brought. "We certainly can't break through now, not when the enemy may nearly equal our remaining numbers. We can only hope Second General Ign destroyed or stalled the main attack at the *nakkle* leg. He *must* somehow cross to aid us in recapturing the palace and the city."

His crest rose as he regarded Sagat once more. "In any event, the Celestial Mother has called the Hij." He gestured around. "I see no Hij but us, such as we are. Sound the recall horns," he told Shelg. "As soon as the Celestial Mother's horn falls silent," he added respectfully. "Bring the army back to the positions we occupied before the final attack. Try to rig as much overhead protection as you can," he added doubtfully.

"Then?" Shelg asked.

Jash whipped his head to the side in a kind of mystified shrug. "Then, Ker-noll Shelg, those of us who are Hij—the senior officers who remain—will present ourselves as the Giver of Life commands, and hear what she has to say."

"This is treason!" Sagat seethed.

Jash rounded on him. "Treason against whom? Against *what*? The Celestial Mother, to whom we owe our highest obedience? Our very existence? Or Esshk—who made us too, but only to support his own ambition to rule an empire that's crumbling around us?" Jash was ranting now. "He's undermined the empire by subverting the Giver of Life and the order her reign guaranteed. He's slaughtered the *real* Hij, the ancient Hij of Old Sofesshk, and the timeless stability they represented. And his arrogantly distant, unsupportable assaults on prey we disdained and no longer understood have resulted in innumerable defeats and brought this reckoning upon us!" Jash wasn't exactly sure the last part was entirely Esshk's fault, but he'd absolutely attempted to capitalize on the chaos that ensued. "You won't speak again," he roared at Sagat, "or you'll be destroyed at once—and *your* master will have no eyes to see what comes to pass when we consult the Celestial Mother . . . and the enemy!"

CHAPTER
45

////// *Southwest bank of the Zambezi River*

The rain was over; all the Sky Priests back on *Big Sal* said so, whenever they managed to get through by radio or get reports from the planes starting to venture overhead. *Wind's still a bitch, though,* grumped General Pete Alden. *An' this damn mud!* He was riding on the back of Taa-leen's tank again, churning, roaring, fishtailing northwest through bloodred, rocky soup. Though menacing clouds lingered to the north, the sky above was mostly clear, admitting the steamy, blistering rays of an afternoon sun intent on reestablishing its presence with a vengeance. Pete pulled his canteen from his belt and took a tiny sip before offering it to Taa-leen. The Lemurian division commander took a grateful gulp of his own, then, with a questioning blink, passed the canteen below. *Water's gonna be a big problem if we don't get to the supply depot soon,* Pete knew. Nobody would drink the rancid runoff hereabouts. *An' that's just to keep the army alive. We need fuel and ammo to keep fighting.*

There were more trees here at least, a few that survived Grik axes scouring the place for wood to shore up or cover trenches. And a lot of that effort had been wasted, since the fourth and final line had already been abandoned when the bedraggled remains of Pete's two corps stormed it just at dawn. Pete wished they could've hit it sooner, but they had to regroup after the bloody, nightmarish melee in front of the third trench. Otherwise, he'd have had nothing left to lead but an utterly exhausted, disorganized mob. And once they had the final trench, he'd been almost desperate to stop, to let his army rest, but the main Repub force coming up from the south was still too far away. The Grik had the numbers to crush either one of them if they put things together. They had to keep pushing, keep them off balance, keep them running. Somehow, they had.

Bouncing as the tank lurched, Pete eyed the few short, fat, clumpy-topped trees he saw as his abbreviated tank column thundered past. Only six machines remained—including one of the slower veterans of Zanzibar that just showed up in the middle of the fighting. Its low speed wasn't a factor now, since between getting stuck and breaking down, it was all any of them could do to keep up with the weary infantry columns, hurriedly and somewhat haphazardly reassembled by divisions, trudging through muck that seemed to stretch to the sea behind and the mountains ahead. Pete knew that wasn't the case. Elements of the Army of the Republic now lay just beyond some low hills to the south, and a great forest—he wondered if the trees were the same as these—wasn't far in front. But the stumps of what had once been forest here as well now jutted up like broken teeth in the mouth of hell.

"The wind will help dry the mud," Muln Rolak offered, seemingly reading his thoughts. The old Lemurian had nimbly joined him on the tank shortly before, though he'd have clearly preferred to ride a me-naak, or even a paalka, despite the discomfort of sitting on one of their broad backs. But neither animal would stay near enough to the bellowing, smoking machine for him to talk to his friend, and Pete flatly refused to ride double with Rolak. "It'd look stupid," he'd insisted. So now they talked—more properly, yelled—at each other, and Taa-leen as the shot-battered tank wallowed onward.

"Fat lotta good that does those poor guys," Pete shouted, nodding out at the troops.

"I'm told it'll dry quite quickly," Rolak insisted. "Though it might seem this is the stormy season, it's appparently not the rainy season. Odd as thaat sounds, there's a distinction."

He waved his hand around them. "All this will be haard as stone again in days."

"Who told you that?"

"Hij Geerki," Rolak confessed, blinking surprise for Pete's benefit. "He came in with a draaft of his Grik from Mada-gaas-gar, just before the storm, to supply gener-aal labor at Arracca Field. A few prisoners haave been taken downriver for him to interview about such things. And, of course, much of whaat the Sky Priests know about the seasonal weather here came from Grik sailors we captured at Zaan-zi-baar."

"We have prisoners?" Pete asked, somewhat shocked. "From *this* fight?"

"Quite a few, I understaand. Perhaps hundreds."

"Huh. I'll be damned."

"I imaagine so." Rolak grinned, blinking genuine humor.

Pete looked sidelong at him. "You're in a awful good mood, considerin'," he grumbled. "An' last night," he added lower, suppressing a shudder. "We came *that* close to losin' the whole damn war."

"But we didn't," Rolak countered simply, "and the plaan—which I considered overly complicated, as you know—seems to haave worked quite well."

"Not that complicated," Pete denied, "just lots of moving parts that went to shit. The basic idea was pretty simple."

"Indeed," Rolak agreed, still cheerful. "But you miss my point. Of course the moving paarts of the plaan went to shit; they were each in intimate contaact with the enemy. Cap-i-taan Reddy, you, and I all expected thaat to haappen, and those directly commaanding those seemingly disassociated aaspects rose to the chaallenge—as we've come to rely on them to. Why do you suppose I raised so little fuss when you younglingly insisted on gaamboling forwaard into the attaack yourself? You *knew* you'd be needed there at some criticaal point, and I trust your instincts enough thaat *I* knew—if you lived long enough—you were probably right." He grinned. "I also knew I'd haave to organize some effort to save your aass."

"You're just making shit up to make yourself look good."

"I need not invent anything to do thaat." Rolak sniffed. "But you digress me. Returning to my aargument: though maany paarts of the plaan haad to be ... modified on the fly, the graand scheme, primarily formulated by Cap-i-taan Reddy and Mr. McFaar-lane—both of whom remain refreshingly modest regaarding their straa-tegic thinking," he jibed, "seems to haave come off raather well."

The tank had been laboring up a slight rise, and as it reached the top, Pete was distracted by the sight of the river on their right. It was surprisingly low down in relation to the advance and Pete realized they must've been on a gently rising grade all along. Green forest still dominated the far shoreline, flanking steep hills that turned to mountains in the distance. *No way we ever could've pushed through there,* Pete realized, *and the Grik knew it too. That's why there'd never been any choice but for us to butt heads here.* His gaze was quickly drawn to the smoldering wreck of a Grik BB in the near shallows, then expanded to encompass the Repub monitors, smoke streaming from their twin funnels as they guarded the cluster of transports gathered behind an impromptu but healthy-looking defense of a broad beach at the bend of the river. They'd reached the Maroons at last, and Pete felt a great weight lift from his shoulders. A handful of me-naaks quickly gathered in the open behind the barricades, mostly constructed of crates, and started galloping uphill in his direction.

"He's right," Taa-Leen agreed. He'd been listening to his headphones with one ear while trying to keep up with the conversation behind him. "A few Naancys is scouting ahead, an' with a few exceptions, all they're seein' is the baacks o' the Grik, runnin' for the forest south o' Sofesshk."

"Swell," Pete said, and meant it. "Now shut this thing down. Have *all* the tanks stop here. We'll never get 'em down that slope, anyway." He grinned. "Well, we *could,* but we'd never get 'em back up here if we did. Fall the crews out an' tell 'em to hit the shade for a while. They've earned it. There's a clump of those dopey trees along the ridge that drops off to the river. We'll get some o' those Shee-ree an' Maroons to lug fuel and ammo up here. They've got wagons an' paalkas."

One by one, the roaring engines died, and a kind of quiet that Pete had forgotten existed descended. At least for a moment. That's when the cheering started, rising from the parched throats of tired troops, eventually stretching down the straggling columns to the southeast. Most of the troops couldn't see the depot yet, but the excitement spread from others who could, and in their minds, just reaching it was a victory. It was, of course, but it would be a while before anyone knew how complete it was.

Pete and Rolak helped Taa-Leen out of the tank, the division commander's legs too rubbery to support his weight at first. Willing members of the Triple I, providing close support for all the tanks, jumped up and hauled all the crews out and half carried them to the meager shade. The tankers were so caked with foamy sweat that Pete could hardly recognize them as 'Cats. Finally, he, Rolak, and Taa-Leen slid to the ground and waited while the me-naak riders approached. The me-naaks themselves balked a few yards away, nostrils flaring at the smell of hot iron, oil, and sweat, but the riders slid off their animals and splashed in the mud, striding forward and saluting.

"Colonel Will, Lieutenant Colonel Durai, Lieutenant Colonel Naasra," Pete greeted the commanders of the Maroons and Shee-ree, as well as the CO of the 5th B'mbaado. He was rarely so specific about rank unless chewing somebody out, but Maroons and Shee-ree had a bumpy history. If he just called them all "colonel," they'd start fighting over who was really in charge. As for Naasra, Pete didn't know her, but she might be one of those 'Cats who didn't like taking orders from Shee-ree or Maroons. Fortunately, no matter how tired he was, he remembered that simply addressing them all formally should squash any bullshit. Regardless how glad he was to see them, however, his eyes had already fastened on to somebody else he hadn't expected at all. "Major," he added with a growing smile.

Bekiaa-Sab-At smiled back, tilting her helmet away from her face. She looked just as worn as anyone in Pete's command, her tattered smock and leather armor as black with dried blood as her brindled fur. She and a human companion stood in stark contrast to the relatively clean troops who'd secured the beachhead depot against minimal, confused resistance. All the me-naaks looked rough, and Bekiaa's in particular practically sagged where it stood. Pete could only guess what Bekiaa had been through, but some inner reserve of energy had animated her eyes with obvious pleasure, and she actually lunged forward to embrace Rolak, Taa-Leen, even Pete. Self-consciously, Pete raised a hand and patted her shoulder.

"Ah, she's *Legate* Bekiaa, in the Army o' the Republic, makin' her senior ta any colonel while she holds the title," said her companion, a tall, tough-looking young man, vaguely familiar. His tone was somewhat sharp and disapproving, and Pete would've sworn it was protective—as if Bekiaa needed protecting! "Ye can take her back, I suppose, an' call her what ye will, but she directly commands the hardest-fightin' division in our army. Now may not be the best time to muck things up."

"Optio!" Bekiaa chided, while Pete and Rolak both laughed. "This is Pete Aalden, *Gener-aal of all the Union Armies and Maa-rines*!"

"An' ye talk ta General Kim any different?" the man accused. "I know who he is."

"Then you should also know we're extremely well aacquainted with Legate Bekiaa and her quaality, and would never dream of mucking things up just now. Though we most emphaatically *do* waant her baack when the time is right," Rolak said evenly.

Bekiaa grinned. "Gener-aals, may I present my aide, Optio Jack Meek."

Pete reached to shake the younger man's hand. "You're Ambassador Meek's boy," he stated. "Interesting guy."

"Aye," Meek grudged, but shook the offered hand.

"Good to meet you . . . Optio." Even Pete knew Meek was more senior in Inquisitor Choon's intelligence service than his army rank implied. He looked back at Bekiaa. "But what're you doing here? *How* did you get here? Where's your division? Where's Courtney?"

"Gener-aal Braadford's safe, coordinating the movement of his corps with Gener-aal Kim, whose main army now lies less than eight miles south. The Grik opposing him haave fled. As best we can tell, except for a pocket of five or six thousaands thaat Colonel Saachic's caaval-ry cut off, all of Second General Ign's Grik are destroyed or in retreat."

"*Gener-aal* Braadford," Rolak observed, blinking surprise.

"So it was Ign after all," Pete muttered. "I suspected as much."

"We only suspect as well," Bekiaa confided, "but raadio reports from your Arracca Field via our airborne Caantets confirm thaat's whaat your prisoners say."

Pete looked at Rolak. "More than they've told us."

Bekiaa diplomatically cleared her throat. "In any event, Gener-aal Faan's Third Corps and Gener-aal Mu-Tai's Twelfth, as well as my own division, are much closer." She pointed at low, brushy hills to the south. "Probably just a couple of miles by now. I expect your scouts haave made contaact already. The Gener-aals provided us with their own and some of their scouts' mounts so I could ride here and make contaact with Col-nol Will." She nodded at the Maroon, then grinned again, blinking mischievously. "Kim and Choon wanted to send Repub caaval-ry, under Gener-aal Taal-Gaak—which would've been very historic, I'm sure—for the first meeting of all Aallied forces in this hemisphere. But judging by the re-aaction of some of Taal's horse caav to meanies"—she blinked amusement at a remembered scene—"I strongly recommended we use Faan's animaals."

"I suspect you also strongly suggested you be the one to make contaact," Rolak said dryly.

"Optio Meek and me," Bekiaa replied sweetly. "We were closest after all, and well . . . I know you."

Colonels Will, Durai, and Naasra had been reduced to whipping their heads back and forth during this exchange, but Will finally got a word in. "What's it all mane, Gan'rals?" he asked. "Are armaes are cambinin' at last, the Gareiks are an tha' ran, an' we hare thare's a truce a' same sart at tha' Gareik Palace at Sofesshk." He hesitated. "Daes it mane we've won?"

Impulsively, Pete hugged Bekiaa again, the stench of her sweaty smock and bloody leather, as well as the filthy me-naak she'd ridden, going unnoticed. No doubt he smelled as bad or worse. "What it means, Colonel, is now we can really push the bastards," he said. "Keep 'em going, keep 'em running, an' wear 'em out. I expect our cavalry"—he glanced at Bekiaa—"horse and meanie, if we can teach 'em to get along or keep 'em apart, will be a big help with that. Grik never have liked cavalry. Probably never even occurred to 'em to break anything to ride—if there's any such thing on Earth that'd let 'em. Maybe a meanie would, raised from an egg. We may never know. Anyway, we keep enough pressure on the lizards, and sooner or later they'll either fall apart—or have to stop and fight. My money's on the second bet." His voice turned harsh. "If it comes to that, though, we'll kick their asses straight to hell." He sobered, looking at a big chunk of a column of infantry that had ground to a halt to hear and see what was happening. They looked dead tired, but his excitement must've been catching because none seemed out of it, none looked ready to quit.

"Have we won?" he repeated Will's question, raising his voice. "Depends on how you look at it, after last night. We kicked the lizards outa their trenches an' sent 'em off with their tails between their legs. An' we're alive. That tells *me* we won a battle, Pete." Satisfied cheers and yips rose around them, but Pete was shaking his head. "Have we won the *war*?" he shouted, and quickly answered himself. "Not yet." He looked at Bekiaa. "But, by God—by the Maker—we ain't lost. An' I'd'a *helluva* lot rather be in our shoes than theirs!"

CHAPTER
46

////// *Palace of Vanished Gods*

T hird Division's General Mersaak himself led Safir Maraan's Silver and Black Battalions of her own personal guard regiment, the fabled 600, in pushing reluctant Grik back from the positions they'd taken near the small dock. That had been the biggest test so far of how compliant the enemy would be to the horns. Quickly, the 600 formed a corridor leading from there, through the Allied perimeter, and to the palace itself. Two companies of the 3rd Baalkpan and what was left of the 1st Battalion, 2nd Marines (about the same number) formed an honor guard carrying the Stainless Banner of the Trees for Baalkpan, the silver and black flag of B'mbaado and Aryaal, the Stars and Stripes of the Marines, and the brightly embroidered flag of the United Homes—all flapping loudly in the whipping wind—out to meet USS *Walker.*

Matt Reddy wished they could've flown the Empire and Republic flags too, but nobody around here had examples and there hadn't been time to have them made. The battered old destroyer gingerly maneuvered around the wrecked Grik BB and hardly kissed the dock, brown river water churning forward from reversing screws, and lines were thrown to ready hands waiting to secure her. Spanky had brought the ship in and Matt, already resplendent in his best whites, hat, and even white gloves, stood near the brow, while Chief Jeek's pipe relayed instructions for final adjustments to the height of the accommodation ladder. Finally, with all engines stopped and lines singled up, Matt briskly descended to the dock and saluted the waiting flags before exchanging salutes with the officers who met him.

"This is crazy," Mersaak muttered through clenched teeth.

"That's what Spanky said," Matt agreed under his breath. He was surrounded by a lot of firepower, but there were also a *lot* of Grik, very close, and his only weapons were the 1911 Colt and Academy sword hanging from the belt that Juan had absolutely insisted he wear. "I don't want to look like I *need* weapons," Matt had complained. "It might spoil the whole effect of what I'm trying to sell."

"But you must look like a *warrior*, Cap-tan," Juan had adamantly replied. "The warrior who leads us all. I don't know much about how these loco lizards think, but I bet that's important." Matt suspected he was right and finally relented.

Now he strode alongside Mersaak, flags and honor guard behind, as they marched to where Safir, Chack, Abel Cook, an Impie officer Matt didn't know, and Enrico Galay (with his arm in a sling), and perhaps a score of men, 'Cats, and Khonashi waited. Matt tried to stare straight ahead but couldn't help taking in all the dead heaped beyond the corridor the 600 made. Granted, most were Grik, but there were an awful lot of *his* people sprawled on the ground in front of the palace. *Thank God all the seriously wounded have been moved inside,* he thought. *And the sooner we get this sorted out, the sooner I can bring more medics and corps-'Cats up from where Second Corps landed.* Almost half the corps was still on the other side of the palace, waiting.

All those present from II Corps and Chack's Brigade saluted, and Matt returned the honor before Safir—suitably cleaned and polished despite the fact that an incredibly grimy Chack couldn't seem to keep from touching her from time to time, as if reassuring himself his beloved was really here—stepped forward and embraced him.

"Are you crazy?" she demanded softly into his chest.

"Why does everybody keep asking me that?"

Safir snorted and clasped him tighter. "I . . . I think we *did it*," she murmured before stepping back.

"I'm just glad you're safe." Matt's eyes encompassed the rest. "All of you. As for how this'll all turn out . . . We'll see."

There was a commotion behind the Grik lines, a large group moving among them and stepping into the open.

"Aallied Expedition-aary Force!" Chack bellowed. "Chaarge baayonets!"

With a single thunderous shout, seven thousand troops, four ranks deep, took one step toward the enemy and lowered their rifles with the well-drilled precision of some immense machine. Bayonets bristled outward, tilted slightly up. The closest Grik recoiled, growling, but the cluster moving toward them kept on coming.

"Thought we'd show 'em how importaant you are to us, and we'll protect you if they try anything," Chack said lowly to Matt, a satisfied grin splitting his face. "Like you said on the raadio, this meeting's as much about perception as anything. Whaat they *think* we'll do, as much as whaat we *caan*. But with respect, Cap-i-taan, I don't think you should'a come either." He gestured around. "This goes south, as Sil-vaa would say, we'll kill every daamn one of them—but they'll get a lot of us too. It'll be . . . baad."

"That's why I wore my fancy duds," Matt said lightly. "To make sure it doesn't come to that." He chuckled. "I've never seen a Grik in white before." He raised an arm displaying a sleeve that Juan had kept conscientiously immaculate. "This alone might shake 'em—and just think how pissed Juan'll be if they get me dirty!"

"He'd kill 'em all, by himself!" Galay agreed.

Matt nodded, but frowned slightly and looked back at Chack and Safir. "Actually, I kind of agree; this *is* nuts. I sure wish Pete and Rolak were here. They're the only ones who've dealt directly with hostile Grik commanders." He shook his head. "But they're too far. And even if they could just drop what they're doing, it'd take too long to get 'em here." He smiled wryly. "Then again, first time they talked to Halik they were just winging it too. And they didn't have the political and spiritual honcho of all the Grik in the bag." He looked at Chack. "You've given me an advantage Pete and Rolak never had. I *better* be able to wing it myself, after the sacrifice your people made to put that in my pocket."

The Grik representatives, fifteen of them, had finally stopped in front of the Allied line. All wore the "uniform" of New Army troops, consisting of iron scales sewn on gray leather, and carried a banner of their own that looked for all the world like a Japanese Rising Sun flag, complete with a big, red "meatball" in the middle. The only real differences were the stylized Grik swords painted on each side of the circle, and the light tan field behind the bloodred rays. Most striking, however, was that nearly all the Grik looked very young, younger even than Lawrence, and few of the bristly crests atop their heads or the plumage on their tails—signs of Grik adulthood—looked fully formed. For all that, they were still full-size, with full-size teeth, taller than a 'Cat and heavy as a man, and looked just as savage and battle ready as any Grik Matt ever saw. More so, since they all carried muskets on slings with bayonets attached, as well as their swords, and moved in a defensive block they'd apparently stepped into without thinking about it.

I haven't seen "wild" Grik this close since Second Grik City, Matt realized, *and they were all the old style Uul warriors. They were plenty deadly, but these are* soldiers, *bred for a new kind of war. Thank God we forced this when we did because superior weapons—breechloaders versus muzzle-loaders—was the only advantage we had left. At least here, for this fight. With just another year or two . . .* He shook the thought away.

Chack looked at Matt, who nodded. "Bring him out," Chack called behind, then faced the backs of the troops barring the enemy's way. He took a long breath. "Let 'em through," he shouted. There was some hesitation, and a bandaged Impie sergeant looked back anxiously. "But Colonel . . . they're *armed*!"

Chack nodded. "So are we," he assured, then lowered his voice. "And how would we tell them to leave their weapons, anyway?"

A squad of Impies peeled back, allowing the deputation through, just as a commotion behind him drew Matt's attention. There at last were Silva and Lawrence, and Silva at least was as heavily armed as usual, as they escorted a short, plump, disheveled Grik between them. The ancient Lemurian, First Sergeant Moe, brought up the rear. Silva and Moe looked pretty ragged. Both were filthy, bloody, and bandaged. Lawrence was comparatively clean but seemed just as tired. Matt knew he'd been up for days, first for the hair-raising parachute drop, then the fight for the city and the palace, and finally for his lengthy conference with the Celestial Mother that brought them this possibility.

The Grik between them just looked . . . weird. As Matt had noted, he was plump—something he'd almost never seen in a Grik—and his crest was artificially stiffened with some kind of hastily applied pomade. Even more bizarre, he seemed to be wearing *makeup* of some sort, to cover the graying feathery fur around his eyes and snout. But the makeup hadn't been freshened and was all the more obvious.

"Howdy, Skipper," Silva said with a grin, as grimy, blood-caked fingers stuffed a wad of yellowish leaves in his cheek. The weariness in his eye and tone was clear. "Glad you could join us. Surprised Pam didn't tag along with you."

"Wouldn't've missed it," Matt replied, "and she tried." He cleared his throat. "How are you, First Sergeant?" he asked Moe.

"Old, sur."

Matt nodded. "And you, Lawrence? It seems we owe you *another* medal—when we get around to making some." There were a few low, ironic chuckles. "Where's the other interpreter?"

"Ol' Pokey's dead, Skipper," Silva said.

"I . . . sad that I all you got, Ca'tain Reddy," Lawrence apologized.

"Nonsense. I'm sorry about Pokey, and that so much still depends on you, but we couldn't be in better hands." He nodded at the Grik between them. "This is the Chooser?"

"Ay, sur."

"He understands English?"

"Hetter than he let on, at first," Lawrence confirmed.

"Good to know." Matt spoke directly to the Chooser for the first time. "You'll tell these"—he gestured at the waiting warriors—"what's happened in the palace and elsewhere, and that your Celestial Mother is alive and unharmed. You'll get their names and ranks so I know who I'm talking to, then you'll speak for me. And you'll tell them *exactly* what I tell you, or Lawrence will let me know." He paused. "I've heard about you, Chooser, so I know what a treacherous turd you are. Your *life* depends on your honesty today, so don't screw it up. Understand?"

The Chooser nodded vigorously. "Yesss."

"Good."

And so, with the Chooser speaking for Matt, and Lawrence only occasionally providing clarifications and translating for the Grik—with Silva sometimes deciphering Lawrence's pronunciation—Captain Reddy and First Kernoll Jash began their historic dialogue in the wreckage of the Holy City of Old Sofesshk at the foot of the Palace of Vanished Gods. And Matt knew exactly what a monumental achievement it was, even if—as he quickly learned—this Kerr-noll Jash had nowhere near the power to stop the war altogether. He did have a very strong, disciplined force, however, as well as a respected reputation among other New Army warriors. He might be very useful. The trick now was to get him to stop fighting and reestablish an example of direct obedience to the Celestial Mother so the Allied Expeditionary Force could consolidate its gains and lick its wounds. The horns and the Chooser's word seemed almost sufficient for that—until Jash made the unprecedented demand to hear the command straight from the Celestial Mother herself.

"I know you too well, Chooser," Jash scoffed, "by reputation and Second General Ign's words. You'd say or do anything to preserve yourself. We'll cease all attempts to retake the palace and withdraw only after I've *seen* that the Giver of Life is safe, and *hear* her command that I do so."

The Chooser bristled, though it was impossible to tell, but with a quick glance over his shoulder, he continued.

"You don't understand, First Kerr-noll. You won't be given the opportunity to *withdraw*."

"Opportunity?" Jash snapped.

The Chooser's tone reflected real regret when he explained. "You fought well here, but while you were occupied with this battle, the one on the river and beyond turned entirely. Not only has the enemy fleet fought its way here, as you see yourself, but Second General Ign's great army is crushed. It flees westward even now, and nothing of consequence stands between the rest of his rampaging swarm"—he nodded at the tall man in white—"and the Holy City."

Jash was taken aback. *How?* "But Second General Ign is *here*, just across the river!" he blurted, forgetting for an instant that the enemy understood him. "He will come!" he added defiantly.

"He can't," the Chooser stated, "not with the enemy so powerful on the water. And *why* is he here? He came for the same reason you did. Seeing he can't cross, he'll continue west along the coast of Lake Nalak. Once around it, perhaps he'll move north, but he can't help you here."

Jash was still stunned, but shook it off. "Then *we* will withdraw north as well. The way is clear and no lake or river blocks our path."

The Chooser was shaking his head. "Regrettably, withdrawal is not one of the three choices the invading prey—and the Celestial Mother—have given you. It wouldn't be an option in any case, now that the storm is passing. Surely you've seen the several flying machines already overhead?"

Jash had. Two or three were up there now, and if what the Chooser said about Ign was true, every machine the enemy had could be devoted to his destruction—as soon as he disengaged here. "Three choices?" he snorted dubiously.

"Yes. First, you may resume your attack. Be warned, however, that such an act will be interpreted as a rebellious assault upon the Giver of Life herself. The enemy will destroy you, and any survivors will receive the traitor's death."

"Second?" Jash quickly demanded before his officers could react.

"You may disarm and become the laboring Uul of the invading prey." The delegation hissed with fury. "It is so," the Chooser hastened to confirm. "She gave the command herself." He paused. "But that isn't the choice she hopes you'll make."

The hissing stopped, and Jash looked first at the tall man in white, then the bloody giant by the Chooser. It was indescribably difficult to restrain himself from snatching out his sword and laying into all of them, then and there. The Gharrichk'k had no notion of inviolate parlay, and that he'd come at all, and with so few, reflected only his strict interpretation of the call summoning the Hij. Personally, he now considered his whole army Hij, but knew that wasn't what the Celestial Mother had in mind. He took a deep, calming breath. Only then did he notice that the giant's primary weapon no longer pointed at the Chooser. The big, dark hole in the end of the thing was aimed, almost casually, directly at Jash's eye. The big man noticed his attention and displayed what would've been a perfect array of teeth, if one of them hadn't been missing.

"The third choice," Jash snarled. "Is that what she wants us to make? What is it?"

"Life," the Chooser stated. "For you and all our people, and the restoration of . . ." The Chooser paused. "A measure of what we've lost."

"How?" Jash demanded, surprised.

"By joining her and these"—he waved around them—"her former enemies, in the Hunt for the greatest traitor the Gharrichk'k have ever known."

"And that is?" Jash asked.

"The former Regent Champion, First General Esshk, of course."

I have him, Matt realized, when he heard Lawrence repeat that and saw Jash's reaction. By all accounts of the prisoners sent to Arracca Field, and forwarded to him as quickly as Hij Geerki could collect them, Esshk had been worshipped by his troops—for a while. Ign still was, apparently, to have kept them fighting as long as he had. But some, including this one, it seemed, had grown to hate Esshk and all he'd done, and blamed him for how the world had so suddenly and violently been turned upside down.

"*She* considers Esshk a traitor?" Jash asked, glancing at Sagat. The garrison trooper wouldn't meet his gaze.

When this was translated for Matt, he looked at Safir. "Is she ready?" They'd suspected they'd have to bring the Celestial Mother out at some point.

"And waiting," Safir confirmed. "I'll take the Chooser and get her. Follow me," she told the fat Grik and turned for the palace. A half dozen Marines and an equal number of the 600 formed around Safir, collecting the Chooser as they went.

"I'll let her tell you that herself," Matt told Jash, through Lawrence. For several moments afterward, Matt and Jash just stared at one another. Jash averted his gaze first, recognizing that if nothing else, the man in white—the talker called him Captain Reddy—was of far greater rank than he. He studied the giant, again speculating whether he could take him, but finally lacking anything better to do while they waited, he turned to Lawrence. "What *are* you?" he asked the shorter, lighter, different-colored version of his own species. He waved at some of the Khonashi. "What are *they*? None of you are prey. I know that now, but neither are you Gharrichk'k."

Lawrence thought about it, trying to form a suitable reply that Jash might understand. Slowly, he began, "All you see here, of any race, are . . . warriors combined in the service of Captain Reddy. Likewise, they represent all the free, united peoples *he* serves, who placed their trust in him . . . and serve us all in turn." He shook his head. "I don't expect you to grasp such unusual notions, so imperfectly explained," he continued simply, "but you must recognize that we—all these various peoples—have defeated yours. In our capacity for violence, we're not that different from you." His tone hardened. "Conversely, we couldn't be *more* different in the most important respects: while your race is bound together solely to conquer and devour, we once led rich, enjoyable lives with little conflict. Your kind would call us prey for that, yet we all came together and brought this war to you to *stop* your attacks on us. If it weren't for the mindless aggression of the culture you protect, you never would've seen us here at all." He waved at all the bodies heaped in death. "Never would've seen this."

He pointed his snout at Matt. "Just as significant, we all *chose* to serve him. Not only because he brings us victory, but because he returns our service with respect, loyalty . . ." He paused, trying to add "honor," but knew no Grik word for it, even though General Alden believed Halik understood the concept. He didn't have time to explain. "And truthfulness," he ended inadequately.

Jash looked confused, as well he might, given how many unusual concepts Lawrence—who wasn't so sure of some of them himself—had thrown at him so quickly. "So, you're saying that, as Captain Reddy serves all your races, he will now serve the Celestial Mother?" he asked skeptically. "How can that be?"

Lawrence spoke with Matt for a moment, and the giant made a few snorting comments. Lawrence turned back to Jash, and Matt regarded him with a steady gaze.

"Captain Reddy swears to *lead* those of your race who'll combine with all of ours *alongside* the Celestial Mother, to destroy what the Gharrichk'k have been—and have come to be under the influence of General Esshk." Lawrence took a breath. "That's the third choice you're given, that your Celestial Mother has already made. We all understand it's the most significant choice you've ever been allowed, but I suggest you make it wisely."

Jash turned to look back at his troops, his division, and pondered the implications of what the little orange-and-brown-striped interpreter said, contemplating the novelty of such a momentous choice. He noticed then that quite a few of the warriors that had joined his division after it came across the river were wearing the black and red slash marks of Esshk's garrison troops, and he wondered a little resentfully where *they'd* been during the initial fighting. *Scattered all over the city, no doubt, and finally drawn to the sound of battle,* he allowed. *At least they haven't turned prey.* Still, even with the additions, his force was sorely depleted—and for what?

No Gharrichk'k he'd heard of had ever fought for his own reasons—except Esshk himself. Yet Jash was living proof that *all* of his race, even Uul, could think if they lived long enough to realize it or were "elevated." He'd been raised to fight for Esshk. As he matured and saw how capricious Esshk could be, he'd devoted himself personally to Ign. But now he was being asked—*asked*!—to re-devote himself to the Celestial Mother, to whom his allegiance had always been instinctively drawn. *There really is no choice at all,* he reflected. *If the offer's real.*

His eyes narrowed briefly when he saw how many garrison troops had shoved their way to the front, closest to where he and his officers came through the line, but suspected it was only natural. *If they heard all that's been said, and the Celestial Mother really is coming out, the garrison will just as instinctively want to be near her, to protect her. Aside from her personal guards, they've been close to her the longest.* He glanced aside. *But Sagat will still not meet my gaze and is acting very strange indeed.*

He looked back at the tall man dressed in white. "You've given me much to think about," he told him, through Lawrence. "Yet the implications of what you offer are so vast, I can hardly comprehend them." He paused and added, almost pleadingly, "I *must* hear what the Giver of Life commands."

Matt nodded and smiled with relief and satisfaction. *Is this really going to work?* he asked himself. "You bet," he agreed, just as a commotion behind him drew his attention to a procession emerging from the palace. Safir and Moe were in the lead, followed by the escort they took, which surrounded the Chooser and the biggest live Grik Matt ever saw. He'd seen a few female Grik—broodmares, Courtney called them—and they were generally a little larger than males. And he'd viewed the beheaded remains of the old Celestial Mother; her massive, bloated corpse lolling on her throne, washed in dried blood, and looking more like some monstrous, blubbery walrus than a deadly reptilian predator. The chamber had stunk so bad, he hadn't lingered long. The lantern light hinted at the same coppery plumage on this daughter, beneath a red, gold-trimmed cloak. And she wasn't bloated, just . . .

really *big*, probably standing six and a half or seven feet tall. He suspected the super lizards around Baalkpan—allosaurs, according to Courtney—probably didn't grow bigger than the Celestial Mother for a year.

There was some unhappy muttering among the Allied troops surrounding the entourage. *Only natural,* Matt thought. *After all they've been through, most would gladly kill the big broad.* Safir apparently sensed the mood and shouted, "Ten-*hut*!" All the troops in earshot instantly obeyed, stiffening to attention. Those farther out did so as soon as the order was repeated.

First Ker-noll Jash had never seen the Celestial Mother either. Probably only a handful of the garrison troops had, from a distance. And at this first glimpse of her bright, radiant beauty, he wondered how anyone, even Es-shk, could ever deny her. As she stopped before him, she began to speak, and the soft tones she uttered—which actually included his *name*—were like the sweet sounds of life awakening with the sunrise. Without thinking, Jash hurled himself to the rubbled paving stones, followed by his officers and most of his troops.

What he didn't realize until too late, in the brief thunder of thousands of Gharrichk'k prostrating themselves before their Giver of Life, was that not everyone followed his example. Sagat and his surviving companion, along with hundreds of Grik gathered tightly just beyond the bristling bayonets, raised the roaring shout of "Esshk!" and charged.

"Shit!" Matt and Silva both yelled, as a short section of the wall of troops in front of them disintegrated under a fusillade of musket fire, stabbing, hacking, and just sheer numbers. Matt pulled his Academy sword and pistol. Chack, his exhaustion vaporizing, whipped out his cutlass and slammed into a whole pack of Grik with nothing else. Abel Cook, Milke, even Galay and half a dozen others were just a step behind. Silva's Thompson rattled, the hot brass falling all over the back of Jash—who suddenly realized what Sagat had planned all along. Leaping to his feet, he only barely avoided Matt's sword—and the bitter, hate-filled glare behind it—before he could bellow, "As-sassins! Protect the Celestial Mother! Destroy those wear-

ing the red and black! Do *not* fight our former enemies!"
Prostrated Grik warriors jumped up and surged against
the tight block of garrison troops even as they fought to
pour through the widening gap in the Allied line.

Lawrence was the only one who understood what Jash
was yelling, and the surprised and vengeful Allied troops
around the palace fired a belated, ragged volley, killing or
wounding any Grik that had risen from cover, attacking
or not. Lawrence was desperately screaming at Matt to
stop the shooting—which clearly bewildered *him*—until
he saw Jash and his officers slam into the initial rush of
garrison troops themselves and start slashing at them
right alongside Chack. Matt's distracted surprise nearly
cost him his life when his sword was deflected by a Grik
musket, but he spun inside beside the barrel just as it went
off. Claws raked painfully down his back, but he turned
again and fired two quick shots into the Grik's face with
his pistol. He spared another quick glance at Jash and
Chack, fighting together, and thought he knew what Lawrence was trying to tell him. He fired at another pair of
Grik trying to bolt past and join the first surge, now fighting around the Celestial Mother as her Lemurian guards
tried to get her back to the palace. Blood spattered his
whites, then flooded his sleeve when he drove his sword
through a leathery Grik throat. "Lawrence!" he shouted.
"What the hell?"

"Re-els!" Lawrence panted. He wasn't even armed
and was fighting the bigger Grik with nothing but the
claws on his feet and one hand. Curiously, as usual, he
wouldn't use his teeth unless he had no choice.

"Rebels," Silva shouted, in case the skipper didn't get
that. He had.

"How can we tell the difference?"

"Damned if I know," Silva replied. "Does it *make* a
difference?"

"Yes!"

Abel Cook reeled back from the thickening, reforming
line, but a couple hundred must've already broken
through, completely ignoring Matt and rushing straight at
the Celestial Mother. A few dozen more of Safir's troops
and Chack's Raiders got there first, but were surrounded

by a seething gaggle of Grik fighting as fanatically as any Matt ever saw—even as more Allied troops rushed up around *them*, bayoneting them in the back.

Matt caught Cook, who just looked dazed, a big, fresh dent in his helmet. "Cease firing outside the perimeter!" he roared, repeating it twice more. "The Grik are fighting rebels. Leave 'em to it!" He shoved Cook away to the right. "Pass the word." He saw Chack looking back, blinking incredulity. Galay was on the ground, stunned. The breach appeared contained, but the troopers there were fighting hard to keep it so. "Not you," he yelled, then blinked irony while he shook his head and pointed at Jash—whom Chack just now seemed to notice. "Just . . . take your lead from him, and kill whoever *he's* killing!"

"Damn," Silva spat, grabbing Lawrence and steadying him. Like Cook, the Sa'aaran was covered in blood and looked dazed, but it might've been simple, utter exhaustion at this point. All the Grik close enough to threaten them were already dead and a platoon with Captain McIntyre had surrounded them, in any case. "Who's that leave for *us* ta kill?"

Matt nodded his gratitude. No matter where he wanted to go or what he wanted to do, it was implicit that Silva wouldn't leave Matt's side. He grabbed McIntyre's arm. "Send a runner to get on the horn as fast as they can and tell any ships and planes in the area not, repeat *not*, to attack. We're sorting this out ourselves." Then he pointed his bloody sword at the quickly withering knot of Grik around the Celestial Mother. "We can still kill *them*, Chief Silva."

There were probably only about a hundred assassins left by the time Matt, Silva, Lawrence, McIntyre, and his platoon of Raiders joined the slaughter, yelling at the troops to *save* the Celestial Mother instead of shoot her, just in case they hadn't already gotten the word. They killed some Grik with their blades, washing themselves in yet more blood, but couldn't add much or really even hasten the rescue because so many were already there. Unfortunately, for a little longer, Safir, Moe, and their small group of guards were still alone inside all that, fighting desperately to protect the giant, coppery Grik.

And the Celestial Mother was fighting too, despite having taken several painful wounds from musket balls. She'd been the primary target of the attack, after all. Only her great size allowed her to absorb the damage and keep going, her long, manicured claws slashing over the helmets of her shorter Lemurian defenders, tearing out throats and literally pulling off heads, showering blood all over herself and everyone around her. Matt could see all this, never losing sight of the giant Grik as her rescuers tightened around her, so he wasn't surprised to find her still standing when all the Grik were slain at last and he finally reached her. He was surprised and heartsick, however, to find her standing alone.

Corps-'Cats were already squeezing through the press while loud, frantic Lemurian voices called for more over the squalls of wounded Grik that were vengefully hacked apart. A swift, mind-numbed survey of the carnage revealed the corpses of nearly all the guards, most half-buried under mangled Grik. And there, lying on his side with a short sword still in his hand and a dead 'Cat draped across his legs, was the body of the Chooser. His eyes were wide, unseeing, and his tongue lolled from open jaws into a pool of blood beneath his head. The only movement in the abattoir surrounding the Celestial Mother, in fact, was her heavy breathing—and the weak rise and fall of a bloody bayonet on the end of a rifle between her widely spaced legs.

"Jesus!" Silva snarled, jumping forward. Pulling the sticky rifle away, he handed it to someone instead of tossing it like he started to, lest the bayonet skewer one of the corps-'Cats inspecting someone nearby. Then, with too many hands trying to help, including Matt's, he dragged two forms out from under the huge Grik.

One was General Queen Safir Maraan, and the other was First Sergeant Moe. With a cry, Chack shouldered through the press and scooped up his mate, even as corps-'Cats fought him to find her wounds and cut the leather straps securing her cuirass. There was at least one large hole in it. Most evident and horrifying of all, however, was the deep sword cut to the side of her face that had caved in her right eye socket. Holding the limp form,

Chack started to moan, and it was the most desolate, heartrending sound Matt ever heard. Slowly, he knelt by his Lemurian friend and put his arm around his shoulders. To his amazement, however, Safir gasped when the cuirass was pulled away, and her left eyelid parted to reveal the bright silver orb beneath. She blinked to focus.

"I hurt," she said simply, softly, under the rain of Chack's tears that soaked her wrecked, bloody face.

"I bet you do," Matt told her gently, anxious worry displacing some of his grief. He motioned for the corps-'Cats to take her. "Get her in the palace, to the surgeons."

"No!" Chack almost snarled. "I'll do it!"

Matt stood, helping his physically and emotionally exhausted friend rise with his burden.

"Moe?" Safir asked weakly. "He saved me." Then her eye focused on the Celestial Mother, watching all this with perplexed interest, along with the pain she must be feeling as well. "She did too," Safir added. Chack only glared up at the Celestial Mother as he started away. He did let the corps-'Cats help support him so he wouldn't drop Safir.

"Ol' Moe's gone," Silva told Matt, his good eye suspiciously damp as well. "Bled out pertectin' Safir, I reckon. Geezer must have a dozen cuts an' holes ineem." Silva sniffed. "Dumb-ass should'a stuck by me."

Matt shook his head, looking up at the Celestial Mother. Her cloak was gone and she was clothed now only in blood. "Thank God he didn't or we would've lost Safir—which probably would've cost us Chack too," he added. It was a cold-blooded statement of fact, but Silva knew how hard the skipper would take losing either of them.

Two more live wounded were found under the bodies and quickly taken away while Matt and the Celestial Mother regarded one another. And with the Giver of Life secure, the fighting elsewhere rapidly dwindled. In mere moments, it seemed, Abel Cook, Randal Milke, and General Mersaak joined them, with Jash and another blood-streaked Grik officer. Except for Abel's soft remarks—"That's First Sergeant Moe, poor fellow. I thought he'd never die. *Couldn't* die. Perhaps you'll think on that yourself, Chief Silva"—Matt ignored the newcomers. "Tell her we can treat her wounds," he told Lawrence. The Sa'aaran complied.

"I have healers of my own," the Celestial Mother answered.

"Not anymore," Lawrence pointed out. "Unless they hid somewhere in the palace where we couldn't find them. And ours are better."

"Then I accept." She was still staring at Matt. "So *he* is your First General," she stated. It wasn't a question. Then she gestured at the Lemurian dead around her. "Who acts as if these are as his own hatchlings—though even toward hatchlings, I've never seen such . . . attachment as I witnessed from him, and that other."

A harried, nervous corps-'Cat started inventorying the Celestial Mother's wounds while Matt contemplated what Lawrence told him she said, considering not only her perspective, but how he should proceed. The guards, corps-'Cat, and Safir, of course, had proven they'd protect her, and Jash's unrestrained presence so soon after the short, sharp fight with the mutineers showed they could cooperate, but Matt knew he had to reinforce the parameters of that cooperation at once. "Tell her I think of all our people as my 'hatchlings.' She should think of hers the same way. For God's sake, they all worship her as their 'mother,' after all!" He started talking directly to her as Lawrence followed his words. "But Chack—the one most attached to the injured female general who led your defense—was extra upset because she's his mate." He shook his head. "I doubt you understand that."

He was right. Some Hij had mates, of course, as specific, reliable conduits for perpetuating their bloodline, but any other significance of the word beyond the brief physical act was utterly alien to Grik. Lawrence, who only imperfectly understood the concept himself, tried to explain it as the most intense of friendships, but lost his way again because Grik had no word for "friend" either. Regardless, the Celestial Mother seemed most fascinated by the fact that Safir was female—and a general. "Are there many such?" she asked.

"Yes," Lawrence confirmed. "Not from my race, or the Khonashi that resemble us, but females of other races in the Union and Grand Alliance often perform the same tasks and duties as males." He didn't go into the cultural differences within the Alliance, and that there were still exceptions. That would only confuse things more, and the Celestial Mother was clearly mystified enough as it was.

"How?" she asked. "Are they all Uul?"

"There *are* no Uul among us, anywhere. If there were, we'd . . . elevate them at once," Lawrence responded adamantly.

Jash had remained silent during this exchange, partly out of awe to be in the presence of the Celestial Mother, but also to hear what was said. Now he had to speak. "Giver of Life," he began, going down to the bloody ground. "If I may?"

"You are?"

"First Ker-noll Jash. I command those that attempted to protect you from the invaders. . . ."

"Poorly," the Celestial Mother commented.

"Perhaps."

"And those who tried to murder me?"

"Garrison troops. The same that slaughtered virtually all the Ancient Hij of this city. *Esshk's* troops and all that wore the red and black slash marks of his service are being destroyed," he assured. He recognized the head of one of the decapitated corpses at her feet right in front of his face and nudged it with his snout. "That was Sagat. Their leader."

The Celestial Mother glanced at the head, looking troubled. Or perhaps the probing of the Lemurian healer pained her? She waved a bloody-clawed hand. "Rise. Speak."

Jash quickly stood. "I would speculate. The attachment we saw, it only now occurs to me . . ." Jash glanced at Matt and in the direction Chack had gone. "If, for whatever reason, these folk become so attached to one another—as you remarked on—is it any wonder they fought so hard when we tried to make them prey? How many *other* prey through the ages have felt the same?" He pointed his snout at Matt. "He *is* something like their First General, as I understand such things, though there's more to it than that. How much safer would our race be if he somehow, eventually, formed an attachment to us?"

The Celestial Mother blinked wide eyes. "Very astute, First Ker-noll Jash. Allow no harm to come to yourself. I'll have need of thoughtful advisors in the time to come." She glanced down at the Chooser's corpse. "And this notion of acquired, preferred attachment requires consideration. Even *he* chose me over Esshk, in the end." She looked back at Jash. "Halt the destruction of the garrison troops. They may adopt the same preferment now, and you might need them."

She turned to Matt with a gust of air from her snout. "So. If you're First General to all your people, will you now be mine?"

It was all Matt could do to choke back a bitter laugh when Lawrence translated this—and all else that was said. *The very idea,* he thought. *Me as First General of the Grik! After all we've been through.* He wondered what Sandra would say, if she'd laugh hysterically or just throw up. And what of Keje? Tassanna? Chack and Safir? *What would Adar have said, in my shoes now?* That sobered him, as did the immediate power play the Celestial Mother just made, because he wasn't sure Adar would've caught it.

"I appreciate your protecting our people," he began cautiously, "who were injured or killed protecting you—after they fought so hard to *beat* you." He turned to Jash. "And make no mistake, you *are* beaten." He rubbed red eyes. He was very tired too. "At the same time, in a sense, we've already fought together against Esshk, and that counts for something. He's still on the loose with most of your empire at his back, but he's our mutual enemy now and a threat to us all. Still, it'll take more than one little scrap, with us on the same side, before we're pals."

He looked at Lawrence. "Try to tell them that—and one more thing. If they've got to associate us with titles they're used to, then General Pete Alden—the man who *wrecked* their army at the Neckbone—is First General to them. Rolak's second, and right on down the line. We'll see where Jash and any others fit in as we get to know them and figure out if we can trust 'em. If we can't, we'll just have to go back to plan A and kill 'em all."

He looked at the Celestial Mother. "As for me—and

whoever else I say—she can think of us as her Regent Champions, like Esshk was, except now she'll do what *we* tell her. How long that lasts depends on how well she behaves, how quick she can cook up a better society—maybe along the lines of North Borno." He paused. "We might need 'King' Tony Scott out here," he mused. "But it mainly depends on how fast she convinces us she's ready to rule responsibly—by *our* definition—and in peace with everybody around her."

"Except Esshk," Silva ground out.

"Right," Matt agreed darkly. "Except Esshk."

"That is . . . acceptable, for now," the Celestial Mother finally replied after Lawrence explained as best he could. "We'll join your Grand Alliance—under your guidance," she hastened to add to Matt, "while you command the Great Hunt." She looked meaningfully at Lawrence. "I must have a worthy senior advisor, however, to describe how I must rule the Gharrichk'k as our ancient ways are rebuilt." Her tone sounded somewhat vulnerable for the first time.

Matt caught the desperation in Lawrence's voice, however, as he completed the translation, and saw the pleading in his eyes. So did Silva, who snorted and smirked and muttered, "Why, you ol' misceggenator! You been schemin' this all along!"

"No!" Lawrence begged. "Don't ditch I 'ith her!"

Matt blinked, surprised. He'd never seen Lawrence afraid, but his terror was unmistakable now. Maybe he thought the responsibility of such an assignment was beyond him? "Major I'Joorka's still unfit to resume command of the First North Borno," he thought aloud, "but should be sufficiently recovered for this duty." He smiled at Lawrence. "Tell her the greatest commander and hero of the Khonashi will be appointed as her . . . Co-Regent Champion and liaison to the Grand Alliance. I'll try to get Hij Geerki to help him," he added to himself.

Then he turned to Jash. "You and I need to figure out how to keep our troops from killing each other and get them working together as soon as possible, because no matter how hard *you* think that's going to be, I guarantee it'll be harder. I don't know if your soldiers'll hold a grudge, but mine sure will, and they've been scared of Grik longer than they reckon time. They're not scared anymore, though; they've replaced their fear with hate." Matt suddenly realized he wasn't at all sure how this arrangement would go down back home. It would've been impossible just a year before; the hate ran too deep. But after all the bloodshed, and with other looming threats . . . It simply wasn't possible to kill every Grik in the world, so they'd have to force a way to get along with some.

He blinked curiosity at Jash in the Lemurian way. "I wonder if you've started to learn what that kind of hate feels like? If so, you better point it at Esshk—and figure out how to brush it off when it's aimed at you, 'cause there'll be a lot. You'll have to *earn* it away," he said forcefully. "Maybe the best start is to have unarmed parties, from both sides, get busy cleaning up around here." He paused before continuing, distaste clear on his face. "You can do what you want with your dead—eat 'em, whatever. But the first lizard that takes a bite out of one of ours'll get his head blown off."

Lawrence told the Celestial Mother and Jash what Matt said, and though he was profoundly relieved he wouldn't get ditched, he couldn't ignore a certain twinge of regret. And was that disappointment he saw in the eyes of the Celestial Mother? He shook his head to clear the thought, but it wouldn't go away. Then again, neither would the memory of what happened to Pokey.

CHAPTER 47

////// *El Palo*
North Coast of Nuevo Granada
Holy Dominion
March 18, 1945

Fred Reynolds and Kari-Faask orbited their lone Nancy twelve hundred feet over the NUS invasion fleet just offshore of El Palo. It wasn't a very impressive place, just a seaside fishing town near the northernmost point of the South American continent. There was no great protected harbor, nor any real defenses—not like El Henal to the west or Puerto del Cielo to the east—and that, as well as the fact that the Doms would never expect them to land there in the first place, was precisely why they had.

There'd been controversy over that. Obviously, the western Allies—the Union and Impies—would've preferred the NUS invade closer to the Pass of Fire, not only to help clear the way for the 2nd Fleet AEF as it marched east, but to ease the supply of modern weapons they hoped to deliver. But only the western approach to the pass had been secured, and it could take time before the whole thing was in Allied hands. Alternatively, a practically unopposed landing of the whole NUS Army would allow it to consolidate its position directly astride the east-west Camino Militar, where it could threaten all of Nuevo Granada just by being there and still distract the

Doms from what was happening in the pass. Moreover, it wasn't much farther from the NUS's primary base of supply in Cuba, sea-lanes in a more open sea should be more secure, and the Republic of Real People—with its base of supply actually closer—had promised modern weapons as well, including the seaplane tenders and its very first squadron of "modern" warships.

Fred didn't know which strategy was best, but it didn't really matter what he and Kari thought. Still flying the only plane east of the pass since the tenders hadn't arrived yet and USS *Donaghey* had only enough fuel for them, their job was spying threats from a distance, on land and sea, and reporting what they saw to Captain Greg Garrett on USS *Donaghey*, or Admiral Duncan aboard his flagship, NUSS *Zachary Taylor*. "Old Zack" was equipped with one of six small radio sets they'd flown over from Dulce. They were also strictly forbidden to fly low enough for anything on the ground or water to damage their plane, and ordered to avoid Grikbirds at any cost. Fred was fine with that, though he knew sometimes you *couldn't* avoid Grikbirds. So far, at least for the past few days, the only ones they spotted were flying hell for leather, low overland, probably bearing dispatches.

"Pretty daamn impressive," Kari shouted behind him. "There's nearly a hundred traansports down there, mostly merchies, but big ones," she allowed, "an' more thaan haaff is steamers." There actually weren't that many now. Quite a few had already sailed back for Santiago and more cargo, but Fred wasn't in the mood to argue for the sake of argument. "Then they got twenty o' their heavy liners," Kari continued, "another twenty-five big-gun frigate DDs, like Cap-i-taan Willis's *Congress*, an' thaat maany more lighter frigates an' sloops." That much was certainly true. "On top o' thaat," Kari continued, "they've put fifty thousaands of men ashore, the Maker knows how maany horses an' guns, an' ever'thing they need to fight a baattle or two."

Fred snorted. Kari made it sound like it had been easy, but it hadn't. The NUS hadn't made a real amphibious assault in decades and never on this scale. Captain Garrett tried to advise them, based on his experience at Raan-

Goon, but the operation had been a study in chaos. If the landing had been opposed, or a Dom fleet of any size appeared during that critical time, the NUS invasion of Nuevo Granada could've been a catastrophe. *And they knew it would be too,* Fred realized, his respect for Semmes, Admiral Duncan, and probably Captain Anson ratcheting up a notch. *Another reason why they chose this spot.*

He waggled his wings at the sailors below and took a last glance at the shoreside town. *El Palo,* he thought. *"Palo" means "stick," I think. Or maybe "mast" or "spar."* He shook his head, looking past the town at the tall, straight timber of the forest beyond. The land looked nothing like he'd imagined it would, being more like the "Mast Tree Forest" near the New Britain Isles colony of Saint Francis—and that answered another question forming in his mind. "Nobody's even gonna miss this joint, with everybody going to steam," he said. "Unless they cut timber for ships' hulls here too. But they can do that just about anywhere down here, I bet."

Banking slightly left, Fred turned out to sea and began the longest leg of their search pattern, back toward Puerto del Cielo, where intelligence last reported the heavy League destroyer *Leopardo* lurked. That information was pretty old, however, and they wouldn't go close enough to confirm it in any case. *Leopardo* didn't have dual-purpose guns—that they knew of—but did mount pom-poms. Regardless, whether she was there or not, Puerto del Cielo was a very dangerous city, probably packed with Grikbirds, and they didn't have the fuel if they were going to search their whole grid.

They flew in silence until they saw El Penon to the south—the closest fairly large Dom city—and they turned due north. That next leg of their scout was relatively uneventful as well, though they saw a lot of fishing boats, and high, gray clouds began to form in the northeast. An hour and a half later, they made their routine turn to the west-northwest. They didn't expect to see anything at all on this stretch—maybe some NUS transports bringing more supplies or heading back to Cuba. The western approach from El Paso del Fuego, Rio Grabacion, or Puerto

Dominio was deemed the most probable direction enemy warships might still come from.

As anticipated, they eventually saw smears of smoke from oil-burning Nussie ships and even passed right over one. Fred waggled his wings again, but a short time later began to settle into a kind of trance. He was tired, and the drone of the in-line engine and vibration of the plane made it almost impossible for him to stay alert on this kind of flight. *Kari'll keep watch,* he told himself. *That's what she's along for.*

"Whaat's thaat?" Kari suddenly demanded through the voice tube by Fred's ear, and he jerked upright from where he'd scrunched down in his seat.

"What? Where?"

"T'ree o'clock, 'bout eighteen, twenny miles. Lotsa smoke! Can't see nothin' else."

At fifteen hundred feet, the horizon was a little over forty-five miles away. That didn't take haze or eye strain into account, however, and even a Lemurian's vision was limited to identifying something the size of, say, an island at that distance. But half that far, thick smoke was easy. Even Fred could see it, now that Kari pointed it out.

"Right," Fred said, turning north. "Let's have a look. Send our position and that we're checking something out."

"Okaay."

The base of the leaning tower of smoke suddenly flashed bright, and the dark line down to the water grew indistinct and faded.

"What the hell?" Fred murmured. "Hey, Kari, send that a Nussie merchie might've caught fire and blown up. I . . . I think I see another one not too far away. We'll make for it and try to lead it to the wreck."

Even at a measly 90 mph, which was all Fred could coax from this older and now somewhat hard-used Nancy, they closed the distance fairly rapidly.

"That's weird," Fred murmured, staring at the Nussie transport ahead.

"Whaat?" Kari demanded.

"Well, those guys *had* to see the other ship go up—no way they didn't—and they've got the bearing. You'd think they'd be heading over there as fast as they can. Nobody'll survive long in the water," he added unnecessarily. "But she isn't going that way at all. She's hauling ass the other way . . . *whoa!*" A cluster of tall waterspouts suddenly erupted around the transport. "What the hell?"

"*Whaat* the hell?" Kari demanded.

"I, uh . . ." Fred's first thought was that Grikbirds carrying bombs had somehow flown way out here and dropped them on the ship. *Or maybe they came off one of those "carriers" we heard about,* he told himself and started scanning the sky. *That's crazy, though,* he realized. *No damn Grikbirds could toss* that *tight a pattern. Could they?*

That left only one alternative. He lowered his gaze and looked beyond where the first ship was demolished. "Shit!" he shouted, just as another salvo of eight 4.7″ shells plunged around—and on—the fleeing sail/steam transport. Fred thought two of them hit, but two was enough. Half the bow was blown away in a blizzard of shattered timbers, and black smoke and silver steam gushed from the funnel as the engineering space was blasted open. The ship stalled, almost right under them now.

"Shit *whaat*?" Kari roared with frustration. She could see the shattered transport, already quickly filling, but not what caused it.

"It's that damn *Leopardo*, that's what. Sure as hell!" Fred called back. He could see the ship clearly now that it had advanced beyond the smoke of the farthest wreck, just smoldering debris on the water now. "Send it!" he shouted. "'League destroyer *Leopardo*'s sinking our transports heading back to Cuba.'"

No more salvos fell around the sinking ship. What would be the point? It was doomed. Swiftly, *Leopardo* accelerated and turned almost due south. She'd apparently veered slightly to starboard to exercise all her guns. *Target practice,* Fred supposed bitterly. Realizing the Leaguers had to see them and they were getting a bit too close, he turned away. "Tell Captain Garrett and Admiral Duncan *Leopardo*'s settled on a heading of"—he paused and glanced at his compass—"about two zero zero. Speed, maybe twenty-five knots. She's making right for the invasion fleet."

Leopardo

"They've seen us," stated Capitano Ciano, disappointed, lowering his binoculars. In the distance, the small plane was easily visible to the naked eye, turning south.

"Excellent," replied Capitaine de Fregate Victor Gravois.

Ciano looked surprised. "How can that be good? I thought you wanted to destroy as much NUS shipping as we can."

Gravois shook his head. "No." His voice took on an official aspect, as if speaking at an inquiry—or award ceremony. "It was our intention to protect the territorial integrity of our Dominion allies without provoking the North American continental power calling itself the New United States. Sadly, numerous"—he smiled tightly and inserted—"we don't know how many yet, of course—NUS merchant vessels and warships chose to defy us. Some actually *fired* on us!" He added that with something that sounded like genuine surprise.

"But, Capitaine," Ciano objected, "we've seen no warships yet, and *nothing* fired on us!"

"Not yet, my dear Capitano Ciano," Gravois said, "but they will."

Ciano was clearly still confused, and Gravois sighed. "Part, if not all the NUS fleet, will meet us as we approach their beachhead. How can they not? I hope the alarm that plane delivers will warn most of them away, but some will surely stay and provide your crew additional exercise. Don't sink *too* many," he cautioned. "If necessary, I'll tell you when to stop."

"But why . . . ?" Ciano shrugged. "Why *all* this? Why not just destroy the entire NUS fleet, and all their transports too?"

Gravois laughed. "You're too new at this, my friend, and Don Hernan *thinks* he's too clever by half. Very well. It's really quite simple: It's my aim to terrorize the NUS, not defeat it, until it better serves my purpose. We must make them cautious, however; afraid to commit too much shipping to supply their forces ashore. It'll take more to defeat their army than Don Hernan thinks, and it might strike deeply indeed if we don't slow its progress. . . ."

"By limiting its supplies," Ciano agreed, but he still looked mystified.

"On the other hand," Gravois practically leered, "His Holiness Don Hernan won't know we limited *ourselves* and will be suitably impressed by the havoc we wreak. Quite appreciative as well, I'm sure. Particularly in light of other possible developments," he mused absently.

They knew an action had commenced at the Pass of Fire, but had no word of its outcome. Gravois suspected Don Hernan's Blood Priests would've already been crowing about a great victory, so either the battle still raged or it hadn't gone as Don Hernan predicted. Gravois smiled. That might serve his purposes as well.

"But with the bulk of the NUS fleet intact," he continued, "he'll understand he still needs us very much. Can't have him thinking one of his little problems has been eliminated entirely. That wouldn't do at all. He *is* quite clever," Gravois warned. "Rather dangerously so. Therefore, we have to keep him dependent on us, and can't allow ourselves to become the *only* problem he has to worry about."

"We have to scatter the fleet!" Greg Garrett said, speaking directly to Admiral Duncan over the radio. Feet thundered on the deck above as *Donaghey*'s crew was already racing to make sail. *Donaghey* was the only warship with the NUS fleet that relied on sails alone. Greg had sent his Dom prize, *Matarife*, on a reconnaissance cruise toward Ascension Island.

"Nonsense," Duncan retorted, "we'll go out and meet her!"

Greg sighed. "At *Leopardo*'s reported speed, she'll get here just at dark, probably coming in so we'll be lit up by the sunset and she can stand off farther than we can even shoot, and pick us off. She'll slaughter the entire fleet! Our only hope is to scatter now. Maybe she'll just get a few of us."

Duncan hesitated. "You're quite sincere, Captain Garrett," he observed, astonished. "But I fail to understand how a single ship can manage that. You yourself destroyed a similar ship with two elderly, outmoded frigates, if I recall. No offense, sir!" he hastily added. "It was quite a feat, I'm sure. But that only proves my point."

Greg looked over at Smitty Smith, his gunnery officer, and rolled his eyes. Smitty was slowly chewing a soggy cigar, but his face remained impassive. Greg's Lemurian XO, Mak-Araa, blinked consternation. "With all due respect, sir," Greg spoke into the microphone, "you just don't get it. Sure, we killed *Atúnez*, but we did it by surprise, at pistol shot, and she was a sitting duck."

"I knew our success would come back and bite us on the ass someday," Smitty grumped aside to Mak.

Greg glared at him. "Admiral," he continued, "*Leopardo*'s bigger, faster, and twice as powerful as *Atúnez*. And she's hunting *us*. *We're* the sitting ducks." He sighed. "Sir," he pleaded, "you just haven't *seen*. You can't possibly know what she's capable of, and I'm begging you to trust me."

There was a longer pause this time. "Captain Garrett, I won't leave our forces ashore unsupported. Even if all you say is true, I'd be drummed out of the service."

Greg's heart sank.

"What I will do," Admiral Duncan continued, "is scatter the bulk of the fleet. Commodore Semmes will arrange a suitable rendezvous. I'll remain here with . . ." He considered. "Six ships of the line. They should be more than sufficient to deal with a single ship, no matter how advanced." Greg began to protest again, but Duncan cut him off. "If they're not, you'll have been proven right, Commodore Semmes will assume command of the fleet, and I'll be dead. Not sure I *want* to live in a world where one ship's equal to half a dozen of our best," he mused darkly. Greg started to point out that his crews might disagree, but knew it was pointless.

"Thank you, sir, and good luck" was all he said. Turning to Mak, he told him, "Signal Commodore Semmes. Tell him the admiral's ordered the fleet to scatter. I'd recommend he send it generally east-northeast, and west-northwest, but the ships need to get out of sight of each other as fast as they can. And don't stop for any they might see in distress. They'll just turn into targets too."

"Any suggestions for the rendezvous?" Mak asked.

Greg rubbed his scalp and shook his head. "We already knew the League had picked a side," he growled, "but now the murdering bastards are in the open. With *Leopardo* on the loose, and God knows what else, no place in the Caribbean'll be safe." He shrugged. "Suggest we rendezvous back at Santiago. *Leopardo* can't do much to the guys ashore; she'll be afraid to deplete her ammo too much, I bet. And she can't just park here either. We'll figure a way to get transports in with food and ammo. Maybe at night. But the time's finally come when Captain Reddy—or *somebody*—is gonna have to send us some *goddamn help.*"

Donaghey dashed northeast that night through a rising sea, stopping just long enough to take Fred and Kari and their tired Nancy aboard. The weather was worsening and that was tricky, but everyone had plenty of experience at it now. They never saw *Leopardo* and, better yet, she didn't spot *Donaghey*. But it was a somber crew indeed that watched the bright, distant flashes light the southwest horizon for a little more than forty minutes. When the flashes faded, there was only a dull red gleam against the gathering clouds to mark the flaming graves of ships. Kari and *Donaghey*'s signal-'Cats tried to contact Admiral Duncan on *Old Zack* far into the night, but there was no response.

Matt Reddy stood on USS *Walker*'s main deck behind the bridge, staring out at the Palace of Vanished Gods and the ruined city beyond. Dennis Silva was beside him, all cleaned up, but wearing enough bandages to cover nearly every inch of skin that would otherwise be exposed. He spoke to Pam occasionally, pointing out things ashore, but mainly he was just there to be by his skipper, as he'd been since that final, crazy fight. Matt didn't know what Pam thought of that, but at least she had him with her for a while. He shook his head and wondered how they'd work through what came next.

All the bodies had been cleared and great pyres burned on the relatively compact battlefield in front of the entrance to the palace, still surrounded by elements of II Corps. First Colonel Jash's Slasher Division—the best translation they'd come up with—was in a large encampment on the northeast outskirts of the city. It was still under arms, but all its ammunition had been collected. And Jash was being watched by more of Safir Maraan's troops brought up to join their comrades by the Repub monitors and Colonel Will's transports from where they'd fallen back to secure the old perimeter after the breakout battle.

Safir wasn't here, of course, and neither was Chack. Jumbo Fisher's Clippers had been coming and going constantly, flying the worst wounded out to *Salissa*, *Madraas*, *Tarakaan Island*, and *Sular*. Shipping them past holdout shore batteries in fragile transports wasn't a good idea, though *Gray* and *Ellie*, and most of their Nancys, were working their way back downriver to clear them out. The Repub monitors stayed to guard against anything approaching from upriver.

Old Sofesshk isn't all ruined, Matt supposed, *and Courtney'll have a ball figuring out the most ancient architecture someday, whether it was built by Grik or somebody earlier that they ran off.* Matt looked fondly at the Australian general, in the fine Republic officer's uniform someone loaned him, talking animatedly with Muln Rolak about that very possibility. Despite the uniform, it was still Courtney, complete with the sombrero he was fanning himself with and Krag rifle supported by a sling.

Walker was crowded amidships, ferrying a large sampling of Allied officers across from the wasteland of New Sofesshk to meet the Celestial Mother. General Kim, Inquisitor Choon, General Taal, and Optio Meek would be the first to represent the Republic, though more would soon follow. And Matt guessed Courtney and Bekiaa were Repubs too, in a way. Pete had stayed with his army, following Colonel Saachic as he chased Second General Ign west, but generals Rolak, Faan, and Mu-Tai were here, along with a small escort from the Triple I sent by General Taa-leen. Captain McIntyre was the senior Impie now, Matt remembered sadly, but he was already ashore. He and Major Cook were doing their best to patch Chack's Brigade back together. Neither begrudged their commander's departure with his wounded mate.

Major I'joorka, here for the Khonashi in addition to being a new Regent Champion, and Hij Geerki had come in on a Clipper. I'joorka was still weak and would bear his burn scars forever, but he assured Matt he was up for this. Lawrence was introducing him and Geerki to the Celestial Mother now—and warning them about her "powers."

Matt suspected Geerki was having the time of his life. He'd been one of the lowest-ranking Hij in the empire, and now he'd help teach the couple thousand ancient Hij who'd finally emerged—and the Celestial Mother herself—how to be "good critchers."

Colonel Will and Lieutenant Colonel Durai represented the Maroons and Shee-ree, and a couple of wide-eyed La-laantis were even present. Matt thought it important that *somebody* from every Allied power actually see the Celestial Mother in Allied hands, and the only ones he could think of that weren't represented at all were the NUS—but they'd never fought the Grik, anyway.

He was glad to meet General Kim at last, and see so many familiar faces. Some, like Courtney and Bekiaa, even Choon, he hadn't seen in a very long time. But the absence of many more, not even lost, who *ought* to be here—like Keje, Tassanna, Pete, Alan Letts, even Rebecca Anne McDonald—left him feeling glum. And of course he missed his wife. She'd *really* earned the right to enjoy this victory. The win was incomplete, of course, but still significant; something to give them hope. And Sandra could probably use some hope right now.

Matt had finally been informed that she was having their child, but the delivery had been very difficult and prolonged. Every radio inquiry he made was answered with "She's doing fine; just having a tough time. Quite normal when it's your first." But Matt was growing increasingly concerned and irritable. "Just how long do these things take?" he'd unreasonably demanded of Ed Palmer at one point. He'd immediately apologized to the young signal officer but remained unhappy and embarrassed by his outburst. Then, of course, news from elsewhere and other fronts began to filter in. Some was cause for satisfaction, and he passed that along, but some gave him even more to worry about, all while the exhausting battle his wife was waging kept a crushing, breathless, racing feeling in his chest and made it difficult to concentrate.

"What's that?" a smiling Courtney Bradford asked, pointing at a folded message form Matt was tapping against the bulwark. Several others, including Rolak, Kim, Choon, and Bekiaa, were with him. "More good news, I hope?

Bloody marvelous about the Pass of Fire!" He chuckled. "Old Shinya! Never thought he'd be so useful or accomplish so much when we fished him from the water like a drowned rat!"

Matt looked at the paper and shook his head. "It's from Shinya, but it isn't so good. A report from Fred and Kari."

Courtney frowned, knowing Matt would tell them what it said in his own time, but then he brightened. "Fascinating rumor about Esshk, though," he enthused. "No one quite seems to know where he is, just 'up north' somewhere. Possibly around a place called Lake Galk. I've heard it described as something like the Western Great Rift Valley, only filled with enough water to be considered an inland sea!"

"Quite faascinating," Rolak grumbled ironically, "since it's more thaan rumor, and the same sources indicate he still commaands a very laarge force of New Aarmy troops." He looked at Matt. "Speaking of surprising usefulness, Hij Geerki continues to impress me with his initiaative. Not only did he supply laborers from his former Uul at Grik City to help build Caamp Simy and Arracca Field, but he also provided a number of traanslators and spies he's appaarently been training. I took the liberty of sending severaal to join Gener-aal Aalden. They've already proven useful—"

"Indeed," Courtney interrupted. "I spoke to one myself, and word is already rampant that as soon as news from here reached Esshk, he grandly, publicly proclaimed himself Supreme Regent with absolute authority—granted by the Celestial Mother herself, mind"—he chuckled again—"to rule the entire Grik Empire in her stead. Only until he can 'snatch her back from the claws of the invading prey and destroy us forever,' of course," he added sarcastically.

Rolak was nodding. "Word of his decrees spread faaster thaan the Celestial Mother's, declaring Esshk a usurper and commaanding every regency in the empire to combine with her—and us—against him." He sighed. "Esshk must've sent runners everywhere, perhaaps extending their range with airships." He blinked significantly. "This came from straagglers following Gener-aal Ign, so Esshk clearly contaacted him. Airships again, at night I presume. In aany event, Esshk's story might be easier for maany to aaccept thaan the Celestiaal Mother's, since she *is* in our 'claws.'"

"Lawrence doesn't think it'll matter much," Matt told them, proving he'd already heard. "Sure, regencies close to wherever Esshk and his army's at will stay loyal to him, but quite a few had already balked and didn't trust Esshk to start with. Maybe they'll come over to the CM now, or at worst, stay uncommitted until they see how things shake out." He reached over and patted Rolak on the shoulder. "I think the biggest wild cards you and Pete"—he looked at Kim—"and Republic troops will have to worry about are Ign and what Halik'll do when he gets here. We know he's coming, but still don't know what his intentions are. We damn sure can't divert anything to go after him, so we just have to hope he stays neutral or the Celestial Mother can sway him. In the meantime, I'd say your best bet is to wreck Esshk before him and Halik ever meet."

They'd drawn a crowd, and nearly everyone in the waist was gathered around as they approached the dock by the Palace of Vanished Gods. "You taalk like we're not gonna be here, Skipper." It was Tabby, standing with Isak and Bernie Sandison, who spoke.

Matt finally raised the message form and shook it. "We're not." He took a long breath. "Everybody knows we took the Pass of Fire from the Doms, and that's swell. But now the League's jumped in with both feet. That damn *Leopardo* shot up the Nussie's invasion fleet after they landed their army, and it's largely on its own hook now. Not an impossible situation by itself," he said, shaking his head, "because the Nussies are getting some local support like Shinya did on the west coast. Covert supply runs can focus on ammunition. On top of that, Shinya will soon be on his way to join them. The problem is," he continued bleakly, "we'd hoped to ship him there, but he's fresh out of ships. And a fighting march might take months." He frowned. "Which brings us to the *real* problem. I don't think Gravois—it *had* to be Gravois on *Leopardo*—would have the guts to start the big dance without all his ducks lined up behind him."

"An' his ducks're half a dozen battlewagons, as many cruisers, an' maybe twenty DDs," Silva stated, matter-of-factly. Matt looked at him darkly, wondering how he knew. Silva had *not* been one of the people in the know. The big chief gunner's mate just shook his head, and that disconcerting, beatific grin began to spread across his face.

"Well, yes," Matt agreed, still irritated. "That's about the size of it"—he looked back at Silva—"and was part of what I was *about* to tell you all. The other part is what it means." He shook his head. "I spoke to Chairman Letts on the radio last night, and he'd already spoken to Governor-Empress McDonald—who's at Respite Island now, thank God, on her way back to the New Britain Isles." Matt looked hard at General Kim. "I even talked directly to your kaiser, Nig-Taak, for the first time. All agree we have no choice but to pull every modern ship and carrier in First Fleet, right now, and steam for the Pass of Fire as fast as we can. We have no idea what the League's timetable is, just guesses by Fiedler and Hoffman. We might already be too late," he added grimly.

"The Repub monitors and Des-Ron 10 will stay," Matt assured the rising voices, "and should be sufficient to deal with anything the Grik can still throw at you on the water. We'll also leave most of *Big Sal*'s and *Madraas*'s planes, after the hit Arracca Field took. I doubt anything like *that'll* ever happen again. COFO Leedom's already doubling the size of the perimeter around the field and will more than double the security force as fresh troops arrive." He smiled slightly at Rolak. "And they're coming, along with more weapons, ammo, and all the supplies you need. You won't be forgotten here. The only thing not coming is more modern ships."

He looked down at *Walker*'s deck and gently shifted his shoe on the pitted steel, as if caressing the old ship, then looked at Kim again. "As for the rest of First Fleet, your kaiser promised me the Republic would join us with some of its new ships. I hope to God it's true, because Second Fleet has precisely *one* operational carrier. Two will be in the yard for who knows how long, and the rest of the fleet is finished. And while Shinya and the Nussies deal with the Doms onshore, we're probably going to have to face the League at sea." He blinked regret at his Lemurian crew members nearby.

"Not to diminish anyone's service—everybody on this ship has been through nine kinds of hell. But only a few of you were with us at Baalkpan Bay when we fought *Amagi*. You know how . . . different that was from anything else we've done." He paused. "Your newer shipmates'll be counting on you to help them train for that—against the equivalent of maybe a dozen *Amagi*s at once."

The ship touched the dock and they felt the engines stop. "We'll do our best to prepare you," he continued. "But nobody on this world"—he glanced at Silva, Pam, Bernie, and Isak, even Courtney; they were the only old hands present (Spanky and Paddy were on the bridge)— "nobody but a *very* few," he qualified, "have any idea at all what a modern surface fleet action's like."

"Nope," Silva said, and grinned. "*I* was there—an' we *lost* that one, bad. Battle o' the Java Sea."

Matt had to force himself not to cover his eyes with his hands. "A fine example of how we *won't* fight this one," he growled through gritted teeth.

Realizing he probably should've kept his mouth shut, Silva barked, "Damn straight!" then eased back behind the skipper—where Pam slugged him in the arm with her sharp middle knuckle protruding from her fist.

Matt exhaled. "My point, I guess, is I know we're leaving you in the lurch, but I'm confident you'll finish the job. And knowing that is why we're free to do our best to keep the League—and Doms—out of the Pass of Fire." He patted Rolak's shoulder again and looked at the others. "None of this'll matter much in the long run if we can't. With the League and Doms together"—he looked intently around—"they'll have the rabid numbers of the Grik, with heavier weapons than we've ever had. They'll choke us off, eventually, and everything we've been through'll be for nothing."

"Damn straight," Silva said again.

"What's the matter with you?" Pam hissed. "You makin' up for that stupid Petey not bein' here?"

"I do kinda miss the little turd," Silva whispered back.

Then he grinned again. "But it looks like I'm back in the Navy for real this time, an' no more o' this sewer-river fightin' either. It's the deep blue sea again for me!"

Matt barely heard him, because just then he saw Ed Palmer standing by Tabby with one of those dreaded yellowish message forms in his hand. He groaned inwardly—until he saw the huge smile splitting the kid's face. Quickly, he motioned him over and looked at the page.

FROM: ADMIRAL KEJE-FRIS-AR CINC-WEST USNRS SALISSA X TO: CAPTAIN M P REDDY CINCAF USS WALKER X EYES ONLY DISTRIBUTE AT DISCRETION X JOKING X HAVE ALREADY DISPATCHED TO ALL FIRST-FLEET ELEMENTS AND CHAIRMAN LETTS X CONGRATULATIONS ON BIRTH OF HEALTHY HIGHLY VOCAL YOUNGLING X MINISTER OF MEDICINE S T REDDY TIRED BUT FINE X MOTHER AND YOUNGLING SEND LOVE TO COURAGEOUS FATHER X SUGGEST COURAGEOUS FATHER MAKE A QUICK AND BOLD DECISION ABOUT NAMES ALREADY DISCUSSED X SURGEON COMMANDS NO FURTHER COMM UNTIL MOTHER RESTS X CONGRATULATIONS AGAIN X MESSAGE ENDS XXX

USS *Walker*'s horn, very close on the battered funnel standing tall above them, suddenly whooped deafeningly, and Matt almost dropped the message. And even as *Walker*'s horn kept sounding, *Mahan*'s joined in, as did those on the steam transports and DDs of Des-Ron 10, even the Repub monitors, *Ancus* and *Servius*, a couple of miles away. All was joined by cheering, and Courtney and Bekiaa both wrapped Matt in a hug.

"The last to know?" Matt shouted at Spanky, who'd slid down the rungs of the ladder to the bridge, a mischievous grin on his bearded face.

"Just this once, Skipper," Spanky yelled back, the grin fading a little. "Things were touch-and-go for a while, and

Lady Sandra *ordered* everybody to keep it mum. Figured you had enough on your mind."

"She would," Matt murmured, looking back at the yellow page, suddenly searching.

"So, what is it, Skipper?" Silva asked. "Boy or girl?"

"I'll be damned," Matt barked with a sudden laugh of his own. It felt strange, but amazingly good. "It doesn't say! She wants a name, but how am I supposed to decide?"

"Relax, Skipper," Silva said. "You got time. Little scudder's eyes prob'ly ain't even open yet." Pam punched him again.

"We all have time now," Courtney agreed, plopping his hat on his head. "A short respite, perhaps, but well earned. And more reasons than not to celebrate for once!"

Carefully, Matt folded the message form and put it in his pocket, vowing to save it. With a smiling nod at a grinning Ed Palmer, glad to deliver good news for a change, Matt looked at all his friends. "You're right. For today, the war's over." He glanced at Spanky and qualified, "By watches, and those on duty will maintain Condition Three. Work it out." He looked back at the others. "But we'll have a Sky Priest say a few words by the funeral pyres tonight and have a *real* party, Lemurian style." Lemurian wakes, when they were at liberty to provide them, often degenerated into drunken revelries, celebrating the ascension of the departed into the Heavens.

"We'll start the war again tomorrow," Matt added a little more somberly, "and we'll kick Esshk's, Don Hernan's, and Gravois's asses straight to hell!"

EPILOGUE

*B*y Fred Reynolds's reckoning, the water off
El Palo's brown-sand beach was unnaturally still and kind of dingy-looking. There
was no surf and hardly any waves. There was a lot of debris in the water, however, and he had to watch for that as
he looked for a place to set his and Kari's Nancy down.
The charred wreck of one of Admiral Duncan's ships lay
in the shallows. Its crew had probably tried to beach it
before it sank, or maybe it just wound up there, adrift and
ablaze. Only flotsam remained of the rest of the ships that
stayed to fight. Interestingly, a lot of that had gone into
the construction of several floating docks extending outward from the beach.

Fred touched down on the water as smoothly as if he
were landing on a lake and motored over to a dock that
looked dangerously overloaded, almost awash. A ship
had come the night before, braving the lurking *Leopardo*
to offload food and ammunition. It left before dawn, but
the supplies were still going ashore to join a great mountain of crates and barrels on the beach. Wagons were being loaded there, and men in tropical white fatigues
carried lighter stuff into the woods like a double line of
ants. Several horses stood nearby, men holding their

reins. Fred flipped the ignition switch off and the engine behind him died. As always, the sudden silence was deafening. Standing in the cockpit, he caught a line somebody threw.

"Look, Fred! It's Caap'n Aanson!" Kari cried. Only then did Fred realize it was Anson himself who tossed the fresh white rope.

"Morning, sir," Fred said, grinning.

Anson smiled. "Good morning to you both. I saw your machine coming in and thought I'd meet you myself. I'm glad to see you well," he added sincerely. After watching what *Leopardo* did to six fine ships of the line and several unidentified frigates or transports on the horizon, he'd been *very* concerned about *Donaghey* and Fred and Kari. He waved at the line of laborers. "A lamentable circumstance we find ourselves in."

"Any trouble with the Doms?"

"Little enough as yet, though there are rumors of a large force assembling at El Henal and a smaller one at El Penon. That might ultimately be the bigger threat, as more troops arrive from Puerto del Cielo." He smiled again. "On the other hand, much as the inhabitants of smaller towns and cities in the west received General Shinya, the locals here also perceive us as liberators, by and large. Many have enlisted. There's debate whether they should form their own units, as Sister Audry's Vengadores did, or be integrated into our existing regiments. The latter is simpler. We've sufficient former Doms in the ranks to translate, and full immersion makes recruits easier to train." His smile faded. "And watch, of course. I have little fear of betrayal at present, however. The Doms had no idea we'd come here and couldn't have positioned many spies." His eyebrows arched. "And the locals are aware that just having *seen* us, they are doomed unless we prevail. So far, they seem happy to assist our scouts and help secure provisions."

"Thaat's somethin'," Kari told him, "'cause it'll be a while before your fleet can keep up with supply. Not with thaat daamn *Leopaardo* runnin' loose."

"Perhaps your Second Fleet might be of assistance?" Anson probed.

"Not likely," Fred grumped. "There's not much left. Hardly any surface element, and nothing that can stand up to *Leopardo*. And the air wings took a helluva beating. It'll take time to get them sorted out." He looked worriedly at the sky. "Seen any Grikbirds around here? Maybe even . . . bigger things?"

"There are a number of unpleasant creatures in the forest, much like those you and I encountered once before, but nothing hostile from the air as yet; just the usual swarms of little lizardbirds. We'll inform you at once if we perceive an aerial threat."

The NUS invasion force had kept transmissions to a minimum because they couldn't be certain their code was secure. Particularly with *Leopardo* and possibly other Leaguers listening. An exception would certainly be made if Grikbirds appeared, especially since the enemy would already know they'd *sent* them.

"Good, because we should at least have more planes pretty soon," Fred said, then brightened. "And Captain Reddy and the First Fleet AEF took the Grik capital at Sofesshk! Bet you hadn't heard that! The war in the west isn't over, maybe not by a long shot," he cautioned, "but First Fleet's on its way!"

"That's wonderful news!" Anson enthused.

Fred's expression clouded. "Maybe not so wonderful, since the scuttlebutt is that a big chunk of the *League* fleet's coming too. Honestly, sir, they've got a lot more metal than us—like *Leopardo*, but even bigger—and I don't see there's much we can do about it." He paused, fumbling in his pocket. "Look, sir, I was told to hand-deliver a message to General Cox. With Admiral Duncan dead and Commodore Semmes back in Santiago, I guess he's the cheese."

"For now, at least," Anson confirmed, holding out his hand. "I'll see he gets it."

Fred gave him the note without hesitation and shrugged. "No secret from *you*, I guess. Basically, since supply's so iffy, they're giving him a choice. Your army can't just sit on the beach forever, so if Cox doesn't think he can carry the fight to the Doms, they want to try to pull everybody out. It'll take time," he warned, "and they'll have to do it sneaky, but they figure they can."

Anson slapped his hand with the note several times, almost angrily, then put it in a pocket as he turned to look at the land behind him. The trees were extremely tall but otherwise there was nothing remarkable about it. Rows and rows of tents could be seen beyond the little town of El Palo and off beneath the trees in the forest, fading in the gloom and blue haze of campfire smoke. Lots of troops were milling around from camp to camp, and others were drilling in the shade on the beach. Fred saw mounted soldiers approaching along the tree line in a long column of twos, Comanches mixed with what he'd come to recognize as Anson's sky blue–uniformed Rangers.

"I shouldn't speak for General Cox," Anson said, "but I know him well enough that I believe I can. I'm certain I speak for almost everyone in the army—and the natives who've joined us, of course." He turned back to Fred and Kari. "Personally, I've been waiting for this opportunity to strike down the hateful Dominion and the evil it nurtures all my life." Smiling sadly, he fondly regarded his two young friends, both of whom had suffered painfully in the hands of the Doms themselves. "No doubt you understand as well as anyone why we must push on." His face brightened. "Come ashore. Things aren't so tight that we can't spare you breakfast!"

Fred glanced at the sky again, but also caught Kari adamantly shaking her head. "Thanks, but we better not. There *will* be Grikbirds sooner or later, and I don't want 'em to catch us with our asses in a puddle." He leaned over toward the pier and shook Anson's hand. "So long, Captain. And good luck!"

Several more Rangers had gathered around Anson, and they helped push the plane away from the pier. Settling back on the parachute padding his wicker seat, Fred flipped a switch and shouted, "Contact!"

"We'll be baack!" Kari shouted as she reached up and propped the engine. It roared to life, and she dropped down in her own seat.

A few minutes later, Anson watched the little plane rise from the water and soar away to the northwest. "God be with you, my friends," he said. Followed by the other Rangers, anxious to make their scouting reports, he picked his way through the dwindling crates and barrels and labored through the sand toward El Palo and General Cox's headquarters.

SW Grik Arabia

"And I thought things couldn't get any weirder," Enaak sighed as he, Dalibor Svec, several of their officers, and a score of troopers threaded their way through Regent General Halik's marching camp after another of their "consultations." Halik's army had pushed most of the way across Arabia, a land of flat, grassy prairies, scarce trees, massive herbivores, and equally substantial predators. The grass eaters generally looked kind of like kravaas, with four legs, big bony frills, and a cluster of lethal-looking horns pointing forward and to the sides. The most striking differences were their size and girth. The predators mostly went on four legs too, kind of like giant me-naaks. It was hard not to watch them fight, and Enaak and Svec wondered if their cavalry mounts were picking up pointers. Any beasts that looked overly interested in Halik's long column were discouraged by his now-impressive artillery train, and provided a steady diet for his army—and Enaak's troopers.

Unfortunately, there were also a lot of Grik, more than might be expected until one considered how many a single large animal would feed. And the fertile plain supported vast numbers of the monsters. The local Grik were understandably protective of their territorial regencies, and sometimes it seemed as if Halik had to fight every group he met. That was bad enough, from Halik's perspective, but the reasons why, besides simple territoriality, were strange and diverse enough to cause him fits.

Some naturally saw Halik and his hundred thousand troops as invaders from another regency. That happened all the time, and such conflicts had historically been encouraged as a means of population control, even sport, among the various regents. In addition, the great war was far away, the details unclear. The Celestial Mother was worshipped as everywhere, but might've been anywhere as far as most knew. A few thought she was still at the Celestial City on Madagascar, and Sofesshk was a myth. This was Enaak's first indication, when Niwa explained it later, that monolithic as the Grik might be, their empire was so extensive that they also tended to be highly insular from one regency to the next.

Ultimately, the Prime Regent of Arabia (the territory had been established longer than Persia), as well as many of his vice regents, summoned sufficiently high opinions of themselves—and a quarter million old-style warriors—to oppose Halik's passage on general, historical principles. They were destroyed.

Other vice regents hesitated. They'd heard of Halik—Esshk had been looking for him long enough, after all—but perceived him as Esshk's direct representative and wanted nothing to do with "Esshk's Hunt." What made these encounters most bizarre was that some might've even joined Halik if he'd unequivocally declared *against* Esshk. Since he couldn't, they'd fought too.

And, oddly, that was an increasingly common theme. For various reasons, to those who knew it, Esshk's name became less esteemed the closer they got to the ancient, sacred lands of Africa itself. A lot of that had to do with what rumor reported he was up to. He'd "slaughtered all the ancient Hij" at Old Sofesshk, he was "failing in the Great Hunt," or he'd "stripped whole regencies for his wasted swarms" and left them open to absorption by regents he favored. One rumor claimed he wasn't even real, that he was a construct of the Chooser. Finally, vaguely related and darkest of all, was that Esshk, or the Chooser, had "usurped the authority of the Celestial Mother herself, and held himself above her."

Colonel Enaak and Dalibor Svec actually knew which of these rumors were based on truth, and General Niwa probably suspected. But Henry Stokes directly ordered them *not* to tell Halik, and his reasons were very simple. They still didn't know what Halik would do when he got to central Africa, and as long as he had to fight all the way, he wasn't just delayed, but weakened. On the other hand, if he learned about Esshk's usurpation and did declare against him, he might show up with an army bigger than anything they'd ever seen. He'd probably destroy Esshk for them then, but what if he decided to "rescue" the Celestial Mother himself? They might wind up right back where they started, with a much more capable adversary. Best for now, Stokes advised, to leave things as they were. I'joorka and Hij Geerki would keep working on the Celestial Mother, and if there came a time when she could command Halik with an authority he'd obey without question, their orders might change.

In the meantime, Enaak and even Svec—a little—felt almost sorry for Halik, and how this whole crusade of his was tearing him apart.

"I couldn't agree with you more," Svec grouched as they finally cleared Halik's camp and quickened the pace of their mounts in the direction of their own. Despite improvements in sanitation that Niwa instigated, Halik's camp still stank. Bad. "He ought to just turn around and go home," Svec added. "Be content with what he's achieved in Persia and be done with it."

"Could you do that?" Major Ondrej Svec asked his father.

The older man looked at him, his great beard whipping in the wind around a sad smile. "You know I had a wife before I came to this world," he reminded his son. "Her name was Darja, and we lived near Kladno." He added this for Enaak's benefit, as if the Lemurian should know where Kladno was. "I still miss her," Svec confessed, but then reached over and roughly ruffled his son's hair. "But I wouldn't go back to her even if I could, and I won't go back to your mother until this war is safely won!"

"I'm in it to the end as well," Major Nika declared.

Enaak refrained from pointing out that Nika hadn't been in it all that long. "So, we all haave our destinies," he said instead. "As does Haalik, it seems. And since we caan't stop him from doing whaatever he waants, we must remain close, be his 'friends,' and hopefully steer his decisions to our benefit." His me-naak hopped a dry gully, and the others joined him. "I'm not sure withholding information as possibly influential as we haave is the proper course of aaction, but we'll do as we're told." He blinked grimly. "Unless thaat conflicts with our ultimate duty: to convince Haalik thaat whaatever he becomes or accomplishes, *his* destiny is not best served by screwing around with the Graand Alliaance. Esshk won't tell him thaat, of course, but he's certainly smaart enough to learn from Esshk's dis-aasters."

"Oh, I'm sure of that," the older Svec growled moodily. "I just hope he doesn't learn enough from Esshk's failures to *beat* us!"

That thought was foremost in all their minds. "He'll be up against Gener-aal Aalden again," Enaak reminded. "And Gener-aal Rolak. That might give him pause."

"If it doesn't only encourage him to seek a second match," Svec cautioned darkly. "Halik's not the same *plazivy* Alden and Rolak forced out of Indiaa. Not only does he know it, but he commands a much better army now as well."

Enaak had nothing to say to that.

CAST OF CHARACTERS

(L)—*Lemurian, or Mi-Anakka*
(G)—*Grik, or Gharrichk'k*
Lt. Cmdr. Matthew Patrick Reddy, USNR—CINCAF (Commander in Chief of All Allied Forces).

First Fleet Elements

USS *Walker* (DD-163)

Lt. Cmdr. Matthew Patrick Reddy

Cmdr. Brad "Spanky" McFarlane—XO and Minister of Naval Engineering.

Cmdr. Bernard Sandison—Torpedo Officer and Minister of Experimental Ordnance.

Cmdr. Toos-Ay-Chil (L)—First Officer.

Lt. Sonny Campeti—Gunnery Officer.

Lt. Ed Palmer—Signals.

Surgeon Lieutenant Pam Cross

Lt. Tab-At "Tabby" (L)—Engineering Officer.

Ensign Min-Sakir "Minnie" (L)—Bridge talker.

Chief Boatswain's Mate Jeek (L)—Former crew chief, Special Air Division.

Chief Engineer Isak Reuben—One of the original Mice.

Chief Quartermaster Patrick "Paddy" Rosen

Juan Marcos—Officer's Steward.

Earl Lanier—Cook.

Wallace Fairchild—Sonarman, Anti–Mountain Fish Countermeasures (AMF-DIC).

Corporal Neely—Imperial Marine and bugler assigned to *Walker*.

USS *Mahan* (DD-102)

Cmdr. Tiaa-Baari (L)

Cmdr. Muraak-Saanga (L)—XO (former *Donaghey* XO and sailing master).

Lt. Sonya—Engineering Officer.

Chief Gunner's Mate Pak-Ras-Ar "Pack Rat" (L)—Gunnery Officer.

Torpedoman 1st Class Fino Saal (L)—Acting Torpedo Officer.

USS *James Ellis* (DD-21)

Cmdr. Perry Brister

Lt. Rolando "Ronson" Rodriguez—XO.

Lt. (jg) Suaa "Suey" Jin (L)—"Sound Man," Anti–Mountain Fish Countermeasures (AMF-DIC).

Lt. (jg) Paul Stites—Gunnery Officer.

Lt. (jg) Johnny Parks—Engineering Officer.

Chief Bosun's Mate Carl Bashear

Taarba-Kaar "Tabasco" (L)—Cook.

U-112

Oberleuitnant Kurt Hoffman (German).

Oberleuitnant Walbert Fiedler (German).

USS *Savoie* (BB-1)

Cmdr. Russ Chappelle

Lt. Michael "Mikey" Monk—XO.

Lt. Naala-Araan (L)—Quartermaster.

Lt. (jg) Dean Laney—Engineering Officer.

Lt. Stanly Raj—Impie First Lieutenant.

Surgeon Cmdr. Kathy McCoy
Stanley "Dobbin" Dobson—Chief Bosun's Mate.
Gunnery Sergeant Arnold Horn, USMC—
   formerly of the 4th (US) Marines.

USS *Fitzhugh Gray* (CL-1)
Cmdr. Toru Miyata
Lt. Cmdr. Ado-Sin (L)—XO.
Lt. Robert Wallace—Gunnery Officer.
Lt. Sainaa-Asa (L)—Engineering Officer.
Lt. (jg) Eno-Sab-Raan (L)—Torpedo Officer.
Ensign Gaat-Rin (L)
CPO Pepper (L)—Chief Bosun's Mate.

USS *Tarakaan Island* (SPD-3)
Self-propelled dry dock.

USS *Sular* (Protected Troopship)
Converted from Grik BB.

Carrier Air
Admiral Keje-Fris-Ar (L)
Commodore Tassanna-Ay-Arracca (L)

USNRS *Salissa* "Big Sal" (CV-1)
Captain Atlaan-Fas (L)
Cmdr. Sandy Newman—XO.
Surgeon Commander Sandra Tucker Reddy—
   Minister of Medicine and wife of Captain
   Reddy.
Diania—Steward's Assistant and Sandra's friend
   and bodyguard.

1st Naval Air Wing
Captain Jis-Tikkar "Tikker" (L)—Commander
   of Flight Operations (COFO) of 1st Naval Air

Wing, including 1st, 2nd, 3rd Bomb Squadrons; 1st, 2nd Pursuit Squadrons.

USS *Madraas* (CV-8) 8th Naval Air Wing.

Frigates (DDs) Attached

Des-Ron 10

USS *Bowles****

USS *Saak-Fas****

USS *Clark***

USS *Kas-Ra-Ar***—Captain Mescus-Ricum (L).

USS *Ramic-Sa-Ar**

MTB-Ron-1 (Motor Torpedo Boat Squadron Number 1)

> 11 x MTBs (Numbers 4, 7, 13, 15, 16, 18–23)
> **Lieutenant Nat Hardee**

Land-Based Air

> **Colonel Ben Mallory**

Arracca Field—Army/Navy air base at the mouth of the Zambezi River

> **Lt. Cmdr. Mark Leedom**—Commander of Flight Operations (COFO), 4th, 7th, 8th Bomb Squadrons; 5th, 6th, 14th Pursuit Squadrons; and the remainder of the 5th Naval Air Wing.
>
> **2nd Lt. Cecil Dixon**—Mallory's Operation Officer.
>
> **2nd Lt. Niaa-Saa "Shirley" (L)**—Mallory's aide and pilot.
>
> **Lt. Araa-Faan (L)**—Commander of Flight Operations (COFO) at Grik City.
>
> **Lt. Walt "Jumbo" Fisher**—Pat-Squad 22.
>
> **Former General of the Sky Hideki Muriname**

AEF-1 (First Fleet Allied Expeditionary Force)
General of the Army and Marines Pete Alden— Former sergeant in USS *Houston* Marine contingent.

I Corps
General Lord Muln-Rolak (L)

1st (Galla) Division
General Taa-leen (L)
1st Marines; 5th, 6th, 7th, 10th Baalkpan

2nd Division
General Rin-Taaka-Ar (L)
1st, 2nd Maa-ni-la; 4th, 6th, 7th Aryaal

II Corps
General Queen Safir Maraan (L)

3rd Division
General Mersaak (L)
"The 600" (B'mbaado Regiment composed of "Silver" and "Black" Battalions); 3rd Baalkpan; 3rd, 10th B'mbaado; 1st, 5th Sular; 1st Battalion, 2nd Marines

6th Division
General Grisa (L)
5th, 6th B'mbaado; 1st, 2nd, 9th Aryaal; 3rd Sular

1st Cavalry Brigade
Lt. Colonel Saachic (L)
3rd and 6th Maa-ni-la Cavalry

"Maroons"
Colonel Will

Consolidated Division of "Maroons," Shee-ree, and Allied Advisors

III Corps
General Faan-Ma-Mar (L)

9th & 11th Divisions
2nd, 3rd, 7th, 8th Maa-ni-la; 8th Baalkpan; 10th Aryaal

Hij Geerki (G)—Rolak's "pet," captured at Rangoon, now "mayor" of Grik POWs at Grik City.

VI Corps

Special Force

1st Allied Raider Brigade—"Chack's Raiders" or "Chack's Brigade"
Lt. Col. Chack-Sab-At (L)
Chief Gunner's Mate Dennis Silva
Lawrence "Larry the Lizard"—Orange-and-brown tiger-striped Grik-like Sa'aaran.

21st (Combined) Allied Regiment
1st, 2nd Battalions of the 9th Maa-ni-la; 2nd Battalion of the 1st Respite

Major Alistair Jindal—Imperial Marine.
Captain McIntyre

7th (Combined) Allied Regiment
19th Baalkpan; 1st Battalion of the 11th Imperial Marines

Major Enrico Galay—Former corporal in the Philippine Scouts.

1st North Borno Regiment
Major Abel Cook—in place of Major I'joorka.
1st Sergeant "Moe" the Hunter
Sergeant "Pokey"—Real Grik who has switched sides.

En route

XII Corps

    General Mu-Tai (L)

    Half-trained Austraal volunteers with rifle-muskets

XIV Corps

    Militia out of Baalkpan, Sular, and B'taava

In Persia

(Detached Duty, shadowing General Halik)

5th Maa-ni-la Cavalry

    Colonel Enaak (L)

Czech Legion

    Colonel Dalibor Svec

    The Czech Legion, or "Brotherhood of Volunteers," is a near-division-level cavalry force of aging Czechs, Slovaks, and their continental Lemurian allies, militarily—if not politically—bound to the Grand Alliance.

The Republic of Real People

    Caesar (Kaiser) Nig-Taak (L)

    General Marcus Kim—Military High Command.

    Inquisitor Kon-Choon (L)—Director of Spies.

    General Taal-Gaak (L)—Republic Cavalry Commander.

    Courtney Bradford—Australian naturalist and engineer. Minister of Science and Plenipotentiary at Large for the Grand Alliance.

    Colonel Bekiaa-Sab-At (L)—Military liaison from the Grand Alliance and Legate under General Kim; now directly commanding the 23rd Legion.

Optio Jack Meek—Bekiaa's aide, Inquisitor Choon's liaison, and Doocy Meek's son.

Prefect Bele—Bekiaa's XO.

TFG-2 (Task Force Garret-2)

Long-Range Reconnaissance and Exploration

USS *Donaghey* (DD-2)

Cmdr. Greg Garrett

Lt. Mak-Araa (L)—XO.

Lt. (jg) Wendel "Smitty" Smith—Gunnery Officer.

Chief Bosun's Mate Jenaar-Laan (L)

Surgeon Lt. (jg) Sori-Maai (L)

Marine Lieutenant Haana-Lin-Naar (L)

Major "Tribune" Pol-Heena (L)

Leutnant Koor-Susk (L)

USS *Matarife* (prize ship)

At Baalkpan

Cmdr. Alan Letts—Chairman of the United Homes and the Grand Alliance.

Leading Seaman Henry Stokes—Director of Office of Strategic Intelligence (OSI); formerly of HMAS *Perth*.

Cmdr. Steve "Sparks" Riggs—Minister of Communications and Electrical Contrivances.

Lord Bolton Forester—Imperial Ambassador.

Lt. Bachman—Forester's aide.

Leftenant (Ambassador) Doocy Meek—British sailor and former POW (WWI), representing the Republic of Real People.

Surgeon Cmdr. Karen Theimer Letts—Assistant Minister of Medicine.

"King" Tony Scott—High Chief and Assembly-person for the Khonashi of North Borno.

Eastern Sea Campaign
High Admiral Harvey Jenks—CINCEAST.

Second Fleet
Fleet Admiral Lelaa-Tal-Cleraan (L)

USS *Maaka-Kakja* (CV-4)
"Flag" Captain Tex Sheider

Gilbert Yeager—Chief Engineer; one of the original Mice.

3rd Naval Air Wing
2nd Lt. Orrin Reddy—Commander of Flight Operations (COFO) 9th, 11th, 12th Bomb Squadrons; 7th, 10th Pursuit Squadrons. Orrin Reddy, though as reluctant as his cousin to assume higher official rank and still stubbornly considering himself a 2nd Lt. in the US Army Air Corps, has been named "Flag" COFO of Second Fleet.

Sgt. Kuaar-Ran-Taak "Seepy" (L)—Orrin Reddy's "backseater."

USS *New Dublin* (CV-6)—6th Naval Air Wing.

USS *Raan-Goon* (CV-7)—7th Naval Air Wing.

Line of Battle
Admiral E. B. Hibbs

9 Ships of the Line including HIMSs *Mars, Centurion, Mithra, Hermes, Diana, Ananke, Feronia, Poena,* and *Nesoi,* plus:

USS *Sword*—Former Dom *Espada de Dios.*

USS *Destroyer*—Former Dom *Deoses Destructor.*
Cmdr. Ruik-Sor-Raa (L)—One-armed former commander of USS *Simms.*

Lt. Parr—XO; former commander of HIMS *Icarus*.

Attached DDs

HIMSs *Ulysses, Euripides, Tacitus*

HIMS *Achilles*

Lt. Grimsley

USS *Pinaa-Tubo*—Ammunition ship.

Lt. Radaa-Nin (L)

USS *Saanga*—Fleet oiler.

USS *Pucot*—Fleet oiler.

Second Fleet Allied Expeditionary Force

Army of the Sisters

General Tomatsu Shinya

Saan-Kakja (L)—High Chief of Maa-ni-la and all the Filpin Lands.

Governor-Empress Rebecca Anne McDonald

Lt. Ezekial Krish—Aide-de-camp.

Surgeon Cmdr. Selass-Fris-Ar (L)—Daughter of Keje-Fris-Ar.

X Corps

Three divisions Lemurian Army and Marines, 6 divisions Imperial Marines, 4 regiments "Frontier Troops"; total 10 divisions w/ heavy artillery and support train.

General James Blair

Colonel Dao Iverson—6th Imperial Marines.

Captain Faal-Pel "Stumpy" (L)—1st Battalion, 8th Maa-ni-la.

Sister's Own Division

"Colonel" Sister Audry—Benedictine nun; nominal command.

Colonel Arano Garcia—"El Vengadores de Dios," a regiment raised from penitent Dominion POWs on New Ireland, augmented by disaffected Dom Christians represented by **Captain Bustos**, who replaced Ximen, KIA.

Captain Jasso—Garcia's XO (Pacal's replacement).

"Lord" Sergeant Major Koratin (L)—Marine protector and advisor to Sister Audry.

Major Blas-Ma-Ar "Blossom" (L)—2nd Battalion, 2nd Marines, and the Ocelomeh (Jaguar Warriors).

Captain Ixtli—Blas's acting XO.

Lt. Anaar-Taar (L)—C Company, 2nd Battalion, 2nd Marines.

Spon-Ar-Aak "Spook" (L)—Gunner's Mate, and 1st Sgt. of C Company, 2nd Battalion, 2nd Marines.

XI Corps and Filpin Scouts
> **General Ansik-Talaa (L)**

XV Corps
> Embarked Imperial Marines.

In contact with "New United States" Forces
> **Lt. Fred Reynolds**—Formerly Special Air Division, USS *Walker.*
>
> **Lt. (jg) Kari-Faask (L)**—Reynolds's friend and "backseater."

"New United States" Forces
> **Admiral Duncan**—Overall operational commander of the NUS naval and land forces in the Caribbean, aboard NUSS *Zachary Taylor.*
>
> **Commodore Semmes**—Commanding NUS Fleet, aboard NUSS *Eric Holland.*

Lt. Ulysses "Ully" Locke—XO.

Captain Ezra Willis—Commanding heavy frigate NUSS *Congress*.

Lt. Samuel Hudgens—XO.

Captain "Anson"—NUS Ranger.

Alferez (Ensign) Tomas Perez Mole—League Prisoner (Spanish).

Enemies

Grik (Gharrichk'k)

Celestial Mother (G)—Absolute, godlike ruler of all the Grik, regardless of the relationships between the various Regencies.

General Esshk (G)—First General of all the Grik, and Regent Champion Consort to the new Celestial Mother.

The Chooser (G)—Highest member of his order at the Court of the Celestial Mother; prior to current policy, "choosers" selected those destined for life—or the cookpots—as well as those eligible for elevation to Hij status.

General of the Sky Mitsuo Ando—Muriname's former XO.

General Ign (G)—Commander of Esshk's New Warriors.

First Ker-noll Jash—Commander of the Slashers.

Ker-noll Naxa

Ker-noll Shelg

In Persia

General Halik

General Shlook

General Ugla (G)

General Orochi Niwa (Japanese)

Holy Dominion

>   **His Supreme Holiness, Messiah of Mexico, and by the Grace of God, Emperor of the World**—"Dom Pope" and absolute ruler.
>
>   **Don Hernan de Divina Dicha**—Blood Cardinal.
>
>   **General Mayta**—Commander of the Army of God.
>
>   **General Allegria**—Blood Drinker and son of Don Hernan.

League of Tripoli

>   **Capitaine de Fregate Victor Gravois** (French)
>
>   **Capitano di Fregata Ciano** (Italian)
>
>   **Contrammiraglio Oriani** (Italian)—Organizations for Vigilance and Repression of Antifascism.

In Allied custody

>   **Capitaine Dupont** (French)

SPECIFICATIONS

American-Lemurian Ships and Equipment

USS *Walker* (DD-163)—Wickes (Little) class four-stacker destroyer. Twin-screw steam turbines; 1,200 tons; 314′ x 30′. Max speed (as designed): 35 knots. 112 officers and enlisted (current) including Lemurians (L). Armament: Main—3 x 4″-50 + 1 x DP 4″-50. Secondary—4 x 25 mm Type 96 AA, 4 x .50 cal MG, 6 x .30 cal MG. 40-60 Mk-6 (or equivalent) depth charges for 2 stern racks and 2 Y guns (with adapters). 2 x 21″ quadruple-tube torpedo mounts. Impulse-activated catapult for PB-1B Nancy seaplane.

USS *Mahan* (DD-102)—Wickes-class four-stacker destroyer. Twin-screw steam turbines; 960 tons; 264′ x 30′ (as rebuilt). Max speed: 25 knots. Rebuild has resulted in shortening, and removal of 2 funnels and boilers. Forward 4″-50 is on a dual-purpose mount. Otherwise, her armament and upgrades are the same as those of USS *Walker*.

USS *James Ellis* (DD-21)—Wickes (Walker) class four-stacker destroyer. Twin-screw steam turbines; 1,300 tons; 314′ x 30′. Max speed: 37 knots. 115 officers and enlisted. Armament: Main—4 x DP 4″-50. Secondary—4 x .50 cal MG, 6 x .30 cal MG. 40-60 Mk-6 (or equivalent) depth charges for 2 stern racks and 2 Y guns (with adapters). 2 x 21″ quadruple-tube torpedo mounts. Impulse-activated catapult for PB-1B Nancy seaplane.

USS *Sular*—Protected troopship converted from Grik BB. 800′ x 100′, 18,000 tons. Twin-screw, triple-expansion

Baalkpan Navy Yard steam engine. Max speed: 16 knots. Crew: 400. 100 stacked motor dories mounted on sliding davits. Armament: 4 x DP 4"-50, 4 x .30 cal MG.

USS *Tarakaan Island* (SPD-3)—Self-propelled dry dock (SPD). Twin-screw, triple-expansion steam engine; 15,990 tons; 800' x 100'. Armament: 3 x DP 4"-50, 6 x .30 cal MG.

USS *Savoie* (BB-1)—26,000 tons; 548' x 88'; 4 screws. Max speed: 20 knots. 1,050 officers and enlisted. Initial armament: 8 x 340 mm (13.5"), 8 x 138.6 mm (5.5"), 8 x DP 75 mm (3"), 5 x quad-mount 13.2 mm, 24 x 8 mm.

USS *Fitzhugh Gray* (CL-1)—Four-stacker light cruiser. Triple-screw steam turbines; 3,800 tons, 440' x 45'. Max speed: 30–35 knots. 211 officers and enlisted. Armament: Main—3 x 2 DP 5.5". Secondary—5 x DP 4"-50, 2 x 21" quadruple-tube torpedo mounts, 6 x twin .50 cal. MG, 6 x Y guns (with adapters), 80 MK-6 (or equivalent) depth charges for 2 stern racks. 2 x impulse-activated catapults for PB-1B Nancy seaplanes.

***U-112* (Type XIB submarine)**—371' x 31', 4,600 tons submerged. Twin-screw, 8 x 12 cyl diesel engines, 2 x electric motors. Max speed: 18 knots surface, 6.5 knots submerged. 110 officers and enlisted. Armament: 6 x 21" torpedo tubes, 4 bow, 2 stern. 4 x 127 mm guns in 2 armored mounts, 2 x 37 mm, 2 x 20 mm.

Carriers

USNRS (US Navy Reserve Ship) *Salissa* (*Big Sal*, CV-1)—Aircraft carrier/tender, converted from seagoing Lemurian Home. Single-screw, triple-expansion steam; 13,000 tons; 1,009' x 200'. Armament: 2 x 5.5", 6 x 4"-50 DP, 4 x twin-mount 25 mm AA, 20 x 50 pdrs (as reduced), 50 aircraft assembled, 80–100 in crates.

USS *Maaka-Kakja* (CV-4)—Purpose-built aircraft carrier/tender. Single-screw, triple-expansion steam; 14,670 tons; 1009' x 210'. Armament: 2 x 4.7" DP, 50 x 50 pdrs. Up to 80 aircraft.

USS *Madras* (CV-8)—Baalkpan Bay–class fleet carrier. 9,000 tons, 850′ x 150′. Twin-screw, triple-expansion steam. Max speed: 15 knots. Armament: 4 x Baalkpan Arsenal 4″-50 DP guns, 2 amidships, 1 each forward and aft. Can carry as many aircraft as *Maaka-Kakja*.

USS *New Dublin* (CV-6)—Same as above.

USS *Raan-Goon* (CV-7)—Same as above.

Frigates (DDs)

USS *Donaghey* (DD-2)—Square-rig sail, 1,200 tons, 168′ x 33′; 200 officers and enlisted. Sole survivor of first new construction. Armament: 24 x 18 pdrs, Y gun, and depth charges.

*Dowden class—Square-rig steamer, 1,500 tons, 185′ x 34′. Max speed: 12–15 knots. Armament: 20 x 32 pdrs, Y gun, and depth charges. 218 officers and enlisted.

**Haakar-Faask class—Square-rig steamer, 1,600 tons, 200′ x 36′. Max speed: 15 knots. Armament: 20 x 32 pdrs, Y gun, and depth charges. 226 officers and enlisted.

***Scott class—Square-rig steamer, 1,800 tons, 210′ x 40′. Max speed: 17 knots. Armament: 20 x 50 pdrs, Y gun, and depth charges. 260 officers and enlisted.

Note: Nearly all of these have been converted to AVDs (destroyer/seaplane tenders), DMs (destroyer/mine layers), fast transports, and auxiliaries.

Auxiliaries—Purpose-built heavy-hauler transports, oilers, tenders, and general cargo vessels. A growing number of steam auxiliaries have joined the fleet, with hull dimensions similar to enlarged Scott-class DDs, but with minimal armament. Some fast clipper-shaped vessels are still employed as long-range oilers. Fore- and aft-rigged feluccas remain in service as fast transports and scouts.

Respite Island–class SPDs—Self-propelled dry dock. Designed along similar hull lines as the new purpose-built carriers, and inspired by the massive seagoing Lemurian Homes. They are intended as rapid-deployment, heavy-lift dry docks, and for bulky transport.

USNRS—*Salaama-Na* Home—Unaltered, other than by emplacement of 50 x 50 pdrs. 8,600 tons, 1014' x 150'. 3 tripod masts support semirigid "junklike" sails or "wings." Max speed: about 6 knots, but capable of short sprints up to 10 knots using 100 long sweeps. In addition to living space in the hull, there are three tall pagoda-like structures within the tripods that cumulatively accommodate up to 6,000 people.

***Woor-Na* Home**—Lightly armed (10 x 32 pdrs) heavy transport, specifications as for *Salaama-Na*.

MTBs—50' long x 16' wide, 14 tons, twin 6-cylinder engines and screws. Max speed: 26 knots. Crew: 12 officers and enlisted. Armament: 2 x 21" torpedoes, 3 x .30 cal MGs.

Aircraft

P-40E Warhawk—Allison V1710, V12, 1,150 hp. Max speed: 360 mph. Ceiling 29,000 ft. Crew: 1. Armament: 6 x .50 cal Browning MG, and up to 1,000-lb bomb.

PB-1B "Nancy"—W/G type, in-line 4 cyl 150 hp. Max speed: 110 mph. Max weight: 1,900 lbs. Crew: 2. Armament: 400-lb bombs.

PB1-F "Nancy"—10 cyl, 410 hp faired in radial. Max speed: 160 mph. Max weight: 2,600 lbs. Crew: 2. Armament: 600-lb bombs, 2 x .30 cal Browning MG in fuselage.

PB-2 "Buzzard"—3 x W/G type, in-line 4 cyl 150 hp. Max speed: 80 mph. Max weight: 3,000 lbs. Crew: 2, and up to 6 passengers. Armament: 600-lb bombs.

PB-5 "Clipper"—4 x W/G type, in-line 4 cyl 150 hp. Max speed: 90 mph. Max weight: 4,800 lbs. Crew: 3, and up to 8 passengers. Armament: 1,500-lb bombs.

PB-5B—As for PB-5, but powered by 4 x MB 5 cyl, 254 hp radials. Max speed: 125 mph. Max weight: 6,200 lbs. Crew: 3, and up to 10 passengers. Armament: 2,000-lb bombs.

PB-5D "Clipper"—4 x 10 cyl, 410 hp radials. Max speed: 145 mph. Max weight: 7,800 lbs. Crew: 5–6, and up to 8 passengers. Armament: 5 x .30 cal, 2,500-lb bombs/torpedoes.

P-1B Mosquito Hawk or "Fleashooter"—MB 5 cyl 254 hp radial. Max speed: 220 mph. Max weight: 1,220 lbs. Crew: 1. Armament: 2 x .45 cal Blitzerbug machine guns in wheel pants.

P-1C—10 cyl, 410 hp radial. Max speed: 265 mph. Max weight: 1,740 lbs. Crew: 1. Armament: 2 x .30 cal Browning MG in wings.

JU-52—3 x BMW Hornet 518 hp radials. Max speed: 160 mph. Max weight: 20,000 lbs.

Field artillery—6 pdr on stock-trail carriage—effective to about 1,500 yds, or 300 yds with canister. 12 pdr on stock-trail carriage—effective to about 1,800 yds, or 300 yds with canister. 3″ mortar—effective to about 800 yds. 4″ mortar—effective to about 1,500 yds.

Primary small arms—Allin-Silva breech-loading rifle (.50–80 cal), Allin-Silva breech-loading smoothbore (20 gauge), 1911 Colt and copies (.45 ACP), Blitzerbug SMG (.45 ACP). M-1917 Navy cutlass, grenades, bayonet.

Secondary small arms—Rifle-musket (.50 cal), 1903 Springfield (.30–06), 1898 Krag-Jorgensen (.30 US), 1918 BAR (.30–06), Thompson SMG (.45 ACP). A small number of other firearms are available.

MGs—1919 water-cooled Browning and copies (.30–06). 41 lbs without mount, 400–600 rpm, 1,500 yds. M2 Browning and copies (.50 cal). 121 lbs (with water jacket). Light-barrel versions from P-40s weigh 60 lbs.

Armored vehicles—Mk-II *Grikoshai* or "Grik Smusher"—16′ long x 10′ wide, 7 tons. Crew: 4+1 (Lemurians). Armament: 2 x .30 cal MG, 1 x .50 cal MG in a top-mounted turret.

Imperial Ships and Equipment

Until recently, few Imperial ships shared enough specifics to be described as classes, but could be grouped by size and capability. Most shared the fundamental similarity of being powered by steam-driven paddle wheels and a complete suit of sails. Copies of Allied Scott-class DDs were briefly made, but all-new construction is being equipped with double- or triple-expansion engines, screw propellers, and iron hulls.

Ships of the line—About 180′–200′ x 52′–58′, 1,900–2,200 tons. 50–80 x 30 pdrs, 20 pdrs, 10 pdrs, 8 pdrs. (8 pdrs are more commonly used as field guns by the Empire.) Speed: about 8–10 knots. 400–475 officers and enlisted.

Frigates—About 160′–180′ x 38′–44′, 1,200–1,400 tons. 24–40 x 20–30 pdrs. Speed: about 13–15 knots. 275–350 officers and enlisted. Example: HIMS *Achilles*, 160′ x 38′, 1,300 tons, 26 x 20 pdrs.

Field artillery—The Empire of the New Britain Isles has adopted the Allied 12 pdr.

Primary small arms—Allin-Silva breech-loading rifle (.50–80 cal), rifle-musket (.50 cal), bayonet. Swords and smoothbore flintlock muskets (.75 cal), are now considered secondary and are issued to native allies in the Dominion.

Republic Ships and Equipment

The Republic is building blue-water Imperator-class protected cruisers, though details of their design have Matt Reddy wondering if they'd be better described as battlecruisers—or targets.

Princeps-class coastal- and harbor-defense monitors— 210′ x 50′, 1,200 tons. Twin-screw, 11 knots, 190 officers and enlisted. Armament: 4 x 8″ guns in two turrets, 4 x MG08 8 x 57 mm (Maxim) MG on flying bridge.

Field artillery—75 mm quick-firing breechloader based on the French 75. Range: 3,000 yds with black powder propellant and time or contact fuse exploding shell. 300 yds with canister.

Primary small arms: Breech-loading bolt action, single-shot rifle, 11.15 x 60R (.43 Mauser) cal.

Secondary small arms: M-1898 Mauser (8 x 57 mm), Mauser and Luger pistols, mostly in 11 and 7.65 mm.

Republic military rank structure is a combination of ancient and new, with a few unique aspects. Each legion, commanded by a colonel, has six cohorts. The senior cohort commander (and XO) is the prefect, and roughly equivalent to a major. The remaining cohorts are led by senior centurions (captains), who still command one of the six centuries in the cohort through their senior optio (2nd lieutenant), who has a junior optio (like an ensign) as his assistant. Other centurions are roughly equivalent to 1st lieutenants. The Republic also has provisions for temporary, special-purpose rank appointments. A military tribune may be given specific tasks requiring them to outrank all prefects and below, as well as single-ship captains. A legate may supersede the colonel of any legion for a specific purpose, unless countermanded by the general of the army the legion is attached to. Likewise, legates act as commodores at sea.

Enemy Warships and Equipment

Grik

New, unnamed class of Grik BBs (ironclad battleships)— 800' x 100', about 27,000 tons. Twin-screw, double-expansion steam. Max speed: 10 knots. Crew: 1,300. Armament: 3 x 15" 400 pdrs (2 forward, 1 aft), 24 x 100 pdrs, 24 x 4" AA mortars.

***Azuma*-class CAs (ironclad cruisers)**—300' x 37', about 3,800 tons. Twin-screw, double-expansion steam, sail auxiliary. Max speed: 12 knots. Crew: 320. Armament: 20 x 40 pdrs or 14 x 50 pdrs, and 1 or 2 x 100 pdrs. 4 x firebomb catapults.

Tatsuta—Kurokawa's double-ended paddle/steam yacht. The pattern for all Grik tugs and light transports.

Aircraft—Hydrogen-filled rigid dirigibles or zeppelins. 300' x 48', 5 x 2 cyl 80 hp engines. Max speed: 60 mph. Useful lift: 3,600 lbs. Crew: 16. Armament: 6 x 2 pdr swivel guns, bombs.

AJ1M1c Fighter—9 cyl 380 hp radial. Max speed: 260 mph. Max weight: 1,980 lbs. Crew: 1. Armament: 2 x Type 89 MG (copies) 7.7 x 58mm SR cal.*

DP1M1 Torpedo Bomber—2 x 9 cyl 380 hp radials. Max speed: 180 mph. Max weight: 3,600 lbs. Crew: 3. Armament: 1 x Type 89 MG (copy) 7.7 x 58 mm SR cal.* 1 torpedo or 1,000-lb bombs.

*Note: Other than those on former Japanese aircraft, no MG of any type is available to the Grik—as yet.

Field artillery—The standard Grik field piece is a 9 pdr, but 4s and 16s are also used, with effective ranges of 1,200, 800, and 1,600 yds, respectively. Powder is satisfactory, but windage is often excessive, resulting in poor accuracy. Grik "field" firebomb throwers fling 10- and 25-lb bombs, depending on the size, for a range of 200 and 325 yds, respectively.

Primary small arms—Copies of Allied .60 Cal smoothbore percussion muskets are now widespread, but swords and spears are still in use—as are teeth and claws.

League of Tripoli

Leopardo—Leone- (Exploratori-) class destroyer. 372' x 34', 2,600 tons. Twin-screw. Max speed: 30 knots. Armament: 8 x 120 mm, 6 x 20 mm, 4 x 21" torpedo tubes. 210 officers and enlisted.

Ramb V—Auxiliary cruiser/tender. 383' x 49', 3,730 tons. Twin-screw. Max speed: 18.5 knots. Armament: 3 x 4.7" guns, 8 x 13.2 mm antiaircraft guns. 1 catapult for observation floatplane. 111 officers and enlisted.

Holy Dominion

Like Imperial vessels, Dominion warships fall in a number of categories difficult to describe as classes, but, again, can be grouped by size and capability. Despite their generally more primitive design, Dom warships run larger and more heavily armed than their Imperial counterparts.

Ships of the line—About 200′ x 60′, 3,400–3,800 tons. 64–98 x 24 pdrs, 16 pdrs, 9 pdrs. Speed: about 7–10 knots. 470–525 officers and enlisted.

Heavy frigates (cruisers)—About 170′ x 50′, 1,400–1,600 tons. 34–50 x 24 pdrs, 9 pdrs. Speed: about 14 knots. 290–370 officers and enlisted.

Aircraft—The Doms have no aircraft yet, but employ dragons or "Grikbirds" for aerial attack.

Field artillery—9 pdrs on split-trail carriages—effective to about 1,500 yds, or 600 yds with grapeshot.

Primary small arms—Flintlock (patilla-style) musket (.69 cal), sword, pike, bayonet. Only officers and cavalry use pistols, which are often quite ornate and of various calibers.